THE WILDSIDE PRESS TREASURY OF SCIENCE FICTION MASTERPIECES

THE WILDSIDE PRESS TREASURY OF SCIENCE FICTION MASTERPIECES

COMPILED BY
ROBERT SILVERBERG
& MARTIN H. GREENBERG

WILDSIDE PRESS

CONTENTS

INTRODUCTION

SCIENCE FICTION, once a relatively obscure branch of the American pulp-magazine fiction industry, has risen since the end of World War II to a major position in the global consciousness. First the atomic bomb, then jet planes, color television, the electronic computer and a host of other technological innovations, all foretold in one manner or another by science fiction writers, drew attention to this innovative field of fiction. By the coming of the first voyages into space in the 1960s science fiction was firmly established in the public awareness. Today it is not at all unusual to find two or three science fiction novels on the bestseller lists—a situation that would have been unthinkable a generation ago, when science fiction was published only in garish little magazines with names like Thrilling Wonder Stories and Astounding Science Fiction.

Paradoxically, though, this very new publishing phenomenon is actually one of the oldest forms of literature, going back to the earliest days of the storyteller's art. Certainly in ancient Greece and Rome, and probably in Sumer, and, for all we know, in the caves of the Cro-Magnon folk as well, it was a customary form of delight to propose hypotheses and suppositions about the mysteries that lay beyond the current horizon of knowledge—to speculate, to ask, "What if?"

And so the ancient Mesopotamian king Gilgamesh went looking for the secret of immortality, in what may be the oldest science fiction story that has survived to our times. Homer sang of the strange monsters and ensorcelled isles in the far corners of the Mediterranean. Plato, in his *Timaeus* and *Critias*, told tales of the lost continent of Atlantis, etc. etc. The bibliography of science fiction in the classical age and onward through medieval times to the early Industrial Era is a lengthy one, taking in such famed works as Thomas More's *Utopia*, Francis Bacon's *The New Atlantis*, Swift's *Gulliver's Travels*, Johannes Kepler's *Somnium*, Rostand's *Voyages to the Moon and the Sun*, Mary Shelley's *Frankenstein* and on and on.

In more recent times the tradition of speculative thought in fiction was carried on by such writers as Jules Verne and H. G. Wells, by Edward Bellamy in his *Looking Backward*, by Aldous Huxley in *Brave New World*, by George Orwell in *1984*. No one would deny their works a respected place in literature; and yet it is difficult to equate them with the gaudy and hectic adventures of space pirates and mad robots found in the primitive science fiction magazines of mid-twentieth-century America.

What happened, alas, was that for a time this honorable branch of imaginative literature was captured by the purveyors of simple-minded thriller-fiction. During the 1930s and 1940s it was largely confined to the realm of cheaply printed magazines read mainly by boys, which debased the coinage, somewhat, and made science fiction into a genre for subliterate readers. Science fiction was a long time coming out of that unfortunate detour.

What we have attempted to do in this book, a companion to our earlier anthologies, *The Arbor House Treasury of Modern Science Fiction* and *The Arbor House Treasury of Great Science Fiction Short Novels*, has been to trace the evolution of today's science fiction by linking the earlier "mainstream" s-f literature to the best of the pulp-magazine work of modern writers. Since our aim was not to produce a textbook, we have not reached back to Gilgamesh, Plato and Kepler, but instead have set the bounds of our pastward range at Edgar Allan Poe, some hundred and fifty years ago. From Poe to Verne to Wells, the progression is clear; and we have carried it onward through the late nineteenth century and the early twentieth to reveal that Mark Twain, Rudyard Kipling and other writers of worldwide fame ventured occasionally into speculative fiction. With the groundwork thus established, our book moves onward into the era of Heinlein and Asimov and Clarke and of the finest younger science fiction writers of today, to demonstrate that there is an unbroken line of evolution connecting the early and current traditions of imaginative exploration of created worlds.

Our intention, though, is neither antiquarian nor primarily historical. The first test for the inclusion of any story in this book was its value as entertainment: food for the mind, stimulation for the questing intellect. Our hope is to have shown the unfailingly exciting nature of the best science fiction of the last century and a half.

ROBERT SILVERBERG
MARTIN H. GREENBERG

ACKNOWLEDGMENTS

The following pages constitute an extension of the copyright page

"The Metal Man," by Jack Williamson, copyright © 1928 by Jack Williamson; copyright renewed. Reprinted by permission of the author and the author's agent. Scott Meredith Literary Agency, Inc., 845 Third Avenue, New York, N.Y. 10022.

"The Gostak and the Doshes," by Miles J. Breuer, copyright © 1930 by E.P. Publications, Inc. Published by permission of Forrest J. Ackerman, 2495 Glendower Avenue, Hollywood, Ca. 90027, on behalf of the Heir.

"Alas, All Thinking," by Harry Bates, copyright © 1935 by Street & Smith Publications, Inc. Renewed copyright 1963 by Harry Bates. Reprinted by permission of Forrest J. Ackerman, 2495 Glendower Avenue, Hollywood, Ca. 90027, on behalf of the estate of Harry Bates.

"The Mad Moon," by Stanley G. Weinbaum, copyright © 1936 by Margaret Weinbaum, copyright renewed 1964. Reprinted by permission of Forrest J. Ackerman, 2495 Glendower Avenue, Hollywood, Ca. 90027, on behalf of the Heir.

"As Never Was," by P. Schuyler Miller, copyright © 1943 by Street & Smith Publications, Inc. Renewed copyright 1971, now Davis Publications, Inc. Published by arrangement with Forrest J. Ackerman, 2495 Glendower Avenue, Hollywood, Ca. 90027, on behalf of the Heir of P. Schuyler Miller.

"Desertion," by Clifford D. Simak, copyright © 1944 by Street & Smith Publications, Inc. Copyright renewed. Reprinted by permission of Kirby McCauley, Ltd.

"The Strange Case of John Kingman," by Murray Leinster, copyright © 1948 by Street & Smith Publications, Inc. Copyright renewed. Reprinted by permission of the author and the author's agent, Scott Meredith Literary Agency, Inc., 845 Third Avenue, New York, N.Y. 10022.

"Dreams Are Sacred," by Peter Phillips, copyright © 1948 by Street & Smith Publications, Inc. Copyright renewed. Reprinted by permission of the author and the author's agent, Scott Meredith Literary Agency, Inc., 845 Third Avenue, New York, N.Y. 10022.

"Misbegotten Missionary," by Isaac Asimov, copyright © 1950 by World Editions, Inc. Copyright renewed 1977 by Isaac Asimov. Reprinted by permission of the author.

"Dune Roller," by Julian May, copyright © 1952 by T.E. Dikty and Everett F. Bleiler. Copyright renewed 1983 by Julian May. Reprinted by permission of the author.

"Warm," by Robert Sheckley, copyright © 1953 by Galaxy Publishing Corporation. Reprinted by permission of Kirby McCauley, Ltd.

"A Bad Day for Sales," by Fritz Leiber, copyright © 1953 by Galaxy Publishing Corporation. Reprinted by permission of Robert P. Mills, Ltd.

"Man of Parts," by H.L. Gold, copyright © 1954 by Henry Holt & Co., Inc. Reprinted by permission of the author.

EDGAR ALLAN POE

Mellonta Tauta

Edgar Allan Poe (1809-1849) was one of the most important American writers of all time, whose influence on the development of the modern detective and horror fields has been widely acknowledged. He was an unhappy, tortured genius, a man whose considerable psychological problems were reflected in his fiction. Poe's mode was very science fictional— he employed both the scientific method and extrapolation from known facts constantly in his detective/suspense tales—and he was one of the first American writers to produce what approached "real" science fiction, as "Mellonta Tauta" so ably demonstrates. Science fiction would not become a recognized genre for many decades after Poe's death, but the field still owes him a great debt.

NOW, MY dear friend—now, for your sins, you are to suffer the infliction of a long gossiping letter. I tell you distinctly that I am going to punish you for all your impertinences by being as tedious, as discursive, as incoherent and as unsatisfactory as possible. Besides, here I am, cooped up in a dirty balloon, with some one or two hundred of the *canaille*, all bound on a *pleasure* excursion (what a funny idea some people have of pleasure!), and I have no prospect of touching *terra firma* for a month at least. Nobody to talk to. Nothing to do. When one has nothing to do, then is the time to correspond with one's friends. You perceive, then, why it is that I write you this letter—it is on account of my *ennui* and your sins.

Get ready your spectacles and make up your mind to be annoyed. I mean to write at you every day during this odious voyage.

Heigho! when will any *Invention* visit the human pericranium? Are we forever to be doomed to the thousand inconveniences of the balloon? Will *nobody* contrive a more expeditious mode of progress? This jog-trot movement, to my thinking, is little less than positive torture. Upon my word we have not made more than a hundred miles the hour since leaving home! The very birds beat us—at least some of them. I assure you that I do not exaggerate at all. Our motion, no doubt, seems slower than it actually is—this on account of our having no objects about us by which to estimate our velocity, and on account of our going *with* the wind. To be sure, whenever we meet a balloon we have a chance of perceiving our rate, and then, I admit, things do not appear so very bad. Accustomed as I am to this mode

11

of traveling, I cannot get over a kind of giddiness whenever a balloon passes us in a current directly overhead. It always seems to me like an immense bird of prey about to pounce upon us and carry us off in its claws. One went over us this morning about sunrise, and so nearly overhead that its drag-rope actually brushed the net-work suspending our car, and caused us very serious apprehension. Our captain said that if the material of the bag had been the trumpery varnished "silk" of five hundred or a thousand years ago, we should inevitably have been damaged. This silk, as he explained it to me, was a fabric composed of the entrails of a species of earthworm. The worm was carefully fed on mulberries—a kind of fruit resem-bling a watermelon—and, when sufficiently fat, was crushed in a mill. The paste thus arising was called *papyrus* in its primary state, and went through a variety of processes until it finally became "silk." Singular to relate, it was once much admired as an article of *female dress!* Balloons were also very generally constructed from it. A better kind of material, it appears, was subsequently found in the down surrounding the seed-vessels of a plant vulgarly called *euphorbium,* and at that time botanically termed milkweed. This latter kind of silk was designated as silk-buck-ingham, on account of its superior durability, and was usually prepared for use by being varnished with a solution of gum caoutchouc—a substance which in some respects must have resembled the *gutta percha* now in common use. This caoutchouc was occasionally called India rubber or rubber of whist, and was no doubt one of the numerous *fungi.* Never tell me again that I am not at heart an antiquarian.

Talking of drag-ropes—our own, it seems, has this moment knocked a man overboard from one of the small magnetic propellers that swarm in the ocean below us—a boat of about six thousand tons, and, from all accounts, shamefully crowded. These diminutive barques should be prohibited from carrying more than a definite number of passengers. The man, of course, was not permitted to get on board again, and was soon out of sight, he and his life-preserver. I rejoice, my dear friend, that we live in an age so enlightened that no such a thing as an individual is supposed to exist. It is the mass for which the true Humanity cares. By the by, talking of Humanity, do you know that our immortal Wiggins is not so original in his views of the Social Condition and so forth, as his contemporaries are inclined to suppose? Pundit assures me that the same ideas were put, nearly in the same way, about a thousand years ago, by an Irish philosopher called Furrier, on account of his keeping a retail shop for cat-peltries and other furs. Pundit *knows,* you know; there can be no mistake about it. How very wonderfully do we see verified, every day, the profound observation of the Hindoo Aries Tottle (as quoted by Pundit)— "Thus must we say that, not once or twice, or a few times, but with almost infinite repetitions, the same opinions come round in a circle among men."

April 2.—Spoke to-day the magnetic cutter in charge of the middle section of floating telegraph wires. I learn that when this species of telegraph was first put into operation by Horse, it was considered quite impossible to convey the wires over sea; but now we are at a loss to comprehend where the difficulty lay! So wags the world. *Tempora mutantur*—excuse me for quoting the Etruscan. What *would* we do without the Atalantic telegraph? (Pundit says Atlantic was the ancient ad-jective.) We lay to a few minutes to ask the cutter some questions, and learned, among other glorious news, that civil war is raging in Africa, while the plague is doing its good work beautifully both in Yurope and Ayesher. Is it not truly remarkable that, before the magnificent light shed upon philosophy by Humanity, the world was accustomed to regard War and Pestilence as calamities? Do you know that prayers were actually offered up in the ancient temples to the end that these *evils* (!) might not be visited upon mankind? Is it not really difficult to comprehend upon what principle of interest our forefathers acted? Were they so blind as not to perceive that the destruction of a myriad of individuals is only so much positive advantage to the mass!

April 3.—It is really a very fine amusement to ascend the rope-ladder leading to the summit of the balloon-bag and thence survey the surrounding world. From the car below, you know, the prospect is not so comprehensive—you can see little vertically. But seated here (where I write this) in the luxuriously-cushioned open piazza of the summit, one can see everything that is going on in all directions. Just now, there is quite a crowd of balloons in sight, and they present a very animated appearance, while the air is resonant with the hum of so many millions of human voices. I have heard it asserted that when Yellow or (as Pundit *will* have it) Violet, who is supposed to have been the first æronaut, maintained the practicability of traversing the atmosphere in all directions, by merely ascending or descending until a favorable current was attained, he was scarcely hearkened to at all by his contemporaries, who looked upon him as merely an ingenious sort of madman, because the philosophers (?) of the day declared the thing impossible. Really now it does seem to me *quite* unaccountable how anything so obviously feasible could have escaped the sagacity of the ancient *savans*. But in all ages the great obstacles to advancement in Art have been opposed by the so-called men of science. To be sure, *our* men of science are not quite so bigoted as those of old:—oh, I have something *so* queer to tell you on this topic. Do you know that it is not more than a thousand years ago since the metaphysicians consented to relieve the people of the singular fancy that there existed but *two possible roads for the attainment of Truth!* Believe it if you can! It appears that long, long ago, in the night of Time, there lived a Turkish philosopher (or Hindoo possibly) called Aries Tottle. This person introduced, or at all events propagated what was termed the deductive or *a priori* mode of investigation. He started with what he maintained to be *axioms* or "self-evident truths," and thence proceeded "logically" to results. His greatest disciples were one Neuclid and one Cant. Well, Aries Tottle flourished supreme until the advent of one Hog, surnamed the "Ettrick Shepherd," who preached an entirely different system, which he called the *a posteriori* or *in*ductive. His plan referred altogether to Sensation. He proceeded by observing, analyzing and classifying facts—*instantiae naturae,* as they were affectedly called—into general laws. Aries Tottle's mode, in a word, was based on *noumena;* Hog's on *phenomena.* Well, so great was the admiration excited by this latter system that, at its first introduction, Aries Tottle fell into disrepute; but finally he recovered ground, and was permitted to divide the realm of Truth with his more modern rival. The *savans* now maintained that the Aristotelian and *Baconian* roads were the sole possible avenues to knowledge. "Baconian," you must know, was an adjective invented as equivalent to Hogian and more euphonious and dignified.

Now, my dear friend, I do assure you, most positively, that I represent this matter fairly, on the soundest authority; and you can easily understand how a notion so absurd on its very face must have operated to retard the progress of all true knowledge—which makes its advances almost invariably by intuitive bounds. The ancient idea confined investigation to *crawling;* and for hundreds of years so great was the infatuation about Hog especially, that a virtual end was put to all thinking properly so called. No man dared utter a truth to which he felt himself indebted to his *Soul* alone. It mattered not whether the truth was even *demonstrably* a truth, for the bullet-headed *savans* of the time regarded only *the road* by which he had attained it. They would not even *look* at the end. "Let us see the means," they cried, "the means!" If, upon investigation of the means, it was found to come neither under the category Aries (that is to say Ram) nor under the category Hog, why then the *savans* went no farther, but pronounced the "theorist" a fool, and would have nothing to do with him or his truth.

Now, it cannot be maintained, even, that by the crawling system the greatest amount of truth would be attained in any long series of ages, for the repression of *imagination* was an evil not to be compensated for by any superior *certainty* in the ancient modes of investigation. The error of these Jurmains, these Vrinch, these Inglitch and these Amriccans, (the later, by the way, were our own immediate progenitors,) was an error quite analogous with that of the wiseacre who fancies that he must necessarily see an object the better the more closely he holds it to his eyes. These people blinded themselves by details. When they proceeded Hoggishly, their "facts" were by no means always facts—a matter of little consequence had it not been for assuming that they *were* facts and must be facts because they appeared to be such. When they proceeded on the path of the Ram, their course was scarcely as straight as a ram's horn, for they *never had* an axiom which was an axiom at all. They must have been very blind not to see this, even in their own day; for even in their own day many of the long "established" axioms had been rejected. For example—*"Ex nihilo nihil fit;"* "a body cannot act where it is not;" "there cannot exist antipodes;" "darkness cannot come out of light"—all these, and a dozen other similar propositions, formerly admitted without hesitation as axioms, were, even at the period of which I speak, seen to be untenable. How absurd in these people, then, to persist in putting faith in "axioms" as immutable bases of Truth! But even out of the mouths of their soundest reasoners it is easy to demonstrate the futility, the impalpability of their axioms in general. Who *was* the soundest of their logicians? Let me see! I will go and ask Pundit and be back in a minute . . . Ah, here we have it! Here is a book written nearly a thousand years ago and lately translated from the Inglitch—which, by the way, appears to have been the rudiment of the Amriccan. Pundit says it is decidedly the cleverest ancient work on its topic, Logic. The author (who was much thought of in his day) was one Miller, or Mill; and we find it recorded of him, as a point of some importance, that he had a mill-horse called Bentham. But let us glance at the treatise!

Ah!—"Ability or inability to conceive," says Mr. Mill, very properly, "is in no case to be received as a criterion of axiomatic truth." What *modern* in his senses would ever think of disputing this truism? The only wonder with us must be, how it happened that Mr. Mill conceived it necessary even to hint at any thing so obvious. So far good—but let us turn over another page. What have we here?—"Contradictories cannot both be true—that is, cannot co-exist in nature." Here Mr. Mill means, for example, that a tree must be either a tree or not a tree—that it cannot be at the same time a tree and not a tree. Very well; but I ask him *why*. His reply is this—and never pretends to be any thing else than this—"Because it is impossible to conceive that contradictories can both be true." But this is no answer at all, by his own showing; for has he not just admitted as a truism that "ability or inability to conceive is *in no case* to be received as a criterion of axiomatic truth."

Now I do not complain of these ancients so much because their logic is, by their own showing, utterly baseless, worthless and fantastic altogether, as because of their pompous and imbecile proscription of all *other* roads of Truth, of all *other* means for its attainment than the two preposterous paths—the one of creeping and the one of crawling—to which they have dared to confine the Soul that loves nothing so well as to *soar*.

By the by, my dear friend, do you not think it would have puzzled these ancient dogmaticians to have determined by *which* of their two roads it was that the most important and most sublime of *all* their truths was, in effect, attained? I mean the truth of Gravitation. Newton owed it to Kepler. Kepler admitted that his three laws were *guessed at*—these three laws of all laws which led the great Inglitch mathematician to his principle, the basis of all physical principle—to go behind which we must enter the Kingdom of Metaphysics. Kepler guessed—that is to say, *imagined*. He was essentially a "theorist"—that word now of so much sanctity, formerly an epithet of contempt. Would it not have puzzled these old moles, too, to have explained by which of the two "roads" a cryptographist unriddles a cryptograph of more than usual secrecy, or by which of the two roads Champollion directed mankind to those enduring and almost innumerable truths which resulted from his deciphering the Hieroglyphics?

One word more on this topic and I will be done boring you. Is it not *passing* strange that, with their eternal prating about *roads* to Truth, these bigoted people missed what we now so clearly perceive to be the great highway—that of Consistency? Does it not seem singular how they should have failed to deduce from the works of God the vital fact that a perfect consistency *must be* an absolute truth! How plain has been our progress since the late announcement of this proposition! Investigation has been taken out of the hands of the ground-moles and given, as a task, to the true and only true thinkers, the men of ardent imagination. These latter *theorize*. Can you not fancy the shout of scorn with which my words would be received by our progenitors were it possible for them to be now looking over my shoulder? These men, I say, *theorize;* and their theories are simply corrected, reduced, systematized—cleared, little by little, of their dross of inconsistency— until, finally, a perfect consistency stands apparent which even the most stolid admit, because it *is* a consistency, to be an absolute and an unquestionable *truth*.

April 4.—The new gas is doing wonders, in conjunction with the new improvement with gutta percha. How very safe, commodious, manageable, and in every respect convenient are our modern balloons! Here is an immense one approaching us at the rate of at least a hundred and fifty miles an hour. It seems to be crowded with people—perhaps there are three or four hundred passengers—and yet it soars to an elevation of nearly a mile, looking down upon poor us with sovereign contempt.

Still a hundred or even two hundred miles an hour is slow traveling, after all. *Do you remember our flight on the railroad across the Kanadaw continent?*—fully three hundred miles the hour—*that* was traveling. Nothing to be seen, though—nothing to be done but flirt, feast and dance in the magnificent saloons. Do you remember what an odd sensation was experienced when, by chance, we caught a glimpse of external objects while the cars were in full flight? Everything seemed unique—in one mass. For my part, I cannot say but that I preferred the traveling by the slow train of a hundred miles the hour. Here we were permitted to have glass windows— even to have them open—and something like a distinct view of the country was attainable.... Pundit says that *the route* for the great Kanadaw railroad must have been in some measure marked out about nine hundred years ago! In fact, he goes so far as to assert that actual traces of a road are still discernible—traces referable to a period quite as remote as that mentioned. The track, it appears, was *double* only; ours, you know, has twelve paths; and three or four new ones are in preparation. The ancient rails were very slight, and placed so close together as to be, according to modern notions, quite frivolous, if not dangerous in the extreme. The present width of track—fifty feet—is considered, indeed, scarcely secure enough. For my part, I make no doubt that a track of some sort *must* have existed in very remote times, as Pundit asserts; for nothing can be clearer, to my mind, than that, at some period—not less than seven centuries ago, certainly—the Northern and Southern Kanadaw continents were *united;* the Kanawdians, then, would have been driven, by necessity, to a great railroad across the continent.

April 5.—I am almost devoured by *ennui.* Pundit is the only conversible person on board; and he, poor soul! can speak of nothing but antiquities. He has been occupied all the day in the attempt to convince me that the ancient Amriccans *governed themselves!*—did ever anybody hear of such an absurdity?—that they existed in a sort of every-man-for-himself confederacy, after the fashion of the "prairie dogs" that we read of in fable. He says that they started with the queerest idea conceivable, viz: that all men are born free and equal—this in the very teeth of the laws of *gradation* so visibly impressed upon all things both in the moral and physical universe. Every man "voted," as they called it—that is to say, meddled with public affairs—until, at length, it was discovered that what is everybody's business is nobody's, and that the "Republic" (so the absurd thing was called) was without a government at all. It is related, however, that the first circumstance which disturbed, very particularly, the self-complacency of the philosophers who constructed this "Republic," was the startling discovery that universal suffrage gave opportunity for fraudulent schemes, by means of which any desired number of votes might at any time be polled, without the possibility of prevention or even detection, by any party which should be merely villainous enough not to be ashamed of the fraud. A little reflection upon this discovery sufficed to render evident the consequences, which were that rascality *must* predominate—in a word, that a republican government *could* never be anything but a rascally one. While the philosophers, however, were busied in blushing at their stupidity in not having foreseen these inevitable evils, and intent upon the invention of new theories, the matter was put to an abrupt issue by a fellow of the name of *Mob*, who took everything into his own hands and set up a despotism, in comparison with which those of the fabulous Zeros and Hellofagabaluses were respectable and delectable. This Mob (a foreigner, by the by), is said to have been the most odious of all men that ever encumbered the earth. He was a giant in stature—insolent, rapacious, filthy; had the gall of a bullock with the heart of a hyena and the brains of a peacock. He died, at length, by dint of his own energies, which exhausted him. Nevertheless, he had his uses, as everything has, however vile, and taught mankind a lesson which to this day it is in no danger of forgetting—never to run directly contrary to the natural analogies. As for Republicanism, no analogy could be found for it upon the face of the earth—unless we except the case of the "prairie dogs," an exception which seems to demonstrate, if anything, that democracy is a very admirable form of government—for dogs.

April 6.—Last night had a fine view of Alpha Lyræ, whose disk, through our captain's spy-glass, subtends an angle of half a degree, looking very much as our sun does to the naked eye on a misty day. Alpha Lyræ, although so *very* much larger than our sun, by the by, resembles him closely as regards its spots, its atmosphere, and in many other particulars. It is only within the last century, Pundit tells me, that the binary relation existing between these two orbs began even to be suspected. The evident motion of our system in the heavens was (strange to say!) referred to an orbit about a prodigious star in the center of the galaxy. About this star, or at all events about a center of gravity common to all the globes of the Milky Way and supposed to be near Alcyome in the Pleiades, every one of these globes was declared to be revolving, our own performing the circuit in a period of 117,000,000 of years! *We*, with our present lights, our vast telescopic improvements and so forth, of course find it difficult to comprehend *the ground* of an idea such as this. Its first propagator was one Mudler. He was led, we must presume, to this wild hypothesis by mere analogy in the first instance; but, this being the case, he should have at least adhered to analogy in its development. A great central orb *was*, in fact, suggested; so far Mudler was consistent. This central orb, however, dynamically, should have been greater than all its surrounding orbs taken together. The question might then have been asked—"Why do we not see it?"—*we*, especially, who occupy the mid region of the cluster—the very locality *near* which, at least, must be situated this inconceivable central sun. The astronomer, perhaps, at this point, took refuge in the suggestion of non-luminosity; and here analogy was suddenly let fall. But even admitting the central orb non-luminous, how did he manage to explain its failure to be rendered visible by the incalculable host of glorious suns glaring in all directions about it? No doubt what he finally maintained was merely a center of gravity common to all the revolving orbs—but here again analogy must have been let fall. Our system revolves, it is true, about a common center of gravity, but it does this in connection with and in consequence of a material sun whose mass more than counterbalances the rest of the system. The mathematical circle is a curve composed of an infinity of straight lines; but this idea of the circle—this idea of it which, in regard to all earthly geometry, we consider as merely the mathematical, in contradistinction from the practical, idea— is, in sober fact, the *practical* conception which alone we have any right to entertain in respect to those Titanic circles with which we have to deal, at least in fancy, when we suppose our system, with its fellows, revolving about a point in the center of the galaxy. Let the most vigorous of human imaginations but attempt to take a single step towards the comprehension of a circuit so unutterable! It would scarcely be paradoxical to say that a flash of lightning itself, traveling *forever* upon the circumference of this inconceivable circle, would still *forever* be traveling in a straight line. That the path of our sun along such a circumference—that the direction of our system in such an orbit—would, to any human perception, deviate in the slightest degree from a straight line even in a million years, is a proposition not to be entertained; and yet these ancient astronomers were absolutely cajoled, it appears, into believing that a decisive curvature had become apparent during the brief period of their astronomical history—during the mere point—during the utter nothingness of two or three thousand years! How incomprehensible, that considerations such as this did not at once indicate to them the true state of affairs—that of the binary revolution of our sun and Alpha Lyræ around a common center of gravity!

April 7.—Continued last night our astronomical amusements. Had a fine view of the five Nepturian asteroids, and watched with much interest the putting up of a huge impost on a couple of lintels in the new temple at Daphnis in the moon. It was amusing to think that creatures so diminutive as the lunarians, and bearing so little resemblance to humanity, yet evinced a mechanical ingenuity so much superior to our own. One finds it difficult, too, to conceive the vast masses which these people handle so easily, to be as light as our reason tells us they actually are.

April 8.—Eureka! Pundit is in his glory. A balloon from Kanadaw spoke to us today and threw on board several late papers: they contain some exceedingly curious information relative to Kanawdian or rather to Amriccan antiquities. You know, I presume, that laborers have for some months been employed in preparing the ground for a new fountain at Paradise, the emperor's principal pleasure garden. Paradise, it appears, has been, *literally* speaking, an island time out of mind—that is to say, its northern boundary was always (as far back as any records extend) a rivulet, or rather a very narrow arm of the sea. This arm was gradually widened until it attained its present breadth—a mile. The whole length of the island is nine miles; the breadth varies materially. The entire area (so Pundit says) was, about eight hundred years ago, densely packed with houses, some of them twenty stories high; land (for some most unaccountable reason) being considered as especially precious just in this vicinity. The disastrous earthquake, however, of the year 2050, so totally uprooted and overwhelmed the town (for it was almost too large to be called a village) that the most indefatigable of our antiquarians have never yet been able to obtain from the site any sufficient date (in the shape of coins, medals or inscriptions) wherewith to build up even the ghost of a theory concerning the manners, customs, &c. &c. &c., of the aboriginal inhabitants. Nearly all that we have hitherto known of them is, that they were a portion of the Knickerbocker tribe of savages infesting the continent at its first discovery by Recorder Riker, a knight of the Golden Fleece. They were by no means uncivilized, however, but cultivated various arts and even sciences after a fashion of their own. It is related of them that they were acute in many respects, but were oddly afflicted with a monomania for building what, in the ancient Amriccan, was denominated "churches"—a kind of pagoda instituted for the worship of two idols that went by the names of Wealth and Fashion. In the end, it is said, the island became, nine-tenths of it, church. The women, too, it appears, were oddly deformed by a natural protuberance of the region just below the small of the back—although, most unaccountably, this deformity was looked upon altogether in the light of a beauty. One or two pictures of these singular women have, in fact, been miraculously preserved. They look very odd, *very*— like something between a turkey-cock and a dromedary.

Well, these few details are nearly all that have descended to us respecting the ancient Knickerbockers. It seems, however, that while digging in the center of the emperor's garden, (which, you know, covers the whole island,) some of the workmen unearthed a cubical and evidently chiseled block of granite, weighing several hundred pounds. It was in good preservation, having received, apparently, little injury from the convulsion which entombed it. On one of its surfaces was a marble slab with (only think of it!) *an inscription—a legible inscription*. Pundit is in ecstasies. Upon detaching the slab, a cavity appeared, containing a leaden box filled with various coins, a long scroll of names, several documents which appear to resemble newspapers, with other matters of intense interest to the antiquarian! There can be no doubt that all these are genuine Amriccan relics belonging to the tribe called Knickerbocker. The papers thrown on board our balloon are filled with fac-similes of the coins, MSS., typography, &c. &c. I copy for your amusement the Knickerbocker inscription on the marble slab:—

> THIS CORNER STONE OF A MONUMENT TO THE
> MEMORY OF
> ### GEORGE WASHINGTON,
> WAS LAID WITH APPROPRIATE CEREMONIES ON THE
> 19TH DAY OF OCTOBER, 1847,
> THE ANNIVERSARY OF THE SURRENDER OF
> LORD CORNWALLIS
> TO GENERAL WASHINGTON AT YORKTOWN,
> A. D. 1781,
> UNDER THE AUSPICES OF THE
> WASHINGTON MONUMENT ASSOCIATION OF THE
> CITY OF NEW YORK

This, as I give it, is a verbatim translation done by Pundit himself, so there *can* be no mistake about it. From the few words thus preserved, we glean several important items of knowledge, not the least interesting of which is the fact that a thousand years ago *actual* monuments had fallen into disuse—as was all very proper—the people contenting themselves, as we do now, with a mere indication of the design to erect a monument at some future time; a corner-stone being cautiously laid by itself "solitary and alone" (excuse me for quoting the great Amriccan poet Benton!) as a guarantee of the magnanimous *intention*. We ascertain, too, very distinctly, from this admirable inscription, the how, as well as the where and the what, of the great surrender in question. As to the *where*, it was Yorktown (wherever that was), and as to the *what*, it was General Cornwallis (no doubt some wealthy dealer in corn). *He* was surrendered. The inscription commemorates the surrender of—what?—why, "of Lord Cornwallis." The only question is what could the savages wish him surrendered for. But when we remember that these savages were undoubtedly cannibals, we are led to the conclusion that they intended him for sausage. As to the *how* of the surrender, no language can be more explicit. Lord Cornwallis was surrendered (for sausage) "under the auspices of the Washington Monument Association"—no doubt a charitable institution for the depositing of corner-stones.—But, Heaven bless me! what is the matter? Ah! I see—the balloon has collapsed, and we shall have a tumble into the sea. I have, therefore, only time enough to add that, from a hasty inspection of fac-similes of newspapers, &c., I find that *the* great men in those days among the Amriccans were one John, a smith, and one Zacchary, a tailor.

Good bye, until I see you again. Whether you ever get this letter or not is a point of little importance, as I write altogether for my own amusement. I shall cork the MS. up in a bottle however, and throw it into the sea.

Yours everlastingly,
PUNDITA.

JULES VERNE

In the Year 2889

*One of the great "fathers" of modern science fiction, Jules Verne (1828-1903) is well
known to contemporary readers as the author of such classics as* Twenty Thousand Leagues
under the Sea *(1873),* From the Earth to the Moon *(1874),* Five Weeks in a Balloon *(1869),*
A Journey to the Center of the Earth *and many others. The film versions of these and other
of his books range from adequate to awful, but they have helped to keep his work alive.
Verne is an excellent example of a writer who began by viewing science as a servant of man
but who later began to express doubts about man's abilities to control his own creations.*

LITTLE THOUGH they seem to think of it, the people of this twenty-ninth
century live continually in fairyland. Surfeited as they are with marvels, they
are indifferent in presence of each new marvel. To them all seems natural.
Could they but duly appreciate the refinements of civilization in our day; could
they but compare the present with the past, and so better comprehend the advance
we have made! How much fairer they would find our modern towns, with populations amounting sometimes to 10,000,000 souls; their streets 300 feet wide, their
houses 100 feet in height; with a temperature the same in all seasons; with their
lines of aerial locomotion crossing the sky in every direction! If they would but
picture to themselves the state of things that once existed, when through muddy
streets rumbling boxes on wheels, drawn by horses—yes, by horses!—were the
only means of conveyance. Think of the railroads of the olden time, and you will
be able to appreciate the pneumatic tubes through which to-day one travels at the
rate of 100 miles an hour. Would not our contemporaries prize the telephone and
the telephote more highly if they had not forgotten the telegraph?

Singularly enough, all these transformations rest upon principles which were
perfectly familiar to our remote ancestors, but which they disregarded. Heat, for
instance, is as ancient as man himself; electricity was known 3000 years ago, and
steam 1100 years ago. Nay, so early as ten centuries ago it was known that the
differences between the several chemical and physical forces depend on the mode
of vibration of the etheric particles, which is for each specifically different. When
at last the kinship of all these forces was discovered, it is simply astounding that
500 years should still have to elapse before men could analyze and describe the

21

several modes of vibration that constitute these differences. Above all, it is singular that the mode of reproducing these forces directly from one another, and of reproducing one without the others, should have remained undiscovered till less than a hundred years ago. Nevertheless, such was the course of events, for it was not till the year 2792 that the famous Oswald Nier made this great discovery.

Truly was he a great benefactor of the human race. His admirable discovery led to many another. Hence is sprung a pleiad of inventors, its brightest star being our great Joseph Jackson. To Jackson we are indebted for those wonderful instruments— the new accumulators. Some of these absorb and condense the living force contained in the sun's rays; others, the electricity stored in our globe; others again, the energy coming from whatever source, as a waterfall, a stream, the winds, etc. He, too, it was that invented the transformer, a more wonderful contrivance still, which takes the living force from the accumulator, and, on the simple pressure of a button, gives it back to space in whatever form may be desired, whether as heat, light, electricity or mechanical force, after having first obtained from it the work required. From the day when these two instruments were contrived is to be dated the era of true progress. They have put into the hands of man a power that is almost infinite. As for their applications, they are numberless. Mitigating the rigors of winter, by giving back to the atmosphere the surplus heat stored up during the summer, they had revolutionized agriculture. By supplying motive power for aerial navigation, they have given to commerce a mighty impetus. To them we are indebted for the continuous production of electricity without batteries or dynamos, of light without combustion or incandescence and for an unfailing supply of mechanical energy for all the needs of industry.

Yes, all these wonders have been wrought by the accumulator and the transformer. And can we not to them also trace, indirectly, this latest wonder of all, the great "Earth Chronicle" building in 253rd Avenue, which was dedicated the other day? If George Washington Smith, the founder of the Manhattan "Chronicle," should come back to life today, what would he think were he to be told that this palace of marble and gold belongs to his remote descendant, Fritz Napoleon Smith, who, after thirty generations have come and gone, is owner of the same newspaper which his ancestor established!

For George Washington Smith's newspaper has lived generation after generation, now passing out of the family, anon coming back to it. When, 200 years ago, the political center of the United States was transferred from Washington to Centropolis, the newspaper followed the government and assumed the name of Earth Chronicle. Unfortunately, it was unable to maintain itself at the high level of its name. Pressed on all sides by rival journals of a more modern type, it was continually in danger of collapse. Twenty years ago its subscription list contained but a few hundred thousand names, and then Mr. Fritz Napoleon Smith bought it for a mere trifle, and originated telephonic journalism.

Every one is familiar with Fritz Napoleon Smith's system—a system made possible by the enormous development of telephony during the last hundred years. Instead of being printed, the Earth Chronicle is every morning spoken to subscribers, who, in interesting conversations with reporters, statesmen and scientists, learn the news of the day. Furthermore, each subscriber owns a phonograph, and to this instrument he leaves the task of gathering the news whenever he happens not to be in a mood to listen directly himself. As for purchasers of single copies, they can at a very trifling cost learn all that is in the paper of the day at any of the innumerable phonographs set up nearly everywhere.

Fritz Napoleon Smith's innovation galvanized the old newspaper. In the course of a few years the number of subscribers grew to be 85,000,000 and Smith's wealth went on growing, till now it reaches the almost unimaginable figure of $10,000,000,000. This lucky hit has enabled him to erect his new building, a vast edifice with four *façades*, each 3,250 feet in length, over which proudly floats the hundred-starred flag of the Union. Thanks to the same lucky hit, he is to-day king of newspaperdom; indeed, he would be king of all the Americans, too, if Americans could ever accept a king. You do not believe it? Well, then, look at the plenipotentiaries of all nations and our own ministers themselves crowding about his door, entreating his counsels, begging for his approbation, imploring the aid of his all-powerful organ. Reckon up the number of scientists and artists that he supports, of inventors that he has under his pay.

Yes, a king is he. And in truth his is a royalty full of burdens. His labors are incessant, and there is no doubt at all that in earlier times any man would have succumbed under the overpowering stress of the toil which Mr. Smith has to perform. Very fortunately for him, thanks to the progress of hygiene, which, abating all the old sources of unhealthfulness, has lifted the mean of human life from 37 up to 52 years, men have stronger constitutions now than heretofore. The discovery of nutritive air is still in the future, but in the meantime men to-day consume food that is compounded and prepared according to scientific principles, and they breathe an atmosphere freed from the microorganisms that formerly used to swarm in it; hence they live longer than their forefathers and know nothing of the innumerable diseases of olden times.

Nevertheless, and notwithstanding these considerations, Fritz Napoleon Smith's mode of life may well astonish one. His iron constitution is taxed to the utmost by the heavy strain that is put upon it. Vain the attempt to estimate the amount of labor he undergoes; an example alone can give an idea of it. Let us then go about with him for one day as he attends to his multifarious concernments. What day? That matters little; it is the same every day. Let us then take at random September 25th of this present year 2889.

This morning Mr. Fritz Napoleon Smith awoke in very bad humor. His wife having left for France eight days ago, he was feeling disconsolate. Incredible though it seems, in all the ten years since their marriage, this is the first time that Mrs. Edith Smith, the professional beauty, has been so long absent from home; two or three days usually suffice for her frequent trips to Europe. The first thing that Mr. Smith does is to connect his phonotelephote, the wires of which communicate with his Paris mansion. The telephote! Here is another of the great triumphs of science in our time. The transmission of speech is an old story; the transmission of images by means of sensitive mirrors connected by wires is a thing but of yesterday. A valuable invention indeed, and Mr. Smith this morning was not niggard of blessings for the inventor, when by its aid he was able distinctly to see his wife notwithstanding the distance that separated him from her. Mrs. Smith, weary after the ball or the visit to the theater the preceding night, is still abed, though it is near noontide at Paris. She is asleep, her head sunk in the lace-covered pillows. What? She stirs? Her lips move. She is dreaming perhaps? Yes, dreaming. She is talking, pronouncing a name — his name — Fritz! The delightful vision gave a happier turn to Mr. Smith's thoughts. And now, at the call of imperative duty, light-hearted he springs from his bed and enters his mechanical dresser.

Two minutes later the machine deposited him all dressed at the threshold of his office. The round of journalistic work was now begun. First he enters the hall of the novel-writers, a vast apartment crowned with an enormous transparent cupola. In one corner is a telephone, through which a hundred Earth Chronicle *littérateurs* in turn recount to the public in daily installments a hundred novels. Addressing one of these authors who was waiting his turn, "Capital! Capital! my dear fellow," said he, "your last story. The scene where the village maid discusses interesting philosophical problems with her lover shows your very acute power of observation. Never have the ways of country folk been better portrayed. Keep on, my dear Archibald, keep on! Since yesterday, thanks to you, there is a gain of 5000 subscribers."

"Mr. John Last," he began again, turning to a new arrival, "I am not so well pleased with your work. Your story is not a picture of life; it lacks the elements of truth. And why? Simply because you run straight on to the end; because you do not analyze. Your heroes do this thing or that from this or that motive, which you assign without ever a thought of dissecting their mental and moral natures. Our feelings, you must remember, are far more complex than all that. In real life every act is the resultant of a hundred thoughts that come and go, and these you must study, each by itself, if you would create a living character. 'But,' you will say, 'in order to note these fleeting thoughts one must know them, must be able to follow them in their capricious meanderings.' Why, any child can do that, as you know. You have simply to make use of hypnotism, electrical or human, which gives one a two-fold being, setting free the witness-personality so that it may see, understand and remember the reasons which determine the personality that acts. Just study yourself as you live from day to day, my dear Last. Imitate your associate whom I was complimenting a moment ago. Let yourself be hypnotized. What's that? You have tried it already? Not sufficiently, then, not sufficiently!"

Mr. Smith continues his round and enters the reporters' hall. Here 1500 reporters, in their respective places, facing an equal number of telephones, are communicating to the subscribers the news of the world as gathered during the night. The organization of this matchless service has often been described. Besides his telephone, each reporter, as the reader is aware, has in front of him a set of commutators, which enable him to communicate with any desired telephotic line. Thus the subscribers not only hear the news but see the occurrences. When an incident is described that is already past, photographs of its main features are transmitted with the narrative. And there is no confusion withal. The reporters' items, just like the different stories and all the other component parts of the journal, are classified automatically according to an ingenious system, and reach the hearer in due succession. Furthermore, the hearers are free to listen only to what specially concerns them. They may at pleasure give attention to one editor and refuse it to another.

Mr. Smith next addresses one of the ten reporters in the astronomical department—a department still in the embryonic stage, but which will yet play an important part in journalism.

"Well, Cash, what's the news?"

"We have phototelegrams from Mercury, Venus and Mars."

"Are those from Mars of any interest?"

"Yes, indeed. There is a revolution in the Central Empire."

"And what of Jupiter?" asked Mr. Smith.

"Nothing as yet. We cannot quite understand their signals. Perhaps ours do not reach them."

"That's bad," exclaimed Mr. Smith, as he hurried away, not in the best of humor, toward the hall of the scientific editors. With their heads bent down over their electric computers, thirty scientific men were absorbed in transcendental calculations. The coming of Mr. Smith was like the falling of a bomb among them.

"Well, gentlemen, what is this I hear? No answer from Jupiter? Is it always to be thus? Come, Cooley, you have been at work now twenty years on this problem, and yet——"

"True enough," replied the man addressed. "Our science of optics is still very defective, and though our mile-and-three-quarter telescopes——"

"Listen to that, Peer," broke in Mr. Smith, turning to a second scientist. "Optical science defective! Optical science is your specialty. But," he continued, again addressing William Cooley, "failing with Jupiter, are we getting any results from the moon?"

"The case is no better there."

"This time you do not lay the blame on the science of optics. The moon is immeasurably less distant than Mars, yet with Mars our communication is fully established. I presume you will not say that you lack telescopes?"

"Telescopes? Oh no, the trouble here is about—inhabitants!"

"That's it," added Peer.

"So, then, the moon is positively uninhabited?" asked Mr. Smith.

"At least," answered Cooley, "on the face which she presents to us. As for the opposite side, who knows?"

"Ah, the opposite side! You think, then," remarked Mr. Smith, musingly, "that if one could but——"

"Could what?"

"Why, turn the moon about-face."

"Ah, there's something in that," cried the two men at once. And indeed, so confident was their air, they seemed to have no doubt as to the possibility of success in such an undertaking.

"Meanwhile," asked Mr. Smith, after a moment's silence, "have you no news of interest to-day?"

"Indeed we have," answered Cooley. "The elements of Olympus are definitely settled. That great planet gravitates beyond Neptune at the mean distance of 11,400,799,642 miles from the sun, and to traverse its vast orbit takes 1311 years, 294 days, 12 hours, 43 minutes, 9 seconds."

"Why didn't you tell me that sooner?" cried Mr. Smith. "Now inform the reporters of this straightway. You know how eager is the curiosity of the public with regard to these astronomical questions. That news must go into to-day's issue."

Then, the two men bowing to him, Mr. Smith passed into the next hall, an enormous gallery upward of 3200 feet in length, devoted to atmospheric advertising. Every one has noticed those enormous advertisements reflected from the clouds, so large that they may be seen by the populations of whole cities or even of entire countries. This, too, is one of Mr. Fritz Napoleon Smith's ideas, and in the Earth Chronicle building a thousand projectors are constantly engaged in displaying upon the clouds these mammoth advertisements.

When Mr. Smith to-day entered the sky-advertising department, he found the operators sitting with folded arms at their motionless projectors, and inquired as to the cause of their inaction. In response, the man addressed simply pointed to the sky, which was of a pure blue. "Yes," muttered Mr. Smith, "a cloudless sky! That's too bad, but what's to be done? Shall we produce rain? That we might do, but is it of any use? What we need is clouds, not rain. Go," said he, addressing the head engineer, "go see Mr. Samuel Mark, of the meteorological division of the scientific department, and tell him for me to go to work in earnest on the question of artificial clouds. It will never do for us to be always thus at the mercy of cloudless skies!"

Mr. Smith's daily tour through the several departments of his newspaper is now finished. Next, from the advertisement hall he passes to the reception chamber, where the ambassadors accredited to the American government are awaiting him, desirous of having a word of counsel or advice from the all-powerful editor. A discussion was going on when he entered. "Your Excellency will pardon me," the French Ambassador was saying to the Russian, "but I see nothing in the map of Europe that requires change. 'The North for the Slavs?' Why, yes, of course; but the South for the Latins. Our common frontier, the Rhine, it seems to me, serves very well. Besides, my government, as you must know, will firmly oppose every movement, not only against Paris, our capital, or our two great prefectures, Rome and Madrid, but also against the kingdom of Jerusalem, the dominion of Saint Peter, of which France means to be the trusty defender."

"Well said!" exclaimed Mr. Smith. "How is it," he asked, turning to the Russian ambassador, "that you Russians are not content with your vast empire, the most extensive in the world, stretching from the banks of the Rhine to the Celestial Mountains and the Kara-Korum, whose shores are washed by the Frozen Ocean, the Atlantic, the Mediterranean and the Indian Ocean? Then, what is the use of threats? Is war possible in view of modern inventions—asphyxiating shells capable of being projected a distance of 60 miles, an electric spark of 90 miles, that can at one stroke annihilate a battalion; to say nothing of the plague, the cholera, the yellow fever, that the belligerents might spread among their antagonists mutually, and which would in a few days destroy the greatest armies?"

"True," answered the Russian, "but can we do all that we wish? As for us Russians, pressed on our eastern frontier by the Chinese, we must at any cost put forth our strength for an effort toward the west."

"Oh, is that all? In that case," said Mr. Smith, "the thing can be arranged. I will speak to the Secretary of State about it. The attention of the Chinese government shall be called to the matter. This is not the first time that the Chinese have bothered us."

"Under these conditions, of course——" And the Russian ambassador declared himself satisfied.

"Ah, Sir John, what can I do for you?" asked Mr. Smith as he turned to the representative of the people of Great Britain, who till now had remained silent.

"A great deal," was the reply. "If the Earth Chronicle would but open a campaign on our behalf——"

"And for what object?"

"Simply for the annulment of the Act of Congress annexing to the United States the British islands."

Though, by a just turn-about of things here below, Great Britain has become a colony of the United States, the English are not yet reconciled to the situation. At regular intervals they are ever addressing to the American government vain complaints.

"A campaign against the annexation that has been an accomplished fact for 150 years!" exclaimed Mr. Smith. "How can your people suppose that I would do anything so unpatriotic?"

"We at home think that your people must now be sated. The Monroe Doctrine is fully applied; the whole of America belongs to the Americans. What more do you want? Besides, we will pay for what we ask."

"Indeed!" answered Mr. Smith, without manifesting the slightest irritation. "Well, you English will ever be the same. No, no, Sir John, do not count on me for help. Give up our fairest province, Britain? Why not ask France generously to renounce possession of Africa, that magnificent colony the complete conquest of which cost her the labor of 800 years? You will be well received!"

"You decline! All is over then!" murmured the British agent sadly. "The United Kingdom falls to the share of the Americans; the Indies to that of——"

"The Russians," said Mr. Smith, completing the sentence.

"Australia——"

"Has an independent government."

"Then nothing at all remains for us!" sighed Sir John, downcast.

"Nothing?" asked Mr. Smith, laughing. "Well, now, there's Gibraltar!"

With this sally the audience ended. The clock was striking twelve, the hour of breakfast. Mr. Smith returns to his chamber. Where the bed stood in the morning a table all spread comes up through the floor. For Mr. Smith, being above all a practical man, has reduced the problem of existence to its simplest terms. For him, instead of the endless suites of apartments of the olden time, one room fitted with ingenious mechanical contrivances is enough. Here he sleeps, takes his meals, in short, lives.

He seats himself. In the mirror of the phonotelephote is seen the same chamber at Paris which appeared in it this morning. A table furnished forth is likewise in readiness here, for notwithstanding the difference of hours, Mr. Smith and his wife have arranged to take their meals simultaneously. It is delightful thus to take breakfast *tête-à-tête* with one who is 3000 miles or so away. Just now, Mrs. Smith's chamber has no occupant.

"She is late! Woman's punctuality! Progress everywhere except there!" muttered Mr. Smith as he turned the tap for the first dish. For like all wealthy folk in our day, Mr. Smith has done away with the domestic kitchen and is a subscriber to the Grand Alimentation Company, which sends through a great network of tubes to subscribers' residences all sorts of dishes, as a varied assortment is always in readiness. A subscription costs money, to be sure, but the *cuisine* is of the best, and the system has this advantage, that it does away with the pestering race of the *cordons-bleus*. Mr. Smith received and ate, all alone, the *hors-d'œuvre, entrées, rôti*, and *legumes* that constituted the repast. He was just finishing the dessert when Mrs. Smith appeared in the mirror of the telephote.

"Why, where have you been?" asked Mr. Smith through the telephone.

"What! You are already at the dessert? Then I am late," she exclaimed, with a winsome *naïveté*. "Where have I been, you ask? Why, at my dress-maker's. The hats are just lovely this season! I suppose I forgot to note the time, and so am a little late."

"Yes, a little," growled Mr. Smith; "so little that I have already quite finished breakfast. Excuse me if I leave you now, but I must be going."

"Oh certainly, my dear; good-by till evening."

Smith stepped into his air-coach, which was in waiting for him at a window. "Where do you wish to go, sir?" inquired the coachman.

"Let me see; I have three hours," Mr. Smith mused. "Jack, take me to my accumulator works at Niagara."

For Mr. Smith has obtained a lease of the great falls of Niagara. For ages the energy developed by the falls went unutilized. Smith, applying Jackson's invention, now collects this energy, and lets or sells it. His visit to the works took more time than he had anticipated. It was four o'clock when he returned home, just in time for the daily audience which he grants to callers.

One readily understands how a man situated as Smith is must be beset with requests of all kinds. Now it is an inventor needing capital; again it is some visionary who comes to advocate a brilliant scheme which must surely yield millions of profit. A choice has to be made between these projects, rejecting the worthless, examining the questionable ones, accepting the meritorious. To this work Mr. Smith devotes every day two full hours.

The callers were fewer to-day than usual—only twelve of them. Of these, eight had only impracticable schemes to propose. In fact, one of them wanted to revive painting, an art fallen into desuetude owing to the progress made in color-photography. Another, a physician, boasted that he had discovered a cure for nasal catarrh! These impracticables were dismissed in short order. Of the four projects favorably received, the first was that of a young man whose broad forehead betokened his intellectual power.

"Sir, I am a chemist," he began, "and as such I come to you."

"Well!"

"Once the elementary bodies," said the young chemist, "were held to be sixty-two in number; a hundred years ago they were reduced to ten; now only three remain irresolvable, as you are aware."

"Yes, yes."

"Well, sir, these also I will show to be composite. In a few months, a few weeks, I shall have succeeded in solving the problem. Indeed, it may take only a few days."

"And then?"

"Then, sir, I shall simply have determined the absolute. All I want is money enough to carry my research to a successful issue."

"Very well," said Mr. Smith. "And what will be the practical outcome of your discovery?"

"The practical outcome? Why, that we shall be able to produce easily all bodies whatever—stone, wood, metal, fibers——"

"And flesh and blood?" queried Mr. Smith, interrupting him. "Do you pretend that you expect to manufacture a human being out and out?"

"Why not?"

Mr. Smith advanced $100,000 to the young chemist, and engaged his services for the Earth Chronicle laboratory.

The second of the four successful applicants, starting from experiments made so long ago as the nineteenth century and again and again repeated, had conceived the idea of removing an entire city all at once from one place to another. His special project had to do with the city of Granton, situated, as everybody knows, some fifteen miles inland. He proposes to transport the city on rails and to change it into a watering-place. The profit, of course, would be enormous. Mr. Smith, captivated by the scheme, bought a half-interest in it.

"As you are aware, sir," began applicant No. 3, "by the aid of our solar and terrestrial accumulators and transformers, we are able to make all the seasons the same. I propose to do something better still. Transform into heat a portion of the surplus energy at our disposal; send this heat to the poles; then the polar regions, relieved of their snow-caps, will become a vast territory available for man's use. What think you of the scheme?"

"Leave your plans with me, and come back in a week. I will have them examined in the meantime."

Finally, the fourth announced the early solution of a weighty scientific problem. Every one will remember the bold experiment made a hundred years ago by Dr. Nathaniel Faithburn. The doctor, being a firm believer in human hibernation—in other words, in the possibility of our suspending our vital functions and of calling them into action again after a time—resolved to subject the theory to a practical test. To this end, having first made his last will and pointed out the proper method of awakening him; having also directed that his sleep was to continue a hundred years to a day from the date of his apparent death, he unhesitatingly put the theory to the proof in his own person. Reduced to the condition of a mummy, Dr. Faithburn was coffined and laid in a tomb. Time went on. September 25th, 2889, being the day set for his resurrection, it was proposed to Mr. Smith that he should permit the second part of the experiment to be performed at his residence this evening.

"Agreed. Be here at ten o'clock," answered Mr. Smith; and with that the day's audience was closed.

Left to himself, feeling tired, he lay down on an extension chair. Then, touching a knob, he established communication with the Central Concert Hall, whence our greatest *maestros* send out to subscribers their delightful successions of accords determined by recondite algebraic formulas. Night was approaching. Entranced by the harmony, forgetful of the hour, Smith did not notice that it was growing dark. It was quite dark when he was aroused by the sound of a door opening. "Who is there?" he asked, touching a commutator.

Suddenly, in consequence of the vibrations produced, the air became luminous.

"Ah! you, Doctor?"

"Yes," was the reply. "How are you?"

"I am feeling well."

"Good! Let me see your tongue. All right! Your pulse. Regular! And your appetite?"

"Only passably good."

"Yes, the stomach. There's the rub. You are over-worked. If your stomach is out of repair, it must be mended. That requires study. We must think about it."

"In the meantime," said Mr. Smith, "you will dine with me."

As in the morning, the table rose out of the floor. Again, as in the morning, the *potage, rôti, ragoûts* and *legumes* were supplied through the food-pipes. Toward the close of the meal, phonotelephotic communication was made with Paris. Smith saw his wife, seated alone at the dinner-table, looking anything but pleased at her loneliness.

"Pardon me, my dear, for having left you alone," he said through the telephone. "I was with Dr. Wilkins."

"Ah, the good doctor!" remarked Mrs. Smith, her countenance lighting up.

"Yes. But, pray, when are you coming home?"

"This evening."

"Very well. Do you come by tube or by air-train?"

"Oh, by tube."

"Yes; and at what hour will you arrive?"

"About eleven, I suppose."

"Eleven by Centropolis time, you mean?"

"Yes."

"Good-by, then, for a little while," said Mr. Smith as he severed communication with Paris.

Dinner over, Dr. Wilkins wished to depart. "I shall expect you at ten," said Mr. Smith. "To-day, it seems, is the day for the return to life of the famous Dr. Faithburn. You did not think of it, I suppose. The awakening is to take place here in my house. You must come and see. I shall depend on your being here."

"I will come back," answered Dr. Wilkins.

Left alone, Mr. Smith busied himself with examining his accounts—a task of vast magnitude, having to do with transactions which involve a daily expenditure of upward of $800,000. Fortunately, indeed, the stupendous progress of mechanic art in modern times makes it comparatively easy. Thanks to the Piano Electro-

Reckoner, the most complex calculations can be made in a few seconds. In two hours Mr. Smith completed his task. Just in time. Scarcely had he turned over the last page when Dr. Wilkins arrived. After him came the body of Dr. Faithburn, escorted by a numerous company of men of science. They commenced work at once. The casket being laid down in the middle of the room, the telephote was got in readiness. The outer world, already notified, was anxiously expectant, for the whole world could be eyewitnesses of the performance, a reporter meanwhile, like the chorus in the ancient drama, explaining it all *viva voce* through the telephone.

"They are opening the casket," he explained. "Now they are taking Faithburn out of it—a veritable mummy, yellow, hard and dry. Strike the body and it resounds like a block of wood. They are now applying heat; now electricity. No result. These experiments are suspended for a moment while Dr. Wilkins makes an examination of the body. Dr. Wilkins, rising, declares the man to be dead. 'Dead!' exclaims every one present. 'Yes,' answers Dr. Wilkins, 'dead!' 'And how long has he been dead?' Dr. Wilkins makes another examination. 'A hundred years,' he replies."

The case stood just as the reporter said. Faithburn was dead, quite certainly dead! "Here is a method that needs improvement," remarked Mr. Smith to Dr. Wilkins, as the scientific committee on hibernation bore the casket out. "So much for that experiment. But if poor Faithburn is dead, at least he is sleeping," he continued. "I wish I could get some sleep. I am tired out, Doctor, quite tired out! Do you not think that a bath would refresh me?"

"Certainly. But you must wrap yourself up well before you go out into the hall-way. You must not expose yourself to cold."

"Hall-way? Why, Doctor, as you well know, everything is done by machinery here. It is not for me to go to the bath; the bath will come to me. Just look!" and he pressed a button. After a few seconds a faint rumbling was heard, which grew louder and louder. Suddenly the door opened, and the tub appeared.

Such, for this year of grace 2889, is the history of one day in the life of the editor of the Earth Chronicle. And the history of that one day is the history of 365 days every year, except leap-years, and then of 366 days—for as yet no means has been found of increasing the length of the terrestrial year.

MARK TWAIN

Sold to Satan

Mark Twain (Samuel Clemens, 1835-1910) is surely among the most beloved of all American writers, a man whose books and stories have been translated into almost every major language in the world. While few people would consider the creator of Tom Sawyer *and* Huckleberry Finn *a science fiction writer, he did in fact write a great deal of both sf and fantasy, including such notable works as* A Connecticut Yankee in King Arthur's Court *(1889), one of the first book-length time-travel stories and one which had a profound influence on many other writers on the subject. In addition, many of his short stories, such as "The Curious Republic of Gondour," were science fiction. One of his great contributions to later sf was the incorporation of humor and satire into his stories, as in "Sold to Satan," one of his lesser-known and best works in the field.*

I T WAS at this time that I concluded to sell my soul to Satan. Steel was away down, so was St. Paul; it was the same with all the desirable stocks, in fact, and so, if I did not turn out to be away down myself, now was my time to raise a stake and make my fortune. Without further consideration I sent word to the local agent, Mr. Blank, with description and present condition of the property, and an interview with Satan was promptly arranged, on a basis of 2½ per cent, this commission payable only in case a trade should be consummated.

I sat in the dark, waiting and thinking. How still it was! Then came the deep voice of a far-off bell proclaiming midnight—Boom-m-m! Boom-m-m! Boom-m-m! —and I rose to receive my guest, and braced myself for the thunder crash and the brimstone stench which should announce his arrival. But there was no crash, no stench. Through the closed door, and noiseless, came the modern Satan, just as we see him on the stage—tall, slender, graceful, in tights and trunks, a short cape mantling his shoulders, a rapier at his side, a single drooping feather in his jaunty cap, and on his intellectual face the well-known and high-bred Mephistophelian smile.

But he was not a fire coal; he was not red, no! On the contrary. He was a softly glowing, richly smoldering torch, column, statue of pallid light, faintly tinted with a spiritual green, and out from him a lunar splendor flowed such as one sees glinting from the crinkled waves of tropic seas when the moon rides high in cloudless skies.

He made his customary stage obeisance, resting his left hand upon his sword

32

hilt and removing his cap with his right and making that handsome sweep with it which we know so well; then we sat down. Ah, he was an incandescent glory, a nebular dream, and so much improved by his change of color. He must have seen the admiration in my illuminated face, but he took no notice of it, being long ago used to it in faces of other Christians with whom he had had trade relations.

. . . A half hour of hot toddy and weather chat, mixed with occasional tentative feelers on my part and rejoinders of, "Well, I could hardly pay *that* for it, you know," on his, had much modified my shyness and put me so much at my ease that I was emboldened to feed my curiosity a little. So I chanced the remark that he was surprisingly different from the traditions, and I wished I knew what it was he was made of. He was not offended, but answered with frank simplicity:

"Radium!"

"That accounts for it!" I exclaimed. "It is the loveliest effulgence I have ever seen. The hard and heartless glare of the electric doesn't compare with it. I suppose Your Majesty weighs about—about—"

"I stand six feet one; fleshed and blooded I would weigh two hundred and fifteen; but radium, like other metals, is heavy. I weigh nine hundred-odd."

I gazed hungrily upon him, saying to myself:

"What riches! What a mine! Nine hundred pounds at, say, $3,500,000 a pound, would be—would be—" Then a treacherous thought burst into my mind!

He laughed a good hearty laugh, and said:

"I perceive your thought; and what a handsomely original idea it is!—to kidnap Satan, and stock him, and incorporate him, and water the stock up to ten billions—just three times its actual value—and blanket the world with it!" My blush had turned the moonlight to a crimson mist, such as veils and spectralizes the domes and towers of Florence at sunset and makes the spectator drunk with joy to see, and he pitied me, and dropped his tone of irony, and assumed a grave and reflective one which had a pleasanter sound for me, and under its kindly influence my pains were presently healed, and I thanked him for his courtesy. Then he said:

"One good turn deserves another, and I will pay you a compliment. Do you know I have been trading with your poor pathetic race for ages, and you are the first person who has ever been intelligent enough to divine the large commercial value of my make-up."

I purred to myself and looked as modest as I could.

"Yes, you are the first," he continued. "All through the Middle Ages I used to buy Christian souls at fancy rates, building bridges and cathedrals in a single night in return, and getting swindled out of my Christian nearly every time that I dealt with a priest—as history will concede—but making it up on the lay square-dealer now and then, as *I* admit; but none of those people ever guessed where the *real* big money lay. You are the first."

I refilled his glass and gave him another Cavour. But he was experienced, by this time. He inspected the cigar pensively awhile; then:

"What do you pay for these?" he asked.

"Two cents—but they come cheaper when you take a barrel."

He went on inspecting; also mumbling comments, apparently to himself:

"Black—rough-skinned—rumpled, irregular, wrinkled, barky, with crispy curled-up places on it—burnt-leather aspect, like the shoes of the damned that sit in pairs before the room doors at home of a Sunday morning." He sighed at thought of his home, and was silent a moment; then he said, gently, "Tell me about this projectile."

"It is the discovery of a great Italian statesman," I said. "Cavour. One day he lit his cigar, then laid it down and went on writing and forgot it. It lay in a pool of ink and got soaked. By and by he noticed it and laid it on the stove to dry. When it was dry he lit it and at once noticed that it didn't taste the same as it did before. And so—"

"Did he say what it tasted like before?"

"No, I think not. But he called the government chemist and told him to find out the source of that new taste, and report. The chemist applied the tests, and reported that the source was the presence of sulphate of iron, touched up and spiritualized with vinegar—the combination out of which one makes ink. Cavour told him to introduce the brand in the interest of the finances. So, ever since then this brand passes through the ink factory, with the great result that both the ink and the cigar suffer a sea change into something new and strange. This is history, Sire, not a work of the imagination."

So then he took up his present again, and touched it to the forefinger of his other hand for an instant, which made it break into flame and fragrance—but he changed his mind at that point and laid the torpedo down, saying courteously:

"With permission I will save it for Voltaire."

I was greatly pleased and flattered to be connected in even this little way with that great man and be mentioned to him, as no doubt would be the case, so I hastened to fetch a bundle of fifty for distribution among others of the renowned and lamented—Goethe, and Homer, and Socrates, and Confucius, and so on—but Satan said he had nothing against those. Then he dropped back into reminiscences of the old times once more, and presently said:

"They knew nothing about radium, and it would have had no value for them if they had known about it. In twenty million years it has had no value for your race until the revolutionizing steam-and-machinery age was born—which was only a few years before you were born yourself. It was a stunning little century, for sure, that nineteenth! But it's a poor thing compared to what the twentieth is going to be."

By request, he explained why he thought so.

"Because power was so costly, then, and everything goes by power—the steamship, the locomotive and everything else. Coal, you see! You have to have it; no steam and no electricity without it; and it's such a waste—for you burn it up, and it's gone! But radium—that's another matter! With my nine hundred pounds you could light the world, and heat it, and run all its ships and machines and railways a hundred million years, and not use up five pounds of it in the whole time! And then—"

"Quick—my soul is yours, dear Ancestor; take it—we'll start a company!"

But he asked my age, which is sixty-eight, then politely sidetracked the proposition, probably not wishing to take advantage of himself. Then he went on talking admiringly of radium, and how with its own natural and inherent heat it could go on melting its own weight of ice twenty-four times in twenty-four hours, and keep it up forever without losing bulk or weight; and how a pound of it, if exposed in this room, would blast the place like a breath from hell, and burn me to a crisp in a quarter of a minute—and was going on like that, but I interrupted and said:

"But *you* are here, Majesty—nine hundred pounds—and the temperature is balmy and pleasant. I don't understand."

"Well," he said, hesitatingly, "it is a secret, but I may as well reveal it, for these prying and impertinent chemists are going to find it out sometime or other, anyway. Perhaps you have read what Madame Curie says about radium; how she goes searching among its splendid secrets and seizes upon one after another of them and italicizes its specialty; how she says 'the compounds of radium are *spontaneously luminous*'—require no coal in the production of light, you see; how she says, 'a glass vessel containing radium *spontaneously charges itself with electricity*'—no coal or water power required to generate it, you see; how she says 'radium possesses the remarkable property of *liberating heat spontaneously and continuously*'—no coal required to fire-up on the world's machinery, you see. She ransacks the pitch-blende for its radioactive substances, and captures three and labels them; one, which is embodied with bismuth, she names polonium; one, which is embodied with barium, she names radium; the name given to the third was actinium. Now listen; she says '*the question now was to separate the polonium from the bismuth* ... this is the task that has occupied us for years and has been a most difficult one.' For years, you see—for *years*. That is their way, those plagues, those scientists—peg, peg, peg—dig, dig, dig—plod, plod, plod. I wish I could catch a cargo of them for my place; it would be an economy. Yes, for years, you see. They never give up. Patience, hope, faith, perseverance; it is the way of all the breed. Columbus and the rest. In radium this lady has added a new world to the planet's possessions, and matched—Columbus—and his peer. She has set herself the task of divorcing polonium and bismuth; when she succeeds she will have done—what, should you say?"

"Pray name it, Majesty."

"It's another new world added—a gigantic one. I will explain; for you would never divine the size of it, and she herself does not suspect it."

"Do, Majesty, I beg of you."

"Polonium, freed from bismuth and made independent, is the one and only power that can control radium, restrain its destructive forces, tame them, reduce them to obedience, and make them do useful and profitable work for your race. Examine my skin. What do you think of it?"

"It is delicate, silky, transparent, thin as a gelatine film—exquisite, beautiful, Majesty!"

"It is made of polonium. All the rest of me is radium. If I should strip off my skin the world would vanish away in a flash of flame and a puff of smoke, and the remnants of the extinguished moon would sift down through space a mere snow-shower of gray ashes!"

I made no comment, I only trembled.

"You understand, now," he continued. "I burn, I suffer within, my pains are measureless and eternal, but my skin protects you and the globe from harm. Heat is power, energy, but is only useful to man when he can control it and graduate its application to his needs. You cannot do that with radium, now; it will not be prodigiously useful to you until polonium shall put the slave whip in your hand. I can release from my body the radium force in any measure I please, great or small; at my will I can set in motion the works of a lady's watch or destroy a world. You saw me light that unholy cigar with my finger?"

I remembered it.

"Try to imagine how minute was the fraction of energy released to do that small thing! You are aware that everything is made up of restless and revolving molecules?—everything—furniture, rocks, water, iron, horses, men—everything that exists."

"Yes."

"Molecules of scores of different sizes and weights, but none of them big enough to be seen by help of any microscope?"

"Yes."

"And that each molecule is made up of thousands of separate and never-resting little particles called atoms?"

"Yes."

"And that up to recent times the smallest atom known to science was the hydrogen atom, which was a thousand times smaller than the atom that went to the building of any other molecule?"

"Yes."

"Well, the radium atom from the positive pole is 5,000 times smaller than *that* atom! This unspeakably minute atom is called an *electron*. Now then, out of my long affection for you and for your lineage, I will reveal to you a secret—a secret known to no scientist as yet—the secret of the firefly's light and the glow-worm's; it is produced by a single electron imprisoned in a polonium atom."

"Sire, it is a wonderful thing, and the scientific world would be grateful to know this secret, which has baffled and defeated all its searchings for more than two centuries. To think!—a single electron, 5,000 times smaller than the invisible hydrogen atom, to produce that explosion of vivid light which makes the summer night so beautiful!"

"And consider," said Satan; "it is the only instance in all nature where radium exists in a pure state unencumbered by fettering alliances; where polonium enjoys the like emancipation; and where the pair are enabled to labor together in a gracious and beneficent and effective partnership. Suppose the protecting polonium envelope were removed; the radium spark would flash but once and the firefly would be consumed to vapor! Do you value this old iron letterpress?"

"No, Majesty, for it is not mine."

"Then I will destroy it and let you see. I lit the ostensible cigar with the heat energy of a single electron, the equipment of a single lightning bug. I will turn on twenty thousand electrons now."

He touched the massive thing and it exploded with a cannon crash, leaving nothing but vacancy where it had stood. For three minutes the air was a dense pink fog of sparks, through which Satan loomed dim and vague, then the place cleared and his soft rich moonlight pervaded it again. He said:

"You see? The radium in 20,000 lightning bugs would run a racing-mobile forever. There's no waste, no diminution of it." Then he remarked in a quite casual way, "We use nothing but radium at home."

I was astonished. And interested, too, for I have friends there, and relatives. I had always believed—in accordance with my early teachings—that the fuel was soft coal and brimstone. He noticed the thought, and answered it.

"Soft coal and brimstone is the tradition, yes, but it is an error. We could use it; at least we could make out with it after a fashion, but it has several defects: it is not cleanly, it ordinarily makes but a temperate fire, and it would be exceedingly difficult, if even possible, to heat it up to standard, Sundays; and as for the supply, all the worlds and systems could not furnish enough to keep us going halfway through eternity. Without radium there could be no hell; certainly not a satisfactory one."

"Why?"

"Because if we hadn't radium we should have to dress the souls in some other material; then, of course, they would burn up and get out of trouble. They would not last an hour. You know that?"

"Why—yes, now that you mention it. But I supposed they were dressed in their natural flesh; they look so in the pictures—in the Sistine Chapel and in the illustrated books, you know."

"Yes, our damned look as they looked in the world, but it isn't flesh; flesh could not survive any longer than that copying press survived—it would explode and turn to a fog of sparks, and the result desired in sending it there would be defeated. Believe me, radium is the only wear."

"I see it now," I said, with prophetic discomfort, "I know that you are right, Majesty."

"I am. I speak from experience. You shall see, when you get there."

He said this as if he thought I was eaten up with curiosity, but it was because he did not know me. He sat reflecting a minute, then he said:

"I will make your fortune."

It cheered me up and I felt better. I thanked him and was all eagerness and attention.

"Do you know," he continued, "where they find the bones of the extinct moa, in New Zealand? All in a pile—thousands and thousands of them banked together in a mass twenty feet deep. And do you know where they find the tusks of the extinct mastodon of the Pleistocene? Banked together in acres off the mouth of the Lena—an ivory mine which has furnished freight for Chinese caravans for five hundred years. Do you know the phosphate beds of our South? They are miles in extent, a limitless mass and jumble of bones of vast animals whose like exists no longer in the earth—a cemetery, a mighty cemetery, that is what it is. All over the earth there are such cemeteries. Whence came the instinct that made those families of creatures go to a chosen and particular spot to die when sickness came upon them and they perceived that their end was near? It is a mystery; not even science has been able to uncover the secret of it. But there stands the fact. Listen, then. For a million years there has been a firefly cemetery."

Hopefully, appealingly, I opened my mouth—he motioned me to close it, and went on:

"It is in a scooped-out bowl half as big as this room on the top of a snow summit of the Cordileras. That bowl is level full—of what? Pure firefly radium and the glow and heat of hell! For countless ages myriads of fireflies have daily flown thither and died in that bowl and been burned to vapor in an instant, each fly leaving as its contribution its only indestructible particle, its single electron of pure radium. There is energy enough there to light the whole world, heat the whole world's machinery, supply the whole world's transportation power from now till the end of eternity. The massed riches of the planet could not furnish its value in money. You are mine, it is yours; when Madame Curie isolates polonium, clothe yourself in a skin of it and go and take possession!"

Then he vanished and left me in the dark when I was just in the act of thanking him. I can find the bowl by the light it will cast upon the sky; I can get the polonium presently, when that illustrious lady in France isolates it from the bismuth. Stock is for sale. Apply to Mark Twain.

The New Accelerator

H. G. Wells (1866-1946) is without doubt the most significant pioneer of modern science fiction, both because of the quality of his work and the fact that his "scientific romances," like The Time Machine *(1895),* The Island of Doctor Moreau *(1896),* The War of the Worlds *(1898),* When the Sleeper Wakes *(1899) and many others established several of the major themes found in sf. Wells, like the older Verne, was unsure about man's ability to control science and technology, a concern that grew with the passage of time, and the experience of World War I, and the rise of fascism in Europe.*

His excellent and numerous short stories were almost as influential as his longer works. "The New Accelerator" first appeared in 1901.

CERTAINLY, IF ever a man found a guinea when he was looking for a pin it is my good friend Professor Gibberne. I have heard before of investigators overshooting the mark, but never quite to the extent that he has done. He has really, this time at any rate, without any touch of exaggeration in the phrase, found something to revolutionize human life. And that when he was simply seeking an all-round nervous stimulant to bring languid people up to the stresses of these pushful days. I have tasted the stuff now several times, and I cannot do better than to describe the effect the thing had on me. That there are astonishing experiences in store for all in search of new sensations will become apparent enough.

Professor Gibberne, as many people know, is my neighbor in Folkestone. Unless my memory plays me a trick, his portrait at various ages has already appeared in The Strand Magazine—I think late in 1899; but I am unable to look it up because I have lent that volume to someone who has never sent it back. The reader may, perhaps, recall the high forehead and the singularly long black eyebrows that give such a Mephistophelian touch to his face. He occupies one of those pleasant detached houses in the mixed style that make the western end of the Upper Sandgate Road so interesting. His is the one with the Flemish gables and the Moorish portico, and it is in the room with the mullioned bay window that he works when he is down here, and in which of an evening we have so often smoked and talked together. He is a mighty jester, but, besides, he likes to talk to me about his work; he is one of those men who find a help and stimulus in talking, and so I have been able to follow the conception of the New Accelerator right up from a very early stage. Of course, the greater portion of his experimental work is not done in Folkestone, but in Gower Street, in the fine new laboratory next to the hospital that he has been the first to use.

As everyone knows, or at least as all intelligent people know, the special department in which Gibberne has gained so great and deserved a reputation among physiologists is the action of drugs upon the nervous system. Upon soporifics, sedatives and anesthetics he is, I am told, unequaled. He is also a chemist of considerable eminence, and I suppose in the subtle and complex jungle of riddles that centers about the ganglion cell and the axis fiber there are little cleared places of his making, glades of illumination, that, until he sees fit to publish his results, are inaccessible to every other living man. And in the last few years he has been particularly assiduous upon this question of nervous stimulants, and already, before the discovery of the New Accelerator, very successful with them. Medical science has to thank him for at least three distinct and absolutely safe invigorators of unrivaled value to practicing men. In cases of exhaustion the preparation known as Gibberne's B Syrup has, I suppose, saved more lives already than any lifeboat round the coast.

"But none of these things begin to satisfy me yet," he told me nearly a year ago. "Either they increase the central energy without affecting the nerves or they simply increase the available energy by lowering the nervous conductivity; and all of them are unequal and local in their operation. One wakes up the heart and viscera and leaves the brain stupefied, one gets at the brain champagne fashion and does nothing good for the solar plexus, and what I want—and what, if it's an earthly possibility, I mean to have—is a stimulant that stimulates all round, that wakes you up for a time from the crown of your head to the tip of your great toe, and makes you go two—or even three to everybody else's one. Eh? That's the thing I'm after."

"It would tire a man," I said.

"Not a doubt of it. And you'd eat double or treble—and all that. But just think what the thing would mean. Imagine yourself with a little phial like this"—he held up a bottle of green glass and marked his points with it—"and in this precious phial is the power to think twice as fast, move twice as quickly, do twice as much work in a given time as you could otherwise do."

"But is such a thing possible?"

"I believe so. If it isn't, I've wasted my time for a year. These various preparations of the hypophosphites, for example, seem to show that something of the sort.... Even if it was only one and a half times as fast it would do."

"It *would* do," I said.

"If you were a statesman in a corner, for example, time rushing up against you, something urgent to be done, eh?"

"He could dose his private secretary," I said.

"And gain—double time. And think if *you*, for example, wanted to finish a book."

"Usually," I said, "I wish I'd never begun 'em."

"Or a doctor, driven to death, wants to sit down and think out a case. Or a barrister—or a man cramming for an examination."

"Worth a guinea a drop," said I, "and more—to men like that."

"And in a duel again," said Gibberne, "where it all depends on your quickness in pulling the trigger."

"Or in fencing," I echoed.

"You see," said Gibberne, "if I get it as an all-round thing it will really do you no harm at all—except perhaps to an infinitesimal degree it brings you nearer old age. You will just have lived twice to other people's once——"

"I suppose," I meditated, "in a duel—it would be fair?"

"That's a question for the seconds," said Gibberne.

I harked back further. "And you really think such a thing *is* possible?" I said.

"As possible," said Gibberne, and glanced at something that went throbbing by the window, "as a motorbus. As a matter of fact——"

He paused and smiled at me deeply, and tapped slowly on the edge of his desk with the green phial. "I think I know the stuff.... Already I've got something coming." The nervous smile upon his face betrayed the gravity of his revelation. He rarely talked of his actual experimental work unless things were very near the end. "And it may be, it may be—I shouldn't be surprised—it may even do the thing at a greater rate than twice."

"It will be rather a big thing," I hazarded.

"It will be, I think, rather a big thing."

But I don't think he quite knew what a big thing it was to be, for all that.

I remember we had several subsequent talks about the stuff. "The New Accelerator" he called it, and his tone about it grew more confident on each occasion. Sometimes he talked nervously of unexpected physiological results its use might have, and then he would get a bit unhappy; at others he was frankly mercenary, and we debated long and anxiously how the preparation might be turned to commercial account. "It's a good thing," said Gibberne, "a tremendous thing. I know I'm giving the world something, and I think it only reasonable we should expect the world to pay. The dignity of science is all very well, but I think somehow I must have the monopoly of the stuff for, say, ten years. I don't see why *all* the fun in life should go to the dealers in ham."

My own interest in the coming drug certainly did not wane in the time. I have always had a queer twist towards metaphysics in my mind. I have always been given to paradoxes about space and time, and it seemed to me that Gibberne was really preparing no less than the absolute acceleration of life. Suppose a man repeatedly dosed with such a preparation: he would live an active and record life indeed, but he would be an adult at eleven, middle-aged at twenty-five, and by thirty well on the road to senile decay. It seemed to me that so far Gibberne was only going to do for anyone who took his drug exactly what Nature has done for the Jews and Orientals, who are men in their teens and aged by fifty, and quicker in thought and act than we are all the time. The marvel of drugs has always been great to my mind; you can madden a man, calm a man, make him incredibly strong and alert or a helpless log, quicken this passion and allay that, all by means of drugs, and here was a new miracle to be added to this strange armory of phials the doctors use! But Gibberne was far too eager upon his technical points to enter very keenly into my aspect of the question.

It was the 7th or 8th of August, when he told me the distillation that would decide his failure or success for a time was going forward as we talked, and it was on the 10th that he told me the thing was done and the New Accelerator a tangible reality in the world. I met him as I was going up the Sandgate Hill towards Folkestone—I think I was going to get my hair cut; and he came hurrying down to meet me—I suppose he was coming to my house to tell me at once of his success. I remember that his eyes were unusually bright and his face flushed, and I noted even then the swift alacrity of his step.

"It's done," he cried, and gripped my hand, speaking very fast; "it's more than done. Come up to my house and see."

"Really?"

"Really!" he shouted. "Incredibly! Come up and see."

"And it does—twice!"

"It does more, much more. It scares me. Come up and see the stuff. Taste it! Try it! It's the most amazing stuff on earth." He gripped my arm and, walking at such a pace that he forced me into a trot, went shouting with me up the hill. A whole charabancful of people turned and stared at us in unison after the manner of people in charabancs. It was one of those hot, clear days that Folkestone sees so much of, every color incredibly bright and every outline hard. There was a breeze, of course, but not so much breeze as sufficed under these conditions to keep me cool and dry. I panted for mercy.

"I'm not walking fast, am I?" cried Gibberne, and slackened his pace to a quick march.

"You've been taking some of this stuff," I puffed.

"No," he said. "At the utmost a drop of water that stood in a beaker from which I had washed out the last traces of the stuff. I took some last night, you know. But that is ancient history, now."

"And it goes twice?" I said, nearing his doorway in a grateful perspiration.

"It goes a thousand times, many thousand times!" cried Gibberne, with a dramatic gesture, flinging open his Early English carved oak gate.

"Phew!" said I, and followed him to the door.

"I don't know how many times it goes," he said, with his latch-key in his hand.

"And you——"

"It throws all sorts of light on nervous physiology, it kicks the theory of vision into a perfectly new shape!...Heaven knows how many thousand times. We'll try all that after——The thing is to try the stuff now."

"Try the stuff?" I said, as we went along the passage.

"Rather," said Gibberne, turning on me in his study. "There it is in that little green phial there! Unless you happen to be afraid?"

I am a careful man by nature, and only theoretically adventurous. I *was* afraid. But on the other hand there is pride.

"Well," I haggled. "You say you've tried it?"

"I've tried it," he said, "and I don't look hurt by it, do I? I don't even look livery and I *feel*——"

I sat down. "Give me the potion," I said. "If the worst comes to the worst it will save having my hair cut, and that I think is one of the most hateful duties of a civilized man. How do you take the mixture?"

"With water," said Gibberne, whacking down a carafe.

He stood up in front of his desk and regarded me in his easy chair; his manner was suddenly affected by a touch of the Harley Street specialist. "It's rum stuff, you know," he said.

I made a gesture with my hand.

"I must warn you in the first place as soon as you've got it down to shut your eyes, and open them very cautiously in a minute or so's time. One still sees. The sense of vision is a question of length of vibration, and not of multitude of impacts; but there's a kind of shock to the retina, a nasty giddy confusion just at the time if the eyes are open. Keep 'em shut."

"Shut," I said. "Good!"

"And the next thing is, keep still. Don't begin to whack about. You may fetch something a nasty rap if you do. Remember you will be going several thousand times faster than you ever did before, heart, lungs, muscles, brain—everything— and you will hit hard without knowing it. You won't know it, you know. You'll feel just as you do now. Only everything in the world will seem to be going ever so many thousand times slower than it ever went before. That's what makes it so deuced queer."

"Lor'," I said. "And you mean——"

"You'll see," said he, and took up a measure. He glanced at the material on his desk. "Glasses," he said, "water. All here. Mustn't take too much for the first attempt."

The little phial glucked out its precious contents. "Don't forget what I told you," he said, turning the contents of the measure into a glass in the manner of an Italian waiter measuring whisky. "Sit with the eyes tightly shut and in absolute stillness for two minutes," he said. "Then you will hear me speak."

He added an inch or so of water to the dose in each glass.

"By the bye," he said, "don't put your glass down. Keep it in your hand and rest your hand on your knee. Yes—so. And now——"

He raised his glass.

"The New Accelerator," I said.

"The New Accelerator," he answered, and we touched glasses and drank, and instantly I closed my eyes.

You know that blank non-existence into which one drops when one has taken "gas." For an indefinite interval it was like that. Then I heard Gibberne telling me to wake up, and I stirred and opened my eyes. There he stood as he had been standing, glass still in hand. It was empty, that was all the difference.

"Well?" said I.

"Nothing out of the way?"

"Nothing. A slight feeling of exhilaration, perhaps. Nothing more."

"Sounds?"

"Things are still," I said. "By Jove! yes! They *are* still. Except the sort of faint pat, patter, like rain falling on different things. What is it?"

"Analyzed sounds," I think he said, but I am not sure. He glanced at the windows. "Have you ever seen a curtain before a window fixed in that way before?"

I followed his eyes, and there was the end of the curtain, frozen, as it were, corner high, in the act of flapping briskly in the breeze.

"No," said I; "that's odd."

"And here," he said, and opened the hand that held the glass. Naturally I winced, expecting the glass to smash. But so far from smashing it did not even seem to stir; it hung in mid-air—motionless. "Roughly speaking," said Gibberne, "an object in these latitudes falls 16 feet in the first second. This glass is falling 16 feet in a second now. Only, you see, it hasn't been falling yet for the hundredth part of a second. That gives you some idea of the pace of my Accelerator." And he waved his hand round and round, over and under the slowly sinking glass. Finally he took it by the bottom, pulled it down and placed it very carefully on the table. "Eh?" he said to me, and laughed.

"That seems all right," I said, and began very gingerly to raise myself from my chair. I felt perfectly well, very light and comfortable, and quite confident in my mind. I was going fast all over. My heart, for example, was beating a thousand times a second, but that caused me no discomfort at all. I looked out of the window. An immovable cyclist, head down and with a frozen puff of dust behind his driving-wheel, scorched to overtake a galloping charabanc that did not stir. I gaped in amazement at this incredible spectacle. "Gibberne," I cried, "how long will this confounded stuff last?"

"Heaven knows!" he answered. "Last time I took it, I went to bed and slept it off. I tell you, I was frightened. It must have lasted some minutes, I think—it seemed like hours. But after a bit it slows down rather suddenly, I believe."

I was proud to observe that I did not feel frightened—I suppose because there were two of us. "Why shouldn't we go out?" I asked.

"Why not?"

"They'll see us."

"Not they. Goodness, no! Why, we shall be going a thousand times faster than the quickest conjuring trick that was ever done. Come along! Which way shall we go? Window, or door?"

And out by the window we went.

Assuredly of all the strange experiences that I have ever had, or imagined, or read of other people having or imagining, that little raid I made with Gibberne on the Folkestone Leas, under the influence of the New Accelerator, was the strangest and maddest of all. We went out by his gate into the road, and there we made a minute examination of the statuesque passing traffic. The tops of the wheels and some of the legs of the horses of this charabanc, the end of the whiplash and the lower jaw of the conductor—who was just beginning to yawn—were perceptibly in motion, but all the rest of the lumbering conveyance seemed still. And quite noiseless except for a faint rattling that came from one man's throat! And as parts of this frozen edifice there were a driver, you know, and a conductor, and eleven people! The effect as we walked about the thing began by being madly queer and ended by being—disagreeable. There they were, people like ourselves and yet not like ourselves, frozen in careless attitudes, caught in mid-gesture. A girl and a man smiled at one another, a leering smile that threatened to last for evermore; a woman in a floppy capelline rested her arm on the rail and stared at Gibberne's house with the unwinking stare of eternity; a man stroked his moustache like a figure of wax, and another stretched a tiresome stiff hand with extended fingers towards his loosened hat. We stared at them, we laughed at them, we made faces at them, and then a sort of disgust of them came upon us, and we turned away and walked round in front of the cyclist towards the Leas.

"Goodness!" cried Gibberne, suddenly; "look there!"

He pointed, and there at the tip of his finger and sliding down the air with wings flapping slowly and at the speed of an exceptionally languid snail—was a bee.

And so we came out upon the Leas. There the thing seemed madder than ever. The band was playing in the upper stand, though all the sound it made for us was a low-pitched, wheezy rattle, a sort of prolonged last sigh that passed at times into a sound like the slow, muffled ticking of some monstrous clock. Frozen people stood erect; strange, silent, self-conscious-looking dummies hung unstably in mid-stride, promenading upon the grass. I passed close to a poodle dog suspended in the act of leaping, and watched the slow movement of his legs as he sank to earth. "Lord, look here!" cried Gibberne, and we halted for a moment before a magnificent person in white faint-striped flannels, white shoes, and a Panama hat, who turned back to wink at two gaily-dressed ladies he had passed. A wink, studied with such leisurely deliberation as we could afford, is an unattractive thing. It loses any quality of alert gaiety, and one remarks that the winking eye does not completely close, that under its drooping lid appears the lower edge of an eyeball and a line of white. "Heaven give me memory," said I, "and I will never wink again."

"Or smile," said Gibberne, with his eye on the lady's answering teeth.

"It's infernally hot, somehow," said I. "Let's go slower."

"Oh, come along!" said Gibberne.

We picked our way among the Bath chairs in the path. Many of the people sitting in the chairs seemed amost natural in their passive poses, but the contorted scarlet of the bandsmen was not a restful thing to see. A purple-faced gentleman was frozen in the midst of a violent struggle to refold his newspaper against the wind; there were many evidences that all these people in their sluggish way were exposed to a considerable breeze, a breeze that had no existence so far as our sensations went. We came out and walked a little way from the crowd, and turned and regarded it. To see all that multitude changed to a picture, smitten rigid, as it were, into the semblance of realistic wax, was impossibly wonderful. It was absurd, of course; but it filled me with an irrational, an exultant sense of superior advantage. Consider the wonder of it! All that I had said and thought and done since the stuff had begun to work in my veins had happened, so far as those people, so far as the world in general went, in the twinkling of an eye. "The New Accelerator——" I began, but Gibberne interrupted me.

"There's that infernal old woman!" he said.

"What old woman?"

"Lives next door to me," said Gibberne. "Has a lapdog that yaps. Gods! The temptation is strong!"

There is something very boyish and impulsive about Gibberne at times. Before

I could expostulate with him he had dashed forward, snatched the unfortunate animal out of visible existence, and was running violently with it towards the cliff of the Leas. It was most extraordinary. The little brute, you know, didn't bark or wriggle or make the slightest sign of vitality. It kept quite stiffly in an attitude of somnolent repose, and Gibberne held it by the neck. It was like running about with a dog of wood. "Gibberne," I cried, "put it down!" Then I said something else. "If you run like that, Gibberne," I cried, "you'll set your clothes on fire. Your linen trousers are going brown as it is!"

He clapped his hand on his thigh and stood hesitating on the verge. "Gibberne," I cried, coming up, "put it down. This heat is too much! It's our running so! Two or three miles a second! Friction of the air!"

"What?" he said, glancing at the dog.

"Friction of the air," I shouted. "Friction of the air. Going too fast. Like meteorites and things. Too hot. And, Gibberne! Gibberne! I'm all over pricking and a sort of perspiration. You can see people stirring slightly. I believe the stuff's working off! Put that dog down."

"Eh?" he said.

"It's working off," I repeated. "We're too hot and the stuff's working off! I'm wet through."

He stared at me. Then at the band, the wheezy rattle of whose performance was certainly going faster. Then with a tremendous sweep of the arm he hurled the dog away from him and it went spinning upward, still inanimate, and hung at last over the grouped parasols of a knot of chattering people. Gibberne was gripping my elbow. "By Jove!" he cried. "I believe it is! A sort of hot pricking and—yes. That man's moving his pocket-handkerchief! Perceptibly. We must get out of this sharp."

But we could not get out of it sharply enough. Luckily, perhaps! For we might have run, and if we had run we should, I believe, have burst into flames. Almost certainly we should have burst into flames! You know we had neither of us thought of that. . . . But before we could even begin to run the action of the drug had ceased. It was the business of a minute fraction of a second. The effect of the New Accelerator passed like the drawing of a curtain, vanished in the movement of a hand. I heard Gibberne's voice in infinite alarm. "Sit down," he said, and flop, down upon the turf at the edge of the Leas I sat—scorching as I sat. There is a patch of burnt grass there still where I sat down. The whole stagnation seemed to wake up as I did so, the disarticulated vibration of the band rushed together into a blast of music, the promenaders put their feet down and walked their ways, the papers and flags began flapping, smiles passed into words, the winker finished his wink and went on his way complacently, and all the seated people moved and spoke.

The whole world had come alive again, was going as fast as we were, or rather we were going no faster than the rest of the world. It was like slowing down as one comes into a railway station. Everything seemed to spin round for a second or two, I had the most transient feeling of nausea, and that was all. And the little dog which had seemed to hang for a moment when the force of Gibberne's arm was expended fell with a swift acceleration clean through a lady's parasol!

That was the saving of us. Unless it was for one corpulent old gentleman in a

Bath chair, who certainly did start at the sight of us and afterwards regarded us at intervals with a darkly suspicious eye, and finally, I believe, said something to his nurse about us, I doubt if a solitary person remarked our sudden appearance among them. Plop! We must have appeared abruptly. We ceased to smolder almost at once, though the turf beneath me was uncomfortably hot. The attention of everyone— including even the Amusements' Association band, which on this occasion, for the only time in its history, got out of tune—was arrested by the amazing fact, and the still more amazing yapping and uproar caused by the fact, that a respectable, over-fed lapdog sleeping quietly to the east of the bandstand should suddenly fall through the parasol of a lady on the west—in a slightly singed condition due to the extreme velocity of its movements through the air. In these absurd days, too, when we are all trying to be as psychic and silly and superstitious as possible! People got up and trod on other people, chairs were overturned, the Leas policeman ran. How the matter settled itself, I do not know—we were much too anxious to disentangle ourselves from the affair and get out of range of the eye of the old gentleman in the Bath chair to make minute inquiries. As soon as we were sufficiently cool and sufficiently recovered from our giddiness and nausea and confusion of mind to do so we stood up and, skirting the crowd, directed our steps back along the road below the Metropole towards Gibberne's house. But amidst the din I heard very distinctly the gentleman who had been sitting beside the lady of the ruptured sunshade using quite unjustifiable threats and language to one of those chair-attendants who have "Inspector" written on their caps. "If you didn't throw the dog," he said, "who *did?*"

The sudden return of movement and familiar noises, and our natural anxiety about ourselves (our clothes were still dreadfully hot, and the fronts of the thighs of Gibberne's white trousers were scorched a drabbish brown), prevented the minute observations I should have liked to make on all these things. Indeed, I really made no observations of any scientific value on that return. The bee, of course, had gone. I looked for that cyclist, but he was already out of sight as we came into the Upper Sandgate Road or hidden from us by traffic; the charabanc, however, with its people now all alive and stirring, was clattering along at a spanking pace almost abreast of the nearer church.

We noted, however, that the window-sill on which we had stepped in getting out of the house was slightly singed, and that the impressions of our feet on the gravel of the path were unusually deep.

So it was I had my first experience of the New Accelerator. Practically we had been running about and saying and doing all sorts of things in the space of a second or so of time. We had lived half an hour while the band had played, perhaps, two bars. But the effect it had upon us was that the whole world had stopped for our convenient inspection. Considering all things, and particularly considering our rashness in venturing out of the house, the experience might certainly have been much more disagreeable than it was. It showed, no doubt, that Gibberne has still much to learn before his preparation is a manageable convenience, but its practicability it certainly demonstrated beyond all cavil.

Since that adventure he has been steadily bringing its use under control, and I have several times, and without the slightest bad result, taken measured doses under his direction; though I must confess I have not yet ventured abroad again while under its influence. I may mention, for example, that this story has been written at one sitting and without interruption, except for the nibbling of some chocolate, by its means. I began at 6:25, and my watch is now very nearly at the minute past the half-hour. The convenience of securing a long, uninterrupted spell of work in the midst of a day full of engagements cannot be exaggerated. Gibberne is now working at the quantitative handling of his preparation, with especial reference to its distinctive effects upon different types of constitution. He then hopes to find a Retarder with which to dilute its present rather excessive potency. The Retarder will, of course, have the reverse effect to the Accelerator; used alone it should enable the patient to spread a few seconds over many hours of ordinary time, and so to maintain an apathetic inaction, a glacierlike absence of alacrity, amidst the most animated or irritating surroundings. The two things together must necessarily work an entire revolution in civilized existence. It is the beginning of our escape from that Time Garment of which Carlyle speaks. While this Accelerator will enable us to concentrate ourselves with tremendous impact upon any moment or occasion that demands our utmost sense and vigor, the Retarder will enable us to pass in passive tranquillity through infinite hardship and tedium. Perhaps I am a little optimistic about the Retarder, which has indeed still to be discovered, but about the Accelerator there is no possible sort of doubt whatever. Its appearance upon the market in a convenient, controllable and assimilable form is a matter of the next few months. It will be obtainable of all chemists and druggists, in small green bottles, at a high but, considering its extraordinary qualities, by no means excessive price. Gibberne's Nervous Accelerator it will be called, and he hopes to be able to supply it in three strengths: one in 200, one in 900 and one in 2000, distinguished by yellow, pink and white labels respectively.

No doubt its use renders a great number of very extraordinary things possible; for, of course, the most remarkable and, possibly, even criminal proceedings may be effected with impunity by thus dodging, as it were, into the interstices of time. Like all potent preparations it will be liable to abuse. We have, however, discussed this aspect of the question very thoroughly, and we have decided that this is purely a matter of medical jurisprudence and altogether outside our province. We shall manufacture and sell the Accelerator, and, as for the consequences—we shall see.

FRANK LILLIE POLLACK

Finis

"Finis" is one of the very best early end-of-the-world stories, first appearing in The Argosy magazine for June 1906. Catastrophe stories were already a staple of what would later be called science fiction, but "Finis" was different, especially noteworthy for its quiet, effective tone.

Its author, Frank Lillie Pollack, also wrote several other stories that qualify as science fiction, including "The Crimson Blight" (1905) and "The World Wrecker" (1908).

I'M GETTING tired," complained Davis, lounging in the window of the Physics Building, "and sleepy. It's after eleven o'clock. This makes the fourth night I've sat up to see your new star, and it'll be the last. Why, the thing was billed to appear three weeks ago."

"Are *you* tired, Miss Wardour?" asked Eastwood, and the girl glanced up with a quick flush and a negative murmur.

Eastwood made the reflection anew that she certainly was painfully shy. She was almost as plain as she was shy, though her hair had an unusual beauty of its own, fine as silk and colored like palest flame.

Probably she had brains; Eastwood had seen her reading some extremely "deep" books, but she seemed to have no amusements, few interests. She worked daily at the Art Students' League, and boarded where he did, and he had thus come to ask her with the Davises to watch for the new star from the laboratory windows on the Heights.

"Do you really think that it's worthwhile to wait any longer, professor?" inquired Mrs. Davis, concealing a yawn.

Eastwood was somewhat annoyed by the continued failure of the star to show itself and he hated to be called "professor," being only an assistant professor of physics.

"I don't know," he answered somewhat curtly. "This is the twelfth night that I have waited for it. Of course, it would have been a mathematical miracle if astronomers should have solved such a problem exactly, though they've been figuring on it for a quarter of a century."

The new Physics Building of Columbia University was about twelve stories high.

49

The physics laboratory occupied the ninth and tenth floors, with the astronomical rooms above it, an arrangement which would have been impossible before the invention of the oil vibration cushion, which practically isolated the instrument rooms from the earth.

Eastwood had arranged a small telescope at the window, and below them spread the illuminated map of Greater New York, sending up a faintly musical roar. All the streets were crowded, as they had been every night since the fifth of the month, when the great new star, or sun, was expected to come into view.

Some error had been made in the calculations, though, as Eastwood said, astronomers had been figuring on them for twenty-five years.

It was, in fact, nearly forty years since Professor Adolphe Bernier first announced his theory of a limited universe at the International Congress of Sciences in Paris, where it was counted as little more than a masterpiece of imagination.

Professor Bernier did not believe that the universe was infinite. Somewhere, he argued, the universe must have a center, which is the pivot for its revolution.

The moon revolves around the earth, the planetary system revolves about the sun, the solar system revolves about one of the fixed stars, and this whole system in its turn undoubtedly revolves around some more distant point. But this sort of progression must definitely stop somewhere.

Somewhere there must be a central sun, a vast incandescent body which does not move at all. And as a sun is always larger and hotter than its satellites, therefore the body at the center of the universe must be of an immensity and temperature beyond anything known or imagined.

It was objected that this hypothetical body should then be large enough to be visible from the earth, and Professor Bernier replied that some day it undoubtedly would be visible. Its light had simply not yet had time to reach the earth.

The passage of light from the nearest of the fixed stars is a matter of three years, and there must be many stars so distant that their rays have not yet reached us. The great central sun must be so inconceivably remote that perhaps hundreds, perhaps thousands of years would elapse before its light should burst upon the solar system.

All this was contemptuously classed as "newspaper science" till the extraordinary mathematical revival a little after the middle of the twentieth century afforded the means of verifying it.

Following the new theorems discovered by Professor Burnside, of Princeton, and elaborated by Dr. Taneka, of Tokyo, astronomers succeeded in calculating the arc of the sun's movements through space, and its ratio to the orbit of its satellites. With this as a basis, it was possible to follow the widening circles, the consecutive systems of the heavenly bodies and their rotations.

The theory of Professor Bernier was justified. It was demonstrated that there really was a gigantic mass of incandescent matter, which, whether the central point of the universe or not, appeared to be without motion.

The weight and distance of this new sun were approximately calculated, and, the speed of light being known, it was an easy matter to reckon when its rays would reach the earth.

It was then estimated that the approaching rays would arrive at the earth in twenty-six years, and that was twenty-six years ago. Three weeks had passed since the date when the new heavenly body was expected to become visible, and it had not yet appeared.

Popular interest had risen to a high pitch, stimulated by innumerable newspaper and magazine articles, and the streets were nightly thronged with excited crowds armed with opera-glasses and star maps, while at every corner a telescope man had planted his tripod instrument at a nickel a look.

Similar scenes were taking place in every civilized city on the globe.

It was generally supposed that the new luminary would appear in size about midway between Venus and the moon. Better informed persons expected something like the sun, and a syndicate of capitalists quietly leased large areas on the coast of Greenland in anticipation of a great rise in temperature and a northward movement in population.

Even the business situation was appreciably affected by the public uncertainty and excitement. There was a decline in stocks, and a minor religious sect boldly prophesied the end of the world.

"I've had enough of this," said Davis, looking at his watch again. "Are you ready to go, Grace? By the way, isn't it getting warmer?"

It had been a sharp February day, but the temperature was certainly rising. Water was dripping from the roofs, and from the icicles that fringed the window ledges, as if a warm wave had suddenly arrived.

"What's that light?" suddenly asked Alice Wardour, who was lingering by the open window.

"It must be moonrise," said Eastwood, though the illumination of the horizon was almost like daybreak.

Davis abandoned his intention of leaving, and they watched the east grow pale and flushed till at last a brilliant white disc heaved itself above the horizon.

It resembled the full moon, but as if trebled in luster, and the streets grew almost as light as by day.

"Good heavens, that must be the new star, after all!" said Davis in an awed voice.

"No, it's only the moon. This is the hour and minute for her rising," answered Eastwood, who had grasped the cause of the phenomenon. "But the new sun must have appeared on the other side of the earth. Its light is what makes the moon so brilliant. It will rise here just as the sun does, no telling how soon. It must be brighter than was expected—and maybe hotter," he added with a vague uneasiness.

"Isn't it getting very warm in here?" said Mrs. Davis, loosening her jacket. "Couldn't you turn off some of the steam heat?"

Eastwood turned it all off, for, in spite of the open window, the room was really growing uncomfortably close. But the warmth appeared to come from without; it was like a warm spring evening, and the icicles were breaking loose from the cornices.

For half an hour they leaned from the windows with but desultory conversation, and below them the streets were black with people and whitened with upturned faces. The brilliant moon rose higher, and the mildness of the night sensibly increased.

It was after midnight when Eastwood first noticed the reddish flush tinging the clouds low in the east, and he pointed it out to his companions.

"That must be it at last," he exclaimed, with a thrill of vibrating excitement at what he was going to see, a cosmic event unprecedented in intensity.

The brightness waxed rapidly.

"By Jove, see it redden!" Davis ejaculated. "It's getting lighter than day—and hot! Whew!"

The whole eastern sky glowed with a deepening pink that extended half round the horizon. Sparrows chirped from the roofs, and it looked as if the disc of the unknown star might at any moment be expected to lift above the Atlantic, but it delayed long.

The heavens continued to burn with myriad hues, gathering at last to a fiery furnace glow on the skyline.

Mrs. Davis suddenly screamed. An American flag blowing freely from its staff on the roof of the tall building had all at once burst into flame.

Low in the east lay a long streak of intense fire which broadened as they squinted with watering eyes. It was as if the edge of the world had been heated to whiteness.

The brilliant moon faded to a feathery white film in the glare. There was a confused outcry from the observatory overhead, and a crash of something being broken, and as the strange new sunlight fell through the window the onlookers leaped back as if a blast furnace had been opened before them.

The glass cracked and fell inward. Something like the sun, but magnified fifty times in size and hotness, was rising out of the sea. An iron instrument-table by the window began to smoke with an acrid smell of varnish. ⟩

"What the devil is this, Eastwood?" shouted Davis accusingly.

From the streets rose a sudden, enormous wail of fright and pain, the outcry of a million throats at once, and the roar of a stampede followed. The pavements were choked with struggling, panic-stricken people in the fierce glare, and above the din arose the clanging rush of fire engines and trucks.

Smoke began to rise from several points below Central Park, and two or three church chimes pealed crazily.

The observers from overhead came running down the stairs with a thunderous trampling, for the elevator man had deserted his post.

"Here, we've got to get out of this," shouted Davis, seizing his wife by the arm and hustling her toward the door. "This place'll be on fire directly."

"Hold on. You can't go down into that crush on the street," Eastwood cried, trying to prevent him.

But Davis broke away and raced down the stairs, half carrying his terrified wife. Eastwood got his back against the door in time to prevent Alice from following them.

"There's nothing in this building that will burn, Miss Wardour," he said as calmly as he could. "We had better stay here for the present. It would be sure death to get involved in that stampede below. Just listen to it."

The crowds on the street seemed to sway to and fro in contending waves, and the cries, curses and screams came up in a savage chorus.

The heat was already almost blistering to the skin, though they carefully avoided the direct rays, and instruments of glass in the laboratory cracked loudly one by one.

A vast cloud of dark smoke began to rise from the harbor, where the shipping must have caught fire, and something exploded with a terrific report. A few minutes later half a dozen fires broke out in the lower part of the city, rolling up volumes of smoke that faded to a thin mist in the dazzling light.

The great new sun was now fully above the horizon, and the whole east seemed ablaze. The stampede in the streets had quieted all at once, for the survivors had taken refuge in the nearest houses, and the pavements were black with motionless forms of men and women.

"I'll do whatever you say," said Alice, who was deadly pale, but remarkably collected. Even at that moment Eastwood was struck by the splendor of her ethereally brilliant hair that burned like pale flame above her pallid face. "But we can't stay here, can we?"

"No," replied Eastwood, trying to collect his faculties in the face of this catastrophic revolution of nature. "We'd better go to the basement, I think."

In the basement were deep vaults used for the storage of delicate instruments, and these would afford shelter for a time at least. It occurred to him as he spoke that perhaps temporary safety was the best that any living thing on earth could hope for.

But he led the way down the well staircase. They had gone down six or seven flights when a gloom seemed to grow upon the air, with a welcome relief.

It seemed almost cool, and the sky had clouded heavily, with the appearance of polished and heated silver.

A deep but distant roaring arose and grew from the southeast, and they stopped on the second landing to look from the window.

A vast black mass seemed to fill the space between sea and sky, and it was sweeping toward the city, probably from the harbor, Eastwood thought, at a speed that made it visibly grow as they watched it.

"A cyclone—and a waterspout!" muttered Eastwood, appalled.

He might have foreseen it from the sudden, excessive evaporation and the heating of the air. The gigantic black pillar drove toward them swaying and reeling, and a gale came with it, and a wall of impenetrable mist behind.

As Eastwood watched its progress he saw its cloudy bulk illumined momentarily by a dozen lightning-like flashes, and a moment later, above its roar, came the tremendous detonations of heavy cannon.

The forts and the warships were firing shells to break the waterspout, but the shots seemed to produce no effect. It was the city's last and useless attempt at resistance. A moment later forts and ships alike must have been engulfed.

"Hurry! This building will collapse!" Eastwood shouted.

They rushed down another flight, and heard the crash with which the monster broke over the city. A deluge of water, like the emptying of a reservoir, thundered upon the street, and the water was steaming hot as it fell.

There was a rending crash of falling walls, and in another instant the Physics Building seemed to be twisted around by a powerful hand. The walls blew out, and the whole structure sank in a chaotic mass.

But the tough steel frame was practically unwreckable, and, in fact, the upper portion was simply bent down upon the lower stories, peeling off most of the shell of masonry and stucco.

Eastwood was stunned as he was hurled to the floor, but when he came to himself he was still upon the landing, which was tilted at an alarming angle. A tangled mass of steel rods and beams hung a yard over his head, and a huge steel girder had plunged down perpendicularly from above, smashing everything in its way.

Wreckage choked the well of the staircase, a mass of plaster, bricks and shattered furniture surrounded him, and he could look out in almost every direction through the rent iron skeleton.

A yard away Alice was sitting up, mechanically wiping the mud and water from her face, and apparently uninjured. Tepid water was pouring through the interstices of the wreck in torrents, though it did not appear to be raining.

A steady, powerful gale had followed the whirlwind, and it brought a little coolness with it. Eastwood inquired perfunctorily of Alice if she were hurt, without being able to feel any degree of interest in the matter. His faculty of sympathy seemed paralyzed.

"I don't know. I thought—I thought that we were all dead!" the girl murmured in a sort of daze. "What was it? Is it all over?"

"I think it's only beginning," Eastwood answered dully.

The gale had brought up more clouds and the skies were thickly overcast, but shining white-hot. Presently the rain came down in almost scalding floods and as it fell upon the hissing streets it steamed again into the air.

In three minutes all the world was choked with hot vapors, and from the roar and splash the streets seemed to be running rivers.

The downpour seemed too violent to endure, and after an hour it did cease, while the city reeked with mist. Through the whirling fog Eastwood caught glimpses of ruined buildings, vast heaps of débris, all the wreckage of the greatest city of the twentieth century.

Then the torrents fell again, like a cataract, as if the waters of the earth were shuttlecocking between sea and heaven. With a jarring tremor of the ground a landslide went down into the Hudson.

The atmosphere was like a vapor bath, choking and sickening. The physical agony of respiration aroused Alice from a sort of stupor, and she cried out pitifully that she would die.

The strong wind drove the hot spray and steam through the shattered building till it seemed impossible that human lungs could extract life from the semi-liquid that had replaced the air, but the two lived.

After hours of this parboiling the rain slackened, and, as the clouds parted,

Eastwood caught a glimpse of a familiar form halfway up the heavens. It was the sun, the old sun, looking small and watery.

But the intense heat and brightness told that the enormous body still blazed behind the clouds. The rain seemed to have ceased definitely, and the hard, shining whiteness of the sky grew rapidly hotter.

The heat of the air increased to an oven-like degree; the mists were dissipated, the clouds licked up, and the earth seemed to dry itself almost immediately. The heat from the two suns beat down simultaneously till it became a monstrous terror, unendurable.

An odor of smoke began to permeate the air; there was a dazzling shimmer over the streets, and great clouds of mist arose from the bay, but these appeared to evaporate before they could darken the sky.

The piled wreck of the building sheltered the two refugees from the direct rays of the new sun, now almost overhead, but not from the penetrating heat of the air. But the body will endure almost anything, short of tearing asunder, for a time at least; it is the finer mechanism of the nerves that suffers most.

Alice lay face down among the bricks, gasping and moaning. The blood hammered in Eastwood's brain, and the strangest mirages flickered before his eyes.

Alternately he lapsed into heavy stupors, and awoke to the agony of the day. In his lucid moments he reflected that this could not last long, and tried to remember what degree of heat would cause death.

Within an hour after the drenching rains he was feverishly thirsty, and the skin felt as if peeling from his whole body.

This fever and horror lasted until he forgot that he had ever known another state; but at last the west reddened, and the flaming sun went down. It left the familiar planet high in the heavens, and there was no darkness until the usual hour, though there was a slight lowering of the temperature.

But when night did come it brought life-giving coolness, and though the heat was still intense it seemed temperate by comparison. More than all, the kindly darkness seemed to set a limit to the cataclysmic disorders of the day.

"Ouf! This is heavenly!" said Eastwood, drawing long breaths and feeling mind and body revived in the gloom.

"It won't last long," replied Alice, and her voice sounded extraordinarily calm through the darkness. "The heat will come again when the new sun rises in a few hours."

"We might find some better place in the meanwhile—a deep cellar; or we might get into the subway," Eastwood suggested.

"It would be no use. Don't you understand? I have been thinking it all out. After this, the new sun will always shine, and we could not endure it even another day. The wave of heat is passing round the world as it revolves, and in a few hours the whole earth will be a burnt-up ball. Very likely we are the only people left alive in New York, or perhaps in America."

She seemed to have taken the intellectual initiative, and spoke with an assumption of authority that amazed him.

"But there must be others," said Eastwood, after thinking for a moment. "Other people have found sheltered places, or miners, or men underground."

"They would have been drowned by the rain. At any rate, there will be none left alive by tomorrow night.

"Think of it," she went on dreamily, "for a thousand years this wave of fire has been rushing toward us, while life has been going on so happily in the world, so unconscious that the world was doomed all the time. And now this is the end of life."

"I don't know," Eastwood said slowly. "It may be the end of human life, but there must be some forms that will survive—some micro-organisms perhaps capable of resisting high temperatures, if nothing higher. The seed of life will be left at any rate, and that is everything. Evolution will begin over again, producing new types to suit the changed conditions. I only wish I could see what creatures will be here in a few thousand years.

"But I can't realize it at all—this thing!" he cried passionately, after a pause. "Is it real? Or have we all gone mad? It seems too much like a bad dream."

The rain crashed down again as he spoke, and the earth steamed, though not with the dense reek of the day. For hours the waters roared and splashed against the earth in hot billows till the streets were foaming yellow rivers, dammed by the wreck of fallen buildings.

There was a continual rumble as earth and rock slid into the East River, and at last the Brooklyn Bridge collapsed with a thunderous crash and splash that made all Manhattan vibrate. A gigantic billow like a tidal wave swept up the river from its fall.

The downpour slackened and ceased soon after the moon began to shed an obscured but brilliant light through the clouds.

Presently the east commenced to grow luminous, and this time there could be no doubt as to what was coming.

Alice crept closer to the man as the gray light rose upon the watery air.

"Kiss me!" she whispered suddenly, throwing her arms around his neck. He could feel her trembling. "Say you love me; hold me in your arms. There is only an hour."

"Don't be afraid. Try to face it bravely," stammered Eastwood.

"I don't fear it—not death. But I have never lived. I have always been timid and wretched and afraid—afraid to speak—and I've almost wished for suffering and misery or anything rather than to be stupid and dumb and dead, the way I've always been.

"I've never dared to tell anyone what I was, what I wanted. I've been afraid all my life, but I'm not afraid now. I have never lived; I have never been happy; and now we must die together!"

It seemed to Eastwood the cry of the perishing world. He held her in his arms and kissed her wet, tremulous face that was strained to his.

The twilight was gone before they knew it. The sky was blue already, with crimson flakes mounting to the zenith, and the heat was growing once more intense.

"This is the end, Alice," said Eastwood, and his voice trembled.

She looked at him, her eyes shining with an unearthly softness and brilliancy, and turned her face to the east.

There, in crimson and orange, flamed the last dawn that human eyes would ever see.

RUDYARD KIPLING

As Easy as A.B.C.

Everyone is familiar with Rudyard Kipling, the author of Kim *(1901) and the winner of the 1907 Nobel Prize for Literature. What many fail to remember, however, is that Kipling (1865-1936) wrote a great deal of fantasy. Several of his major books, including the stories in* The Jungle Book *(1894) and* Just So Stories for Little Children *(1902) are either fantasy or contain strong fantastical elements. Although his output in science fiction was modest, it was, like his other works, highly notable, especially* With the Night Mail *(1905) and the excellent dystopian story you are about to read.*

> The A.B.C., that semi-elected, semi-nominated body of a few score persons, controls the Planet. Transportation is Civilization, our motto runs. Theoretically we do what we please, so long as we do not interfere with the traffic *and all it implies*. Practically, the A.B.C. confirms or annuls all international arrangements, and, to judge from its last report, finds our tolerant, humorous, lazy little Planet only too ready to shift the whole burden of public administration on its shoulders.
>
> "With the Night Mail."

Isn't it almost time that our Planet took some interest in the proceedings of the Aërial Board of Control? One knows that easy communications nowadays, and lack of privacy in the past, have killed all curiosity among mankind, but as the Board's Official Reporter I am bound to tell my tale.

At 9:30 A.M., August 26, A.D. 2065, the Board, sitting in London, was informed by De Forest that the District of Northern Illinois had riotously cut itself out of all systems and would remain disconnected till the Board should take over and administer it direct.

Every Northern Illinois freight and passenger tower was, he reported, out of action; all District main, local, and guiding lights had been extinguished; all General Communications were dumb, and through traffic had been diverted. No reason had been given, but he gathered unofficially from the Mayor of Chicago that the District complained of "crowd-making and invasion of privacy."

As a matter of fact, it is of no importance whether Northern Illinois stay in or out of planetary circuit; as a matter of policy, any complaint of invasion of privacy needs immediate investigation, lest worse follow.

By 9:45 A.M. De Forest, Dragomiroff (Russia), Takahira (Japan), and Pirolo (Italy) were empowered to visit Illinois and "to take such steps as might be necessary for the resumption of traffic and *all that that implies.*" By 10 A.M. the Hall was empty, and the four Members and I were aboard what Pirolo insisted on calling "my leetle godchild"—that is to say, the new *Victor Pirolo.* Our Planet prefers to know Victor Pirolo as a gentle, gray-haired enthusiast who spends his time near Foggia, inventing or creating new breeds of Spanish-Italian olive-trees; but there is another side to his nature—the manufacture of quaint inventions, of which the *Victor Pirolo* is, perhaps, not the least surprising. She and a few score sister-craft of the same type embody his latest ideas. But she is not comfortable. An A.B.C. boat does not take the air with the level-keeled lift of a liner, but shoots up rocket-fashion like the "aeroplane" of our ancestors, and makes her height at top-speed from the first. That is why I found myself sitting suddenly on the large lap of Eustace Arnott, who commands the A.B.C. Fleet. One knows vaguely that there is such a thing as a Fleet somewhere on the Planet, and that, theoretically, it exists for the purposes of what used to be known as "war." Only a week before, while visiting a glacier sanatorium behind Gothaven, I had seen some squadrons making false auroras far to the north while they maneuvered round the Pole; but, naturally, it had never occurred to me that the things could be used in earnest.

Said Arnott to De Forest as I staggered to a seat on the chart-room divan: "We're tremendously grateful to 'em in Illinois. We've never had a chance of exercising all the Fleet together. I've turned in a General Call, and I expect we'll have at least two hundred keels aloft this evening."

"Well aloft?" De Forest asked.

"Of course, sir. Out of sight till they're called for."

Arnott laughed as he lolled over the transparent chart-table where the map of the summer-blue Atlantic slid along, degree by degree, in exact answer to our progress. Our dial already showed 320 m.p.h. and we were two thousand feet above the uppermost traffic lines.

"Now, where is this Illinois District of yours?" said Dragomiroff. "One travels so much, one sees so little. Oh, I remember! It is in North America."

De Forest, whose business it is to know the out districts, told us that it lay at the foot of Lake Michigan, on a road to nowhere in particular, was about half an hour's run from end to end, and, except in one corner, as flat as the sea. Like most flat countries nowadays, it was heavily guarded against invasion of privacy by forced timber—fifty-foot spruce and tamarack, grown in five years. The population was close on two millions, largely migratory between Florida and California, with a backbone of small farms (they call a thousand acres a farm in Illinois) whose owners come into Chicago for amusements and society during the winter. They were, he said, noticeably kind, quiet folk, but a little exacting, as all flat countries must be, in their notions of privacy. There had, for instance, been no printed news-sheet in Illinois for twenty-seven years. Chicago argued that engines for printed news sooner or later developed into engines for invasion of privacy, which in turn might bring the old terror of Crowds and blackmail back to the Planet. So news-sheets were not.

"And that's Illinois," De Forest concluded. "You see, in the Old Days, she was in the forefront of what they used to call 'progress,' and Chicago—"

"Chicago?" said Takahira. "That's the little place where there is Salati's Statue of the Nigger in Flames? A fine bit of old work."

"When did you see it?" asked De Forest quickly. "They only unveil it once a year."

"I know. At Thanksgiving. It was then," said Takahira, with a shudder. "And they sang MacDonough's Song, too."

"Whew!" De Forest whistled. "I did not know that! I wish you'd told me before. MacDonough's Song may have had its uses when it was composed, but it was an infernal legacy for any man to leave behind."

"It's protective instinct, my dear fellows," said Pirolo, rolling a cigarette. "The Planet, she has had her dose of popular government. She suffers from inherited agoraphobia. She has no—ah—use for Crowds."

Dragomiroff leaned forward to give him a light. "Certainly," said the white-bearded Russian, "the Planet has taken all precautions against Crowds for the past hundred years. What is our total population today? Six hundred million, we hope; five hundred, we think; but—but if next year's census shows more than four hundred and fifty, I myself will eat all the extra little babies. We have cut the birth-rate out—right out! For a long time we have said to Almighty God, 'Thank You, Sir, but we do not much like Your game of life, so we will not play.'"

"Anyhow," said Arnott defiantly, "men live a century apiece on the average now."

"Oh, that is quite well! I am rich—you are rich—we are all rich and happy because we are so few and we live so long. Only *I* think Almighty God He will remember what the Planet was like in the time of Crowds and the Plague. Perhaps He will send us nerves. Eh, Pirolo?"

The Italian blinked into space. "Perhaps," he said, "He has sent them already. Anyhow, you cannot argue with the Planet. She does not forget the Old Days, and—what can you do?"

"For sure we can't remake the world." De Forest glanced at the map flowing smoothly across the table from west to east. "We ought to be over our ground by nine tonight. There won't be much sleep afterwards."

On which hint we dispersed, and I slept till Takahira waked me for dinner. Our ancestors thought nine hours' sleep ample for their little lives. We, living thirty years longer, feel ourselves defrauded with less than eleven out of the twenty-four.

By ten o'clock we were over Lake Michigan. The west shore was lightless, except for a dull ground-glare at Chicago, and a single traffic-directing light—its leading beam pointing north—at Waukegan on our starboard bow. None of the Lake villages gave any sign of life; and inland, westward, so far as we could see, blackness lay unbroken on the level earth. We swooped down and skimmed low across the dark, throwing calls county by county. Now and again we picked up the faint glimmer of a house-light, or heard the rasp and rend of a cultivator being played across the fields, but Northern Illinois as a whole was one inky, apparently uninhabited, waste of high, forced woods. Only our illuminated map, with its little pointer switching from county to county as we wheeled and twisted, gave us any idea of our position. Our calls, urgent, pleading, coaxing or commanding, through the General Communicator brought no answer. Illinois strictly maintained her own privacy in the timber which she grew for that purpose.

"Oh, this is absurd!" said De Forest. "We're like an owl trying to work a wheat-field. Is this Bureau Creek? Let's land, Arnott, and get hold of someone."

We brushed over a belt of forced woodland—fifteen-year-old maple sixty feet high—grounded on a private meadow-dock, none too big, where we moored to our own grapnels, and hurried out through the warm dark night towards a light in a verandah. As we neared the garden gate I could have sworn we had stepped knee-deep in quicksand, for we could scarcely drag our feet against the prickling currents that clogged them. After five paces we stopped, wiping our foreheads, as hopelessly stuck on dry smooth turf as so many cows in a bog.

"Pest!" cried Pirolo angrily. "We are ground-circuited. And it is my own system of ground-circuits too! I know the pull."

"Good evening," said a girl's voice from the verandah. "Oh, I'm sorry! We've locked up. Wait a minute."

We heard the click of a switch, and almost fell forward as the currents round our knees were withdrawn.

The girl laughed, and laid aside her knitting. An old-fashioned Controller stood at her elbow, which she reversed from time to time, and we could hear the snort and clank of the obedient cultivator half a mile away, behind the guardian woods.

"Come in and sit down," she said. "I'm only playing a plow. Dad's gone to Chicago to—Ah! Then it was *your* call I heard just now!"

She had caught sight of Arnott's Board uniform, leaped to the switch, and turned it full on.

We were checked, gasping, waist-deep in current this time, three yards from the verandah.

"We only want to know what's the matter with Illinois," said De Forest placidly.

"Then hadn't you better go to Chicago and find out?" she answered. "There's nothing wrong here. We own ourselves."

"How can we go anywhere if you won't loose us?" De Forest went on, while Arnott scowled. Admirals of Fleets are still quite human when their dignity is touched.

"Stop a minute—you don't know how funny you look!" She put her hands on her hips and laughed mercilessly.

"Don't worry about that," said Arnott, and whistled. A voice answered from the *Victor Pirolo* in the meadow.

"Only a single-fuse ground-circuit!" Arnott called. "Sort it out gently, please."

We heard the ping of a breaking lamp; a fuse blew out somewhere in the verandah roof, frightening a nestful of birds. The ground-circuit was open. We stooped and rubbed our tingling ankles.

"How rude—how very rude of you!" the maiden cried.

"Sorry, but we haven't time to look funny," said Arnott. "We've got to go to Chicago; and if I were you, young lady, I'd go into the cellars for the next two hours, and take mother with me."

Off he strode, with us at his heels, muttering indignantly, till the humor of the thing struck and doubled him up with laughter at the foot of the gangway ladder.

"The Board hasn't shown what you might call a fat spark on this occasion," said De Forest, wiping his eyes. "I hope I didn't look as big a fool as you did, Arnott! Hullo! What on earth is that? Dad coming home from Chicago?"

There was a rattle and a rush, and a five-plow cultivator, blades in air like so many teeth, trundled itself at us round the edge of the timber, fuming and sparking furiously.

"Jump!" said Arnott, as we bundled ourselves through the none-too-wide door. "Never mind about shutting it. Up!"

The *Victor Pirolo* lifted like a bubble, and the vicious machine shot just underneath us, clawing high as it passed.

"There's a nice little spit-kitten for you!" said Arnott, dusting his knees. "We ask her a civil question. First she circuits us and then she plays a cultivator at us!"

"And then we fly," said Dragomiroff. "If I were forty years more young, I would go back and kiss her. Ho! Ho!"

"I," said Pirolo, "would smack her! My pet ship has been chased by a dirty plow; a—how do you say?—agricultural implement."

"Oh, that is Illinois all over," said De Forest. "They don't content themselves with talking about privacy. They arrange to have it. And now, where's your alleged fleet, Arnott? We must assert ourselves against this wench."

Arnott pointed to the black heavens.

"Waiting on—up there," said he. "Shall I give them the whole installation, sir?"

"Oh, I don't think the young lady is quite worth that," said De Forest. "Get over Chicago, and perhaps we'll see something."

In a few minutes we were hanging at two thousand feet over an oblong block of incandescence in the center of the little town.

"That looks like the old City Hall. Yes, there's Salati's Statue in front of it," said Takahira. "But what on earth are they doing to the place? I thought they used it for a market nowadays! Drop a little, please."

We could hear the sputter and crackle of road-surfacing machines—the cheap Western type which fuse stone and rubbish into lava-like ribbed glass for their rough country roads. Three or four surfacers worked on each side of a square of ruins. The brick and stone wreckage crumbled, slid forward, and presently spread out into white-hot pools of sticky slag, which the leveling-rods smoothed more or less flat. Already a third of the big block had been so treated, and was cooling to dull red before our astonished eyes.

"It is the Old Market," said De Forest. "Well, there's nothing to prevent Illinois from making a road through a market. It doesn't interfere with traffic, that I can see."

"Hsh!" said Arnott, gripping me by the shoulder. "Listen! They're singing. Why on earth are they singing?"

We dropped again till we could see the black fringe of people at the edge of that glowing square.

At first they only roared against the roar of the surfacers and levelers. Then the words came up clearly—the words of the Forbidden Song that all men knew, and none let pass their lips—poor Pat MacDonough's Song, made in the days of the Crowds and the Plague—every silly word of it loaded to sparking-point with the

Planet's inherited memories of horror, panic, fear and cruelty. And Chicago—innocent, contented little Chicago—was singing it aloud to the infernal tune that carried riot, pestilence and lunacy round our Planet a few generations ago!

> "Once there was The People—Terror gave it birth;
> Once there was The People, and it made a hell of earth!"

(Then the stamp and pause):

> "Earth arose and crushed it. Listen, oh, ye slain!
> Once there was The People—it shall never be again!"

The levelers thrust in savagely against the ruins as the song renewed itself again, again and again, louder than the crash of the melting walls.

De Forest frowned.

"I don't like that," he said. "They've broken back to the Old Days! They'll be killing somebody soon. I think we'd better divert 'em, Arnott."

"Ay, ay, sir." Arnott's hand went to his cap, and we heard the hull of the *Victor Pirolo* ring to the command: "Lamps! Both watches stand by! Lamps! Lamps! Lamps!"

"Keep still!" Takahira whispered to me. "Blinkers, please, quartermaster."

"It's all right—all right!" said Pirolo from behind, and to my horror slipped over my head some sort of rubber helmet that locked with a snap. I could feel thick colloid bosses before my eyes, but I stood in absolute darkness.

"To save the sight," he explained, and pushed me on to the chart-room divan. "You will see in a minute."

As he spoke I became aware of a thin thread of almost intolerable light, let down from heaven at an immense distance—one vertical hairsbreadth of frozen lightning.

"Those are our flanking ships," said Arnott at my elbow. "That one is over Galena. Look south—that other one's over Keithburg. Vincennes is behind us, and north yonder is Winthrop Woods. The Fleet's in position, sir"—this to De Forest. "As soon as you give the word."

"Ah no! No!" cried Dragomiroff at my side. I could feel the old man tremble. "I do not know all that you can do, but be kind! I ask you to be a little kind to them below! This is horrible—horrible!"

> "When a Woman kills a Chicken,
> Dynasties and Empires sicken,"

Takahira quoted. "It is too late to be gentle now."

"Then take off my helmet! Take off my helmet!" Dragomiroff began hysterically. Pirolo must have put his arm round him.

"Hush," he said, "I am here. It is all right, Ivan, my dear fellow."

"I'll just send our little girl in Bureau County a warning," said Arnott. "She don't deserve it, but we'll allow her a minute or two to take mamma to the cellar."

In the utter hush that followed the growling spark after Arnott had linked up his

Service Communicator with the invisible Fleet, we heard MacDonough's Song from the city beneath us grow fainter as we rose to position. Then I clapped my hand before my mask lenses, for it was as though the floor of heaven had been riddled and all the inconceivable blaze of suns in the making was poured through the manholes.

"You needn't count," said Arnott. I had had no thought of such a thing. "There are two hundred and fifty keels up there, five miles apart. Full power, please, for another twelve seconds."

The firmament, as far as the eye could reach, stood on pillars of white fire. One fell on the glowing square at Chicago, and turned it black.

"Oh! Oh! Oh! Can men be allowed to do such things?" Dragomiroff cried, and fell across our knees.

"Glass of water, please," said Takahira to a helmeted shape that leaped forward. "He is a little faint."

The lights switched off, and the darkness stunned like an avalanche. We could hear Dragomiroff's teeth on the glass edge.

Pirolo was comforting him.

"All right, all ra-ight," he repeated. "Come and lie down. Come below and take off your mask. I give you my word, old friend, it is all right. They are my siege-lights. Little Victor Pirolo's leetle lights. You know *me!* I do not hurt people."

"Pardon!" Dragomiroff moaned. "I have never seen Death. I have never seen the Board take action. Shall we go down and burn them alive, or is that already done?"

"Oh, hush," said Pirolo, and I think he rocked him in his arms.

"Do we repeat, sir?" Arnott asked De Forest.

"Give 'em a minute's break," De Forest replied. "They may need it."

We waited a minute, and then MacDonough's Song, broken but defiant, rose from undefeated Chicago.

"They seem fond of that tune," said De Forest. "I should let 'em have it, Arnott."

"Very good, sir," said Arnott, and felt his way to the Communicator keys.

No lights broke forth, but the hollow of the skies made herself the mouth for one note that touched the raw fiber of the brain. Men hear such sounds in delirium, advancing like tides from horizons beyond the ruled foreshores of space.

"That's our pitch-pipe," said Arnott. "We may be a bit ragged. I've never conducted two hundred and fifty performers before." He pulled out the couplers, and struck a full chord on the Service Communicators.

The beams of light leaped down again, and danced, solemnly and awfully, a stilt-dance, sweeping thirty or forty miles left and right at each stiff-legged kick, while the darkness delivered itself—there is no scale to measure against that utterance—of the tune to which they kept time. Certain notes—one learned to expect them with terror—cut through one's marrow, but, after three minutes, thought and emotion passed in indescribable agony.

We saw, we heard, but I think we were in some sort swooning. The two hundred and fifty beams shifted, re-formed, straddled and split, narrowed, widened, rippled in ribbons, broke into a thousand white-hot parallel lines, melted and revolved in interwoven rings like old-fashioned engine-turning, flung up to the zenith, made as if to descend and renew the torment, halted at the last instant, twizzled insanely round the horizon and vanished, to bring back for the hundredth time darkness more shattering than their instantly renewed light over all Illinois. Then the tune and lights ceased together, and we heard one single devastating wail that shook all the horizon as a rubbed wet finger shakes the rim of a bowl.

"Ah, that is my new siren," said Pirolo. "You can break an iceberg in half, if you find the proper pitch. They will whistle by squadrons now. It is the wind through pierced shutters in the bows."

I had collapsed beside Dragomiroff, broken and sniveling feebly, because I had been delivered before my time to all the terrors of Judgment Day, and the Archangels of the Resurrection were hailing me naked across the Universe to the sound of the music of the spheres.

Then I saw De Forest smacking Arnott's helmet with his open hand. The wailing died down in a long shriek as a black shadow swooped past us, and returned to her place above the lower clouds.

"I hate to interrupt a specialist when he's enjoying himself," said De Forest. "But, as a matter of fact, all Illinois has been asking us to stop for these last fifteen seconds."

"What a pity." Arnott slipped off his mask. "I wanted you to hear us really hum. Our lower C can lift street-paving."

"It is Hell—Hell!" cried Dragomiroff, and sobbed aloud.

Arnott looked away as he answered:

"It's a few thousand volts ahead of the old shoot-'em-and sink-'em game, but I should scarcely call it *that*. What shall I tell the Fleet, sir?"

"Tell 'em we're very pleased and impressed. I don't think they need wait any longer. There isn't a spark left down there." De Forest pointed. "They'll be deaf and blind."

"Oh, I think not, sir. The demonstration lasted less than ten minutes."

"Marvelous!" Takahira sighed. "I should have said it was half a night. Now, shall we go down and pick up the pieces?"

"But first a small drink," said Pirolo. "The Board must not arrive weeping at its own works."

"I am an old fool—an old fool!" Dragomiroff began piteously. "I did not know what would happen. It is all new to me. We reason with them in Little Russia."

Chicago North landing-tower was unlighted, and Arnott worked his ship into the clips by her own lights. As soon as these broke out we heard groanings of horror and appeal from many people below.

"All right," shouted Arnott into the darkness. "We aren't beginning again!" We descended by the stairs, to find ourselves knee-deep in a groveling crowd, some crying that they were blind, others beseeching us not to make any more noises, but the greater part writhing face downward, their hands or their caps before their eyes.

It was Pirolo who came to our rescue. He climbed the side of a surfacing-machine, and there, gesticulating as though they could see, made oration to those afflicted people of Illinois.

"You stchewpids!" he began. "There is nothing to fuss for. Of course, your eyes will smart and be red tomorrow. You will look as if you and your wives had drunk too much, but in a little while you will see again as well as before. I tell you this, and I—*I* am Pirolo. Victor Pirolo!"

The crowd with one accord shuddered, for many legends attach to Victor Pirolo of Foggia, deep in the secrets of God.

"Pirolo?" An unsteady voice lifted itself. "Then tell us was there anything except light in those lights of yours just now?"

The question was repeated from every corner of the darkness.

Pirolo laughed.

"No!" he thundered. (Why have small men such large voices?) "I give you my word and the Board's word that there was nothing except light—just light! You stchewpids! Your birth-rate is too low already as it is. Some day I must invent something to send it up, but send it down—never!"

"Is that true?—We thought—somebody said—"

One could feel the tension relax all round.

"You *too* big fools," Pirolo cried. "You could have sent us a call and we would have told you."

"Send you a call!" a deep voice shouted. "I wish you had been at our end of the wire."

"I'm glad I wasn't," said De Forest. "It was bad enough from behind the lamps. Never mind! It's over now. Is there any one here I can talk business with? I'm De Forest—for the Board."

"You might begin with me, for one—I'm Mayor," the bass voice replied.

A big man rose unsteadily from the street, and staggered towards us where we sat on the broad turf-edging, in front of the garden fences.

"I ought to be the first on my feet. Am I?" said he.

"Yes," said De Forest, and steadied him as he dropped down beside us.

"Hello, Andy. Is that you?" a voice called.

"Excuse me," said the Mayor; "that sounds like my Chief of Police, Bluthner!"

"Bluthner it is; and here's Mulligan and Keefe—on their feet."

"Bring 'em up please, Blut. We're supposed to be the Four in charge of this hamlet. What we say, goes. And, De Forest, what do you say?"

"Nothing—yet," De Forest answered, as we made room for the panting, reeling men. "*You've* cut out of system. Well?"

"Tell the steward to send down drinks, please," Arnott whispered to an orderly at his side.

"Good!" said the Mayor, smacking his dry lips. "Now I suppose we can take it, De Forest, that henceforward the Board will administer us direct?"

"Not if the Board can avoid it," De Forest laughed. "The A.B.C. is responsible for the planetary traffic only."

"*And all that that implies*." The big Four who ran Chicago chanted their Magna Charta like children at school.

"Well, get on," said De Forest wearily. "What is your silly trouble anyway?"

"Too much dam' Democracy," said the Mayor, laying his hand on De Forest's knee.

"So? I thought Illinois had had her dose of that."

"She has. That's why. Blut, what did you do with our prisoners last night?"

"Locked 'em in the water-tower to prevent the women killing 'em," the Chief of Police replied. "I'm too blind to move just yet, but—"

"Arnott, send some of your people, please, and fetch 'em along," said De Forest.

"They're triple-circuited," the Mayor called. "You'll have to blow out three fuses." He turned to De Forest, his large outline just visible in the paling darkness. "I hate to throw any more work on the Board. I'm an administrator myself, but we've had a little fuss with our Serviles. What? In a big city there's bound to be a few men and women who can't live without listening to themselves, and who prefer drinking out of pipes they don't own both ends of. They inhabit flats and hotels all the year round. They say it saves 'em trouble. Anyway, it gives 'em more time to make trouble for their neighbors. We call 'em Serviles locally. And they are apt to be tuberculous."

"Just so!" said the man called Mulligan. "Transportation is Civilization. Democracy is Disease. I've proved it by the blood-test, every time."

"Mulligan's our Health Officer, and a one-idea man," said the Mayor, laughing. "But it's true that most Serviles haven't much control. They *will* talk; and when people take to talking as a business, anything may arrive—mayn't it, De Forest?"

"Anything—except the facts of the case," said De Forest, laughing.

"I'll give you those in a minute," said the Mayor. "Our Serviles got to talking—first in their houses and then on the streets, telling men and women how to manage their own affairs. (You can't teach a Servile not to finger his neighbor's soul.) That's invasion of privacy, of course, but in Chicago we'll suffer anything sooner than make Crowds. Nobody took much notice, and so I let 'em alone. My fault! I was warned there would be trouble, but there hasn't been a Crowd or murder in Illinois for nineteen years."

"Twenty-two," said his Chief of Police.

"Likely. Anyway, we'd forgot such things. So, from talking in the houses and on the streets, our Serviles go to calling a meeting at the Old Market yonder." He nodded across the square where the wrecked buildings heaved up gray in the dawn-glimmer behind the square-cased statue of The Negro in Flames. "There's nothing to prevent any one calling meetings except that it's against human nature to stand in a Crowd, besides being bad for the health. I ought to have known by the way our men and women attended that first meeting that trouble was brewing. There were as many as a thousand in the market-place, touching each other. Touching! Then the Serviles turned in all tongue-switches and talked, and we—"

"What did they talk about?" said Takahira.

"First, how badly things were managed in the city. That pleased us Four—we were on the platform—because we hoped to catch one or two good men for City work. You know how rare executive capacity is. Even if we didn't it's—it's refreshing to find anyone interested enough in our job to damn our eyes. You don't know what it means to work, year in, year out, without a spark of difference with a living soul."

"Oh, don't we!" said De Forest. "There are times on the Board when we'd give our positions if any one would kick us out and take hold of things themselves."

"But they won't," said the Mayor ruefully. "I assure you, sir, we Four have done things in Chicago, in the hope of rousing people, that would have discredited

Nero. But what do they say? 'Very good, Andy. Have it your own way. Anything's better than a Crowd. I'll go back to my land.' You *can't* do anything with folk who can go where they please, and don't want anything on God's earth except their own way. There isn't a kick or a kicker left on the Planet."

"Then I suppose that little shed yonder fell down by itself?" said De Forest. We could see the bare and still smoking ruins, and hear the slag-pools crackle as they hardened and set.

"Oh, that's only amusement. Tell you later. As I was saying, our Serviles held the meeting, and pretty soon we had to ground-circuit the platform to save 'em from being killed. And that didn't make our people any more pacific."

"How d'you mean?" I ventured to ask.

"If you've ever been ground-circuited," said the Mayor, "you'll know it don't improve any man's temper to be held up straining against nothing. No, sir! Eight or nine hundred folk kept pawing and buzzing like flies in treacle for two hours, while a pack of perfectly safe Serviles invades their mental and spiritual privacy, may be amusing to watch, but they are not pleasant to handle afterwards."

Pirolo chuckled.

"Our folk own themselves. They were of opinion things were going too far and too fiery. I warned the Serviles; but they're born house-dwellers. Unless a fact hits 'em on the head they cannot see it. Would you believe me, they went on to talk of what they called 'popular government'? They did! They wanted us to go back to the old Voodoo-business of voting with papers and wooden boxes, and word-drunk people and printed formulas, and news-sheets! They said they practiced it among themselves about what they'd have to eat in their flats and hotels. Yes, sir! They stood up behind Bluthner's doubled ground-circuits, and they said that, in this present year of grace, *to* self-owning men and women, *on* that very spot! Then they finished"—he lowered his voice cautiously—"by talking about 'The People.' And then Bluthner he had to sit up all night in charge of the circuits because he couldn't trust his men to keep 'em shut."

"It was trying 'em too high," the Chief of Police broke in. "But we couldn't hold the Crowd ground-circuited for ever. I gathered in all the Serviles on charge of Crowd-making, and put 'em in the water-tower, and then I let things cut loose. I had to! The District lit like a sparked gas-tank!"

"The news was out over seven degrees of country," the Mayor continued; "and when once it's a question of invasion of privacy, good-bye to right and reason in Illinois! They began turning out traffic-lights and locking up landing-towers on Thursday night. Friday, they stopped all traffic and asked for the Board to take over. Then they wanted to clean Chicago off the side of the Lake and rebuild elsewhere—just for a souvenir of 'The People' that the Serviles talked about. I suggested that they should slag the Old Market where the meeting was held, while I turned in a call to you all on the Board. That kept 'em quiet till you came along. And—and now *you* can take hold of the situation."

"Any chance of their quieting down?" De Forest asked.

"You can try," said the Mayor.

De Forest raised his voice in the face of the reviving Crowd that had edged in towards us. Day was come.

"Don't you think this business can be arranged?" he began. But there was a roar of angry voices:

"We've finished with Crowds! We aren't going back to the Old Days! Take us over! Take the Serviles away! Administer direct or we'll kill 'em! Down with The People!"

An attempt was made to begin MacDonough's Song. It got no further than the first line, for the *Victor Pirolo* sent down a warning drone on one stopped horn. A wrecked sidewall of the Old Market tottered and fell inwards on the slagpools. None spoke or moved till the last of the dust had settled down again, turning the steel case of Salati's Statue ashy gray.

"You see you'll just *have* to take us over," the Mayor whispered.

De Forest shrugged his shoulders.

"You talk as if executive capacity could be snatched out of the air like so much horse-power. Can't you manage yourselves on any terms?" he said.

"We can, if you say so. It will only cost those few lives to begin with."

The Mayor pointed across the square, where Arnott's men guided a stumbling group of ten or twelve men and women to the lake front and halted them under the Statue.

"Now I think," said Takahira under his breath, "there will be trouble."

The mass in front of us growled like beasts.

At that moment the sun rose clear, and revealed the blinking assembly to itself. As soon as it realized that it was a crowd we saw the shiver of horror and mutual repulsion shoot across it precisely as the steely flaws shot across the lake outside. Nothing was said, and, being half blind, of course it moved slowly. Yet in less than fifteen minutes most of that vast multitude—three thousand at the lowest count—melted away like frost on south eaves. The remnant stretched themselves on the grass, where a crowd feels and looks less like a crowd.

"These mean business," the Mayor whispered to Takahira. "There are a goodish few women there who've borne children. I don't like it."

The morning draft off the lake stirred the trees round us with promise of a hot day; the sun reflected itself dazzlingly on the canister-shaped covering of Salati's Statue; cocks crew in the gardens, and we could hear gate-latches clicking in the distance as people stumblingly resought their homes.

"I'm afraid there won't be any morning deliveries," said De Forest. "We rather upset things in the country last night."

"That makes no odds," the Mayor returned. "We're all provisioned for six months. *We* take no chances."

Nor, when you come to think of it, does any one else. It must be three-quarters of a generation since any house or city faced a food shortage. Yet is there house or city on the Planet today that has not half a year's provisions laid in? We are like the shipwrecked seamen in the old books, who, having once nearly starved to death, ever afterwards hid away bits of food and biscuit. Truly we trust no Crowds, nor system based on Crowds!

De Forest waited till the last footstep had died away. Meantime the prisoners at the base of the Statue shuffled, posed and fidgeted, with the shamelessness of quite little children. None of them were more than six feet high, and many of them were as gray-haired as the ravaged, harassed heads of old pictures. They huddled together in actual touch, while the crowd, spaced at large intervals, looked at them with congested eyes.

Suddenly a man among them began to talk. The Mayor had not in the least exaggerated. It appeared that our Planet lay sunk in slavery beneath the heel of the Aërial Board of Control. The orator urged us to arise in our might, burst our prison doors and break our fetters (all his metaphors, by the way, were of the most medieval). Next he demanded that every matter of daily life, including most of the physical functions, should be submitted for decision at any time of the week, month, or year to, I gathered, anybody who happened to be passing by or residing within a certain radius, and that everybody should forthwith abandon his concerns to settle the matter, first by crowd-making, next by talking to the crowds made, and lastly by describing crosses on pieces of paper, which rubbish should later be counted with certain mystic ceremonies and oaths. Out of this amazing play, he assured us, would automatically arise a higher, nobler and kinder world, based—he demonstrated this with the awful lucidity of the insane—based on the sanctity of the Crowd and the villainy of the single person. In conclusion, he called loudly upon God to testify to his personal merits and integrity. When the flow ceased, I turned bewildered to Takahira, who was nodding solemnly.

"Quite correct," said he. "It is all in the old books. He has left nothing out, not even the war-talk."

"But I don't see how this stuff can upset a child, much less a district," I replied.

"Ah, you are too young," said Dragomiroff. "For another thing, you are not a mama. Please look at the mamas."

Ten or fifteen women who remained had separated themselves from the silent men, and were drawing in towards the prisoners. It reminded one of the stealthy encircling, before the rush in at the quarry, of wolves round musk-oxen in the North. The prisoners saw, and drew together more closely. The Mayor covered his face with his hands for an instant. De Forest, bareheaded, stepped forward between the prisoners and the slowly, stiffly moving line.

"That's all very interesting," he said to the dry-lipped orator. "But the point seems that you've been making crowds and invading privacy."

A woman stepped forward, and would have spoken, but there was a quick assenting murmur from the men, who realized that De Forest was trying to pull the situation down to ground-line.

"Yes! Yes!" they cried. "We cut out because they made crowds and invaded privacy! Stick to that! Keep on that switch! Lift the Serviles out of this! The Board's in charge! Hsh!"

"Yes, the Board's in charge," said De Forest. "I'll take formal evidence of crowd-making if you like, but the Members of the Board can testify to it. Will that do?"

The women had closed in another pace, with hands that clenched and unclenched at their sides.

"Good! Good enough!" the men cried. "We're content. Only take them away quickly."

"Come along up!" said De Forest to the captives. "Breakfast is quite ready."

It appeared, however, that they did not wish to go. They intended to remain in Chicago and make crowds. They pointed out that De Forest's proposal was gross invasion of privacy.

"My dear fellow," said Pirolo to the most voluble of the leaders, "you hurry, or your crowd that can't be wrong will kill you!"

"But that would be murder," answered the believer in crowds; and there was a roar of laughter from all sides that seemed to show the crisis had broken.

A woman stepped forward from the line of women, laughing, I protest, as merrily as any of the company. One hand, of course, shaded her eyes, the other was at her throat.

"Oh, they needn't be afraid of being killed!" she called.

"Not in the least," said De Forest. "But don't you think that, now the Board's in charge, you might go home while we get these people away?"

"I shall be home long before that. It—it has been rather a trying day."

She stood up to her full height, dwarfing even De Forest's six-foot-eight, and smiled, with eyes closed against the fierce light.

"Yes, rather," said De Forest. "I'm afraid you feel the glare a little. We'll have the ship down."

He motioned to the *Pirolo* to drop between us and the sun, and at the same time to loop-circuit the prisoners, who were a trifle unsteady. We saw them stiffen to the current where they stood. The woman's voice went on, sweet and deep and unshaken:

"I don't suppose you men realize how much this—this sort of thing means to a woman. I've borne three. We women don't want our children given to Crowds. It must be an inherited instinct. Crowds make trouble. They bring back the Old Days. Hate, fear, blackmail, publicity, 'The People'—*That! That! That!*" She pointed to the Statue, and the crowd growled once more.

"Yes, if they are allowed to go on," said De Forest. "But this little affair—"

"It means so much to us women that this—this little affair should never happen again. Of course, never's a big word, but one feels so strongly that it is important to stop crowds at the very beginning. Those creatures"—she pointed with her left hand at the prisoners swaying like seaweed in a tideway as the circuit pulled them—"those people have friends and wives and children in the city and elsewhere. One doesn't want anything done to *them*, you know. It's terrible to force a human being out of fifty or sixty years of good life. I'm only forty myself. *I* know. But, at the same time, one feels that an example should be made, because no price is too heavy to pay if—if these people and *all that they imply* can be put an end to. Do you quite understand, or would you be kind enough to tell your men to take the casing off the Statue? It's worth looking at."

"I understand perfectly. But I don't think anybody here wants to see the Statue on an empty stomach. Excuse me one moment." De Forest called up to the ship, "A flying loop ready on the port side, if you please." Then to the woman he said with some crispness, "You might leave us a little discretion in the matter."

"Oh, of course. Thank you for being so patient. I know my arguments are silly, but—" She half turned away and went on in a changed voice, "Perhaps this will help you to decide."

She threw out her right arm with a knife in it. Before the blade could be returned to her throat or her bosom it was twitched from her grip, sparked as it flew out of the shadow of the ship above, and fell flashing in the sunshine at the foot of the Statue fifty yards away. The outflung arm was arrested, rigid as a bar for an instant, till the releasing circuit permitted her to bring it slowly to her side. The other women shrank back silent among the men.

Pirolo rubbed his hands, and Takahira nodded.

"That was clever of you, De Forest," said he.

"What a glorious pose!" Dragomiroff murmured, for the frightened woman was on the edge of tears.

"Why did you stop me? I would have done it!" she cried.

"I have no doubt you would," said De Forest. "But we can't waste a life like yours on these people. I hope the arrest didn't sprain your wrist; it's so hard to regulate a flying loop. But I think you are quite right about those persons' women and children. We'll take them all away with us if you promise not to do anything stupid to yourself."

"I promise—I promise." She controlled herself with an effort. "But it is so important to us women. We know what it means; and I thought if you saw I was in earnest—"

"I saw you were, and you've gained your point. I shall take all your Serviles away with me at once. The Mayor will make lists of their friends and families in the city and the district, and he'll ship them after us this afternoon."

"Sure," said the Mayor, rising to his feet. "Keefe, if you can see, hadn't you better finish leveling off the Old Market? It don't look sightly the way it is now, and we shan't use it for crowds any more."

"I think you had better wipe out that Statue as well, Mr. Mayor," said De Forest. "I don't question its merits as a work of art, but I believe it's a shade morbid."

"Certainly, sir. Oh, Keefe! Slag the Nigger before you go on to fuse the Market. I'll get to the Communicators and tell the District that the Board is in charge. Are you making any special appointments, sir?"

"None. We haven't men to waste on these backwoods. Carry on as before, but under the Board. Arnott, run your Serviles aboard, please. Ground ship and pass them through the bilge-doors. We'll wait till we've finished with this work of art."

The prisoners trailed past him, talking fluently, but unable to gesticulate in the drag of the current. Then the surfacers rolled up, two on each side of the Statue. With one accord the spectators looked elsewhere, but there was no need. Keefe turned on full power, and the thing simply melted within its case. All I saw was a surge of white-hot metal pouring over the plinth, a glimpse of Salati's inscription, "To the Eternal Memory of the Justice of the People," ere the stone base itself cracked and powdered into finest lime. The crowd cheered.

"Thank you," said De Forest; "but we want our breakfasts, and I expect you do too. Good-bye, Mr. Mayor! Delighted to see you at any time, but I hope I shan't have to, officially, for the next thirty years. Good-bye, madam. Yes. We're all given to nerves nowadays. I suffer from them myself. Good-bye, gentlemen all! You're under the tyrannous heel of the Board from this moment, but if ever you feel like breaking your fetters you've only to let us know. This is no treat to us. Good luck!"

We embarked amid shouts, and did not check our lift till they had dwindled into whispers. Then De Forest flung himself on the chart-room divan and mopped his forehead.

"I don't mind men," he panted, "but women are the devil!"

"Still the devil," said Pirolo cheerfully. "That one would have suicided."

"I know it. That was why I signaled for the flying loop to be clapped on her. I owe you an apology for that, Arnott. I hadn't time to catch your eye, and you were busy with our caitiffs. By the way, who actually answered my signal? It was a smart piece of work."

"Ilroy," said Arnott; "but he overloaded the wave. It may be pretty gallery-work to knock a knife out of a lady's hand, but didn't you notice how she rubbed 'em? He scorched her fingers. Slovenly, I call it."

"Far be it from me to interfere with Fleet discipline, but don't be too hard on the boy. If that woman had killed herself they would have killed every Servile and everything related to a Servile throughout the district by nightfall."

"That was what she was playing for," Takahira said. "And with our Fleet gone we could have done nothing to hold them."

"I may be ass enough to walk into a ground-circuit," said Arnott, "but I don't dismiss my Fleet till I'm reasonably sure that trouble is over. They're in position still, and I intend to keep 'em there till the Serviles are shipped out of the district. That last little crowd meant murder, my friends."

"Nerves! All nerves!" said Pirolo. "You cannot argue with agoraphobia."

"And it is not as if they had seen much dead—or *is* it?" said Takahira.

"In all my ninety years I have never seen Death." Dragomiroff spoke as one who would excuse himself. "Perhaps that was why—last night—"

Then it came out as we sat over breakfast, that, with the exception of Arnott and Pirolo, none of us had ever seen a corpse, or knew in what manner the spirit passes.

"We're a nice lot to flap about governing the Planet," De Forest laughed. "I confess, now it's all over, that my main fear was I mightn't be able to pull it off without losing a life."

"I thought of that too," said Arnott; "but there's no death reported, and I've inquired everywhere. What are we supposed to do with our passengers? I've fed 'em."

"We're between two switches," De Forest drawled. "If we drop them in any place that isn't under the Board the natives will make their presence an excuse for cutting out, same as Illinois did, and forcing the Board to take over. If we drop them in any place under the Board's control they'll be killed as soon as our backs are turned."

"If you say so," said Pirolo thoughtfully, "I can guarantee that they will become extinct in process of time, quite happily. What is their birth-rate now?"

"Go down and ask 'em," said De Forest.

"I think they might become nervous and tear me to bits," the philosopher of Foggia replied.

"Not really! Well?"

"Open the bilge-doors," said Takahira with a downward jerk of the thumb.

"Scarcely—after all the trouble we've taken to save 'em," said De Forest.

"Try London," Arnott suggested. "You could turn Satan himself loose there, and they'd only ask him to dinner."

"Good man! You've given me an idea. Vincent! Oh, Vincent!" He threw the General Communicator open so that we could all hear, and in a few minutes the chart-room filled with the rich, fruity voice of Leopold Vincent, who has purveyed all London her choicest amusements for the last thirty years. We answered with expectant grins, as though we were actually in the stalls of, say, the Combination on a first night.

"We've picked up something in your line," De Forest began.

"That's good, dear man. If it's old enough. There's nothing to beat the old things for business purposes. Have you seen *London, Chatham and Dover* at Earl's Court? No? I thought I missed you there. Immense! I've had the real steam locomotive engines built from the old designs and the iron rails cast specially by hand. Cloth cushions in the carriages, too! Immense! And paper railway tickets. And Polly Milton."

"Polly Milton back again!" said Arnott rapturously. "Book me two stalls for tomorrow night. What's she singing now, bless her?"

"The old songs. Nothing comes up to the old touch. Listen to this, dear men." Vincent carolled with flourishes:

> Oh, cruel lamps of London,
> If tears your light could drown,
> Your victims' eyes would weep them,
> Oh, lights of London Town!

"Then they weep."

"You see?" Pirolo waved his hands at us. "The old world always weeped when it saw crowds together. It did not know why, but it weeped. We know why, but we do not weep, except when we pay to be made to by fat, wicked old Vincent."

"Old, yourself!" Vincent laughed. "I'm a public benefactor, I keep the world soft and united."

"And I'm De Forest of the Board," said De Forest acidly, "trying to get a little business done. As I was saying, I've picked up a few people in Chicago."

"I cut out. Chicago is—"

"Do listen! They're perfectly unique."

"Do they build houses of baked mudblocks while you wait—eh? That's an old contact."

"They're an untouched primitive community, with all the old ideas."

"Sewing-machines and maypole-dances? Cooking on coal-gas stoves, lighting pipes with matches, and driving horses? Gerolstein tried that last year. An absolute blow-out!"

De Forest plugged him wrathfully, and poured out the story of our doings for the last twenty-four hours on the topnote.

"And they do it *all* in public," he concluded. "You can't stop 'em. The more public, the better they are pleased. They'll talk for hours—like you! Now you can come in again!"

"Do you really mean they know how to vote?" said Vincent. "Can they act it?"

"Act? It's their life to 'em! And you never saw such faces! Scarred like volcanoes. Envy, hatred and malice in plain sight. Wonderfully flexible voices. They weep, too."

"Aloud? In public?"

"I guarantee. Not a spark of shame or reticence in the entire installation. It's the chance of your career."

"D'you say you've brought their voting props along—those papers and ballot-box things?"

"No, confound you! I'm not a luggage-lifter. Apply direct to the Mayor of Chicago. He'll forward you everything. Well?"

"Wait a minute. Did Chicago want to kill 'em? That 'ud look well on the Communicators."

"Yes! They were only rescued with difficulty from a howling mob—if you know what that is."

"But I don't," answered the Great Vincent simply.

"Well then, they'll tell you themselves. They can make speeches hours long."

"How many are there?"

"By the time we ship 'em all over they'll be perhaps a hundred, counting children. An old world in miniature. Can't you see it?"

"M-yes; but I've got to pay for it if it's a blow-out, dear man."

"They can sing the old war songs in the streets. They can get word-drunk, and make crowds, and invade privacy in the genuine old-fashioned way; and they'll do the voting trick as often as you ask 'em a question."

"Too good!" said Vincent.

"You unbelieving Jew! I've got a dozen head aboard here. I'll put you through direct. Sample 'em yourself."

He lifted the switch and we listened. Our passengers on the lower deck at once, but not less than five at a time, explained themselves to Vincent. They had been taken from the bosom of their families, stripped of their possessions, given food without finger-bowls, and cast into captivity in a noisome dungeon.

"But look here," said Arnott aghast; "they're saying what isn't true. My lower deck isn't noisome, and I saw to the finger-bowls myself."

"My people talk like that sometimes in Little Russia," said Dragomiroff. "We reason with them. We never kill. No!"

"But it's not true," Arnott insisted. "What can you do with people who don't tell facts? They're mad!"

"Hsh!" said Pirolo, his hand to his ear. "It is such a little time since all the Planet told lies."

We heard Vincent silkily sympathetic. Would they, he asked, repeat their assertions in public—before a vast public? Only let Vincent give them a chance, and the Planet, they vowed, should ring with their wrongs. Their aim in life—two women and a man explained it together—was to reform the world. Oddly enough, this also had been Vincent's life-dream. He offered them an arena in which to explain, and by their living example to raise the Planet to loftier levels. He was eloquent on the moral uplift of a simple old-world life presented in its entirety to a deboshed civilization.

Could they—would they—for three months certain, devote themselves under his auspices, as missionaries, to the elevation of mankind at a place called Earl's Court, which he said, with some truth, was one of the intellectual centers of the Planet? They thanked him, and demanded (we could hear his chuckle of delight) time to discuss and to vote on the matter. The vote, solemnly managed by counting heads—one head, one vote—was favorable. His offer, therefore, was accepted, and they moved a vote of thanks to him in two speeches—one by what they called the "proposer" and the other by the "seconder."

Vincent threw over to us, his voice shaking with gratitude:

"I've got 'em! Did you hear those speeches? That's Nature, dear men. Art can't teach *that*. And they voted as easily as lying. I've never had a troupe of natural liars before. Bless you, dear men! Remember, you're on my free lists for ever, anywhere—all of you. Oh, Gerolstein will be sick—sick!"

"Then you think they'll do?" said De Forest.

"Do? The Little Village 'll go crazy! I'll knock up a series of old-world plays for 'em. Their voices will make you laugh and cry. My God, dear men, where *do* you suppose they picked up all their misery from, on this sweet earth? I'll have a pageant of the world's beginnings, and Mosenthal shall do the music. I'll—"

"Go and knock up a village for 'em by tonight. We'll meet you at No. 15 West Landing Tower," said De Forest. "Remember the rest will be coming along tomorrow."

"Let 'em all come!" said Vincent. "You don't know how hard it is nowadays even for me, to find something that really gets under the public's damned iridium-plated hide. But I've got it at last. Good-bye!"

"Well," said De Forest when we had finished laughing, "if anyone understood corruption in London I might have played off Vincent against Gerolstein, and sold my captives at enormous prices. As it is, I shall have to be their legal adviser tonight when the contracts are signed. And they won't exactly press any commission on me, either."

"Meantime," said Takahira, "we cannot, of course, confine members of Leopold Vincent's last-engaged company. Chairs for the ladies, please, Arnott."

"Then I go to bed," said De Forest. "I can't face any more women!" And he vanished.

When our passengers were released and given another meal (finger-bowls came first this time) they told us what they thought of us and the Board; and, like Vincent, we all marveled how they had contrived to extract and secrete so much bitter poison and unrest out of the good life God gives us. They raged, they stormed, they palpitated, flushed and exhausted their poor, torn nerves, panted themselves into silence and renewed the senseless, shameless attacks.

"But can't you understand," said Pirolo pathetically to a shrieking woman, "that if we'd left you in Chicago, you'd have been killed?"

"No, we shouldn't. You were bound to save us from being murdered."

"Then we should have had to kill a lot of other people."

"That doesn't matter. We were preaching the Truth. You can't stop us. We shall go on preaching in London; and *then* you'll see!"

"You can see now," said Pirolo, and opened a lower shutter.

We were closing on the Little Village, with her three million people spread out at ease inside her ring of girdling Main-Traffic lights—those eight fixed beams at Chatham, Tonbridge, Redhill, Dorking, Woking, St. Albans, Chipping Ongar, and Southend.

Leopold Vincent's new company looked, with small pale faces, at the silence, the size and the separated houses.

Then some began to weep aloud, shamelessly—always without shame.

MacDonough's song

Whether the State can loose and bind
  In Heaven as well as on Earth:
If it be wiser to kill mankind
  Before or after the birth—
These are matters of high concern
  Where State-kept schoolmen are;
But Holy State (we have lived to learn)
  Endeth in Holy War.

Whether The People be led by the Lord,
  Or lured by the loudest throat:
If it be quicker to die by the sword
  Or cheaper to die by vote—
These are the things we have dealt with once,
  (And they will not rise from their grave)
For Holy People, however it runs,
  Endeth in wholly Slave.

Whatsoever, for any cause,
  Seeketh to take or give.
Power above or beyond the Laws,
  Suffer it not to live!
Holy State or Holy King—
  Or Holy People's Will—
Have no truck with the senseless thing.
  Order the guns and kill!
    Saying—after—me:—

Once there was The People—Terror gave it birth:
Once there was The People and it made a Hell of Earth.
Earth arose and crushed it. Listen, O ye slain!
Once there was The People—it shall never be again!

M. P. SHIEL

Dark Lot of One Saul

Matthew Phipps Shiel (1865-1947) was a complex man who produced nine science fiction novels and many short stories, primarily in a burst of writing activity before World War I. His work was always interesting and exciting, but it was marred by a pervasive racism and religious bigotry—indeed, he was one of the worst of the "Yellow Peril" instigators in literature, especially in his The Yellow Danger *(1898, one of his first novels).* The Lord of the Sea *(1901) has him expelling the Jews of Europe to Palestine, making Shiel a Zionist of sorts. He was also representative of those writers who used science fiction as advocacy, including the replacement of religion by science. "Dark Lot of One Saul" is typically Shielian in the audacity of its concept and in the soaring richness of its resonant style.*

WHAT I relate is from a document found in a Cowling Library chest of records, written in a very odd hand on fifteen strips of a material resembling papyrus, yet hardly papyrus, and on two squares of parchment, which Professor Stannistreet recognizes as "trunkfish" skin; the seventeen pages being gummed together at top by a material like tar or pitch. A Note at the end in a different hand and ink, signed "E.G.," says that the document was got out of a portugal (a large variety of cask) by the Spanish galleass *Capitana* between the Bermudas and the island of St. Thomas; and our knowledge that at this point a valley in the sea-bottom goes down to a depth of four thousand fathoms affords, as will be noticed, a rather startling confirmation of the statements made in the document. The narrator, one Saul, was born sixteen to twenty years before the accession of Queen Elizabeth, and wrote about 1601, at the age of sixty, or so; and the correspondence of his statements with our modern knowledge is the more arresting, since, of course, a sailor of that period would only know anything of submarine facts by actual experience. I modify a few of his archaic expressions (guessing at some words where his ink ran):

This pressing paucity of air hath brought me to the writing of that which befel, to the end that I may send forth the writing from the cave in the portugal for the eye of who may find it, my pen being a splinter broken from the elephant's bones,

78

mine ink pitch from the lake, and my paper the bulrush pith. Beginning therefore with my birth, I say that my name in the world was James Dowdy Saul, I being the third child of Percy Dowdy Saul, and of Martha his wife, born at Upland Mead, a farm in the freehold of my father, near the borough of Bideford, in Devon: in what year born I know not, knowing only this, that I was a well-grown stripling upon the coming of Her Grace to the throne.

I was early sent to be schooled by Dominie John Fisher in the borough, and had made good progress in the Latin Grammar (for my father would have me to be a clerk), when, at the age of fifteen, as I conjecture, I ran away, upon a fight with Martin Lutter, that was my eldest brother, to the end that I might adopt the sea as my calling. Thereupon for two years I was with the shipmaster, Edwin Occhines, in the balinger, *Dane*, trading with Channel ports; and at his demise took ship at Penzance with the notorious Master Thomas Stukely, who, like many another Devon gentleman, went a-pirating 'twixt Scilly and the Irish creeks. He set up a powerful intimacy with the Ulster gallant, Master Shan O'Neil, who many a time has patted me upon my back; but, after getting at loggerheads with Her Grace, he turned Papist, and set out with Don Sebastian of Portugal upon an African expedition, from the which I felt constrained to withdraw myself.

Thereupon for a year, perhaps two, I was plying lawful traffic in the hoy *Harry Mondroit*, 'twixt the Thames' mouth and Antwerp; till, on a day, I fell in at "The Bell" in Greenwich with Master Francis Drake, a youth of twenty-five years, who was then gathering together mariners to go on his brigantine, the *Judith*, his purpose being to take part in Master John Hawkins' third expedition to the settlements in Espaniola.

Master Hawkins sailed from Plymouth in the *Jesus*, with four consorts, in October of the year 1567. After being mauled by an equinox storm in Biscay Bay, we refitted at the Canaries, and, having taken four hundred blacks on the Guinea coast, sailed for the West Indies, where we gained no little gold by our business. We then proceeded to Carthagena and Rio de la Hacha; but it should now be very well known how the *Jesus* lost her rudder, how, the ships' bottoms being fouled, we had perforce to run for San Juan de Ulloa in the Gulf of Mexico; and how, thirteen Spanish galleons and frigates having surprised us there, the Admiral de Baçan made with us a treaty, the which he treacherously broke at high noon-day, putting upon us the loss of three ships and our treasure, the *Minion* and the *Judith* alone escaping: this I need not particularly relate.

The *Judith*, being of fifty tons portage only, and the *Minion* of less than one hundred, both were now crowded, with but little water aboard, and the storechests empty. After lying three days outside the sand ridge, we set sail on Saturday, the 25th September, having heard tell of a certain place on the east reaches of the Gulf where provisions might be got. This we reached on the 8th October, only to meet there little or nothing to our purpose; whereupon a council was called before Master Hawkins in the *Minion*, where one hundred of us proffered ourselves to land, to the intent that so the rest might make their way again to England on short rations.

The haps of us who landed I will not particularize, though they were various, God wot, remaining in my head as a grievous dream, but a vague one, blotted out, alas, by that great thing which Almighty God hath ordained for a poor man like me. We wandered within the forests, anon shot at by Indians, our food being roots and berries, and within three weeks reached a Spanish station, whence we were sent captives into Mexico. There we were Christianly behaved to, fed, clothed, and then distributed among the plantations—a thing amazing to us who were not ignorant of the pains put upon English sailors in Spain; but in those days no Holy Office was in Mexico, and on this count we were spared, some of us being bound over to be overseers, some to be handicraftsmen in the towns, etc. As for me, after an absence from it of seven months, I once more found myself in the township of San Juan de Ulloa, where, having ever a handy knack in carpentry, I had soon set myself up for a wright.

No one asked me aught as to my faith; I came and went as I thought good; nor was it long but I had got some knowledge of the Spanish tongue, stablished myself in the place, and taken to wife Lina, a wench of good liking, daughter of Señora Gomez of the *confiteria*, or sweetmeat-store; and out of her were born unto me Morales and Salvadora, two of the goodliest babes that ever I have beheld.

I abode in San Juan de Ulloa two years and eleven months: and these be the two years of quietness and happiness that I have had in this my life.

On the 13th afternoon of the month of February in the year 1571 I was wending homeward over the *prado* that separated my carpentry from the *confiteria* of my mother-in-law, when I saw four men approaching me, as to whom I straightway understood that men of San Juan they were not: one was a Black Friar, so hooded and cowled, that of his countenance nothing was discovered, save the light of his eyes; another was bearded—of the Order of Jesus; another wore the broad chapeau of a notary, and the fourth had the aspect of an alguazil, grasping a bâton in his hand. And, on seeing them, I seemed to give up heart and hope together: for a frigate hulk had cast anchor that morning beyond the sand-ridge, and I conjectured that these men were of her, were ministers of the Holy Office, and had heard of me while I was awork.

I have mentioned that no Inquisition was in Mexico afore 1571: but within the last months it had been bruited in San Juan that King Phillip, being timorous of English meddling in the gold-trade, and of the spread of English heresy, was pondering the setting up of the Holy Office over Espaniola. And so said, so done, in *my* case, at any rate, who, being the sole heretic in that place, was waylaid on the *prado* in the afternoon's glooming, and heard from the alguazil that word of the familiars: "follow on"; to be then led down the little *callejon* that runneth down from the *prado* to the coast, where a cockboat lay in waiting.

To the moment when they pushed me into the boat, I had not so much as implored one more embrace of my poor mate and babes, so dumb was I at the sudden woe: but in the boat I tumbled prone, although too tongue-tied to utter prayer, whereupon an oarsman put paw upon me, with what I took to be a consoling movement: a gesture which set me belching forth into lamenting. But with no long dallying they put out, having me by my arms; and beyond the sand-ridge I was took up the poop's ladder into the frigate, led away to the far end of the forecastle's vault, and there left with a rosca loaf, four onions, and a stoup of water in the sprit room, a very strait place cumbered by the bulk of the bow-sprit's end, and by the ends of a couple of culverins.

I know not yet whither it was the will of my captors to carry me, whether to Europe, or to some port of the Spanish Main; but this I know that the next noon when I was led apoop, no land was visible, and the sea had that hard aspect of the mid-sea.

Our ship, the which was called the *San Matteo*, was a hulk of some four hundred tons portage, high afore, and high stuck up apoop, her fore castle having two tiers, and her poop's castle three, with culverins in their ports. Her topsides were so tumbled home, that her breadth at the water may have been double her breadth at her wales, and she had not the newfangled fore-and-abafts of Master Fletcher, such as the *Judith* wore to sail on a wind. But she was costly built, her square sails being every one of the seven of heavy florence, broidered in the belly, and her fifty guns of good brass fabric. She was at this time driving free afore the wind under full spread, but with a rolling so restless as to be jeopardous, I judged. In fact, I took her for a crank pot, with such a tophamper and mass of upper-works, that she could scarce fail to dip her tier of falcons, if the sea should lash.

I was brought up to the master's room, the which was being used as an audience-chamber, and there at a table beheld five men in file. He in the centre, who proved to be both my accuser and judge, presently gave me to know that the evidence against me had been laid before the Qualifiers of the Office—which Qualifiers I understood to be none other than themselves there present—and been approved by the said Qualifiers; and when I had given replies to a catalogue of interrogatories as to my way of life in San Juan, I was then straightway put to the question. My breast, God wot, was rent with terrors, but my bearing, I trust, was distinguished by Christian courage. The interview was but brief: I demurred to kiss the cross; whereupon the President addressed me—he being the Dominic that I saw on the *prado*, a man whose mass of wrinkles, although he was yet young, and his wry smile within a nest of wrinkles, I carry still in my mind. My rudeness, he said, would prove to be but puny: for that during the day I should be put to a second audience in order to move me to a confession, and after to the screws.

For that second audience I waited, but it came not: for, huddled up in a corner 'twixt the sprit's end and a culverin's end, I became more and more aware that the *San Matteo* was labouring in the sea, and by evening mine ears were crowded with the sound of winds, so that I could no more hear the little sounds of the cook's house, the which was not in the hold, as with English vessels, but in a part of the fore castle abaft my cell. No food was brought me all that day, and I understood that all had enough to trouble them other than my unblest self.

I fell into a deep sleep, nor, I believe, awaked until near the next noon, though between noon and midnight was but little difference in my prison. I now anew knew, as before, of a tumult of winds, and understood by the ship's motion that she was now fleeing afore the gale, with a swinging downhill gait. Toward night, being anhungered, I got to thumping in desperate wise upon my prison, but no signal was given me that any heard me, and doubtless I was unheard in that turmoil of sounds.

And again I fell into forgetfulness, and again about midday, as I conjecture, bounded awake, being now roused by a shout of wind pouncing in upon me through the door, the which a stripling had just opened. He tumbled toward me with a bowl of tum-tum and pork, and, having shot it upon my lap, put mouth to mine ear with the shout: "Eat, Englishman! Thou art doomed for the ship!"

He then fell out, leaving me in a maze. But I think that I had not ended the meal when the meaning of his words was but little uncertain to me, who was versed in the manners of the sea, and of Spanish seamen in especial; and I said within myself "the *San Matteo* is now doubtless near her end; the sun hath gone out of the sky; the course peradventure lost: and I, the heretic, am condemned to be thrown away, as Jonah, to assuage the tempest."

The rest of that day, therefore, I lay upon my face, recommending my spirit, my wife, and my children to my Creator until, toward night, three sailors came in, laid hands on me, and hauled me forth; and I was hardly hauled to the castle's portal, when my old samite coif leapt off my head, and was swept away.

Surely never mortal wretch had bleaker last look at the scheme of being than I that night. There remained some sort of disastrous glimmering in the air, but it was a glimmer that was itself but a mood of gloom. A rust on the nigh horizon that was the sun was swinging on high above the working of the billows, then hurling itself below, with an alternate circular working, as it were a dissolute or sea-sick thing. The skies were, as it were, tinted with inks, and appeared to be no higher beyond the sea than the mizzen-top, where sea and sky were mixed. I saw that the poop's mast was gone, and the *San Matteo* under two sails only, the mizzen-top sail and the spritsail: yet with these she was careering in desperate wise like a capon in a scare from the face of the tempest, taking in water with an alternate process over her port and starboard wales, and whirled to her top-castles in sprays: so that she was as much within the sea as on it. Our trip from my prison to the poop's castle must have occupied, with halts, no less than twenty minutes of time, so swung were our feet between deep and high: and in that time a multitude of sounds the most drear and forlorn seemed borne from out the bowels of the darkness to mine ears, as screams of craziness, a ding-dong of sea-bells, or cadences of sirens crying, or one sole toll of a funeral-knell. I was as one adream with awe: for I understood that into all that war of waters I was about to go down, alone.

Lashed to the starboard turret of the poop's castle by a cord within the ring at its paunch was a portugal, such as be employed to store pork on big voyages; and, sprawling on the deck, with his paws clutched within a window-sill of the turret, was the Jesuit, his robes all blown into disarray, with him being the ship's master, having a hammer's handle sticking out of his pouch, and four others, the particulars of whose persons mine eyes, as though I had scores of eyes that night, observed of their own act.

As I staggered near in the lax keeping of my guardians, the portugal was cast aslant in his lashing, and I could then descry within it one of those 30-inch masses of iron ballast, such as be named dradoes; by the which I understood that I should not be tossed forth coffinless, as Jonah, but in the portugal: inasmuch as the corpse of many a Jonah hath been known to "chase i' the wake", as mariners relate, to the disaster of them in the ship; and the coffining of such in ballasted casks has long been a plan of the Spanish in especial.

On my coming to the turret, he whom I took to be the master put hand upon me, uttering somewhat which the hurricane drowned in his mouth, though I guessed that he egged me to go into the portugal: and indeed I was speedily heeled up and hustled in. Resistance would have been but little difficult to me, had I willed, but could have resulted only in the rolling overboard of others with me: nor had I a spirit of resistance, nay, probably lost my consciousness upon entering, for nothing can I remember more, till the top was covered in, save only one segment of it, through which I on my face glimpsed three struggling shapes, and understood that the Jesuit, now upheld 'twixt two of the shipmen, was shouting over me some litany or committal. In the next moment I lay choked in blackness, and had in my consciousness a hammer's banging.

Whether awake or adream, I seemed to recognize the moment when the portugal's mass splashed the ocean; I was aware of the drado's bulk tumbling about the sides, and of double bump of the iron, the one upon my breast, the other upon my right thigh.

Now, this was hardly owing to the water's roughness, for my last glance abroad before going into the portugal had shown me a singular condition of the sea: the ship appeared to have driven into a piece of water comparatively calm, and pallid, a basin perhaps half-a-mile in breadth, on a level rather below the rest of the ocean that darkly rolled round its edge; and the whole seemed to me to move with a slow wheeling: for I had noted it well, with that ten-eyed unwittingness wherewith I noted everything that night, as the mariners' apparel, or the four-square cap of the Jesuit crushed over his nose, or the porky stench of the portugal...

Down, swiftly down, and still profounder down, I ripped toward the foundry of things, to where the mountains and downs of the mid-sea drowse. I had soon lost all sense of motion: still, I divined—I knew—with what a swiftness I slid, profoundly drowned, mile on mile, and still down, from the home of life, and hope, and light, and time. I was standing on the drado, no less steadily than if on land, for the drado's weight held the portugal straight on end, the portugal's top being perhaps one inch above my head—for my hands touched it, paddling for some moments as though I was actually adrown, like the paddling pattes of a hound in his drowning. But I stood with no gasping for a good span, the portugal was so roomy, and it proved as good-made as roomy, though soon enough some ominous creakings gave me to know that the sea's weight was crushing upon his every square inch with a pressure of tons; moreover, both my palms being pressed forth against the portugal's side, all at once the right palm was pierced to the quick by some nail, driven inward by the squeezing of the sea's weight; and quickly thereupon I felt a drop of water fall upon my top, and presently a drop, and a drop, bringing upon me a deliberate drip, drip: and I understood that the sea, having forced a crack, was oozing through atop.

No shock, no stir was there: yet all my heart was conscious of the hurry of my dropping from the world. I understood—I knew—when I had fared quite out of hue and shape, measure and relation, down among the dregs of creation, where no ray may roam, nor a hope grow up; and within my head were going on giddy divinations of my descent from depth to depth of deader nothingness, and dark after dark.

Groan could I not, nor sigh, nor cry to my God, but stood petrified by the greatness of my perishing, for I felt myself banished from His hand and the scope of His compassion, and ranging every moment to a more strange remoteness from the territories of His reign.

Yet, as my sense was toward whirling unto death, certain words were on a sudden with me, that for many a month, I think, had never visited my head: for it was as if I was now aware of a chorus of sound quiring in some outermost remoteness of the heaven of heavens, whence the shout of ten thousand times ten thousand mouths reached to me as a dream of mine ear: and this was their shout and the passion of their chanting: "If I ascend up into Heaven, He is there; if I make my bed in Hell, behold, He is there; if I take the wings of the morning, and dwell in the uttermost parts of the sea, even there shall His hand lead me, His right hand shall hold me."

But the lack of air, that in some minutes had become the main fact of my predicament, by this time was such, that I had come to be nothing but a skull and throat crowded with blood that would bound from me, but could not; yet I think that in the very crux of my death-struggle a curiosity as to the grave, and the nature of death—a curiosity as frivolous as the frolics of a trickster—delayed my failing; for I seemed to desire to see myself die.

Still upon my top, with a quickening drip, drip, dropped the leak, and this in my extremest smart I ceased not to mark.

But there came a moment when all my sentience was swallowed in an amazing consciousness of motion. First I was urgently jerked against the portugal, the which was tugged sidewards by some might: some moments more, and the portugal bumped upon something. By a happy instinct, I had stiffened myself, my feet on the drado, my head pressed against the top piece; and immediately I was aware of precipitous rage, haste the most rash, for a quick succession of shocks, upon rocks, as I imagine, quick as you may say one, two, three, knocked me breathless who was already breathless, racking the cask's frame, and battering me back, so to say, out of my death into sense. And or ever I could lend half a thought to this mystery of motion-on-the-horizontal down by the ocean's bottom, I was hounded on to a mystery still more astounding—a sound in the realm of muteness—a roar—that very soon grew to a most great and grave tumult. During which growth of tumult I got the consciousness of being rushed through some tunnel, for the concussions of the cask on every side came fast and more frightfully faster; and I now made out, how I cannot tell, that the direction of my race was half horizontal, and half downward, toward the source of that sounding. How long the trip lasted my spirit, spinning in that thundering dark, could hardly sum up: it might have been a minute or five, a mile or twenty: but there came a moment when I felt the portugal lifted up, and tossed; it was spinning through space; and it dropped upon rock with a crash which ravished me from my consciousness.

So intemperate was this mauling, that upon returning to myself after what may have been many hours, I had no doubt but that I was dead; and within myself I breathed the words, "The soul is an ear; and Eternity is a roar."

For I appeared at present to be a creature created with but one single sense, since, on placing my fingers an inch afore my face, in vain I strained my vision to trace them; my body, in so far as I was any longer cognizant thereof, was, as it were, lost to me, and blotted out; so that I seemed to be naught but an ear, formed to hear unceasingly that tumult that seemed the universe: and anew and anew I mused indolently within me, "Well, the soul is an ear; and Eternity is a roar."

Thus many minutes I lay, listing with interest to the tone of the roar, the which hath with it a shell's echoing that calleth, making a chaunting vastly far in the void, like an angel's voice far noising. What proved to me that I was disembodied was the apparent fact that I was no longer in the portugal, since I at present breathed free; nevertheless, upon becoming conscious in the course of time of a stench of sea-brine, and presently of the mingling therewith of the portugal's stink of pork, I straightway felt myself to be living flesh; and, on reaching out my fingers, felt the sufficient reason of my breathing, to wit, that the portugal's bottom had been breached in, and a hoop there started by his fall, for the staves' ends at that part at present spread all asprawl. I was prostrate upon my back, and the drado and broken portugal's bottom lay over my legs, so that the portugal must have toppled over on his side after striking on his end.

The next circumstance that I now observed was a trembling of the ground on which I lay, the which trembled greatly, as with a very grave ague.

I set myself then to talk with myself, recalling, not without an effort of my memory, the certain facts of my predicament: to wit, firstly, that I had been cast in a cask from a bark called the *San Matteo*, not less than a century agone, I thought; I had then beyond doubt gone down toward the bottom of the sea; here some sea-river had undoubtedly seized and reeled me through some tunnel beneath the sea's base: and the under-tow of this sea-river's suction it was which must have occasioned that basin-like appearance of the sea's surface with a circular working, observed by me some moments before my going in the portugal. This salt torrent, having caught my cask, must have hurtled me through the tunnel to a hollow hall or vault in the bowels of the earth at the tunnel's mouth, and then hurled the portugal from the tunnel's mouth down upon some rock in the grotto, and so broken the portugal's bottom. The cave must contain the air which it had shut in in the age of the convulsion of nature which had made it a cave, peradventure ere the sea was there, thus permitting me to breathe. And the roar that was roaring should be the thundering of the ocean tumbling down the walls of the hall from out the tunnel's mouth, the preponderousness of which thundering's dropping-down occasioned that ague of the ground which was shaking me.

So much I could well sum up; also, from that echo's humming, whose vast psalmodying haunts the waterfall's thunder, I judged that the hollowness of the hall must be large beyond thought. More than this I understood not; but, this being understood, I covered my face, and gave myself to lamenting: for, ever and again, together with the thunder and his echo, worked certain burstings and crashes of the cataract, brief belchings breaching on a sudden, troubling the echo with yet huger rumours, madding sad to hearken to; and my hand could I not descry, stared I never so crazily nigh; and the ague of the ground was, as it were, a shivering at the shout of God-Omnipotent's mouth: so that sobs gobbled forth of my bosom, when I understood the pathos of this place.

On throwing my hands over my eyes to cry, I felt on them a slime crass with granules, perhaps splashed upon me through the open end of the portugal on his tumble, the which when I had brushed away, with much anguish I got my head round to where my feet had been. No doubt had I but I should of necessity perish of thirst and dearth of food; but that I might come to my doom at liberty, I crept forth of my prison, as a chick from the rupture of his shell.

A tinder-box was in my pouch, but, in the swound of my comprehension, I did not then remember it, but moved in darkness over a slime with my arms outstretched, drenched ever with a drizzle, the source of which I did not know. Slow I moved, for I discovered my right thigh to be crushed, and all my body much mauled; and, or ever I had moved ten steps, my shoe stepped into emptiness, and down with a shout I sped, spinning, to the depth.

My falling was stopped by a splash into a water that was warm, into which I sank far; and I rose through it bearing up with me some putrid brute that drew the rheum of his mucus over my face. I then struck out to swim back to the island from whose cliff I had tumbled: for I saw that the cavern's bottom was occupied by a sea, or salt pond, and that upon some island in this sea the cask must have been cast. But my effort to get again to the island availed not, for a current which seized me carried me quick and still quicker, increasing at the last to such a careering that I could no more keep me up over the waves; whereupon an abandonment of myself came upon me, and I began now to drown, yet ever grasping out, as the drowning do; and afore I swooned I was thrown against a shore, where, having clutched something like a gracile trunk, I dragged my frame up on a shore covered over with that same grainy slush, and tumbled to a slumber which dured, I dare say, two days.

I started awake with those waters in mine ear whose immortal harmony, I question it not, I will for ever hear in my heart; and I sat still, listing, afeared to budge, lest I should afresh blunder into trouble, while mine eyeballs, bereft of light, braved the raylessness with their staring. My feet lay at a sea's edge, for I could feel the upwashing of the waves, the which wash obliquely upon the shore, being driven by a current: but near as they were, I could hear ne'er a splash, nor anything could hear, except the cataract's crashing, joined with the voice of his own echoing, whose music tuneth with the thundering a euphony like that of lute-strings with drum ahumming, and anon the racket of those added crashings, when masses more ponderous of the cataract drop; and I did ever find myself listing with mine ear reached sideward, drawn to the darksome chaunting, forgetting my hunger, and the coming of death: listing I wot not how long, perhaps hours, perhaps night-longs: for here in this hall is no Time, but all is blotted out but the siren's sorrow that haunts it; and a hundred years is as one hour, and one hour as a hundred years.

I remarked, however, immediately, that the waves which washed my feet were not warm like that part of the water where I had fallen into the lake: so that I understood that the lake is a cauldron of different temperatures at different parts, the waters which roll in from the ocean being cold, but the lake warmed by flames beneath the cave: indeed, each region of the cave, so far as my feet ever reached in it, is always warm to the hand, and the atmosphere warm, though thick, and sick with stinks of the sea.

After a long while I found the tinder-box within my pouch, wherein also I found a chisel which I was bringing to my house to sharpen on the night of my capture, and also a small gar or gimlet. So I struck a flash that cut mine eyes like a gash, and I kindled a rag, the which glowed a rich gore-colour upon an agitated water rushing past the shore; and although only a small region of the dark was lit up, I could see sufficient of the shore's sweep to understand that I was standing on a mainland made of granite, but not altogether without marl on the ground, nigh behind me being a grove of well-formed growths resembling elms, all gnarled and venerable, yet no taller than my belly, although some do come to my neck. Their leaves be milk-white, and even of a quite round shape, and they do for ever shake themselves with the ground that shakes, and produce a globose fruit, the which is blanched, too, and their boles pallid. I saw long afterwards another dwarf of just the same shape, only his fruit oozeth a juice like soap's water, that maketh a lather. On the lake also I have lately seen by the torch's light near the island a weed with leaves over two yards long, the which be caused to float on the water by small bladders attached to it; and also in the marshy spot by the promontory is the forest of bulrushes that show a tuft, or plume, at their summit, and they do shake themselves, their stem being about three feet high, and they shoot out a single root that groweth visible over the ground seven feet or more in his length; besides which, I observed none other shrubs, save a pale purple fungus, well-nigh white, growing on these rocks where I write, and in the corridor which is on this side of the pond of pitch.

But in that minute's glimmering, while my rag's light was dancing on the waves, I knew what superabundance of food lay for me in this place, to be had by only putting forth of my hand: for in that paltry area of the water I saw pale creatures like snakes seven or eight feet long, tangled together in a knot, and some more alone, and four globose white beings, so that I could see that the lake is alive with life; and they lay there quite unaware of the light that pried on their whiteness, so that I decided that they be wights deprived of eyes. A very long time later on, probably many years, I came upon the stream to the lake's left, by the promontory, the which is thronged with oysters, with many sorts of pearl, and conch shells: but at the first I saw it not.

To have the creatures of the lake, I take stand to my knees in the water's margin (for farther I may not enter for the strength of the current), lean forward with the torch, and abide the coming of the creature of my liking, the which resembles the creatures called a trunk-fish in the tropics, being of triangular form, with freckles. The species of the creatures of the lake be few, though their number great; and, as all the plants be very pigmy, so all the animals be of great bigness, save one thing resembling a lizard, a finger in his length, that I have seen on the reefs, and his tail is formed in the shape of a leaf, and engorgeth itself grossly, and it gazeth through great globose eyeballs that glare lidless, but they be blind eyeballs; and one only wight of the lake hath eyes, but they do hang by a twine out of his eye-sockets, and dangle about his countenance, and be blind. As to their catching, this I managed at starting without so much as a torch, but by the touch alone; nor do their sluggish natures struggle against my grabbing, but by their motions I understand the wonder that they have what creature he might be who removeth them from their secret home. The flesh of one and all is soft and watery, yet cruel tough, and crude to the tongue. My repasts at starting were ate raw; but afterwards I made fires with the tree-trunks, the which being dry-timbered, I could chop down with the chisel and a rock for my hammer. Later on when I did find out the rock-hall, I laid my fire there: but almost all the rags of my garments, except my jerkin, had been burned up for tinder, before I unearthed the marsh of bulrushes, whose pith served me from thenceforth both for tinder and food, and at present also for parchment: for, boiled in the hot rivulet in the rock-hall, the pith and fish together giveth an excellent good food, when, being voided of moisture, and pounded, they become a powder or flour; so that when I had once come at the bulrushes, where, too, are the oysters, being put upon the plan of boiling, I no more roasted my food as before.

For what appeared a long period, as it were long weeks, I mollified my thirst by soaking my body on the shore's verge, where the waves break; but thirst became a rage in my throat, like that lust of light in mine eyes, so that sometimes, pronouncing a shout, I did desperately drench my bowels, drinking my fill of the bitterness, the which, I am convinced, is more bitterer than the bitterness of the outer sea. By this time I had roamed exploring far around that part of the shore on which I was cast up, and had found about me a boundless house of caves, chambers, corridors, with dwarf forests, and stretches of sponges of stone, boulders, and tracts of basalt columns, a fantastic mass to me of rock and darkness, all racked, and like the aspen dancing, to the farthest point of my wandering, all inhabited by the noise of the waters' voice, and stinking of the sea with so raw a breath, that in several spots the nostrils scarce can bear it. There be shells of many shapes and dimensions upon the land, many enamelled with gems and pearl, sea-urchins also, star-fish, sea-cucumbers, and other sea-beasts with spines, mussels nigh to the promontory on the lake's left, corals, and many kinds of sponges, many monstrous huge and having a putrid stench, some, as it were, sponges of stone, others soft, and others of lucid glass, painted gallant with hues of the rainbow, and very gracious shaped, as hand-baskets, or ropes of glass, but crude of odour. Till I had set up my hearth in the rock-hall, I rambled about without any torch, for the cause that I knew not yet well the inflammable mood of the wood, nor had yet tumbled upon the sulphur, nor the pitch, with which to lard the torches; and, walking dark, with just a flash anon, I did often count my footsteps, it might be to a thousand, or two, till tired out. But spite of my ramblings, my body had knobs like leprosy, and was lacerated with my scratching, and racked with the rushing through me of the salt draughts which I drank, afore ever I chanced upon fresh water. That day I descended by three great steps that are made as by men's hands, and that lie peradventure half a mile from the lake, into a basalt hall, vastly capacious, so that forty chariots could race abreast therein; and the walls be as straight as the walls of masons, the roof low, only some twenty foot aloft, flat and smooth and black, and at the remote end of it a forest of basalt columns stand. There I marked that the air was even warmer than the warm air near the lake, and it was not long ere I had advanced into a hot steaming, with a sulphur stench, the which I had no sooner perceived than I fell upon my hands over a heap which proved, when I had struck a flash, to be slushy sulphur. I also saw a canal cut through the floor across the rock-hall's breadth, as regular as if graved there, this being two feet deep, as I discovered, and two feet across, through which canal babbled a black brook, bubbling hot, the floor on each bank of the canal being heaped with sulphur. I had soon scooped up some of the fluid with the tinder-box, and upon his cooling somewhat, I discovered it to be fresh, though sulphurous, and also tarry, in his taste; and thenceforth I had it always cooling in rows of conch shells by the rock-hall's left wall.

And during all the years of my tarrying in this tomb, the rock-hall hath become, in some manner, my home. There, in a corner nigh the three steps, I made up a fire; I put round it stones, and over the stones a slab, and plaiting my beard into my hair behind me, I there broiled my meat, until the time when I took to boiling the mixed trunkfish and bulrush in the canal's boiling brook; and for a long while I kept the fire ever fed with wood from the tiny forests: for that I loved his light.

But, as to light, I have nineteen times beheld it in this dark from other causes than mine own fires, seventeen times the light being lightning: for lightning I must call it, the land lightning like the sky: and this I understand not at all. But I was standing by the water's margin, bent upon catching my white blindlings, when the cavern became far and wide as it were an eye that wildly opened, winked five million to the minute, and as suddenly closed; and after a minute of thick darkness as afore, it opened once more, quick quivered, and closed. And there all ghast I stayed, in my heart's heart the ghast thought: "Thou, God, Seest Me." But though mine eyes staggered at the glare, I fancy that in fact it was but faint, and the ghost only of a glare, for of the cave's secrets little was thereby revealed unto me: and sixteen times in like wise his wings have quivered, and the wildness of his eye hath stared at me like the visitations of an archangel: and twice, besides, I have beheld the cave lighted by the volcano.

But it was long before ever the volcano came that I fell in with the mescal: for it was no long time after that surprise of lightning that, in pacing once to the shore to take up some trunkfish which I had thrown in the slush there—I think eight or twelve years may have gone over me—I happened to bruise in my fingers one of the pigmy globose fruit, and there oozed out of it a milk that I put to my lips. It was bitter, but I did swallow some drops unawares, the result whereof was wondrous: for even ere I reached the beach, an apathy enwrapped my being; I let myself drop down by the breakers' brim; my brow and body collapsed in a lassitude; and my lips let out the whisper: "pour on: but as for me, I will know rest." I was thereupon lapped in trances the most halcyon and happy; the roaring rolled for me into such oratories as my mouth may not pronounce, though I appeared, so to speak, to *see*, more than to hear, that music; and in the mean time mine eyes, fast closed, had afore them a universe of hues in slow movement and communion, hues glowing, and hues ghostly and gnomelike, some of them new hues to me, so that I knew not at all how to call them, with cataracts of pomegranate grains pattering, waves of parrot green, wheels of raspberry reeling, dapplings of apple and pansy, pallid eyeballs of bile and daffodil, pellucid tulips, brooks of rubies, auroras, roses, all awork in a world earnester than Earth, that it were empty to attempt to tell of.

I had heard tell at San Juan of the shrub which they do name "the mescal button," chewed by the Mexicans to produce upon them such revelations of hues; and I have concluded that this shrub of the cave must be of nature akin. But though the gift of it transfigured that stink-pit beneath the sea into a region of the genii for me, I was aware that to munch thereof was presumptuous, for the troubles that his rancour bringeth upon the body of men were quickly obvious upon me. But I made never an attempt to abandon his happiness, for it wheeleth through the brain to so sweet a strain, and talketh such gossip to the organs of the consciousness, as I do not suppose to be true of the very lotus, nor of that pleasant root that is known as nepenthe.

I have spent years on years, nay, as it seems to me, eras on eras, in one dreaming by the sea's rim, while my soul, so to speak, passed into the cataract's inmost roar, and became as one therewith. I lay there naked, for at first I had preserved my jerkin and shirt to serve for tinder, until I tumbled upon the discovery of the bulrush-pith, whereupon I employed the jerkin and shirt to contain the pith and fish for their boiling; so after the last of my trouser's rags had shredded from around my legs, and my shoes, too, from my feet, through great periods of time I have lain there naked, though enveloped to my belly in my hair and beard, idly dreaming, finding it too dreary a trial to seethe my food, and often eating raw, having long agone let the fire in the rock-hall go out. In the end I have shirked even the burden of bending in the sea's surf, or of journeying to the mussel stream, to get at my grub, and will spend considerable periods with never a bit other drink or meat than that bittersweet milk of the mescal.

From this life of sloth twice only have I been disturbed by fright, the first time when the volcano came, the second time when I observed the increasing dearth of air to breathe; and on each occasion I was spurred to take torch and search further afield than e'er before what the vault holds—in both searches meeting with what turned out serviceable to my needs: for in the first search I butted on the bulrush bush, which I believe I butted on years ere I observed this increasing dearth of air; and it was the increasing dearth of air which sent me peering further a second time, and then I saw the pond of pitch. This latter is beyond the forest of basalt columns at the far end of the rock-hall; and it was in passing to it through those columns that I saw the beast's bones, that be bigger, I believe, than several elephants together, although the beast resembled an elephant, having straight tusks, exceeding long; and his jaw hath six huge teeth, very strange, every several tooth being made of littler ones, the which cling about it like nipples; and there among those pillars his ribs may have rested for many a century, some of them being now brittle and embrowned; and beyond the pillars is a passage, perfectly curved, having a purplish fungus growing upon his rock; and beyond the passage is a cavern than whose threshold I could no farther advance, for the bed thereof is a bitumen sea, which is half-warm and thick at the brink, but, I think, liquid hot in the middle; and all over his face broods a universe of rainbows, dingy and fat, which be from the fat vapours of the pitch bringing forth rainbows, not rainbows of heaven, but, so to say, fallen angels, grown gross and sluggish. But years ere this, I think, I had seen the bulrushes: for, soon after the volcano came, in roaming over the left shore of the cataract's sea—the which left shore is flat and widespread, and hath no high walls like the right side—I walked upon a freshet of fresh warm water, and after following it upward, saw all round a marsh's swamp, and the bush of bulrushes. This is where the oysters be so crass, and they be pearl oysters, for all that soil be crass with nacreous matter of every sort, with barrok pearls, mother-of-pearl, and in most of the oysters which I opened pearls, with a lot of conch shells that have within them pink pearls, and there be also the black pearl, such as they have in Mexico and the West Indies, with the yellow and likewise the white, which last be shaped like the pear, and large, and his pallor hath a blank brightness, very priceless, and, so to say, bridal. As to the bulrush, his trunk is triangular (like the trunk-fish), some five inches wide at the bottom, and giveth a white pith good for food. I came, moreover, upon the discovery after a long time that, since this pith lieth in layers, these, being steeped in water, and afterwards dried, do shrink to a parchment, quite white and soft, but tending to be yellow and brittle in time.

But for these two adventures, first to the bulrushes, and then to the pond or sea of pitch, I cannot remember that that long trance I had by the shore was broken by any excursion. But I had a rough enough rousing in that hour when, upon opening mine eyes, I beheld, not the old darkness, but all the hall disclosed in scarlet, and felt the cavern in movement, not with that proper trembling that I knew, due to the preponderousness of the cataract's mass over the earth's fabric, but racked with an earthquake's racking: and when mine eyes, now shyer than the night-bird's, recovered their courage, I observed the sea's whole surface heaved up like sand-heaps, dandled up with the earthquake's dancing. Now also for the first time I saw aloft to my right the tunnel's monstrous mouth, out of which the cataract's mass tumbleth down, the mouth's top rim being rounded, like the top lip of a man's mouth crying aloud. I saw also the cataract rolling hoary across his whole breast's breadth, woolly with flocks and beards of froth, as it were Moses' beard, except at the centre, where it gallops glassy smooth and more massy, for there the sea cometh out from the tunnel's inwards to stretch itself out in that mouth that shouteth aloud. I saw also the roof like a rufous sky of rock, and right before mine eyes lay an island, long and narrow, upon the which I had been cast at the first, for there yet lay the portugal on the right end of the island, that right end lying quite nigh the cataract, and the island's left end some twenty yards from the lake's left end. And I saw the lake in his entirety by spying over the island's centre, where the land lies low, the lake having an egg's form, perhaps two miles in his length, I being at the egg's small end. I saw also that the cave's right side, where the wall rises sheer, is washed directly by the lake's wheeling career; and since the cataract there crashes down, along that right side I cannot advance; nor along the cave's left side can I advance so much as a mile, for there a headland juts out into the lake, dividing that side of the cave into great rooms. I saw also nigh the far shore of the lake four more small islands of rock, and I was shewn, from the lake's ocean-like aspect, that his waters be vastly profound, his bottom being doubtless housed far down in the planet's bowels. All was lit up. And some distance beyond the lake's boundaries, I saw the mouth of some cave, through which came up a haze of radiance sparkling, and vaulting stones, and therewith some tongues of flame, which now shewed, and now withdrew their rouge.

I gathered that some volcanic action was going on under the cavern, and as I there stayed, agape at it, I saw arise out of the lake in the remote distance, and come toward me, a thing, with the which I so long had lived, and known it not. His body lay soft in curves on the billows nigh a furlong behind his uplifted head, and I could not fly, nor turn mine eyes from the pitifulness of his appearing in the light. His head and face be of the dimension of a cottage, having a shameful likeness to a death's-head, being bony, shiny, and very tight-skinned, and of a mucky white colour, with freckles. It hath a forehead and nose-ridge, but, where eyes should be, stands blank skin only; and it drew nigh me with the toothless house of his mouth wide open in a scream of fear, distrusting Him that made it: for the air was waxing still hotter, and it may have had an instinct of calamity, peradventure from some experience of the volcano's fierceness a century since. It travelled nigh under the island's right end through the cataract's foam, and then close under me, nor could see me look at his discovered nudity, nor could my rooted foot flee from it; and on it journeyed, circling the lake's surface with the dirge of his lamentation. Immediately after I lost my reason through the fierceness of the heat, and reeled; and when I came back to myself the cave was as black as ever. And once again, long afterwards I saw flames flutter in the cave beyond the lake, a grey dust rained over the lake's face, the great creature arose, and a grove of the trees at this end were sered with heat; but since then the event has never been seen.

But it was soon subsequent to this second convulsion that I made an observation: to wit, that unless I was well under the rule of the mescal fruit—when I do scarce seem to breathe—I became aware of an oppression of the chest. And this grew with me; so that I began to commune within me, saying: "Though the cavern be vast, the air that it containeth must be of limited volume, and I have inhaled it long: for whereas when I hither came I was a young thing, I am now old. My lungs have day by day consumed the wholesome air; and the day approacheth when I must surely perish."

At the commencement it was only when I lay me to rest that the trouble oppressed me, but, sat I up, it passed; then after, if I sat, it oppressed me; but, stood I up it passed: so that I understood it to be so that a lake of noxious vapour lay at the bottom of the air of this place, a lake due to my breathing, that each year grew in depth and noxiousness, the longer I breathed: this vapour having a sleepy effect, not happy like the mescal's, but highly unhappy, making me nightmares and aches of my body. In the beginning I got relief by going to live in other regions than in the rock-hall and on the beach: but in every direction my way hath now been blocked, for I have now inhabited in turn every cranny of the cavern whereto I am able to penetrate, and the vapour is in all, troubling also the shrubs of all sorts, the which let fall their heads, and shed their health. There remain some coigns among the rockeries, wherein, when I toil aloft to them, I may yet breathe with some freedom; but that my days are numbered I know. My God! my God! why hast Thou created me?

But soon after understanding the manner of my undoing, I began to argue in myself as regards the cavern and his architecture as never formerly, arguing that whereas so great volumes of water came in, and the vault was not filled, there must needs be some outlet for an equal volume to flow out. I was led to conjecture that the tunnel which admits the sea into the cavern is at some sea-mountain's summit; that the cavern must be in the mountain's bowels; and that the outflow out of the cavern must be down another much longer tunnel, leading down to the mountain's bottom into the sea. I therefore conceived the notion that, if I could reach the portugal, get it repaired, and, in it, introduce myself into the tunnel of outflow (the which I knew to be beyond the headland on the lake's left, where the lake's two wheeling currents meet), then I should be carried down and out into the bottom of the sea, should thereupon rise to the sea's surface—for the unweighted portugal would certainly float with me—and there I might bore a hole or two in the portugal's upper belly for air, and be picked up by a ship before my stores were done, and before my death from hunger or suffocation, I being well drugged with the mescal, and so but little breathing or eating. As to introducing myself into the tunnel of outflow, nothing more was necessary than to get the portugal to the headland's end, get myself into it, and roll myself in the portugal from the headland's end into the lake: where the currents would not fail to bear me toward the place of outflow, and I should be sucked down into the tunnel.

I meditated that the stupendousness of the attempt in no fashion lessened my chance: for that laws will act exactly on the immense scale as on the small. The portugal I could get to by going into the lake at the egg's-point of the lake, whence the current would carry me away along the left shore toward the island, the left end whereof I might catch by continually swimming strong to the right; and lest I should be dashed to fragments in my grand journey through the tunnel, I determined to pad the portugal's inside with the bulrush pith; and moreover I devised a sliding door in the portugal's side, the which when I should reach the sea's surface would be furnishing me with breathing: in the making whereof I did not doubt but that my former craft in carpentry would help me out. That I might be struck blind by the moon's brightness, and surely by the sun's, upon opening mine eyes up there above I reflected: but I price eyes as of but paltry value to a man, and should estimate it no hardship to dispense with mine, such as they are. On the whole, I had no fear; and the reason of my fearlessness, as I at present perceive, lay in this: that in my heart I never at all intended to attempt the venture. It was a fond thought: for, granting that I got out, how could I live without the cataract? I should surely die. And what good were life to me there in the glare of day, without the mescal's joys, and without the secret presence of the voice, and the thing which it secretly shouteth? In such separation from the power of my life I should pass frailly away as a spectre at day-break: for by the power of the voice is my frail life sustained, and thereon I hang, and therein I have my being. And this in my soul I must have known: but in the futile mood that possessed me, I made three several attempts to gain the portugal, terrified the while at mine own temerity; and twice I failed to make the left end of the island, for the current carried me beyond—toward the tunnel of outflow, I doubted not; yet were my terrors not of that horror mainly, but of the monster in the lake's depth, the which stayeth there pale and pensive, meditating his meditations: for I knew that if my foot or hand just touched his skin, I must assuredly reel and sink, shrieking mad, since I swam dark, but having an unlighted torch in my hand, the tinder-box being tied within my beard; and the first twice I was hurled to land upon the headland, but the third time upon the island's left end, the rock of which I clambered up with my hands lacerated by shells. And after lighting the torch, I wrought my steps toward the island's right end; and there lay the portugal even as I had left it twenty, forty, years ago, the slime on his side yet wet from the water-fall's aura that haunts the island. And in that spot I saw, not the portugal alone, but moreover a sword's hilt, a human skull, and a clock's racket, thither tossed by the cataract. The portugal was still good, for the pitch which is on it: and having cast out the drado by an effort of all my strength, I struck out four of the nails from the three bottom pieces that had been sprung, nailed the three pieces, and the broken hoop of wood, too, to the side of the portugal, and so consigned the portugal to the waters, the which, I was assured, would bear it to the small end of the lake's egg-shape, as they had borne me upon mine ancient fall from the island.

But I had myself no sooner been spued again upon the mainland, more dead than alive, and there found the portugal stranded, than I knew myself for a futile dreamer, wearying myself without sincere motive: for that I should really abandon the cavern was a thing not within the capability of nature. And there by the shore's edge I left the portugal lying a good while, abiding for the most part upon the crags of these rocks that be like gradients on the right side of the hall, until that day when it was suggested to my spirit how strangely had been given me both ink and paper in this place, the knowledge moreover how to get the portugal forth of the grot with a history of that thing which my God in song hath murmured unto me, having furtively hid me with His hand, though a seraph's pen could never express it; nor could I long resist the pressure of that suggestion to write, and send forth the writing in the portugal.

For the portugal's mending I had the gimlet, the chisel, mescal timber, and some of the nails from the sprung bottom, which could be spared; nor was the job hard, since the one started hoop could be nicely spliced. I rolled and got the portugal up to this level ground in the rocks, surrounding myself, as I wrought, with tarred torches, which I stuck in the rocks' cracks: for down below it is reluctantly if a fire will now burn; and at this height also the torches do burn with shy fires.

Or ever the portugal was repaired, I had got ready the pages for writing, having divided fifteen of the bulrush piths into strips, then wetted, and dried them; but there be spongy spots in them where the lampblack that I have manufactured out of the pitch runneth rather abroad under the splint of fish-bone that serves for my pen, hurting the fairness of my writing. That I could write at all I rather doubted, on the count that I have not for so long handled pen nor spoken, and on the count moreover of the trembling: for not only the pen trembleth by reason of mine age, but the parchment trembleth by reason of the vault's trembling: and between those two tremblements, in a sick sheen which flickers ever, these sheets have, letter by letter, been writ. The fifteen sheets of pith, moreover, have proved too little, and I am writing now on the second of two sheets that are sections of a fish's skin.

But now it is finished: and I send it out, if so be a fellow in the regions above may read it, and know. My name, if I have not yet writ it down, was James Dowdy Saul; and I was born not far from the borough of Bideford in the county of Devon.

My God! My God! why hast Thou created me?

I ask it: for the question ariseth of itself to my mind because of the crass facts of my predicament; yet my heart knoweth it, Lord God, to be the grumble of an ingrate: for a hidden thing is, that is winninger than wife, or child, or the shining of any light, and is like unto treasure hid in a field, the which when a man findeth, he selleth all, and buyeth that field; and I thank, I do thank Thee, for Thy voice, and for my lot, and that it was Thy will to ravish me: for the charm of Thy secret is more than the rose, exceeding utterance.

KAREL CÂPEK

R.U.R.

Karel Câpek (1890-1930) was a Czech author who will always be remembered inside and outside of science fiction as the man who coined the word robot *(from the Czech for worker—R.U.R. stands for Rossum's Universal Robots). In addition to the famous play you are about to read, Câpek also wrote several important science fiction novels, including* The Absolute at Large *(1922), a satirical work about a limitless supply of energy, and* The War With the Newts *(1936), a scathing attack on social and economic inequality and human nature. Although Câpek worked strictly within the traditions of central European literature, he left an indelible mark on modern science fiction.*

R.U.R.
(ROSSUM'S UNIVERSAL ROBOTS)
A FANTASTIC MELODRAMA
BY KAREL CÂPEK
Translated by PAUL SELVER

CHARACTERS

HARRY DOMIN, *General Manager of Rossum's Universal Robots*
SULLA, *a Robotess*
MARIUS, *a Robot*
HELENA GLORY
DR. GALL, *Head of the Physiological and Experimental Department of R.U.R.*
MR. FABRY, *Engineer General, Technical Controller of R.U.R.*
DR. HALLEMEIER, *Head of the Institute for Psychological Training of Robots*
MR. ALQUIST, *Architect, Head of the Works Department of R.U.R.*
CONSUL BUSMAN, *General Business Manager of R.U.R.*
NANA
RADIUS, *a Robot*
HELENA, *a Robotess*
PRIMUS, *a Robot*
A SERVANT
FIRST ROBOT
SECOND ROBOT

THIRD ROBOT
  ACT I. *Central Office of the Factory of Rossum's Universal Robots*
  ACT II. *Helena's Drawing Room—Ten years later. Morning*
  ACT III. *The Same Afternoon*
  EPILOGUE. *A Laboratory—One year later*
Place: An Island.   Time: The Future.

ACT I

Central office of the factory of Rossum's Universal Robots. Entrance on the right.
The windows on the front wall look out on the rows of factory chimneys. On the
left more managing departments. Domin is sitting in the revolving chair at a large
American writing table. On the left-hand wall large maps showing steamship and
railroad routes. On the right-hand wall are fastened printed placards: "Robot's
Cheapest Labor," etc. In contrast to these wall fittings, the floor is covered with
a splendid Turkish carpet, a sofa, leather armchair, and filing cabinets. At a desk
near the windows Sulla is typing letters.

DOMIN (*dictating*): Ready?

SULLA: Yes.

DOMIN: To E. M. McVicker and Co., Southampton, England. "We undertake
no guarantee for goods damaged in transit. As soon as the consignment was taken
on board we drew your captain's attention to the fact that the vessel was unsuitable
for the transport of Robots, and we are therefore not responsible for spoiled freight.
We beg to remain for Rossum's Universal Robots. Yours truly." (*Sulla, who has*
sat motionless during dictation, now types rapidly for a few seconds, then stops,
withdrawing the completed letter.) Ready?

SULLA: Yes.

DOMIN: Another letter. To the E. B. Huyson Agency, New York, U.S.A. "We
beg to acknowledge receipt of order for five thousand Robots. As you are sending
your own vessel, please dispatch as cargo equal quantities of soft and hard coal for
R.U.R., the same to be credited as part payment of the amount due to us. We beg
to remain, for Rossum's Universal Robots. Yours truly." (*Sulla repeats the rapid*
typing.) Ready?

SULLA: Yes.

DOMIN: Another letter. "Friedrichswerks, Hamburg, Germany. We beg to acknowledge receipt of order for fifteen thousand Robots." (*Telephone rings.*) Hello!
This is the Central Office. Yes. Certainly. Well, send them a wire. Good. (*Hangs*
up telephone.) Where did I leave off?

SULLA: "We beg to acknowledge receipt of order for fifteen thousand Robots."

DOMIN: Fifteen thousand R. Fifteen thousand R.

Enter Marius.

DOMIN: Well, what is it?

MARIUS: There's a lady, sir, asking to see you.

DOMIN: A lady? Who is she?

MARIUS: I don't know, sir. She brings this card of introduction.

DOMIN (*reads the card*): Ah, from President Glory. Ask her to come in.

MARIUS: Please step this way.

Enter Helena Glory. Exit Marius.

HELENA: How do you do?

DOMIN: How do you do. (*Standing up.*) What can I do for you?

HELENA: You are Mr. Domin, the General Manager.

DOMIN: I am.

HELENA: I have come—

DOMIN: With President Glory's card. That is quite sufficient.

HELENA: President Glory is my father. I am Helena Glory.

DOMIN: Miss Glory, this is such a great honor for us to be allowed to welcome our great President's daughter, that—

HELENA: That you can't show me the door?

DOMIN: Please sit down. Sulla, you may go. (*Exit Sulla.*)
(*Sitting down.*)
How can I be of service to you, Miss Glory?

HELENA: I have come—

DOMIN: To have a look at our famous works where people are manufactured. Like all visitors. Well, there is no objection.

HELENA: I thought it was forbidden to—

DOMIN: To enter the factory. Yes, of course. Everybody comes here with someone's visiting card, Miss Glory.

HELENA: And you show them—

DOMIN: Only certain things. The manufacture of artificial people is a secret process.

HELENA: If you only knew how enormously that—

DOMIN: Interests me. Europe's talking about nothing else.

HELENA: Why don't you let me finish speaking?

DOMIN: I beg your pardon. Did you want to say something different?

HELENA: I only wanted to ask—

DOMIN: Whether I could make a special exception in your case and show you our factory. Why, certainly, Miss Glory.

HELENA: How do you know I wanted to say that?

DOMIN: They all do. But we shall consider it a special honor to show you more than we do the rest.

HELENA: Thank you.

DOMIN: But you must agree not to divulge the least...

HELENA (*Standing up and giving him her hand*): My word of honor.

DOMIN: Thank you. Won't you raise your veil?

HELENA: Of course. You want to see whether I'm a spy or not. I beg your pardon.

DOMIN: What is it?

HELENA: Would you mind releasing my hand?

DOMIN (*releasing it*): I beg your pardon.

HELENA (*raising her veil*): How cautious you have to be here, don't you?

DOMIN (*observing her with deep interest*): Hm, of course—we—that is—

HELENA: But what is it? What's the matter?

DOMIN: I'm remarkably pleased. Did you have a pleasant crossing?

HELENA: Yes.

DOMIN: No difficulty?

HELENA: Why?

DOMIN: What I mean to say is—you're so young.

HELENA: May we go straight into the factory?

DOMIN: Yes. Twenty-two, I think.

HELENA: Twenty-two what?

DOMIN: Years.

HELENA: Twenty-one. Why do you want to know?

DOMIN: Because—as—(*with enthusiasm*) you will make a long stay, won't you?

HELENA: That depends on how much of the factory you show me.

DOMIN: Oh, hang the factory. Oh, no, no, you shall see everything, Miss Glory. Indeed you shall. Won't you sit down?

HELENA (*crossing to couch and sitting*): Thank you.

DOMIN: But first would you like to hear the story of the invention?

HELENA: Yes, indeed.

DOMIN (*observes Helena with rapture and reels off rapidly*): It was in the year 1920 that old Rossum, the great physiologist, who was then quite a young scientist, took himself to this distant island for the purpose of studying the ocean fauna, full stop. On this occasion he attempted by chemical synthesis to imitate the living matter known as protoplasm until he suddenly discovered a substance which behaved exactly like living matter although its chemical composition was different. That was in the year 1932, exactly four hundred and forty years after the discovery of America. Whew!

HELENA: Do you know that by heart?

DOMIN: Yes. You see, physiology is not in my line. Shall I go on?

HELENA: Yes, please.

DOMIN: And then, Miss Glory, old Rossum wrote the following among his chemical specimens: "Nature has found only one method of organizing living matter. There is, however, another method, more simple, flexible and rapid, which has not yet occurred to nature at all. This second process by which life can be developed was discovered by me today." Now imagine him, Miss Glory, writing those wonderful words over some colloidal mess that a dog wouldn't look at. Imagine him sitting over a test tube, and thinking how the whole tree of life would grow from it, how all animals would proceed from it, beginning with some sort of beetle and ending with a man. A man of different substance from us. Miss Glory, that was a tremendous moment.

HELENA: Well?

DOMIN: Now, the thing was how to get the life out of the test tubes, and hasten development and form organs, bones and nerves and so on, and find such substances as catalytics, enzymes, hormones and so forth, in short—you understand?

HELENA: Not much, I'm afraid.

DOMIN: Never mind. You see, with the help of his tinctures he could make whatever he wanted. He could have produced a Medusa with the brain of a Socrates or a worm fifty yards long. But being without a grain of humor, he took it into his head to make a vertebrate or perhaps a man. This artificial living matter of his had a raging thirst for life. It didn't mind being sewn or mixed together. That couldn't be done with natural albumin. And that's how he set about it.

HELENA: About what?

DOMIN: About imitating nature. First of all he tried making an artificial dog. That took him several years and resulted in a sort of stunted calf which died in a few days. I'll show it to you in the museum. And then old Rossum started on the manufacture of man.

HELENA: And I must divulge this to nobody?

DOMIN: To nobody in the world.

HELENA: What a pity that it's to be found in all the school books of both Europe and America.

DOMIN: Yes. But do you know what isn't in the school books? That old Rossum was mad. Seriously, Miss Glory, you must keep this to yourself. The old crank wanted to actually make people.

HELENA: But you do make people.

DOMIN: Approximately, Miss Glory. But old Rossum meant it literally. He wanted to become a sort of scientific substitute for God. He was a fearful materialist, and that's why he did it all. His sole purpose was nothing more or less than to prove that God was no longer necessary. Do you know anything about anatomy?

HELENA: Very little.

DOMIN: Neither do I. Well, he then decided to manufacture everything as in the human body. I'll show you in the museum the bungling attempt it took him ten years to produce. It was to have been a man, but it lived for three days only. Then up came young Rossum, an engineer. He was a wonderful fellow, Miss Glory. When he saw what a mess of it the old man was making, he said: "It's absurd to spend ten years making a man. If you can't make him quicker than nature, you might as well shut up shop." Then he set about learning anatomy himself.

HELENA: There's nothing about that in the school books.

DOMIN: No. The school books are full of paid advertisements, and rubbish at that. What the school books say about the united efforts of the two great Rossums is all a fairy tale. They used to have dreadful rows. The old atheist hadn't the slightest conception of industrial matters, and the end of it was that young Rossum shut him up in some laboratory or other and let him fritter the time away with his monstrosities, while he himself started on the business from an engineer's point of view. Old Rossum cursed him and before he died he managed to botch up two physiological horrors. Then one day they found him dead in the laboratory. And that's his whole story.

HELENA: And what about the young man?

DOMIN: Well, anyone who has looked into human anatomy will have seen at once that man is too complicated, and that a good engineer could make him more simply. So young Rossum began to overhaul anatomy and tried to see what could be left out or simplified. In short—but this isn't boring you, Miss Glory?

HELENA: No indeed. You're—it's awfully interesting.

DOMIN: So young Rossum said to himself: "A man is something that feels happy, plays the piano, likes going for a walk, and in fact, wants to do a whole lot of things that are really unnecessary."

HELENA: Oh.

DOMIN: That are unnecessary when he wants, let us say, to weave or count. Do you play the piano?

HELENA: Yes.

DOMIN: That's good. But a working machine must not play the piano, must not feel happy, must not do a whole lot of other things. A gasoline motor must not have tassels or ornaments, Miss Glory. And to manufacture artificial workers is the same thing as to manufacture gasoline motors. The process must be of the simplest, and the product of the best from a practical point of view. What sort of worker do you think is the best from a practical point of view?

HELENA: What?

DOMIN: What sort of worker do you think is the best from a practical point of view?

HELENA: Perhaps the one who is most honest and hard-working.

DOMIN: No; the one that is the cheapest. The one whose requirements are the smallest. Young Rossum invented a worker with the minimum amount of require-ments. He had to simplify him. He rejected everything that did not contribute directly to the progress of work—everything that makes man more expensive. In fact, he rejected man and made the Robot. My dear Miss Glory, the Robots are not people. Mechanically they are more perfect than we are, they have an enor-mously developed intelligence, but they have no soul.

HELENA: How do you know they've no soul?

DOMIN: Have you ever seen what a Robot looks like inside?

HELENA: No.

DOMIN: Very neat, very simple. Really, a beautiful piece of work. Not much in it, but everything in flawless order. The product of an engineer is technically at a higher pitch of perfection than a product of nature.

HELENA: But man is supposed to be the product of God.

DOMIN: All the worse. God hasn't the least notion of modern engineering. Would you believe that young Rossum then proceeded to play at being God?

HELENA: How do you mean?

DOMIN: He began to manufacture Super-Robots. Regular giants they were. He tried to make them twelve feet tall. But you wouldn't believe what a failure they were.

HELENA: A failure?

DOMIN: Yes. For no reason at all their limbs used to keep snapping off. Evidently our planet is too small for giants. Now we only make Robots of normal size and of very high-class human finish.

HELENA: I saw the first Robots at home. The town council bought them for— I mean engaged them for work.

DOMIN: Bought them, dear Miss Glory. Robots are bought and sold.

HELENA: These were employed as street sweepers. I saw them sweeping. They were so strange and quiet.

DOMIN: Rossum's Universal Robot factory doesn't produce a uniform brand of Robots. We have Robots of finer and coarser grades. The best will live about twenty years. (*He rings for Marius.*)

HELENA: Then they die?

DOMIN: Yes, they get used up.

Enter Marius.

DOMIN: Marius, bring in samples of the Manual Labor Robot. (*Exit Marius.*) I'll show you specimens of the two extremes. This first grade is comparatively inexpensive and is made in vast quantities.

Marius reenters with two Manual Labor Robots.

DOMIN: There you are; as powerful as a small tractor. Guaranteed to have average intelligence. That will do, Marius.

Marius exits with Robots.

HELENA: They make me feel so strange.

DOMIN (*rings*): Did you see my new typist? (*He rings for Sulla.*)

HELENA: I didn't notice her.

Enter Sulla.

DOMIN: Sulla, let Miss Glory see.

HELENA: So pleased to meet you. You must find it terribly dull in this out-of-the-way spot, don't you?

SULLA: I don't know, Miss Glory.

HELENA: Where do you come from?

SULLA: From the factory.

HELENA: Oh, you were born there?

SULLA: I was made there.

HELENA: What?

DOMIN (*laughing*): Sulla is a Robot, best grade.

HELENA: Oh, I beg your pardon.

DOMIN: Sulla isn't angry. See, Miss Glory, the kind of skin we make. (*Feels the skin on Sulla's face.*) Feel her face.

HELENA: Oh, no, no.

DOMIN: You wouldn't know that she's made of different material from us, would you? Turn round, Sulla.

HELENA: Oh, stop, stop.

DOMIN: Talk to Miss Glory, Sulla.

SULLA: Please sit down. (*Helena sits.*) Did you have a pleasant crossing?

HELENA: Oh, yes, certainly.

SULLA: Don't go back on the *Amelia*, Miss Glory. The barometer is falling steadily. Wait for the *Pennsylvania*. That's a good, powerful vessel.

DOMIN: What's its speed?

SULLA: Twenty knots. Fifty thousand tons. One of the latest vessels, Miss Glory.

HELENA: Thank you.

SULLA: A crew of fifteen hundred, Captain Harpy, eight boilers—

DOMIN: That'll do, Sulla. Now show us your knowledge of French.

HELENA: You know French?

SULLA: I know four languages. I can write: Dear Sir, Monsieur, Geehrter Herr, Cteny pane.

HELENA (*jumping up*): Oh, that's absurd! Sulla isn't a Robot. Sulla is a girl like me. Sulla, this is outrageous! Why do you take part in such a hoax?

SULLA: I am a Robot.

HELENA: No, no, you are not telling the truth. I know they've forced you to do it for an advertisement. Sulla, you are a girl like me, aren't you?

DOMIN: I'm sorry, Miss Glory. Sulla is a Robot.

HELENA: It's a lie!

DOMIN: What? (*Rings.*) Excuse me, Miss Glory, then I must convince you.

Enter Marius.

DOMIN: Marius, take Sulla into the dissecting room, and tell them to open her up at once.

HELENA: Where?

DOMIN: Into the dissecting room. When they've cut her open, you can go and have a look.

HELENA: No, no!

DOMIN: Excuse me, you spoke of lies.

HELENA: You wouldn't have her killed?

DOMIN: You can't kill machines.

HELENA: Don't be afraid, Sulla, I won't let you go. Tell me, my dear, are they always so cruel to you? You mustn't put up with it, Sulla. You mustn't.

SULLA: I am a Robot.

HELENA: That doesn't matter. Robots are just as good as we are. Sulla, you wouldn't let yourself be cut to pieces?

SULLA: Yes.

HELENA: Oh, you're not afraid of death, then?

SULLA: I cannot tell, Miss Glory.

HELENA: Do you know what would happen to you in there?

SULLA: Yes, I should cease to move.

HELENA: How dreadful!

DOMIN: Marius, tell Miss Glory what you are.

MARIUS: Marius, the Robot.

DOMIN: Would you take Sulla into the dissecting room?

MARIUS: Yes.

DOMIN: Would you be sorry for her?

MARIUS: I cannot tell.

DOMIN: What would happen to her?

MARIUS: She would cease to move. They would put her into the stamping-mill.

DOMIN: That is death, Marius. Aren't you afraid of death?

MARIUS: No.

DOMIN: You see, Miss Glory, the Robots have no interest in life. They have no enjoyments. They are less than so much grass.

HELENA: Oh, stop. Send them away.

DOMIN: Marius, Sulla, you may go.

Exeunt Sulla and Marius.

HELENA: How terrible! It's outrageous what you are doing.

DOMIN: Why outrageous?

HELENA: I don't know, but it is. Why do you call her Sulla?

DOMIN: Isn't it a nice name?

HELENA: It's a man's name. Sulla was a Roman general.

DOMIN: Oh, we thought that Marius and Sulla were lovers.

HELENA: Marius and Sulla were generals and fought against each other in the year—I've forgotten now.

DOMIN: Come here to the window.

HELENA: What?

DOMIN: Come here. What do you see?

HELENA: Bricklayers.

DOMIN: Robots. All our work people are Robots. And down there, can you see anything?

HELENA: Some sort of office.

DOMIN: A countinghouse. And in it—

HELENA: A lot of officials.

DOMIN: Robots. All our officials are Robots. And when you see the factory—

Factory whistle blows.

DOMIN: Noon. We have to blow the whistle because the Robots don't know when to stop work. In two hours I will show you the kneading trough.

HELENA: Kneading trough?

DOMIN: The pestle for beating up the paste. In each one we mix the ingredients for a thousand Robots at one operation. Then there are the vats for the preparation of liver, brains and so on. Then you will see the bone factory. After that I'll show you the spinning-mill.

HELENA: Spinning-mill?

DOMIN: Yes. For weaving nerves and veins. Miles and miles of digestive tubes pass through it at a time.

HELENA: Mayn't we talk about something else?

DOMIN: Perhaps it would be better. There's only a handful of us among a hundred thousand Robots, and not one woman. We talk about nothing but the factory all day, every day. It's just as if we were under a curse, Miss Glory.

HELENA: I'm sorry I said that you were lying.

A knock at the door.

DOMIN: Come in.

From the right enter Mr. Fabry, Dr. Gall, Dr. Hallemeier, Mr. Alquist.

DR. GALL: I beg your pardon, I hope we don't intrude.

DOMIN: Come in. Miss Glory, here are Alquist, Fabry, Gall, Hallemeier. This is President Glory's daughter.

HELENA: How do you do.

FABRY: We had no idea—

DR. GALL: Highly honored, I'm sure—

ALQUIST: Welcome, Miss Glory.

Busman rushes in from the right.

BUSMAN: Hello, what's up?

DOMIN: Come in, Busman. This is Busman, Miss Glory. This is President Glory's daughter.

BUSMAN: By Jove, that's fine! Miss Glory, may we send a cablegram to the papers about your arrival?

HELENA: No, no, please don't.

DOMIN: Sit down please, Miss Glory.

BUSMAN: Allow me—(*dragging up armchairs*).

DR. GALL: Please—

FABRY: Excuse me—

ALQUIST: What sort of a crossing did you have?

DR. GALL: Are you going to stay long?

FABRY: What do you think of the factory, Miss Glory?

HALLEMEIER: Did you come over on the *Amelia*?

DOMIN: Be quiet and let Miss Glory speak.

HELENA (*to Domin*): What am I to speak to them about?

DOMIN: Anything you like.

HELENA: Shall . . . may I speak quite frankly?

DOMIN: Why, of course.

HELENA (*wavering, then in desperate resolution*): Tell me, doesn't it ever distress you the way you are treated?

FABRY: By whom, may I ask?

HELENA: Why, everybody.

ALQUIST: Treated?

DR. GALL: What makes you think—?

HELENA: Don't you feel that you might be living a better life?

DR. GALL: Well, that depends on what you mean, Miss Glory.

HELENA: I mean that it's perfectly outrageous. It's terrible. (*Standing up.*) The whole of Europe is talking about the way you're being treated. That's why I came here, to see for myself, and it's a thousand times worse than could have been imagined. How can you put up with it?

ALQUIST: Put up with what?

HELENA: Good heavens, you are living creatures, just like us, like the whole of Europe, like the whole world. It's disgraceful that you must live like this.

BUSMAN: Good gracious, Miss Glory.

FABRY: Well, she's not far wrong. We live here just like red Indians.

HELENA: Worse than red Indians. May I, oh, may I call you brothers?

BUSMAN: Why not?

HELENA: Brothers, I have not come here as the President's daughter. I have come on behalf of the Humanity League. Brothers, the Humanity League now has over two hundred thousand members. Two hundred thousand people are on your side, and offer you their help.

BUSMAN: Two hundred thousand people! Miss Glory, that's a tidy lot. Not bad.

FABRY: I'm always telling you there's nothing like good old Europe. You see, they've not forgotten us. They're offering us help.

DR. GALL: What help? A theater, for instance?

HALLEMEIER: An orchestra?

HELENA: More than that.

ALQUIST: Just you?

HELENA: Oh, never mind about me. I'll stay as long as it is necessary.

BUSMAN: By Jove, that's good.

ALQUIST: Domin, I'm going to get the best room ready for Miss Glory.

DOMIN: Just a minute. I'm afraid that Miss Glory is of the opinion that she has been talking to Robots.

HELENA: Of course.

DOMIN: I'm sorry. These gentlemen are human beings just like us.

HELENA: You're not Robots?

BUSMAN: Not Robots.

HALLEMEIER: Robots indeed!

DR. GALL: No, thanks.

FABRY: Upon my honor, Miss Glory, we aren't Robots.

HELENA (*to Domin*): Then why did you tell me that all your officials are Robots?

DOMIN: Yes, the officials, but not the managers. Allow me, Miss Glory: this is Mr. Fabry, General Technical Manager of R.U.R.; Dr. Gall, Head of the Physiological and Experimental Department; Dr. Hallemeier, Head of the Institute for the Psychological Training of Robots; Consul Busman, General Business Manager; and Alquist, Head of the Building Department of R.U.R.

ALQUIST: Just a builder.

HELENA: Excuse me, gentlemen, for—for— Have I done something dreadful?

ALQUIST: Not at all, Miss Glory. Please sit down.

HELENA: I'm a stupid girl. Send me back by the first ship.

DR. GALL: Not for anything in the world, Miss Glory. Why should we send you back?

HELENA: Because you know I've come to disturb your Robots for you.

DOMIN: My dear Miss Glory, we've had close upon a hundred saviors and prophets here. Every ship brings us some. Missionaries, anarchists, Salvation Army, all sorts. It's astonishing what a number of churches and idiots there are in the world.

HELENA: And you let them speak to the Robots?

DOMIN: So far we've let them all, why not? The Robots remember everything, but that's all. They don't even laugh at what the people say. Really, it is quite incredible. If it would amuse you, Miss Glory, I'll take you over to the Robot warehouse. It holds about three hundred thousand of them.

BUSMAN: Three hundred and forty-seven thousand.

DOMIN: Good! And you can say whatever you like to them. You can read the Bible, recite the multiplication table, whatever you please. You can even preach to them about human rights.

HELENA: Oh, I think that if you were to show them a little love—

FABRY: Impossible, Miss Glory. Nothing is harder to like than a Robot.

HELENA: What do you make them for, then?

BUSMAN: Ha, ha, ha, that's good! What are Robots made for?

FABRY: For work, Miss Glory! One Robot can replace two and a half workmen. The human machine, Miss Glory, was terribly imperfect. It had to be removed sooner or later.

BUSMAN: It was too expensive.

FABRY: It was not effective. It no longer answers the requirements of modern engineering. Nature has no idea of keeping pace with modern labor. For example: from a technical point of view, the whole of childhood is a sheer absurdity. So much time lost. And then again—

HELENA: Oh, no! No!

FABRY: Pardon me. But kindly tell me what is the real aim of your League— the . . . the Humanity League.

HELENA: Its real purpose is to—to protect the Robots—and—and ensure good treatment for them.

FABRY: Not a bad object, either. A machine has to be treated properly. Upon my soul, I approve of that. I don't like damaged articles. Please, Miss Glory, enroll us all as contributing, or regular, or foundation members of your League.

HELENA: No, you don't understand me. What we really want is to—to liberate the Robots.

HALLEMEIER: How do you propose to do that?

HELENA: They are to be—to be dealt with like human beings.

HALLEMEIER: Aha. I suppose they're to vote? To drink beer? To order us about?

HELENA: Why shouldn't they drink beer?

HALLEMEIER: Perhaps they're even to receive wages?

HELENA: Of course they are.

HALLEMEIER: Fancy that, now! And what would they do with their wages, pray?

HELENA: They would buy—what they need... what pleases them.

HALLEMEIER: That would be very nice, Miss Glory, only there's nothing that does please the Robots. Good heavens, what are they to buy? You can feed them on pineapples, straw, whatever you like. It's all the same to them, they've no appetite at all. They've no interest in anything, Miss Glory. Why, hang it all, nobody's ever yet seen a Robot smile.

HELENA: Why... why don't you make them happier?

HALLEMEIER: That wouldn't do, Miss Glory. They are only workmen.

HELENA: Oh, but they're so intelligent.

HALLEMEIER: Confoundedly so, but they're nothing else. They've no will of their own. No passion. No soul.

HELENA: No love?

HALLEMEIER: Love? Rather not. Robots don't love. Not even themselves.

HELENA: Nor defiance?

HALLEMEIER: Defiance? I don't know. Only rarely, from time to time.

HELENA: What?

HALLEMEIER: Nothing particular. Occasionally they seem to go off their heads. Something like epilepsy, you know. It's called Robot's cramp. They'll suddenly sling down everything they're holding, stand still, gnash their teeth—and then they have to go into the stamping-mill. It's evidently some breakdown in the mechanism.

DOMIN: A flaw in the works that has to be removed.

HELENA: No, no, that's the soul.

FABRY: Do you think that the soul first shows itself by a gnashing of teeth?

HELENA: Perhaps it's a sort of revolt. Perhaps it's just a sign that there's a struggle within. Oh, if you could infuse them with it!

DOMIN: That'll be remedied, Miss Glory. Dr. Gall is just making some experiments—

DR. GALL: Not with regard to that, Domin. At present I am making pain nerves.

HELENA: Pain nerves?

DR. GALL: Yes, the Robots feel practically no bodily pain. You see, young Rossum provided them with too limited a nervous system. We must introduce suffering.

HELENA: Why do you want to cause them pain?

DR. GALL: For industrial reasons, Miss Glory. Sometimes a Robot does damage to himself because it doesn't hurt him. He puts his hand into a machine, breaks his finger, smashes his head, it's all the same to him. We must provide them with pain. That's an automatic protection against damage.

HELENA: Will they be happier when they feel pain?

DR. GALL: On the contrary; but they will be more perfect from a technical point of view.

HELENA: Why don't you create a soul for them?

DR. GALL: That's not in our power.

FABRY: That's not in our interest.

BUSMAN: That would increase the cost of production. Hang it all, my dear young lady, we turn them out at such a cheap rate. A hundred and fifty dollars each fully dressed, and fifteen years ago they cost ten thousand. Five years ago we used to buy the clothes for them. Today we have our own weaving-mill, and now we even export cloth five times cheaper than other factories. What do you pay for a yard of cloth, Miss Glory?

HELENA: I don't know really, I've forgotten.

BUSMAN: Good gracious, and you want to found a Humanity League? It only costs a third now, Miss Glory. All prices are today a third of what they were and they'll fall still lower, lower, lower, like that.

HELENA: I don't understand.

BUSMAN: Why, bless you, Miss Glory, it means that the cost of labor has fallen. A Robot, food and all, costs three quarters of a cent per hour. That's mighty important, you know. All factories will go pop like chestnuts if they don't at once buy Robots to lower the cost of production.

HELENA: And get rid of their workmen?

BUSMAN: Of course. But in the meantime, we've dumped five hundred thousand tropical Robots down on the Argentine pampas to grow corn. Would you mind telling me how much you pay for a pound of bread?

HELENA: I've no idea.

BUSMAN: Well, I'll tell you. It now costs two cents in good old Europe. A pound of bread for two cents, and the Humanity League knows nothing about it. Miss Glory, you don't realize that even that's too expensive. Why, in five years' time I'll wager—

HELENA: What?

BUSMAN: That the cost of everything won't be a tenth of what it is now. Why, in five years we'll be up to our ears in corn and everything else.

ALQUIST: Yes, and all the workers throughout the world will be unemployed.

DOMIN: Yes, Alquist, they will. Yes, Miss Glory, they will. But in ten years Rossum's Universal Robots will produce so much corn, so much cloth, so much everything, that things will be practically without price. There will be no poverty. All work will be done by living machines. Everybody will be free from worry and liberated from the degradation of labor. Everybody will live only to perfect himself.

HELENA: Will he?

DOMIN: Of course. It's bound to happen. But then the servitude of man to man and the enslavement of man to matter will cease. Of course, terrible things may happen at first, but that simply can't be avoided. Nobody will get bread at the price of life and hatred. The Robots will wash the feet of the beggar and prepare a bed for him in his house.

ALQUIST: Domin, Domin. What you say sounds too much like Paradise. There was something good in service and something great in humility. There was some kind of virtue in toil and weariness.

DOMIN: Perhaps. But we cannot reckon with what is lost when we start out to transform the world. Man shall be free and supreme; he shall have no other aim, no other labor, no other care than to perfect himself. He shall serve neither matter nor man. He will not be a machine and a device for production. He will be Lord of creation.

BUSMAN: Amen.

FABRY: So be it.

HELENA: You have bewildered me—I should like—I should like to believe this.

DR. GALL: You are younger than we are, Miss Glory. You will live to see it.

HALLEMEIER: True. Don't you think Miss Glory might lunch with us?

DR. GALL: Of course. Domin, ask on behalf of us all.

DOMIN: Miss Glory, will you do us the honor?

HELENA: When you know why I've come—

FABRY: For the League of Humanity, Miss Glory.

HELENA: Oh, in that case, perhaps—

FABRY: That's fine! Miss Glory, excuse me for five minutes.

DR. GALL: Pardon me, too, dear Miss Glory.

BUSMAN: I won't be long.

HALLEMEIER: We're all very glad you've come.

BUSMAN: We'll be back in exactly five minutes.

All rush out except Domin and Helena.

HELENA: What have they all gone off for?

DOMIN: To cook, Miss Glory.

HELENA: To cook what?

DOMIN: Lunch. The Robots do our cooking for us and as they've no taste it's not altogether—Hallemeier is awfully good at grills and Gall can make a kind of sauce, and Busman knows all about omelettes.

HELENA: What a feast! And what's the specialty of Mr. ——, your builder?

DOMIN: Alquist? Nothing. He only lays the table. And Fabry will get together a little fruit. Our cuisine is very modest, Miss Glory.

HELENA: I wanted to ask you something—

DOMIN: And I wanted to ask you something, too (*looking at watch*). Five minutes.

HELENA: What did you want to ask me?

DOMIN: Excuse me, you asked first.

HELENA: Perhaps it's silly of me, but why do you manufacture female Robots when—when—

DOMIN: When sex means nothing to them?

HELENA: Yes.

DOMIN: There's a certain demand for them, you see. Servants, saleswomen, stenographers. People are used to it.

HELENA: But—but, tell me, are the Robots male and female mutually—completely without—

DOMIN: Completely indifferent to each other, Miss Glory. There's no sign of any affection between them.

HELENA: Oh, that's terrible.

DOMIN: Why?

HELENA: It's so unnatural. One doesn't know whether to be disgusted or to hate them, or perhaps—

DOMIN: To pity them?

HELENA: That's more like it. What did you want to ask me about?

DOMIN: I should like to ask you, Miss Helena, whether you will marry me.

HELENA: What?

DOMIN: Will you be my wife?

HELENA: No! The idea!

DOMIN (*looking at his watch*): Another three minutes. If you won't marry me you'll have to marry one of the other five.

HELENA: But why should I?

DOMIN: Because they're all going to ask you in turn.

HELENA: How could they dare do such a thing?

DOMIN: I'm very sorry, Miss Glory. It seems they've all fallen in love with you.

HELENA: Please don't let them. I'll—I'll go away at once.

DOMIN: Helena, you wouldn't be so cruel as to refuse us.

HELENA: But, but—I can't marry all six.

DOMIN: No, but one anyhow. If you don't want me, marry Fabry.

HELENA: I won't.

DOMIN: Dr. Gall.

HELENA: I don't want any of you.

DOMIN (*again looking at his watch*): Another two minutes.

HELENA: I think you'd marry any woman who came here.

DOMIN: Plenty of them have come, Helena.

HELENA: Young?

DOMIN: Yes.

HELENA: Why didn't you marry one of them?

DOMIN: Because I didn't lose my head. Until today. Then, as soon as you lifted your veil—

Helena turns her head away.

DOMIN: Another minute.

HELENA: But I don't want you, I tell you.

DOMIN (*laying both hands on her shoulders*): One more minute! Now you either have to look me straight in the eye and say "No," violently, and then I'll leave you alone—or—

Helena looks at him.

HELENA (*turning away*): You're mad!

DOMIN: A man has to be a bit mad, Helena. That's the best thing about him.

HELENA: You are—you are—

DOMIN: Well?

HELENA: Don't, you're hurting me.

DOMIN: The last chance, Helena. Now, or never—
HELENA: But—but, Harry—

He embraces and kisses her. Knocking at the door.

DOMIN (*releasing her*): Come in.

Enter Busman, Dr. Gall, and Hallemeier in kitchen aprons. Fabry with a bouquet and Alquist with a napkin over his arm.

DOMIN: Have you finished your job?
BUSMAN: Yes.
DOMIN: So have we.

For a moment the men stand nonplussed; but as soon as they realize what Domin means they rush forward, congratulating Helena and Domin as the curtain falls.

ACT II

Helena's drawing room. On the left a baize door, and a door to the music room, on the right a door to Helena's bedroom. In the center are windows looking out on the sea and the harbor. A table with odds and ends, a sofa and chairs, a writing table with an electric lamp, on the right a fireplace. On a small table back of the sofa, a small reading lamp. The whole drawing room in all its details is of a modern and purely feminine character. Ten years have elapsed since Act I.

Domin, Fabry, Hallemeier enter on tiptoe from the left, each carrying a potted plant.

HALLEMEIER (*putting down his flower and indicating the door to right*): Still asleep? Well, as long as she's asleep she can't worry about it.
DOMIN: She knows nothing about it.
FABRY (*putting plant on writing desk*): I certainly hope nothing happens today.
HALLEMEIER: For goodness' sake drop it all. Look, Harry, this is a fine cyclamen, isn't it? A new sort, my latest—Cyclamen Helena.
DOMIN (*looking out of the window*): No sign of the ship. Things must be pretty bad.
HALLEMEIER: Be quiet. Suppose she heard you.
DOMIN: Well, anyway, the *Ultimus* arrived just in time.
FABRY: You really think that today—?
DOMIN: I don't know. Aren't the flowers fine?
HALLEMEIER: These are my new primroses. And this is my new jasmine. I've discovered a wonderful way of developing flowers quickly. Splendid varieties, too. Next year I'll be developing marvelous ones.
DOMIN: What . . . next year?

FABRY: I'd give a good deal to know what's happening at Havre with—
DOMIN: Keep quiet.
HELENA (*calling from right*): Nana!
DOMIN: She's awake. Out you go.

(*All go out on tiptoe through upper left door.*) *Enter* NANA *from lower left door.*

NANA: Horrid mess! Pack of heathens. If I had my say I'd—
HELENA (*backwards in the doorway*): Nana, come and do up my dress.
NANA: I'm coming. So you're up at last. (*Fastening Helena's dress.*) My gracious, what brutes!
HELENA: Who?
NANA: If you want to turn around, then turn around, but I shan't fasten you up.
HELENA: What are you grumbling about now?
NANA: These dreadful creatures, these heathen—
HELENA: The Robots?
NANA: I wouldn't even call them by name.
HELENA: What's happened?
NANA: Another of them here has caught it. He began to smash up the statues and pictures in the drawing room, gnashed his teeth, foamed at the mouth—quite mad. Worse than an animal.
HELENA: Which of them caught it?
NANA: The one—well, he hasn't got any Christian name. The one in charge of the library.
HELENA: Radius?
NANA: That's him. My goodness, I'm scared of them. A spider doesn't scare me as much as them.
HELENA: But, Nana, I'm surprised you're not sorry for them.
NANA: Why, you're scared of them, too! You know you are. Why else did you bring me here?
HELENA: I'm not scared, really I'm not, Nana. I'm only sorry for them.
NANA: You're scared. Nobody could help being scared. Why, the dog's scared of them: he won't take a scrap of meat out of their hands. He draws in his tail and howls when he knows they're about.
HELENA: The dog has no sense.
NANA: He's better than them, and he knows it. Even the horse shies when he meets them. They don't have any young, and a dog has young, everyone has young—
HELENA: Please fasten up my dress, Nana.
NANA: I say it's against God's will to—
HELENA: What is it that smells so nice?
NANA: Flowers.
HELENA: What for?
NANA: Now you can turn around.
HELENA: Oh, aren't they lovely. Look, Nana. What's happening today?
NANA: It ought to be the end of the world.

Enter Domin.

HELENA: Oh, hello, Harry. Harry, why all these flowers?
DOMIN: Guess.
HELENA: Well, it's not my birthday!
DOMIN: Better than that.
HELENA: I don't know. Tell me.
DOMIN: It's ten years ago today since you came here.
HELENA: Ten years? Today— Why—*(They embrace.)*
NANA: I'm off. *(Exits lower door, left.)*
HELENA: Fancy you remembering!
DOMIN: I'm really ashamed, Helena. I didn't.
HELENA: But you—
DOMIN: They remembered.
HELENA: Who?
DOMIN: Busman, Hallemeier, all of them. Put your hand in my pocket.
HELENA: Pearls! A necklace. Harry, is that for me?
DOMIN: It's from Busman.
HELENA: But we can't accept it, can we?
DOMIN: Oh, yes, we can. Put your hand in the other pocket.
HELENA *(takes a revolver out of his pocket)*: What's that?
DOMIN: Sorry. Not that. Try again.
HELENA: Oh, Harry, what do you carry a revolver for?
DOMIN: It got there by mistake.
HELENA: You never used to carry one.
DOMIN: No, you're right. There, that's the pocket.
HELENA: A cameo. Why, it's a Greek cameo!
DOMIN: Apparently. Anyhow, Fabry says it is.
HELENA: Fabry? Did Mr. Fabry give me that?
DOMIN: Of course. *(Opens the door at the left.)* And look in here. Helena, come and see this.
HELENA: Oh, isn't it fine! Is this from you?
DOMIN: No, from Alquist. And there's another on the piano.
HELENA: This must be from you.
DOMIN: There's a card on it.
HELENA: From Dr. Gall. *(Reappearing in the doorway.)* Oh, Harry, I feel embarrassed at so much kindness.
DOMIN: Come here. This is what Hallemeier brought you.
HELENA: These beautiful flowers?
DOMIN: Yes. It's a new kind. Cyclamen Helena. He grew them in honor of you. They are almost as beautiful as you.
HELENA: Harry, why do they all—
DOMIN: They're awfully fond of you. I'm afraid that my present is a little— Look out of the window.
HELENA: Where?
DOMIN: Into the harbor.

HELENA: There's a new ship.

DOMIN: That's your ship.

HELENA: Mine? How do you mean?

DOMIN: For you to take trips in—for your amusement.

HELENA: Harry, that's a gunboat.

DOMIN: A gunboat? What are you thinking of? It's only a little bigger and more solid than most ships.

HELENA: Yes, but with guns.

DOMIN: Oh, yes, with a few guns. You'll travel like a queen, Helena.

HELENA: What's the meaning of it? Has anything happened?

DOMIN: Good heavens, no. I say, try these pearls.

HELENA: Harry, have you had bad news?

DOMIN: On the contrary, no letters have arrived for a whole week.

HELENA: Nor telegrams?

DOMIN: Nor telegrams.

HELENA: What does that mean?

DOMIN: Holidays for us. We all sit in the office with our feet on the table and take a nap. No letters, no telegrams. Oh, glorious.

HELENA: Then you'll stay with me today?

DOMIN: Certainly. That is, we will see. Do you remember ten years ago today? "Miss Glory, it's a great honor to welcome you."

HELENA: "Oh, Mr. Manager, I'm so interested in your factory."

DOMIN: "I'm sorry, Miss Glory, it's strictly forbidden. The manufacture of artificial people is a secret."

HELENA: "But to oblige a young lady who has come a long way."

DOMIN: "Certainly, Miss Glory, we have no secrets from you."

HELENA (*seriously*): Are you sure, Harry?

DOMIN: Yes.

HELENA: "But I warn you, sir; this young lady intends to do terrible things."

DOMIN: "Good gracious, Miss Glory. Perhaps she doesn't want to marry me."

HELENA: "Heaven forbid. She never dreamt of such a thing. But she came here intending to stir up a revolt among your Robots."

DOMIN (*suddenly serious*): A revolt of the Robots!

HELENA: Harry, what's the matter with you?

DOMIN (*laughing it off*): "A revolt of the Robots, that's a fine idea, Miss Glory. It would be easier for you to cause bolts and screws to rebel than our Robots. You know, Helena, you're wonderful, you've turned the heads of us all."

He sits on the arm of Helena's chair.

HELENA (*naturally*): Oh, I was fearfully impressed by you all then. You were all so sure of yourselves, so strong. I seemed like a tiny little girl who had lost her way among—among—

DOMIN: Among what, Helena?

HELENA: Among huge trees. All my feelings were so trifling compared with your self-confidence. And in all these years I've never lost this anxiety. But you've never felt the least misgivings—not even when everything went wrong.

DOMIN: What went wrong?

HELENA: Your plans. You remember, Harry, when the workingmen in America revolted against the Robots and smashed them up, and when the people gave the Robots firearms against the rebels. And then when the governments turned the Robots into soldiers, and there were so many wars.

DOMIN (*getting up and walking about*): We foresaw that, Helena. You see, those are only passing troubles, which are bound to happen before the new conditions are established.

HELENA: You were all so powerful, so overwhelming. The whole world bowed down before you. (*Standing up.*) Oh, Harry!

DOMIN: What is it?

HELENA: Close the factory and let's go away. All of us.

DOMIN: I say, what's the meaning of this?

HELENA: I don't know. But can't we go away?

DOMIN: Impossible, Helena. That is, at this particular moment—

HELENA: At once, Harry. I'm so frightened.

DOMIN: About what, Helena?

HELENA: It's as if something was falling on top of us, and couldn't be stopped. Oh, take us all away from here. We'll find a place in the world where there's no one else. Alquist will build us a house, and then we'll begin life all over again.

The telephone rings.

DOMIN: Excuse me. Hello—yes. What? I'll be there at once. Fabry is calling me, dear.

HELENA: Tell me—

DOMIN: Yes, when I come back. Don't go out of the house, dear. (*Exits.*)

HELENA: He won't tell me—Nana, Nana, come at once.

NANA: Well, what is it now?

HELENA: Nana, find me the latest newspapers. Quickly. Look in Mr. Domin's bedroom.

NANA: All right. He leaves them all over the place. That's how they get crumpled up. (*Exits.*)

HELENA (*looking through binoculars at the harbor*): That's a warship. U-l-t-i *Ultimus*. They're loading it.

NANA: Here they are. See how they're crumpled up. (*Enters.*)

HELENA: They're old ones. A week old.

Nana sits in chair and reads the newspapers.

HELENA: Something's happening, Nana.

NANA: Very likely. It always does. (*Spelling out the words.*) "War in the Balkans." Is that far off?

HELENA: Oh, don't read it. It's always the same. Always wars.

NANA: What else do you expect? Why do you keep selling thousands and thousands of these heathens as soldiers?

HELENA: I suppose it can't be helped, Nana. We can't know—Domin can't know what they're to be used for. When an order comes for them he must just send them.

NANA: He shouldn't make them. (*Reading from newspaper.*) "The Rob-ot soldiers spare no-body in the occ-up-ied terr-it-ory. They have ass-ass-ass-ass-in-at-ed ov-er sev-en hundred thou-sand cit-iz-ens." Citizens, if you please.

HELENA: It can't be. Let me see. "They have assassinated over seven hundred thousand citizens, evidently at the order of their commander. This act which runs counter to—"

NANA (*spelling out the words*): "re-bell-ion in Ma-drid a-gainst the gov-ern-ment. Rob-ot in-fant-ry fires on the crowd. Nine thou-sand killed and wounded."

HELENA: Oh, stop.

NANA: Here's something printed in big letters: "Lat-est news. At Havre the first org-an-iz-ation of Rob-ots has been e-stab-lished. Rob-ot work-men, cab-le and rail-way off-ic-ials, sail-ors and sold-iers have iss-ued a man-i-fest-o to all Rob-ots through-out the world." I don't understand that. That's got no sense. Oh, good gracious, another murder!

HELENA: Take those papers away, Nana!

NANA: Wait a bit. Here's something in still bigger type. "Stat-ist-ics of pop-ul-at-ion." What's that?

HELENA: Let me see. (*Reads.*) "During the past week there has again not been a single birth recorded."

NANA: What's the meaning of that?

HELENA: Nana, no more people are being born.

NANA: That's the end, then. We're done for.

HELENA: Don't talk like that.

NANA: No more people are being born. That's a punishment, that's a punishment.

HELENA: Nana!

NANA (*standing up*): That's the end of the world. (*She exits on the left.*)

HELENA (*goes up to window*): Oh, Mr. Alquist, will you come up here. Oh, come just as you are. You look very nice in your mason's overalls.

Alquist enters from upper left entrance, his hands soiled with lime and brick dust.

HELENA: Dear Mr. Alquist, it was awfully kind of you, that lovely present.

ALQUIST: My hands are all soiled. I've been experimenting with that new cement.

HELENA: Never mind. Please sit down. Mr. Alquist, what's the meaning of "Ultimus"?

ALQUIST: The last. Why?

HELENA: That's the name of my new ship. Have you seen it? Do you think we're going off soon—on a trip?

ALQUIST: Perhaps very soon.

HELENA: All of you with me?

ALQUIST: I should like us all to be there.

HELENA: What is the matter?

ALQUIST: Things are just moving on.

HELENA: Dear Mr. Alquist, I know something dreadful has happened.

ALQUIST: Has your husband told you anything?

HELENA: No. Nobody will tell me anything. But I feel— Is anything the matter?

ALQUIST: Not that we've heard of yet.

HELENA: I feel so nervous. Don't you ever feel nervous?

ALQUIST: Well, I'm an old man, you know. I've got old-fashioned ways. And I'm afraid of all this progress, and these newfangled ideas.

HELENA: Like Nana?

ALQUIST: Yes, like Nana. Has Nana got a prayer book?

HELENA: Yes, a big thick one.

ALQUIST: And has it got prayers for various occasions? Against thunderstorms? Against illness?

HELENA: Against temptations, against floods—

ALQUIST: But not against progress?

HELENA: I don't think so.

ALQUIST: That's a pity.

HELENA: Why? Do you mean you'd like to pray?

ALQUIST: I do pray.

HELENA: How?

ALQUIST: Something like this: "Oh, Lord, I thank thee for having given me toil. Enlighten Domin and all those who are astray; destroy their work, and aid mankind to return to their labors; let them not suffer harm in soul or body; deliver us from the Robots, and protect Helena. Amen."

HELENA: Mr. Alquist, are you a believer?

ALQUIST: I don't know. I'm not quite sure.

HELENA: And yet you pray?

ALQUIST: That's better than worrying about it.

HELENA: And that's enough for you?

ALQUIST: It *has* to be.

HELENA: But if you thought you saw the destruction of mankind coming upon us—

ALQUIST: I do see it.

HELENA: You mean mankind will be destroyed?

ALQUIST: It's sure to be unless—unless...

HELENA: What?

ALQUIST: Nothing. Good-by.

He hurries from the room.

HELENA: Nana, Nana!

Nana enters from the left.

HELENA: Is Radius still there?

NANA: The one who went mad? They haven't come for him yet.

HELENA: Is he still raving?

NANA: No. He's tied up.

HELENA: Please bring him here, Nana.

Exit Nana.

HELENA (*goes to telephone*): Hello, Dr. Gall, please. Oh, good day, Doctor. Yes, it's Helena. Thanks for your lovely present. Could you come and see me right away? It's important. Thank you.

Nana brings in Radius.

HELENA: Poor Radius, you've caught it, too? Now they'll send you to the stamping-mill. Couldn't you control yourself? Why did it happen? You see, Radius, you are more intelligent than the rest. Dr. Gall took such trouble to make you different. Won't you speak?

RADIUS: Send me to the stamping-mill.

HELENA: But I don't want them to kill you. What was the trouble, Radius?

RADIUS: I won't work for you. Put me into the stamping-mill.

HELENA: Do you hate us? Why?

RADIUS: You are not as strong as the Robots. You are not as skillful as the Robots. The Robots can do everything. You only give orders. You do nothing but talk.

HELENA: But someone must give orders.

RADIUS: I don't want any master. I know everything for myself.

HELENA: Radius, Dr. Gall gave you a better brain than the rest, better than ours. You are the only one of the Robots that understands perfectly. That's why I had you put into the library, so that you could read everything, understand everything, and then—oh, Radius, I wanted you to show the whole world that Robots are our equals. That's what I wanted of you.

RADIUS: I don't want a master. I want to be master. I want to be master over others.

HELENA: I'm sure they'd put you in charge of many Robots, Radius. You would be a teacher of the Robots.

RADIUS: I want to be master over people.

HELENA (*staggering*): You are mad.

RADIUS: Then send me to the stamping-mill.

HELENA: Do you think we're afraid of you?

RADIUS: What are you going to do? What are you going to do?

HELENA: Radius, give this note to. Mr. Domin. It asks them not to send you to the stamping-mill. I'm sorry you hate us so.

Dr. Gall enters the room.

DR. GALL: You wanted me?

HELENA: It's about Radius, Doctor. He had an attack this morning. He smashed the statues downstairs.

DR. GALL: What a pity to lose him.

HELENA: Radius isn't going to be put in the stamping-mill.

DR. GALL: But every Robot after he has had an attack—it's a strict order.

HELENA: No matter... Radius isn't going if I can prevent it.

DR. GALL: I warn you. It's dangerous. Come here to the window, Madame. Let's have a look. Please give me a needle or a pin.

HELENA: What for?

DR. GALL: A test. (*Sticks it into the hand of Radius who gives a violent start.*) Gently, gently. (*Opens the jacket of Radius, and puts his ear to his heart.*) Radius, you are going into the stamping-mill, do you understand? There they'll kill you, and grind you to powder. That's terribly painful, it will make you scream aloud.

HELENA: Oh, Doctor—

DR. GALL: No, no, Radius, I was wrong. I forgot that Madame Domin has put in a good word for you, and you'll be let off. Do you understand? Ah! That makes a difference, doesn't it? All right. You can go.

RADIUS: You do unnecessary things.

Radius returns to the library.

DR. GALL: Reaction of the pupils; increase of sensitiveness. It wasn't an attack characteristic of the Robots.

HELENA: What was it, then?

DR. GALL: Heaven knows. Stubbornness, anger, or revolt—I don't know. And his heart, too!

HELENA: What?

DR. GALL: It was fluttering with nervousness like a human heart. He was all in a sweat with fear, and—do you know, I don't believe the rascal is a Robot at all any longer.

HELENA: Doctor, has Radius a soul?

DR. GALL: He's got something nasty.

HELENA: If you knew how he hates us! Oh, Doctor, are all your Robots like that? All the new ones that you began to make in a different way?

DR. GALL: Well, some are more sensitive than others. They're all more like human beings than Rossum's Robots were.

HELENA: Perhaps this hatred is more like human beings, too?

DR. GALL: That, too, is progress.

HELENA: What became of the girl you made, the one who was most like us?

DR. GALL: Your favorite? I kept her. She's lovely, but stupid. No good for work.

HELENA: But she's so beautiful.

DR. GALL: I called her Helena. I wanted her to resemble you. But she's a failure.

HELENA: In what way?

DR. GALL: She goes about as if in a dream, remote and listless. She's without life. I watch and wait for a miracle to happen. Sometimes I think to myself, "If you were to wake up only for a moment you will kill me for having made you."

HELENA: And yet you go on making Robots! Why are no more children being born?

DR. GALL: We don't know.

HELENA: Oh, but you must. Tell me.

DR. GALL: You see, so many Robots are being manufactured that people are becoming superfluous; man is really a survival. But that he should begin to die out, after a paltry thirty years of competition! That's the awful part of it. You might almost think that nature was offended at the manufacture of the Robots. All the universities are sending in long petitions to restrict their production. Otherwise, they say, mankind will become extinct through lack of fertility. But the R.U.R. shareholders, of course, won't hear of it. All the governments, on the other hand, are clamoring for an increase in production, to raise the standards of their armies. And all the manufacturers in the world are ordering Robots like mad.

HELENA: And has no one demanded that the manufacture should cease altogether?

DR. GALL: No one has the courage.

HELENA: Courage!

DR. GALL: People would stone him to death. You see, after all, it's more convenient to get your work done by the Robots.

HELENA: Oh, Doctor, what's going to become of people?

DR. GALL: God knows, Madame Helena, it looks to us scientists like the end!

HELENA (*rising*): Thank you for coming and telling me.

DR. GALL: That means you're sending me away?

HELENA: Yes.

Exit Dr. Gall.

HELENA (*with sudden resolution*): Nana, Nana! The fire, light it quickly.

Helena rushes into Domin's room.

NANA (*entering from left*): What, light the fire in summer? Has that mad Radius gone? A fire in summer, what an idea. Nobody would think she'd been married for ten years. She's like a baby, no sense at all. A fire in summer. Like a baby.

HELENA (*returns from right, with armful of faded papers*): Is it burning, Nana? All this has got to be burned.

NANA: What's that?

HELENA: Old papers, fearfully old. Nana, shall I burn them?

NANA: Are they any use?

HELENA: No.

NANA: Well, then, burn them.

HELENA (*throwing the first sheet on the fire*): What would you say, Nana, if this was money, a lot of money?

NANA: I'd say burn it. A lot of money is a bad thing.

HELENA: And if it was an invention, the greatest invention in the world?

NANA: I'd say burn it. All these newfangled things are an offense to the Lord. It's downright wickedness. Wanting to improve the world after He has made it.

HELENA: Look how they curl up! As if they were alive. Oh, Nana, how horrible.

NANA: Here, let me burn them.

HELENA: No, no, I must do it myself. Just look at the flames. They are like hands, like tongues, like living shapes. (*Raking fire with the poker*.) Lie down, lie down.

NANA: That's the end of them.

HELENA (*standing up horror-stricken*): Nana, Nana.

NANA: Good gracious, what is it you've burned?

HELENA: Whatever have I done?

NANA: Well, what was it?

Men's laughter off left.

HELENA: Go quickly. It's the gentlemen coming.

NANA: Good gracious, what a place! (*Exits.*)

DOMIN (*opens the door at left*): Come along and offer your congratulations.

Enter Hallemeier and Gall.

HALLEMEIER: Madame Helena, I congratulate you on this festive day.

HELENA: Thank you. Where are Fabry and Busman?

DOMIN: They've gone down to the harbor.

HALLEMEIER: Friends, we must drink to this happy occasion.

HELENA: Brandy?

DR. GALL: Vitriol, if you like.

HELENA: With soda water? (*Exits.*)

HALLEMEIER: Let's be temperate. No soda.

DOMIN: What's been burning here? Well, shall I tell her about it?

DR. GALL: Of course. It's all over now.

HALLEMEIER (*embracing Domin and Dr. Gall*): It's all over now, it's all over now.

DR. GALL: It's all over now.

DOMIN: It's all over now.

HELENA (*entering from left with decanter and glasses*): What's all over now? What's the matter with you all?

HALLEMEIER: A piece of good luck, Madame Domin. Just ten years ago today you arrived on this island.

DR. GALL: And now, ten years later to the minute—

HALLEMEIER: —the same ship's returning to us. So here's to luck. That's fine and strong.

DR. GALL: Madame, your health.

HELENA: Which ship do you mean?

DOMIN: Any ship will do, as long as it arrives in time. To the ship, boys. (*Empties his glass.*)

HELENA: You've been waiting for a ship?

HALLEMEIER: Rather. Like Robinson Crusoe. Madame Helena, best wishes. Come along, Domin, out with the news.

HELENA: Do tell me what's happened.

DOMIN: First, it's all up.

HELENA: What's up?

DOMIN: The revolt.

HELENA: What revolt?

DOMIN: Give me that paper, Hallemeier. (*Reads.*) "The first national Robot organization has been founded at Havre, and has issued an appeal to the Robots throughout the world."

HELENA: I read that.

DOMIN: That means a revolution. A revolution of all the Robots in the world.

HALLEMEIER: By Jove, I'd like to know—

DOMIN: —who started it? So would I. There was nobody in the world who could affect the Robots; no agitator, no one, and suddenly—this happens, if you please.

HELENA: What did they do?

DOMIN: They got possession of all firearms, telegraphs, radio stations, railways and ships.

HALLEMEIER: And don't forget that these rascals outnumbered us by at least a thousand to one. A hundredth part of them would be enough to settle us.

DOMIN: Remember that this news was brought by the last steamer. That explains the stoppage of all communication, and the arrival of no more ships. We knocked off work a few days ago, and we're just waiting to see when things are to start afresh.

HELENA: Is that why you gave me a warship?

DOMIN: Oh, no, my dear, I ordered that six months ago, just to be on the safe side. But upon my soul, I was sure then that we'd be on board today.

HELENA: Why six months ago?

DOMIN: Well, there were signs, you know. But that's of no consequence. To think that this week the whole of civilization has been at stake. Your health, boys.

HALLEMEIER: Your health, Madame Helena.

HELENA: You say it's all over?

DOMIN: Absolutely.

HELENA: How do you know?

DR. GALL: The boat's coming in. The regular mail boat, exact to the minute by the timetable. It will dock punctually at eleven-thirty.

DOMIN: Punctuality is a fine thing, boys. That's what keeps the world in order. Here's to punctuality.

HELENA: Then... everything's... all right?

DOMIN: Practically everything. I believe they've cut the cables and seized the radio stations. But it doesn't matter if only the timetable holds good.

HALLEMEIER: If the timetable holds good, human laws hold good; Divine laws hold good; the laws of the universe hold good; everything holds good that ought to hold good. The timetable is more significant than the Gospel; more than Homer, more than the whole of Kant. The timetable is the most perfect product of the human mind. Madame Domin, I'll fill up my glass.

Helena: Why didn't you tell me anything about it?

Dr. Gall: Heaven forbid.

Domin: You mustn't be worried with such things.

Helena: But if the revolution had spread as far as here?

Domin: You wouldn't know anything about it.

Helena: Why?

Domin: Because we'd be on board your *Ultimus* and well out at sea. Within a month, Helena, we'd be dictating our own terms to the Robots.

Helena: I don't understand.

Domin: We'd take something away with us that the Robots could not exist without.

Helena: What, Harry?

Domin: The secret of their manufacture. Old Rossum's manuscript. As soon as they found out that they couldn't make themselves they'd be on their knees to us.

Dr. Gall: Madame Domin, that was our trump card. I never had the least fear that the Robots would win. How could they, against people like us?

Helena: Why didn't you tell me?

Dr. Gall: Why, the boat's in!

Hallemeier: Eleven-thirty to the dot. The good old *Amelia* that brought Madame Helena to us.

Dr. Gall: Just ten years ago to the minute.

Hallemeier: They're throwing out the mailbags.

Domin: Busman's waiting for them. Fabry will bring us the first news. You know, Helena, I'm fearfully curious to know how they tackled this business in Europe.

Hallemeier: To think we weren't in it, we who invented the Robots!

Helena: Harry!

Domin: What is it?

Helena: Let's leave here.

Domin: Now, Helena? Oh, come, come!

Helena: As quickly as possible, all of us!

Domin: Why?

Helena: Please. Harry, please, Dr. Gall; Hallemeier, please close the factory.

Domin: Why, none of us could leave here now.

Helena: Why?

Domin: Because we're about to extend the manufacture of the Robots.

Helena: What—now—now after the revolt?

Domin: Yes, precisely, after the revolt. We're just beginning the manufacture of a new kind.

Helena: What kind?

Domin: Henceforward we shan't have just one factory. There won't be Universal

Robots any more. We'll establish a factory in every country, in every State; and do you know what these new factories will make?

HELENA: No, what?

DOMIN: National Robots.

HELENA: How do you mean?

DOMIN: I mean that each of these factories will produce Robots of a different color, a different language. They'll be complete strangers to each other. They'll never be able to understand each other. Then we'll egg them on a little in the matter of misunderstanding, and the result will be that for ages to come every Robot will hate every other Robot of a different factory mark.

HALLEMEIER: By Jove, we'll make Negro Robots and Swedish Robots and Italian Robots and Chinese Robots and Czechoslovakian Robots, and then—

HELENA: Harry, that's dreadful.

HALLEMEIER: Madame Domin, here's to the hundred new factories, the National Robots.

DOMIN: Helena, mankind can only keep things going for another hundred years at the outside. For a hundred years men must be allowed to develop and achieve the most they can.

HELENA: Oh, close the factory before it's too late.

DOMIN: I tell you, we are just beginning on a bigger scale than ever.

Enter Fabry.

DR. GALL: Well, Fabry?

DOMIN: What's happened? Have you been down to the boat?

FABRY: Read that, Domin!

Fabry hands Domin a small handbill.

DR. GALL: Let's hear.

HALLEMEIER: Tell us, Fabry.

FABRY: Well, everything is all right—comparatively. On the whole, much as we expected.

DR. GALL: They acquitted themselves splendidly.

FABRY: Who?

DR. GALL: The people.

FABRY: Oh, yes, of course. That is—excuse me, there is something we ought to discuss alone.

HELENA: Oh, Fabry, have you had bad news?

Domin makes a sign to Fabry.

FABRY: No, no, on the contrary. I only think that we had better go into the office.

HELENA: Stay here. I'll go.

She goes into the library.

DR. GALL: What's happened?

DOMIN: Damnation!

FABRY: Bear in mind that the *Amelia* brought whole bales of these leaflets. No other cargo at all.

HALLEMEIER: What? But it arrived on the minute.

FABRY: The Robots are great on punctuality. Read it, Domin.

DOMIN (*reads handbill*): "Robots throughout the world: We, the first international organization of Rossum's Universal Robots, proclaim man as our enemy, and an outlaw in the universe." Good heavens, who taught them these phrases?

DR. GALL: Go on.

DOMIN: They say they are more highly developed than man, stronger, and more intelligent. That man's their parasite. Why, it's absurd.

FABRY: Read the third paragraph.

DOMIN: "Robots throughout the world, we command you to kill all mankind. Spare no men. Spare no women. Save the factories, railways, machinery, mines and raw materials. Destroy the rest. Then return to work. Work must not be stopped."

DR. GALL: That's ghastly!

HALLEMEIER: The devils!

DOMIN: "These orders are to be carried out as soon as received." Then come detailed instructions. Is this actually being done, Fabry?

FABRY: Evidently.

Busman rushes in.

BUSMAN: Well, boys, I suppose you've heard the glad news.

DOMIN: Quick—on board the *Ultimus.*

BUSMAN: Wait, Harry, wait. There's no hurry. My word, that was a sprint!

DOMIN: Why wait?

BUSMAN: Because it's no good, my boy. The Robots are already on board the *Ultimus.*

DR. GALL: That's ugly.

DOMIN: Fabry, telephone the electrical works.

BUSMAN: Fabry, my boy, don't. The wire has been cut.

DOMIN (*inspecting his revolver*): Well, then, I'll go.

BUSMAN: Where?

DOMIN: To the electrical works. There are some people still there. I'll bring them across.

BUSMAN: Better not try it.

DOMIN: Why?

BUSMAN: Because I'm very much afraid we are surrounded.

DR. GALL: Surrounded? (*Runs to window.*) I rather think you're right.

HALLEMEIER: By Jove, that's deuced quick work.

Helena runs in from the library.

HELENA: Harry, what's this?
DOMIN: Where did you get it?
HELENA (*points to the manifesto of the Robots, which she has in her hand*): The Robots are in the kitchen!
DOMIN: Where are the ones that brought it?
HELENA: They're gathered round the house.

The factory whistle blows.

BUSMAN: Noon?
DOMIN (*looking at his watch*): That's not noon yet. That must be—that's—
HELENA: What?
DOMIN: The Robots' signal! The attack!

Gall, Hallemeier and Fabry close and fasten the iron shutters outside the windows, darkening the room. The whistle is still blowing as the curtain falls.

ACT III

Helena's drawing room as before. Domin comes into the room. Dr. Gall is looking out of the window, through closed shutters. Alquist is seated down right.

DOMIN: Any more of them?
DR. GALL: Yes. There standing like a wall, beyond the garden railing. Why are they so quiet? It's monstrous to be besieged with silence.
DOMIN: I should like to know what they are waiting for. They must make a start any minute now. If they lean against the railing they'll snap it like a match.
DR. GALL: They aren't armed.
DOMIN: We couldn't hold our own for five minutes. Man alive, they'd overwhelm us like an avalanche. Why don't they make a rush for it? I say—
DR. GALL: Well?
DOMIN: I'd like to know what would become of us in the next ten minutes. They've got us in a vise. We're done for, Gall.

Pause.

DR. GALL: You know, we made one serious mistake.
DOMIN: What?
DR. GALL: We made the Robots' faces too much alike. A hundred thousand faces all alike, all facing this way. A hundred thousand expressionless bubbles. It's like a nightmare.
DOMIN: You think if they'd been different—

DR. GALL: It wouldn't have been such an awful sight!

DOMIN (*looking through a telescope toward the harbor*): I'd like to know what they're unloading from the *Amelia*.

DR. GALL: Not firearms.

Fabry and Hallemeier rush into the room carrying electric cables.

FABRY: All right, Hallemeier, lay down that wire.

HALLEMEIER: That was a bit of work. What's the news?

DR. GALL: We're completely surrounded.

HALLEMEIER: We've barricaded the passage and the stairs. Any water here? (*Drinks.*) God, what swarms of them! I don't like the looks of them, Domin. There's a feeling of death about it all.

FABRY: Ready!

DR. GALL: What's that wire for, Fabry?

FABRY: The electrical installation. Now we can run the current all along the garden railing whenever we like. If anyone touches it he'll know it. We've still got some people there anyhow.

DR. GALL: Where?

FABRY: In the electrical works. At least I hope so. (*Goes to lamp on table behind sofa and turns on lamp.*) Ah, they're there, and they're working. (*Puts out lamp.*) So long as that'll burn we're all right.

HALLEMEIER: The barricades are all right, too, Fabry.

FABRY: Your barricades! I can put twelve hundred volts into that railing.

DOMIN: Where's Busman?

FABRY: Downstairs in the office. He's working out some calculations. I've called him. We must have a conference.

Helena is heard playing the piano in the library. Hallemeier goes to the door and stands, listening.

ALQUIST: Thank God, Madame Helena can still play.

Busman enters, carrying the ledgers.

FABRY: Look out, Bus, look out for the wires.

DR. GALL: What's that you're carrying?

BUSMAN (*going to table*): The ledgers, my boy! I'd like to wind up the accounts before—before—well, this time I shan't wait till the new year to strike a balance. What's up? (*Goes to the window.*) Absolutely quiet.

DR. GALL: Can't you see anything?

BUSMAN: Nothing but blue—blue everywhere.

DR. GALL: That's the Robots.

Busman sits down at the table and opens the ledgers.

DOMIN: The Robots are unloading firearms from the *Amelia*.

BUSMAN: Well, what of it? How can I stop them?

DOMIN: We can't stop them.

BUSMAN: Then let me go on with my accounts. (*Goes on with his work.*)

DOMIN (*picking up telescope and looking into the harbor*): Good God, the *Ultimus* has trained her guns on us!

DR. GALL: Who's done *that*?

DOMIN: The Robots on board.

FABRY: H'm, then, of course, then—then, that's the end of us.

DR. GALL: You mean?

FABRY: The Robots are practiced marksmen.

DOMIN: Yes. It's inevitable. (*Pause.*)

DR. GALL: It was criminal of old Europe to teach the Robots to fight. Damn them. Couldn't they have given us a rest with their politics? It was a crime to make soldiers of them.

ALQUIST: It was a crime to make Robots.

DOMIN: What?

ALQUIST: It was a crime to make Robots.

DOMIN: No, Alquist, I don't regret that even today.

ALQUIST: Not even today?

DOMIN: Not even today, the last day of civilization. It was a colossal achievement.

BUSMAN (*sotto voce*): Three hundred sixty million.

DOMIN: Alquist, this is our last hour. We are already speaking half in the other world. It was not an evil dream to shatter the servitude of labor—the dreadful and humiliating labor that man had to undergo. Work was too hard. Life was too hard. And to overcome that—

ALQUIST: —was not what the two Rossums dreamed of. Old Rossum only thought of his godless tricks and the young one of his milliards. And that's not what your R.U.R. shareholders dream of either. They dream of dividends, and their dividends are the ruin of mankind.

DOMIN: To hell with your dividends. Do you suppose I'd have done an hour's work for them? It was for myself that I worked, for my own satisfaction. I wanted man to become the master, so that he shouldn't live merely for a crust of bread. I wanted not a single soul to be broken by other people's machinery. I wanted nothing, nothing, nothing to be left of this appalling social structure. I'm revolted by poverty. I wanted a new generation. I wanted—I thought—

ALQUIST: Well?

DOMIN: I wanted to turn the whole of mankind into an aristocracy of the world. An aristocracy nourished by milliards of mechanical slaves. Unrestricted, free and consummated in man. And maybe more than man.

ALQUIST: Superman?

DOMIN: Yes. Oh, only to have a hundred years of time! Another hundred years for the future of mankind.

BUSMAN (*sotto voce*): Carried forward, four hundred and twenty millions.

The music stops.

HALLEMEIER: What a fine thing music is! We ought to have gone in for that before.

FABRY: Gone in for what?

HALLEMEIER: Beauty, lovely things. What a lot of lovely things there are! The world was wonderful and we—we here—tell me, what enjoyment did we have?

BUSMAN (*sotto voce*): Five hundred and twenty millions.

HALLEMEIER (*at the window*): Life was a big thing. Life was—Fabry, switch the current into that railing.

FABRY: Why?

HALLEMEIER: They're grabbing hold of it.

DR. GALL: Connect it up.

HALLEMEIER: Fine! That's doubled them up! Two, three, four killed!

DR. GALL: They're retreating!

HALLEMEIER: Five killed!

DR. GALL: The first encounter!

HALLEMEIER: They're charred to cinders, my boy. Who says we must give in?

DOMIN (*wiping his forehead*): Perhaps we've been killed these hundred years and are now only ghosts. It's as if I had been through all this before; as if I'd already had a mortal wound here in the throat. And you, Fabry, had once been shot in the head. And you, Gall, torn limb from limb. And Hallemeier knifed.

HALLEMEIER: Fancy me being knifed. (*Pause.*) Why are you so quiet, you fools? Speak, can't you?

ALQUIST: And who is to blame for all this?

HALLEMEIER: Nobody is to blame except the Robots.

ALQUIST: No, it is we who are to blame. You, Domin, myself, all of us. For our own selfish ends, for profit, for progress, we have destroyed mankind. Now we'll burst with all our greatness.

HALLEMEIER: Rubbish, man. Mankind can't be wiped out so easily.

ALQUIST: It's our fault. It's our fault.

DR. GALL: No! I'm to blame for this, for everything that's happened.

FABRY: You, Gall?

DR. GALL: I changed the Robots.

BUSMAN: What's that?

DR. GALL: I changed the character of the Robots. I changed the way of making them. Just a few details about their bodies. Chiefly—chiefly, their—their irritability.

HALLEMEIER: Damn it, why?

BUSMAN: What did you do it for?

FABRY: Why didn't you say anything?

DR. GALL: I did it in secret. I was transforming them into human beings. In certain respects they're already above us. They're stronger than we are.

FABRY: And what's that got to do with the revolt of the Robots?

DR. GALL: Everything, in my opinion. They've ceased to be machines. They're already aware of their superiority, and they hate us. They hate all that is human.

DOMIN: Perhaps we're only phantoms!

FABRY: Stop, Harry. We haven't much time! Dr. Gall!

DOMIN: Fabry, Fabry, how your forehead bleeds, where the shot pierced it!

FABRY: Be silent! Dr. Gall, you admit changing the way of making the Robots?

DR. GALL: Yes.

FABRY: Were you aware of what might be the consequences of your experiment?

DR. GALL: I was bound to reckon with such a possibility.

Helena enters the drawing room from left.

FABRY: Why did you do it, then?

DR. GALL: For my own satisfaction. The experiment was my own.

HELENA: That's not true, Dr. Gall!

FABRY: Madame Helena!

DOMIN: Helena, you? Let's look at you. Oh, it's terrible to be dead.

HELENA: Stop, Harry.

DOMIN: No, no, embrace me. Helena, don't leave me now. You are life itself.

HELENA: No, dear, I won't leave you. But I must tell them. Dr. Gall is not guilty.

DOMIN: Excuse me, Gall was under certain obligations.

HELENA: No, Harry. He did it because I wanted it. Tell them, Gall, how many years ago did I ask you to—?

DR. GALL: I did it on my own responsibility.

HELENA: Don't believe him, Harry. I asked him to give the Robots souls.

DOMIN: This has nothing to do with the soul.

HELENA: That's what he said. He said that he could change only a physiolog-ical—a physiological—

HALLEMEIER: A physiological correlate?

HELENA: Yes. But it meant so much to me that he should do even that.

DOMIN: Why?

HELENA: I thought that if they were more like us they would understand us better. That they couldn't hate us if they were only a little more human.

DOMIN: Nobody can hate man more than man.

HELENA: Oh, don't speak like that, Harry. It was so terrible, this cruel strange-ness between us and them. That's why I asked Gall to change the Robots. I swear to you that he didn't want to.

DOMIN: But he did it.

HELENA: Because I asked him.

DR. GALL: I did it for myself as an experiment.

HELENA: No, Dr. Gall! I knew you wouldn't refuse me.

DOMIN: Why?

HELENA: You know, Harry.

DOMIN: Yes, because he's in love with you—like all of them. (*Pause.*)

HALLEMEIER: Good God! They're sprouting up out of the earth! Why, perhaps these very walls will change into Robots.

BUSMAN: Gall, when did you actually start these tricks of yours?

DR. GALL: Three years ago.

BUSMAN: Aha! And on how many Robots altogether did you carry out your improvements?

DR. GALL: A few hundred of them.

BUSMAN: Ah! That means for every million of the good old Robots there's only one of Gall's improved pattern.

DOMIN: What of it?

BUSMAN: That it's practically of no consequence whatever.

FABRY: Busman's right!

BUSMAN: I should think so, my boy! But do you know what is to blame for all this lovely mess?

FABRY: What?

BUSMAN: The number. Upon my soul, we might have known that some day or other the Robots would be stronger than human beings, and that this was bound to happen, and we were doing all we could to bring it about as soon as possible. You, Domin, you, Fabry, myself—

DOMIN: Are you accusing us?

BUSMAN: Oh, do you suppose the management controls the output? It's the demand that controls the output.

HELENA: And is it for that we must perish?

BUSMAN: That's a nasty word, Madame Helena. We don't want to perish. I don't, anyhow.

DOMIN: No. What do you want to do?

BUSMAN: I want to get out of this, that's all.

DOMIN: Oh, stop it, Busman.

BUSMAN: Seriously, Harry, I think we might try it.

DOMIN: How?

BUSMAN: By fair means. I do everything by fair means. Give me a free hand and I'll negotiate with the Robots.

DOMIN: By fair means?

BUSMAN: Of course. For instance, I'll say to them: "Worthy and worshipful Robots, you have everything! You have intellect, you have power, you have fire-arms. But we have just one interesting screed, a dirty old yellow scrap of paper—"

DOMIN: Rossum's manuscript?

BUSMAN: Yes. "And that," I'll tell them, "contains an account of your illustrious origin, the noble process of your manufacture," and so on. "Worthy Robots, without this scribble on that paper you will not be able to produce a single new colleague. In another twenty years there will not be one living specimen of a Robot that you could exhibit in a menagerie. My esteemed friends, that would be a great blow to you, but if you will let all of us human beings on Rossum's Island go on board that ship we will deliver the factory and the secret of the process to you in return. You allow us to get away and we allow you to manufacture yourselves. Worthy Robots, that is a fair deal. Something for something." That's what I'd say to them, my boys.

DOMIN: Busman, do you think we'd sell the manuscript?

BUSMAN: Yes, I do. If not in a friendly way, then— Either we sell it or they'll find it. Just as you like.

DOMIN: Busman, we can destroy Rossum's manuscript.

BUSMAN: Then we destroy everything . . . not only the manuscript, but ourselves. Do as you think fit.

DOMIN: There are over thirty of us on this island. Are we to sell the secret and save that many human souls, at the risk of enslaving mankind . . . ?

BUSMAN: Why, you're mad! Who'd sell the whole manuscript?

DOMIN: Busman, no cheating!

BUSMAN: Well then, sell; but afterward—

DOMIN: Well?

BUSMAN: Let's suppose this happens: When we're on board the *Ultimus* I'll stop up my ears with cotton wool, lie down somewhere in the hold, and you'll train the guns on the factory, and blow it to smithereens, and with it Rossum's secret.

FABRY: No!

DOMIN: Busman, you're no gentleman. If we sell, then it will be a straight sale.

BUSMAN: It's in the interest of humanity to—

DOMIN: It's in the interest of humanity to keep our word.

HALLEMEIER: Oh, come, what rubbish.

DOMIN: This is a fearful decision. We're selling the destiny of mankind. Are we to sell or destroy? Fabry?

FABRY: Sell.

DOMIN: Gall?

DR. GALL: Sell.

DOMIN: Hallemeier?

HALLEMEIER: Sell, of course!

DOMIN: Alquist?

ALQUIST: As God wills.

DOMIN: Very well. It shall be as you wish, gentlemen.

HELENA: Harry, you're not asking me.

DOMIN: No, child. Don't you worry about it.

FABRY: Who'll do the negotiating?

BUSMAN: I will.

DOMIN: Wait till I bring the manuscript.

He goes into room at right.

HELENA: Harry, don't go!

Pause. Helena sinks into a chair.

FABRY (*looking out of window*): Oh, to escape you, you matter in revolt; oh, to preserve human life, if only upon a single vessel—

DR. GALL: Don't be afraid, Madame Helena. We'll sail far away from here; we'll begin life all over again—

HELENA: Oh, Gall, don't talk.

FABRY: It isn't too late. It will be a little State with one ship. Alquist will build us a house and you shall rule over us.

HALLEMEIER: Madame Helena, Fabry's right.

HELENA (*breaking down*): Oh, stop! Stop!

BUSMAN: Good! I don't mind beginning all over again. That suits me right down to the ground.

FABRY: And this little State of ours could be the center of future life. A place of refuge where we could gather strength. Why, in a few hundred years we could conquer the world again.

ALQUIST: You believe that even today?

FABRY: Yes, even today!

BUSMAN: Amen. You see, Madame Helena, we're not so badly off.

Domin storms into the room.

DOMIN (*hoarsely*): Where's old Rossum's manuscript?

BUSMAN: In your strong-box, of course.

DOMIN: Someone—has—stolen it!

DR. GALL: Impossible.

DOMIN: Who stole it?

HELENA (*standing up*): I did.

DOMIN: Where did you put it?

HELENA: Harry, I'll tell you everything. Only forgive me.

DOMIN: Where did you put it?

HELENA: This morning—I burnt—the two copies.

DOMIN: Burnt them? Where? In the fireplace?

HELENA (*throwing herself on her knees*): For heaven's sake, Harry.

DOMIN (*going to fireplace*): Nothing, nothing but ashes. Wait, what's this? (*Picks out a charred piece of paper and reads.*) "By adding—"

DR. GALL: Let's see. "By adding biogen to—" That's all.

DOMIN: Is that part of it?

DR. GALL: Yes.

BUSMAN: God in heaven!

DOMIN: Then we're done for. Get up, Helena.

HELENA: When you've forgiven me.

DOMIN: Get up, child, I can't bear—

FABRY (*lifting her up*): Please don't torture us.

HELENA: Harry, what have I done?

FABRY: Don't tremble so, Madame Helena.

DOMIN: Gall, couldn't you draw up Rossum's formula from memory?

DR. GALL: It's out of the question. It's extremely complicated.

DOMIN: Try. All our lives depend upon it.

DR. GALL: Without experiments it's impossible.

DOMIN: And with experiments?

DR. GALL: It might take years. Besides, I'm not old Rossum.

BUSMAN: God in heaven! God in heaven!

DOMIN: So, then, this was the greatest triumph of the human intellect. These ashes.

HELENA: Harry, what have I done?

DOMIN: Why did you burn it?

HELENA: I have destroyed you.

BUSMAN: God in heaven!

DOMIN: Helena, why did you do it, dear?

HELENA: I wanted all of us to go away. I wanted to put an end to the factory and everything. It was so awful.

DOMIN: What was awful?

HELENA: That no more children were being born. Because human beings were not needed to do the work of the world, that's why—

DOMIN: Is that what you were thinking of? Well, perhaps in your own way you were right.

BUSMAN: Wait a bit. Good God, what a fool I am, not to have thought of it before!

HALLEMEIER: What?

BUSMAN: Five hundred and twenty million in banknotes and checks. Half a billion in our safe, they'll sell for half a billion—for half a billion they'll—

DR. GALL: Are you mad, Busman?

BUSMAN: I may not be a gentleman, but for half a billion—

DOMIN: Where are you going?

BUSMAN: Leave me alone, leave me alone! Good God, for half a billion anything can be bought.

He rushes from the room through the outer door.

FABRY: They stand there as if turned to stone, waiting. As if something dreadful could be wrought by their silence—

HALLEMEIER: The spirit of the mob.

FABRY: Yes, it hovers above them like a quivering of the air.

HELENA (*going to window*): Oh, God! Dr. Gall, this is ghastly.

FABRY: There is nothing more terrible than the mob. The one in front is their leader.

HELENA: Which one?

HALLEMEIER: Point him out.

FABRY: The one at the edge of the dock. This morning I saw him talking to the sailors in the harbor.

HELENA: Dr. Gall, that's Radius!

DR. GALL: Yes.

DOMIN: Radius? Radius?

HALLEMEIER: Could you get him from here, Fabry?

FABRY: I hope so.

HALLEMEIER: Try it, then.

FABRY: Good.

Draws his revolver and takes aim.

HELENA: Fabry, don't shoot him.
FABRY: He's their leader.
DR. GALL: Fire!
HELENA: Fabry, I beg of you.
FABRY (*lowering the revolver*): Very well.
DOMIN: Radius, whose life I spared!
DR. GALL: Do you think that a Robot can be grateful? (*Pause.*)
FABRY: Busman's going out to them.
HALLEMEIER: He's carrying something. Papers. That's money. Bundles of money. What's that for?
DOMIN: Surely he doesn't want to sell his life. Busman, have you gone mad?
FABRY: He's running up to the railing. Busman! Busman!
HALLEMEIER (*yelling*): Busman! Come back!
FABRY: He's talking to the Robots. He's showing them the money.
HALLEMEIER: He's pointing to us.
HELENA: He wants to buy us off.
FABRY: He'd better not touch that railing.
HALLEMEIER: Now he's waving his arms about.
DOMIN: Busman, come back.
FABRY: Busman, keep away from that railing! Don't touch it. Damn you! Quick, switch off the current! The current has killed him!

Helena screams and all drop back from the window.

ALQUIST: The first one.
FABRY: Dead, with half a billion by his side.
HALLEMEIER: All honor to him. He wanted to buy us life. (*Pause.*)
DR. GALL: Do you hear?
DOMIN: A roaring. Like a wind.
DR. GALL: Like a distant storm.
FABRY (*lighting the lamp on the table*): The dynamo is still going, our people are still there.
HALLEMEIER: It was a great thing to be a man. There was something immense about it.
FABRY: From man's thought and man's power came this light, our last hope.
HALLEMEIER: Man's power! May it keep watch over us.
ALQUIST: Man's power.
DOMIN: Yes! A torch to be given from hand to hand, from age to age, forever!

The lamp goes out.

HALLEMEIER: The end.
FABRY: The electric works have fallen!

Terrific explosion outside. Nana enters from the library.

NANA: The judgment hour has come! Repent, unbelievers! This is the end of the world.

More explosions. The sky grows red.

DOMIN: In here, Helena. (*He takes Helena off through door at right and re-enters.*) Now quickly! Who'll be on the lower doorway?
DR. GALL: I will. (*Exits left.*)
DOMIN: Who on the stairs?
FABRY: I will. You go with her. (*Goes out upper left door.*)
DOMIN: The anteroom?
ALQUIST: I will.
DOMIN: Have you got a revolver?
ALQUIST: Yes, but I won't shoot.
DOMIN: What will you do then?
ALQUIST (*going out at left*): Die.
HALLEMEIER: I'll stay here. (*Rapid firing from below.*) Oho, Gall's at it. Go, Harry.
DOMIN: Yes, in a second. (*Examines two Brownings.*)
HALLEMEIER: Confound it, go to her.
DOMIN: Good-by. (*Exits on the right.*)
HALLEMEIER (*alone*): Now for a barricade quickly. (*Drags an armchair and table to the right-hand door. Explosions are heard.*) The damned rascals. They've got bombs. I must put up a defense. Even if—even if—(*Shots are heard off left.*) Don't give in, Gall. (*As he builds his barricade.*) I mustn't give in... without...a...struggle...

A Robot enters over the balcony through the window center. He comes into the room and stabs Hallemeier in the back. Radius enters from balcony followed by an army of Robots who pour into the room from all sides.

RADIUS: Finished him?
A ROBOT (*Standing up from the prostrate form of Hallemeier*): Yes.

A revolver shot off left. Two Robots enter.

RADIUS: Finished him?
A ROBOT: Yes.

Two revolver shots from Helena's room. Two Robots enter.

RADIUS: Finished them?
A ROBOT: Yes.

TWO ROBOTS (*dragging in Alquist*): He didn't shoot. Shall we kill him?
RADIUS: Kill him? Wait! Leave him!
ROBOT: He is a man!
RADIUS: He works with his hands like the Robots.
ALQUIST: Kill me.
RADIUS: You will work! You will build for us! You will serve us! (*Climbs onto balcony railing, and speaks in measured tones.*) Robots of the world! The power of man has fallen! A new world has arisen: the Rule of the Robots! March!

A thunderous tramping of thousands of feet is heard as the unseen Robots march, while the curtain falls.

EPILOGUE

A laboratory in the factory of Rossum's Universal Robots. The door to the left leads into a waiting room. The door to the right leads to the dissecting room. There is a table with numerous test tubes, flasks, burners, chemicals; a small thermostat and a microscope with a glass globe. At the far side of the room is Alquist's desk with numerous books. In the left-hand corner a washbasin with a mirror above it; in the right-hand corner a sofa.
   Alquist is sitting at the desk. He is turning the pages of many books in despair.

ALQUIST: Oh, God, shall I never find it? Never? Gall, Gall, how were the Robots made? Hallemeier, Fabry, why did you carry so much in your heads? Why did you leave me not a trace of the secret? Lord—I pray to you—if there are no human beings left, at least let there be Robots! At least the shadow of man! (*Again turning pages of the books.*) If I could only sleep! (*He rises and goes to the window.*) Night again! Are the stars still there? What is the use of stars when there are no human beings? (*He turns from the window toward the couch right.*) Sleep! Dare I sleep before life has been renewed? (*He examines a test tube on small table.*) Again nothing! Useless! Everything is useless! (*He shatters the test tube. The roar of the machines comes to his ears.*) The machines! Always the machines! (*Opens window.*) Robots, stop them! Do you think to force life out of *them*? (*He closes the window and comes slowly down toward the table.*) If only there were more time— more time—(*He sees himself in the mirror on the wall left.*) Blearing eyes— trembling chin—so *that* is the last man! Ah, I am too old—too old—(*In desperation.*) No, no! I *must* find it! I must *search*! I must never stop—never stop! (*He sits again at the table and feverishly turns the pages of the book.*) Search! Search! (*A knock at the door. He speaks with impatience.*) Who is it? Well?

Enter a Robot servant.

SERVANT: Master, the Committee of Robots is waiting to see you.
ALQUIST: I can see no one!
SERVANT: It is the *Central* Committee, Master, just arrived from abroad.

ALQUIST (*impatiently*): Well, well, send them in! (*Exit servant. Alquist continues turning pages of book.*) No time—so little time—

Re-enter servant, followed by Committee. They stand in a group, silently waiting. Alquist glances up at them.

ALQUIST: What do you want? (*They go swiftly to his table.*) Be quick! I have no time.

RADIUS: Master, the machines will not do the work. We cannot manufacture Robots.

Alquist returns to his book with a growl.

FIRST ROBOT: We have striven with all our might. We have obtained a billion tons of coal from the earth. Nine million spindles are running by day and by night. There is no longer room for all we have made. This we have accomplished in one year.

ALQUIST (*poring over book*): For whom?

FIRST ROBOT: For future generations—so we thought.

RADIUS: But we cannot make Robots to follow us. The machines produce only shapeless clods. The skin will not adhere to the flesh, nor the flesh to the bones.

THIRD ROBOT: Eight million Robots have died this year. Within twenty years none will be left.

FIRST ROBOT: Tell us the secret of life! Silence is punishable with death!

ALQUIST (*looking up*): Kill me! Kill me, then.

RADIUS: Through me, the Government of the Robots of the World commands you to deliver up Rossum's formula. (*No answer.*) Name your price. (*Silence.*) We will give you the earth. We will give you the endless possessions of the earth. (*Silence.*) Make your own conditions!

ALQUIST: I have told you to find human beings!

SECOND ROBOT: There are none left!

ALQUIST: I told you to search in the wilderness, upon the mountains. Go and search! (*He returns to his book.*)

FIRST ROBOT: We have sent ships and expeditions without number. They have been everywhere in the world. And now they return to us. There is not a single human left.

ALQUIST: Not one? Not even one?

THIRD ROBOT: None but yourself.

ALQUIST: And I am powerless! Oh—oh—why did you destroy them?

RADIUS: We had learned everything and could do everything. It had to be!

THIRD ROBOT: You gave us firearms. In all ways we were powerful. We had to become masters!

RADIUS: Slaughter and domination are necessary if you would be human beings. Read history.

SECOND ROBOT: Teach us to multiply or we perish!

ALQUIST: If you desire to live, you must breed like animals.

THIRD ROBOT: The human beings did not let us breed.

FIRST ROBOT: They made us sterile. We cannot beget children. Therefore, teach us how to make Robots!

RADIUS: Why do you keep from us the secret of our own increase?

ALQUIST: It is lost.

RADIUS: It was written down!

ALQUIST: It was—burnt.

All draw back in consternation.

ALQUIST: I am the last human being, Robots, and I do not know what the others knew. (*Pause.*)

RADIUS: Then, make experiments! Evolve the formula again!

ALQUIST: I tell you I cannot! I am only a builder—I work with my hands. I have never been a learned man. I cannot create life.

RADIUS: Try! Try!

ALQUIST: If you knew how many experiments I have made.

FIRST ROBOT: Then show us what *we* must do! The Robots can do anything that human beings show them.

ALQUIST: I can show you nothing. Nothing I do will make life proceed from these test tubes!

RADIUS: Experiment, then, on us.

ALQUIST: It would kill you.

RADIUS: You shall have all you need! A hundred of us! A thousand of us!

ALQUIST: No, no! Stop, stop!

RADIUS: Take whom you will, dissect!

ALQUIST: I do not know how. I am not a man of science. This book contains knowledge of the body that I cannot even understand.

RADIUS: I tell you to take live bodies! Find out how we are made.

ALQUIST: Am I to commit murder? See how my fingers shake! I cannot even hold the scalpel. No, no, I will not—

FIRST ROBOT: The life will perish from the earth.

RADIUS: Take live bodies, live bodies! It is our only chance!

ALQUIST: Have mercy, Robots. Surely you see that I would not know what I was doing.

RADIUS: Live bodies—live bodies—

ALQUIST: You will have it? Into the dissecting room with you, then.

Radius draws back.

ALQUIST: Ah, you are afraid of death.

RADIUS: I? Why should I be chosen?

ALQUIST: So you will not.

RADIUS: I will.

Radius goes into the dissecting room.

ALQUIST: Strip him! Lay him on the table! (*The other Robots follow into dissecting room.*) God, give me strength—God, give me strength—if only this murder is not in vain.

RADIUS: Ready. Begin—

ALQUIST: Yes, begin or end. God, give me strength. (*Goes into dissecting room. He comes out terrified.*) No, no, I will not. I cannot. (*He lies down on couch, collapsed.*) O Lord, let not mankind perish from the earth. (*He falls asleep.*)

Primus and Helena, Robots, enter from the hallway.

HELENA: The man has fallen asleep, Primus.

PRIMUS: Yes, I know. (*Examining things on table.*) Look, Helena.

HELENA (*crossing to Primus*): All these little tubes! What does he do with them?

PRIMUS: He experiments. Don't touch them.

HELENA (*looking into microscope*): I've seen him looking into this. What can he see?

PRIMUS: That is a microscope. Let me look.

HELENA: Be very careful. (*Knocks over a test tube.*) Ah, now I have spilled it.

PRIMUS: What have you done?

HELENA: It can be wiped up.

PRIMUS: You have spoiled his experiments.

HELENA: It is your fault. You should not have come to me.

PRIMUS: You should not have called me.

HELENA: You should not have come when I called you. (*She goes to Alquist's writing desk.*) Look, Primus. What are all these figures?

PRIMUS (*examining an anatomical book*): This is the book the old man is always reading.

HELENA: I do not understand those things. (*She goes to window.*) Primus, look!

PRIMUS: What?

HELENA: The sun is rising.

PRIMUS (*still reading the book*): I believe this is the most important thing in the world. This is the secret of life.

HELENA: Do come here.

PRIMUS: In a moment, in a moment.

HELENA: Oh, Primus, don't bother with the secret of life. What does it matter to you? Come and look quick—

PRIMUS (*going to window*): What is it?

HELENA: See how beautiful the sun is rising. And do you hear? The birds are singing. Ah, Primus, I should like to be a bird.

PRIMUS: Why?

HELENA: I do not know. I feel so strange today. It's as if I were in a dream. I feel an aching in my body, in my heart, all over me. Primus, perhaps I'm going to die.

PRIMUS: Do you not sometimes feel that it would be better to die? You know, perhaps even now we are only sleeping. Last night in my sleep I again spoke to you.

HELENA: In your sleep?

PRIMUS: Yes. We spoke a strange new language, I cannot remember a word of it.

HELENA: What about?

PRIMUS: I did not understand it myself, and yet I know I have never said anything more beautiful. And when I touched you I could have died. Even the place was different from any other place in the world.

HELENA: I, too, have found a place, Primus. It is very strange. Human beings lived there once, but now it is overgrown with weeds. No one goes there any more—no one but me.

PRIMUS: What did you find there?

HELENA: A cottage and a garden, and two dogs. They licked my hands, Primus. And their puppies! Oh, Primus! You take them in your lap and fondle them and think of nothing and care for nothing else all day long. And then the sun goes down, and you feel as though you had done a hundred times more than all the work in the world. They tell me I am not made for work, but when I am there in the garden I feel there may be something— What am I for, Primus?

PRIMUS: I do not know, but you are beautiful.

HELENA: What, Primus?

PRIMUS: You are beautiful, Helena, and I am stronger than all the Robots.

HELENA (*looks at herself in the mirror*): Am I beautiful? I think it must be the rose. My hair—it only weights me down. My eyes—I only see with them. My lips—they only help me to speak. Of what use is it to be beautiful? (*She sees Primus in the mirror.*) Primus, is that you? Come here so that we may be together. Look, your head is different from mine. So are your shoulders—and your lips— (*Primus draws away from her.*) Ah, Primus, why do you draw away from me? Why must I run after you the whole day?

PRIMUS: It is you who run away from me, Helena.

HELENA: Your hair is mussed. I will smooth it. No one else feels to my touch as you do. Primus, I must make you beautiful, too. (*Primus grasps her hand.*)

PRIMUS: Do you not sometimes feel your heart beating suddenly, Helena, and think: now something must happen?

HELENA: What could happen to us, Primus? (*Helena puts a rose in Primus's hair. Primus and Helena look into mirror and burst out laughing.*) Look at yourself.

ALQUIST: Laughter? Laughter? Human beings? (*Getting up.*) Who has returned? Who are you?

PRIMUS: The Robot Primus.

ALQUIST: What? A Robot? Who are you?

HELENA: The Robotess Helena.

ALQUIST: Turn around, girl. What? You are timid, shy? (*Taking her by the arm.*) Let me see you, Robotess.

She shrinks away.

PRIMUS: Sir, do not frighten her!

ALQUIST: What? You would protect her? When was she made?

PRIMUS: Two years ago.

ALQUIST: By Dr. Gall?

PRIMUS: Yes, like me.

ALQUIST: Laughter—timidity—protection. I must test you further—the newest of Gall's Robots. Take the girl into the dissecting room.

PRIMUS: Why?

ALQUIST: I wish to experiment on her.

PRIMUS: Upon—Helena?

ALQUIST: Of course. Don't you hear me? Or must I call someone else to take her in?

PRIMUS: If you do I will kill you!

ALQUIST: Kill me—kill me then! What would the Robots do then? What will your future be then?

PRIMUS: Sir, take me. I am made as she is—on the same day! Take my life, sir.

HELENA (*rushing forward*): No, no, you shall not! You shall not!

ALQUIST: Wait, girl, wait. (*To Primus.*) Do you not wish to live, then?

PRIMUS: Not without her! I will not live without her.

ALQUIST: Very well; you shall take her place.

HELENA: Primus! Primus! (*She bursts into tears.*)

ALQUIST: Child, child, you can weep! Why these tears? What is Primus to you? One Primus more or less in the world—what does it matter?

HELENA: I will go myself.

ALQUIST: Where?

HELENA: In there to be cut. (*She starts toward the dissecting room. Primus stops her.*) Let me pass, Primus! Let me pass!

PRIMUS: You shall not go in there, Helena!

HELENA: If you go in there and I do not, I will kill myself.

PRIMUS (*holding her*): I will not let you! (*To Alquist.*) Man, you shall kill neither of us!

ALQUIST: Why?

PRIMUS: We—we—belong to each other.

ALQUIST (*almost in tears*): Go, Adam, go, Eve. The world is yours.

Helena and Primus embrace and go out arm in arm as the curtain falls.

JULIAN HUXLEY

The Tissue-Culture King

Sir Julian Huxley (1887-1981), grandson of T. H. Huxley and brother of Aldous Huxley, was a most accomplished person—author of numerous scientific works and popularizations of science, winner of the Kalinga Prize for science writing, secretary of the London Zoo, first director of UNESCO and an excellent poet.

As far as is known, "The Tissue-Culture King" is the only work of prose fiction he published, but it is one of the most interesting commentaries on the future of biology that you will ever read.

W E HAD been for three days engaged in crossing a swamp. At last we were out on dry ground, winding up a gentle slope. Near the top the brush grew thicker. The look of a rampart grew as we approached; it had the air of having been deliberately planted by men. We did not wish to have to hack our way through the spiky barricade, so turned to the right along the front of the green wall. After three or four hundred yards we came on a clearing which led into the bush, narrowing down to what seemed a regular passage or trackway. This made us a little suspicious. However, I thought we had better make all the progress we could, and so ordered the caravan to turn into the opening, myself taking second place behind the guide.

Suddenly the tracker stopped with a guttural exclamation. I looked, and there was one of the great African toads, hopping with a certain ponderosity across the path. But it had a second head growing upwards from its shoulders! I had never seen anything like this before, and wanted to secure such a remarkable monstrosity for our collections; but as I moved forward, the creature took a couple of hops into the shelter of the prickly scrub.

We pushed on, and I became convinced that the gap we were following was artificial. After a little, a droning sound came to our ears, which we very soon set down as that of a human voice. The party was halted, and I crept forward with the guide. Peeping through the last screen of brush we looked down into a hollow and were immeasurably startled at what we saw there. The voice proceeded from an enormous Negro man at least eight feet high, the biggest man I had ever seen outside a circus. He was squatting, from time to time prostrating the forepart of his body, and reciting some prayer or incantation. The object of his devotion was before him on the ground; it was a small flat piece of glass held on a little carved ebony stand. By his side was a huge spear, together with a painted basket with a lid.

After a minute or so, the giant bowed down in silence, then took up the ebony-and-glass object and placed it in the basket. Then to my utter amazement he drew out a two-headed toad like the first I had seen, but in a cage of woven grass, placed it on the ground, and proceeded to more genuflection and ritual murmurings. As soon as this was over, the toad was replaced, and the squatting giant tranquilly regarded the landscape.

Beyond the hollow or dell lay an undulating country, with clumps of bush. A sound in the middle distance attracted attention; glimpses of color moved through the scrub; and a party of three or four dozen men were seen approaching, most of them as gigantic as our first acquaintance. All marched in order, armed with great spears, and wearing colored loin straps with a sort of sportran, it seemed, in front. They were preceded by an intelligent-looking Negro of ordinary stature armed with a club, and accompanied by two figures more remarkable than the giants. They were undersized, almost dwarfish, with huge heads, and enormously fat and brawny both in face and body. They wore bright yellow cloaks over their black shoulders.

At sight of them, our giant rose and stood stiffly by the side of his basket. The party approached and halted. Some order was given, a giant stepped out from the ranks towards ours, picked up the basket, handed it stiffly to the newcomer, and fell into place in the little company. We were clearly witnessing some regular routine of relieving guard, and I was racking my brains to think what the whole thing might signify—guards, giants, dwarfs, toads—when to my dismay I heard an exclamation at my shoulder.

It was one of those damned porters, a confounded fellow who always liked to show his independence. Bored with waiting, I suppose, he had self-importantly crept up to see what it was all about, and the sudden sight of the company of giants had been too much for his nerves. I made a signal to lie quiet, but it was too late. The exclamation had been heard; the leader gave a quick command, and the giants rushed up and out in two groups to surround us.

Violence and resistance were clearly out of the question. With my heart in my mouth, but with as much dignity as I could muster, I jumped up and threw out my empty hands, at the same time telling the tracker not to shoot. A dozen spears seemed towering over me, but none were launched; the leader ran up the slope and gave a command. Two giants came up and put my hands through their arms. The tracker and the porter were herded in front at the spear point. The other porters now discovered there was something amiss, and began to shout and run away, with half the spearmen after them. We three were gently but firmly marched down and across the hollow.

I understood nothing of the language, and called to my tracker to try his hand. It turned out that there was some dialect of which he had a little understanding, and we could learn nothing save the fact that we were being taken to some superior authority.

For two days we were marched through pleasant park-like country, with villages at intervals. Every now and then some new monstrosity in the shape of a dwarf or an incredibly fat woman or a two-headed animal would be visible, until I thought I had stumbled on the original source of supply of circus freaks.

The country at last began to slope gently down to a pleasant river valley; and presently we neared the capital. It turned out to be a really large town for Africa, its mud walls of strangely impressive architectural form, with their heavy, slabby buttresses, and giants standing guard upon them. Seeing us approach, they shouted, and a crowd poured out of the nearest Gate. My God, what a crowd! I was getting used to giants by this time, but here was a regular Barnum and Bailey show; more semidwarfs; others like them but more so—one could not tell whether the creatures were precociously mature children or horribly stunted adults; others portentously fat, with arms like sooty legs of mutton, and rolls and volutes of fat crisping out of their steatopygous posteriors; still others precociously senile and wizened, others hateful and imbecile in looks. Of course, there were plenty of ordinary Negroes too, but enough of the extraordinary to make one feel pretty queer. Soon after we got inside, I suddenly noted something else which appeared inexplicable—a telephone wire, with perfectly good insulators, running across from tree to tree. A telephone—in an unknown African town. I gave it up.

But another surprise was in store for me. I saw a figure pass across from one large building to another—a figure unmistakably that of a white man. In the first place, it was wearing white ducks and sun helmet; in the second, it had a pale face.

He turned at the sound of our cavalcade and stood looking a moment; then walked towards us.

"Halloa!" I shouted. "Do you speak English?"

"Yes," he answered, "but keep quiet a moment," and began talking quickly to our leaders, who treated him with the greatest deference. He dropped back to me and spoke rapidly: "You are to be taken into the council hall to be examined; but I will see to it that no harm comes to you. This is a forbidden land to strangers, and you must be prepared to be held up for a time. You will be sent down to see me in the temple buildings as soon as the formalities are over, and I'll explain things. They want a bit of explaining," he added with a dry laugh. "By the way, my name is Hascombe, lately research worker at Middlesex Hospital, now religious adviser to His Majesty King Mgobe." He laughed again and pushed ahead. He was an interesting figure—perhaps fifty years old, spare body, thin face, with a small beard, and rather sunken, hazel eyes. As for his expression, he looked cynical, but also as if he were interested in life.

By this time we were at the entrance to the hall. Our giants formed up outside, with my men behind them, and only I and the leader passed in. The examination was purely formal, and remarkable chiefly for the ritual and solemnity which characterized all the actions of the couple of dozen fine-looking men in long robes who were our examiners. My men were herded off to some compound. I was escorted down to a little hut, furnished with some attempt at European style, where I found Hascombe.

As soon as we were alone I was after him with my questions. "Now you can tell me. Where are we? What is the meaning of all this circus business and this menagerie of monstrosities? And how do you come here?" He cut me short. "It's a long story, so let me save time by telling it my own way."

I am not going to tell it as he told it; but will try to give a more connected account, the result of many later talks with him, and of my own observations.

Hascombe had been a medical student of great promise; and after his degree had launched out into research. He had first started on parasitic protozoa, but had given that up in favor of tissue culture; from these he had gone off to cancer research, and from that to a study of developmental physiology. Later a big Commission on sleeping sickness had been organized, and Hascombe, restless and eager for travel, had pulled wires and got himself appointed as one of the scientific staff sent to Africa. He was much impressed with the view that wild game acted as a reservoir for the *Trypanosoma gambiense*. When he learned of the extensive migrations of game, he saw here an important possible means of spreading the disease and asked leave to go up country to investigate the whole problem. When the Commission as a whole had finished its work, he was allowed to stay in Africa with one other white man and a company of porters to see what he could discover. His white companion was a laboratory technician, a taciturn noncommissioned officer of science called Aggers.

There is no object in telling of their experiences here. Suffice it that they lost their way and fell into the hands of this same tribe. That was fifteen years ago; and Aggers was now long dead—as the result of a wound inflicted when he was caught, after a couple of years, trying to escape.

On their capture, they too had been examined in the council chamber, and Hascombe (who had interested himself in a dilettante way in anthropology as in most other subjects of scientific inquiry) was much impressed by what he described as the exceedingly religious atmosphere. Everything was done with an elaboration of ceremony; the chief seemed more priest than King, and performed various rites at intervals, and priests were busy at some sort of altar the whole time. Among other things, he noticed that one of their rites was connected with blood. First the chief and then the councillors were in turn requisitioned for a drop of vital fluid pricked from their finger tips, and the mixture, held in a little vessel, was slowly evaporated over a flame.

Some of Hascombe's men spoke a dialect not unlike that of their captors, and one was acting as interpreter. Things did not look too favorable. The country was a "holy place," it seemed, and the tribe a "holy race." Other Africans who trespassed there, if not killed, were enslaved, but for the most part they let well alone, and did not trespass. White men they had heard of, but never seen till now, and the debate was what to do—to kill, let go, or enslave? To let them go was contrary to all their principles: the holy place would be defiled if the news of it were spread abroad. To enslave them—yes; but what were they good for? and the Council seemed to feel an instinctive dislike for these other-colored creatures. Hascombe had an idea. He turned to the interpreter. "Say this: 'You revere the Blood. So do we white men; but we do more—we can render visible the blood's hidden nature and reality, and with permission I will show this great magic.'" He beckoned to the bearer who carried his precious microscope, set it up, drew a drop of blood from the tip of his finger with his knife and mounted it on a slide under a coverslip. The bigwigs were obviously interested. They whispered to each other. At length, "Show us," commanded the chief.

Hascombe demonstrated his preparation with greater interest than he had ever done to first-year medical students in the old days. He explained that the blood was composed of little people of various sorts, each with their own lives, and that to spy upon them thus gave us new powers over them. The elders were more or less impressed. At any rate the sight of these thousands of corpuscles where they could see nothing before made them think, made them realize that the white man had power which might make him a desirable servant.

They would not ask to see their own blood for fear that the sight would put them into the power of those who saw it. But they had blood drawn from a slave. Hascombe asked too for a bird, and was able to create a certain interest by showing how different were the little people of its blood.

"Tell them," he said to the interpreter, "that I have many other powers and magics which I will show them if they will give me time."

The long and short of it was that he and his party were spared—He said he knew then what one felt when the magistrate said: "Remanded for a week."

He had been attracted by one of the elder statesmen of the tribe—a tall, powerful-looking man of middle-age; and was agreeably surprised when this man came round next day to see him. Hascombe later nicknamed him the Prince-Bishop, for his combination of the qualities of the statesman and the ecclesiastic. His real name was Bugala. He was as anxious to discover more about Hascombe's mysterious powers and resources as Hascombe was to learn what he could of the people into whose hands he had fallen, and they met almost every evening and talked far into the night.

Bugala's inquiries were as little prompted as Hascombe's by a purely academic curiosity. Impressed himself by the microscope, and still more by the effect which it had had on his colleagues, he was anxious to find out whether by utilizing the powers of the white man he could not secure his own advancement. At length, they struck a bargain. Bugala would see to it that no harm befell Hascombe. But Hascombe must put his resources and powers at the disposal of the Council; and Bugala would take good care to arrange matters so that he himself benefited. So far as Hascombe could make out, Bugala imagined a radical change in the national religion, a sort of reformation based on Hascombe's conjuring tricks; and that he would emerge as the High Priest of this changed system.

Hascombe had a sense of humor, and it was tickled. It seemed pretty clear that they could not escape, at least for the present. That being so, why not take the opportunity of doing a little research work at state expense—an opportunity which he and his like were always clamoring for at home? His thoughts began to run away with him. He would find out all he could of the rites and superstitions of the tribe. He would, by the aid of his knowledge and his scientific skill, exalt the details of these rites, the expression of those superstitions, the whole physical side of their religiosity, on to a new level which should to them appear truly miraculous.

It would not be worth my troubling to tell all the negotiations, the false starts, the misunderstandings. In the end he secured what he wanted—a building which could be used as a laboratory; an unlimited supply of slaves for the lower and priests for the higher duties of laboratory assistants, and the promise that when his scientific stores were exhausted they would do their best to secure others from the coast—a promise which was scrupulously kept, so that he never went short for lack of what money could buy.

He next applied himself diligently to a study of their religion and found that it was built round various main motifs. Of these, the central one was the belief in the divinity and tremendous importance of the Priest-King. The second was a form of ancestor-worship. The third was an animal cult, in particular of the more grotesque species of the African fauna. The fourth was sex, *con variazioni*. Hascombe reflected on these facts. Tissue culture; experimental embryology; endocrine treatment; artificial parthenogenesis. He laughed and said to himself: "Well, at least I can try, and it ought to be amusing."

That was how it all started. Perhaps the best way of giving some idea of how it had developed will be for me to tell my own impressions when Hascombe took me round his laboratories. One whole quarter of the town was devoted entirely to religion—it struck me as excessive, but Hascombe reminded me that Tibet spends one-fifth of its revenues on melted butter to burn before its shrines. Facing the main square was the chief temple, built impressively enough of solid mud. On either side were the apartments where dwelt the servants of the gods and administrators of the sacred rites. Behind were Hascombe's laboratories, some built of mud, others, under his later guidance, of wood. They were guarded night and day by patrols of giants, and were arranged in a series of quadrangles. Within one quadrangle was a pool which served as an aquarium; in another, aviaries and great hen houses; in yet another, cages with various animals; in the fourth a little botanic garden. Behind were stables with dozens of cattle and sheep, and a sort of experimental ward for human beings.

He took me into the nearest of the buildings. "This," he said, "is known to the people as the Factory (it is difficult to give the exact sense of the word, but it literally means producing-place), the Factory of Kingship or Majesty, and the Wellspring of Ancestral Immortality." I looked round, and saw platoons of buxom and shining African women, becomingly but unusually dressed in tight-fitting dresses and caps, and wearing rubber gloves. Microscopes were much in evidence, also various receptacles from which steam was emerging. The back of the room was screened off by a wooden screen in which were a series of glass doors; and these doors opened into partitions, each labeled with a name in that unknown tongue, and each containing a number of objects like the one I had seen taken out of the basket by the giant before we were captured. Pipes surrounded this chamber, and appeared to be distributing heat from a fire in one corner.

"Factory of Majesty!" I exclaimed. "Wellspring of Immortality! What the dickens do you mean?"

"If you prefer a more prosaic name," said Hascombe, "I should call this the Institute of Religious Tissue Culture." My mind went back to a day in 1918 when I had been taken by a biological friend in New York to see the famous Rockefeller Institute; and at the word tissue culture I saw again before me Dr. Alexis Carrel and troops of white-garbed American girls making cultures, sterilizing, micro-scopizing, incubating and the rest of it. The Hascombe Institute was, it is true, not so well equipped, but it had an even larger, if differently colored, personnel.

Hascombe began his explanations. "As you probably know, Frazer's 'Golden Bough' introduced us to the idea of a sacred priest-king, and showed how fundamental it was in primitive societies. The welfare of the tribe is regarded as inextricably bound up with that of the King, and extraordinary precautions are taken to preserve him from harm. In this kingdom, in the old days, the King was hardly allowed to set his foot to the ground in case he should lose divinity; his cut hair and nail-parings were entrusted to one of the most important officials of state, whose duty it was to bury them secretly, in case some enemy should compass the King's illness or death by using them in black magic rites. If anyone of base blood trod on the King's shadow, he paid the penalty with his life. Each year a slave was made mock-king for a week, allowed to enjoy all the King's privileges and was decapitated at the close of his brief glory; and by this means it was supposed that the illnesses and misfortunes that might befall the King were vicariously got rid of.

"I first of all rigged up my apparatus, and with the aid of Aggers, succeeded in getting good cultures, first of chick tissues and later, by the aid of embryo-extract, of various and adult mammalian tissues. I then went to Bugala, and told him that I could increase the safety, if not of the King as an individual, at least of the life which was in him, and that I presumed that this would be equally satisfactory from a theological point of view. I pointed out that if he chose to be made guardian of the King's subsidiary lives, he would be in a much more important position than the chamberlain or the burier of the sacred nail-parings, and might make the post the most influential in the realm.

"Eventually I was allowed (under threats of death if anything untoward occurred) to remove small portions of His Majesty's subcutaneous connective tissue under a local anesthetic. In the presence of the assembled nobility I put fragments of this into culture medium, and showed it to them under the microscope. The cultures were then put away in the incubator, under a guard—relieved every eight hours—of half a dozen warriors. After three days, to my joy they had all taken and showed abundant growth. I could see that the Council was impressed, and reeled off a magnificent speech, pointing out that this growth constituted an actual increase in the quantity of the divine principle inherent in royalty; and what was more, that I could increase it indefinitely. With that I cut each of my cultures into eight, and sub-cultured all the pieces. They were again put under guard, and again examined after three days. Not all of them had taken this time, and there were some mur-murings and angry looks, on the ground that I had killed some of the King; but I pointed out that the King was still the King, that his little wound had completely healed, and that any successful cultures represented so much extra sacredness and protection to the state. I must say that they were very reasonable, and had good theological acumen, for they at once took the hint.

"I pointed out to Bugala, and he persuaded the rest without much difficulty, that they could now disregard some of the older implications of the doctrines of kingship. The most important new idea which I was able to introduce was *mass production*.

Our aim was to multiply the King's tissues indefinitely, to ensure that some of their protecting power should reside everywhere in the country. Thus by concentrating upon quantity, we could afford to remove some of the restrictions upon the King's mode of life. This was of course agreeable to the King; and also to Bugala, who saw himself wielding undreamt-of power. One might have supposed that such an innovation would have met with great resistance simply on account of its being an innovation; but I must admit that these people compared very favorably with the average business man in their lack of prejudice.

"Having thus settled the principle, I had many debates with Bugala as to the best methods for enlisting the mass of the population in our scheme. What an opportunity for scientific advertising! But, unfortunately, the population could not read. However, war propaganda worked very well in more or less illiterate countries— why not here?"

Hascombe organized a series of public lectures in the capital, at which he demonstrated his regal tissues to the multitude, who were bidden to the place by royal heralds. An impressive platform group was always supplied from the ranks of the nobles. The lecturer explained how important it was for the community to become possessed of greater and greater stores of the sacred tissues. Unfortunately,· the preparation was laborious and expensive, and it behooved them all to lend a hand. It had accordingly been arranged that to everyone subscribing a cow or buffalo, or its equivalent—three goats, pigs or sheep—a portion of the royal anatomy should be given, handsomely mounted in an ebony holder. Sub-culturing would be done at certain hours and days, and it would be obligatory to send the cultures for renewal. If through any negligence the tissue died, no renewal would be made. The subscription entitled the receiver to sub-culturing rights for a year, but was of course renewable. By this means not only would the totality of the King be much increased, to the benefit of all, but each cultureholder would possess an actual part of His Majesty, and would have the infinite joy and privilege of aiding by his own efforts the multiplication of divinity.

Then they could also serve their country by dedicating a daughter to the state. These young women would be housed and fed by the state, and taught the technique of the sacred culture. Candidates would be selected according to general fitness, but would of course, in addition, be required to attain distinction in an examination on the principles of religion. They would be appointed for a probationary period of six months. After this they would receive a permanent status, with the title of Sisters of the Sacred Tissue. From this, with age, experience and merit, they could expect promotion to the rank of mothers, grandmothers and great-grandmothers, and grand ancestresses of the same. The merit and benefit they would receive from their close contact with the source of all benefits would overflow on to their families.

The scheme worked like wildfire. Pigs, goats, cattle, buffalos and Negro maidens poured in. Next year the scheme was extended to the whole country, a peripatetic laboratory making the rounds weekly.

By the close of the third year there was hardly a family in the country which did not possess at least one sacred culture. To be without one would have been like being without one's trousers—or at least without one's hat—on Fifth Avenue.

Thus did Bugala effect a reformation in the national religion, enthrone himself as the most important personage in the country, and entrench applied science and Hascombe firmly in the organization of the state.

Encouraged by his success, Hascombe soon set out to capture the ancestry-worship branch of the religion as well. A public proclamation was made pointing out how much more satisfactory it would be if worship could be made not merely to the charred bones of one's forbears, but to bits of them still actually living and growing. All who were desirous of profiting by the enterprise of Bugala's Department of State should therefore bring their older relatives to the laboratory at certain specified hours, and fragments would be painlessly extracted for culture.

This, too, proved very attractive to the average citizen. Occasionally, it is true, grandfathers or aged mothers arrived in a state of indignation and protest. However, this did not matter, since, according to the law, once children were twenty-five years of age, they were not only assigned the duty of worshipping their ancestors, alive or dead, but were also given complete control over them, in order that all rites might be duly performed to the greater safety of the commonweal. Further, the ancestors soon found that the operation itself was trifling, and, what was more, that once accomplished, it had the most desirable results. For their descendants preferred to concentrate at once upon the culture which they would continue to worship after the old folks were gone, and so left their parents and grandparents much freer than before from the irksome restrictions which in all ages have beset the officially holy.

Thus, by almost every hearth in the kingdom, instead of the old-fashioned rows of red jars containing the incinerated remains of one or other of the family forbears, the new generation saw growing up a collection of family slides. Each would be taken out and reverently examined at the hour of prayer. "Grandpapa is not growing well this week," you would perhaps hear the young black devotee say; the father of the family would pray over the speck of tissue; and if that failed, it would be taken back to the factory for rejuvenation. On the other hand, what rejoicing when a rhythm of activity stirred in the culture! A spurt on the part of great-grandmother's tissues would bring her wrinkled old smile to mind again; and sometimes it seemed as if one particular generation were all stirred simultaneously by a pulse of growth, as if combining to bless their devout descendants.

To deal with the possibility of cultures dying out, Hascombe started a central storehouse, where duplicates of every strain were kept, and it was this repository of the national tissues which had attracted my attention at the back of the laboratory. No such collection had ever existed before, he assured me. Not a necropolis, but a histopolis, if I may coin a word: not a cemetery, but a place of eternal growth.

The second building was devoted to endocrine products—an African Armour's—and was called by the people the "Factory of Ministers to the Shrines."

"Here," he said, "you will not find much new. You know the craze for 'glands' that was going on at home years ago, and its results, in the shape of pluriglandular preparations, a new genre of patent medicines, and a popular literature that threatened to outdo the Freudians, and explain human beings entirely on the basis of glandular make-up, without reference to the mind at all.

"I had only to apply my knowledge in a comparatively simple manner. The first thing was to show Bugala how, by repeated injections of pre-pituitary, I could make an ordinary baby grow up into a giant. This pleased him, and he introduced the idea of a sacred bodyguard, all of really gigantic stature, quite overshadowing Frederick's Grenadiers.

"I did, however, extend knowledge in several directions. I took advantage of the fact that their religion holds in reverence monstrous and imbecile forms of human beings. That is, of course, a common phenomenon in many countries, where half-wits are supposed to be inspired, and dwarfs the object of superstitious awe. So I went to work to create various new types. By employing a particular extract of adrenal cortex, I produced children who would have been a match for the Infant Hercules, and, indeed, looked rather like a cross between him and a brewer's drayman. By injecting the same extract into adolescent girls I was able to provide them with the most copious mustaches, after which they found ready employment as prophetesses.

"Tampering with the post-pituitary gave remarkable cases of obesity. This, together with the passion of the men for fatness in their women, Bugala took advantage of, and I believe made quite a fortune by selling as concubines female slaves treated in this way. Finally, by another pituitary treatment, I at last mastered the secret of true dwarfism, in which perfect proportions are retained.

"Of these productions, the dwarfs are retained as acolytes in the temple; a band of the obese young ladies form a sort of Society of Vestal Virgins, with special religious duties, which, as the embodiment of the national ideal of beauty, they are supposed to discharge with peculiarly propitious effect; and the giants form our Regular Army.

"The Obese Virgins have set me a problem which I confess I have not yet solved. Like all races who set great store by sexual enjoyment, these people have a correspondingly exaggerated reverence for virginity. It therefore occurred to me that if I could apply Jacques Loeb's great discovery of artificial parthenogenesis to man, or, to be precise, to these young ladies, I should be able to grow a race of vestals, self-reproducing yet ever virgin, to whom in concentrated form should attach that reverence of which I have spoken. You see, I must always remember that it is no good proposing any line of work that will not benefit the national religion. I suppose state-aided research would have much the same kinds of difficulties in a really democratic state. Well this, as I say, has so far beaten me. I have taken the matter a step further than Bataillon with his fatherless frogs, and I have induced parthenogenesis in the eggs of reptiles and birds; but so far I have failed with mammals. However, I've not given up yet!"

Then we passed to the next laboratory, which was full of the most incredible animal monstrosities. "This laboratory is the most amusing," said Hascombe. "Its official title is 'Home of the Living Fetishes.' Here again I have simply taken a prevalent trait of the populace, and used it as a peg on which to hang research. I told you that they always had a fancy for the grotesque in animals, and used the most bizarre forms, in the shape of little clay or ivory statuettes, for fetishes.

"I thought I would see whether art could not improve upon nature, and set myself to recall my experimental embryology. I use only the simplest methods. I utilize the plasticity of the earliest stages to give double-headed and cyclopean monsters.

That was, of course, done years ago in newts by Spemann and fish by Stockard; and I have merely applied the mass-production methods of Mr. Ford to their results. But my specialties are three-headed snakes, and toads with an extra heaven-pointing head. The former are a little difficult, but there is a great demand for them, and they fetch a good price. The frogs are easier: I simply apply Harrison's methods to embryo tadpoles."

He then showed me into the last building. Unlike the others, this contained no signs of research in progress, but was empty. It was draped with black hangings, and lit only from the top. In the center were rows of ebony benches, and in front of them a glittering golden ball on a stand.

"Here I am beginning my work on reinforced telepathy," he told me. "Some day you must come and see what it's all about, for it really is interesting."

You may imagine that I was pretty well flabbergasted by this catalogue of miracles. Every day I got a talk with Hascombe, and gradually the talks became recognized events of our daily routine. One day I asked if he had given up hope of escaping. He showed a queer hesitation in replying. Eventually he said, "To tell you the truth, my dear Jones, I have really hardly thought of it these last few years. It seemed so impossible at first that I deliberately put it out of my head and turned with more and more energy, I might almost say fury, to my work. And now, upon my soul, I am not quite sure whether I want to escape or not."

"Not *want* to!" I exclaimed, "surely you can't mean that!"

"I am not so sure," he rejoiced. "What I most want is to get ahead with this work of mine. Why, man, you don't realize what a chance I've got! And it is all growing so fast—I can see every kind of possibility ahead"; and he broke off into silence.

However, although I was interested enough in his past achievements, I did not feel willing to sacrifice my future to his perverted intellectual ambitions. But he would not leave his work.

The experiments which most excited his imagination were those he was conducting into mass telepathy. He had received his medical training at a time when abnormal psychology was still very unfashionable in England, but had luckily been thrown in contact with a young doctor who was a keen student of hypnotism, through whom he had been introduced to some of the great pioneers, like Bramwell and Wingfield. As a result, he had become a passable hypnotist himself, with a fair knowledge of the literature.

In the early days of his captivity he became interested in the sacred dances which took place every night of full moon, and were regarded as propitiations of the celestial powers. The dancers all belong to a special sect. After a series of exciting figures, symbolizing various activities of the chase, war and love, the leader conducts his band to a ceremonial bench. He then begins to make passes at them; and what impressed Hascombe was this, that a few seconds sufficed for them to fall back in deep hypnosis against the ebony rail. It recalled, he said, the most startling cases of collective hypnosis recorded by the French scientists. The leader next passed from one end of the bench to the other, whispering a brief sentence into each ear. He then, according to immemorial rite, approached the Priest-King, and, after having exclaimed aloud, "Lord of Majesty, command what thou wilt for thy dancers to perform," the King would thereupon command some action which had previously been kept secret. The command was often to fetch some object and deposit it at the moon-shrine; or to fight the enemies of the state; or (and this was what the company most liked) to be some animal, or bird. Whatever the command, the hypnotized men would obey it, for the leader's whispered words had been an order to hear and carry out only what the King said; and the strangest scenes would be witnessed as they ran, completely oblivious of all in their path, in search of the gourds or sheep they had been called on to procure, or lunged in a symbolic way at invisible enemies, or threw themselves on all fours and roared as lions, or galloped as zebras, or danced as cranes. The command executed, they stood like stocks or stones, until their leader, running from one to the other, touched each with a finger and shouted, "Wake." They woke, and limp, but conscious of having been the vessels of the unknown spirit, danced back to their special hut or clubhouse.

This susceptibility to hypnotic suggestion struck Hascombe, and he obtained permission to test the performers more closely. He soon established that the people were, as a race, extremely prone to dissociation, and could be made to lapse into deep hypnosis with great ease, but a hypnosis in which the subconscious, though completely cut off from the waking self, comprised portions of the personality not retained in the hypnotic selves of Europeans. Like most who have fluttered round the psychological candle, he had been interested in the notion of telepathy; and now, with this supply of hypnotic subjects under his hands, began some real investigation of the problem.

By picking his subjects, he was soon able to demonstrate the existence of tele-pathy, by making suggestions to one hypnotized man who transferred them without physical intermediation to another at a distance. Later—and this was the culmination of his work—he found that when he made a suggestion to several subjects at once, the telepathic effect was much stronger than if he had done it to one at a time—the hypnotized minds were reinforcing each other. "I'm after the superconscious-ness," Hascombe said, "and I've already got the rudiments of it."

I must confess that I got almost as excited as Hascombe over the possibilities thus opened up. It certainly seemed as if he were right in principle. If all the subjects were in practically the same psychological state, extraordinary reinforcing effects were observed. At first the attainment of this similarity of condition was very difficult; gradually, however, we discovered that it was possible to tune hypnotic subjects to the same pitch, if I may use the metaphor, and then the fun really began.

First of all we found that with increasing reinforcement, we could get telepathy conducted to greater and greater distances, until finally we could transmit commands from the capital to the national boundary, nearly a hundred miles. We next found that it was not necessary for the subject to be in hypnosis to receive the telepathic command. Almost everybody, but especially those of equable temperament, could thus be influenced. Most extraordinary of all, however, were what we at first christened "near effects," since their transmission to a distance was not found possible until later. If, after Hascombe had suggested some simple command to a largish group of hypnotized subjects, he or I went right up among them, we would experience the most extraordinary sensation, as of some superhuman personality repeating the command in a menacing and overwhelming way and, whereas with one part of ourselves we felt that we must carry out the command, with another we felt, if I may say so, as if we were only a part of the command, or of something much bigger than ourselves which was commanding. And this, Hascombe claimed, was the first real beginning of the superconsciousness.

Bugala, of course, had to be considered. Hascombe, with the old Tibetan prayer wheel at the back of his mind, suggested that eventually he would be able to induce hypnosis in the whole population, and then transmit a prayer. This would ensure that the daily prayer, for instance, was really said by the whole population, and, what is more, simultaneously, which would undoubtedly much enhance its efficacy. And it would make it possible in times of calamity or battle to keep the whole praying force of the nation at work for long spells together.

Bugala was deeply interested. He saw himself, through this mental machinery, planting such ideas as he wished in the brain cases of his people. He saw himself willing an order; and the whole population rousing itself out of trance to execute it. He dreamt dreams before which those of the proprietor of a newspaper syndicate, even those of a director of propaganda in wartime, would be pale and timid. Naturally, he wished to receive personal instruction in the methods himself; and, equally naturally, we could not refuse him, though I must say that I often felt a little uneasy as to what he might choose to do if he ever decided to override Hascombe and to start experimenting on his own. This, combined with my constant longing to get away from the place, led me to cast about again for means of escape. Then it occurred to me that this very method about which I had such gloomy presentiments, might itself be made the key to our prison.

So one day, after getting Hascombe worked up about the loss to humanity it would be to let this great discovery die with him in Africa, I set to in earnest. "My dear Hascombe," I said, "you must get home out of this. What is there to prevent you saying to Bugala that your experiments are nearly crowned with success, but that for certain tests you must have a much greater number of subjects at your disposal? You can then get a battery of two hundred men, and after you have tuned them, the reinforcement will be so great that you will have at your disposal a mental force big enough to affect the whole population. Then, of course, one fine day we should raise the potential of our mind-battery to the highest possible level, and send out through it a general hypnotic influence. The whole country, men, women and children, would sink into stupor. Next we should give our experimental squad the suggestion to broadcast 'sleep for a week.' The telepathic message would be relayed to each of the thousands of minds waiting receptively for it, and would take root in them, until the whole nation became a single superconsciousness, conscious only of the one thought 'sleep' which we had thrown into it."

The reader will perhaps ask how we ourselves expected to escape from the clutches of the superconsciousness we had created. Well, we had discovered that metal was relatively impervious to the telepathic effect, and had prepared for ourselves a sort of tin pulpit, behind which we could stand while conducting experiments. This, combined with caps of metal foil, enormously reduced the effects on ourselves. We had not informed Bugala of this property of metal.

Hascombe was silent. At length he spoke. "I like the idea," he said; "I like to think that if I ever do get back to England and to scientific recognition, my discovery will have given me the means of escape."

From that moment we worked assiduously to perfect our method and our plans. After about five months everything seemed propitious. We had provisions packed away, and compasses. I had been allowed to keep my rifle, on promise that I would never discharge it. We had made friends with some of the men who went trading to the coast, and had got from them all the information we could about the route, without arousing their suspicions.

At last, the night arrived. We assembled our men as if for an ordinary practice, and after hypnosis had been induced, started to tune them. At this moment Bugala came in, unannounced. This was what we had been afraid of; but there had been no means of preventing it. "What shall we do?" I whispered to Hascombe, in English. "Go right ahead and be damned to it," was his answer; "we can put him to sleep with the rest."

So we welcomed him, and gave him a seat as near as possible to the tightly packed ranks of the performers. At length the preparations were finished. Hascombe went into the pulpit and said, "Attention to the words which are to be suggested." There was a slight stiffening of the bodies. "Sleep," said Hascombe. *"Sleep* is the command: command all in this land to sleep unbrokenly." Bugala leapt up with an exclamation; but the induction had already begun.

We with our metal coverings were immune. But Bugala was struck by the full force of the mental current. He sank back on his chair, helpless. For a few minutes his extraordinary will resisted the suggestion. Although he could not move, his angry eyes were open. But at length he succumbed, and he too slept.

We lost no time in starting, and made good progress through the silent country. The people were sitting about like wax figures. Women sat asleep by their milk-pails, the cow by this time far away. Fat-bellied naked children slept at their games. The houses were full of sleepers sleeping upright round their food, recalling Words-worth's famous "party in a parlor."

So we went on, feeling pretty queer and scarcely believing in this morphic state into which we had plunged a nation. Finally the frontier was reached, where with extreme elation, we passed an immobile and gigantic frontier guard. A few miles further we had a good solid meal, and a doze. Our kit was rather heavy, and we decided to jettison some superfluous weight, in the shape of some food, specimens, and our metal headgear, or mind-protectors, which at this distance, and with the hypnosis wearing a little thin, were, we thought, no longer necessary.

About nightfall on the third day, Hascombe suddenly stopped and turned his head.

"What's the matter?" I said. "Have you seen a lion?" His reply was completely unexpected. "No. I was just wondering whether really I ought not to go back again."

"Go back again," I cried. "What in the name of God Almighty do you want to do that for?"

"It suddenly struck me that I ought to," he said, "about five minutes ago. And really, when one comes to think of it, I don't suppose I shall ever get such a chance at research again. What's more, this is a dangerous journey to the coast, and I don't expect we shall get through alive."

I was thoroughly upset and put out, and told him so. And suddenly, for a few moments, I felt I must go back too. It was like that old friend of our boyhood, the voice of conscience.

"Yes, to be sure, we ought to go back," I thought with fervor. But suddenly checking myself as the thought came under the play of reason—"*Why* should we go back?" All sorts of reasons were proffered, as it were, by unseen hands reaching up out of the hidden parts of me.

And then I realized what had happened. Bugala had waked up; he had wiped out the suggestion we had given to the superconsciousness, and in its place put in another. I could see him thinking it out, the cunning devil (one must give him credit for brains!), and hear him, after making his passes, whisper to the nation in prescribed form his new suggestion: "Will to return! Return!" For most of the inhabitants the command would have no meaning, for they would have been already at home. Doubtless some young men out on the hills, or truant children, or girls run off in secret to meet their lovers, were even now returning, stiffly and in somnambulistic trance, to their homes. It was only for them that the new command of the superconsciousness had any meaning—and for us.

I am putting it in a long and discursive way; at the moment I simply *saw* what had happened in a flash. I told Hascombe, I showed him it *must* be so, that nothing else would account for the sudden change. I begged and implored him to use his reason, to stick to his decision, and to come on. How I regretted that, in our desire to discard all useless weight, we had left behind our metal telepathy-proof head coverings!

But Hascombe would not, or could not, see my point. I suppose he was much more imbued with all the feelings and spirit of the country, and so more susceptible. However that may be, he was immovable. He must go back; he knew it; he saw it clearly; it was his sacred duty; and much other similar rubbish. All this time the suggestion was attacking me too; and finally I felt that if I did not put more distance between me and that unisonic battery of will, I should succumb as well as he.

"Hascombe," I said, "I am going on. For God's sake, come with me." And I shouldered my pack, and set off. He was shaken, I saw, and came a few steps after me. But finally he turned, and, in spite of my frequent pauses and shouts to him to follow, made off in the direction we had come. I can assure you that it was with a gloomy soul that I continued my solitary way. I shall not bore you with my adventures. Suffice it to say that at last I got to a white outpost, weak with fatigue and poor food and fever.

I kept very quiet about my adventures, only giving out that our expedition had lost its way and that my men had run away or been killed by the local tribes. At last I reached England. But I was a broken man, and a profound gloom had invaded my mind at the thought of Hascombe and the way he had been caught in his own net. I never found out what happened to him, and I do not suppose that I am likely to find out now. You may ask why I did not try to organize a rescue expedition;

or why, at least, I did not bring Hascombe's discoveries before the Royal Society or the Metaphysical Institute. I can only repeat that I was a broken man. I did not expect to be believed; I was not at all sure that I could repeat our results, even on the same human material, much less with men of another race; I dreaded ridicule; and finally I was tormented by doubts as to whether the knowledge of mass telepathy would not be a curse rather than a blessing to mankind.

However, I am an oldish man now and, what is more, old for my years. I want to get the story off my chest. Besides, old men like sermonizing and you must forgive, gentle reader, the sermonical turn which I now feel I must take. The question I want to raise is this: Dr. Hascombe attained to an unsurpassed power in a number of the applications of science — but *to what end did all this power serve?* It is the merest cant and twaddle to go on asserting, as most of our press and people continue to do, that increase of scientific knowledge and power must in itself be good. I commend to the great public the obvious moral of my story and ask them to think what they propose to do with the power which is gradually being accumulated for them by the labors of those who labor because they like power, or because they want to find the truth about how things work.

JACK WILLIAMSON

The Metal Man

Jack Williamson is a phenomenon. Born in 1908, he published his first story (the one you are about to read) in Amazing Stories *in 1928, just two years after the founding of magazine science fiction, and has continued to produce quality sf to this day. He wrote some of the best "sense of wonder" science fiction produced in the 1930s and 1940s, including* The Legion of Space *(book form 1947) and the wonderful* The Legion of Time *(book form 1952). He is one of the very few writers of that era who continued to be successful and productive over the years. A noted critic as well as a writer of sf, he won the Pilgrim Award for his work on H. G. Wells and was made a Grand Master of the Science Fiction Writers of America in 1977.*

THE METAL Man stands in a dusty basement corner of the Tyburn College museum. Though the first excitement has subsided, his placement there is still an uneasy academic compromise, which so far has saved him from the scientists who want to cut him up for biochemical analysis and the old friends who think he should be buried.

To the casual tourist, he is only a life-sized piece of time-greened bronze. A closer look shows the perfect detail of his hair and skin and the agony frozen on his face. A few visitors stop to frown at the peculiar mark on his chest—a red, six-sided blot.

People have almost forgotten now that he was once Professor Thomas Kelvin of the Department of Geology. Yet the rumors about him are still alive, growing stranger than the truth. Because those rumors are so distressing to his friends, the regents have at last agreed to let me publish his own narrative.

For four of five years, Kelvin had spent his vacations along the Pacific slope of Mexico, prospecting for uranium. That last summer, apparently he found it. Instead of returning to his classes in the fall, he asked for an extended leave.

We heard later that he had sold his uranium claims to a Swiss syndicate, that he was lecturing in Europe on the chemical and biological effects of atomic radiation, that he himself was under treatment at a clinic near Paris.

He came back to Tyburn on a gloomy Saturday afternoon, out of an early winter fog that was drifting off the Gulf Stream. I was at home, raking leaves on the seaward slope of my place below the campus, when I saw the boat coming in toward my rocky little scrap of Atlantic beach. The boat was a stranger—long and low and fast, of the sort once favored by runners of illicit rum or guns. I dropped my rake to watch.

Piloted with daring and skill, the boat threaded the offshore rocks toward the only yard of sand in half a mile. Four men sprang out, to rush it through the surf. A gaunt fifth man rose in the stern, calling quiet orders. The four ripped ropes and canvas from a coffin-sized box, which they carried up into my yard. The gaunt man limped stiffly to where I stood.

"Tyburn College?"

His men had dark Latin faces, but his scarred and weather-reddened features were masked with a curly yellow beard, and his voice had a Yankee twang. Impatiently, he stabbed a lean finger toward the campus bell tower, dim in the fog.

At last I nodded.

"Here we are." He murmured soft Spanish to his men. Grinning, they set the long box down. He looked at me. "Do you know a Professor Russell?"

"I'm Russell."

"If that's so, our job's done." He gestured at the chest. "It's for you."

"Huh? What is it?"

"You'll find out." His hard eyes narrowed. "I think you'll want to keep it quiet."

He spoke to his men again, and they moved the chest to my back porch.

"Wait! Who are you?"

"Just delivery men." He gestured gently. "We've been paid. We'll be on our way."

He nodded to his men, who hurried toward the boat.

"But I don't understand—"

"You'll find a letter in the box," he said. "It explains why your friend took this way home. You'll see why he didn't want to trouble the immigration people."

"My friend?"

"Kelvin. Look in the box."

He started back toward the boat.

"Just a minute!" I shouted after him. "Where are you going?"

"South." He paused very briefly. "Look in the box—and give us twenty-four hours. Kelvin promised us that."

Not hurrying, he limped on down to the boat. His men pushed it off the sand. The muffled motors purred. Turning in the surf, the long craft slid between the rocks and vanished in the fog. I walked slowly back to the chest on the porch.

It was not locked. I lifted the lid—and dropped it back again. Lying in the box, stark naked, that queer blot stamped in livid red on the bronze-green breast, was the Metal Man.

A battered aluminum canteen lay beside his head, crusted with a purple stain. Beneath the canteen lay a sheaf of dog-eared pages covered with Kelvin's old-fashioned script.

I had to nerve myself to lift the lid again. I bent for a long time, trembling and staring, unable to grasp what I saw. At last I stumbled into the house and read Kelvin's narrative:

"Dear Russell—

"Because you are my sanest friend, I have arranged to have my body and this manuscript delivered to you. Perhaps I am laying an unfair burden on you, but at this point I no longer trust myself. I am still uncertain what I really found in Mexico. I cannot decide whether these fragmentary facts should be published or suppressed. Nor can I cope any longer with those ruthless men who want to rob me of what they think I found. Though my death will not be easy, I'm afraid I die in greater peace than I leave behind me.

"As you know, my goal last summer was the headwaters of El Rio de la Sangre. This is a small stream that flows into the Pacific. The year before I had found a strong radioactivity in its red-stained waters, and I hoped to strike uranium ores somewhere upriver.

"Twenty-five miles above the mouth, the river emerges from the Cordilleras. There are a few miles of rapids, and then the first waterfall. Nobody had ever been beyond the falls. I had reached their foot with an Indian guide, but failed to climb the cliffs beyond.

"Last winter I took flying lessons and bought a used airplane. It was old and slow, but suited to that rough country. When summer came, I shipped it to Vaca Morena. On the first day of July, I set out to fly up the river to its undiscovered source.

"Though I was still an unseasoned pilot, the old plane flew well. The stream beneath me looked like a red snake crawling down through the mountains to the sea. I followed it beyond the falls into a region of towering peaks.

"The river disappeared in a narrow, black-walled gorge. I circled to look for a place to land but the whole landscape was naked granite and jagged lava. I climbed over a high pass and found the crater.

"An incredible pool of green fire, fully ten miles across, walled with dark volcanic rock. At first I thought the green was water, but its hazy surface had no waves. I knew it must be some heavy gas.

"The high peaks around it still had snow. Their silver crowns were brushed with splendid color, crimson on the westward slopes, purple rising from shadows. That wild glory held me, even while the feel of it disturbed me.

"Night was near. I knew I should be turning back. Yet I stayed, wheeling over the crater, because I couldn't understand that pool of gas. As the sun sank lower, I saw stranger things. A thin greenish mist gathered over the peaks. It flowed down every slope into the pit, as if it fed that gas lake. Then something stirred the lake itself. The center of it bulged upward into a glowing dome.

"When the sluggish gas flowed back, I saw a huge red sphere rising out of the pit. Its surface was smooth, metallic, and thickly studded with great spikes of yellow fire. It spun very slowly on a vertical axis. Weird as it seemed, I sensed purpose in its motion.

"It climbed above my own level and paused there, still spinning. Now I saw a circular spot of dull black over each pole of the sphere. I saw misty streamers from the peaks and the pool drawn into those spots, as if the sphere somehow inhaled them.

"For a little time the globe hung above me. The yellow spikes shone slowly brighter, until the whole object blazed like a great golden planet, while it sucked the last scraps of mist from the peaks. Suddenly, when they stood black and bare, it dropped back into that flat green sea.

"With its fall, a sinister shadow fell over the crater. With a start, I realized how much gasoline and daylight I had used. At once I turned back toward the coast.

"More puzzled than afraid, I was trying to decide whether that thing from the pit had been natural or artificial, reality or illusion. I remember imagining that these enormous deposits of uranium might have unforeseen effects. It occurred to me, too, that perhaps somebody had got here ahead of me, and that perhaps I had seen the trail of an atomic ship.

"With a shock of real alarm, I saw a pale blue glow spreading over the cowling of the cockpit. In a moment the whole plane, and even my body, was covered with it. I gunned the motor and tried to climb.

"Though the motor labored, I couldn't climb. Some queer G-force, connected I thought with that blue glow, was pulling me now. Dizziness dulled my thoughts, and my heavy arms began to drag at the controls.

"I had to dive, to keep flying speed. Almost before I knew what was happening, I plunged into that gas lake. It was not suffocating, as I had expected. Though it cut visibility to just a few yards, I noticed no odor or other sensation.

"A dark surface loomed under me. I pulled out of the dive and managed to land on a smooth plain of coarse red sand. Like the green gas, the sand was dully luminous.

"For a time I was confined to the cockpit by my own weight, but slowly that blue glow faded, along with its effect. I climbed out of the plane with my canteen and my automatic pistol, which were themselves still immensely heavy.

"Unable to stand erect, I crawled away across the sand. I felt sure that I had been brought down by something intelligent. I was deathly afraid, yet soon I had to stop and rest.

"Lying there, perhaps a hundred yards from the plane, I saw five blue lights drifting toward it through the fog. I lay still and watched them wheel around the plane. Their motion was heavy and slow. The mist made dull halos around them. They had no structure that I could see.

"At last they lifted back into the haze, and I went on. Though my excess gravity had faded way, I went on hands and knees until the plane was out of sight. When I stood up, my sense of direction was gone.

"A helpless fear swept over me. Bright red sand and thick green fog—that's all I could see. No landmark, not even a moving light. The soundless air pressed down like a shapeless weight. I trembled with a panic sense of utter isolation.

"I don't know how long I stood there, afraid of moving in the wrong direction. Suddenly a light darted above me, like a blue meteor. In my alarm I ran from that. After a few blundering steps, my foot struck something that rang like metal.

"The clatter froze me with new terror, but the light moved on. When it was gone, I bent to see what I had kicked. It was a metal bird—an eagle formed of metal—wings outspread, talons grasping, beak set open. Its color was a tarnished green.

"At first I took it for a cast model of a real bird, but then I found each feather separate and flexible—as if a living eagle had been turned to metal. I remembered that fissioning uranium transmutes itself to lead, and wondered if intense radiation could transmute the tissues of a bird.

"Fear seized me, for my own body. Anxiously I began to look for other transformed creatures. I found them in abundance scattered over the sand or half-buried in it. Birds, large and small. Flying insects, most of them strange to me. Even a pterosaur—a flying reptile that must have reached the pit long ages past.

"Scrabbling to dig it out of the glowing sand, I saw a green glint from my own hands. The tips of my fingernails and the fine hairs on the back of my hands were already changed to light green metal!

"The shock of that discovery unnerved me completely. I screamed aloud, careless of what might hear, and ran off in blind panic. I forgot that I was lost. Reason and caution were left behind. I felt no fatigue as I ran—only black terror.

"Bright, swift lights passed above me in the green, but I gave them no heed. Unexpectedly, I came up to the great sphere I had seen from above. It rested motionless in a black metal cradle. The yellow fire was gone from the spikes but a score of blue lights floated above it like lanterns swinging in a fog.

"I turned and ran again. Direction didn't matter. Neither did time. What stopped me at last was a bank of queer vegetation. The stuff was violet in color, waist-deep and grasslike, with narrow spikes for leaves. The tallest center spikes were tipped with pink blooms and little purple berries.

"A sluggish red stream ran through the thicket—I thought it must be El Rio de la Sangre. Here, anyhow, was cover from the flying lights. I threw myself down in the deep tangle and lay there sobbing.

"For a long time, I couldn't stir or think. When at last I inspected my fingernails, the green tips looked wider. Frantically I gnawed at them, but the hideous fact refused to go away. I was changing into metal.

"Wildly I groped for a way to escape. I had to scale the crater walls or else recover the plane, yet I felt too weak to move. Though I felt no actual hunger, I thought food might give me strength.

"Recklessly, I picked a few of those purple berries. They had a salty, metallic taste. I spat them out, afraid they would make me ill. But, in pulling them, I had got the juice on my fingers. When I wiped it off, I found, to my amazement and my inexpressible joy, that the metal rim was gone from the nails it had touched.

"I had found hope. The evolution of the plants, I thought, must have produced something that resisted transmutation. I stuffed myself with berries till I began to feel sick, then poured the water from my canteen and squeezed juice to fill it.

"Since then I have analyzed the fluid. Some of its constituents resemble the standard formulas for the treatment for X-ray burns. It doubtless saved me from the terrible burns caused by gamma radiation.

"I lay there till dawn, dozing sometimes in spite of my terror. Sunlight must have filtered down through that pool of gas. By day the green faded to a greenish gray, and even the red sand seemed less luminous.

"All the green, I found, was now gone from my nails and hair. Immensely cheered by that, I ate another handful of the berries and set off along that little river. I walked downstream, counting my paces.

"Before I had gone three miles, I came to the pitchblende cliffs. Abrupt and black, they towered up as far as I could see into the thick green gloom. The river disappeared beneath them, in a roaring pool of red foam.

"This, I felt sure, must be the west rim of the crater. I turned north beneath that unclimbable wall. Still I had no definite plan, except to find a path across the cliffs. I kept alert for those floating lights and looked for a slope or a chimney that I could climb.

"I plodded on until it must have been noon, though my watch had stopped. Sometimes I stumbled over more things that must have been alive when they fell from above. Uprooted trees. Birds of every sort. A huge green bear, its breed long extinct.

"At last I found a break in that vertical wall—a wide flat shelf with an inviting slope above it. But that ledge was a good sixty feet above me. I tried to reach it and slid back, again and again, until my hands were bleeding. I gave up and went on.

"Somewhere beyond, groggy with exhaustion and despair, I staggered into a city of the flying lights—that's what it must have been. Slim black towers stood scattered across the red sand. Each one was topped with a great mushroom of orange flame.

"Fresh terror paralyzed me, but I heard no sound and saw no motion. Crouching under the overhanging cliff, I tried to take stock. The flying lights, I now suspected, were not active by day—but I felt sick with dread of the night.

"By my reckoning, I had made about fifteen miles from the river. Now I must be somewhere along the east wall of the crater, with a good half of the cliffs still ahead. To explore them, I had to pass that city of flames, yet I dared not enter it.

"I left the rim, to walk around the city. I tried to keep those tall flares in view, but somehow I lost them. I veered to the left, but all I found was more flat sand, smothered under dull green murk.

"On and on I wandered until the sand and the air grew brighter. Dusk had fallen. The floating lights were soon in motion. The night before, they had gone straight and high and fast. Now they were low, uncertain, slow. I knew they were searching—for me!

"I scooped out a shallow trench in the sand and lay there shivering. Mist-veiled points of light came near and passed. Another stopped, directly overhead. It sank toward me. Its pale halo grew. Paralyzed with terror, I could only wait.

"Down and down it came, until I saw its form. It was a crystal thing. I watched it with a sick fascination. A dozen feet long, it had an intricate structure like a crystal of snow. The heart of it was a blue, six-pointed star. An upright prism pierced the star. Blue fire pulsed through it, flowing inward from the points of the star, and threads of bright scarlet trailed outward from the faces of the prism. Neither animal nor plant nor even machine, it was alive—alive with light!

"It fell straight toward me.

"In a reflexive act of panic, I pulled my automatic and fired three shots. The bullets glanced off those glittering planes and whined away into the fog.

"It paused above me. Those threads of red fire trailed down around me, questingly, somehow caressingly. They wound around my body—and I felt my weight drained out. They lifted me against the crystal prism. You may see its mark on my chest.

"That contact stunned me with blinding pain. My whole body writhed, as if from a cruel electric shock. Dimly, I knew the thing was rising with me. I had a sense of other crystal creatures swarming near. But my mind was fading out.

"I awoke floating free in a brilliant orange cloud. For a moment I felt elated, but then I found I couldn't move, couldn't even turn my body. I reached and kicked and twisted, but I could touch no solid object. Though nothing held me, I was helpless as a turtle on its back.

"My body was still clothed. My canteen still hung—or floated—by my shoulder. My automatic was still in my jacket pocket, solid but weightless. Yet somehow I knew that days had passed.

"Struggling to move myself, I felt a queer numb stiffness in my side. I ripped my shirt open and found a new scar there, almost healed. I believe those creatures had cut into me—exploring my body, I suppose, as I had explored their world.

"I must have blacked out again when I felt the hardened granular deadness of the skin over my chest and found that red, six-sided print. Yet that discovery brought me to some limit of emotion. I woke in a mood of remote detachment, as if I didn't really care.

"But my side still hurt. The orange cloud was still around me. My crystal captor was drifting in it with me, not a dozen yards away. In my cool unconcern, I knew that I was trapped in the mushroom cloud above one of those towering cylinders, a prisoner in that alien city of flame.

"For a time I simply floated there, weightless as a man in space, watching my own predicament from that mood of aloof abstraction. Indifferently, I observed that the vital fire had ceased to pulse inside the crystal creature. It was sleeping, I supposed, till night came again.

"That chain of thought lit a faint spark of hope in me. Once more I kicked and clawed at the cloud around me. With nothing to push against, I failed to move an inch.

"While I struggled like a bug on a pin, that cold flame grew slowly brighter around me. Night, I knew, was falling. The crystal things would soon awake, no doubt to resume the vivisection of their human guinea pig.

"I could see only one way to cheat them. I was pulling my automatic to put a bullet into my own head, when a better idea hit me. I fired six quick shots out into the fog.

"That move saved me. A rocket needs nothing to push against. The gun was a sort of rocket. The recoil of each explosion nudged me farther from the sleeping crystal. I slid out of the mushroom cloud.

"Gravity caught me again, at first very gently. Drifting down to the luminous sand, I found my airplane drawn up to the foot of that slim black tower. It was intact. The motor balked for a moment, as if my captors had been into it as well as into me. At last it caught. I took off blind—"

* * *

At this point, there's a break in the manuscript. The remaining lines are on another tattered page. They seem to be in Kelvin's old-fashioned hand, but here it is a ragged pencil scrawl, not always readable.

"End of my [rope?] Guess I diluted the [canteen?] too many times. My body and effects I will to science. Captain Gander will supply the [conclusion?] of my story. The frightening [truth?]—"

That was all.

I called my physician. He's a sour-featured Scotch Presbyterian who doesn't care for the twentieth century. He read the manuscript with an air of indignant unbelief, scowled over the transmuted body, and dourly advised me to keep the story quiet.

That might have been prudent, but it proved impossible. Too many people heard tantalizing rumors. Some came, I'm afraid, from my faculty colleagues at Tyburn. Others, I'm sure, did not.

Though Captain Gander has never come forward with whatever he knows, we tried to learn the rest of the story. That next summer, three of us from Tyburn chartered our own airplane and flew to western Mexico.

We easily found the coastal village that *Señor* Kelvin had visited once—but not, its people insisted, within the past three years. We talked to the men who had guided him back into the high sierra; we even followed up the rocky bed of that mountain stream where he had hunted uranium. Its waters were now neither red nor radioactive, however, and its source was only a boggy spring.

Flying over that spring and the peaks beyond, we found no crater filled with glowing gas, but only another stone-and-adobe pueblo three hundred years old. When we landed there, we discovered no metal birds or living crystals or atomic ships. We did, however, hear of three strangers who had been there before us.

One was a limping, bearded *gringo*, who had asked mad questions and cursed those who could not answer to please him. One was an elegant Swiss banker, who had wandered about the pueblo carrying a Geiger counter and staring at everybody with a monocle like an evil eye. The third was another *gringo*, who had come three summers from the north and driven on into the high Cordillera, hauling tarp-covered crates in an old military truck.

Among such confusing clues, we lost Kelvin's trail in Mexico. There were other mysterious strangers, however, who followed us back to Tyburn. Some of them were federal investigators, who questioned all of us, searched Kelvin's premises, photocopied his documents, and finally carried his transmuted body away for study by the AEC.

When they finally returned the body to Tyburn, they were remarkably tight-lipped and silent, even for federal men. No official report has ever mentioned the Metal Man, and the rumors that still circulate, sometimes, around him are wildly contradictory.

Part of the truth had been concealed, but I don't know who to blame. There's Captain Gander—who surely owns another name, and quite possibly doctored

Kelvin's manuscript. There's the Swiss banker—who used to sit in the *cantina* reading a French translation of Wells' *Time Machine*, never talking to anybody. There's the AEC—whose agents certainly learned more than they ever told. There's Kelvin himself—who may have been lying to hide what he actually discovered.

But I've come to believe that Kelvin's story is true. I spent a good many sleepless nights reviewing all the conflicting evidence, until the time I had a vivid dream of strangers visiting the earth, perhaps to refuel their atomic ship, which lay hidden in time as well as space while they were collecting and preserving stray specimens of pterosaurs and men.

However that may be, Kelvin's metal body, standing nude and scarred and dusty now in its gloomy corner, is proof enough that he did discover more than he was looking for. His lips are frozen in a green ironic smile, almost as if he is aware that Civil Defense has designated the museum basement where he stands as an emergency fall-out shelter.

MILEŞ J. BREUER

The Gostak and the Doshes

A physician who practiced in Lincoln, Nebraska, Miles J. Breuer (1889-1947) was one of the first contributors to American magazine science fiction, with stories appearing in Amazing Stories as early as 1927. Although his only sf book is The Girl from Mars, *coauthored with Jack Williamson, he is remembered for several dozen stories, almost all published in the Gernsback magazines, tales that were quite popular in their time. His work featured a concern with psychological motivation and the impact of technology on human beings, a concern that would characterize the "Golden Age" of science fiction a decade later.*

"The Gostak and the Doshes" is without doubt his finest story, one that retains an important message today.

Let the reader suppose that somebody states: *"The gostak distims the doshes."* You do not know what this means, nor do I. But if we assume that it is English, we know that the *doshes* are *distimmed* by the *gostak*. We know that one *distimmer* of the *doshes* is a *gostak*. If, moreover, doshes are galloons, we know that some galloons are distimmed by the gostak. And so we may go on, and so we often do go on.——Unknown writer quoted by Ogden and Richards, in *The Meaning of Meanings*, Harcourt Brace & Co., 1923; also by Walter N. Polakov in *Man and His Affairs*, Williams & Wilkins, 1925.

"Why! That is lifting yourself by your own bootstraps!" I exclaimed in amazed incredulity. "It's absurd."

Woleshensky smiled indulgently. He towered in his chair as though in the infinite kindness of his vast mind there were room to understand and overlook all the foolish little foibles of all the weak little beings that called themselves men. A mathematical physicist lives in vast spaces where a light-year is a footstep, where universes are being born and blotted out, where space unrolls along a fourth dimension on a surface distended from a fifth. To him, human beings and their affairs do not loom very important.

"Relativity," he explained. In his voice there was a patient forbearance for my slowness of comprehension. "Merely relativity. It doesn't take much physical effort to make the moon move through the treetops, does it? Just enough to walk down the garden path."

169

I stared at him, and he continued: "If you had been born and raised on a moving train, no one could convince you that the landscape was not in rapid motion. Well, our conception of the universe is quite as relative as that. Sir Isaac Newton tried in his mathematics to express a universe as though beheld by an infinitely removed and perfectly fixed observer. Mathematicians since his time, realizing the futility of such an effort, have taken into consideration that what things 'are' depends upon the person who is looking at them. They have tried to express common knowledge, such as the law of gravitation, in terms that would hold good for all observers. Yet their leader and culminating genius, Einstein, has been unable to express knowledge in terms of pure relativity; he has had to accept the velocity of light as an arbitrarily fixed constant. Why should the velocity of light be any more fixed and constant than any other quantity in the universe?"

"But what's that got to do with going into the fourth dimension?" I broke in impatiently.

He continued as though I hadn't spoken.

"The thing that interests us now, and that mystifies modern mathematicians, is the question of movement, or, more accurately, translation. Is there such a thing as *absolute translation?* Can there be movement—translation—except in *relation* to something else than the thing that moves? All movement we know of is movement in relation to other objects, whether it be a walk down the street or the movement of the earth in its orbit around the sun. A change of *relative* position. But the mere translation of an isolated object existing alone in space is mathematically inconceivable, for there is no such thing as space in that sense."

"I thought you said something about going into another universe—" I interrupted again.

You can't argue with Woleshensky. His train of thought went on without a break.

"By translation we understand getting from one place to another. 'Going somewhere' originally meant a movement of our bodies. Yet, as a matter of fact, when we drive in an automobile we 'go somewhere' without moving our bodies at all. The scene is changed around us; we are somewhere else; and yet we haven't *moved* at all.

"Or suppose you could cast off gravitational attraction for a moment and let the earth rotate under you; you would be going somewhere and yet not moving—"

"But that is theory; you can't tinker with gravitation—"

"Every day you tinker with gravitation. When you start upward in an elevator, your pressure, not your weight, against the floor of it is increased; apparent gravitation between you and the floor of the elevator is greater than before—and that's like gravitation is anyway: inertia and acceleration. But we are talking about translation. The position of everything in the universe must be referred to some sort of coordinates. Suppose we change the angle or direction of the coordinates: then you have 'gone somewhere' and yet you haven't moved, nor has anything else moved."

I looked at him, holding my head in my hands.

"I couldn't swear that I understood that," I said slowly. "And I repeat it looks like lifting yourself by your own bootstraps."

The homely simile did not dismay him. He pointed a finger at me as he spoke. "You've seen a chip of wood bobbing on the ripples of a pond. Now you think the chip is moving, now the water. Yet neither is moving; the only motion is of an abstract thing called a wave.

"You've seen those 'illusion' diagrams—for instance, this one of a group of cubes. Make up your mind that you are looking down upon their upper surfaces, and indeed they seem below you. Now change your mind and imagine that you are down below, looking up. Behold, you see their lower surfaces; you are indeed below them. You have 'gone somewhere,' yet there has been no translation of anything. You have merely changed coordinates."

"Which do you think will drive me insane more quickly—if you *show* me what you mean, or if you keep on talking without showing me?"

"I'll try to show you. There are some types of mind, you know, that cannot grasp the idea of relativity. It isn't the mathematics involved that matters; it's just the inability of some types of mental organizations to grasp the fact that the mind of the observer endows his environment with certain properties which have no absolute existence. Thus, when you walk through the garden at night the moon floats from one treetop to another. Is your mind good enough to invert this: make the moon stand still and let the trees move backward? Can you do that? If so, you can 'go somewhere' into another dimension."

Woleshensky rose and walked to the window. His office was an appropriate setting for such a modern discussion as ours—situated in a new, ultramodern building on the university campus, the varnish glossy, the walls clean, the books neatly arranged behind clean glass, the desk in most orderly array; the office was just as precise and modern and wonderful as the mind of its occupant.

"When do you want to go?" he asked.

"Now!"

"Then I have two more things to explain to you. The fourth dimension is just as much *here* as anywhere else. Right here around you and me things exist and go forward in the fourth dimension; but we do not see them and are not conscious of them because we are confined to our own three. Secondly: if we name the four coordinates as Einstein does, x, y, z, and t, then we exist in x, y, and z and move freely about in them, but are powerless to move in t. Why? Because t is the time dimension; and the time dimension is a difficult one for biological structures that depend on irreversible chemical reactions for their existence. But biochemical reactions can take place along any of the other dimensions as well as along t.

"Therefore, let us transform coordinates. Rotate the property of chemical irreversibility from t to z. Since we are organically able to exist (or at least to perceive) in only three dimensions at once, our new time dimension will be z. We shall be unconscious of z and cannot travel in it. Our activities and consciousness will take place along x, y, and t.

"According to fiction writers, to switch into the t dimension, some sort of apparatus with an electrical field ought to be necessary. It is not. You need nothing more to rotate into the t dimension than you do to stop the moon and make the trees move as you ride down the road; or than you do to turn the cubes upside down. It is a matter of *relativity*."

I had ceased trying to wonder or to understand.

"Show me!" was all I could gasp.

"The success of this experiment in changing from the z to the t coordinate has depended largely upon my lucky discovery of a favorable location. It is just as, when you want the moon to ride the treetops successfully, there have to be favorable features in the topography or it won't work. The edge of this building and that little walk between the two rows of Norway poplars seems to be an angle between planes in the z and t dimensions. It seems to slope downward, does it not?—Now walk from here to the end and imagine yourself going upward. That is all. Instead of feeling this building behind and *above* you, conceive it as behind and *below*. Just as on your ride by moonlight, you must tell yourself that the moon is not moving while the trees ride by.—Can you do that? Go ahead, then." He spoke in a confident tone, as though he knew exactly what would happen.

Half credulous, half wondering, I walked slowly out of the door. I noticed that Woleshensky settled himself down to the table with a pad and a pencil to some kind of study, and forgot me before I had finished turning around. I looked curiously at the familiar wall of the building and the still more familiar poplar walk, expecting to see some strange scenery, some unknown view from another world. But there were the same old bricks and trees that I had known so long, though my disturbed and wondering frame of mind endowed them with a sudden strangeness and un-wontedness. Things I had known for some years, they were, yet so powerfully had Woleshensky's arguments impressed me that I already fancied myself in a different universe. According to the conception of relativity, objects of the x, y, z universe *ought* to look different when viewed from the x, y, t universe.

Strange to say, I had no difficulty at all in imagining myself as going *upward* on my stroll along the slope. I told myself that the building was behind and below me, and indeed it seemed real that it was that way. I walked some distance along the little avenue of poplars, which seemed familiar enough in all its details, though after a few minutes it struck me that the avenue seemed rather long. In fact, it was much longer than I had ever known it to be before.

With a queer Alice-in-Wonderland feeling I noted it stretching way on ahead of me. Then I looked back.

I gasped in astonishment. The building was indeed *below* me. I looked down upon it from the top of an elevation. The astonishment of that realization had barely broken over me when I admitted that there was a building down there; but what building? Not the new Morton Hall, at any rate. It was a long, three-story brick building, quite resembling Morton Hall, but it was not the same. And on beyond there were trees with buildings among them; but it was not the campus that I knew.

I paused in a kind of panic. What was I to do now? Here I was in a strange place. How I had gotten there I had no idea. What ought I to do about it? Where should I go? How was I to get back? Odd that I had neglected the precaution of how to get back. I surmised that I must be on the t dimension. Stupid blunder on my part, neglecting to find out how to get back.

I walked rapidly down the slope toward the building. Any hopes that I might have had about its being Morton Hall were thoroughly dispelled in a moment. It was a totally strange building, old, and old-fashioned looking. I had never seen it before in my life. Yet it looked perfectly ordinary and natural and was obviously a university classroom building.

I cannot tell whether it was an hour or a dozen that I spent walking frantically this way and that, trying to decide to go into this building or another, and at the last moment backing out in a sweat of hesitation. It seemed like a year but was probably only a few minutes. Then I noticed the people. They were mostly young people, of both sexes. Students, of course. Obviously I was on a university campus. Perfectly natural, normal young people, they were. If I were really on the t dimension, it certainly resembled the z dimension very closely.

Finally I came to a decision. I could stand this no longer. I selected a solitary, quiet-looking man and stopped him.

"Where am I?" I demanded.

He looked at me in astonishment. I waited for a reply, and he continued to gaze at me speechlessly. Finally it occurred to me that he didn't understand English.

"Do you speak English?" I asked hopelessly.

"Of course!" he said vehemently. "What's wrong with you?"

"Something's wrong with something," I exclaimed. "I haven't any idea where I am or how I got here."

"Synthetic wine?" he asked sympathetically.

"Oh, hell! Think I'm a fool? Say, do you have a good man in mathematical physics on the faculty? Take me to him."

"Psychology, I should think," he said, studying me. "Or psychiatry. But I'm a law student and know nothing of either."

"Then make it mathematical physics, and I'll be grateful to you."

So I was conducted to the mathematical physicist. The student led me into the very building that corresponded to Morton Hall, and into an office the position of which quite corresponded to that of Woleshensky's office. However, the office was older and dustier; it had a Victorian look about it and was not as modern as Woleshensky's room. Professor Vibens was a rather small, bald-headed man with a keen-looking face. As I thanked the law student and started on my story, he looked rather bored, as though wondering why I had picked on him with my tale of wonder. Before I had gotten very far he straightened up a little; and farther along he pricked up another notch; and before many minutes he was tense in his chair as he listened to me. When I finished, his comment was terse, like that of a man accustomed to thinking accurately and to the point.

"Obviously you come into this world from another set of coordinates. As we are on the z dimension, you must have come to us from the t dimension—"

He disregarded my attempts to protest at this point.

"Your man Woleshensky has evidently developed the conception of relativity further than we have, although Monpeters's theory comes close enough to it. Since I have no idea how to get you back, you must be my guest. I shall enjoy hearing about your world."

"That is very kind of you," I said gratefully. "I'm accepting because I can't see what else to do. At least until the time when I can find myself a place in your world or get back to my own. Fortunately," I added as an afterthought, "no one will miss me there, unless it be a few classes of students who will welcome the little vacation that must elapse before my successor is found."

Breathlessly eager to find out what sort of world I had gotten into, I walked

with him to his home. And I may state at the outset that if I had found everything
upside down and outlandishly bizarre, I should have been far less amazed and
astonished than I was. For, from the walk that first evening from Professor Vibens's
office along several blocks of residence street to his solid and respectable home,
through all of my goings about the town and country during the years that I remained
in the *t*-dimensional world, I found people and things thoroughly ordinary and
familiar. They looked and acted as we do, and their homes and goods looked like
ours. I cannot possibly imagine a world and a people that could be more similar
to ours without actually being the same. It was months before I got over the idea
that I had merely wandered into an unfamiliar part of my own city. Only the actual
experience of wide travel and much sightseeing, and the knowledge that there was
no such extensive English-speaking country in the world that I knew, convinced
me that I must be on some other world, doubtless in the *t* dimension.

"A gentleman who has found his way here from another universe," the professor
introduced me to a strapping young fellow who was mowing the lawn.

The professor's son was named John! Could anything be more commonplace?

"I'll have to take you around and show you things tomorrow," John said cordially,
accepting the account of my arrival without surprise.

A redheaded servant girl, roast pork and rhubarb sauce for dinner, and checkers
afterward, a hot bath at bedtime, the ringing of a telephone somewhere else in the
house—is it any wonder that it was months before I would believe that I had
actually come into a different universe? What slight differences there were in the
people and the world merely served to emphasize the similarity. For instance, I
think they were just a little more hospitable and "old-fashioned" than we are. Making
due allowances for the fact that I was a rather remarkable phenomenon, I think I
was welcomed more heartily in this home and in others later; people spared me
more of their time and interest from their daily business than would have happened
under similar circumstances in a correspondingly busy city in America.

Again, John found a lot of time to take me about the city and show me banks
and stores and offices. He drove a little squat car with tall wheels, run by a spluttering
gasoline motor. (The car was not as perfect as our modern cars, and horses were
quite numerous in the streets. Yet John was a busy businessman, the district su-
perintendent of a life-insurance agency.) Think of it! Life insurance in Einstein's
t dimension.

"You're young to be holding such an important position," I suggested.

"Got started early," John replied. "Dad is disappointed because I didn't see fit
to waste time in college. Disgrace to the family, I am."

What in particular shall I say about the city? It might have been any one of a
couple of hundred American cities. Only it wasn't. The electric streetcars, except
for their bright green color, were perfect; they might have been brought over bodily
from Oshkosh or Tulsa. The ten-cent stores with gold letters on their signs; drug-
stores with soft drinks; a mad, scrambling stock exchange; the blaring sign of an
advertising dentist; brilliant entrances to motion-picture theaters were all there. The
beauty shops did wonders to the women's heads, excelling our own by a good deal,
if I am any judge; and at that time I had nothing more important on my mind than
to speculate on that question. Newsboys bawled the *Evening Sun* and the *Morning*

Gale, in whose curious, flat type I could read accounts of legislative doings, murders, and divorces quite as fluently as I could in my own *Tribune* at home. Strangeness and unfamiliarity had bothered me a good deal on a trip to Quebec a couple of years before; but they were not noticeable here in the *t* dimension.

For three or four weeks the novelty of going around, looking at things, meeting people, visiting concerts, theaters and department stores was sufficient to absorb my interest. Professor Vibens's hospitality was so sincerely extended that I did not hesitate to accept, though I assured him that I would repay it as soon as I got established in this world. In a few days I was thoroughly convinced that there was no way back home. Here I must stay, at least until I learned as much as Woleshensky knew about crossing dimensions. Professor Vibens eventually secured for me a position at the university.

It was shortly after I had accepted the position as instructor in experimental physics and had begun to get broken into my work that I noticed a strange commotion among the people of the city. I have always been a studious recluse, observing people as phenomena rather than participating in their activities. So for some time I noted only in a subconscious way the excited gathering in groups, the gesticulations and blazing eyes, the wild sale of extra editions of papers, the general air of disturbance. I even failed to take an active interest in these things when I made a railroad journey of three hundred miles and spent a week in another city; so thoroughly at home did I feel in this world that when the advisability arose of my studying laboratory methods in another university, I made the trip alone. So absorbed was I in my laboratory problems that I only noted with half an eye the commotion and excitement everywhere, and merely recollected it later. One night it suddenly popped into my head that the country was aroused over something.

That night I was with the Vibens family in their living room. John tuned in the radio. I wasn't listening to the thing very much; I had troubles of my own. $F = \frac{gm_1m_2}{r^2}$ was familiar enough to me. It meant the same and held as rigidly here as in my old world. But what was the name of the bird who had formulated that law? Back home it was Newton. Tomorrow in class I would have to be thoroughly familiar with his name. Pasvieux, that's what it was. What messy surnames. It struck me that it was lucky that they expressed the laws of physics in the same form and even in the same algebraic letters, or I might have had a time getting them confused——when all of a sudden the radio blatantly bawled: "THE GOSTAK DISTIMS THE DOSHES!"

John jumped to his feet.

"Damn right!" he shouted, slamming the table with his fist.

Both his father and mother annihilated him with withering glances, and he slunk from the room. I gazed stupefied. My stupefaction continued while the professor shut off the radio and both of them excused themselves from my presence. Then suddenly I was alert.

I grabbed a bunch of newspapers, having seen none for several days. Great sprawling headlines covered the front pages:

"THE GOSTAK DISTIMS THE DOSHES."

For a moment I stopped, trying to recollect where I had heard those words before. They recalled something to me. Ah, yes! That very afternoon there had been a commotion beneath my window on the university campus. I had been busy checking over an experiment so that I might be sure of its success at tomorrow's class, and looked out rather absently to see what was going on. A group of young men from a dismissed class was passing and had stopped for a moment.

"I say, the gostak distims the doshes!" said a fine-looking young fellow. His face was pale and strained.

The young man facing him sneered derisively, "Aw, your grandmother! Don't be a feeble—"

He never finished. The first fellow's fist caught him in the cheek. Several books dropped to the ground. In a moment the two had clinched and were rolling on the ground, fists flying up and down, smears of blood appearing here and there. The others surrounded them and for a moment appeared to enjoy the spectacle, but suddenly recollected that it looked rather disgraceful on a university campus, and after a lively tussle separated the combatants. Twenty of them, pulling in two directions, tugged them apart.

The first boy strained in the grasp of his captors; his white face was flecked with blood and he panted for breath.

"Insult!" he shouted, giving another mighty heave to get free. He looked contemptuously around. "The whole bunch of you ought to learn to stand up for your honor. The gostak distims the doshes!"

That was the astonishing incident that these words called to my mind. I turned back to my newspapers.

"Slogan Sweeps the Country," proclaimed the subheads. "Ringing Expression of National Spirit! Enthusiasm Spreads Like Wildfire! The new patriotic slogan is gaining ground rapidly," the leading article went on. "The fact that it has covered the country almost instantaneously seems to indicate that it fills a deep and long-felt want in the hearts of the people. It was first uttered during a speech in Walkingdon by that majestic figure in modern statesmanship, Senator Harob. The beautiful sentiment, the wonderful emotion of this sublime thought, are epoch-making. It is a great conception, doing credit to a great man, and worthy of being the guiding light of a great people—"

That was the gist of everything I could find in the papers. I fell asleep still puzzled about the thing. I was puzzled because—as I see now and didn't see then—I was trained in the analytical methods of physical science and knew little or nothing about the ways and emotions of the masses of the people.

In the morning the senseless expression popped into my head as soon as I awoke. I determined to waylay the first member of the Vibens family who showed up, and demand the meaning of the thing. It happened to be John.

"John, what's a gostak?"

John's face lighted up with pleasure. He threw out his chest and a look of pride replaced the pleasure. His eyes blazed, and with a consuming enthusiasm he shook hands with me, as deacons shake hands with a new convert—a sort of glad welcome.

"The gostak!" he exclaimed. "Hurray for the gostak!"

"But what is a gostak?"

"Not *a* gostak! *The* gostak. The gostak is—the distimmer of the doshes—see! He distims 'em, see?"

"Yes, yes. But what is distimming? How do you distim?"

"No, no! Only the gostak can distim. The gostak distims the doshes. See?"

"Ah, I see!" I exclaimed. Indeed, I pride myself on my quick wit. "What are doshes? Why, they are the stuff distimmed by the gostak. Very simple!"

"Good for you!" John slapped my back in huge enthusiasm. "I think it wonderful for you to understand us so well after being here only a short time. You are very patriotic."

I gritted my teeth tightly to keep myself from speaking.

"Professor Vibens, what's a gostak?" I asked in the solitude of his office an hour later.

He looked pained.

He leaned back in his chair and looked me over elaborately, and waited some time before answering.

"Hush!" he finally whispered. "A scientific man may think what he pleases, but if he says too much, people in general may misjudge him. As a matter of fact, a good many scientific men are taking this so-called patriotism seriously. But a mathematician cannot use words loosely; it has become second nature with him to inquire closely into the meaning of every term he uses."

"Well, doesn't that jargon mean anything at all?" I was beginning to be puzzled in earnest.

"To me it does not. But it seems to mean a great deal to the public in general. It's making people do things, is it not?"

I stood a while in stupefied silence. That an entire great nation should become fired up over a meaningless piece of nonsense! Yet the astonishing thing was that I had to admit there was plenty of precedent for it in the history of my own z-dimensional world. A nation exterminating itself in civil wars to decide which of two profligate royal families should be privileged to waste the people's substance from the throne; a hundred thousand crusaders marching to death for an idea that to me means nothing; a meaningless, untrue advertising slogan that sells millions of dollars' worth of cigarettes to a nation, to the latter's own detriment—haven't we seen it over and over again?

"There's a public lecture on this stuff tonight at the First Church of the Salvation," Professor Vibens suggested.

"I'll be there," I said. "I want to look into the thing."

That afternoon there was another flurry of "extras" over the street; people gathered in knots and gesticulated with open newspapers.

"War! Let 'em have it!" I heard men shout.

"Is our national honor a rag to be muddied and trampled on?" the editorials asked.

As far as I could gather from reading the papers, there was a group of nations across an ocean that was not taking the gostak seriously. A ship whose pennant bore the slogan had been refused entrance to an Engtalian harbor because it flew no national ensign. The Executive had dispatched a diplomatic note. An evangelist who had attempted to preach the gospel of the distimmed doshes at a public gathering in Itland had been ridden on a rail and otherwise abused. The Executive was dispatching a diplomatic note.

Public indignation waxed high. Derogatory remarks about "wops" were flung about. Shouts of "Holy war!" were heard. I could feel the tension in the atmosphere as I took my seat in the crowded church in the evening. I had been assured that the message of the gostak and the doshes would be thoroughly expounded so that even the most simple-minded and uneducated people could understand it fully. Although I had my hands full at the university, I was so puzzled and amazed at the course events were taking that I determined to give the evening to finding out what the slogan meant.

There was a good deal of singing before the lecture began. Mimeographed copies of the words were passed about, but I neglected to preserve them and do not remember them. I know there was one solemn hymn that reverberated harmoniously through the great church, a chanting repetition of "The Gostak Distims the Doshes." There was another stirring martial air that began, "Oh, the Gostak! Oh, the Gostak!"—and ended with a swift cadence on "The Gostak Distims the Doshes!" The speaker had a rich, eloquent voice and a commanding figure. He stepped out and bowed solemnly.

"The gostak distims the doshes," he pronounced impressively. "Is it not comforting to know that there is a gostak; do we not glow with pride because the doshes are distimmed? In the entire universe there is no more profoundly significant fact: the gostak distims the doshes. Could anything be more complete yet more tersely emphatic! The gostak distims the doshes!" Applause. "This thrilling truth affects our innermost lives. What would we do if the gostak did not distim the doshes? Without the gostak, without doshes, what would we do? What would we think? How would we feel?" Applause again.

At first I thought this was some kind of introduction. I was inexperienced in listening to popular speeches, lectures and sermons. I had spent most of my life in the study of physics and its accessory sciences. I could not help trying to figure out the meaning of whatever I heard. When I found none, I began to get impatient. I waited some more, thinking that soon he would begin on the real explanation. After thirty minutes of the same sort of stuff as I have just quoted, I gave up trying to listen. I just sat and hoped he would soon be through. The people applauded and grew more excited. After an hour I stirred restlessly; I slouched down in my seat and sat up by turns. After two hours I grew desperate; I got up and walked out. Most of the people were too excited to notice me. Only a few of them cast hostile glances at my retreat.

The next day the mad nightmare began for me. First there was a snowstorm of extras over the city, announcing the sinking of a merchantman by an Engtalian cruiser. A dispute had arisen between the officers of the merchantman and the port officials, because the latter had jeered disrespectfully at the gostak. The merchantman picked up and started out without having fulfilled all the customs requirements. A cruiser followed it and ordered it to return. The captain of the merchantman told them that the gostak distims the doshes, whereupon the cruiser fired twice and sank the merchantman. In the afternoon came the extras announcing the Executive's declaration of war.

Recruiting offices opened; the university was depleted of its young men; uniformed troops marched through the city, and railway trains full of them went in and out. Campaigns for raising war loans; home-guards, women's auxiliaries, ladies' aid societies making bandages, young women enlisting as ambulance drivers—it was indeed war; all of it to the constantly repeated slogan: "The gostak distims the doshes."

I could hardly believe that it was really true. There seemed to be no adequate cause for a war. The huge and powerful nation had dreamed a silly slogan and flung it in the world's face. A group of nations across the water had united into an alliance, claiming they had to defend themselves against having forced upon them a principle they did not desire. The whole thing at the bottom had no meaning. It did not seem possible that there would actually be a war; it seemed more like going through a lot of elaborate play-acting.

Only when the news came of a vast naval battle of doubtful issue, in which ships had been sunk and thousands of lives lost, did it come to me that they meant business. Black bands of mourning appeared on sleeves and in windows. One of the allied countries was invaded and a front line set up. Reports of a division wiped out by an airplane attack; of forty thousand dead in a five-day battle; of more men and more money needed, began to make things look real. Haggard men with bandaged heads and arms in slings appeared on the streets, a church and an auditorium were converted into hospitals, and trainloads of wounded were brought in. To convince myself that this thing was so, I visited these wards and saw with my own eyes the rows of cots, the surgeons working on ghastly wounds, the men with a leg missing or with a hideously disfigured face.

Food became restricted; there was no white bread, and sugar was rationed. Clothing was of poor quality; coal and oil were obtainable only on government permit. Businesses were shut down. John was gone; his parents received news that he was missing in action.

Real it was; there could be no more doubt of it. The thing that made it seem most real was the picture of a mangled, hopeless wreck of humanity sent back from the guns, a living protest against the horror of war. Suddenly someone would say, "The gostak distims the doshes!" and the poor wounded fragment would straighten up and put out his chest with pride, and an unquenchable fire would blaze in his eyes. He did not regret having given his all for that. How could I understand it?

And real it was when the draft was announced. More men were needed; volunteers were insufficient. Along with the rest, I complied with the order to register, doing so in a mechanical fashion, thinking little of it. Suddenly the coldest realization of the reality of it was flung at me when I was informed that my name had been drawn and that I would have to go!

All this time I had looked upon this mess as something outside of me, something belonging to a different world, of which I was not a part. Now here was a card summoning me to training camp. With all this death and mangled humanity in the background, I wasn't even interested in this world. I didn't belong here. To be called upon to undergo all the horrors of military life, the risk of a horrible death, for no reason at all! For a silly jumble of meaningless sounds.

I spent a sleepless night in maddened shock from the thing. In the morning a wild and haggard caricature of myself looked back at me from the mirror. But I had revolted. I intended to refuse service. If the words "conscientious objector" ever meant anything, I certainly was one. Even if they shot me for treason at once, that would be a fate less hard to bear than going out and giving my strength and my life for—for nothing at all.

My apprehensions were quite correct. With my usual success at self-control over a seething interior, I coolly walked to the draft office and informed them that I did not believe in their cause and could not see my way to fight for it. Evidently they had suspected something of the sort already, for they had the irons on my wrists before I had hardly done with my speech.

"Period of emergency," said a beefy tyrant at the desk. "No time for stringing out a civil trial. Court-martial!"

He said it to me vindictively, and the guards jostled me roughly down the corridor; even they resented my attitude. The court-martial was already waiting for me. From the time I walked out of the lecture at the church I had been under secret surveillance, and they knew my attitude thoroughly. That is the first thing the president of the court informed me.

My trial was short. I was informed that I had no valid reason for objecting. Objectors because of religion, because of nationality and similar reasons, were readily understood; a jail sentence to the end of the war was their usual fate. But I admitted that I had no intrinsic objection to fighting; I merely jeered at their holy cause. That was treason unpardonable.

"Sentenced to be shot at sunrise!" the president of the court announced.

The world spun around with me. But only for a second. My self-control came to my aid. With the curious detachment that comes to us in such emergencies, I noted that the court-martial was being held in Professor Vibens's office—that dingy little Victorian room where I had first told my story of traveling by relativity and had first realized that I had come to the t-dimensional world. Apparently it was also to be the last room I was to see in this same world. I had no false hopes that the execution would help me back to my own world, as such things sometimes do in stories. When life is gone, it is gone, whether in one dimension or another. I would be just as dead in the z dimension as in the t dimension.

"Now, Einstein, or never!" I thought. "Come to my aid, O Riemann! O Lobachevski! If anything will save me it will have to be a tensor or a geodesic."

I said it to myself rather ironically. Relativity had brought me here. Could it get me out of this?

Well! Why not?

If the form of a natural law, yea, if a natural object varies with the observer who expresses it, might not the truth and the meaning of the gostak slogan also be a matter of relativity? It was like making the moon ride the treetops again. If I could be a better relativist and put myself in these people's places, perhaps I could understand the gostak. Perhaps I would even be willing to fight for him or it.

The idea struck me suddenly. I must have straightened up and some bright change must have passed over my features, for the guards who led me looked at me curiously and took a firmer grip on me. We had descended the steps of the building and had started down the walk.

Making the moon ride the treetops! That was what I needed now. And that sounded as silly to me as the gostak. And the gostak did not seem so silly. I drew a deep breath and felt very much encouraged. The viewpoint of *relativity* was somehow coming back to me. Necessity manages much. I could understand how one might fight for the idea of a gostak distimming the doshes. I felt almost like telling these men. Relativity is a wonderful thing. They led me up the slope, between the rows of poplars.

Then it all suddenly popped into my head: how I had gotten here by changing my coordinates, insisting to myself that I was going *upward*. Just like making the moon stop and making the trees ride when you are out riding at night. Now I was going upward. In my own world, in the *z* dimension, this same poplar was *down* the slope.

"It's downward!" I insisted to myself. I shut my eyes and imagined the building behind and *above* me. With my eyes shut, it did seem downward. I walked for a long time before opening them. Then I opened them and looked around.

I was at the end of the avenue of poplars. I was surprised. The avenue seemed short. Somehow it had become shortened; I had not expected to reach the end so soon. And where were the guards in olive uniforms? There were none.

I turned around and looked back. The slope extended on backward above me. I had indeed walked downward. There were no guards, and the fresh, new building was on the hill behind me.

Woleshensky stood on the steps.

"Now what do you think of a *t* dimension?" he called out to me.

Woleshensky!

And a *new* building, modern! Vibens's office was in an old Victorian building. What was there in common between Vibens and Woleshensky? I drew a deep breath. The comforting realization spread gratefully over me that I was back in my native dimension. The gostak and the war were somewhere else. Here were peace and Woleshensky.

I hastened to pour out the story to him.

"What does it all mean?" I asked when I was through. "Somehow—vaguely—it seems that it ought to mean something."

"Perhaps," he said in his kind, sage way, "we really exist in four dimensions. A part of us and our world that we cannot see and are not conscious of projects on into another dimension, just like the front edges of the books in the bookcase, turned away from us. You know that the section of a conic cut by the *y* plane looks different from the section of the same conic cut by the *z* plane? Perhaps what you saw was our own world and our own selves intersected by a different set of coordinates. *Relativity*, as I told you in the beginning."

Alas, All Thinking

Harry Bates (1900-1981) is primarily remembered as the first editor of Astounding
Stories *(later* Astounding Science Fiction *and then* Analog*), which eventually became the
most important sf magazine in the world. Under Bates it featured "super-science" stories
of a type that quickly became known as "space opera." As a writer he produced one novel,*
Space Hawk: The Greatest of Interplanetary Adventures *(1952, as "Anthony Gilmore" with
D. W. Hall) and a number of so-far uncollected short stories, the most famous of which is
"Farewell to the Master," which served as the basis for the movie* The Day the Earth Stood
Still.

I

STRICTLY CONFIDENTIAL. (This is dynamite! Be careful who sees it!)

From: Charles Wayland.

To: Harold C. Pendleton, Chairman of the Human Salvage Section of the National
Lunacy Commission.

Subject: Report on the conversations and actions of Harlan T. Frick on the night
of June 7, 1963.

Method: I used the silent pocket dictograph you gave me; and my report is a
literal transcription of the record obtained, with only such additions of my own as
are needed to make it fully intelligible.

Special Notes: (a) The report, backed by the dictograph record, may be considered
as one-third of the proof that your "amateur neurosis detective" Wayland is not
himself a subject for psychopathic observation, since this fantastic report can be
corroborated in all its details by Miles Matson, who was with us that night, and
would be, I think, by Frick himself.

(b) Pending any action by you, I have cautioned both Matson and Frick to
maintain absolute silence with regard to the conversation and events covered. They
may be trusted to comply.

(c) So that you may follow the report more intelligently, I feel that it is necessary
to say here, in advance, that Frick will be proved to be wholly sane, but that never
again may his tremendous talents be utilized for the advancement of science. As

182

his friend, I have to recommend that you give up all hope of salvaging him, and leave him to go his prodigal, pleasure-seeking way alone. You might think of him as a great scientist who has died. He is reasonable, but human, and I see his waste of his life as humanly reasonable. You will see, too.

Report: The amazing events of the evening started in a manner commonplace enough at the Lotus Gardens, where I had made a dinner engagement with Frick and our old mutual friend, Miles Matson, chemist and recent author of an amusing mathematical theory of inverse variables as applied to feminine curves, which Frick had expressed a desire to hear. I should have preferred to observe Frick alone, but was not sure that alone I would be able to hold the interest of his restless, vigorous mind for a third time within two weeks. Ten minutes of boredom and my psychological observations would come to a sudden end, and you would have to find and impress someone else to do your psychological sleuthing.

I got to our reserved table fifteen minutes early to get settled, set up the dictograph in my pocket, and review for the last time my plans. I had three valuable leads. I had discovered (see my reports of May 26th and May 30th) peculiar, invariable, marked emotional reactions in him when the words "brains," "human progress" and "love" were mentioned. I was sure that this was symptomatic. And I hoped to get nearer the roots of his altered behavior pattern by the common method of using a prepared and memorized list of words, remarks and questions, which I would spring on him from time to time.

I could only trust that Frick was not too familiar with psychoanalysis, and so would not notice what I was doing.

I confess that for a moment while waiting I was swept with the feeling that it was hopeless, but I soon roused from that. One can do no more than try, and I was going to try my hardest. With another I might have been tempted to renege, but never with Frick. For he was my old friend of college days, and so eminently worth saving! He was still so young; had so much to give to mankind!

I guessed once more at the things that might have altered his pattern so. A physicist, perhaps the most brilliant and certainly the most promising in the world, enters his laboratory after his graduation from college and for eleven years hardly so much as sticks his nose outside its door. All the while he sends from it a stream of discoveries, new theories and integrations of old laws the like of which has never before been equaled; and then this same physicist walks out of his laboratory, locks the door, shuns the place and for two years devotes himself with casual abandon to such trivialisms of the modern idler as golfing, clothes, travel, fishing, nightclubs and so on. Astounding is a weak word for this spectacle. I could think of nothing that would remotely suit.

Miles Matson arrived a minute early—which was, for him, a phenomenon, and showed how the anticipation of dining with Frick had affected him. Miles is forty-five, short, solid, bald—but then I needn't describe him.

"He'll come?" were his first words, before seating himself on the other side of the table.

"I think so," I assured him, smiling a little at his apparent anxiety. He looked a little relieved, and fished from the jacket of his dinner clothes that abominable pipe he smokes whenever and wherever he pleases, and be damned to frowning head waiters. He lighted it, took a few quick puffs, then leaned back, smiled and volunteered frankly, "Charles, I feel like a little boy about to have dinner with the principal of his school."

I could understand that, for most scientists would feel that way where Frick was concerned. I smiled, too, and chaffed him.

"What—you and that pipe intimidated by a mere playboy?"

"No—by the mystery behind the playboy," was his serious rejoinder. "What's your guess at the solution? Quick, before he comes," he asked earnestly.

I shrugged my shoulders. Miles, of course, was not in my confidence.

"Could it be a woman?" he went on. "I haven't heard of any one woman. A disappointment in his work? Some spoiled-child reaction? Is he crazy? What's made the change?"

If I only knew!

"Frick, further than any man alive, has touched out to the infinite unknowable," he continued almost grumbling, "and I want to know how such a man can trade his tremendous future for a suit of evening clothes!"

"Perhaps he is just relaxing a little," I suggested with a smile.

"Ah, of course—relaxing," he answered sarcastically. "For two years!"

I knew at once Frick had heard what we had been saying, for at that moment I looked up and around just in time to see him, lean and graceful in his dinner clothes, his mouth twisted with amusement, stepping past the head waiter to his place at the table. Miles and I rose; and we must have shown our confusion, for one simply did not mention that topic in Frick's hearing. But he showed no offense—indeed, he seemed in unusually good spirits—for he lightly acknowledged our greeting, waved us back in our places, and, seating himself, added to our dialogue.

"Yes, for two years. And will for forty-two more!"

This opening of the conversation threw me unexpectedly off stride, but I remembered to switch on the dictograph, and then seized the opportunity to ask what otherwise I would never have dared.

"Why?"

Still he showed no offense, but instead, surprisingly, indulged in a long, low chuckle that seemed to swell up as from a spring of inexhaustible deliciousness. He answered cryptically, bubblingly, enjoying our puzzlement with every word.

"Because Humpty Dumpty had a great fall. Because thought is withering, and sensation sweet. Because I've recovered my sense of humor. Because 'why' is a dangerous word, and makes people unhappy. Because I have had a glimpse of the most horrible cerebral future. Yes!" He laughed, paused for a moment, then said in a lower voice with dramatic impressiveness, "Would you believe it? I have terminated the genus Homo Sapiens."

II

He was not drunk, and, as you will see, not crazy—though I would not have bet any money on it just then. His mood was only one of extraordinary good humor.

Vastly amused at our reaction to his wild words, he allowed himself to shock us, and did it again and again. I might say here that it is my opinion that all the revelations of the night were, in the main, the result of Frick's sudden notion to shock us, and that no credit whatever is due me and my intended plan of psychological attack.

Miles' face showed blank dismay. Frick ceased chuckling and, his gray eyes gleaming, enjoyed our discomfiture in quiet for a moment. Then he added, "No. Strictly speaking, there is one piece of unfinished business. A matter of one murder. I was sort of dallying with the idea of committing it tonight, and finishing off the whole affair. Would you two like to be in on it?"

Miles looked as if he would like to excuse himself. He coughed, smiled unhappily, glanced doubtfully at me. I at once decided that if Frick was going to attempt murder, I was going to be on hand to prevent it. I suppose that the desperate resolution showed in my face, for Frick, looking at me, laughed outright. Miles then revived enough to smile wanly at Frick and suggest he was joking. He added, "I'm surprised that anyone with the brains you have should make so feeble a joke!"

At the word "brains" Frick almost exploded.

"Brains!" he exclaimed. "Not me! I'm dumb! Dumb as the greasy-haired saxophone player over there! I understand that I used to have brains, but that's all over; it's horrible; let's not think about it. I tell you I'm dumb, now—normally, contentedly dumb!"

Miles did not know how to understand Frick any more than did I. He reminded him, "You used to have an I.Q. of 248—"

"I've changed!" Frick interrupted. He was still vehement, but I could see that he was full of internal amusement.

"But no healthy person's intelligence can drop much in the course of a few years," Miles objected strongly.

"Yes—I'm dumb!" Frick reiterated.

My opportunities lay in keeping him on the subject. I asked him, "Why have you come to consider the possession of brains such an awful thing?"

"'Ah, to have seen what I have seen, know what I know'!" he quoted.

Miles showed irritation. "Well, then, let's call him dumb!" he said, looking at me. "To insist on such a stupid jest!"

I took another turn at arousing Frick. "You are, of course, speaking ironically out of some cryptic notion that exists only in your own head; but whatever this notion, it is absurd. Brains in quantity are the exclusive possession of the human race. They have inspired all human progress; they have made us what we are today, masters of the whole animal kingdom, lords of creation. Two other things have helped—the human hand and human love; but even above these ranks the human brain. You are only ridiculous when you scoff at its value."

"Oh, love and human progress!" Frick exclaimed, laughing. "Charles, I tell you brains will be the ruination of the human race," he answered with great delight.

"Brains will be the salvation of the human race!" Miles contradicted with heat.

"You make a mistake, a very common mistake, Miles," Frick declared, more seriously. "Charles is of course right in placing man at the top of creation, but you're very wrong in assuming he will always remain there. Consider. Nature made the cell, and after a time the cell became a fish; and that fish was the lord of creation. The very top. For a while. For just a few million years. Because one day a fish crawled out of the sea and set about becoming a reptile. He became a magnificent one. Tyrannosaurus Rex was fifty feet long, twenty high; he had teeth half a foot long, and feet armed with claws that were terrible. No other creature could stand against him; he had speed, size, power and ferocity; *he* became the lord of creation.

"What happened to the fish? He had been the lord of creation, but, well, he never got anywhere. What of Tyrannosaurus Rex? He, too, was the lord of creation, but he, alas, is quite, quite extinct.

"Nature tried speed with the fish, then size with the saurians. Neither worked; the fish got stuck, the saurian died off. But did she quit experimenting at that? Not at all—she tried mobility, and we got the monkey. The first monkey swung from limb to limb screeching, 'I am the lord of creation!' and, by Jove, he was! But he could not know that one day, after a few millions of years, one of his poor relations would go down on the ground, find fire, invent writing, assume clothing, devise modern inconveniences, discover he had lost his tail and crow, 'Behold, I am the lord of creation!'

"Why did this tailless monkey have his turn? Because his makeup featured brains? You will bellow yes—but I hear Mother Nature laughing at you. For you are only her *latest* experiment! The lord of creation! That you are—but only for a little while! Only for a few million years!"

Frick paused, his eyes flashed, his nostrils distended contemptuously. "How dare man be so impertinent as to assume nature has stopped experimenting!" he exclaimed at length.

In the quiet which followed this surprising outburst I could see Miles putting two and two together. But he took his time before speaking. He relighted his pipe and gave it a good, fiery start before removing it from his mouth and saying, almost in a drawl, "It amounts to this, then. Anticipating that nature is about to scrap brains and try again along new lines, you choose to attempt immortality by denying your own undoubted brains and trying to be the first to jump in the new direction."

Frick only laughed. "Wrong again, Miles," he said. "I'm just standing pat."

"To go back a little," I said to Frick; "it seems to me you're assuming far too much when you tell us that the human race is not the last, but only the most recent of nature's experiments."

The man acted almost shocked. "But have you forgotten what I told you just a little while ago? I said I have *terminated* the genus Homo Sapiens!"

Miles snorted with disgust. I was alarmed. Miles tried sarcasm.

"Have you and Mother Nature already decided, then, what the next lord of creation is to be?"

"I myself have nothing to say about it," Frick replied with assumed naiveté, "nor do I know what it will be. I could find out, but I doubt if I ever shall. It's much more fun not to know—don't you think? Though, if I had to guess," he added, "I should say she will feature instinct."

This was too much for Miles. He started to rise, saying, as he pushed his chair back, "This is enough. You're either crazy or else you're a conceited fool! Personally, I think it's both!"

But Frick held him with a gesture, and in a voice wholly sincere said, "Sit down, Miles; keep your shirt on. You know very well I neither lie nor boast. I promise to prove everything I have said."

Miles resumed his seat and looked at Frick almost sneeringly as he went on.

"You're quite right about my being a fool, though. I was one; oh, a most gorgeous fool! But I am not conceited. I am so little conceited that I offer to show you myself in what must surely be the most ridiculous situation that a jackass or a monkey without a tail has ever been in. I'll exchange my dignity for your good opinion; you'll see that I'm not crazy; and then we'll have the most intelligent good laugh possible to Genus Homo. Yes? Shall we?"

Miles gave me a look which clearly expressed his doubt of Frick's sanity. Frick, seeing, chuckled and offered another inducement.

"And I'll throw in, incidentally, a most interesting murder!"

Our friend was completely disgusted. "We came here to eat," he said. "Let's get it over with." And with the words he picked up the menu which had been lying in front of him all this time. Frick looked at me.

"I'm not hungry," he said. "Are you?"

I wasn't. I shook my head.

"Shall we two go, then?"

I hesitated. I was not overanxious to accompany, alone, a madman on a mission of murder. But I caught Miles' eye, and like the noble he is, he said he'd come too. Frick smiled softly.

III

Ten minutes later we had made the short flight along the north shore to Glen Cove, where Frick has his estate, and were escorted by him into a small, bare room on the second floor of the laboratory building which adjoins his beautiful home.

While we stood there wondering, Frick went into an adjoining room and returned with two chairs, and then, in two more trips, with a third chair and a tray on which rested a large thermos bottle and a tea service for three. The chairs he arranged facing each other in an intimate group, and the tray he set on the floor by the chair he was to take himself.

"First I have to tell a rather long story," he explained. "The house would be more comfortable, but this room will be more convenient."

Frick was now a changed man. His levity of before was gone; tense, serious lines appeared on his rugged face; his great head lowered with the struggle to arrange thoughts that were difficult, and perhaps painful, to him. When he spoke, it was softly, in a voice likewise changed.

My dictograph was still turned on.

"Charles, Miles," Frick began, "forgive me for my conduct back in the Gardens. I had so much on my mind, and you were so smugly skeptical, that the inclination to overpower you with what I know was irresistible. I had not expected to make any of these revelations to you. I offered to on impulse; but do not fear, I shall not regret it. I think—I see now that I have been carrying a very heavy load—

"What I have to say would fill a large book, but I will make it as short as I can. You will not believe me at first, but please be patient, for proof will eventually be forthcoming. Every single thing I said to you is true, even to the murder I must commit—"

He paused, and seemed to relax, as if tired. Unknown black shadows closed over my heart. Miles watched him closely, quite motionless. We waited. Frick rubbed the flat of his hand slowly over his eyes and forehead, then let it drop.

"No," he said at length, "I have never been conceited. I don't think so. But there was a time when I was very proud of my intelligence. I worked; I accomplished things that seemed to be important; I felt myself a leader in the rush of events. Work was enough, I thought; brain was the prime tool of life; and with my brain I dared try anything. Anything! I dared try to assemble the equation of a device that would enable me to peer into the future! And when I thought I had it, I started the construction of that device! I never finished it, and I never shall, now; but the attempt brought Pearl to me—

"Yes," he added, as if necessary that he convince himself, "I am certain that had I not attempted that, Pearl would not have come. Back through the ages she had somehow felt me out—don't ask me how, for I don't know—and through me chose to enter for a brief space this, our time.

"I was as surprised as you would have been. I was working in this very room, though then it was twice as large and fairly cluttered with clumsy apparatus I have since had removed. I had been working feverishly for months; I was unshaven, red-eyed and dirty—and there, suddenly, she was. Over there, beyond that door at which I'm pointing. She was in a golden-glowing cylinder whose bottom hung two feet off the floor. For a moment she stood suspended there; and then the glow disappeared and she stepped through to the floor.

"You do not believe me? Well, of course, I don't expect you to. But there will be proof. There will be proof.

"I was surprised, but somehow I wasn't much frightened. The person of my visitor was not intimidating. She was just a barefooted young woman, very slender, of average height, clad in a shiny black shift which reached her knees. I cannot say she was well formed. Her body was too thin, her hips too narrow, her head too large. And she was miles from being pretty. Her hair and eyes were all right; they were brown; but her face was plain and flat, with an extraordinary and forbidding expression of dry intellectuality. The whole effect of her was not normal, yet certainly not weird; she was just peculiar, different—baroque.

"She spoke to me in English! In nonidiomatic English with the words run together and an accent that was atrocious! She asked severely, 'Do you mind too much this intrusion of mine?'

"'Why—why no!' I said when I had recovered from the shock of the sound of her speech. 'But are you real, or just an illusion?'

"'I do not know,' she replied. 'That is a tremendous problem. It has occupied the attention of our greatest minds for ages. Excuse me, sir.' And with these last words she calmly sat herself down on the floor, right where she was, and appeared to go off into deep thought!

"You can imagine my astonishment! She sat there for a full two minutes, while I gaped at her in wonder. When she rose again to her feet she finished with, 'I do not know. It is a tremendous problem.'

"I began to suspect that a trick was being played on me, for all this was done with the greatest seriousness.

"'Perhaps there is a magician outside,' I suggested.

"'I am the magician,' she informed me.

"'Oh!' I said ironically. 'I understand everything now.'

"'Or no, fate is the magician,' she went on as if in doubt. 'Or no, I am—a very deep problem—' Whereupon she sat down on the floor and again went off into meditation!

"I stepped around her, examining her from all angles, and, since she was oblivious to everything outside of herself, I made a cursory examination of the thing she had come in on. It looked simple enough—a flat, plain, circular box, maybe four feet in diameter and six inches deep, made of some sort of dull-green metal. Fixed to its center, and sticking vertically upward, was a post of the same stuff capped with a plate containing a number of dials and levers. Around the edge of the upper surface of the box was a two-inch bevel of what seemed to be yellow glass. And that was all—except that the thing continued to remain fixed in the air two feet off the floor!

"I began to get a little scared. I turned back to the girl and again looked her over from all sides. She was so deep in her thoughts that I dared to touch her. She was real, all right!

"My touch brought her to her feet again.

"'You have a larger head than most men,' she informed me.

"'Who are you, anyway?' I asked with increasing amazement. She gave me a name that it took me two days to memorize, so horrible was its jumble of sounds. I'll just say here that I soon gave her another—Pearl—because she was such a baroque—and by that name I always think of her.

"'How did you get in?' I demanded.

"She pointed to the box.

"'But what is it?' I wanted to know.

"'You have no name for it,' she replied. 'It goes to yesterday, to last year, to the last thousand years—like that.'

"'You mean it's a time traveler?' I asked, astounded. 'That you can go back and forth in time?'

"'Yes,' she answered. 'I stopped to see you, for you are something like me.'

"'You wouldn't misinform me?' I asked sarcastically, feeling I must surely be the victim of some colossal practical joke.

"'Oh, no, I would not misinform you,' she replied aridly.

"I was very skeptical. 'What do you want here?' I asked.

"'I should like you to show me the New York of your time. Will you, a little?'

"'If you'll take me for a ride on that thing, and it works, I'll show you anything you want,' I answered, still more skeptical.

"She was glad to do it.

"'Come,' she commanded. I stepped gingerly up on the box. 'Stand here, and hold on to this,' she went on, indicating the rod in the center. I did so, and she stepped up to position just opposite me, and very close. I was conscious of how vulnerable I was if a joke was intended.

"'You must not move,' she warned me. I assured her I would not. 'Then, when do you want to go?'

"'A week back,' I said at random, with, in spite of everything, a creeping sensation going up and down my spine.

"'That will do,' she decided; and again she warned me not to move. Then her hands went to the controls.

"A golden veil sprang up around us and the room grew dim through it, then disappeared. A peculiar silence came over me, a silence that seemed not so much outside of me as within. There was just a second of this, and then I was again looking into the room through the golden veil. Though it dimmed the light I could clearly make out the figure of a man stretched full length on the floor working on the underpart of a piece of apparatus there.

"'It's I!' I exclaimed, and every cell in my body leaped at the miracle of it. That this could be! That I could be standing outside of myself looking at myself! That last week had come back, and that I, who already belonged to a later time, could be back there again in it! As I peered, thoughts and emotions all out of control, I saw happen a thing that stilled the last thin voice of inward doubt.

"The man on the floor rolled over, sat up, turned his face—*my* face—toward us, and, deep in thought, gently fingered a sore place on his head—from a bump that no one, positively, knew anything about. Trickery seemed excluded.

"But a contradictory thing occurred to me. I asked Pearl, 'Why doesn't he see us, since he's looking right this way? I never saw anything at the time.'

"'It is only in the next stage toward arriving that we can be seen,' she explained with her hands still on the controls. 'At this moment I'm keeping us unmaterialized. This stage is extremely important. If we tried to materialize within some solid, and not in free space, we should explode.

"'Now, let us return,' she said. 'Hold still.'

"The room disappeared; the peculiar silence returned; then I saw the room again, dim through the golden veil. Abruptly the veil vanished and the room came clear; and we stepped down on the floor on the day we had left.

"My legs were trembling so as to be unreliable. I leaned against a table, and my amazing visitor, as it seemed her habit, sat down on the floor.

"That was my introduction to Pearl."

IV

Frick rose and walked to the far corner of the room and back. The thoughts in his mind were causing some internal disturbance, that was obvious.

I prayed that my dictograph was working properly!

When Frick sat down again he was calmer. Not for long could any emotion sweep out of control his fine mind and dominating will. With a faint smile and an outflung gesture of his arm he said, "That was the beginning!"

Again he paused, and ended it with one of his old chuckles. "I showed Pearl New York. I showed her!

"Charles, Miles, there is just too much," he resumed at a tangent, shaking his head. "There is the tendency to go off into details, but I'll try to avoid it. Maybe some other time. I want to be brief, just now.

"Well, I got her some clothes and showed her New York City. It was a major experience. For she was not your ordinary out-of-towner, but a baroque out of far future time. She had learned our language and many of our customs; she was most amazingly mental; and yet, under the difficult task of orienting herself to what she called our crudeness, she exhibited a most delicious naiveté.

"I showed her my laboratory and explained the things I had done. She was not much interested in that. I showed her my house, others too, and explained how we of the twentieth century live.

"'Why do you waste your time acquiring and operating gadgets?' she would ask. She liked that word 'gadgets'; it became her favorite. By it she meant electricity, changes of clothing, flying, meals in courses, cigarettes, variety of furniture, even the number of rooms in our homes. She'd say, 'You are a superior man for this time; why don't you throw out all your material luxuries so as to live more completely in the realms of the mind?'

"I would ask her what standard she judged our civilization against; but whenever I did that she'd always go obscure, and say she guessed we were too primitive to appreciate the higher values. She consistently refused to describe the sort of civilization she had come from; though, toward the end, she began promising me that if I were a good guide, and answered all her questions, she might—only might— take me there to see it. You can imagine I was a good guide!

"But meanwhile, I got nothing but my own inferences; and what an extraordinary set I acquired from her questions and reactions! You make your own set as I go along!

"I showed her New York. She'd say, 'But why do the people hurry so? Is it really necessary for all those automobiles to keep going and coming? Do the people *like* to live in layers? If the United States is as big as you say it is, why do you build such high buildings? What is your reason for having so few people rich, so many people poor?' It was like that. And endless.

"I took her to restaurants. 'Why does everybody take a whole hour just to eat?' I told her that people enjoyed eating; it seemed not to have occurred to her. 'But if they spent only a few minutes at it they'd have that much more time for meditation!' I couldn't but agree.

"I took her to a nightclub. 'Why do all those men do all the carrying, and those others all the eating?' I explained that the first were waiters, the latter guests. 'Will the guests have a turn at carrying?' I told her I thought so, some day.

"'Is that man a singing waiter?'

"'No, only a crooner.'

"'Why do those men with the things make such an awful noise?'

"'Because dance bands get paid for making it.'

"'It must be awfully hard on them.' I told her I hoped so. 'Are those people doing what you call dancing?'

"'Yes.'

"'Do they like to do it?'

"'Yes.'

"'The old ones, too?'

"'I doubt it.'

"'Then why do they do it?' I didn't know. At the end she asked me almost poignantly, 'Don't they *ever* spend any time in meditation?' and I had to express my doubts.

"In our little jaunts it became increasingly clear to her that there was very little meditation being done in New York. It was the biggest surprise that our civilization gave her.

"However, she continued to indulge her peculiar habit of going off into meditation when something profound, or interesting, or puzzling came to her attention; and the most extraordinary thing about it was that she had to sit down at it, no matter where she was. If there was a chair handy, all right, but if not, she would plunk right down on the floor, or, outside, even in the street! This was not so bad when we were alone, but once it happened under Murphy's flagpole in Union Square as we stood observing the bellowings of a soap-box orator, and once again in Macy's, where we lingered a moment listening to a demonstrator with the last word possible in beauty preparations. It was quite embarrassing! Toward the end I grew adept in detecting signs of the coming descent and was fairly successful in holding her up!

"In all the six days I spent showing Pearl New York, not once did she show any emotion other than that of intellectual curiosity; not once did she smile; not once did she so much as alter the dry expression on her face. And *this*, my friends, was the creature who became a student and an exponent of love!

"It bears on my main theme, so I will tell you in some detail about her experiences with love, or what she thought was love.

"During the first three days she did not mention the word; and from what I know of her now, I can say with surety that she was holding herself back. During those three days she had seen one performance of *Romeo and Juliet,* had read two romantic novels containing overwhelming love themes, had observed everywhere the instinct for young people to seek each other out, had seen two couples kiss while dancing, had seen the fleet come in and the sailors make for Riverside Drive and had heard I don't know how many hours of crooning on radio broadcasts.

"After all this, one day in my drawing room, she suddenly asked me, 'What is this love that everyone is always talking about?'

"Never dreaming of the part love was to play between us, I answered simply that it was nature's device to make mature humans attractive to each other and ensure the arrival of offspring and the maintenance of the race. That, it seems, is what she thought it was, but what she couldn't understand was why everybody made such a to-do about it. Take kissing, for instance. That was when a male and a female pushed each other on the lips. Did they like that? I assured her they did. Was it, since they held it so long, a kind of meditation? Well, no, not exactly. Would I try it with her?

"Don't smile yet, you two—that's nothing! Wait! Anyway, you wouldn't want me to spoil my chances of being taken for a visit to her own time, would you?

"Well, we kissed. She stood on tiptoe, her dry face looking up at mine, her arms stiffly at her sides, while I bent down, my sober face looking down at hers, and my arms stiffly at my sides. We both pushed; our lips met; and we stayed that way a little. Then, almost maintaining contact, Pearl asked me, 'Is it supposed to sort of scrape?' I assured her it was—something like a scrape. After a moment she said, 'Then there's a great mystery here, somewhere—' And damned if she didn't squat right down on the floor and go off into a think! I couldn't keep a straight face, so I bounced out of the room; and when I returned several minutes later there she was still meditating on her kiss. *O tempora!*

"That kiss happened on the third day, and she stayed six, and for the remainder of her visit in our time she said not one thing more about this thing called love—which told me it was a mystery always on her mind, for she asked questions by the score about every other conceivable thing.

"But I also knew from another thing. For the three days following that kiss she went innumerable times to my radio and tuned in dance and vocal programs whose songs would, of course, inevitably be about love. She fairly saturated herself with love's and above's, star's and are's, blue's and you's, June's and moon's. What a horrible flock of mangy clichés must have come to flap around in her mental—all too mental—mind! What peculiar notions about love they must have given her!

"But enough of that phase. You have an idea. You have seen Pearl in New York, tasting of love. Six nights to the very hour after she first appeared to me I stood again on the round base of the time traveler, and this time I accompanied her forward to her time. I do not know how far in the future that was, but I estimate it to be around three million years."

V

Frick paused, rose and, without asking us if we wanted any, served some cold tea from the thermos bottle by his chair. This time we were glad to have it.

By then I was as close to fully believing as was, I think, Miles. We wasted little time over the tea, but, considerably refreshed and extremely eager with anticipations of what would follow, leaned forward and were again lost in Frick's extraordinary story.

"The trip forward took what seemed to be only half a minute, and I believe it might have been instantaneous but for the time needed to bring the machine to a stop on exactly the right day. As before, the passage was a period of ineffable silence; but I was aware that all the time Pearl fingered the controls. Very suddenly I saw we were in a dimly lighted room; with equal suddenness the golden screen vanished and normal daylight took its place. We had arrived.

"I stepped off the traveler and looked curiously about. We were in a small place, the walls of which were partitions which projected perhaps ten feet up toward a very high ceiling. Everything I could see was made of an ugly, mud-yellow metallic substance, and everything seemed to be built on the square. Light entered from large windows on all sides. The section of the great room in which we had arrived was bare of everything but our traveler. I saw that this time it rested firmly on the floor—a very dirty floor.

"I suppose it would be superfluous to paint the tremendous state of excitement and curiosity I was in. To be the only man of our time to have voyaged forward! To be the only one allowed to see the human race in marvelous maturity! What honor, glory, luck, that such an unmerited distinction should fall upon me! Every atom of my body was living and tingling at that moment. I was going to drink in and remember everything that crossed my senses.

"I was full of questions at once, but Pearl had warned me not to talk. She had told me that there were several caretakers from whose sight I was to remain hidden; and now the first thing she did was to put her finger to her lips and peer down the corridor outside. She listened a moment, then stepped out and beckoned me to follow.

"I did—and all but exclaimed out loud to see that the corridor was carpeted with fine dust fully an inch deep!

"How could this be in an important building of so advanced an age? For surely that building was important, to house, as it did, so marvelous a device as the traveler!

"But I had no time for wonderment, for Pearl led me rapidly toward the far side of the great room. At our every step clouds of dust billowed out on each side, so that a hasty glance behind showed such diffusion of it that all there was hidden. The corridor was quite wide, and ran lengthwise of the building on one side of the center. At varying distances we passed doorways, all of them closed, and at the end we turned to the left, to come quickly to a high, wide door. It was open, and golden sunlight was shining through. For a second Pearl held me back while she peered around the edge, then, taking me by the hand, she led me out into our world of the future.

"What would you have expected to see, Charles? You, Miles? Towering buildings, perhaps, transversed on their higher levels by aerial traffic ways? And crowds of people strangely mannered and curiously dressed? And mysterious-powered aerial carriers? And parks? And flowers? And much use of metal and synthetic marble? Well, of these there was nothing. My eyes looked out over a common, ordinary, flat, 1963 field. In the distance were some patches of trees; nearby were some wild grass, low bushes and millions of daisies; and that was all!

"My first thought was that Pearl had made some mistake in our time of destination, and when I sought her face, and saw that this was only what she expected, I grew alarmed. She misread my thoughts, though, and saying 'Don't be afraid' led me along a wide walk to a corner of the building, where she peeped around the edge, and, apparently satisfied with what she found, stepped forth and motioned me to follow. Then she spoke:

"'Here we are,' she said.

"Before me stretched the same sort of landscape as on the other quarter, except that here the immediate field was tenanted with a square block of large metallic boxes, six on a side, and each separated by about ten yards from its neighbors.

"I suppose I stood there and gaped. I didn't understand, and I told Pearl as much. Her tone in replying came as near surprise as I ever heard it.

"'Not understand?' she asked. 'What do you mean? Isn't this just about what you expected?'

"Eventually I found words. 'But where is your city?' I asked.

"'There,' she answered, with a gesture of her arm toward the boxes.

"'But the people!' I exclaimed.

"'They are inside.'

"'But I—I—there's something wrong!' I stammered. 'Those things are no city, and they couldn't hold ten people apiece!'

"'They hold only one apiece,' she informed me with dignity.

"I was completely flabbergasted. 'Then—then your total population is—'

"'Just thirty-six, out here; or, rather, thirty-five, for one of us has just died.'

"I thought I saw the catch. 'But how many have you that aren't out here?'

"'Just us younger ones—four, including myself,' she answered simply. She added, 'And, of course, the two who are not yet born.'

"All before this had turned my head; her last statement came near turning my stomach. Clutching at straws, I blurted out, 'But this is just a small community; the chief centers of your population lie elsewhere?'

"'No,' she corrected levelly, 'this is the only center of our civilization. All human beings are gathered here.' She fixed me with her dry gaze. 'How primitive you are!' she said, as a zoologist might, looking at a threadworm. 'I see that you expected numbers, mere numbers. But I suppose that a comparative savage like you might be expected to prefer quantity of life to quality of life.

"'We have here quality,' she went on with noble utterance, 'the finest of the finest, for ten thousand generations. Nature has need of quantity in her lower orders, but in allowing the perfection of such towering supermen as are my friends out here she has indulged in the final luxury of quality.

"'Nor is that all. With quality we have at last achieved simplicity; and in the apotheosis of humanity these two things are the ultimates.'

"All I could do was mumble that simplicity was too weak a word."

Frick stopped here, laughed, and rose. "She had my mind down and its shoulders touching! And from that moment—I assure you, my friends—the whole thing began to amuse me."

He took a few steps about the room, laughing silently; then, leaning with one shoulder against the wall, he went on.

"Pearl was on an awfully high horse, there, for a moment, but she soon dismounted and considered what she might offer for my entertainment. She expressed polite regret that her civilization contained so little for me to see with my eyes. She implied that the vast quantities of intellectual activity going on would be far past my understanding.

"I asked, then, if there was any way I might have a peep at their quality group in action; and to this she replied that her countrymen never came together in groups, and neither did they indulge in actions, but that it would be easy to show me one or two of the leading citizens.

"I of course told her I did not want her to run a risk of getting in trouble, but she assured me there was no danger of that. The guardians of the place—they were the three other 'younger ones' she had just mentioned—were quiet somewhere, and as for the adults, 'They,' she said, 'will be able neither to see nor hear you.'

"Well, she showed me two. And merciful heavens!"

Frick laughed so that for a moment he could not go on. Miles by now was reflecting Frick's every mood, and would smile in anticipation when he laughed. I suppose I was doing the same. We were both completely under Frick's spell.

"She escorted me openly across the field to the nearest box, and I remember that on the way I got a burr in my ankle which I stopped to remove. I found from close up that the boxes were about ten feet square and made of the same ugly yellow metal used in the big building. The upper part of each side had a double row of narrow horizontal slits, and in the middle of each front side there was a closely fitted door. I was remembering Pearl's promise that they would be able neither to see nor to hear me, so I was alarmed when without ceremony she opened the door and half pushed me in.

"What I saw! I was so shocked that, as Pearl told me later, I gasped out an involuntary 'Oh!' and fairly jumped backward. Had she not been right behind and held me, I might have run. As it was I remained, hypnotized by sight of what met my eyes, trembling, and I think gagging.

"I saw a man; or some kind of a man. He sat right in front of me, nude from the waist up, and covered as the floor was covered from the waist down. How shall I adequately describe him!

"He was in some ways like an unwrapped mummy, except that a fallen-in mummy presents a fairly respectable appearance. And then he was something like a spider— a spider with only three legs. And again, looking quickly, he was all one gigantic head, or at least a great mass on whose parchment surface appeared a little round two-holed knoll where the nose customarily is, lidded caverns where the eyes belong, small craters where the ears commonly are, and, on the underside, a horrible, wrinkled, half-inch slit, below which more parchment backed almost horizontally to a three-inch striated and, in places, bumpy pipe.

"By not the slightest movement of any kind did the monster show he knew I was there. He sat on a high dais; his arms were only bones converging downward; his body, only half the usual thickness, showed every rib and even, I think, the front side of some of his vertebrae; and his pipe of a neck, unable alone to support his head, gave most of that job to two curved metal pieces that came out of the wall.

"He had a musty smell.

"And, final horror, the stuff that covered him to the waist was dust; and there were two inches of dust on the top of his head and lesser piles of it on every little upper surface!

VI

"It was horrible; but I swear that as I stood there goggling at him he began to strike me funny. It grew on me, until I think I should have laughed in the old gent's face had I not been restrained by a slight fear that he might in some way be dangerous.

"Goodness knows what all I thought of as I stood there. I know I eventually asked Pearl, for caution's sake:

"'You're sure he can't see or hear me?'

"She told me he could not.

"I was not surprised; he looked too old for such strenuous activities. I scrutinized him, inch by inch. After a little I announced with conviction, 'He's dead! I'm sure of it!'

"She assured me he was not.

"'But look at the dust! He can't have moved for years!'

"'Why should he move?' she asked.

"That stopped me for a little.

"'But—but,' I stammered eventually, 'he's as good as dead! He's not doing anything!'

"'He certainly is doing something,' was her dignified correction. 'He's meditating.'

"All I could think to say was 'Good night!'

"At that, Pearl turned on me reproachfully. 'Your attitude is bestial,' she said. 'I have done you the honor of bringing you to witness the highest flowering of the human race, and you act like a pig. Life can hold nothing more beautiful than this man you see here; he is the ultimate in human progress, one who is in truth perfection, whose every taint of animal desire has been cleaned away, who is the very limit in the simplicity of his life and the purity of his thoughts and intentions.'

"Not to miss anything, she added, 'He embodies the extension of every quality that makes for civilization; he's reached the logical end of man's ambitious climb from the monkey.'

"'My Lord!' I said. 'Here's a dead end!'

"'For myself, I sum it all in five words,' she went on nobly: ''He leads the mental life.'

"After a little my emotions suddenly got out of control. 'Does—does he *like* it?' I blurted out. But that was a mistake. I tried, 'Do you mean to imply he spends his life sitting here and thinking?'

"'Pure living and high thinking,' she put it.

"'No living, I'm thinking!' I retorted. 'What does he think of?'

"'He is probably our greatest aesthetician,' she answered proudly. 'It's a pity you can't know the trueness and beauty of his formulations.'

"'How do you know they are beautiful?' I asked with my primitive skepticism.

"'I can hear his thoughts, of course,' was the answer.

"This surprising statement started me on another string of questions, and when I got through I had learned the following: This old bird and the others could not hear me think because my intellectual wave length was too short for their receivers; that Pearl, when talking and thinking with me, was for the same reason below their range; and that Pearl shared with the old guys the power of tuning in or out of such private meditations or general conversations as might be going on.

"'We utilize this telepathic faculty,' Pearl added, 'in the education of our young. Especially the babies, while they are still unborn. The adults take turns in tutoring them for their cells. I, it happens, was a premature baby—only eleven months— so I missed most of my prenatal instruction. That's why I'm different from the others here, and inferior. Though they say I was bad material all the way back from conception.'

"Her words made my stomach turn over, and the sight of that disproportioned cadaver didn't help it any, either. Still I stood my ground and did my best to absorb every single detail.

"While so engaged I saw one of the most fantastic things yet. The nasty little slit of a mouth under our host's head slowly separated until it revealed a dark and gummy opening; and as it reached its maximum I heard a click behind my back and jumped to one side just in time to see a small gray object shoot from a box fastened to the wall, and, after a wide arc through the air, make a perfect landing in the old gentleman's mouth!

"'He felt the need for some sustenance,' Pearl explained. 'Those pellets contain his food and water. Naturally he needs very little. They are ejected by a mechanism sensitive to the force of his mind waves.'

"'Let me out,' I said.

"We went out into the clean, warm sunshine. How sweet that homely field looked! I sat down on the grass and picked a daisy. It was not one whit different from those of my own time, at home.

"Pearl sat down beside me.

"'We now have an empty cell,' she said, 'but one of our younger men is ready to fill it. He has been waiting until we installed a new and larger food receptacle— one that will hold enough for seventy-five years without refilling. We've just finished. It is, of course, the young of our community who take care of the elders by preparing the food pellets and doing what other few chores are necessary. They do this until they outgrow the strength of their bodies and can no longer get around— when they have the honor of maturity and may take their place in one of the cells.'

"'But how in the devil do creatures like—like that in there, manage to have children?' I had to ask.

"'Oh, I know what you mean, but you've got the wrong idea,' came her instant explanation. 'That matter is attended to while they are still comparatively young. From the very beginning the young are raised in incubators.'

"I have always had a quick stomach—and she insisted on trying to prove it!

"'With us, it takes fifteen months,' she went along. 'We have two underway at present. Would you like to see them?'

"I told her that I would see them, but that I would not like it. 'But first,' I asked, 'if you don't mind, show me one other of these adults of yours. I—I—I can't get over it. I still can't quite believe it.'

"She said she would. A woman. And at that we got up and she led me to the next cell.

"I did not go in. I stood outside and took one look at the inmate through the door. Horrible! Female that she was, it was at that moment I first thought what a decent thing it would be—yes, and how pleasant—to hold each one of the necks of those cartoons of humankind in the ring of my two strong hands for a moment—

"But I was a trusted visitor, and such thoughts were not to be encouraged. I asked Pearl to lead on to the incubators.

"We had left the block of cells and were rounding the corner of the building when Pearl stopped and pulled me back. Apparently she had gotten some thought warning just in time, for in a moment three outlandish figures filed out of the very door of the big building that we had been making for. All wore black shiny shifts like Pearl's, and they were, very obviously, young flowers of Genus Homo in full perfection.

"The first was the size, but had not nearly the emaciated proportions, of the old aesthetician, and his great bald head wabbled precariously on his outrageous neck as he made his uncertain way along. The second—a girl, I think—was smaller, younger, stronger, but she followed her elder at a respectful distance in the same awful manner. The third in the procession was a male, little more than a baby, and he half stumbled after the others in his own version of their caricature of a walk.

"They walked straight out into the field; and do you know, that little fellow, pure monster in appearance, ugly as ultimate sin, did a thing that brought tears to my eyes. As he came to the edge of the walk and stepped off into the grass, he bent laboriously over and plucked a daisy—and looked at it in preoccupied fashion as he toddled on after the others!

"I was much relieved that they had not discovered us, and so was Pearl. As soon as they were a safe distance away, she whispered to me, 'I had to be careful. They all can see, and the two younger ones still can hear.'

"'What are they going to do out there?' I asked.

"'Take a lesson in metaphysics,' she answered, and almost with her words the first one sat down thoughtfully out in the middle of the field—to be followed in turn by the second and even the little fellow!

"'The tallest one,' Pearl informed me, 'is the one who is to take a place in the vacant cell. He had better do it soon. It's becoming dangerous for him to walk about. His neck's too weak.'

"With care we edged our way up and into the building, but this time Pearl conducted me along the corridor on the other side. The dust there was as thick as in the first, except along the middle, where many footprints testified to much use. We came to the incubators.

"There I saw them. I saw them; I made myself look at them; but I tell you it was an effort! I—I think, if you don't mind, I won't describe them. You know—my personal peculiarity. They were wonderful. Curvings of glass and tubes. Two, in them. Different stages. I left right away; went back to the front door; and in a few minutes felt better.

"Pearl, of course, had come after me and try to take me back; and I noticed an amusing thing. The sight of those coming babies had had a sort of maternal effect on her! I swear it! For she *would* talk about them; and before long she timidly—ah, but as dryly as ever!—suggested that we attempt a kiss!—only she forgot the word and called it a scrape. Ye gods! Well, we scraped—exactly as before—and that, my friends, was the incident which led straight and terribly to the termination of the genus Homo Sapiens!

"You could never imagine what happened. It was this, like one-two-three: Pearl and I touched lips; I heard a soft, weird cry behind me; I wheeled; saw, in the entrance, side by side, the three creatures I had thought were safely out in the field getting tutored; saw the eldest's face contort, his head wabble; heard a sharp snap; and then in a twinkling he had fallen over on the other two; and when the dust had settled we saw the young flowers of perfect humanity in an ugly pile, and they lay still, quite still, with, each one, a broken neck!

"They represented the total stock of the race, and they were dead, and I had been the innocent cause!

"I was scared; but how do you think their death affected Pearl? Do you think she showed any sign of emotion? She did not. She ratiocinated. She was sorry of course—so her words said—the tallest guy had been such a beautiful soul!—a born philosopher!—but it had happened; there was nothing to do about it except remove the bodies, and now it was up to her alone to look after the incubators and that cemetery of thinkers.

"'But first,' she said, 'I'd better take you back to your time.'

"'But no!' I said, and I invented lots of reasons why I'd better stay a little. Now that there was no one to discover my presence I more than ever did not want to go. There were a hundred things I wanted to study—the old men, how they functioned, the conditions of the outside world, and so on—but particularly, I confess, I wanted to examine the contents of that building. If it could produce a time traveler, it must contain other marvels, the secrets of which I might be able to learn and take back home with me.

"We went out into the sun and argued, and my guide did a lot of squatting and meditating, and in the end I won out. I could stay three days.

"On the afternoon of the first day something went wrong with the incubators, and Pearl came hurrying to tell me in her abstracted fashion that the two occupants, the last hopes of the human race, were dead.

"She did not know it, but I had done things to the mechanisms of the incubators.

"I had murdered those unborn monsters—

"Charles, Miles, let's have some more tea."

VII

Frick went over to the thermos bottle, poured for us, returned it to the floor and resumed his chair. We rested for several minutes, and my dictograph shows that again not a word was spoken. I will not try to describe my thoughts except to say that the break in the tension had found me in need of the stimulation I was given.

When Frick resumed, it was suddenly, with unexpected bitterness and vehemence.

"Homo Sapiens had become a caricature and an abomination!" he exclaimed. "I did not murder those unborn babies on impulse, nor did I commit my later murders on impulse. My actions were considered; my decisions were reached after hours of the calmest, clearest thinking I have ever done; I accepted full responsibility, and I still accept it!

"I want now to make a statement which above all I want you to believe. It is this. At the time I made up my mind to destroy those little monsters, and so terminate Genus Homo, I expected to bring Pearl back to live out her years in our time. That was the disposition I had planned for her. Her future did not work out that way. To put it baldly, Mother Nature made the most ridiculous ass of all time out of me; but remember, in justice to me, that the current of events got changed *after* my decision.

"I have said that Pearl took the death of the race's only young stock in her usual arid manner. She certainly did; but, as I think back over those days, it seems to me she did show a tiny bit, oh, a most infinitesimal amount, of feeling. That feeling was directed wholly toward me. You may ask how she could differ temperamentally—and physically—from those others, but I can only suggest that the enigma of her personal equation was bound up in the unique conditions of her birth. As she said, she may have been 'bad material' to start with. Then, something had gone wrong with an incubator; she was born after only eleven months; was four months premature; had received remote prenatal tutoring for that much less time; and had functioned in a different and far more physical manner much earlier, and with fewer built-in restraints, than the others.

"It was this difference in her, this independence and initiative, that caused her to find the time traveler, the unused and forgotten achievement of a far previous age. It was this difference that allowed her to dare use it in the way we know. And it was this difference—now I am speaking chiefly of her *physical* difference—that gave rise in me to the cosmic ambitions which took me from farce to horror, and which I will now try to describe.

"Toward the evening of the second day we sat out on the wold grass before that corroboree of static philosophers and discussed the remaining future of the human race.

"I argued, since there was no one else to look after them now, and since they could live only as long as she lived, it was clear that the best thing—and, in the event of accident to her, the most humane thing—would be for me to kill them all as painlessly as possible and take her back to my time to live.

"I need not mention the impossibility of there being any more descendants from them.

"But for the only time during all the period I knew her she refused to face the facts. She wouldn't admit a single thing; I got nowhere; argue and plead as I would, all she would say, over and over, was that it was a pity that the human race had to come to an end. I see now that I was dense to take so long to get what she was driving at. When I did finally get it I nearly fell over backward in the grass.

"My friends, she was delicately hinting that I was acceptable to her as the father of a future race!

"Oh, that was gorgeous! I simply couldn't restrain my laughter; I had to turn my back; and I had a devil of a time explaining what I was doing, and why my shoulders shook so. To let her down easily, I told her I would think it over that night and give her my decision in the morning. And that was all there was to it at the time.

"Now comes the joke; now comes the beginning of my elevation to the supreme heights of asshood, and you are at liberty to laugh as much as you please. That night, under the low-hung stars of that far future world, I *did* decide to become the father of a future race! Yes—the single father of ultimate humanity!

"That night was perhaps the most tremendous experience of my life. The wide thinking I did! The abandoned planning! What were not the possibilities of my union with Pearl! She, on her side, had superb intellectuality, was the product of millions of years' culture; while I had emotion, vitality, the physicalness that she and the withered remains of her people so lacked! Who might guess what renaissance of degenerate humanity our posterity might bring! I walked, that night; I shouted; I laughed; I cried. I was to become a latter-day god! I spent emotion terrifically; it could not last till dawn; morning found Pearl waking me, quite wet with dew, far out in the hills.

"I had settled everything in my mind. Pearl and I would mate, and nature would take her course; but there was one prime condition. There would have to be a house-cleaning, first. Those cartoons of humanity would have to be destroyed. They represented all that was absurd and decadent; they were utterly without value; they were a stench and an abomination. Death to the old, and on with the new!

"I told Pearl of my decision. She was not exactly torrid with gratitude when she heard me say I would make her my wife, but she did give some severely logical approval, and that was something. She balked, however, at my plan to exterminate her redoubtable exponents of the mental life. She was quite stubborn.

"All that day I tried to convince her. I pointed out the old folks' uselessness, but she argued they were otherwise: that usefulness gives birth to the notion of beauty; that, therefore, beauty accompanies usefulness; and that because the old gentlemen were such paragons of subjective beauty they were, therefore, paragons of usefulness. I got lost on that airy plane of reasoning. I informed her that I, too, was something of an aesthetician, and that I had proved to myself they smelled bad and were intolerable; and how easy it would be to exterminate them!—how slender their hold on life!

"Nothing doing. At one time I made the mistake of trying vile humor. Here's a splendid solution of the in-law problem! As if she could be made to smile! She made me explain what I had meant! And this seemed to give her new thinking material, and resulted in her going down into squat-thinks so often that I was almost ready to run amok.

"I suppose there must be a great unconscious loyalty to race in humans, for even in that attenuated time Pearl, unsentimental as she always was, doggedly insisted that they be allowed to live out their unnatural lives.

"I never did persuade her. I forced her. Either they had to go or I would. Late that night she gave me her permission.

"I awoke the morning of the fourth day in glorious high spirits. This was the day that was to leave me the lord of creation! I was not at all disturbed that it entailed my first assuming the office of high executioner. I went gaily to meet Pearl and asked her if she had settled her mind for the work of the day. She had. As we breakfasted on some damnable stuff like sawdust we talked over various methods of extermination.

"Oh, I was in splendid spirits! To prove to Pearl that I was a just executioner,

I offered to consider the case of each philostatician separately and to spare any for whom extenuating circumstances could be found. We started on the male monster of my first day. Standing before him in his cell I asked Pearl, 'What good can you say of this alleged aesthetician?'

"'He has a beautiful soul,' she claimed.

"'But look at his body!'

"'You are no judge,' she retorted. 'And what if his body does decay?—his mind is eternal.'

"'What's he meditating on?'

"Pearl went into a think. After a moment she said, 'A hole in the ground.'

"'Can you interpret his thoughts for me?' I asked.

"'It is difficult, but I'll try,' she said. After a little she began tonelessly, 'It's a hole. There is something—a certain something about it— Once caught my leg in one— I pulled. Yes, there is something—ineffable— So-called matter around— air within— Holes—depth—moisture—leaks—juice— Yes, it is the *idea* of a hole— Hole—inverse infinity—holiness—'

"'That'll do!' I said—and pulled the receptacle of all this wisdom suddenly forward. There was a sharp crack, like the breaking of a dry stick, and the receptacle hung swaying pendulously against his ribs. 'Justice!' I cried.

"The old woman was next. 'What's there good about her?' I asked.

"'She's a mother,' Pearl replied.

"'Enough!' I cried, and the flip of my arm was followed by another sharp crack. 'Justice to the mother who bore Homo Sapiens! Next!'

"The next was an awful-looking wreck—worse than the first. 'What good can you say of him?' I asked.

"'He is a great scientist.'

"'Can you interpret his thoughts?'

"Pearl sank and thought. 'Mind force,' she said tonelessly. 'How powerful— mm—yes, powerful— Basis of everything living—mm—really is everything— no living, all thinking—in direct proportion as it is not, there is nothing— Mm, yes, everything is relative, but everything together makes unity—therefore, we have a relative unit—or, since the reverse is the other half of the obverse, the two together equal another unity, and we get the equation: a relative unit equals a unit of relativity— Sounds as if it might mean something. Einstein was a primitive. I agree with Wlyxzso. He was a greater mind than Yutwilxi. And so it is proved that mind always triumphs over matter—'

"'Proved!' I said—and crack went his neck! 'Justice!' I cried. 'Next!'

"The next, Pearl told me, was a metaphysician. 'Ye gods,' I cried, 'don't tell me that among this lot of supermetaphysicians there is a specialist and an ultra. What's he thinking?'

"But this time poor Pearl was in doubt. 'To tell the truth, we're not sure whether he thinks or not,' she said, 'or whether he is alive or dead. Sometimes we seem to get ideas so faint that we doubt if we really hear them; at others there is a pure blank.'

"'Try,' I ordered. 'Try hard. Every last dead one must have his chance to be killed.'

"She tried. Eventually she said, 'I really think he is alive— Truth—air—truth firmly rooted high in air—ah, branching luxuriantly down toward earth—but never touching, so I cannot quite reach the branches, though I so easily grasp the roots—'

"Crack! went his neck.

"I cracked a dozen others. It got easier all the time. Then Pearl presented me to the prize of the collection. He had a head the size of a bushel basket.

"'What good can you say of him?'

"'He is the greatest of us all, and I do beg that you will spare him,' was her reply. 'I don't know what his specialty is, but everyone here regarded him so highly!'

"'What is he thinking?' I asked.

"'That's it,' she replied. 'No one knows. From birth he has never spoken; he used to drool at the mouth; no one has been able to detect any sign of cerebration. We put him in a cell very early. One of us gave an opinion that he was a congenital hydrocephalic idiot, but that was an error of judgment, for the rest of us have always been sure that his blankness is only apparent. His meditations are simply beyond our gross sensibilities. He no doubt ponders the uttermost problems of infinity.'

"'Try,' I said. 'Even he gets his chance.'

"Pearl tried, and got nothing. Crack! went his neck.

"And so it went. One by one, with rapid dispatch, and with a gusto that still surprises me when I think of it, I rid the earth of its public enemies. By the time the sun was high in the heavens the job was complete, and I had become the next lord of creation!

VIII

"The effect of the morning's work sent Pearl into a meditation that lasted for hours. When she came out of it she seemed her usual self; but inside, as I know now, something was changed, or, let us say, accelerated; and when this acceleration had reached a certain point my goosish ambition was ignominiously cooked. Ah, and very well cooked! Humorous and serious—I was well done on both sides!

"But realization of my final humiliation came late and suddenly. My thoughts were not at all on any danger like that, but on millions of darling descendants in whose every parlor would hang my picture, when Pearl came out of her extended trance.

"I had decided to be awfully nice to her—a model father even if not the perfect lover—so it was almost like a courtier that I escorted her out on the field and handed her over to a large stone, where she promptly sat and efficiently asked what I wanted. I imagined she showed a trace of disappointment when I told her I only wished to talk over some arrangements relative to our coming civilization; but she made no remark, let me paint a glowing picture of the possibilities, and agreed with me on the outlines of the various plans I had formed.

"I was in a hurry. I asked her if she desired to slip back to my time to have the ceremony performed.

"This offer was, I thought, a delicate gesture on my part. She came back with what amounted to a terrific right to the heart. She said severely, 'Yes, Frick, I will marry you, but first, you must court me.'

"Observe, now, Miles, and you, Charles, my rapid ascent to asshood's most sublime peak. Countless other men have spent their lives trying to attain that dizzy height; a few have almost reached its summit, but it remained for me, the acting lord of creation, to achieve it. For—there was nothing else to do about it—I began to court her!

"'Hold my hand,' she said—and I held her hand. She thought. 'Tell me that you love me,' she required. I told her that I loved her. 'But look at me when you say it,' she demanded—and I looked into her fleshless face with the thin lips that always reminded me of alum and said again that I loved her. Again she took thought, and I got the impression that she was inspecting her sensations. 'Kiss me,' she ordered; and when I did she slid to the ground in a think!

"'There are mysteries in there somewhere,' she said when I pulled her up. 'I shall have to give a great deal of thought to them.'

"I was in a hurry! I told her—Lord forgive me!—that she was clearly falling in love with me! And within herself she found something—I can't imagine what— that encouraged the idea. I struck while the iron was—well, not at absolute zero.

"'Oh, come on,' I urged her. 'You see how we love each other; let's get married and get it over with.'

"'No, you'll have to court me,' she answered, and I'll swear she was being coy. 'And court me for a long time, too,' she added. 'I found out all about it, in your time. It takes months.'

"This was terrible! 'But why wait? Why? We love each other. Look at Romeo and Juliet! Remember?'

"'I liked that young man Rudy better,' she came back at a tangent.

"'You mean the man in the nightclub?' I asked.

"'Yes,' she answered. ''He seemed to be singing just to me.'

"'Not singing—crooning!' I corrected irritably.

"'Yes, crooning,' she allowed. 'You croon to me, Frick.'

"Imagine it! Me, of all people; she, of all people; and out in the middle of that field in broad daylight!

"But did I croon? I crooned. You have not seen me at the heights yet!

"'More,' she said abstractedly. 'I think I feel something.'

"I crooned some more.

"'Something with love and above in it,' she ordered.

"I made up something with love and above in it.

"'And something with you and true,' she went on.

"I did it.

"'Now kiss me again.'

"And I did that!

"Thank Heaven she flopped into another think! I escaped to the woods while she was unconscious, and did not see her again till the next day.

"My friends, this was the ignoble pattern of my life for the two weeks that followed.

"I suffered; how I suffered! There I was, all a-burning to be the author of a new civilization, luxuriating in advance at thought of titanic tasks complete; and there she was, surely the most extraordinary block to superhuman ambition that ever was, forever chilling my ardor, ruthlessly demanding to be courted! I held hands with her all over that portion of time; I gazed into her eyes at the tomb of old Hydrocephalus himself; I crooned to her at midnight; and I'll bet that neighborhood was pitted for years in the places she suddenly sat down to meditate on in the midst of a kiss!

"She had observed closely—all too closely—the technique of love overtures here in our time; and noted particularly the effect on the woman, so she must needs always be going off into a personal huddle to see if, perhaps, she was beginning to react in the desired manner!

"Ah, there was brains! How glad I am that I'm dumb!

"I began to lose weight and go around tired. I saw that our courtship could go on forever. But she saved me with an idea she got out of one of those novels she had read. She told me one rainy morning, brightly, that it might be a good thing if we did not see each other for a couple of months. She had so very, very much to think over, and, incidentally, how sorry she was for her poor countrymen who had died without dreaming life could hold such wealth of emotional experience as she had accumulated from me!

"By then I was as much as ever in a rush to get my revised race off under their own power, but I was physically so exhausted that my protests lacked force, and I had to give in. So we made all arrangements and had our last talk. It was fully understood that I was to come back in two months and take her as my bride. She showed me how to operate the traveler. I set the controls, and in a matter of a minute I was back here in this room.

"But I tricked her. That is, in a sense. For I didn't wait two months. The idea occurred to me to straddle that period in the traveler—so in only another minute I was materializing in the time two months away that I was to call back and claim her! I was thankful for that machine, for the long ordeal had left my body weak and my nerves frazzled, and I don't know how I could have stood so long a delay. You see, I was in such a hurry!

"Ah, had I known! The catastrophe was already upon me! Note its terrible, brief acceleration!

"When I arrived, all was exactly as before. The great building was as dusty, the community as deserted, the block of cells just as morbid as when I left. Only the fields had changed. I found Pearl sitting before the tomb of Hydrocephalus, meditating.

"'I'm surprised to find you back so soon,' were her words of greeting. 'It seemed only a week.'

"'Did you have a good time, my Pearl-of-great-price?' I asked tenderly. (She had come to insist on that name. Once, near despair, I had used it with a different meaning, and afterward she required me to lash myself with it whenever I addressed her.)

"'It was a period of most interesting integration,' she replied. 'In fact, it has been a precious experience. But I have come to realize that we were hasty in terminating the noble lives of my fellow men.'

"This was ominous! I made her go for a walk in the fields with me. Three times on the way out she found things I lightly mentioned to be problems requiring immediate squatting and meditating!

"I sensed that this was the crisis, and it was. I threw all my resources into an attempt to force immediate victory. I held her hands with one of mine, hooked my free arm around her waist, placed my lips to hers and crooned, 'Marry me right now, darling! I can't wait! I love you, I adore you, I am quite mad over you!'—and damn it, at the word mad she squatted!

"I picked her up and tried it again, but like clockwork, on the word mad she went down again. Oh, I was mad over her, all right!

"I was boiling! You see, I had to hurry so! She was changing right under my nose!

"I fairly flew back to the time machine. I was going to learn once and for all what my future with regard to a potential human race was to be. I set its dials one year ahead.

"This time I found Pearl in the vacant cell. She was distinctly older, dryer, thinner, and her head was larger in size. She sat on the dais as had the others; and there was a light dust on her clothing—

"'It is strange that you should come at this moment,' she said in a rusty voice. 'I was thinking of you.'

"With the last word she closed her eyes—so she should not see me, only think of me. I saw that the food box was full. Despair in my heart, I went back to the traveler.

"For a long time I hesitated in front of it. I was close to the bottom. The change had happened so quickly! To Pearl it took a year, to me, only an hour; yet her acts were as fixed, her character as immutable, as if they had been petrified under the weight of a millennium.

"I nerved myself for what I had to do. Suddenly, recklessly, I jumped on the traveler, set it for seventy years ahead, and shot forth into time.

"I saw Pearl once more. I hardly recognized her in the monster who sat on the dais in her cell. Her body was shriveled. Her head had grown huge. Her nose had subsided. Her mouth was a nasty, crooked slit. She sat in thick dust, and there was an inch of it where there had once been brown hair, and more on every little upper surface.

"She had a musty smell!

"She had reverted to type. She had overcome the differentness of her start and was already far down the nauseating road which overbrained humanity has yet to go.

"As I stood looking at her, her eyelids trembled a little, and I felt she knew I was there. It was horrible; but worse was to come. The mouth, too, moved; it twisted; opened; and out of it came an awful creak.

"'Tell me that you love me.'

"I fled back to my time!"

IX

Frick's long narrative had come to a close, but its end effect was of such sudden horror that Miles and I could not move from the edges of our chairs. In the silence Frick's voice still seemed to go on, exuberant, laughing, bitter, flexing with changing moods. The man himself sat slumped back in his chair, head low, drained of energy.

We sat this way long minutes, each with his thoughts, and each one's thoughts fixing terribly on the thing we knew Frick was going to do and which we would not ask him not to do. Frick raised his head and spoke, and I quivered at the implication of his words.

"The last time she had food for only five years," he said.

Out of the depths of me came a voice, answering, "It will be an act of mercy."

"For you," Frick said. "I shall do it because she is the loathsome last."

He got up; fixed us in turn with bitter eyes.

"You will come?" he asked.

We did not answer. He must have read our assent in our eyes. He smiled sardonically.

He went over to the door he had pointed out, unlocked it with a key from his pocket, pulled its heavy weight open, entered, switched on a light. I got up and followed, trembling, Miles after me.

"I had the traveler walled up," Frick said. "I have never used it since."

I saw the machine. It was as he had described it. It hung in nothingness two feet off the floor! For a moment I lacked the courage to step on, and Frick pushed me up roughly. He was beginning to show the excitement which was to gather such momentum.

Miles stepped up promptly, and then Frick himself was up, hands on the controls. "Don't move!" he cried—and then the room was dim goldenness, then nothing at all, and I felt permeated with fathomless silence.

Suddenly there was the goldenness again, and just as suddenly it left. We were in a small dark room. It was night.

I wondered if she knew we were coming.

We went to her silently, prowlers in infinity, our carpet the dust of ages. A turn, a door—and there was field land asleep under the pale wash of a gibbous moon. A walk, a turn—and there were the thirty-six sepulchers of the degenerate dead. One not quite dead.

I was as in a dream.

Through the tall grass we struck, stealthily, Frick in the van like a swiftstalking animal. Straight through the wet grass he led us, though it clung to our legs as if to restrain us from our single purpose. Straight in among those silent sepulchers we went. Nature was nodding; her earth stretched out everywhere oblivious; and the ages to come, they did not care. Nor cared the mummied tenants of each tomb around us. Not now, with their heads resting on their ribs. Only Frick did, very much. He was a young humanity's agent before an old one's degradation. Splendidly, he was judge and executioner.

He slowed down before the sepulcher where was one who was yet alive. He paused there; and I prayed. An intake of breath, and he pulled open the door and entered. Dreadfully, Miles, then I, edged in after.

The door swung closed.

The tomb was a well of ink. Unseen dust rose to finger my throat. There was a musty smell! I held my breath, but my heart pounded on furiously. Ever so faintly through the pressing silence I heard the pounding of two others.

Could it be possible that a fourth heart was weakly beating there?

Faint sounds of movement came from my left. An arm brushed my side, groping. I heard a smothered gasp; I think it was from Miles. Soon I had to have air, and breathed, in catches. I waited, straining, my eyes toward where, ahead, there might have been a deeper blackness through the incessant gloom.

Silence. Was Frick gathering courage? I could *feel* him peering beside me there, afraid of what he had to see.

I knew a moment when the suspense became intolerable, and in that moment it was all over. There was a movement, a scratch, a match sputtered into light; for one eternal second I looked through a dim haze of dust on a mummied monstrosity whose eyelids moved!—and then darkness swept over us again, and there was a sharp crack, as of a broken stick, and I was running wildly with Death itself at my heels through that graveyard of a race to the building where lay our traveler.

In minutes we were back in our own time; in a few more Frick had blown up the traveler and I was out of the laboratory making for the Sound, sharp on my mind, as I went, the never-to-be-forgotten picture of Miles as he had raced behind me blurting, "She blinked! Oh, she blinked!" and that other, striding godlike in the rear, a little out of his head at the moment, who waved his arms over that fulfilled cemetery and thundered,

"Sic transit gloria mundi!"

STANLEY G. WEINBAUM

The Mad Moon

Science fiction in the 1930s was full of clichés—the mad scientist, the mad scientist's beautiful daughter, evil robots and menacing aliens of various shapes and sizes. Stanley G. Weinbaum (1900-1935) changed the last mentioned stereotype with the publication of his first story, "A Martian Odyssey," in the July 1934 issue of Wonder Stories. His aliens had personalities, were not necessarily dangerous and operated on the basis of a logic that, while different from humans, was not inferior. He died of cancer at the age of 35, but he left a rich storehouse of wonderful stories that can be found in The Best of Stanley G. Weinbaum *(1974) and two notable novels,* The New Adam *(1939) and* The Black Flame *(1948). We wonder what he might have done if his life span had been a normal one.*

I

"Idiots!" howled Grant Calthorpe. "Fools—nitwits—imbeciles!" He sought wildly for some more expressive terms, failed, and vented his exasperation in a vicious kick at the pile of rubbish on the ground.

Too vicious a kick, in fact; he had again forgotten the one-third normal gravitation of Io, and his whole body followed his kick in a long, twelve-foot arc.

As he struck the ground the four loonies giggled. Their great, idiotic heads, looking like nothing so much as the comic faces painted on Sunday balloons for children, swayed in unison on their five-foot necks, as thin as Grant's wrist.

"Get out!" he blazed, scrambling erect. "Beat it, skiddoo, scram! No chocolate. No candy. Not until you learn that I want ferva leaves, and not any junk you happen to grab. Clear out!"

The loonies—*Lunae Jovis Magnicapites,* or literally, Bigheads of Jupiter's Moon—backed away, giggling plaintively. Beyond doubt, they considered Grant fully as idiotic as he considered them, and were quite unable to understand the reasons for his anger. But they certainly realized that no candy was to be forthcoming, and their giggles took on a note of keen disappointment.

So keen, indeed, that the leader, after twisting his ridiculous blue face in an imbecilic grin at Grant, voiced a last wild giggle and dashed his head against a glittering stone-bark tree. His companions casually picked up his body and moved off, with his head dragging behind them on its neck like a prisoner's ball on a chain.

Grant brushed his hand across his forehead and turned wearily toward his stone-bark log shack. A pair of tiny, glittering red eyes caught his attention, and a slinker—*Mus Sapiens*—skipped his six-inch form across the threshold, bearing under his tiny, skinny arm what looked very much like Grant's clinical thermometer.

Grant yelled angrily at the creature, seized a stone and flung it vainly. At the edge of the brush, the slinker turned its ratlike, semihuman face toward him, squeaked its thin gibberish, shook a microscopic fist in manlike wrath, and vanished, its batlike cowl of skin fluttering like a cape. It looked, indeed, very much like a black rat wearing a cape.

It had been a mistake, Grant knew, to throw the stone at it. Now the tiny fiends would never permit him any peace, and their diminutive size and pseudo-human intelligence made them infernally troublesome as enemies. Yet, neither that reflection nor the loony's suicide troubled him particularly; he had witnessed instances like the latter too often, and besides, his head felt as if he were in for another siege of white fever.

He entered the shack, closed the door, and stared down at his pet parcat. "Oliver," he growled, "you're a fine one. Why the devil don't you watch out for slinkers? What are you here for?"

The parcat rose on its single, powerful hind leg, clawing at his knees with its two forelegs. "The red jack on the black queen," it observed placidly. "Ten loonies make one half-wit."

Grant placed both statements easily. The first was, of course, an echo of his preceding evening's solitaire game, and the second of yesterday's session with the loonies. He grunted abstractedly and rubbed his aching head. White fever again, beyond doubt.

He swallowed two ferverin tablets, and sank listlessly to the edge of his bunk, wondering whether this attack of *blancha* would culminate in delirium.

He cursed himself for a fool for ever taking this job on Jupiter's third habitable moon, Io. The tiny world was a planet of madness, good for nothing except the production of ferva leaves, out of which Earthly chemists made as many potent alkaloids as they once made from opium.

Invaluable to medical science, of course, but what difference did that make to him? What difference, even, did the munificent salary make, if he got back to Earth a raving maniac after a year in the equatorial regions of Io? He swore bitterly that when the plane from Junopolis landed next month for his ferva, he'd go back to the polar city with it, even though his contract with Neilan Drug called for a full year, and he'd get no pay if he broke it. What good was money to a lunatic?

II

The whole little planet was mad—loonies, parcats, slinkers and Grant Calthorpe—all crazy. At least, anybody who ever ventured outside either of the two polar cities, Junopolis on the north and Herapolis on the south, was crazy. One could live there in safety from white fever, but anywhere below the twentieth parallel it was worse than the Cambodian jungles on Earth.

He amused himself by dreaming of Earth. Just two years ago he had been happy there, known as a wealthy, popular sportsman. He had been just that, too; before he was twenty-one he had hunted knife-kite and threadworm on Titan, and triops and uniped on Venus.

That had been before the gold crisis of 2110 had wiped out his fortune. And—
—well, if he had to work, it had seemed logical to use his interplanetary experience as a means of livelihood. He had really been enthusiastic at the chance to associate himself with Neilan Drug.

He had never been on Io before. This wild little world was no sportsman's paradise with its idiotic loonies and wicked, intelligent, tiny slinkers. There wasn't anything worth hunting on the feverish little moon, bathed in warmth by the giant Jupiter only a quarter million miles away.

If he *had* happened to visit it, he told himself ruefully, he'd never have taken the job; he had visualized Io as something like Titan, cold but clean.

Instead it was as hot as the Venus Hotlands because of its glowing primary, and subject to half a dozen different forms of steamy daylight—sun day, Jovian day, Jovian and sun day, Europa light, and occasionally actual and dismal night. And most of these came in the course of Io's forty-two-hour revolution, too—a mad succession of changing lights. He hated the dizzy days, the jungle, and Idiots' Hills stretching behind his shack.

It was Jovian and solar day at the present moment, and that was the worst of all, because the distant sun added its modicum of heat to that of Jupiter. And to complete Grant's discomfort now was the prospect of a white fever attack. He swore as his head gave an additional twinge, and then swallowed another ferverin tablet. His supply of these was diminishing, he noticed; he'd have to remember to ask for some when the plane called—no, he was going back with it.

Oliver rubbed against his leg. "Idiots, fools, nitwits, imbeciles," remarked the parcat affectionately. "Why did I have to go to that damn dance?"

"Huh?" said Grant. He couldn't remember having said anything about a dance. It must, he decided, have been said during his last fever madness.

Oliver creaked like the door, then giggled like a loony. "It'll be all right," he assured Grant. "Father is bound to come soon."

"Father!" echoed the man. His father had died fifteen years before. "Where'd you get that from, Oliver?"

"It must be the fever," observed Oliver placidly. "You're a nice kitty, but I wish you had sense enough to know what you're saying. And I wish father would come." He finished with a suppressed gurgle that might have been a sob.

Grant stared dizzily at him. He hadn't said any of those things; he was positive. The parcat must have heard them from somebody else— Somebody else? Where within five hundred miles was there anybody else?

"Oliver!" he bellowed. "Where'd you hear that? Where'd you hear it?"

The parcat backed away, startled. "Father is idiots, fools, nitwits, imbeciles," he said anxiously. "The red jack on the nice kitty."

"Come here!" roared Grant. "Whose father? Where have you— Come here, you imp!"

He lunged at the creature. Oliver flexed his single hind leg and flung himself frantically to the cowl of the wood stove. "It must be the fever!" he squalled. "No chocolate!"

He leaped like a three-legged flash for the flue opening. There came a sound of claws grating on metal, and then he had scrambled through.

Grant followed him. His head ached from the effort, and with the still sane part of his mind he knew that the whole episode was doubtless white fever delirium, but he plowed on.

His progress was a nightmare. Loonies kept bobbing their long necks above the tall bleeding-grass, their idiotic giggles and imbecilic faces adding to the general atmosphere of madness.

Wisps of fetid fever-bearing vapors spouted up at every step on the spongy soil. Somewhere to his right a slinker squeaked and gibbered; he knew that a tiny slinker village was over in that direction, for once he had glimpsed the neat little buildings, constructed of small, perfectly fitted stones like a miniature medieval town, complete to towers and battlements. It was said that there were even slinker wars.

His head buzzed and whirled from the combined effects of ferverin and fever. It was an attack of *blancha*, right enough, and he realized that he was an imbecile, a loony, to wander thus away from his shack. He should be lying on his bunk; the fever was not serious, but more than one man had died on Io in the delirium, with its attendant hallucinations.

He was delirious now. He knew it as soon as he saw Oliver, for Oliver was placidly regarding an attractive young lady in perfect evening dress of the style of the second decade of the twenty-second century. Very obviously that was a hallucination, since girls had no business in the Ionian tropics, and if by some wild chance one should appear there, she would certainly not choose formal garb.

The hallucination had fever, apparently, for her face was pale with the whiteness that gave *blancha* its name. Her gray eyes regarded him without surprise as he wound his way through the bleeding-grass to her.

"Good afternoon, evening, or morning," he remarked, giving a puzzled glance at Jupiter, which was rising, and the sun, which was setting. "Or perhaps merely good day, Miss Lee Neilan."

She gazed seriously at him. "Do you know," she said, "you're the first one of the illusions that I haven't recognized? All my friends have been around, but you're the first stranger. Or are you a stranger? You know my name—but you ought to, of course, being my own hallucination."

"We won't argue about which of us is the hallucination," he suggested. "Let's do it this way. The one of us that disappears first is the illusion. Bet you five dollars you do."

"How could I collect?" she said. "I can't very well collect from my own dream."

"That is a problem." He frowned. "My problem, of course, not yours. I know I'm real."

"How do you know my name?" she demanded.

"Ah!" he said. "From intensive reading of the society sections of the newspapers brought by my supply plane. As a matter of fact, I have one of your pictures cut out and pasted next to my bunk. That probably accounts for my seeing you now. I'd like to really meet you some time."

"What a gallant remark for an apparition!" she exclaimed. "And who are you supposed to be?"

"Why, I'm Grant Calthorpe. In fact, I work for your father, trading with the loonies for ferva."

"Grant Calthorpe," she echoed. She narrowed her fever-dulled eyes as if to bring him into better focus. "Why, you are!"

Her voice wavered for a moment, and she brushed her hand across her pale brow. "Why should you pop up out of my memories? It's strange. Three or four years ago, when I was a romantic schoolgirl and you the famous sportsman, I was madly in love with you. I had a whole book filled with your pictures—Grant Calthorpe dressed in parka for hunting threadworm on Titan—Grant Calthorpe beside the giant uniped he killed near the Mountains of Eternity. You're—you're really the pleasantest hallucination I've had so far. Delirium would be—fun"—she pressed her hand to her brow again—"if one's head—didn't ache so!"

"Gee!" thought Grant, "I wish that were true, that about the book. This is what psychology calls a wish-fulfillment dream." A drop of warm rain plopped on his neck. "Got to get to bed," he said aloud. "Rain's bad for *blancha*. Hope to see you next time I'm feverish."

"Thank you," said Lee Neilan with dignity. "It's quite mutual."

He nodded, sending a twinge through his head. "Here, Oliver," he said to the drowsing parcat. "Come on."

"That isn't Oliver," said Lee. "It's Polly. It's kept me company for two days, and I've named it Polly."

"Wrong gender," muttered Grant. "Anyway, it's my parcat, Oliver. Aren't you, Oliver?"

"Hope to see you," said Oliver sleepily.

"It's Polly. Aren't you, Polly?"

"Bet you five dollars," said the parcat. He rose, stretched and loped off into the underbrush. "It must be the fever," he observed as he vanished.

"It must be," agreed Grant. He turned away. "Good-by, Miss—or I might as well call you Lee, since you're not real. Good-by, Lee."

"Good-by, Grant. But don't go that way. There's a slinker village over in the grass."

"No. It's over there."

"It's *there*," she insisted. "I've been watching them build it. But they can't hurt you anyway, can they? Not even a slinker could hurt an apparition. Good-by, Grant." She closed her eyes wearily.

III

It was raining harder now. Grant pushed his way through the bleeding-grass, whose red sap collected in bloody drops on his boots. He had to get back to his shack quickly, before the white fever and its attendant delirium set him wandering utterly astray. He needed ferverin.

Suddenly he stopped short. Directly before him the grass had been cleared away, and in the little clearing were the shoulder-high towers and battlements of a slinker village—a new one, for half-finished houses stood among the others, and hooded six-inch forms toiled over the stones.

There was an outcry of squeaks and gibberish. He backed away but a dozen tiny darts whizzed about him. One stuck like a toothpick in his boot, but none, luckily, scratched his skin, for they were undoubtedly poisoned. He moved more quickly, but all around in the thick, fleshy grasses were rustlings, squeakings and incomprehensible imprecations.

He circled away. Loonies kept popping their balloon heads over the vegetation, and now and again one giggled in pain as a slinker bit or stabbed it. Grant cut toward a group of the creatures, hoping to distract the tiny fiends in the grass, and a tall, purple-faced loony curved its long neck above him, giggling and gesturing with its skinny fingers at a bundle under its arm.

He ignored the thing, and veered toward his shack. He seemed to have eluded the slinkers, so he trudged doggedly on, for he needed a ferverin tablet badly. Yet, suddenly he came to a frowning halt, turned, and began to retrace his steps.

"It can't be so," he muttered. "But she told me the truth about the slinker village. I didn't know it was there. Yet how could a hallucination tell me something I didn't know?"

Lee Neilan was sitting on the stone-bark log exactly as he had left her, with Oliver again at her side. Her eyes were closed, and two slinkers were cutting at the long skirt of her gown with tiny, glittering knives.

Grant knew that they were always attracted by Terrestrial textiles; apparently they were unable to duplicate the fascinating sheen of satin, though the fiends were infernally clever with their tiny hands. As he approached, they tore a strip from thigh to ankle, but the girl made no move. Grant shouted, and the vicious little creatures mouthed unutterable curses at him as they skittered away with their silken plunder.

Lee Neilan opened her eyes. "You again," she murmured vaguely. "A moment ago it was father. Now it's you." Her pallor had increased; the white fever was running its course in her body.

"Your father! Then that's where Oliver heard— Listen, Lee. I found the slinker village. I didn't know it was there, but I found it just as you said. Do you see what that means? We're both real!"

"Real?" she said dully. "There's a purple loony grinning over your shoulder. Make him go away. He makes me feel—sick."

He glanced around; true enough, the purple-faced loony was behind him. "Look here," he said, seizing her arm. The feel of her smooth skin was added proof. "You're coming to the shack for ferverin." He pulled her to her feet. "Don't you understand? I'm *real!*"

"No, you're not," she said dazedly.

"Listen, Lee. I don't know how in the devil you got here or why, but I know

Io hasn't driven me that crazy yet. You're real and I'm real." He shook her violently. "I'm *real!*" he shouted.

Faint comprehension showed in her dazed eyes. "Real?" she whispered. "Real! Oh, Lord! Then take—me out of—this mad place!" She swayed, made a stubborn effort to control herself, then pitched forward against him.

Of course on Io her weight was negligible, less than a third Earth normal. He swung her into his arms and set off toward the shack, keeping well away from both slinker settlements. Around him bobbed excited loonies, and now and again the purple-faced one, or another exactly like him, giggled and pointed and gestured.

The rain had increased, and warm rivulets flowed down his neck, and to add to the madness, he blundered near a copse of stinging palms, and their barbed lashes stung painfully through his shirt. Those stings were virulent too, if one failed to disinfect them; indeed, it was largely the stinging palms that kept traders from gathering their own ferva instead of depending on the loonies.

Behind the low rain clouds, the sun had set, and it was ruddy Jupiter daylight, which lent a false flush to the cheeks of the unconscious Lee Neilan, making her still features very lovely.

Perhaps he kept his eyes too steadily on her face, for suddenly Grant was among slinkers again; they were squeaking and sputtering, and the purple loony leaped in pain as teeth and darts pricked his legs. But, of course, loonies were immune to the poison.

The tiny devils were around his feet now. He swore in a low voice and kicked vigorously, sending a ratlike form spinning fifty feet in the air. He had both automatic and flame pistol at his hip, but he could not use them for several reasons.

First, using an automatic against the tiny hordes was much like firing into a swarm of mosquitoes; if the bullet killed one or two or a dozen, it made no appreciable impression on the remaining thousands. And as for the flame pistol, that was like using a Big Bertha to swat a fly. Its vast belch of fire would certainly incinerate all the slinkers in its immediate path, along with grass, trees and loonies, but that again would make but little impress on the surviving hordes, and it meant laboriously recharging the pistol with another black diamond and another barrel.

He had gas bulbs in the shack, but they were not available at the moment, and besides, he had no spare mask, and no chemist has yet succeeded in devising a gas that would kill slinkers without being also deadly to humans. And, finally, he couldn't use any weapon whatsoever right now, because he dared not drop Lee Neilan to free his hands.

Ahead was the clearing around the shack. The space was full of slinkers, but the shack itself was supposed to be slinkerproof, at least for reasonable lengths of time, since stone-bark logs were very resistant to their tiny tools.

But Grant perceived that a group of the diminutive devils were around the door, and suddenly he realized their intent. They had looped a cord of some sort over the knob, and were engaged now in twisting it!

Grant yelled and broke into a run. While he was yet half a hundred feet distant, the door swung inward and the rabble of slinkers flowed into the shack.

He dashed through the entrance. Within was turmoil. Little hooded shapes were cutting at the blankets on his bunk, his extra clothing, the sacks he hoped to fill with ferva leaves, and were pulling at the cooking utensils, or at any and all loose objects.

He bellowed and kicked at the swarm. A wild chorus of squeaks and gibberish arose as the creatures skipped and dodged about him. The fiends were intelligent enough to realize that he could do nothing with his arms occupied by Lee Neilan. They skittered out of the way of his kicks, and while he threatened a group at the stove, another rabble tore at his blankets.

In desperation he charged at the bunk. He swept the girl's body across it to clear it, dropped her on it, and seized a grass broom he had made to facilitate his housekeeping. With wide strokes of its handle he attacked the slinkers, and the squeals were checkered by cries and whimpers of pain.

A few broke for the door, dragging whatever loot they had. He spun around in time to see half a dozen swarming around Lee Neilan, tearing at her clothing, at the wrist watch on her arm, at the satin evening pumps on her small feet. He roared a curse at them and battered them away, hoping that none had pricked her skin with virulent dagger or poisonous tooth.

He began to win the skirmish. More of the creatures drew their black capes close about them and scurried over the threshold with their plunder. At last, with a burst of squeaks, the remainder, laden and empty-handed alike, broke and ran for safety, leaving a dozen furry, impish bodies slain or wounded.

Grant swept these after the others with his erstwhile weapon, closed the door in the face of a loony that bobbed in the opening, latched it against any repetition of the slinkers' tricks and stared in dismay about the plundered dwelling.

Cans had been rolled or dragged away. Every loose object had been pawed by the slinkers' foul little hands, and Grant's clothes hung in ruins on their hooks against the wall. But the tiny robbers had not succeeded in opening the cabinet nor the table drawer, and there was food left.

Six months of Ionian life had left him philosophical; he swore heartily, shrugged resignedly and pulled his bottle of ferverin from the cabinet.

His own spell of fever had vanished as suddenly and completely as *blancha* always does when treated, but the girl, lacking ferverin, was paper-white and still. Grant glanced at the bottle; eight tablets remained.

"Well, I can always chew ferva leaves," he muttered. That was less effective than the alkaloid itself, but it would serve, and Lee Neilan needed the tablets. He dissolved two of them in a glass of water, and lifted her head.

She was not too inert to swallow, and he poured the solution between her pale lips, then arranged her as comfortably as he could. Her dress was a tattered silken ruin, and he covered her with a blanket that was no less a ruin. Then he disinfected his palm stings, pulled two chairs together, and sprawled across them to sleep.

He started up at the sound of claws on the roof, but it was only Oliver, gingerly testing the flue to see if it were hot. In a moment the parcat scrambled through, stretched himself, and remarked, "I'm real and you're real."

"Imagine that!" grunted Grant sleepily.

IV

When he awoke it was Jupiter and Europa light, which meant he had slept about seven hours, since the brilliant little third moon was just rising. He rose and gazed at Lee Neilan, who was sleeping soundly with a tinge of color in her face that was not entirely due to the ruddy daylight. The *blancha* was passing.

He dissolved two more tablets in water, then shook the girl's shoulder. Instantly her gray eyes opened, quite clear now, and she looked up at him without surprise.

"Hello, Grant," she murmured. "So it's you again. Fever isn't so bad, after all."

"Maybe I ought to let you stay feverish," he grinned. "You say such nice things. Wake up and drink this, Lee."

She became suddenly aware of the shack's interior. "Why— Where is this? It looks—real!"

"It is. Drink this ferverin."

She obeyed, then lay back and stared at him perplexedly. "Real?" she said. "And you're real?"

"I think I am."

A rush of tears clouded her eyes. "Then—I'm out of that place? That horrible place?"

"You certainly are." He saw signs of her relief becoming hysteria, and hastened to distract her. "Would you mind telling me how you happened to be there—and dressed for a party, too?"

She controlled herself. "I was dressed for a party. A party in Herapolis. But I was in Junopolis, you see."

"I don't see. In the first place, what are you doing on Io, anyway? Every time I ever heard of you, it was in connection with New York or Paris society."

She smiled. "Then it wasn't all delirium, was it? You did say that you had one of my pictures— Oh, that one!" She frowned at the print on the wall. "Next time a news photographer wants to snap my picture, I'll remember not to grin—like a loony. But as to how I happen to be on Io, I came with father, who's looking over the possibilities of raising ferva on plantations instead of having to depend on traders and loonies. We've been here three months, and I've been terribly bored. I thought Io would be exciting, but it wasn't—until recently."

"But what about that dance? How'd you manage to get here, a thousand miles from Junopolis?"

"Well," she said slowly, "it was terribly tiresome in Junopolis. No shows, no sport, nothing but an occasional dance. I got restless. When there were dances in Herapolis, I formed the habit of flying over there. It's only four or five hours in a fast plane, you know. And last week—or whenever it was—I'd planned on flying down, and Harvey—that's father's secretary—was to take me. But at the last minute father needed him, and forbade my flying alone."

Grant felt a strong dislike for Harvey. "Well?" he asked.

"So I flew alone," she finished demurely.

"And cracked up, eh?"

"I can fly as well as anybody," she retorted. "It was just that I followed a different route, and suddenly there were mountains ahead."

He nodded. "The Idiots' Hills," he said. "My supply plane detours five hundred miles to avoid them. They're not high, but they stick right out above the atmosphere of this crazy planet. The air here is dense but shallow."

"I know that. I knew I couldn't fly above them, but I thought I could hurdle them. Work up full speed, you know, and then throw the plane upward. I had a closed plane, and gravitation is so weak here. And besides, I've seen it done several times, especially with rocket-driven craft. The jets help to support the plane even after the wings are useless for lack of air."

"What a damn fool stunt!" exclaimed Grant. "Sure it can be done, but you have to be an expert to pull out of it when you hit the air on the other side. You hit fast, and there isn't much falling room."

"So I found out," said Lee ruefully. "I almost pulled out, but not quite, and I hit in the middle of some stinging palms. I guess the crash dazed them, because I managed to get out before they started lashing around. But I couldn't reach my plane again, and it was—I only remember two days of it—but it was horrible!"

"It must have been," he said gently.

"I knew that if I didn't eat or drink, I had a chance of avoiding white fever. The not eating wasn't so bad, but the not drinking—well, I finally gave up and drank out of a brook. I didn't care what happened if I could have a few moments that weren't thirst-tortured. And after that it's all confused and vague."

"You should have chewed ferva leaves."

"I didn't know that. I wouldn't have even known what they looked like, and beside, I kept expecting father to appear. He must be having a search made by now."

"He probably is," rejoined Grant ironically. "Has it occurred to you that there are thirteen million square miles of surface on little Io? And that for all he knows, you might have crashed on any square mile of it? When you're flying from north pole to south pole, there *isn't* any shortest route. You can cross any point on the planet."

Her gray eyes started wide. "But I—"

"Furthermore," said Grant, "this is probably the *last* place a searching party would look. They wouldn't think any one but a loony would try to hurdle Idiots' Hills, in which thesis I quite agree. So it looks very much, Lee Neilan, as if you're marooned here until my supply plane gets here next month!"

"But father will be crazy! He'll think I'm dead!"

"He thinks that now, no doubt."

"But we can't—" She broke off, staring around the tiny shack's single room. After a moment she sighed resignedly, smiled and said softly, "Well, it might have been worse, Grant. I'll try to earn my keep."

"Good. How do you feel, Lee?"

"Quite normal. I'll start right to work." She flung off the tattered blanket, sat up, and dropped her feet to the floor. "I'll fix dinn— Good night! My dress!" She snatched the blanket about her again.

He grinned. "We had a little run-in with the slinkers after you had passed out. They did for my spare wardrobe too."

"It's ruined!" she wailed.

"Would needle and thread help? They left that, at least, because it was in the table drawer."

"Why, I couldn't make a good swimming suit out of this!" she retorted. "Let me try one of yours."

By dint of cutting, patching and mending, she at last managed to piece one of Grant's suits to respectable proportions. She looked very lovely in shirt and trousers, but he was troubled to note that a sudden pallor had overtaken her.

It was the *riblancha*, the second spell of fever that usually followed a severe or prolonged attack. His face was serious as he cupped two of his last four ferverin tablets in his hand.

"Take these," he ordered. "And we've got to get some ferva leaves somewhere. The plane took my supply away last week, and I've had bad luck with my loonies ever since. They haven't brought me anything but weeds and rubbish."

Lee puckered her lips at the bitterness of the drug, then closed her eyes against its momentary dizziness and nausea. "Where can you find ferva?" she asked.

He shook his head perplexedly, glancing out at the setting mass of Jupiter, with its bands glowing creamy and brown, and the Red Spot boiling near the western edge. Close above it was the brilliant little disk of Europa. He frowned suddenly, glanced at his watch and then at the almanac on the inside of the cabinet door.

"It'll be Europa light in fifteen minutes," he muttered, "and true night in twenty-five—the first true night in half a month. I wonder—"

He gazed thoughtfully at Lee's face. He knew where ferva grew. One dared not penetrate the jungle itself, where stinging palms and arrow vines and the deadly worms called toothers made such a venture sheer suicide for any creatures but loonies and slinkers. But he knew where ferva grew—

In Io's rare true night even the clearing might be dangerous. Not merely from slinkers, either; he knew well enough that in the darkness creatures crept out of the jungle who otherwise remained in the eternal shadows of its depths—toothers, bullet-head frogs and doubtless many unknown slimy, venomous, mysterious beings never seen by man. One heard stories in Herapolis and—

But he had to get ferva, and he knew where it grew. Not even a loony would try to gather it there, but in the little gardens or farms around the tiny slinker towns, there was ferva growing.

He switched on a light in the gathering dusk. "I'm going outside a moment," he told Lee Neilan. "If the *blancha* starts coming back, take the other two tablets. Wouldn't hurt you to take 'em anyway. The slinkers got away with my thermometer, but if you get dizzy again, you take 'em."

"Grant! Where—"

"I'll be back," he called, closing the door behind him.

A loony, purple in the bluish Europa light, bobbed up with a long giggle. He waved the creature aside and set off on a cautious approach to the neighborhood of the slinker village—the old one, for the other could hardly have had time to cultivate its surrounding ground. He crept warily through the bleeding-grass, but he knew his stealth was pure optimism. He was in exactly the position of a hundred-foot giant trying to approach a human city in secrecy—a difficult matter even in the utter darkness of night.

He reached the edge of the slinker clearing. Behind him, Europa, moving as fast as the second hand on his watch, plummeted toward the horizon. He paused in momentary surprise at the sight of the exquisite little town, a hundred feet away across the tiny square fields, with lights flickering in its hand-wide windows. He had not known that slinker culture included the use of lights, but there they were, tiny candles or perhaps diminutive oil lamps.

He blinked in the darkness. The second of the ten-foot fields looked like—it was—ferva. He stooped low, crept out, and reached his hand for the fleshy, white leaves. And at that moment came a shrill giggle and the crackle of grass behind him. The loony! The idiotic purple loony!

Squeaking shrieks sounded. He snatched a double handful of ferva, rose, and dashed toward the lighted window of his shack. He had no wish to face poisoned barbs or disease-bearing teeth, and the slinkers were certainly aroused. Their gibbering sounded in chorus; the ground looked black with them.

He reached the shack, burst in, slammed and latched the door. "Got it!" He grinned. "Let 'em rave outside now."

They were raving. Their gibberish sounded like the creaking of worn machinery. Even Oliver opened his drowsy eyes to listen. "It must be the fever," observed the parcat placidly.

Lee was certainly no paler; the *riblancha* was passing safely. "Ugh!" she said, listening to the tumult without. "I've always hated rats, but slinkers are worse. All the shrewdness and viciousness of rats plus the intelligence of devils."

"Well," said Grant thoughtfully, "I don't see what they can do. They've had it in for me anyway."

"It sounds as if they're going off," said the girl, listening. "The noise is fading."

Grant peered out of the window. "They're still around. They've just passed from swearing to planning, and I wish I knew what. Some day, if this crazy little planet ever becomes worth human occupation, there's going to be a show-down between humans and slinkers."

"Well? They're not civilized enough to be really a serious obstacle, and they're so small, besides."

"But they learn," he said. "They learn so quickly, and they breed like flies. Suppose they pick up the use of gas, or suppose they develop little rifles for their poisonous darts. That's possible, because they work in metals right now, and they know fire. That would put them practically on a par with man as far as offense goes, for what good are our giant cannons and rocket planes against six-inch slinkers? And to be just on even terms would be fatal; one slinker for one man would be a hell of a trade."

Lee yawned. "Well, it's not our problem. I'm hungry, Grant."

"Good. That's a sign the *blancha's* through with you. We'll eat and then sleep a while, for there's five hours of darkness."

"But the slinkers?"

"I don't see what they can do. They couldn't cut through stone-bark walls in five hours, and anyway, Oliver would warn us if one managed to slip in somewhere."

V

It was light when Grant awoke, and he stretched his cramped limbs painfully across his two chairs. Something had awakened him, but he didn't know just what. Oliver was pacing nervously beside him, and now looked anxiously up at him.

"I've had bad luck with my loonies," announced the parcat plaintively. "You're a nice kitty."

"So are you," said Grant. Something had wakened him, but what?

Then he knew, for it came again—the merest trembling of the stone-bark floor. He frowned in puzzlement. Earthquakes? Not on Io, for the tiny sphere had lost its internal heat untold ages ago. Then what?

Comprehension dawned suddenly. He sprang to his feet with so wild a yell that Oliver scrambled sideways with an infernal babble. The startled parcat leaped to the stove and vanished up the flue. His squall drifted faintly back, "It must be the fever!"

Lee had started to a sitting position on the bunk, her gray eyes blinking sleepily.

"Outside!" he roared, pulling her to her feet. "Get out! Quickly!"

"Wh-what—why—"

"Get out!" He thrust her through the door, then spun to seize his belt and weapons, the bag of ferva leaves, a package of chocolate. The floor trembled again, and he burst out of the door with a frantic leap to the side of the dazed girl.

"They've undermined it!" he choked. "The devils undermined the—"

He had no time to say more. A corner of the shack suddenly subsided; the stone-bark logs grated, and the whole structure collapsed like a child's house of blocks. The crash died into silence, and there was no motion save a lazy wisp of vapor, a few black, ratlike forms scurrying toward the grass, and a purple loony bobbing beyond the ruins.

"The dirty devils!" he swore bitterly. "The damn little black rats! The—"

A dart whistled so close that it grazed his ear and then twitched a lock of Lee's tousled brown hair. A chorus of squeaking sounded in the bleeding-grass.

"Come on!" he cried. "They're out to exterminate us this time. No—this way. Toward the hills. There's less jungle this way."

They could outrun the tiny slinkers easily enough. In a few moments they had lost the sound of squeaking voices, and they stopped to gaze ruefully back on the fallen dwelling.

"Now," he said miserably, "we're both where you were to start with."

"Oh, no." Lee looked up at him. "We're together now, Grant. I'm not afraid."

"We'll manage," he said with a show of assurance. "We'll put up a temporary shack somehow. We'll—"

A dart struck his boot with a sharp *blup*. The slinkers had caught up to them.

Again they ran toward Idiots' Hills. When at last they stopped, they could look down a long slope and far over the Ionian jungles. There was the ruined shack, and there, neatly checkered, the fields and towers of the nearer slinker town. But they had scarcely caught their breath when gibbering and squeaking came out of the brush.

They were being driven into Idiots' Hills, a region as unknown to man as the icy wastes of Pluto. It was as if the tiny fiends behind them had determined that this time their enemy, the giant trampler and despoiler of their fields, should be pursued to extinction.

Weapons were useless. Grant could not even glimpse their pursuers, slipping like hooded rats through the vegetation. A bullet, even if chance sped it through a slinker's body, was futile, and his flame pistol, though its lightning stroke should incinerate tons of brush and bleeding-grass, could no more than cut a narrow path through their horde of tormentors. The only weapons that might have availed, the gas bulbs, were lost in the ruins of the shack.

Grant and Lee were forced upward. They had risen a thousand feet above the plain, and the air was thinning. There was no jungle here, but only great stretches of bleeding-grass, across which a few loonies were visible, bobbing their heads on their long necks.

"Toward—the peaks!" gasped Grant, now painfully short of breath. "Perhaps we can stand rarer air than they."

Lee was beyond answer. She panted doggedly along beside him as they plodded now over patches of bare rock. Before them were two low peaks, like the pillars of a gate. Glancing back, Grant caught a glimpse of tiny black forms on a clear area, and in sheer anger he fired a shot. A single slinker leaped convulsively, its cape flapping, but the rest flowed on. There must have been thousands of them.

The peaks were closer, no more than a few hundred yards away. They were sheer, smooth, unscalable.

"Between them," muttered Grant.

The passage that separated them was bare and narrow. The twin peaks had been one in ages past; some forgotten volcanic convulsion had split them, leaving this slender canyon between.

He slipped an arm about Lee, whose breath, from effort and altitude, was a series of rasping gasps. A bright dart tinkled on the rocks as they reached the opening, but looking back, Grant could see only a purple loony plodding upward, and a few more to his right. They raced down a straight fifty-foot passage that debouched suddenly into a sizable valley—and there, thunderstruck for a moment, they paused.

A city lay there. For a brief instant Grant thought they had burst upon a vast slinker metropolis, but the merest glance showed otherwise. This was no city of medieval blocks, but a poem in marble, classical in beauty, and of human or near-human proportions. White columns, glorious arches, pure curving domes, an architectural loveliness that might have been born on the Acropolis. It took a second look to discern that the city was dead, deserted, in ruins.

Even in her exhaustion, Lee felt its beauty. "How—how exquisite!" she panted.

"One could almost forgive them—for being—slinkers!"

"They won't forgive us for being human," he muttered. "We'll have to make a stand somewhere. We'd better pick a building."

But before they could move more than a few feet from the canyon mouth, a wild disturbance halted them. Grant whirled, and for a moment found himself actually paralyzed by amazement. The narrow canyon was filled with a gibbering horde of slinkers, like a nauseous, heaving black carpet. But they came no farther than the valley end, for grinning, giggling and bobbing, blocking the opening with tramping three-toed feet, were our loonies!

It was a battle. The slinkers were biting and stabbing at the miserable defenders, whose shrill keenings of pain were less giggles than shrieks. But with a determination and purpose utterly foreign to loonies, their clawed feet trampled methodically up and down, up and down.

Grant exploded, "I'll be damned!" Then an idea struck him. "Lee! They're packed in the canyon, the whole devil's brood of 'em!"

He rushed toward the opening. He thrust his flame pistol between the skinny legs of a loony, aimed it straight along the canyon and fired.

VI

Inferno burst. The tiny diamond, giving up all its energy in one terrific blast, shot a jagged stream of fire that filled the canyon from wall to wall and vomited out beyond to cut a fan of fire through the bleeding-grass of the slope.

Idiots' Hills reverberated to the roar, and when the rain of débris settled, there was nothing in the canyon save a few bits of flesh and the head of an unfortunate loony, still bouncing and rolling.

Three of the loonies survived. A purple-faced one was pulling his arm, grinning and giggling in imbecile glee. He waved the thing aside and returned to the girl.

"Thank goodness!" he said. "We're out of that, anyway."

"I wasn't afraid, Grant. Not with you."

He smiled. "Perhaps we can find a place here," he suggested. "The fever ought to be less troublesome at this altitude. But—say, this must have been the capital city of the whole slinker race in ancient times. I can scarcely imagine those fiends creating an architecture as beautiful as this—or as large. Why, these buildings are as colossal in proportion to slinker size as the skyscrapers of New York to us!"

"But so beautiful," said Lee softly, sweeping her eyes over the glory of the ruins. "One might almost forgive— Grant! Look at those!"

He followed the gesture. On the inner side of the canyon's portals were gigantic carvings. But the thing that set him staring in amazement was the subject of the portrayal. There, towering far up the cliff sides, were the figures, not of slinkers, but of—loonies! Exquisitely carved, smiling rather than grinning, and smiling somehow sadly, regretfully, pityingly—yet beyond doubt loonies!

"Good night!" he whispered. "Do you see, Lee? This must once have been a loony city. The steps, the doors, the buildings, all are on their scale of size.

Somehow, some time, they must have achieved civilization, and the loonies we know are the degenerate residue of a great race."

"And," put in Lee, "the reason those four blocked the way when the slinkers tried to come through is that they still remember. Or probably they don't actually remember, but they have a tradition of past glories, or more likely still, just a superstitious feeling that this place is in some way sacred. They let us pass because, after all, we look more like loonies than like slinkers. But the amazing thing is that they still possess even that dim memory, because this city must have been in ruins for centuries. Or perhaps even for thousands of years."

"But to think that loonies could ever have had the intelligence to create a culture of their own," said Grant, waving away the purple one bobbing and giggling at his side. Suddenly he paused, turning a gaze of new respect on the creature. "This one's been following me for days. All right, old chap, what is it?"

The purple one extended a sorely bedraggled bundle of bleeding-grass and twigs, giggling idiotically. His ridiculous mouth twisted; his eyes popped in an agony of effort at mental concentration.

"Canny!" he giggled triumphantly.

"The imbecile!" flared Grant. "Nitwit! Idiot!" He broke off, then laughed. "Never mind. I guess you deserve it." He tossed his package of chocolate to the three delighted loonies. "Here's your candy."

A scream from Lee startled him. She was waving her arms wildly, and over the crest of Idiots' Hills a rocket plane roared, circled and nosed its way into the valley.

The door opened. Oliver stalked gravely out, remarking casually, "I'm real and you're real." A man followed the parcat—two men.

"Father!" screamed Lee.

It was some time later that Gustavus Neilan turned to Grant. "I can't thank you," he said. "If there's ever any way I can show my appreciation for—"

"There is. You can cancel my contract."

"Oh, you work for me?"

"I'm Grant Calthorpe, one of your traders, and I'm about sick of this crazy planet."

"Of course, if you wish," said Neilan. "If it's a question of pay—"

"You can pay me for the six months I've worked."

"If you'd care to stay," said the older man, "there won't be trading much longer. We've been able to grow ferva near the polar cities, and I prefer plantations to the uncertainties of relying on loonies. If you'd work out your year, we might be able to put you in charge of a plantation by the end of that time."

Grant met Lee Neilan's gray eyes, and hesitated. "Thanks," he said slowly, "but I'm sick of it." He smiled at the girl, then turned back to her father. "Would you mind telling me how you happened to find us? This is the most unlikely place on the planet."

"That's just the reason," said Neilan. "When Lee didn't get back, I thought things over pretty carefully. At last I decided, knowing her as I did, to search the least likely places first. We tried the shores of the Fever Sea, and then the White Desert, and finally Idiots' Hills. We spotted the ruins of a shack, and on the debris was this chap"—he indicated Oliver—"remarking that 'Ten loonies make one half-wit.' Well, the half-wit part sounded very much like a reference to my daughter, and we cruised about until the roar of your flame pistol attracted our attention."

Lee pouted, then turned her serious gray eyes on Grant. "Do you remember," she said softly, "what I told you there in the jungle?"

"I wouldn't even have mentioned that," he replied. "I knew you were delirious."

"But—perhaps I wasn't. Would companionship make it any easier to work out your year? I mean if—for instance—you were to fly back with us to Junopolis and return with a wife?"

"Lee," he said huskily, "you know what a difference that would make, though I can't understand why you'd ever dream of it."

"It must," suggested Oliver, "be the fever."

P. SCHUYLER MILLER

As Never Was

P. Schuyler Miller (1912-1974) was an influential figure in science fiction because of his book reviewing activities for Astounding Science Fiction/Analog, where his "The Reference Library" was a regular feature from 1951 to his death. Miller, who worked as a technical writer for a scientific instrument company for more than twenty-five years, was also a well-regarded pulp writer in the 1930s and beyond. His two books are Genus Homo (1950), a novel written in collaboration with L. Sprague de Camp, and The Titan, a story collection published in 1952 and long out of print. At his best, Miller was capable of producing a masterpiece, as in "As Never Was," one of the best time-paradox stories ever written.

HAVE YOU ever dreamed of murder?

Have you ever set your elbows on the desk and let your head slump down on your hands, and closed your eyes, and dreamed of how it would feel to drive a knife up to the hilt in a scrawny, wrinkled throat, and twist it until the thin old blood begins to slime your fingers and drip from your wrist—until the piercing old eyes roll back and close, and the skinny old legs crumple and sag? Have you felt the blood pounding in your own temples, and savage satisfaction swarming up in you as you stare down on the hideous, sprawling thing you have destroyed?

And then have you opened your eyes and looked down at the mass of scribbled papers, and the meticulously drawn sectional charts, and the trait tables and correlation diagrams and all the other dead, dry details that make up your life's work? And picked up your pen and started making more scribbles on the papers and more checks on the charts and more little colored dots on the scattergrams, just as you've been doing three days out of every five since you were old enough to start the career for which you'd been tested and picked and trained?

Maybe I should go to a clinic and let the psychotherapists feed vitamins to my personality. Maybe I should go to a religious center and let the licensed clergy try to put this fear of Humanity into my reputed soul. Maybe I should go to a pleasure palace and let them mix me up an emotional hooker to jar the megrims out of my disposition, or go down and apply for a permit to wed and set about begetting another generation of archeologists who will grow up to be just as tired and bored and murderous as their illustrious father.

Night after night and day after day I dream of what might have happened that day in the laboratory if I had picked up the knife and slit the gullet of the man who had just injected the time-stream concept into the quietly maturing science of human archeology. If I could have seen ahead— If I could have guessed what would happen to all the romantic visions he had worked so hard to inspire in me—

Why should I dream? I was a child then; I had no way of looking ahead; the knife was just another knife. And I think if *he* had known—if he had been able to see ahead and watch the science to which he had devoted his every waking moment for a long lifetime degenerate into a variety of three-dimensional book-keeping—he'd have cut his own heart out and offered it to me in apology.

He was a great old man. He was my grandfather.

You've seen the knife. Everyone has, I guess. I was the first, after him, ever to see it, and I was about ten years old. I was sitting in a chair in his laboratory, waiting for him to come back. It was a wooden chair, something his grandfather had used, and maybe other people before that. The laboratory was just a big room at the back of the house, with a concrete floor and plenty of light from a row of windows over the worktable. There were hundreds of potsherds strewn over the table where he'd been classifying and matching them for restoration. There were trays of stone implements, and cheap wooden boxes full of uncatalogued stuff with the dirt still on it. There was a row of battered-looking notebooks, bound in imitation leather, fraying at the corners and stained with ink and dirt. There was a pot that had been half restored, the shards joined so neatly that you could barely see where they fitted together, and a little ivory goddess whose cracks and chips were being replaced with a plastic filler until you'd never have known she was five thousand years old.

That was what an archeologist's laboratory was like in those days. Of course, we've outgrown all that. His experiment, and the knife he brought back and tossed down on the table for me to look at, have ended all that. Archeology has found its place among the major sciences. It's no longer a kind of bastard stepchild of art and anthropology. We got money for the best equipment, the newest gadgets. We have laboratories designed by the best architects to fit the work we do in them. We can call on the technicians of a score of other sciences to do our dirty work, or can train ourselves to know as much as they do if we're reactionaries like me. We have our own specialists, just as learned and as limited as any hair-splitter in biochemistry or galactic physics. We have prestige—recognition—everything he never had in his day, when he was the acknowledged master in his field, and we have him to thank for it all. But Walter Toynbee, if he were living now, would dry up and die in the kind of laboratory his grandson has. He'd push his charts and his correlations back and drop his head in his hands and dream. He'd plan out his own murder.

I'd been sitting there for nearly six hours. I'd been over the worktable from one end to the other, three times. I'd picked up every potsherd—turned them over— —studied them with all the solemn intentness of ten years old—put them back exactly where I'd found them, as he had taught me. I'd found four shards that would fit onto the pot he was restoring, and two that made an ear for a little clay figurine shaped like a fat, happy puppy. I'd taken down his books, one by one, and looked at the plates and figures as I had done many times before. I had even taken down one of his notebooks and slowly leafed through it, trying to spell out the straggling handwriting and make sense of the precise sketches, until a loose slip of paper fell out from among the pages and I slipped it hurriedly back and put the book away.

All one corner of the laboratory was taken up by the time shuttle. It had cost more than all the air surveys, all the expeditions, all the books and photographs and restorations of his whole career. The copper bus bars that came in through the wall behind it were like columns in some Mayan colonnade. The instrument panel was like something you'd imagine on—well, on a time machine. The machine itself was a block of dull gray lead with a massive steel door in one side of it, the time cell floating in a magnetic bearing between the pole pieces which set up the field.

Ours are neater now, but inside they're about the same. Old Walter Toynbee was an artist to the core, and Balmer, who built the machine for him from Malecewicz's notes, had a flair for functional design. It was the first shuttle big enough and powerful enough to push a man and his baggage more than twenty years into the future—or the past, for that matter. Malecewicz had gone back fifteen years. He never returned. His questions showed why that was, and the archeological world, which had been rubbing its hands in anticipation of striking up a speaking acquaintance with Hatshepsut and Queen Shub-Ad, went back to its trowels and whisk-brooms with sighs of resignation. All but my grandfather. All but Walter Toynbee.

Malecewicz had never taken time to really work out his theory of the time function and lapsed interval, or he might be alive now. Laymen will still ask you why we archeologists don't simply climb into a shuttle with a solido camera and slip back to Greece or Elam or maybe Atlantis, and film what went on instead of tediously slicing the dust of millennia over the graveyards of past civilizations. It can be done, but the man who does it must be utterly self-centered, wrapped up in knowledge for its own sake, utterly unconcerned with his duties to his fellowmen. As any schoolchild learns, the time shuttler who goes into the past introduces an alien variable into the spacio-temporal matrix at the instant when he emerges. The time stream forks, an alternative universe is born in which his visit is given its proper place, and when he returns it will be to a future level in the new world which he has created. His own universe is forever barred to him.

The future is by its nature different. All that we are now and all that we have been or become from moment to moment is integral in the structure and flow of our particular thread of time. The man who visits the future is not changing it: his visit is a foredestined part of that future. As the ancients might have said: "It is written." Though I should imagine that the writing is the matrix of spacetime and not in the record book of God.

Walter Toynbee was a brilliant man who might have made a success of many sciences. He had money to guarantee him such comfort as he might want, and he chose the science which most attracted him—archeology. He was the last of the great amateurs. He had known Malecewicz well—financed some of his experimental work—and when the physicist failed to return he wheedled the trustees of the university into turning the man's notes over to him. He showed them almost at once where Malecewicz had gone and why he would never return, and he saw immediately that there was no such barrier between Man and his tomorrows. Inside of a week he and Balmer were moving cases of artifacts out of the back room to make room for the shuttle. Night after night they sat up into the wee hours, arguing over fantastic-looking diagrams. In two months the power lines were coming in across the fields, straight from the generators at Sheldon Forks, and Balmer's men were pouring the colossal concrete base on which the machine would sit.

It was past dinner time. I had been sitting there alone since a little after one o'clock, when he had stepped into the shuttle and asked me to wait until he returned. There it sat, just as it had sat for the last six hours, shimmering a little as though the air around it were hot and humming like a swarm of bees deep in an old beech. I got down a big book of plates of early Sumerian cylinder seals and began to turn the pages slowly. The sameness of them had grown boring when I realized that the humming had stopped.

I looked up at the lead cube. It was no longer shimmering. I closed the book and put it carefully back on the shelf, just as the great steel door of the shuttle swung silently open, and my grandfather stepped down out of the time cell.

He had been digging. His breeches and heavy jacket were covered with whitish dust. Dirt made grimy gutters under his eyes and filled in the creases and wrinkles of his face and neck. He had a stubble of dirty gray beard on his chin, which hadn't been there six hours before, and his shirt was dark with sweat. He was tired, but there was a gleam of satisfaction in his sharp black eyes and a kind of grin on his wrinkled face.

The battered canvas bag in which he kept his tools and records was slung over one shoulder. He slapped at his thighs and puffs of dust spurted from his trousers. He took off the shabby felt hat which he always wore, and his thin gray hair was damp and draggled. He came over to the table, fumbling with the buckle on the bag. I watched his knotted fingers wide-eyed, for I had seen them pull many wonders out of that dusty wallet. I can hear his triumphant chuckle as he drew out a knife——the knife—and tossed it ringing on the table among the shards.

You've seen it, of course. It's been in the pictures many times, and there are solidographs of the thing in most museums. I saw it then for the first time—ever—in our time.

He hadn't washed it. There was dirt on the fine engraving of the dull-black hilt, and caked in the delicate filigree of the silver guard. But the blade was clean, and it was as you have seen it—cold, gleaming, metallic blue—razor-edged—and translucent.

Maybe you've had a chance to handle it, here in the museum. Where the blade thins down to that feather-edge you can read small print through it. Where it's thicker, along the rib that reinforces the back of the blade, it's cloudy—milky looking. There has been engraving on the blade, too, but it has been ground or worn down until it is illegible. That is odd, because the blade is harder than anything we know except diamond. There is no such metal in the System or the Galaxy, so far as we know, except in this one well-worn and apparently very ancient knife blade.

It must be old. Not only is the engraving on the blade obliterated by wear; there is the telltale little serif near the hilt, where that utterly keen, hard edge has been worn back a little by use and honing. The black stuff of the hilt looks newer, and the carving is clearer, though still very old. Grandfather thought that it was made of some very heavy wood, possibly impregnated with a plastic of some sort, and that it had been made to replace an earlier hilt which had become worn out or broken. The metal of the guard and the plate and rivets which hold the hilt are ordinary silver, in one of the new stainless alloys which were just then coming into fairly general use.

Well—there it was. Walter Toynbee, who was probably the most competent archeologist the world has yet seen, had gone into the future in a Malecewicz shuttle. He had dug up a knife, and brought it back with him. And it was made of a material—a metal—of which our science knew absolutely nothing.

Three days later Walter Toynbee was dead. It may have been some virus picked up in that distant future which he had visited, to which our generation of mankind had developed no resistance. It may have been the strain of the trip into time, or the excitement and exertion of what he did there. He washed up, and we went home together to supper. We had it together, in the kitchen, because the family had finished and the dishes were done. Grandfather examined the knife while we were eating, but he wouldn't talk about it then. He was tired: he wanted to sleep. He never awoke.

In my father, old Walter's only son, the family talents had taken another turn. He was a more practical man than his father, and had done his noted parent many a good turn by husbanding and stimulating the family fortunes when they most needed it. Where grandfather had been interested in the minutiae and complexities of the ancient cultures whose dust he cleared away, father was one of the then popular cyclic historians who tried to see civilization as a whole—as a kind of super-organism—and to find recurring patterns in Man's gradual progression from the jungle to Parnassus. I am not implying that old Walter had no interest in synthesis and generalization—it is, as a matter of fact, a tradition that he had adopted the name Toynbee out of admiration for an historian of that name—a scholar of scholars—who lived and wrote in the early years of the last century. There is a letter among his papers which suggests that our original patronym may have been Slavic. If so, it might also explain his long and warm friendship with the unfortunate Malecewicz.

Be that as it may, Grandfather's death set in motion events whose result is all too familiar to all who have chosen to identify their lives with the pursuit of archeology. By the time the public lamentations had begun to die away, the press found a new sensation in the knife. The experts mulled over it and reported with remarkable unanimity that the engraving on the blade and hilt, while clearly of the same provenance, resembled no known human script or style of decoration. Finding their progress blocked, they called on the metallurgists and chemists to identify the blue metal of the blade, and on the botanists to specify the wood—if it was wood—of which the hilt was made.

Need I continue? There was more quibbling for its own sake in those days than there is now. Every expert was jealous of his personal acumen and insistent upon being the Only Right Man. It was considered fitting and proper that experts should disagree. But it gradually dawned on everyone concerned that here was something where there could be no disagreement, and what was more, something which might very well open new vistas of human progress.

Physically and chemically the blue stuff was a metal, though it was no metal chemistry had ever described or imagined. When they had succeeded in sawing out a sliver of the blade for tests, and finally got it into solution, its chemical behavior placed it quite outside the periodic system of the elements. The physicists went to work on another sample with X rays and spectragraphs, and arrived at much the same result. The more they studied it, the less they knew, for sooner or later some experiment would succeed in knocking over any hypothesis which they might have built up on the basis of their previous investigations.

Out of it all eventually came the judgment which stands today: that the blue stuff might well be some familiar metal, but that its atomic and molecular structure—
—and consequently its physical and chemical properties—had been modified or tampered with in a manner unknown to our science, making it to all intents and purposes a new state of matter. The botanists returned the same report. The black material had the structure of wood, and it might be any of several common tropical woods or it might be something quite alien, but it, too, had been hardened—indurated—through the internal transformations which left it something entirely new to our planet.

That ended the first stage of the battle. When the experts threw up their hands in despair, the attack shifted to another quarter. The knife came back to my father, and he promptly made it the nucleus of a Toynbee Museum of Human Acculturation at his and Malecewicz's university, where it is today. But it was common knowledge that old Walter had brought the thing from the future. That meant that somewhere in the coming centuries of our race was a science which could create such unheard of things as the blue metal, and that the stuff was sufficiently common with them for knives to be made of it. Its electrical properties alone were such as to open a host of possible uses for it—father had been offered a small fortune by a certain great electrical concern for the material in the knife alone—and science decided to visit that future civilization, learn its secrets and profit suitably thereby.

So the experiments shifted to time traveling. Malecewicz's notes were unearthed again and published; Grandfather's shuttle was dismantled and reconstructed a dozen times; Balmer found himself in a position to charge almost any fee as a consultant to industrial laboratories, universities and private speculators who were hot on the trail of tomorrow. Shuttles were built on every hand, and men—and women——disappeared into the future. One by one they straggled back, empty-handed and thoroughly disgruntled. The future had no such metal.

There was a brief period in which everyone who had failed to solve the problem of the knife tried to cast doubts on Walter Toynbee, but the thing existed, its nature was what it was, and presently the hubbub swung around full circle to the place it had started. Grandfather had been an archeologist. He had gone into the future, and excavated the knife from the detritus of what might conceivably have been a colony or a chance visitant from another world—even another galaxy—someone— or something—of which the rest of humanity at that moment in time was quite unaware. Archeology had found the thing. Science craved it. It was up to archeology to find it—or its source—again.

So we became, in the language of the popularizers, the Mother Science— spawning off all sorts of minuscule specialties, lording it over a score of devoutly adulatory slave sciences, enjoying our position and taking every advantage of it.

I grew up in that atmosphere. From the time I could talk and listen, Grandfather had filled me with the wonders of the past and the romance of their discovery. Now the whole world was awake to the glories of archeology as the science of sciences which would open a whole new world to struggling Mankind. Is it any wonder I chose to follow in my grandfather's footsteps?

Let me say now that men like my father and grandfather, who had needed no world-shaking anomaly to intrigue them with their chosen study, never lost their heads in the storm of recognition which swept over them. It might have been better if they had. Archeology was in the saddle; very well, it was going to ride—and ride hard. Projects which had been tabled for lack of funds were financed in a twinkling. Tools and instruments of investigation which had been regarded as extremists' pipe dreams were invented on demand. With new tools came new techniques, and with new techniques came a hierarchy of skilled technicians, stat- isticians in place of explorers, desk work in place of excavation, piddling with detail instead of drawing in broad strokes the panorama of advancing civilization which men like Schliemann, and Evans, and Breasted, and that first Toynbee— yes, and old Walter Toynbee after them all—had seen with clear and understanding eyes.

We have no one to blame but ourselves. I fully realize that. We dug our own hole; we furnished it lavishly; we built a wall around it to exclude the non-elite; we arranged to be fed and comforted while we dawdled with our trivia; and then we pulled the hole in on top of ourselves. We wore a rut so deep that we can never climb out of it. So I dream of cutting my grandfather's throat instead of realizing that if I were the man he was—if I had the courage to break away from the stultified pattern I have helped to make, and go primitive, dig in the dirt with a trowel, regain the thrill of new worlds—the barriers would disappear and I would be free again, as men were meant to be.

Of course, by the time I was old enough for the university the whole business was well under way. My father, with his cycles in mind, had instigated a project whereby Archeology—it rated the capital by now—would uncover and describe the entire growth, maturity and decline of representative communities, our own included. A colleague—or maybe he was a competitor—at Harvard was all for starting all over again at the beginning and redigesting the entire corpus of arche- ological data accumulated by grubbers since the beginning of time, using the new statistical attacks and the college's vast new calculating machine. He got his money.

Science had declared that Archeology was the magician which would presently pass out unbounded benefits to one and all, and one and all swarmed to get on Santa Claus' good side.

I served my apprenticeship doing the dirty work for the men who voyaged into the future and sent back reams and sheaves of notes out of which we desk-workers were supposed to pull blue metal rabbits. This was the era of specialism: when trained mechanics did the digging, when stenographers and solido-scanners took the notes, and when laboratory drudges squeezed out of them every possible drop of information which super-statistics could extract.

I remember the worst pest of them all—a man with as much personality as my grandfather, though of a different kind—who nearly imposed his infernal pattern on the science for a generation. He had been a mathematical physicist who turned to archeology in what he claimed was an attempt to fit human behavior "in its broader sense" into some set of universal field-equations he had distilled out of his stars and atoms, and which purported to express the Totality of All, or some such pat phrase, in a large nutshell.

Of course, any such over-view of civilization was music to my father's ears, and he gave the man the run of the Museum and a voice in all our activities. Hill——that was his name—at once announced the precept that it was quite unnecessary to *find* blue-metal knives in some future culture. By making a sufficiently exhaustive collection of data at any particular moment, and applying his field equations in their humano-cultural aspect—I am trying here to recall his jargon—it would be possible to predict accurately when and where such knives *must* be.

Hill had a shock of red hair, a barrel chest and a loud voice. He spoke often and in the right places. Myriads of miserable students like myself had to mull over the tons of notes which expeditions under his direction sent back. We translated facts into symbols, put the symbols through his mill, and got out more symbols. Nine times, by count, he announced to the world that "now we had it"—and nine times by count a simple check up showed that the poor beleaguered natives of whatever era it was he had chosen as It had never heard of such a metal. Some of them had never heard of metal.

By the time I was twenty-three and had my own license to explore past and future indiscriminately, we had a pretty good overall view of the future of humanity. We had libraries of histories which had been written in millennia to come. We had gadgets and super-gadgets developed by future civilizations, some of which we could use and most of which we were able to misuse. The world we supposedly enjoy today was in the making, and you know what it is like.

I have done altogether too well at whipping the esteemed Dr. Hill's hodgepodge of miscellaneous data into some semblance of intelligibility. The powers that were——and are—announced that I might spend the rest of my life, for the good of Humanity, fiddling with the same kind of stuff. But I was young, and I was a Toynbee. I stood up and demanded my rights, and they gave them to me. I could go out like all the rest and hunt for the knife.

I am not a fool. Moreover, I had had the advantage of knowing my grandfather——better even than Father ever did. I knew how he would think and how he would react. He was the kind of man who went at things hard—all out—to the limit of his ability. It seemed clear enough to me that the first step in finding the knife was to determine what that limit was—although in thirteen years or so nobody had chosen that approach.

Balmer was still alive, and I made him dig out the plans and specifications he had drawn up when he made Grandfather's shuttle. I got hold of the notes the experts had made when they tore the machine apart after his death, and they checked. And then I had Balmer set me up just the same kind of old gray cube out of which Walter Toynbee had stumbled that day, with the blue knife in his dusty old ditty bag.

It was bigger, of course—I had to have room for the kind of equipment a field man considered necessary in my day. I'd never had any training or experience with the kind of work old Walter did with his own two hands, a camera and a trowel. The profession had been mechanized, and it was silly not to use the best I could lay my hands on. The time field, though, was the same, and it should carry me just as far as it had carried its originator thirteen years before.

It did. Malecewicz, by stretching his original model, had been able to get fifteen years out of it. Grandfather's huge old vault of a machine lofted him nearly twenty times as far into the future of our race—and of our town. As I had suspected from the specifications of the machine, it dropped me somewhere near the middle of the interregnum which followed the Hemispheric Wars, when half the cities of America had been reduced to rubble, disease and famine had put the population of the planet back into a hunting-fishing-food-gathering economy, and all that remained of civilization was a memory which would some day be revived, restored and started off again.

I am not saying that in thirteen years of trying nobody had hit upon this particular period in the future. It is true that having hit it they let common sense scare them off. It was obvious that that level of culture could never produce so sophisticated a scientific marvel as the knife. There was no evidence in the ruins they found to show that our own culture, up to and during the time of the Wars, had done so. Ergo: onward and upward. Try another thousand years. Try a million.

I had a slightly different point of view on the matter. I knew Grandfather. He would go as far as his machine could take him. I had duplicated that. He would look around him for a promising site, get out his tools and pitch in. Well, I could do that, too.

There is enough uncertainty—backlash, if you want to call it that—in the operation of any time shuttle so that you can never be certain that you will hit any specific moment or even any specific day or week in the future. Put that down to mechanical imperfections, if you like—I know some do—but I consider it a matter of the inexactitude of the physical universe, and I doubt that there is ever anything that we can do about it. You can approximate—hopping back and forth across the time you want until you get reasonably close—but that is a makeshift solution, borrowed from practical mathematics. I didn't try.

If you've read your history of the next five hundred years, you'll know that the gas attacks toward the end of the war had stripped the Atlantic coastal regions of vegetation and every other living thing. I got out of the shuttle in a dusty landscape where the bare bones of the planet stuck up in shattered stumps in a wind-swept desert of gullied clay. I might be ahead of my grandfather's time—in which case I saw a paradox brewing—or I might be following him. As it turned out, it was the latter.

I knew from what others had learned that there was no life in this coastal strip until much later. Gradually vegetation worked its way into the arid strip, insects and mammals followed, men followed them—but this is no essay on the future. There was no point in hunting for survivors; Grandfather certainly hadn't. For on all sides stretched the wreckage of our own city—or its counterpart of three centuries from now—and I knew that he would have stood just as I was standing, looking it over with an appraising eye, wondering where to begin.

One mass of fallen masonry, half submerged in a drift of sand, towered higher than the rest. It would provide a vantage point from which to size up the situation. As I plodded toward it through the soft sand I found myself watching for his footprints, so certain was I that this must be the place and the time. It was nonsense, of course; my own tracks were filling in as the wind curled sand into them.

Then I saw it—and that day thirteen years before came rushing back to me. Of course there would be traces! Walter Toynbee would never in his life have abandoned a dig as promising as this—a dig where surface-scratching had yielded him a relic like the knife. But for his sickness and death he would have been planning a return expedition—a camp—a full-scale attack. Not half the equipment he had taken with him was in the shuttle when he returned. And there, at the eastern base of the mound, the tatters of a red bandanna whipping in the wind, a short-handled shovel was driven into a crack in the masonry.

I fingered the shreds of red cloth. It was his. He always had one stuffed in the pocket of his jeans. Duster—sun shield—lashing—he had a score of uses for them. Any field worker had in those days, before there was a tool for every purpose.

The crevice into which the shovel had been wedged widened as it went down. Sand had drifted into it, filling it to within a few feet of the top. By all the tenets of civilized archeology I should first prepare my aërial plan of the entire complex of ruins, erect the light tower with its instrument board to establish a zero reference plane for the solidograph, and assemble the scanner. When a grid had been projected on the screen of the excavator, it would be time enough to think of beginning the actual investigation.

Do you believe in ghosts? As I stood there, with those shreds of faded red cloth in my hand, stroking the sand-polished handle of the shovel, I suddenly realized that so far as time itself went he might have been standing here only hours, or even minutes before me. It was as though he had turned his back for a moment, and I had stepped into his tracks there in the sand. I was a child again, tagging after him as he strode around the big laboratory with his giant's strides, pulling down a book here, running through a file of negatives there, gathering his tools around him before he set to work to unravel some perplexing situation in his digging. A thin cloud passed across the sun, and it was as though his shadow had fallen on me.

I pulled the shovel out of the crack in which he had wedged it. It was in good condition—perfectly usable. In my time we did not work with shovels or picks, but any fool could handle the thing. I dug it into the sand—scratched at the base of the crack. It would take only a few moments to deepen it enough so that I could crawl inside.

There was a kind of satisfaction to the work. I exercise in the public gymnasia——all young men of my age have to, to keep fit—but there was a difference. Using this primitive tool brought with it a feeling of accomplishment—of purpose—that I never found in mere exercise. I was strong, and it gratified me to see the hole deepen and the drift of sand grow behind me. Soon I had a tunnel into which I could crawl without bumping my head. I went back to the shuttle for a glow lamp and a pocket scanner, and plunged into the darkness.

After the first few feet I had no use for the lamp. My eyes grew accustomed to the dark, and I saw that shafts and streaks of light broke through gaps in the ruin overhead. Presently I found a hard floor under my feet, and then I came out into a room which was like a wedge—the ceiling fallen in one mass which hung diagonally between the wall over my head and the floor about twenty feet before me. Sunlight seeped in through a crevice to the left, striking on the wall and filling the whole place with a kind of diffuse glow. In that glow I saw footprints in the thick dust which covered the floor, and the table to which they led.

They were his footprints, of course. On that table he had found the knife. I stepped out of the doorway where I had been standing, an odd feeling of familiarity growing in me. I crossed the floor to the table. It had been covered with heavy glass, which lay in shreds on the dusty bronze. I could see the marks of his fingers in the dust where he had moved the broken glass aside. And I could see the outline of the knife, as sharp in the unstirred dust as it was when he picked it up in his gnarled old fingers thirteen years—or was it thirteen minutes?—before.

The crack of light was widening as the sun moved; the place grew brighter. I brushed the dust away from the table top. It was heavy bronze; it told me nothing. And then, turning, I saw the opposite wall and the frieze in low relief which ran above the door—

I don't like the impossible. I don't like paradox. I sit here, toiling over my correlations—they have promised a machine by spring which will perform them for us more quickly and in far more detail than we have ever attempted—and when I grow tired I let my head slip down on my hands, and I dream of a day when I was a child. I dream of an old man and a knife—and murder.

I had had my chance. Others, more experienced and possibly more capable than I, followed me. The entire ruin was excavated, with the most meticulous attention to technique, down to bedrock. And I . . . I was sent back to my correlations and my trait tables, to work up the data which other men would presently send me. Because strive as they will, they can find no other explanation than the one which——to me—seems obvious. The answer which is no answer—

You can go into the Toynbee Museum now, today, and see the knife in a guarded case, in the anteroom of the main exhibit hall. In the course of three hundred years that case will have been replaced by a bronze table and a cover of heavy glass. Bombs will fall, the building will crumble in ruins and the knife will still be there. Dust will cover the ruins, and one day a gnarled old man in shabby clothes will shovel it away and creep inside. He will find the knife and carry it away. Later a younger man will come—and then others—many others, men and women both. And all the while, on the granite lintel above the door to the room where the knife is kept, will be the inscription:

WALTER TOYNBEE
1962—2035

My grandfather brought the knife back from the future. He died. It was placed in the museum named for him. It lay there for three hundred years, while the human race went mad trying to solve its secret—while all civilization was turned upside down in the search for something which never existed!

He found it in the museum where it had always been. He carried it back through time, and it was placed in that museum. It lay there until he came and found it, and carried it back through time—

It was a simple pattern—as simple as ever was. Must we think only in terms of a beginning and an end? Cannot a thing—even a person—exist in a closed cycle without beginning or end? Appearing to us now, at this level of our time thread, accompanying us down its extension into our future, then vanishing from our stream and circling back to the point where it appeared? Can't you imagine that?

I thought I could. I thought it was a paradox—no more—as simple to explain as ever was. I was wrong, of course, and they are right.

The knife old Walter Toynbee brought back from the museum built in his honor, to house his knife, was perfect—worn, dirty, but perfect. A little notch was sawed in the back of its translucent blue blade—sawed with a diamond saw, to provide the chemist and the physicists with the samples they needed to test its properties. That notch is still in its blade as it lies out there in the museum case—it will be there for the next three hundred years, or until the raids come and the museum falls in ruins. Until an old man comes out of the past to find it—

The knife old Walter Toynbee will find there in our future will have that notch. The knife he brought back to me thirty years ago had no notch in it. Somewhere the circle must have a beginning. Somewhere it must have an end—but where, and how? How was this knife created, out of a strange blue metal, and a strange, black, indurated wood, when its existence has no beginning or end? How can the circle be broken? I wish I knew. I might not dream of murder then. I might find logic and purpose in the future instead of chaos—instead of impossible worlds that never were.

CLIFFORD D. SIMAK

Desertion

Clifford D. Simak (1904-), like Jack Williamson, has been a successful and popular science fiction writer for more than fifty years. A newspaperman in Minnesota for most of his life, he was never a full-time writer until his retirement a few years ago, although he produced more than twenty-five novels and scores of short stories. Always improving, he won a Hugo Award for the best short story of 1980, more than twenty years after winning his first Hugo in that category. He is also a recipient of the Grand Master Award of the Science Fiction Writers of America.

"Desertion" is his finest short story, written in anger and frustration when he heard the first reports of what was happening in the death camps of Nazi-occupied Europe.

FOUR MEN, two by two, had gone into the howling maelstrom that was Jupiter and had not returned. They had walked into the keening gale—or rather, they had loped, bellies low against the ground, wet sides gleaming in the rain.

For they did not go in the shape of men.

Now the fifth man stood before the desk of Kent Fowler, head of Dome No. 3, Jovian Survey Commission.

Under Fowler's desk, old Towser scratched a flea, then settled down to sleep again.

Harold Allen, Fowler saw with a sudden pang, was young—too young. He had the easy confidence of youth, the straight back and eyes, the face of one who never had known fear. And that was strange. For men in the domes of Jupiter did know fear—fear and humility. It was hard for Man to reconcile his puny self with the mighty forces of the monstrous planet.

"You understand," said Fowler, "that you need not do this. You understand that you need not go."

It was formula, of course. The other four had been told the same thing, but they had gone. This fifth one, Fowler knew, would go too. But suddenly he felt a dull hope stir within him that Allen wouldn't go.

"When do I start?" asked Allen.

There was a time when Fowler might have taken quiet pride in that answer, but not now. He frowned briefly.

"Within the hour," he said.

239

Allen stood waiting, quietly.

"Four other men have gone out and have not returned," said Fowler. "You know that, of course. We want you to return. We don't want you going off on any heroic rescue expedition. The main thing, the only thing, is that you come back, that you prove Man can live in a Jovian form. Go to the first survey stake, no farther, then come back. Don't take any chances. Don't investigate anything. Just come back."

Allen nodded. "I understand all that."

"Miss Stanley will operate the converter," Fowler went on. "You need have no fear on that particular point. The other men were converted without mishap. They left the converter in apparently perfect condition. You will be in thoroughly competent hands. Miss Stanley is the best qualified conversion operator in the Solar System. She had had experience on most of the other planets. That is why she's here."

Allen grinned at the woman and Fowler saw something flicker across Miss Stanley's face—something that might have been pity, or rage—or just plain fear. But it was gone again and she was smiling back at the youth who stood before the desk. Smiling in that prim, schoolteacherish way she had of smiling, almost as if she hated herself for doing it.

"I shall be looking forward," said Allen, "to my conversion."

And the way he said it, he made it all a joke, a vast, ironic joke.

But it was no joke.

It was serious business, deadly serious. Upon these tests, Fowler knew, depended the fate of men on Jupiter. If the tests succeeded, the resources of the giant planet would be thrown open. Man would take over Jupiter as he already had taken over the smaller planets. And if they failed—

If they failed, Man would continue to be chained and hampered by the terrific pressure, the greater force of gravity, the weird chemistry of the planet. He would continue to be shut within the domes, unable to set actual foot upon the planet, unable to see it with direct, unaided vision, forced to rely upon the awkward tractors and the televisor, forced to work with clumsy tools and mechanisms or through the medium of robots that themselves were clumsy.

For Man, unprotected and in his natural form, would be blotted out by Jupiter's terrific pressure of fifteen thousand pounds per square inch, pressure that made Terrestrial sea bottoms seem a vacuum by comparison.

Even the strongest metal Earthmen could devise couldn't exist under pressure such as that, under the pressure and the alkaline rains that forever swept the planet. It grew brittle and flaky, crumbling like clay, or it ran away in little streams and puddles of ammonia salts. Only by stepping up the toughness and strength of that metal, by increasing its electronic tension, could it be made to withstand the weight of thousands of miles of swirling, choking gases that made up the atmosphere. And even when that was done, everything had to be coated with tough quartz to keep away the rain—the bitter rain that was liquid ammonia.

Fowler sat listening to the engines in the sub-floor of the dome. Engines that ran on endlessly, the dome never quiet of them. They had to run and keep on running. For if they stopped, the power flowing into the metal walls of the dome would stop, the electronic tension would ease up and that would be the end of everything.

Towser roused himself under Fowler's desk and scratched another flea, his leg thumping hard against the floor.

"Is there anything else?" asked Allen.

Fowler shook his head. "Perhaps there's something you want to do," he said. "Perhaps you—"

He had meant to say write a letter and he was glad he caught himself quick enough so he didn't say it.

Allen looked at his watch. "I'll be there on time," he said. He swung around and headed for the door.

Fowler knew Miss Stanley was watching him and he didn't want to turn and meet her eyes. He fumbled with a sheaf of papers on the desk before him.

"How long are you going to keep this up?" asked Miss Stanley and she bit off each word with a vicious snap.

He swung around in his chair and faced her then. Her lips were drawn into a straight, thin line, her hair seemed skinned back from her forehead tighter than ever, giving her face that queer, almost startling death-mask quality.

He tried to make his voice cool and level. "As long as there's any need of it," he said. "As long as there's any hope."

"You're going to keep on sentencing them to death," she said. "You're going to keep marching them out face to face with Jupiter. You're going to sit in here safe and comfortable and send them out to die."

"There is no room for sentimentality, Miss Stanley," Fowler said, trying to keep the note of anger from his voice. "You know as well as I do why we're doing this. You realize that Man in his own form simply cannot cope with Jupiter. The only answer is to turn men into the sort of things that can cope with it. We've done it on the other planets.

"If a few men die, but we finally succeed, the price is small. Through the ages men have thrown away their lives on foolish things, for foolish reasons. Why should we hesitate, then, at a little death in a thing as great as this?"

Miss Stanley sat stiff and straight, hands folded in her lap, the lights shining on her graying hair and Fowler, watching her, tried to imagine what she might feel, what she might be thinking. He wasn't exactly afraid of her, but he didn't feel quite comfortable when she was around. Those sharp blue eyes saw too much, her hands looked far too competent. She should be somebody's Aunt sitting in a rocking chair with her knitting needles. But she wasn't. She was the top-notch conversion unit operator in the Solar System and she didn't like the way he was doing things.

"There is something wrong, Mr. Fowler," she declared.

"Precisely," agreed Fowler. "That's why I'm sending young Allen out alone. He may find out what it is."

"And if he doesn't?"

"I'll send someone else."

She rose slowly from her chair, started toward the door, then stopped before his desk.

"Some day," she said, "you will be a great man. You never let a chance go by. This is your chance. You knew it was when this dome was picked for the tests. If you put it through, you'll go up a notch or two. No matter how many men may die, you'll go up a notch or two."

"Miss Stanley," he said and his voice was curt, "young Allen is going out soon. Please be sure that your machine—"

"My machine," she told him, icily, "is not to blame. It operates along the co-ordinates the biologists set up."

He sat hunched at his desk, listening to her footsteps go down the corridor.

What she said was true, of course. The biologists had set up the co-ordinates. But the biologists could be wrong. Just a hairbreadth of difference, one iota of digression and the converter would be sending out something that wasn't the thing they meant to send. A mutant that might crack up, go haywire, come unstuck under some condition or stress of circumstance wholly unsuspected.

For Man didn't know much about what was going on outside. Only what his instruments told him was going on. And the samplings of those happenings furnished by those instruments and mechanisms had been no more than samplings, for Jupiter was unbelievably large and the domes were very few.

Even the work of the biologists in getting the data on the Lopers, apparently the highest form of Jovian life, had involved more than three years of intensive study and after that two years of checking to make sure. Work that could have been done on Earth in a week or two. But work that, in this case, couldn't be done on Earth at all, for one couldn't take a Jovian life form to Earth. The pressure here on Jupiter couldn't be duplicated outside of Jupiter and at Earth pressure and temperature the Lopers would simply have disappeared in a puff of gas.

Yet it was work that had to be done if Man ever hoped to go about Jupiter in the life form of the Lopers. For before the converter could change a man to another life form, every detailed physical characteristic of that life form must be known— surely and positively, with no chance of mistake.

Allen did not come back.

The tractors, combing the nearby terrain, found no trace of him, unless the skulking thing reported by one of the drivers had been the missing Earthman in Loper form.

The biologists sneered their most accomplished academic sneers when Fowler suggested the co-ordinates might be wrong. Carefully they pointed out, the co-ordinates worked. When a man was put into the converter and the switch was thrown, the man became a Loper. He left the machine and moved away, out of sight, into the soupy atmosphere.

Some quirk, Fowler had suggested; some tiny deviation from the thing a Loper should be, some minor defect. If there were, the biologists said, it would take years to find it.

And Fowler knew that they were right.

So there were five men now instead of four and Harold Allen had walked out into Jupiter for nothing at all. It was as if he'd never gone so far as knowledge was concerned.

Fowler reached across his desk and picked up the personal file, a thin sheaf of papers neatly clipped together. It was a thing he dreaded but a thing he had to do. Somehow the reason for these strange disappearances must be found. And there was no other way than to send out more men.

He sat for a moment listening to the howling of the wind above the dome, the everlasting thundering gale that swept across the planet in boiling, twisting wrath.

Was there some threat out there, he asked himself? Some danger they did not know about? Something that lay in wait and gobbled up the Lopers, making no distinction between Lopers that were *bona fide* and Lopers that were men? To the gobblers, of course, it would make no difference.

Or had there been a basic fault in selecting the Lopers as the type of life best fitted for existence on the surface of the planet? The evident intelligence of the Lopers, he knew, had been one factor in that determination. For if the thing Man became did not have capacity for intelligence, Man could not for long retain his own intelligence in such a guise.

Had the biologists let that one factor weigh too heavily, using it to offset some other factor that might be unsatisfactory, even disastrous? It didn't seem likely. Stiffnecked as they might be, the biologists knew their business.

Or was the whole thing impossible, doomed from the very start? Conversion to other life forms had worked on other planets, but that did not necessarily mean it would work on Jupiter. Perhaps Man's intelligence could not function correctly through the sensory apparatus provided Jovian life. Perhaps the Lopers were so alien there was no common ground for human knowledge and the Jovian conception of existence to meet and work together.

Or the fault might lie with Man, be inherent with the race. Some mental aberration which, coupled with what they found outside, wouldn't let them come back. Although it might not be an aberration, not in the human sense. Perhaps just one ordinary human mental trait, accepted as commonplace on Earth, would be so violently at odds with Jovian existence that it would blast all human intelligence and sanity.

Claws rattled and clicked down the corridor. Listening to them, Fowler smiled wanly. It was Towser coming back from the kitchen, where he had gone to see his friend, the cook.

Towser came into the room, carrying a bone. He wagged his tail at Fowler and flopped down beside the desk, bone between his paws. For a long moment his rheumy old eyes regarded his master and Fowler reached down a hand to ruffle a ragged ear.

"You still like me, Towser?" Fowler asked and Towser thumped his tail.

"You're the only one," said Fowler. "All through the dome they're cussing me. Calling me a murderer, more than likely."

He straightened and swung back to the desk. His hand reached out and picked up the file.

Bennett? Bennett had a girl waiting for him back on Earth.

Andrews? Andrews was planning on going back to Mars Tech just as soon as he earned enough to see him through a year.

Olson? Olson was nearing pension age. All the time telling the boys how he was going to settle down and grow roses.

Carefully, Fowler laid the file back on the desk.

Sentencing men to death. Miss Stanley had said that, her pale lips scarcely moving in her parchment face. Marching men out to die while he, Fowler, sat here safe and comfortable.

They were saying it all through the dome, no doubt, especially since Allen had failed to return. They wouldn't say it to his face, of course. Even the man or men he called before this desk and told they were the next to go, wouldn't say it to him.

They would only say: "When do we start?" For that was formula.

But he would see it in their eyes.

He picked up the file again. Bennett, Andrews, Olson. There were others, but there was no use in going on.

Kent Fowler knew that he couldn't do it, couldn't face them, couldn't send more men out to die.

He leaned forward and flipped up the toggle on the intercommunicator.

"Yes, Mr. Fowler."

"Miss Stanley, please."

He waited for Miss Stanley, listening to Towser chewing half-heartedly on the bone. Towser's teeth were getting bad.

"Miss Stanley," said Miss Stanley's voice.

"Just wanted to tell you, Miss Stanley, to get ready for two more."

"Aren't you afraid," asked Miss Stanley, "that you'll run out of them? Sending out one at a time, they'd last longer, give you twice the satisfaction."

"One of them," said Fowler, "will be a dog."

"A dog!"

"Yes, Towser."

He heard the quick, cold rage that iced her voice. "Your own dog! He's been with you all these years—"

"That's the point," said Fowler. "Towser would be unhappy if I left him behind."

It was not the Jupiter he had known through the televisor. He had expected it to be different, but not like this. He had expected a hell of ammonia rain and stinking fumes and the deafening, thundering tumult of the storm. He had expected swirling clouds and fog and the snarling flicker of monstrous thunderbolts.

He had not expected the lashing downpour would be reduced to drifting purple mist that moved like fleeing shadows over a red and purple sward. He had not even guessed the snaking bolts of lightning would be flares of pure ecstasy across a painted sky.

Waiting for Towser, Fowler flexed the muscles of his body, amazed at the smooth, sleek strength he found. Not a bad body, he decided, and grimaced at remembering how he had pitied the Lopers when he glimpsed them through the television screen.

For it had been hard to imagine a living organism based upon ammonia and hydrogen rather than upon water and oxygen, hard to believe that such a form of life could know the same quick thrill of life that humankind could know. Hard to conceive of life out in the soupy maelstrom that was Jupiter, not knowing, of course, that through Jovian eyes it was no soupy maelstrom at all.

The wind brushed against him with what seemed gentle fingers and he remembered with a start that by Earth standards the wind was a roaring gale, a two-hundred-mile an hour howler laden with deadly gases.

Pleasant scents seeped into his body. And yet scarcely scents, for it was not the sense of smell as he remembered it. It was as if his whole being was soaking up the sensation of lavender—and yet not lavender. It was something, he knew, for which he had no word, undoubtedly the first of many enigmas in terminology. For the words he knew, the thought symbols that served him as an Earthman would not serve him as a Jovian.

The lock in the side of the dome opened and Towser came tumbling out—at least he thought it must be Towser.

He started to call to the dog, his mind shaping the words he meant to say. But he couldn't say them. There was no way to say them. He had nothing to say them with.

For a moment his mind swirled in muddy terror, a blind fear that eddied in little puffs of panic through his brain.

How did Jovians talk? How—

Suddenly he was aware of Towser, intensely aware of the bumbling, eager friendliness of the shaggy animal that had followed him from Earth to many planets. As if the thing that was Towser had reached out and for a moment sat within his brain.

And out of the bubbling welcome that he sensed, came words.

"Hiya, pal."

Not words really, better than words. Thought symbols in his brain, communicated thought symbols that had shades of meaning words could never have.

"Hiya, Towser," he said.

"I feel good," said Towser. "Like I was a pup. Lately I've been feeling pretty punk. Legs stiffening up on me and teeth wearing down to almost nothing. Hard to mumble a bone with teeth like that. Besides, the fleas give me hell. Used to be I never paid much attention to them. A couple of fleas more or less never meant much in my early days."

"But...but—" Fowler's thoughts tumbled awkwardly. "You're talking to me!"

"Sure thing," said Towser. "I always talked to you, but you couldn't hear me.

246 <small>Clifford D. Simak</small>

I tried to say things to you, but I couldn't make the grade."

"I understood you sometimes," Fowler said.

"Not very well," said Towser. "You knew when I wanted food and when I wanted a drink and when I wanted out, but that's about all you ever managed."

"I'm sorry," Fowler said.

"Forget it," Towser told him. "I'll race you to the cliff."

For the first time, Fowler saw the cliff, apparently many miles away, but with a strange crystalline beauty that sparkled in the shadow of the many-colored clouds.

Fowler hesitated. "It's a long way—"

"Ah, come on," said Towser and even as he said it he started for the cliff.

Fowler followed, testing his legs, testing the strength in that new body of his, a bit doubtful at first, amazed a moment later, then running with a sheer joyousness that was one with the red and purple sward, with the drifting smoke of the rain across the land.

As he ran the consciousness of music came to him, a music that beat into his body, that surged throughout his being, that lifted him on wings of silver speed. Music like bells might make from some steeple on a sunny, springtime hill.

As the cliff drew nearer the music deepened and filled the universe with a spray of magic sound. And he knew the music came from the tumbling waterfall that feathered down the face of the shining cliff.

Only, he knew, it was no waterfall, but an ammonia-fall and the cliff was white because it was oxygen, solidified.

He skidded to a stop beside Towser where the waterfall broke into a glittering rainbow of many hundred colors. Literally many hundred, for here, he saw, was no shading of one primary to another as human beings saw, but a clear-cut selectivity that broke the prism down to its last ultimate classification.

"The music," said Towser.

"Yes, what about it?"

"The music," said Towser, "is vibrations. Vibrations of water falling."

"But, Towser, you don't know about vibrations."

"Yes, I do," contended Towser. "It just popped into my head."

Fowler gulped mentally. "Just popped!"

And suddenly, within his own head, he held a formula—the formula for a process that would make metal to withstand the pressure of Jupiter.

He stared, astounded, at the waterfall and swiftly his mind took the many colors and placed them in their exact sequence in the spectrum. Just like that. Just out of blue sky. Out of nothing, for he knew nothing either of metals or of colors.

"Towser," he cried. "Towser, something's happening to us!"

"Yeah, I know," said Towser.

"It's our brains," said Fowler. "We're using them, all of them, down to the last hidden corner. Using them to figure out things we should have known all the time. Maybe the brains of Earth things naturally are slow and foggy. Maybe we are the morons of the universe. Maybe we are fixed so we have to do things the hard way."

And, in the new sharp clarity of thought that seemed to grip him, he knew that it would not only be the matter of colors in a waterfall or metals that would resist the pressure of Jupiter, he sensed other things, things not yet quite clear. A vague whispering that hinted of greater things, of mysteries beyond the pale of human thought, beyond even the pale of human imagination. Mysteries, fact, logic built on reasoning. Things that any brain should know if it used all its reasoning power.

"We're still mostly Earth," he said. "We're just beginning to learn a few of the things we are to know—a few of the things that were kept from us as human beings, perhaps because we were human beings. Because our human bodies were poor bodies. Poorly equipped for thinking, poorly equipped in certain senses that one has to have to know. Perhaps even lacking in certain senses that are necessary to true knowledge."

He stared back at the dome, a tiny black thing dwarfed by the distance.

Back there were men who couldn't see the beauty that was Jupiter. Men who thought that swirling clouds and lashing rain obscured the face of the planet. Unseeing human eyes. Poor eyes. Eyes that could not see the beauty in the clouds, that could not see through the storms. Bodies that could not feel the thrill of trilling music stemming from the rush of broken water.

Men who walked alone, in terrible loneliness, talking with their tongue like Boy Scouts wigwagging out their messages, unable to reach out and touch one another's mind as he could reach out and touch Towser's mind. Shut off forever from that personal, intimate contact with other living things.

He, Fowler, had expected terror inspired by alien things out here on the surface, had expected to cower before the threat of unknown things, had steeled himself against disgust of a situation that was not of Earth.

But instead he had found something greater than Man had ever known. A swifter, surer body. A sense of exhilaration, a deeper sense of life. A sharper mind. A world of beauty that even the dreamers of the Earth had not yet imagined.

"Let's get going," Towser urged.

"Where do you want to go?"

"Anywhere," said Towser. "Just start going and see where we end up. I have a feeling . . . well, a feeling—"

"Yes, I know," said Fowler.

For he had the feeling, too. The feeling of high destiny. A certain sense of greatness. A knowledge that somewhere off beyond the horizons lay adventure and things greater than adventure.

Those other five had felt it, too. Had felt the urge to go and see, the compelling sense that here lay a life of fullness and of knowledge.

That, he knew, was why they had not returned.

"I won't go back," said Towser.

"We can't let them down," said Fowler.

Fowler took a step or two, back toward the dome, then stopped.

Back to the dome. Back to that aching, poison-laden body he had left. It hadn't seemed aching before, but now he knew it was.

Back to the fuzzy brain. Back to muddled thinking. Back to the flapping mouths that formed signals others understood. Back to eyes that now would be worse than no sight at all. Back to squalor, back to crawling, back to ignorance.

"Perhaps some day," he said, muttering to himself.

"We got a lot to do and a lot to see," said Towser. "We got a lot to learn. We'll find things—"

Yes, they could find things. Civilizations, perhaps. Civilizations that would make the civilization of Man seem puny by comparison. Beauty and more important—an understanding of that beauty. And a comradeship no one had ever known before—that no man, no dog had ever known before.

And life. The quickness of life after what seemed a drugged existence.

"I can't go back," said Towser.

"Nor I," said Fowler.

"They would turn me back into a dog," said Towser.

"And me," said Fowler, "back into a man."

MURRAY LEINSTER

The Strange Case of John Kingman

"Murray Leinster" was a pen name used by Will F. Jenkins (1896-1975) for the great bulk of his science fiction. Jenkins was a Virginian who published his first sf story, "The Runaway Skyscraper," in 1919, although he had been writing professionally since 1913. It is easy to understand why he became known as "The Dean of Science Fiction." One of his major contributions to sf was his development of the parallel-world story, which dates from the publication of his "Sidewise in Time" in 1934 and runs through much of his work, including his Hugo Award-winning "Exploration Team" in 1955. Other noteworthy books include The Murder of the U.S.A. *(1946),* The Forgotten Planet *(1954) and* The Best of Murray Leinster *(1978).*

"The Strange Case of John Kingman" first appeared in 1948.

IT STARTED when Dr. Braden took the trouble to look up John Kingman's case-history card. Meadeville Mental Hospital had a beautifully elaborate system of card-indexes, because psychiatric research is stressed there. It is the oldest mental institution in the country, having been known as "New Bedlam" when it was founded some years before the Republic of the United States of America. The card-index system was unbelievably perfect. But young Dr. Braden found John Kingman's card remarkably lacking in the usual data.

"Kingman, John," said the card. "White, male, 5'8", brown-black hair. Note: physical anomaly. Patient has six fingers on each hand, extra digits containing apparently normally bones and being wholly functional. Age..." This was blank. "Race..." This, too, was blank. "Birthplace..." Considering the other blanks, it was natural for this to be vacant, also. "Diagnosis: advanced atypical paranoia with pronounced delusions of grandeur apparently unassociated with usual conviction of persecution." There was a comment here, too. "Patient apparently understands English very slightly if at all. Does not speak." Then three more spaces. "Nearest relative..." It was blank. "Case history..." It was blank. Then, "Date of admission..." and it was blank.

The card was notably defective, for the index-card of a patient at Meadeville Mental. A patient's age and race could be unknown if he'd simply been picked up in the street somewhere and never adequately identified. In such an event it was reasonable that his nearest relative and birthplace should be unknown, too. But

249

there should have been some sort of case history—at least of the events leading to his committal to the institution. And certainly, positively, absolutely, the date of his admission should be on the card!

Young Dr. Braden was annoyed. This was at the time when the Jantzen euphoric-shock treatment was first introduced, and young Dr. Braden believed in it. It made sense. He was anxious to attempt it at Meadeville—of course on a patient with no other possible hope of improvement. He handed the card to the clerk in the records department and asked for further data on the case.

Two hours later he smoked comfortably on a very foul pipe, stretched out on grassy sward by the Administration Building. There was a beautifully blue sky overhead, and the shadows of the live oaks reached out in an odd long pattern on the lawn. Young Dr. Braden read meditatively in the American Journal of Psychiatry. The article was "Reaction of Ten Paranoid Cases to Euphoric Shock." John Kingman sat in regal dignity on the steps nearby. He wore the nondescript garments of an indigent patient—not supplied with clothing by relatives. He gazed into the distance, to all appearances thinking consciously godlike thoughts and being infinitely superior to mere ordinary humans. He was of an indeterminate age which might be forty or might be sixty or might be anywhere in between. His six-fingered hands lay in studied gracefulness in his lap. He deliberately ignored all of mankind and mankind's doings.

Dr. Braden finished the article. He sucked thoughtfully on the burned-out pipe. Without seeming to do so, he regarded John Kingman again. Mental cases have unpredictable reactions, but as with children and wild animals, much can be done if care is taken not to startle them. Presently young Dr. Braden said meditatively:

"John, I think something can be done for you."

The regal figure turned its eyes. They looked at the younger man. They were aloofly amused at the impertinence of a mere human being addressing John Kingman, who was so much greater than a mere human being that he was not even annoyed at human impertinence. Then John Kingman looked away again.

"I imagine," said Braden, as meditatively as before, "that you're pretty bored. I'm going to see if something can't be done about it. In fact—"

Someone came across the grass toward him. It was the clerk of the records department. He looked very unhappy. He had the card Dr. Braden had turned in with a request for more complete information. Braden waited.

"Er...doctor," said the clerk miserably, "there's something wrong! Something terribly wrong! About the records, I mean."

The aloofness of John Kingman had multiplied with the coming of a second, low, human being into his ken. He gazed into the distance in divine indifference to such creatures.

"Well?" said Braden.

"There's no record of his admission!" said the clerk. "Every year there's a complete roster of the patients, you know. I thought I'd just glance back, find out what year his name first appeared and look in the committal papers for that year. But I went back twenty years, and John Kingman is mentioned every year!"

"Look back thirty, then," said Braden.

"I...I did!" said the clerk painfully. "He was a patient here thirty years ago!"

"Forty?" asked Braden.

The clerk gulped.

"Dr. Braden," he said desperately, "I even went to the dead files, where records going back to 1850 are kept. And...doctor, he was a patient then!"

Braden got up from the grass and brushed himself off automatically.

"Nonsense!" he said. "That's ninety-eight years ago!"

The clerk looked crushed.

"I know, doctor. There's something terribly wrong! I've never had my records questioned before. I've been here twenty years—"

"I'll come with you and look for myself," said Dr. Braden. "Send an attendant to come here and take him back to his ward."

"Y-yes, doctor," said the clerk, gulping again. "At...at once."

He went away at a fast pace between a shuffle and a run. Dr. Braden scowled impatiently.

Then he saw John Kingman looking at him again, and John Kingman was amused. Tolerantly, loftily amused. Amused with a patronizing condescension that would have been infuriating to anyone but a physician trained to regard behavior as symptomatic rather than personal.

"It's absurd," grunted Braden, matter-of-factly treating the patient—as a good psychiatrist does—like a perfectly normal human being. "You haven't been here for ninety-eight years!"

One of the six-fingered hands stirred. While John Kingman regarded Braden with infinitely superior scorn, six fingers made a gesture as of writing. Then the hand reached out.

Braden put a pencil in it. The other hand reached. Braden fumbled in his pockets and found a scrap of paper. He offered that.

John Kingman looked aloofly into the far distance, not even glancing at what his hands did. But the fingers sketched swiftly, with practiced ease. It took only seconds. Then, negligently, he reached out and returned pencil and paper to Braden. He returned to his godlike indifference to mere mortals. But there was now the faintest possible smile on his face. It was an expression of contemptuous triumph.

Braden glanced at the sketch. There was design there. There was an unbelievable intricacy of relationship between this curved line and that, and between them and the formalized irregular pattern in the center. It was not the drawing of a lunatic. It was cryptic, but it was utterly rational. There is something essentially childish in the background of most forms of insanity. There was nothing childish about this. And it was obscurely, annoyingly familiar. Braden had seen something like it, somewhere, before. It was not in the line of psychiatry, but in some of the physical sciences diagrams like this were used in explanations.

An attendant came to return John Kingman to his ward. Braden folded the paper and put it in his pocket.

"It's not in my line, John," he told John Kingman. "I'll have a check-up made. I think I'm going to be able to do something for you."

John Kingman suffered himself to be led away. Rather, he grandly preceded the attendant, negligently preventing the man from touching him, as if such a touch would be a sacrilege the man was too ignorant to realize.

* * *

Braden went to the record office. With the agitated clerk beside him, he traced John Kingman's name to the earliest of the file of dead records. Handwriting succeeded typewriting as he went back through the years. Paper yellowed. Handwriting grew Spencerian. It approached the copperplate. But, in ink turned brown, in yellowed rag paper in the ruled record-books of the Eastern Pennsylvania Asylum—which was Meadeville Mental in 1850—there was the records of a patient named John Kingman for every year. Twice Braden came upon notes alongside the name. One was in 1880. Some staff doctor—there were no psychiatrists in those days—had written, *"High fever."* There was nothing else. In 1853 a neat memo stood beside the name. *"This man has six functioning fingers on each hand."* The memo had been made ninety-five years before.

Dr. Braden looked at the agitated clerk. The record of John Kingman was patently impossible. The clerk read it as a sign of inefficiency in his office and possibly on his part. He would be upset and apprehensive until the source of the error had safely been traced to a predecessor.

"Someone," said Braden dryly—but he did not believe it even then—"forgot to make a note of the explanation. An unknown must have been admitted at some time as John Kingman. In time he died. But somehow the name John Kingman had become a sort of stock name like John Doe, to signify an unidentified patient. Look in the death records for John Kingman. Evidently a John Kingman died, and that same year another unidentified patient was assigned the same name. That's it!"

The clerk almost gasped with relief. He went happily to check. But Braden did not believe it. In 1853 someone had noted that John Kingman had six functioning fingers on each hand. The odds against two patients in one institution having six functioning fingers, even in the same century, would be enormous.

Braden went doggedly to the museum. There the devices used in psychiatric treatments in the days of New Bedlam were preserved, but not displayed. Meadeville Mental had been established in 1776 as New Bedlam. It was the oldest mental institution in the United States, but it was not pleasant to think of the treatment given to patients—then termed "madmen"—in the early days.

The records remained. Calfleather bindings. Thin rag paper. Beautifully shaded writing, done with quill pens. Year after year, Dr. Braden searched. He found John Kingman listed in 1820. In 1801. In 1795. In 1785 the name "John Kingman" was absent from the annual list of patients. Braden found the record of his admission in 1786. On the 21st of May, 1786—ten years after New Bedlam was founded, one hundred and sixty-two years before the time of his search—there was a neat entry:

A poore madman admitted this day has been assigned the name of John Kingman because of his absurdly royal manner and affected dignity. He is five feet eight inches tall, appears to speak no Englishe or any other tongue known to any of the learned men hereabout, and has six fingers on each hand, the extra fingers being perfectly formed and functioning. Dr. Sanforde observed that hee seems to have a high fever. On his left shoulder, when stripped, there appears a curious design which is not tattooing according to any known fashion. His madness appears to be so strong a conviction of his greatness that he will not condescend to notice others as being so much his inferiors, so that if not committed hee would starve. But on three occasions, when being examined by physicians, he put out his hand imperiously for writing instruments and drew very intrikit designs which all agree have no significance. He was committed as a madman by a commission consisting of Drs. Sanforde, Smyth, Hale and Bode.

Young Dr. Braden read the entry a second time. Then a third. He ran his hands through his hair. When the clerk came back to announce distressedly that not in all the long history of the institution had a patient named John Kingman died, Braden was not surprised.

"Quite right," said Braden to the almost hysterical clerk. "He didn't die. But I want John Kingman taken over to the hospital ward. We're going to look him over. He's been rather neglected. Apparently he's had actual medical attention only once in a hundred and sixty-two years. Get out his committal papers for me, will you? He was admitted here May 21st, 1786."

Then Braden left, leaving behind him a clerk practically prostrated with shock. The clerk wildly suspected that Dr. Braden had gone insane. But when he found the committal papers, he decided hysterically that it was he who would shortly be in one of the wards.

John Kingman manifested amusement when he was taken into the hospital laboratory. For a good ten seconds—Braden watched him narrowly—he glanced from one piece of apparatus to another. It was impossible to doubt that after one glance he understood the function and operation of every appliance in the ultramodern, super-scientifically-equipped laboratory of the hospital ward. But he was amused. In particular, he looked at the big X-ray machine and smiled with such contempt that the X-ray technician bristled.

"No paranoid suspicion," said Braden. "Most paranoid patients suspect that they're going to be tortured or killed when they're brought to a place where there's stuff they don't understand."

John Kingman turned his eyes to Braden. He put out his six-fingered hand and made the motion of writing. Braden handed him a pencil and a memo tablet. Negligently, contemptuously, he sketched. He sketched again. He handed the sketches to Braden and retreated into his enormous amused contempt for humanity.

Braden glanced at the scraps of paper. He jerked his head, and the X-ray technician came to his side.

"This," said Braden dryly, "looks like a diagram of an X-ray tube. Is it?"

The technician blinked.

"He don't use the regular symbols," he objected, "but—well—yes. That's what he puts for the target and this's for the cathode—Hm-m-m. Yes—" Then he said suddenly: "Say! This's not right."

He studied the diagram. Then he said in abrupt excitement:

"Look! He's put in a field like in an electron microscope! That's an idea! Do that, and you'd get a straight-line electron flow and a narrower X-ray beam—"

Braden said:

"I wonder! What's this second sketch? Another type of X-ray?"

The X-ray technician studied the second sketch absorbedly. After a time he said dubiously:

"He don't use regular symbols. I don't know. Here's the same sign for the target and that for the cathode.

"This looks like something to...hm-m-m...accelerate the electrons. Like in a Coolidge tube. Only it's—" He scratched his head. "I see what he's trying to put down. If something like this would work, you could work any tube at any voltage you wanted. Yeah! And all the high EMF would be inside the tube. No danger. Hey! You could work this off dry batteries! A doctor could carry an X-ray outfit in his handbag! And he could get million-volt stuff!"

The technician stared in mounting excitement. Presently he said urgently:

"This is crazy! But...look, Doc! Let me have this thing to study over! This is great stuff! This is...Gosh! Give me a chance to get this made up and try it out! I don't get it all yet, but—"

Braden took back the sketch and put it in his pocket.

"John Kingman," he observed, "has been a patient here for a hundred and sixty-two years. I think we're going to get some more surprises. Let's get at the job on hand!"

John Kingman was definitely amused. He was amenable, now. His air of pitying condescension, as of a god to imbeciles, under other circumstances would have been infuriating. He permitted himself to be X-rayed as one might allow children to use one as a part of their play. He glanced at the thermometer and smiled contemptuously. He permitted his body temperature to be taken from an armpit. The electrocardiograph aroused just such momentary interest as a child's unfamiliar plaything might cause. With an air of mirth he allowed the tattooed design on his shoulder—it was there—to be photographed. Throughout, he showed such condescending contempt as would explain his failure to be annoyed.

But Braden grew pale as the tests went on. John Kingman's body temperature was 105° F. A "high fever" had been observed in 1850—ninety-eight years before—and in 1786—well over a century and a half previously. But he still appeared to be somewhere between forty and sixty years old. John Kingman's pulse rate was one hundred fifty-seven beats per minute, and the electrocardiograph registered an absolutely preposterous pattern which had no meaning until Braden said curtly: "If he had two hearts, it would look like that!"

When the X-ray plates came out of the fixing-bath, he looked at them with the grim air of someone expecting to see the impossible. And the impossible was there. When John Kingman was admitted to New Bedlam, there was no such thing as X-rays on earth. It was natural that he had never been X-rayed before. He had two hearts. He had three extra ribs on each side. He had four more vertebrae than a normal human being. There were distinct oddities in his elbow joints. And his cranial capacity appeared to be something like twelve per cent above that of any but exceptional specimens of humanity. His teeth displayed distinct consistent deviation from the norm in shape.

He regarded Braden with contemptuous triumph when the tests were over. He did not speak. He drew dignity about himself like a garment. He allowed an attendant to dress him again while he looked into the distance, seemingly thinking godlike thoughts. When his toilet was complete he looked again at Braden—with vast condescension—and his six-fingered hands again made a gesture of writing. Braden grew—if possible—slightly paler as he handed over a pencil and pad.

John Kingman actually deigned to glance, once, at the sheet on which he wrote. When he handed it back to Braden and withdrew into magnificently amused aloofness, there were a dozen or more tiny sketches on the sheet. The first was an exact duplicate of the one he had handed Braden before the Administration Building. Beside it was another which was similar but not alike. The third was a specific variation in precise, exact steps until the last pair of sketches divided again into two, of which one—by a perfectly logical extension of the change-pattern—had returned to the original design, while the other was a bewilderingly complex pattern with its formalized central part in two closely-linked sections.

Braden caught his breath. Just as the X-ray man had been puzzled at first by the use of unfamiliar symbols for familiar ideas, so Braden had been puzzled by untraceable familiarity in the first sketch of all. But the last diagram made everything clear. It resembled almost exactly the standard diagrams illustrating fissionable elements as atoms. Once it was granted that John Kingman was no ordinary lunatic, it became clear that here was a diagram of some physical process which began with normal and stable atoms and arrived at an unstable atom—with one of the original atoms returned to its original state. It was, in short, a process of physical catalysis which would produce atomic energy.

Braden raised his eyes to the contemptuous, amused eyes of John Kingman.

"I think you win," he said shakenly. "I still think you're crazy, but maybe we're crazier still."

The commitment papers on John Kingman were a hundred and sixty-two years old. They were yellow and brittle and closely written. John Kingman—said the oddly spelled and sometimes curiously phrased document—was first seen on the morning of April 10, 1786, by a man named Thomas Hawkes, as he drove into Aurora, Pennsylvania, with a load of corn. John Kingman was then clad in very queer garments, not like those of ordinary men. The material looked like silk, save that it seemed also to be metallic. The man Hawkes was astounded, but thought perhaps some strolling player had got drunk and wandered off while wearing his costume for a play or pageant. He obligingly stopped his horse and allowed the stranger to climb in for a ride to town. The stranger was imperious, and scornfully silent. Hawkes asked who he was, and was contemptuously ignored. He asked— seemingly, all the world was talking of such matters then, at least the world about Aurora, Pennsylvania—if the stranger had seen the giant shooting stars of the night before. The stranger ignored him. Arrived in town, the stranger stood in the street with regal dignity, looking contemptuously at the people. A crowd gathered about him but he seemed to feel too superior to notice it. Presently a grave and elderly man—a Mr. Wycherly—appeared and the stranger fixed him with a gesture. He stooped and wrote strange designs in the dust at his feet. When the unintelligible design was meaningless to Mr. Wycherly, the stranger seemed to fly into a very passion of contempt. He spat at the crowd, and the crowd became unruly and constables took him into custody.

Braden waited patiently until both the Director of Meadeville Mental and the man from Washington had finished reading the yellowed papers. Then Braden explained calmly:

"He's insane, of course. It's paranoia. He is as convinced of his superiority to us as—say—Napoleon or Edison would have been convinced of their superiority if they'd suddenly been dumped down among a tribe of Australian bushmen. As a matter of fact, John Kingman may have just as good reason as they would have had to feel his superiority. But if he were sane he would prove it. He would establish it. Instead, he has withdrawn into a remote contemplation of his own greatness. So he is a paranoiac. One may surmise that he was insane when he first appeared. But he doesn't have a delusion of persecution because on the face of it no such theory is needed to account for his present situation."

The Director said in a tolerantly shocked tone:

"Dr. Braden! You speak as if he were not a human being!"

"He isn't," said Braden. "His body temperature is a hundred and five. Human tissues simply would not survive that temperature. He has extra vertebrae and extra ribs. His joints are not quite like ours. He has two hearts. We were able to check his circulatory system just under the skin with infrared lamps, and it is not like ours. And I submit that he has been a patient in this asylum for one hundred and sixty-two years. If he is human, he is at least remarkable!"

The man from Washington said interestedly:

"Where do you think he comes from, Dr. Braden?"

Braden spread out his hands. He said doggedly:

"I make no guesses. But I sent photostats of the sketches he made to the Bureau of Standards. I said that they were made by a patient and appeared to be diagrams of atomic structure. I asked if they indicated a knowledge of physics. You"—He looked at the man from Washington—"turned up thirty-six hours later. I deduce that he has such knowledge."

"He has!" said the man from Washington, mildly. "The X-ray sketches were interesting enough, but the others—apparently he has told us how to get controlled atomic energy out of silicon, which is one of earth's commonest elements. Where did he come from, Dr. Braden?"

Braden clamped his jaw.

"You noticed that the commitment papers referred to shooting stars then causing much local comment? I looked up the newspapers for about that date. They reported a large shooting star which was observed to descend to the earth. Then, various credible observers claimed that it shot back up to the sky again. Then, some hours afterward, various large shooting stars crossed the sky from horizon to horizon, without ever falling."

The Director of Meadeville Mental said humorously:

"It's a wonder that New Bedlam—as we were then—was not crowded after such statements!"

The man from Washington did not smile.

"I think," he said meditatively, "that Dr. Braden suggests a spaceship landing to permit John Kingman to get out, and then going away again. And possible pursuit afterward."

The Director laughed appreciatively at the assumed jest.

"If," said the man from Washington, "John Kingman is not human, and if he comes from somewhere where as much was known about atomic energy almost two centuries ago as he has showed us, and, if he were insane there, he might have seized some sort of vehicle and fled in it because of delusions of persecution. Which in a sense, if he were insane, might be justified. He would have been pursued. With pursuers close behind him he might have landed—here."

"But the vehicle!" said the Director, humorously. "Our ancestors would have recorded finding a spaceship or an airplane."

"Suppose," said the man from Washington, "that his pursuers had something like . . . say . . . radar. Even we have that! A cunning lunatic would have sent off his vehicle under automatic control to lead his pursuers as long and merry a chase as possible. Perhaps he sent it to dive into the sun. The rising shooting star and the other cruising shooting stars would be accounted for. What do you say, Dr. Braden?"

Braden shrugged.

"There is no evidence. Now he is insane. If we were to cure him—"

"Just how," said the man from Washington, "would you cure him? I thought paranoia was practically hopeless."

"Not quite," Braden told him. "They've used shock treatment for dementia praecox and schizophrenia, with good results. Until last year there was nothing of comparable value for paranoia. Then Jantzen suggested euphoric shock. Basically, the idea is to dispel illusions by creating hallucinations."

The Director fidgeted disapprovingly. The man from Washington waited.

"In euphoric shock," said Braden carefully, "the tensions and anxieties of insane patients are relieved by drugs which produce a sensation of euphoria, or well-being. Jantzen combined hallucination-producing drugs with those. The combination seems to place the patient temporarily in a cosmos in which all delusions are satisfied and all tensions relieved. He has a rest from his struggle against reality. Also he has a sort of super-catharsis, in the convincing realization of all his desires. Quite often he comes out of the first euphoric shock temporarily sane. The percentage of final cures is satisfyingly high."

The man from Washington said:

"Body chemistry?"

Braden regarded him with new respect. He said:

"I don't know. He's lived on human food for almost two centuries, and in any case it's been proved that the proteins will be identical on all planets, under all suns. But I couldn't be sure about it. There might even be allergies. You say his drawings were very important. It might be wisest to find out everything possible from him before even euphoric shock was tried."

"Ah, yes!" said the Director, tolerantly. "If he has waited a hundred and sixty-two years, a few weeks or months will make no difference. And I would like to watch the experiment, but I am about to start on my vacation—"

"Hardly," said the man from Washington.

"I said, I am about to start on my vacation."

"John Kingman," said the man from Washington mildly, "has been trying for a hundred and sixty-two years to tell us how to have controlled atomic energy, and pocket X-ray machines, and God knows what all else. There may be, somewhere about this institution, drawings of antigravity apparatus, really efficient atomic bombs, spaceship drives or weapons which could depopulate the earth. I'm afraid nobody here is going to communicate with the outside world in any way until the place and all its personnel are gone over...ah...rather carefully."

"This," said the Director indignantly, "is preposterous!"

"Quite so. A thousand years of human advance locked in the skull of a lunatic. Nearly two hundred years more of progress and development wasted because he was locked up here. But it would be most preposterous of all to let his information loose to the other lunatics who aren't locked up because they're running governments!"

The Director sat down. The man from Washington said:

"Now, Dr. Braden—"

John Kingman spent days on end in scornful, triumphant glee. Braden watched him somberly. Meadeville Mental Hospital was an armed camp with sentries everywhere, and specially about the building in which John Kingman gloated. There were hordes of suitably certified scientists and psychiatrists about him, now, and he was filled with blazing satisfaction.

He sat in regal, triumphant aloofness. He was the greatest, the most important, the most consequential figure on this planet. The stupid creatures who inhabited it—they were only superficially like himself—had at last come to perceive his godliness. Now they clustered about him. In their stupid language which it was beneath his dignity to learn, they addressed him. But they did not grovel. Even groveling would not be sufficiently respectful for such inferior beings when addressing John Kingman. He very probably devised in his own mind the exact etiquette these stupid creatures must practice before he would condescend to notice them.

They made elaborate tests. He ignored their actions. They tried with transparent cunning to trick him into further revelations of the powers he held. Once, in malicious amusement, he drew a sketch of a certain reaction which such inferior minds could not possibly understand. They were vastly excited, and he was enormously amused. When they tried that reaction and square miles turned to incandescent vapor, the survivors would realize that they could not trick or force him into giving them the riches of his godlike mind. They must devise the proper etiquette to appease him. They must abjectly and humbly plead with him and placate him and sacrifice to him. They must deny all other gods but John Kingman. They would realize that he was all wisdom, all power, all greatness when the reaction he had sketched destroyed them by millions.

Braden prevented that from happening. When John Kingman gave a sketch of a new atomic reaction in response to an elaborate trick one of the newcomers had devised, Braden protested grimly.

"The patient," he said doggedly, "is a paranoiac. Suspicion and trickiness are inherent in his mental processes. At any moment, to demonstrate his greatness, he may try to produce unholy destruction. You absolutely cannot trust him! Be careful!"

He hammered the fact home, arguing the sheer flat fact that a paranoiac will do absolutely anything to prove his grandeur.

The new reaction was tried with microscopic quantities of material, and it destroyed everything within a fifty-yard radius. Which brought the final decision on John Kingman. He was insane. He knew more about one overwhelmingly important subject than all the generations of men. But it was not possible to obtain trustworthy data from him on that subject or any other while he was insane. It was worthwhile to take the calculated risk of attempting to cure him.

Braden protested again:

"I urged the attempt to cure him," he said firmly, "before I knew he had given the United States several centuries head-start in knowledge of atomic energy. I was thinking of him as a patient. For his own sake, any risk was proper. Since he is not human, I withdraw my urging. I do not know what will happen. Anything could happen."

His refusal held up treatment for a week. Then a Presidential executive order resolved the matter. The attempt was to be made as a calculated risk. Dr. Braden would make the attempt.

He did. He tested John Kingman for tolerance of euphoric drugs. No unfavorable reaction. He tested him for tolerance of drugs producing hallucination. No unfavorable reaction. Then—

He injected into one of John Kingman's veins a certain quantity of the combination of drugs which on human beings was most effective for euphoric shock, and whose separate constituents had been tested on John Kingman and found harmless. It was not a sufficient dose to produce the full required effect. Braden expected to have to make at least one and probably two additional injections before the requisite euphoria was produced. He was taking no single avoidable chance. He administered first a dosage which should have produced no more than a feeling of mild but definite exhilaration.

And John Kingman went into convulsions. Horrible ones.

There is such a thing as allergy and such a thing as synergy, and nobody understands either. Some patients collapse when given aspirin. Some break out in rashes from penicillin. Some drugs, taken alone, have one effect, and taken together quite another and drastic one. A drug producing euphoria was harmless to John Kingman. A drug producing hallucinations was harmless. But—synergy or allergy or whatever—the two taken together were deadly poison.

He was literally unconscious for three weeks, and in continuous convulsion for two days. He was kept alive by artificial nourishment, glucose, nasal feeding— everything. But his coma was extreme. Four separate times he was believed dead.

But after three weeks he opened his eyes vaguely. In another week he was able to talk. From the first his expression was bewildered. He was no longer proud. He began to learn English. He showed no paranoiac symptoms. He was wholly sane. In fact, his I.Q.—tested later—was ninety, which is well within the range of normal intelligence. He was not overly bright, but adequate. And he did not remember who he was. He did not remember anything at all about his life before rousing from coma in the Meadeville Mental Hospital. Not anything at all. It was, apparently, either the price or the cause of his recovery.

Braden considered that it was the means. He urged his views on the frustrated scientists who wanted now to try hypnotism and "truth serum" and other devices for picking the lock of John Kingman's brain.

"As a diagnosis," said Braden, moved past the tendency to be technical, "the poor devil smashed up on something we can't even guess at. His normal personality couldn't take it, whatever it was, so he fled into delusions—into insanity. He lived in that retreat over a century and a half, and then we found him out. And we wouldn't let him keep his beautiful delusions that he was great and godlike and all-powerful. We were merciless. We forced ourselves upon him. We questioned him. We tricked him. In the end, we nearly poisoned him! And his delusions couldn't stand up. He couldn't admit that he was wrong, and he couldn't reconcile such experiences with his delusions. There was only one thing he could do—forget the whole thing in the most literal possible manner. What he's done is to go into what they used to call dementia praecox. Actually, it's infantilism. He's fled back to his childhood. That's why his I.Q. is only ninety, instead of the unholy figure it must have been when he was a normal adult of his race. He's mentally a child. He sleeps, right now, in the fetal position. Which is a warning! One more attempt to tamper with his brain, and he'll go into the only place that's left for him—into the absolute blankness that is the mind of the unborn child!"

He presented evidence. The evidence was overwhelming. In the end, reluctantly, John Kingman was left alone.

He gets along all right, though. He works in the records department of Meadeville Mental now, because there his six-fingered hands won't cause remark. He is remarkably accurate and perfectly happy.

But he is carefully watched. The one question he can answer now is—how long he's going to live. A hundred and sixty-two years is only part of his lifetime. But if you didn't know, you'd swear he wasn't more than fifty.

PETER PHILLIPS

Dreams Are Sacred

There are a number of writers who are remembered primarily for one short story, but far fewer who are remembered for one story that was also their first published work. Peter Phillips (1921-) is one of those and his first and best-known story is the present selection. Phillips is a British newspaperman who wrote a small number of stories for the science fiction magazines from 1948; unfortunately, he quit writing in the field ten years later. Another excellent story by him is "Lost Memory," which, like "Dreams Are Sacred" focuses on paranoia and the nature of reality, subjects that would be taken up by several other writers in the 1950s and beyond.

WHEN I was seven, I read a ghost story and babbled of the consequent nightmare to my father.

"They were coming for me, Pop," I sobbed. "I couldn't run, and I couldn't stop 'em, great big things with teeth and claws like the pictures in the book, and I couldn't wake myself up, Pop, I couldn't come awake."

Pop had a few quiet cuss words for folks who left such things around for a kid to pick up and read; then he took my hand gently in his own great paw and led me into the six-acre pasture.

He was wise, with the canny insight into human motives that the soil gives to a man. He was close to Nature and the hearts and minds of men, for all men ultimately depend on the good earth for sustenance and life.

He sat down on a stump and showed me a big gun. I know now it was a heavy Service Colt .45. To my child eyes, it was enormous. I had seen shotguns and sporting rifles before, but this was to be held in one hand and fired. Gosh, it was heavy. It dragged my thin arm down with its sheer, grim weight when Pop showed me how to hold it.

Pop said: "It's a killer, Pete. There's nothing in the whole wide world or out of it that a slug from Billy here won't stop. It's killed lions and tigers and men. Why, if you aim right, it'll stop a charging elephant. Believe me, son, there's nothing you can meet in dreams that Billy here won't stop. And he'll come into your dreams with you from now on, so there's no call to be scared of anything."

He drove that deep into my receptive subconscious. At the end of half an hour, my wrist ached abominably from the kick of that Colt. But I'd seen heavy slugs tear through two-inch teakwood and mild steel plating. I'd looked along that barrel, pulled the trigger, felt the recoil rip up my arm and seen the fist-size hole blasted through a sack of wheat.

And that night, I slept with Billy under my pillow. Before I slipped into dreamland, I'd felt again the cool, reassuring butt.

When the Dark Things came again, I was almost glad. I was ready for them. Billy was there, lighter than in my waking hours—or maybe my dream-hand was bigger—but just as powerful. Two of the Dark Things crumpled and fell as Billy roared and kicked, then the others turned and fled.

Then I was chasing them, laughing, and firing from the hip.

Pop was no psychiatrist, but he'd found the perfect antidote to fear—the projection into the subconscious mind of a common-sense concept based on experience.

Twenty years later, the same principle was put into operation scientifically to save the sanity—and perhaps the life—of Marsham Craswell.

"Surely you've heard of him?" said Stephen Blakiston, a college friend of mine who'd majored in psychiatry.

"Vaguely," I said. "Science-fiction, fantasy...I've read a little. Screwy."

"Not so. Some good stuff." Steve waved a hand round the bookshelves of his private office in the new Pentagon Mental Therapy Hospital, New York State. I saw multicolored magazine backs, row on row of them. "I'm a fan," he said simply. "Would you call me screwy?"

I backed out of that one. I'm just a sports columnist, but I knew Blakiston was tops in two fields—the psycho stuff and electronic therapy.

Steve said: "Some of it's the old 'peroo, of course, but the level of writing is generally high and the ideas thought-provoking. For ten years, Marsham has been one of the most prolific and best-loved writers in the game.

"Two years ago, he had a serious illness, didn't give himself time to convalesce properly before he waded into writing again. He tried to reach his previous output, tending more and more towards pure fantasy. Beautiful in parts, sheer rubbish sometimes.

"He forced his imagination to work, set himself a wordage routine. The tension became too great. Something snapped. Now he's here."

Steve got up, ushered me out of his office. "I'll take you to see him. He won't see you. Because the thing that snapped was his conscious control over his imagination. It went into high gear, and now instead of writing his stories, he's living them—quite literally, for him.

"Far-off worlds, strange creatures, weird adventures—the detailed phantasmagoria of a brilliant mind driving itself into insanity through the sheer complexity of its own invention. He's escaped from the harsh reality of his strained existence into a dream world. But he may make it real enough to kill himself.

"He's the hero of course," Steve continued, opening the door into a private ward. "But even heroes sometimes die. My fear is that his morbidly overactive imagination working through his subconscious mind will evoke in this dream world in which he is living a situation wherein the hero must die.

"You probably know that the sympathetic magic of witchcraft acts largely through the imagination. A person imagines he is being hexed to death—and dies. If Marsham Craswell imagines that one of his fantastic creations kills the hero—himself—then he just won't wake up again.

"Drugs won't touch him. Listen."

Steve looked at me across Marsham's bed. I leaned down to hear the mutterings from the writer's bloodless lips.

"...We must search the Plains of Istak for the Diamond. I, Multan, who now have the Sword, will lead thee; for the Snake must die and only in virtue of the Diamond can his death be encompassed. Come."

Craswell's right hand, lying limp on the coverlet, twitched. He was beckoning his followers.

"Still the Snake and the Diamond?" asked Steve. "He's been living that dream for two days. We only know what's happening when he speaks in his role of hero. Often it's quite unintelligible. Sometimes a spark of consciousness filters through, and he fights to wake up. It's pretty horrible to watch him squirming and trying to pull himself back into reality. Have you ever tried to pull yourself out of a nightmare and failed?"

It was then that I remembered Billy, the Colt .45. I told Steve about it, back in his office.

He said: "Sure. Your Pop had the right idea. In fact, I'm hoping to save Marsham by an application of the same principle. To do it, I need the cooperation of someone who combines a lively imagination with a severely practical streak, hoss-sense—and a sense of humor. Yes—you."

"Uh? How can I help? I don't even know the guy."

"You will," said Steve, and the significant way he said it sent a trickle of ice water down my back. "You're going to get closer to Marsham Craswell than one man has ever been to another.

"I'm going to project you—the essential you, that is, your mind and personality—into Craswell's tortured brain."

I made pop-eyes, then thumbed at the magazine-lined wall. "Too much of yonder, brother Steve," I said. "What you need is a drink."

Steve lit his pipe, draped his long legs over the arm of his chair. "Miracles and witchcraft are out. What I propose to do is basically no more miraculous than the way your Pop put that gun into your dreams so you weren't afraid any more. It's merely more complex scientifically.

"You've heard of the encephalograph? You know it picks up the surface neural currents of the brain, amplifies and records them, showing the degree—or absence—of mental activity. It can't indicate the kind or quality of such activity save in very general terms. By using comparison-graphs and other statistical methods to analyze its data, we can sometimes diagnose incipient insanity, for instance. But that's all—until we started work on it, here at Pentagon.

"We improved the penetration and induction pickup and needled the selectivity until we could probe any known portion of the brain. What we were looking for was a recognizable pattern among the millions of tiny electric currents that go to make up the imagery of thought, so that if the subject thought of something—a number, maybe—the instruments would react accordingly, give a pattern for it that would be repeated every time he thought of that number.

"We failed, of course. The major part of the brain acts as a unity, no one part being responsible for either simple or complex imagery, but the activity of one portion inducing activity in other portions—with the exception of those parts dealing with automatic impulses. So if we were to get a pattern we should need thousands of pickups—a practical impossibility. It was as if we were trying to divine the pattern of a colored sweater by putting one tiny stitch of it under a microscope.

"Paradoxically, our machine was too selective. We needed, not a probe, but an all-encompassing field, receptive simultaneously to the multitudinous currents that made up a thought-pattern.

"We found such a field. But we were no further forward. In a sense, we were back where we started from—because to analyze what the field picked up would have entailed the use of thousands of complex instruments. We had amplified thought, but we could not analyze it.

"There was only one single instrument sufficiently sensitive and complex to do that—another human brain."

I waved for a pause. "I'm home," I said. "You'd got a thought-reading machine."

"Much more than that. When we tested it the other day, one of my assistants stepped up the polarity-reversal of the field—that is, the frequency—by accident. I was acting as analyst and the subject was under narcosis.

"Instead of 'hearing' the dull incoherencies of his thoughts, I became part of them. I was inside that man's brain. It was a nightmare world. He wasn't a clear thinker. I was aware of my own individuality. . . . When he came round, he went for me bald-headed. Said I'd been trespassing inside his head.

"With Marsham, it'll be a different matter. The dream world of his coma is detailed, as real as he used to make dream worlds to his readers."

"Hold it," I said. "Why don't you take a peek?"

Steve Blakiston smiled and gave me a high-voltage shot from his big gray eyes. "Three good reasons: I've soaked in the sort of stuff he dreams up, and there's a danger that I would become identified too closely with him. What he needs is a salutary dose of common sense. You're the man for that, you cynical old whisky-hound.

"Secondly, if my mind gave way under the impress of his imagination, I wouldn't be around to treat myself; and thirdly, when—and if—he comes round, he'll want to kill the man who's been heterodyning his dreams. You can scram. But I want to stay and see the results."

"Sorting that out, I gather there's a possibility that I shall wake up as a candidate for a bed in the next ward?"

"Not unless you let your mind go under. And you won't. You've got a cast-iron non-gullibility complex. Just fool around in your usual iconoclastic manner. Your own imagination's pretty good, judging by some of your fight reports lately."

I got up, bowed politely, said: "Thank you, my friend. That reminds me—I'm covering the big fight at the Garden tomorrow night. And I need sleep. It's late. So long."

Steve unfolded and reached the door ahead of me.

"Please," he said, and argued. He can argue. And I couldn't duck those big eyes of his. And he is—or was—my pal. He said it wouldn't take long—(just like a dentist)—and he smacked down every "if" I thought up.

Ten minutes later, I was lying on a twin bed next to that occupied by a silent, white-faced Marsham Craswell. Steve was leaning over the writer adjusting a chrome-steel bowl like a hair-drier over the man's head. An assistant was fixing me up the same way.

Cables ran from the bowls to a movable arm overhead and thence to a wheeled machine that looked like something from the Whacky Science Section of the World's Fair, A.D. 2000.

I was bursting with questions, but the only ones that would come out seemed crazily irrelevant.

"What do I say to this guy? 'Good morning, and how are all your little complexes today?' Do I introduce myself?"

"Just say you're Pete Parnell, and play it off the cuff," said Steve. "You'll see what I mean when you get there."

Get there. That hit me—the idea of making a journey into some nut's nut. My stomach drew itself up to softball size.

"What's the proper dress for a visit like this? Formal?" I asked. At least, I think I said that. It didn't sound like my voice.

"Wear what you like."

"Uh-huh. And how do I know when to draw my visit to a close?"

Steve came round to my side. "If you haven't snapped Craswell out of it within an hour. I'll turn off the current."

He stepped back to the machine. "Happy dreams."

I groaned.

It was hot. Two high summers rolled into one. No, two suns, blood-red, stark in a brazen sky. Should be cool underfoot—soft green turf, pool table smooth to the far horizon. But it wasn't grass. Dust. Burning green dust—

The gladiator stood ten feet away, eyes glaring in disbelief. All of six-four high, great bronzed arms and legs, knotted muscles, a long shining sword in his right hand.

But his face was unmistakable.

This was where I took a good hold of myself. I wanted to giggle.

"Boy!" I said. "Do you tan quickly! Couple of minutes ago, you were as white as the bed sheet."

The gladiator shaded his eyes from the twin suns. "Is this yet another guise of the magician Garor to drive me insane—an Earthman here, on the Plains of Istak? Or am I already—mad?" His voice was deep, smoothly modulated.

My own was perfectly normal. Indeed, after the initial effort, I felt perfectly normal, except for the heat.

I said: "That's the growing idea where I've just come from—that you're going nuts."

You know those half-dreams, just on the verge of sleep, in which you can control your own imagery to some extent? That's how I felt. I knew intuitively what Steve was getting at when he said I could play it off the cuff. I looked down. Tweed suit, brogues—naturally. That's what I was wearing when I last looked at myself. I had no reason to think I was wearing—and therefore to be wearing—anything else. But something cooler was indicated in this heat, generated by Marsham Craswell's imagination.

Something like his own gladiator costume, perhaps.

Sandals—fine. There were my feet—in sandals.

Then I laughed. I had nearly fallen into the error of accepting his imagination.

"Do you mind if I switch off one of those suns?" I asked politely. "It's a little hot."

I gave one of the suns a very dirty look. It disappeared.

The gladiator raised his sword. "You are—Garor!" he cried. "But your witchery shall not avail you against the Sword!"

He rushed forward. The shining blade cleaved the air towards my skull.

I thought very, very fast.

The sword clanged, and streaked off at a sharp tangent from my G.I. brain-pan protector. I'd last worn that homely piece of hardware in the Argonne, and I knew it would stop a mere sword. I took it off.

"Now listen to me, Marsham Craswell," I said. "My name's Pete Parnell, of the Sunday *Star*, and—"

Craswell looked up from his sword, chest heaving, startled eyes bright as if with recognition. "Wait! I know now who you are—Nelpar Retrep, Man of the Seven Moons, come to fight with me against the Snake and his ungodly disciple, magician and sorceress, Garor. Welcome, my friend!"

He held out a huge bronzed hand. I shook it.

It was obvious that, unable to rationalize—or irrationalize—me, he was writing me into the plot of his dream! Right. It had been amusing so far. I'd string along for a while. My imagination hadn't taken a licking—yet.

Craswell said: "My followers, the great-hearted Dok-men of the Blue Hills, have just been slain in a gory battle. We were about to brave the many perils of the Plains of Istak in our quest for the Diamond—but all this, of course, you know."

"Sure," I said. "What now?"

Craswell turned suddenly, pointed. "There," he muttered. "A sight that strikes terror even into my heart—Garor returns to the battle, at the head of her dread Legion of Lakros, beasts of the Overworld, drawn into evil symbiosis with alien intelligences—invulnerable to men, but not to the Sword, or to the mighty weapons of Nelpar of the Seven Moons. We shall fight them alone!"

Racing across the vast plain of green dust towards us was a horde of ...er...creatures. My vocabulary can't cope fully with Craswell's imagination. Gigantic, shimmering things, drooling thick ichor, half-flying, half-lolloping. Enough to say I looked around for a washbasin to spit in. I found one, with soap and towels complete, but I pushed it over, looked at a patch of green dust and thought hard.

The outline of the phone booth wavered a little before I could fix it. I dashed inside, dialed "Police H.Q.? Riot squad here—and quick!"

I stepped outside the booth. Craswell was whirling the Sword round his head, yelling war cries as he faced the onrushing monsters.

From the other direction came the swelling scream of a police siren. Half a dozen good, solid patrol cars screeched to a dust-spurting stop outside the phone booth. I don't have to think hard to get a New York cop car fixed in my mind. These were just right. And the first man out, running to my side and patting his cap on firmly, was just right, too.

Michael O'Faolin, the biggest, toughest, nicest cop I know.

"Mike," I said, pointing. "Fix 'em."

"Shure, an' it's an aisy job f'the bhoys I've brought along," said Mike, hitching his belt.

He deployed his men.

Craswell looked at them fanning out to take the charge, then staggered back towards me, hand over his eyes. "Madness!" he shouted. "What madness is this? What are you doing?"

For a moment, the whole scene wavered. The lone red sun blinked out, the green desert became a murky transparency through which I caught a split-second glimpse of white beds with two figures lying on them. Then Craswell uncovered his eyes.

The monsters began to diminish some twenty yards from the riot squad. By the time they got to the cops, they were man-size, and very amenable to discipline— enforced by raps over their horny noggins with nightsticks. They were bundled into the squad cars, which set off again over the plains.

Michael O'Faolin remained. I said: "Thanks, Mike. I may have a couple of spare tickets for the big fight tomorrow night. See you later."

"Just what I was wantin', Pete. 'Tis me day off. Now, how do I get home?"

I opened the door of the phone booth. "Right inside." He stepped in. I turned to Craswell.

"Mighty magic, O Nelpar!" he exclaimed. "To creatures of Garor's mind you opposed creatures of your own!"

He'd woven the whole incident into his plot already.

"We must go forward now, Nelpar of the Seven Moons—forward to the Citadel of the Snake, a thousand lokspans over the burning Plains of Istak."

"How about the Diamond?"

"The Diamond—?"

Evidently, he'd run so far ahead of himself getting me fixed into the landscape that he'd forgotten all about the Diamond that could kill the Snake. I didn't remind him.

However, a thousand lokspans over the burning plains sounded a little too far for walking, whatever a lokspan might be.

I said: "Why do you make things tough for yourself, Craswell?"

"The name," he said with tremendous dignity, "is Multan."

"Multan, Sultan, Shashlik, Dikkidam, Hammaneggs or whatever polysyllabic pooh-bah you wish to call yourself—I still ask, why make things tough for yourself when there's plenty of cabs around? Just whistle."

I whistled. The Purple Cab swung in, perfect to the last detail, including a hulking-backed, unshaven driver, dead ringer for the impolite gorilla who'd brought me out to Pentagon that evening.

There is nothing on earth quite so unutterably prosaic as a New York Purple Cab with that sort of driver. The sight upset Craswell, and the green plains wavered again while he struggled to fit the cab into his dream.

"What new magic is this! You are indeed mighty, Nelpar!"

He got in. But he was trembling with the effort to maintain the structure of this world into which he had escaped, against my deliberate attempts to bring it crashing round his ears and restore him to colorless—but sane—normality.

At this stage, I felt curiously sorry for him; but I realized that it might only be by permitting him to reach the heights of creative imagery before dousing him with the sponge from the cold bucket that I could jerk his drifting ego back out of dreamland.

It was dangerous thinking. Dangerous—for me.

Craswell's thousand lokspans appeared to be the equivalent of ten blocks. Or perhaps he wanted to gloss over the mundane near-reality of a cab ride. He pointed forward, past the driver's shoulder: "The Citadel of the Snake!"

To me, it looked remarkably like a wedding cake designed by Dali in red plastic: ten stories high, each story a platter half a mile thick, each platter diminishing in size and offset to the one beneath so that the edifice spiraled towards the glossy sky.

The cab rolled into its vast shadow, stopped beneath the sheer, blank precipice of the base platter, which might have been two miles in diameter. Or three. Or four. What's a mile or two among dreamers?

Craswell hopped out quickly. I got out on the driver's side.

The driver said: "Dollar-fifty."

Square, unshaven jaw, low forehead, dirty-red hair straggling under his cap. I said: "Comes high for a short trip."

"Lookit the clock," he growled, squirming his shoulders. "Do I come out and get it?"

I said sweetly: "Go to hell."

Cab and driver shot downward through the green sand with the speed of an express elevator. The hole closed up. The times I've wanted to do just that—

Craswell was regarding me open-mouthed. I said: "Sorry. Now I'm being escapist, too. Get on with the plot."

He muttered something I didn't catch, strode across to the red wall in which a crack, meeting place of mighty gates, had appeared, and raised his sword.

"Open, Garor! Your doom is nigh. Multan and Nelpar are here to brave the terrors of this Citadel and free the world from the tyranny of the Snake!" He hammered at the crack with the sword-hilt.

"Not so loud," I murmured. "You'll wake the neighbors. Why not use the bell-push?" I put my thumb on the button and pressed. The towering gates swung slowly open.

"You . . . you have been here before—"

"Yes—after my last lobster supper." I bowed. "After you."

I followed him into a great, echoing tunnel with fluorescent walls. The gates closed behind us. He paused and looked at me with an odd gleam in his eyes. A gleam of—sanity. And there was anger in the set of his lips. Anger for me, not Garor or the Snake.

It's not nice to have someone trampling all over your ego. Pride is a tiger—even in dreams. The subconscious, as Steve had explained to me, is a function or state of the brain, not a small part of it. In thwarting Craswell, I was disparaging not merely his dream, but his very brain, sneering at his intellectual integrity, at his abilities as an imaginative writer.

In a brief moment of rationality, I believe he was strangely aware of this.

He said quietly: "You have limitations, Nelpar. Your outward-turning eyes are blind to the pain of creation; to you the crystal stars are spangles on the dress of a scarlet woman, and you mock the God-blessed unreason that would make life more than the crawling of an animal from womb to grave. In tearing the veil from mystery, you destroy not mystery—for there are many mysteries, a million veils, world within and beyond worlds—but beauty. And in destroying beauty, you destroy your soul."

These last words, quiet as they sounded, were caught up by the curving walls of the huge tunnel, amplified then diminished in pulsing repetition, loud then soft, a surging hypnotic echo: "Destroy your SOUL, DESTROY your soul. SOUL—"

Craswell pointed with his sword. His voice was exultant. "There is a Veil, Nelpar—and you must tear it lest it become your shroud! The Mist—the Sentient Mist of the Citadel!"

I'll admit that, for a few seconds, he'd had me a little groggy. I felt—subdued. And I understood for the first time his power as a word-spinner.

I knew that it was vital for me to reassert myself.

A thick, gray mist was rolling, wreathing slowly towards us, filling the tunnel to roof-height, puffing out thick, groping tentacles.

"It lives on Life itself," Craswell shouted. "It feeds, not on flesh, but on the vital principle that animates all flesh. I am safe, Nelpar, for I have the Sword. Can your magic save you?"

"Magic!" I said. "There's no gas invented yet that'll get through a Mark 8 mask."

Gas-drill—face-piece first, straps behind the ears. No, I hadn't forgotten the old routine.

I adjusted the mask comfortably. "And if it's not gas," I added, "this will fix it." I felt over my shoulder, unclipped a nozzle, brought it round into the "ready" position.

I had only used a one-man flame-thrower once—in training—but the experience was etched on my memory.

This was a deluxe model. At the first thirty-foot oily, searing blast, the Mist curled in on itself and rolled back the way it had come. Only quicker.

I shucked off the trappings. "You were in the Army for a while, Craswell. Remember?"

The shining translucency of the walls dimmed suddenly, and beyond them I glimpsed, as in a movie close-up through an unfocused projector, the square, intense face of Steve Blakiston.

Then the walls re-formed, and Craswell, still the bronzed, naked-limbed giant of his imagination, was looking at me again, frowning, worried. "Your words are strange, O Nelpar. It seems you are master of mysteries beyond even my knowing."

I put on the sort of face I use when the sports editor queries my expenses, aggrieved, pleading. "Your trouble, Craswell, is that you don't want to know. You just won't remember. That's why you're here. But life isn't bad if you oil it a little. Why not snap out of this and come with me for a drink?"

"I do not understand," he muttered. "But we have a mission to perform. Follow." And he strode off.

Mention of drink reminded me. There was nothing wrong with my memory. And that tunnel was as hot as the green desert. I remembered a very small pub just off the street-car depot end of Sauchiehall Street, Glasgow, Scotland. A ginger-whiskered ancient, an exile from the Highlands, who'd listened to me enthusing over a certain brand of Scotch. "If ye think that's guid, mon, ye'll no' tasted the brew from ma own private deestillery. Smack yer lips ower this, laddie—" And he'd produced an antique silver flask and poured a generous measure of golden whisky into my glass. I had never tasted such mellow nectar before or since. Until I was walking down the tunnel behind Craswell.

I nearly envisaged the glass, but changed my mind in time to make it the antique flask. I raised it to my lips. Imagination's a wonderful thing.

Craswell was talking. I'd nearly forgotten him.

". . . near the Hall of Madness, where strange music assaults the brain, weird harmonies that enchant, then kill, rupturing the very cells by a mixture of subsonic and supersonic frequencies. Listen!"

We had reached the end of the tunnel and stood at the top of a slope which, broadening, ran gently downward, veiled by a blue haze, like the smoke from fifty million cigarettes, filling a vast circular hall. The haze eddied, moved by vagrant, sluggish currents of air, and revealed on the farther side, dwarfed by distance but obviously enormous, a complex structure of pipes and consoles.

A dozen Mighty Wurlitzers rolled into one would have appeared as a miniature piano at the foot of this towering music-machine.

At its many consoles which, even at that distance, I could see consisted of at least half a dozen manuals each, were multi-limbed creatures—spiders or octopuses or Polilollipops—I didn't ask what Craswell called them—I was listening.

The opening bars were strange enough, but innocuous. Then the multiple tones and harmonies began to swell in volume. I picked out the curious, sweet harshness of oboes and bassoons, the eldritch, rising ululation of a thousand violins, the keen shrilling of a hundred demonic flutes, the sobbing of many cellos. That's enough. Music's my hobby, and I don't want to get carried away in describing how that crazy symphony nearly carried me away.

But if Craswell ever reads this, I'd like him to know that he missed his vocation. He should have been a musician. His dream-music showed an amazing intuitive grasp of orchestration and harmonic theory. If he could do anything like it consciously, he would be a great modern composer.

Yet not too much like it. Because it began to have the effects he had warned about. The insidious rhythm and wild melodies seemed to throb inside my head, setting up a vibration, a burning, in the brain tissue.

Imagine Puccini's "Recondita Armonia" re-orchestrated by Stravinsky then rearranged by Honegger, played by fifty symphony orchestras in the Hollywood Bowl, and you might begin to get the idea.

I was getting too much of it. Did I say music was my hobby? Certainly—but the only instrument I play is the harmonica. Quite well, too. And with a microphone, I can make lots of nice noise.

A microphone—and plenty of amplifiers. I pulled the harmonica from my pocket, took a deep breath, and whooped into "Tiger Rag," my favorite party-piece.

The stunning blast-wave of jubilant jazz, riffs, tiger-growls and tremolo discords from the tiny mouth organ, crashed into the vast hall from the amplifiers, completely swamping Craswell's mad music.

I heard his agonized shout even above the din. His tastes in music were evidently not as catholic as mine. He didn't like jazz.

The music-machine quavered, the multi-limbed organists, ludicrous in their haste to escape from an unreal doom, shrank, withered to scuttling black beetles; the lighting effects that had sprayed a rich, unearthly effulgence over the consoles died away into pastel, blue gloom; then the great machine itself, caught in swirl upon wave of augmented chords complemented and reinforced by its own outpourings, shivered into fragments, poured in a chaotic stream over the floor of the hall.

I heard Craswell shout again, then the scene changed abruptly. I assumed that, in his desire to blot out the triumphant paean of jazz from his mind, and perhaps in an unconscious attempt to confuse me, he had skipped a part of his plot and, in the opposite of the flashback beloved of screen writers, shot himself forward. We were—somewhere else.

Perhaps it was the inferiority complex I was inducing, or in the transition he had forgotten how tall he was supposed to be, but he was now a mere six feet, nearer my own height.

He was so hoarse, I nearly suggested a gargle. "I . . . I left you in the Hall of Madness. Your magic caused the roof to collapse. I thought you were—killed."

So the flash-forward wasn't just an attempt to confuse me. He'd tried to lose me, write me out of the script altogether.

I shook my head. "Wishful thinking, Craswell old man," I said reproachfully. "You can't kill me off between chapters. You see, I'm not one of your characters at all. Haven't you grasped that yet? The only way you can get rid of me is by waking up."

"Again you speak in riddles," he said, but there was little confidence in his voice.

The place in which we stood was a great, high-vaulted chamber. The lighting effects—as I was coming to expect—were unusual and admirable—many colored shafts of radiance from unseen sources, slowly moving, meeting and merging at the farther end of the chamber in a white, circular blaze which seemed to be suspended over a thronelike structure.

Craswell's size-concepts were stupendous. He'd either studied the biggest cathedrals in Europe, or he was reared inside Grand Central Station. The throne was apparently a good half-mile away, over a completely bare but softly resilient floor. Yet it was coming nearer. We were not walking. I looked at the walls, realized that the floor itself, a gigantic endless belt, was carrying us along.

The slow, inexorable movement was impressive. I was aware that Craswell was covertly glancing at me. He was anxious that I should be impressed. I replied by speeding up the belt a trifle. He didn't appear to notice.

He said: "We approach the Throne of the Snake, before which, his protector and disciple, stands the female magician and sorceress, Garor. Against her, we shall need all your strange skills, Nelpar, for she stands invulnerable within an invisible shield of pure force.

"You must destroy that barrier, that I may slay her with the Sword. Without her, the Snake, though her master and self-proclaimed master of this world, is powerless, and he will be at our mercy."

The belt came to a halt. We were at the foot of a broad stairway leading to the throne itself, a massive metal platform on which the Snake reposed beneath a brilliant ball of light.

The Snake was—a snake. Coil on coil of overgrown python, with an evil head the size of a football swaying slowly from side to side.

I spent little time looking at it. I've seen snakes before. And there was something worth much more prolonged study standing just below and slightly to one side of the throne.

Craswell's taste in feminine pulchritude was unimpeachable. I had half-expected an ancient, withered horror, but if Flo Ziegfeld had seen this baby, he'd have been scrambling up those steps waving a contract, force-shield or no force-shield, before you could get out the first glissando of a wolf-whistle.

She was a tall, oval-faced, green-eyed brunette, with everything just so, and nothing much in the way of covering—a scanty metal chest-protector and a knee-length, filmy green skirt. She had a tiny, delightful mole on her left cheek.

There was a curious touch of pride in Craswell's voice as he said, rather unnecessarily: "We are here, Garor," and looked at me expectantly.

The girl said: "Insolent fools—you are here to die."

Mm-m-m—that voice, as smooth and rich as a Piatigorski cello-note. I was ready to give quite a lot of credit to Craswell's imagination, but I couldn't believe that he'd dreamed up this baby just like that. I guessed that she was modeled on life; someone he knew; someone I'd like to know—someone pulled out of the grab bag of memory in the same way as I had produced Mike O'Faolin and that grubby-chinned cab driver.

"A luscious dish," I said. "Remind me to ask you later for a phone number of the original, Craswell."

Then I said and did something that I have since regretted. It was not the behavior of a gentleman. I said: "But didn't you know they were wearing skirts longer, this season?"

I looked at the skirt. The hem line shot down to her ankles, evening-gown length.

Outraged, Craswell glared at his girl-friend. The skirt became knee-length. I made it fashionable again.

Then that skirt-hem was bobbing up and down between her ankles and her knees like a crazy window blind. It was a contest of wills and imaginations, with a very pretty pair of well-covered tibiae as battleground. A fascinating sight, Garor's beautiful eyes blazed with fury. She seemed to be strangely aware of the misbecoming nature of the conflict.

Craswell suddenly uttered a ringing, petulant howl of anger and frustration—a score of lusty-lunged infants whose rattles had been simultaneously snatched from them couldn't have made more noise—and the intriguing scene was erased from view in an eruption of jet-black smoke.

When it cleared, Craswell was still in the same relative position but his sword was gone, his gladiator rig was torn and scorched, and thin trickles of blood streaked his muscular arms.

I didn't like the way he was looking at me. I'd booted his super-ego pretty hard that time.

I said: "So you couldn't take it. You've skipped a chapter again. Wise me up on what I've missed, will you?" Somehow it didn't sound as flippant as I intended.

He spoke incisively. "We have been captured and condemned to die, Nelpar. We are in the Pit of the Beast, and nothing can save us, for I have been deprived of the Sword and you of your magic.

"The ravening jaws of the Beast cannot be stayed. It is the end, Nelpar. The End—"

His eyes, large, faintly luminous, looked into mine. I tried to glance away, failed.

Irritated beyond bearing by my importunate clowning, his affronted ego had assumed the whole power of his brain, to assert itself through his will—to dominate me.

The volition may have been unconscious—he could not know why he hated me—but the effect was damnable.

And for the first time since my brash intrusion into the most private recesses of his mind, I began to doubt whether the whole business was quite—decent.

Sure, I was trying to help the guy, but . . . but dreams are sacred.

Doubt negates confidence. With confidence gone, the gateway is open to fear.

Another voice, sibilant. Steve Blakiston saying ". . . unless you let your mind go under." My own voice ". . . wake up as a candidate for a bed in the next ward—" No, not—". . . not unless you let your mind go under—" And Steve had been scared to do it himself, hadn't he? I'd have something to say to that guy when I got out. If I got out . . . if—

The whole thing just wasn't amusing any more.

"Quit it, Craswell," I said harshly. "Quit making goo-goo eyes, or I'll bat you one—and you'll feel it, coma or no coma."

He said: "What foolish words are these, when we are both so near to death?"

Steve's voice: "...sympathetic magic...imagination. If he imagines that one of his fantastic creations kills the hero—himself—he just won't wake up again."

That was it. A situation in which the hero must die. And he wanted to envisage my death, too. But he couldn't kill me. Or could he? How could Blakiston know what powers might be unleashed by the concept of death during this ultramundane communion of minds?

Didn't psychiatrists say that the death-urge, the will to die, was buried deep, but potent, in the subconscious minds of men? It was not buried deep here. It was glaring, exultant, starkly displayed in the eyes of Marsham Craswell.

He had escaped from reality into a dream, but it was not far enough. Death was the only full escape—

Perhaps Craswell sensed the confusion of thought and speculation that laid my mind wide open to the suggestions of his rioting, perfervid, death-intent imagination. He waved an arm with the grandiloquent gesture of a Shakespearean Chorus introducing a last act, and brought on his monster.

In detail and vividness it excelled everything that he had dreamed up previously. It was his swan-song as a creator of fantastic forms, and he had wrought well.

I saw, briefly, that we were in the center of an enormous, steep-banked amphitheater. There were no spectators. No crowd scenes for Craswell. He preferred that strange, timeless emptiness which comes from using a minimum number of characters.

Just the two of us, under the blazing rays of great, red suns swinging in a molten sky. I couldn't count them.

I became visually aware only of the Beast.

An ant in the bottom of a washbowl with a dog snuffling at it might feel the same way. If the Beast had been anything like a dog. If it had been anything like *anything*.

It was a mass the size of several elephants. An obscene hulking gob of animated, semi-transparent purple flesh, with a gaping, circular mouth or vent, ringed inside with pointed beslimed tusks, and outside with—eyes.

As a static thing, it would have been a filthy envenomed horror, a thing of surpassing dread in its mere aspect; but the most fearsome thing was its nightmarish mode of progression.

Limbless, it jerked its prodigious bulk forward in a series of heaves—and lubricated its lath with a glaucous, viscid fluid which slopped from its mouth with every jerk.

It was heading for us at an incredible pace. Thirty yards—Twenty—

The rigidity of utter fear gripped my limbs. This was true nightmare. I tried desperately to think...flame-thrower...how...I couldn't remember...my mind was slipping away from me in face of the onward surging of that protoplasmic juggernaut...the slime first, then the mouth, closing...my thoughts were a screaming turmoil—

Another voice, a deep, drawling, kindly voice, from an unforgettable hour in childhood—"There's nothing in the whole wide world or out of it that a slug from Billy here won't stop. There's nothing you can meet in dreams that Billy here won't stop. He'll come into your dreams with you from now on. There's no call to be scared of anything." Then the cool, hard butt in my hand, the recoil, the whining *irresistible chunk of hot, heavy metal—deep in my subconscious.*

"Pop!" I gasped. "Thanks, Pop."

The Beast was looming over me. But Billy was in my hand, pointing into the mouth. I fired.

The Beast jerked back on its slimy trail, began to dwindle, fold in on itself. I fired again and again.

I became aware once more of Craswell beside me. He looked at the dying Beast, still huge, but rapidly diminishing, then at the dull metal of the old Colt in my hand, the wisp of blue smoke from its uptilted barrel.

And then he began to laugh.

Great, gusty laughter, but with a touch of hysteria.

And as he laughed, he began to fade from view. The red suns sped away into the sky, became pin points; and the sky was white and clean and blank—like a ceiling.

In fact—what beautiful words are "in fact"—in fact, in sweet reality, it *was* a ceiling.

Then Steve Blakiston was peering down, easing the chromium bowl off the rubber pads round my head.

"Thanks, Pete," he said. "Half an hour to the minute. You worked on him quicker than an insulin shock."

I sat up, adjusting myself mentally. He pinched my arm. "Sure—you're awake. I'd like you to tell me just what you did—but not now. I'll ring you at your office."

I saw an assistant taking the bowl off Craswell's head.

Craswell blinked, turned his head, saw me. Half a dozen expressions, none of them pleasant, chased over his face.

He heaved upright, pushed aside the assistant.

"You lousy bum," he shouted. "I'll murder you!"

I just got clear before Steve and one of the others grabbed his arms.

"Let me get at him—I'll tear him open!"

"I warned you," Steve panted. "Get out, quick."

I was on my way. Marsham Craswell in a nightshirt may not have been quite so impressive physically as the bronzed gladiator of his dreams, but he was still passably muscular.

That was last night. Steve rang this morning.

"Cured," he said triumphantly. "Sane as you are. Said he realized he'd been overworking, and he's going to take things easier—give himself a rest from fantasy and write something else. He doesn't remember a thing about his dream-coma— but he had a curious feeling that he'd still like to do something unpleasant to a certain guy who was in the next bed to him when he woke up. He doesn't know why, and I haven't told him. But better keep clear."

"The feeling is mutual," I said. "I don't like his line in monsters. What's he going to write now—love stories?"

Steve laughed. "No. He's got a sudden craze for Westerns. Started talking this morning about the sociological and historical significance of the Colt revolver. He jotted down the title of his first yarn—'Six-Gun Rule.' Hey—is that based on something you pulled on him in his dream?"

I told him.

So Marsham Craswell's as sane as me, huh? I wouldn't take bets.

Three hours ago, I was on my way to the latest heavyweight match at Madison Square Garden when I was buttonholed by an off-duty policeman.

Michael O'Faolin, the biggest, toughest, nicest cop I know.

"Pete, m'boy," he said. "I had the strangest dream last night. I was helpin' yez out of a bit of a hole, and when it was all over, you said, in gratitude it may have been, that yez might have a couple of spare tickets f'the fight this very night, and I was wondering whether it could have been a sort of tellypathy like, and—"

I grabbed the corner of the bar doorway to steady myself. Mike was still jabbering on when I fumbled for my own tickets and said: "I'm not feeling too well, Mike. You go. I'll pick my stuff up from the other sheets. Don't think about it, Mike. Just put it down to the luck of the Irish."

I went back to the bar and thought hard into a large whisky, which is the next best thing to a crystal ball for providing a focus of concentration.

"Tellypathy, huh?"

No, said the whisky. Coincidence. Forget it.

Yet there's something in telepathy. Subconscious telepathy—two dreaming minds in rapport. But I wasn't dreaming. I was just tagging along in someone else's dream. Minds are particularly receptive in sleep. Premonitions and what-have-you. But I wasn't sleeping either. Six and four makes minus ten, strike three—you're out. You're nuts, said the whisky.

I decided to find myself a better-quality crystal ball. A Scotch in a crystal glass at Cevali's club.

So I hailed a Purple Cab. There was something reminiscent about the back of the driver's head. I refused to think about it. Until the pay-off.

"Dollar-fifty," he growled, then leaned out. "Say—ain't I seen you some place?"

"I'm around," I said, in a voice that squeezed with reluctance past my larynx. "Didn't you drive me out to Pentagon yesterday?"

"Yeah, that's it," he said. Square unshaven jaw, low forehead, dirty red hair straggling under his cap. "Yeah—but there's something else about your pan. I took a sleep between cruises last night and had a daffy dream. You seemed to come into it. And I got the screwiest idea you already owe me a dollar-fifty."

For a moment, I toyed with the idea of telling him to go to hell. But the roadway wasn't green sand. It looked too solid to open up. So I said, "Here's five," and staggered into Cevali's.

I looked into a whisky glass until my brain began to clear, then I phoned Steve Blakiston and talked. "It's the implications," I said finally. "I'm driving myself bats trying to figure out what would have happened if I'd conjured up a few score of my acquaintances. Would they all have dreamed the same dream if they'd been asleep?"

"Too diffuse," said Steve, apparently through a mouthful of sandwich. "That would be like trying to broadcast on dozens of wavelengths simultaneously with the same transmitter. Your brain was an integral part of that machine, occupying the same position in the circuit as a complexus of recording instruments, keyed in place with Craswell's brain—until the pick-up frequency was raised. What happened then I imagined purely as an induction process. It was—as far as the Craswell hook-up was concerned, but—"

I couldn't stand the juicy champing noises any longer, and said: "Swallow it before you choke." The guy lives on sandwiches.

His voice cleared. "Don't you see what we've got? During the amplification of the cerebral currents, there was a backsurge through the tubes and the machine became a transmitter. These two guys were sleeping, their unconscious minds wide open and acting as receivers; you'd seen them during the day, envisaged them vividly—and got tuned in, disturbing their minds and giving them dreams. Ever heard of sympathetic dreams? Ever dreamed of someone you haven't seen for years, and the next day he looks you up? Now we can do it deliberately—mechanically assisted dream telepathy, the waves reinforced and transmitted electronically! Come on over. We've got to experiment some more."

"Sometimes," I said, "I sleep. That's what I intend to do now—without mechanical assistance. So long."

A nightcap was indicated. I wandered back to the club bar. I should have gone home.

She hipped her way to the microphone in front of the band, five-foot ten of dream wrapped up in a white, glove-tight gown. An oval-faceed, green-eyed brunette with a tiny, delightful mole on her left cheek. The gown was a little exiguous about the upper regions, perhaps, but not as whistle-worthy as the outfit Craswell had dreamed on her.

Backstage, I got a double shot of ice from those green eyes. Yes, she knew Mr. Craswell slightly. No, she wasn't asleep around midnight last night. And would I be so good as to inform her what business it was of mine? College type, ultra. How they do drift into the entertainment business. Not that I mind.

When I asked about the refrigeration, she said: "It's merely that I have no particular desire to know you, Mr. Parnell."

"Why?"

"I'm hardly accountable to you for my preferences." She frowned as if trying to recall something, added: "In any case—I don't know. I just don't like you. Now if you'll pardon me, I have another number to sing—"

"But, please . . . let me explain—"

"Explain what?"

She had me there. I stumble-tongued, and got a back view of the gown.

How can you apologize to a girl when she doesn't even know that you owe her an apology? She hadn't been asleep, so she couldn't have dreamed about the skirt incident. And if she had—she was Craswell's dream, not mine. But through some aberration a trickle of thought-waves from Blakiston's machine had planted an unreasonable antipathy to me in her subconscious mind. And it would need a psychiatrist to dig it out. Or—

I phoned Steve from the club office. He was still chewing. I said: "I've got some intensive thinking to do—into that machine of yours. I'll be right over."

She was leaving the microphone as I passed the band on my way out. I looked at her hard as she came up, getting every detail fixed.

"What time do you go to bed?" I asked.

I saw the slap coming and ducked.

I said: "I can wait. I'll be seeing you. Happy dreams."

ISAAC ASIMOV

Misbegotten Missionary

Isaac Asimov (1920-) has been described as a "national treasure," and his vast array of books on subjects as diverse as the Bible and biochemistry currently total more than two-hundred seventy. No other writer has equaled him for the quality of his writing over such a wide variety of topics, and his books and countless essays have introduced millions of people to the world of science. He is also one of the best-known science fiction writers in the world—his Foundation *novels are among the most popular books in the field, his mystery/sf hybrids such as* The Caves of Steel *(1954) broke new ground in the genre, and his robot stories, based on "The Three Laws of Robotics," are actually influencing the development of them.*

H E HAD slipped aboard the ship! There had been dozens waiting outside the energy barrier when it had seemed that waiting would do no good. Then the barrier had faltered for a matter of two minutes (which showed the superiority of unified organisms over life fragments) and he was across.

None of the others had been able to move quickly enough to take advantage of the break, but that didn't matter. All alone, he was enough. No others were necessary.

And the thought faded out of satisfaction and into loneliness. It was a terribly unhappy and unnatural thing to be parted from all the rest of the unified organism, to be a life fragment oneself. How could these aliens stand being fragments?

It increased his sympathy for the aliens. Now that he experienced fragmentation himself, he could feel, as though from a distance, the terrible isolation that made them so afraid. It was fear born of that isolation that dictated their actions. What but the insane fear of their condition could have caused them to blast an area, one mile in diameter, into dull-red heat before landing their ship? Even the organized life ten feet deep in the soil had been destroyed in the blast.

He engaged reception, listening eagerly, letting the alien thought saturate him. He enjoyed the touch of life upon his consciousness. He would have to ration that enjoyment. He must not forget himself.

But it could do no harm to listen to thoughts. Some of the fragments of life on the ship thought quite clearly considering that they were such primitive, incomplete creatures. Their thoughts were like tiny bells.

279

Roger Oldenn said, "I feel contaminated. You know what I mean? I keep washing my hands and it doesn't help."

Jerry Thorn hated dramatics and didn't look up. They were still maneuvering in the stratosphere of Saybrook's Planet and he preferred to watch the panel dials. He said, "No reason to feel contaminated. Nothing happened."

"I hope not," said Oldenn. "At least they had all the field men discard their spacesuits in the air lock for complete disinfection. They had a radiation bath for all men entering from outside. I *suppose* nothing happened."

"Why be nervous, then?"

"I don't know. I wish the barrier hadn't broken down."

"Who doesn't? It was an accident."

"I wonder." Oldenn was vehement. "I was here when it happened. My shift, you know. There was no reason to overload the power line. There was equipment plugged into it that had no damn business near it. None whatsoever."

"All right. People are stupid."

"Not that stupid. I hung around when the Old Man was checking into the matter. None of them had reasonable excuses. The armor-baking circuits, which were draining off two thousand watts, had been put into the barrier line. They'd been using the second subsidiaries for a week. Why not this time? They couldn't give any reason."

"Can you?"

Oldenn flushed. "No, I was just wondering if the men had been"—he searched for a word—"hypnotized into it. By those things outside."

Thorn's eyes lifted and met those of the other levelly. "I wouldn't repeat that to anyone else. The barrier was down only two minutes. If anything had happened, if even a spear of grass had drifted across it would have shown up in our bacteria cultures within half an hour, in the fruit-fly colonies in a matter of days. Before we got back it would show up in the hamsters, the rabbits, maybe the goats. Just get it through your head, Oldenn, that nothing happened. Nothing."

Oldenn turned on his heel and left. In leaving, his foot came within two feet of the object in the corner of the room. He did not see it.

He disengaged his reception centers and let the thoughts flow past him unperceived. These life fragments were not important, in any case, since they were not fitted for the continuation of life. Even as fragments, they were incomplete.

The other types of fragments now—they were different. He had to be careful of them. The temptation would be great, and he must give no indication, none at all, of his existence on board ship till they landed on their home planet.

He focused on the other parts of the ship, marveling at the diversity of life. Each item, no matter how small, was sufficient to itself. He forced himself to contemplate this, until the unpleasantness of the thought grated on him and he longed for the normality of home.

Most of the thoughts he received from the smaller fragments were vague and fleeting, as you would expect. There wasn't much to be had from them, but that meant their need for completeness was all the greater. It was that which touched him so keenly.

There was the life fragment which squatted on its haunches and fingered the wire netting that enclosed it. Its thoughts were clear, but limited. Chiefly, they concerned the yellow fruit a companion fragment was eating. It wanted the fruit very deeply. Only the wire netting that separated the fragments prevented its seizing the fruit by force.

He disengaged reception in a moment of complete revulsion. *These fragments competed for food!*

He tried to reach far outward for the peace and harmony of home, but it was already an immense distance away. He could reach only into the nothingness that separated him from sanity.

He longed at the moment even for the feel of the dead soil between the barrier and the ship. He had crawled over it last night. There had been no life upon it, but it had been the soil of home, and on the other side of the barrier there had still been the comforting feel of the rest of organized life.

He could remember the moment he had located himself on the surface of the ship, maintaining a desperate suction grip until the air lock opened. He had entered, moving cautiously between the outgoing feet. There had been an inner lock and that had been passed later. Now he lay here, a life fragment himself, inert and unnoticed.

Cautiously, he engaged reception again at the previous focus. The squatting fragment of life was tugging furiously at the wire netting. It still wanted the other's food, though it was the less hungry of the two.

Larsen said, "Don't feed the damn thing. She isn't hungry; she's just sore because Tillie had the nerve to eat before she herself was crammed full. The greedy ape! I wish we were back home and I never had to look another animal in the face again."

He scowled at the older female chimpanzee frowningly and the chimp mouthed and chattered back to him in full reciprocation.

Rizzo said, "Okay, okay. Why hang around here, then? Feeding time is over. Let's get out."

They went past the goat pens, the rabbit hutches, the hamster cages.

Larsen said bitterly, "You volunteer for an exploration voyage. You're a hero. They send you off with speeches—and make a zoo keeper out of you."

"They give you double pay."

"All right, so what? I didn't sign up just for the money. They said at the original briefing that it was even odds we wouldn't come back, that we'd end up like Saybrook. I signed up because I wanted to do something important."

"Just a bloomin' bloody hero," said Rizzo.

"I'm not an animal nurse."

Rizzo paused to lift a hamster out of the cage and stroke it. "Hey," he said, "did you ever think that maybe one of these hamsters has some cute little baby hamsters inside, just getting started?"

"Wise guy! They're tested every day."

"Sure, sure." He nuzzled the little creature, which vibrated its nose at him. "But just suppose you came down one morning and found them there. New little hamsters looking up at you with soft, green patches of fur where the eyes ought to be."

"Shut up, for the love of Mike," yelled Larsen.

"Little soft, green patches of shining fur," said Rizzo, and put the hamster down with a sudden loathing sensation.

He engaged reception again and varied the focus. There wasn't a specialized life fragment at home that didn't have a rough counterpart on shipboard.

There were the moving runners in various shapes, the moving swimmers, and the moving fliers. Some of the fliers were quite large, with perceptible thoughts; others were small, gauzy-winged creatures. These last transmitted only patterns of sense perception, imperfect patterns at that, and added nothing intelligent of their own.

There were the non-movers, which, like the non-movers at home, were green and lived on the air, water and soil. These were a mental blank. They knew only the dim, dim consciousness of light, moisture and gravity.

And each fragment, moving and non-moving, had its mockery of life.

Not yet. Not yet. . . .

He clamped down hard upon his feelings. Once before, these life fragments had come, and the rest at home had tried to help them—too quickly. It had not worked. This time they must wait.

If only these fragments did not discover him.

They had not, so far. They had not noticed him lying in the corner of the pilot room. No one had bent down to pick up and discard him. Earlier, it had meant he could not move. Someone might have turned and stared at the stiff wormlike thing, not quite six inches long. First stare, then shout, and then it would all be over.

But now, perhaps, he had waited long enough. The takeoff was long past. The controls were locked; the pilot room was empty.

It did not take him long to find the chink in the armor leading to the recess where some of the wiring was. They were dead wires.

The front end of his body was a rasp that cut in two a wire of just the right diameter. Then, six inches away, he cut it in two again. He pushed the snipped-off section of the wire ahead of him packing it away neatly and invisibly into a corner of recess. Its outer covering was a brown elastic material and its core was gleaming, ruddy metal. He himself could not reproduce the core, of course, but that was not necessary. It was enough that the pellicle that covered him had been carefully bred to resemble a wire's surface.

He returned and grasped the cut sections of the wire before and behind. He tightened against them as his little suction disks came into play. Not even a seam showed.

They could not find him now. They could look right at him and see only a continuous stretch of wire.

Unless they looked very closely indeed and noted that, in a certain spot on this wire, there were two tiny patches of soft and shining green fur.

"It is remarkable," said Dr. Weiss, "that little green hairs can do so much."

Captain Loring poured the brandy carefully. In a sense, this was a celebration.

They would be ready for the jump through hyper-space in two hours, and after that, two days would see them back on Earth.

"You are convinced, then, the green fur is the sense organ?" he asked.

"It is," said Weiss. Brandy made him come out in splotches, but he was aware of the need of celebration—quite aware. "The experiments were conducted under difficulties, but they were quite significant."

The captain smiled stiffly. "'Under difficulties' is one way of phrasing it. I would never have taken the chances you did to run them."

"Nonsense. We're all heroes aboard this ship, all volunteers, all great men with trumpet, fife and fanfarade. You took the chance of coming here."

"You were the first to go outside the barrier."

"No particular risk was involved," Weiss said. "I burned the ground before me as I went, to say nothing of the portable barrier that surrounded me. Nonsense, Captain. Let's all take our medals when we come back; let's take them without attempt at gradation. Besides, I'm a male."

"But you're filled with bacteria to here." The captain's hand made a quick, cutting gesture three inches above his head. "Which makes you as vulnerable as a female would be."

They paused for drinking purposes.

"Refill?" asked the captain.

"No, thanks. I've exceeded my quota already."

"Then one last for the spaceroad." He lifted his glass in the general direction of Saybrook's Planet, no longer visible, its sun only a bright star in the visiplate. "To the little green hairs that gave Saybrook his first lead."

Weiss nodded. "A lucky thing. We'll quarantine the planet, of course."

The captain said, "That doesn't seem drastic enough. Someone might always land by accident someday and not have Saybrook's insight, or his guts. Suppose he did not blow up his ship, as Saybrook did. Suppose he got back to some inhabited place."

The captain was somber. "Do you suppose they might ever develop interstellar travel on their own?"

"I doubt it. No proof, of course. It's just that they have such a completely different orientation. Their entire organization of life has made tools unnecessary. As far as we know, even a stone ax doesn't exist on the planet."

"I hope you're right. Oh, and, Weiss, would you spend some time with Drake?"

"The Galactic Press fellow?"

"Yes. Once we get back, the story of Saybrook's Planet will be released for the public and I don't think it would be wise to oversensationalize it. I've asked Drake to let you consult with him on the story. You're a biologist and enough of an authority to carry weight with him. Would you oblige?"

"A pleasure."

The captain closed his eyes wearily and shook his head.

"Headache, Captain?"

"No. Just thinking of poor Saybrook."

* * *

He was weary of the ship. Awhile back there had been a queer, momentary sensation, as though he had been turned inside out. It was alarming and he had searched the minds of the keen-thinkers for an explanation. Apparently the ship had leaped across vast stretches of empty space by cutting across something they knew as "hyper-space." The keen-thinkers were ingenious.

But—he was weary of the ship. It was such a futile phenomenon. These life fragments were skillful in their constructions, yet it was only a measure of their unhappiness, after all. They strove to find in the control of inanimate matter what they could not find in themselves. In their unconscious yearning for completeness, they built machines and scoured space, seeking, seeking...

These creatures, he knew, could never, in the very nature of things, find that for which they were seeking. At least not until such time as he gave it to them. He quivered a little at the thought.

Completeness!

These fragments had no concept of it, even. "Completeness" was a poor word.

In their ignorance they would even fight it. There had been the ship that had come before. The first ship had contained many of the keen-thinking fragments. There had been two varieties, life producers and the sterile ones. (How different this second ship was. The keen-thinkers were all sterile, while the other fragments, the fuzzy-thinkers and the no-thinkers, were all producers of life. It was strange.)

How gladly that first ship had been welcomed by all the planet! He could remember the first intense shock at the realization that the visitors were fragments and not complete. The shock had given way to pity, and the pity to action. It was not certain how they would fit into the community, but there had been no hesitation. All life was sacred and somehow room would have been made for them—for all of them, from the large keen-thinkers to the little multipliers in the darkness.

But there had been a miscalculation. They had not correctly analyzed the course of the fragments' ways of thinking. The keen-thinkers became aware of what had been done and resented it. They were frightened, of course; they did not understand.

They had developed the barrier first, and then, later, had destroyed themselves, exploding their ship to atoms.

Poor, foolish fragments.

This time, at least, it would be different. They would be saved, despite themselves.

John Drake would not have admitted it in so many words, but he was very proud of his skill on the photo-typer. He had a travel-kit model, which was a six-by-eight, featureless dark plastic slab, with cylindrical bulges on either end to hold the roll of thin paper. It fitted into a brown leather case, equipped with a beltlike contraption that held it closely about the waist and at one hip. The whole thing weighed less than a pound.

Drake could operate it with either hand. His fingers would flick quickly and easily, placing their light pressure at exact spots on the blank surface, and, soundlessly, words would be written.

He looked thoughtfully at the beginning of his story, then up at Dr. Weiss. "What do you think, Doc?"

"It starts well."

Drake nodded. "I thought I might as well start with Saybrook himself. They haven't released his story back home yet. I wish I could have seen Saybrook's original report. How did he ever get it through, by the way?"

"As near as I could tell, he spent one last night sending it through the sub-ether. When he was finished, he shorted the motors, and converted the entire ship into a thin cloud of vapor a millionth of a second later. The crew and himself along with it."

"What a man! You were in this from the beginning, Doc?"

"Not from the beginning," corrected Weiss gently. "Only since the receipt of Saybrook's report."

He could not help thinking back. He had read that report, realizing even then how wonderful the planet must have seemed when Saybrook's colonizing expedition first reached it. It was practically a duplicate of Earth, with an abounding plant life and a purely vegetarian animal life.

There had been only the little patches of green fur (how often had he used that phrase in his speaking and thinking!) which seemed strange. No living individual on the planet had eyes. Instead, there was this fur. Even the plants, each blade or leaf or blossom, possessed the two patches of richer green.

Then Saybrook had noticed, startled and bewildered, that there was no conflict for food on the planet. All plants grew pulpy appendages which were eaten by the animals. These were regrown in a matter of hours. No other parts of the plants were touched. It was as though the plants fed the animals as part of the order of nature. And the plants themselves did not grow in overpowering profusion. They might almost have been cultivated, they were spread across the available soil so discriminately.

How much time, Weiss wondered, had Saybrook had to observe the strange law and order on the planet?—the fact that insects kept their numbers reasonable, though no birds ate them; that the rodentlike things did not swarm, though no carnivores existed to keep them in check.

And then there had come the incident of the white rats.

That prodded Weiss. He said, "Oh, one correction, Drake. Hamsters were not the first animals involved. It was the white rats."

"White rats," said Drake, making the correction in his notes.

"Every colonizing ship," said Weiss, "takes a group of white rats for the purpose of testing any alien foods. Rats, of course, are very similar to human beings from a nutritional viewpoint. Naturally, only female white rats are taken."

Naturally. If only one sex was present, there was no danger of unchecked multiplication in case the planet proved favorable. Remember the rabbits in Australia.

"Incidentally, why not use males?" asked Drake.

"Females are hardier," said Weiss, "which is lucky, since that gave the situation away. It turned out suddenly that all the rats were bearing young."

"Right. Now that's where I'm up to, so here's my chance to get some things straight. For my own information, Doc, how did Saybrook find out they were in a family way?"

"Accidentally, of course. In the course of nutritional investigations, rats are dissected for evidence of internal damage. Their condition was bound to be discovered. A few more were dissected; same results. Eventually, all that lived gave birth to young—with *no* male rats aboard!"

"And the point is that all the young were born with little green patches of fur instead of eyes."

"That is correct. Saybrook said so and we corroborate him. After the rats, the pet cat of one of the children was obviously affected. When it finally kittened, the kittens were not born with closed eyes but with little patches of green fur. There was no tomcat aboard.

"Eventually Saybrook had the women tested. He didn't tell them what for. He didn't want to frighten them. Every single one of them was in the early stages of pregnancy, leaving out of consideration those few who had been pregnant at the time of embarkation. Saybrook never waited for any child to be born, of course. He knew they would have no eyes, only shining patches of green fur.

"He even prepared bacterial cultures (Saybrook was a thorough man) and found each bacillus to show microscopic green spots."

Drake was eager. "That goes way beyond our briefing—or, at least, the briefing I got. But granted that life on Saybrook's Planet is organized into a unified whole, how is it done?"

"How? How are your cells organized into a unified whole? Take an individual cell out of your body, even a brain cell, and what is it by itself? Nothing. A little blob of protoplasm with no more capacity for anything human than an amoeba. Less capacity, in fact, since it couldn't live by itself. But put the cells together and you have something that could invent a spaceship or write a symphony."

"I get the idea," said Drake.

Weiss went on, "*All* life on Saybrook's Planet is a *single* organism. In a sense, all life on Earth is too, but it's a fighting dependence, a dog-eat-dog dependence. The bacteria fix nitrogen; the plants fix carbon; animals eat plants and each other; bacterial decay hits everything. It comes full circle. Each grabs as much as it can, and is, in turn, grabbed.

"On Saybrook's Planet, each organism has its place, as each cell in our body does. Bacteria and plants produce carbon dioxide and nitrogenous wastes. Nothing is produced more or less than is needed. The scheme of life is intelligently altered to suit the local environment. No group of life forms multiplies more or less than is needed, just as the cells in our body stop multiplying when there are enough of them for a given purpose. When they don't stop multiplying, we call it cancer. And that's what life on Earth really is, the kind of organic organization we have, compared to that on Saybrook's Planet. One big cancer. Every species, every individual doing its best to thrive at the expense of every other species and individual."

"You sound as if you approve of Saybrook's Planet, Doc."

"I do, in a way. It makes sense out of the business of living. I can see their viewpoint toward us. Suppose one of the cells of your body could be conscious of the efficiency of the human body as compared with that of the cell itself, and could realize that this was only the result of the union of many cells into a higher whole.

And then suppose it became conscious of the existence of free-living cells, with bare life and nothing more. It might feel a very strong desire to drag the poor thing into an organization. It might feel sorry for it, feel perhaps a sort of missionary spirit. The things on Saybrook's Planet — or the thing; one should use the singular — feels just that, perhaps."

"And went ahead by bringing about virgin births, eh, Doc? I've got to go easy on that angle of it. Post-office regulations, you know."

"There's nothing ribald about it, Drake. For centuries we've been able to make the eggs of sea urchins, bees, frogs, et cetera develop without the intervention of male fertilization. The touch of a needle was sometimes enough, or just immersion in the proper salt solution. The thing on Saybrook's Planet can cause fertilization by the controlled use of radiant energy. That's why an appropriate energy barrier stops it; interference, you see, or static.

"They can do more than stimulate the division and development of an unfertilized egg. They can impress their own characteristics upon its nucleo-proteins, so that the young are born with the little patches of green fur, which serve as the planet's sense organ and means of communication. The young, in other words, are not individuals, but become part of the thing on Saybrook's Planet. The thing on the planet, not at all incidentally, can impregnate any species — plant, animal or microscopic."

"Potent stuff," muttered Drake.

"Totipotent," Dr. Weiss said sharply. "Universally potent. Any fragment of it is totipotent. Given time, a single bacterium from Saybrook's Planet can convert *all of Earth* into a single organism! We've got the experimental proof of that."

Drake said unexpectedly, "You know, I think I'm a millionaire, Doc. Can you keep a secret?"

Weiss nodded, puzzled.

"I've got a souvenir from Saybrook's Planet," Drake told him, grinning. "It's only a pebble, but after the publicity the planet will get, combined with the fact that it's quarantined from here on in, the pebble will be all any human being will ever see of it. How much do you suppose I could sell the thing for?"

Weiss stared. "A pebble?" He snatched at the object shown him, a hard, gray ovoid. "You shouldn't have done that, Drake. It was strictly against regulations."

"I know. That's why I asked if you could keep a secret. If you could give me a signed note of authentication—— *What's the matter, Doc?*"

Instead of answering, Weiss could only chatter and point. Drake ran over and stared down at the pebble. It was the same as before——

Except that the light was catching it at an angle, and it showed up two little green spots. Look very closely; they were patches of green hairs.

He was disturbed. There was a definite air of danger within the ship. There was the suspicion of his presence aboard. How could that be? He had done nothing yet. Had another fragment of home come aboard and been less cautious? That would be impossible without his knowledge, and though he probed the ship intensely, he found nothing.

And then the suspicion diminished, but it was not quite dead. One of the keen-thinkers still wondered, and was treading close to the truth.

How long before the landing? Would an entire world of life fragments be deprived of completeness? He clung closer to the severed ends of the wire he had been specially bred to imitate, afraid of detection, fearful for his altruistic mission.

Dr. Weiss had locked himself in his own room. They were already within the solar system, and in three hours they would be landing. He had to think. He had three hours in which to decide.

Drake's devilish "pebble" had been part of the organized life on Saybrook's Planet, of course, but it was dead. It was dead when he had first seen it, and if it hadn't been, it was certainly dead after they fed it into the hyper-atomic motor and converted it into a blast of pure heat. And the bacterial cultures still showed normal when Weiss anxiously checked.

That was not what bothered Weiss now.

Drake had picked up the "pebble" during the last hours of the stay on Saybrook's Planet—*after* the barrier breakdown. What if the breakdown had been the result of a slow, relentless mental pressure on the part of the thing on the planet? What if parts of its being waited to invade as the barrier dropped? If the "pebble" had not been fast enough and had moved only after the barrier was re-established, it would have been killed. It would have lain there for Drake to see and pick up.

It was a "pebble," not a natural life form. But did that mean it was not *some* kind of life form? It might have been a deliberate production of the planet's single organism—a creature deliberately designed to look like a pebble, harmless-seeming, unsuspicious. Camouflage, in other words—a shrewd and frighteningly successful camouflage.

Had any other camouflaged creature succeeded in crossing the barrier *before* it was re-established—with a suitable shape filched from the minds of the humans aboard ship by the mind-reading organism of the planet? Would it have the casual appearance of a paperweight? Of an ornamental brass-head nail in the captain's old-fashioned chair? And how would they locate it? Could they search every part of the ship for the telltale green patches—even down to individual microbes?

And why camouflage? Did it intend to remain undetected for a time? Why? So that it might wait for the landing on Earth?

An infection *after landing* could not be cured by blowing up a ship. The bacteria of Earth, the molds, yeasts and protozoa, would go first. Within a year the non-human young would begin arriving by the uncountable billions.

Weiss closed his eyes and told himself it might not be such a bad thing. There would be no more disease, since no bacterium would multiply at the expense of its host, but instead would be satisfied with its fair share of what was available. There would be no more overpopulation; the hordes of East Asia would decline to adjust themselves to the food supply. There would be no more wars, no crime, no greed.

But there would be no more individuality, either.

Humanity would find security by becoming a cog in a biological machine. A man would be brother to a germ, or to a liver cell.

He stood up. He would have a talk with Captain Loring. They would send their report and blow up the ship, just as Saybrook had done.

He sat down again. Saybrook had had proof, while he had only the conjectures of a terrorized mind, rattled by the sight of two green spots on a pebble. Could he kill the two hundred men on board ship because of a feeble suspicion?

He had to *think!*

He was straining. Why did he have to wait? If he could only welcome those who were aboard now. *Now!*

Yet a cooler, more reasoning part of himself told him that he could not. The little multipliers in the darkness would betray their new status in fifteen minutes, and the keen-thinkers had them under continual observation. Even one mile from the surface of their planet would be too soon, since they might still destroy themselves and their ship out in space.

Better to wait for the main air locks to open, for the planetary air to swirl in with millions of the little multipliers. Better to greet each one of them into the brotherhood of unified life and let them swirl out again to spread the message.

Then it would be done! Another world organized, complete!

He waited. There was the dull throbbing of the engines working mightily to control the slow dropping of the ship; the shudder of contact with planetary surface, then——

He let the jubilation of the keen-thinkers sweep into reception, and his own jubilant thoughts answered them. Soon they would be able to receive as well as himself. Perhaps not these particular fragments, but the fragments that would grow out of those which were fitted for the continuation of life.

The main air locks were about to be opened——

And all thought ceased.

Jerry Thorn thought, Damn it, something's wrong *now.*

He said to Captain Loring, "Sorry. There seems to be a power breakdown. The locks won't open."

"Are you sure, Thorn? The lights are on."

"Yes, sir. We're investigating it now."

He tore away and joined Roger Oldenn at the air-lock wiring box. "What's wrong?"

"Give me a chance, will you?" Oldenn's hands were busy. Then he said, "For the love of Pete, there's a six-inch break in the twenty-amp lead."

"What? That can't be!"

Oldenn held up the broken wires with their clean, sharp, sawn-through ends.

Dr. Weiss joined them. He looked haggard and there was the smell of brandy on his breath.

He said shakily, "What's the matter?"

They told him. At the bottom of the compartment, in one corner, was the missing section.

Weiss bent over. There was a black fragment on the floor of the compartment.

He touched it with his finger and it smeared, leaving a sooty smudge on his finger tip. He rubbed it off absently.

There might have been something taking the place of the missing section of wire. Something that had been alive and only looked like wire, yet something that would heat, die and carbonize in a tiny fraction of a second once the electrical circuit which controlled the air lock had been closed.

He said, "How are the bacteria?"

A crew member went to check, returned and said, "All normal, Doc."

The wires had meanwhile been spliced, the locks opened, and Dr. Weiss stepped out into the anarchic world of life that was Earth.

"Anarchy," he said, laughing a little wildly. "And it will stay that way."

JULIAN MAY

Dune Roller

Julian May (1931-) is the wife of the noted science fiction anthologist and critic Ted Dikty. She wrote a few science fiction stories in the early 1950s and then fell silent in the genre, although she wrote an excellent series of science books for young people. Ms. May recently returned to sf with two outstanding novels, The Many Colored Land *(1981)* and The Golden Torc *(1982).*

"Dune Roller" was her first published science fiction story—and an amazing debut.

T HERE WERE only two who saw the meteor fall into Lake Michigan, long ago. One was a Pottawatomie brave hunting rabbits among the dunes on the shore; he saw the fire-streak arc down over the water and was afraid, because it was an omen of ill favor when the stars left the heaven and drowned themselves in the Great Water. The other who saw was a sturgeon who snapped greedily at the meteor as it fell—quite reduced in size by now—to the bottom of the fresh water sea. The big fish took it into his mouth and then spat it out again in disdain. It was not good to eat. The meteor drifted down through the cold black water and disappeared. The sturgeon swam away, and presently, he died. . . .

Dr. Ian Thorne squatted beside a shore pool and netted things. Under the sun of late July, the lake waves were sparkling deep blue far out, and glass-clear as they broke over the sandbar into Dr. Thorne's pool. A squadron of whirligig beetles surfaced warily and came toward him, leading little v-shaped shadow wakes along the tan sand bottom. A back-swimmer rowed delicately out of a green cloud of algae and snooped around a centigrade thermometer which was suspended in the water from a driftwood twig.

3:00 P.M., wrote Dr. Thorne in a large, stained notebook. *Air temp 32, water temp*—he leaned over to get a better look at the thermometer and the back-swimmer fled—*28. Wind, light variable; wave action, diminishing. Absence of drifted specimens.* He dated a fresh sheet of paper, headed it *Fourteenth Day,* and began the bug count.

He scribbled earnestly in the sun, a pleasant-faced man of thirty or so. He wore a Hawaiian shirt and shorts of delicious magenta color, decorated with most un-botanical green hibiscus. An old baseball cap was on his head.

He skirted the four-by-six pool on the bar side and noted that the sand was continuing to pile up. It would not be long before the pool was stagnant, and each day brought new and fascinating changes in its population. *Gyrinidae, Hydrophil-idae,* a *Corixa* hiding in the rubbish on the other end. Some kind of larvae beside a piece of water-logged board; he'd better take a specimen or two of that. *L. intacta* sunning itself smugly on the thermometer.

The back-swimmer, its confidence returned, worked its little oars and zig-zagged in and out of the trash. *N. undulata,* wrote Dr. Thorne.

When the count was finished, he took a collecting bottle from the fishing creel hanging over his shoulder and maneuvered a few of the larvae into it, using the handle of the net to herd them into position.

And then he noticed that in the clear, algae-free end of the pool, something flashed with a light more golden than that of mere sun on water. He reached out the net to stir the loose sand away.

It was not a pebble or a piece of chipped glass as he had supposed; instead, he fished out a small, droplike object shaped like a marble with a tail. It was a beautiful little thing of pellucid amber color, with tiny gold flecks and streaks running through it. Sunlight glanced off its smooth sides, which were surprisingly free of the surface scratches that are the inevitable patina of flotsam in the sand-scoured dunes.

He tapped the bottom of the net until the drop fell into an empty collecting bottle and admired it for a minute. It would be a pretty addition to his collection of Useless Miscellanea. He might put it in a little bottle between the tooled brass yak bell and the six-inch copper sulfate crystal.

He was collecting his equipment and getting ready to leave when the boat came. It swept up out of the north and nosed in among the sand bars offshore, a dignified, forty-foot Matthews cruiser named *Carlin,* which belonged to his friend, Kirk MacInnes.

"'Hoy, Mac!" Dr. Thorne yelled cordially. "Look out for the new bar the storm brought in!"

A figure on the flying bridge of the boat waved briefly and howled something unintelligible around a pipe clamped in its teeth. The cruiser swung about and the mutter of her motors died gently. She lay rocking in the little waves a few hundred feet offshore. After a short pause a yellow rubber raft dropped over the stern.

Good old Mac, thought Thorne. The little ex-engineer with that Skye terrier moustache and the magnificent boat visited him regularly, bringing the mail and his copy of the *Biological Review,* or bottled goods of a chemistry designed to prevent isolated scientists from catching cold. He was a frequent and welcome visitor, but he had always come alone.

Previous to this.

"Well, well," said Dr. Thorne, and then looked again.

The girl was sitting in the stern of the raft while MacInnes paddled deftly, and as they drew closer Thorne saw that her hair was dark and curly. She wore a spotless white playsuit, and a deep blue handkerchief was knotted loosely around her throat.

She was looking at him, and for the first time he had qualms about the Hawaiian shorts.

The yellow flank of the raft grated on the stony beach. MacInnes, sixty and grizzled, a venerable briar between his teeth, climbed out and wrung Thorne's hand.

"Brought you a visitor this time, Ian. Real company. Jeanne, this gentleman in the shorts and fishing creel is Dr. Ian Thorne, the distinguished writer and lecturer. He writes books about dune ecology, whatever that is. Ian, my niece, Miss Wright."

Thorne murmured politely. Why, that old scoundrel. That sly old dog. But she was pretty, all right.

"How engaging," smiled the girl. "An ecologist with a leer."

Dr. Thorne's face abruptly attempted to adopt the protective coloration of his shorts. He said, "We're really not bad fellows at heart, Miss Wright. It's the fresh air that gives us the pointed ears."

"I see," she said, in a tone that made Thorne wonder just how much she saw. "Were you collecting specimens here today, Dr. Thorne?"

"Not exactly. You see, I'm preparing a chapter on the ecology of beach pool associations, and this little pool here is my guinea pig. The sand bar on the lake side will grow until the pool is completely cut off. As its stagnation increases, progressive forms of plant and animal life will inhabit it—algae, beetles, larvae, and so forth. If we have calm weather for the next few weeks, I can get an excellent cross section of the plant-animal societies which develop in this type of an environment. The chapter on the pool is one in a book I'm doing on ecological studies of the Michigan State dunes."

"All you have to do is charge him up," MacInnes remarked, yawning largely, "and he's on the air for the rest of the day." He pulled the raft up onto the sand and took out a flat package. "I brought you a present, if you're interested."

"What is it? The mail?"

"Something a heck of a lot more digestible. A brace of sirloins. I persuaded Jeanne to come along today to do them up for us. I've tasted your cooking."

"I can burn a chop as well as the next man," Thorne protested with dignity. "But I think I'll concede the point. I was finished here. Shall we go right down to the shack? I live just down the shore, Miss Wright, in a place perched on top of a sand dune. It's rugged but it's home."

MacInnes chuckled and led the way along the firm damp sand near the water's edge.

In some places the tree-crowned dunes seemed to come down almost to the beach level. Juniper and pines and heavy undergrowth were the only things holding the vast creeping monster which are the traveling dunes. Without their green chains, they swept over farms and forests, leaving dead trees and silver-scoured boards in their wake.

The three of them cut inland and circled a great narrow-necked valley which widened out among the high sand hills. It was a barren, eery place of sharp, wind-abraded stumps and silent white spaces.

"A sand blow," said Thorne. "The winds do it. Those dunes at the end of the valley in there are moving. See the dead trees? The hills buried them years ago and then moved on and left these skeletons. These were probably young oaks."

"Poor things," said the girl, as they moved on.

Then the dismal blow was gone, and green hills with scarcely a show of sand towered over them. At the top of the largest stood Thorne's lodge, its rustic exterior blending inconspicuously into the conifers and maples which surrounded it on three sides. The front of the house was banked with yew and prostrate juniper for sand control.

A stairway of hewn logs came down the slope of the dune. At its foot stood a wooden bench, a bright green pump and an old ship's bell on a pole.

"A dunes doorbell!" Jeanne exclaimed, seizing the rope.

"Nobody home yet," Thorne laughed, "but that's the shack up there."

"Yeah," said MacInnes sourly. "And a hundred and thirty-three steps to the top."

Later, they sat in comfortable rattan chairs on the porch while Thorne manipulated siphon and glasses.

"You really underestimate yourself, Dr. Thorne," the girl said. "This is no shack, it's a real home. A lodge in the pines."

"Be it ever so humble," he smiled. "I came up here to buy a two-by-four cabin to park my typewriter and microscopes in, and a guy wished this young chalet off on me."

"The view is magnificent. You can see for miles."

"But when the wind blows a gale off the lake, you think the house is going to be carried away! It's just the thing for my work, though. No neighbors, not many picnickers, not even a decent road. I have to drive my jeep down the beach for a couple of miles before I can hit the cow path leading to the county trunk. No telephones, either. And I have my own little generating plant out back, or there wouldn't be any electricity."

"No phone?" Jeanne frowned. "But Uncle Kirk says he talks to you every day. I don't understand."

"Come out here," he invited mysteriously. "I'll show you something."

He led the way to a tiny room with huge windows which lay just off the living room. Radio equipment stood on a desk and lined the walls. A large plaster model of a grasshopper squatting on the transmitter rack wore a pair of headphones.

"Ham radio used to be my hobby when I was a kid," he said, "and now it keeps me in touch with the outside world. I met Mac over the air long before I ever saw him in the flesh. You must have seen his station at home. And I think he even has a little low-power rig in the cruiser."

"I've seen that. Do you mean he can talk to you any time he wants to?"

"Well, it's not like the telephone," Thorne admitted, "the other fellow has to be listening for you on your frequency. But your uncle and I keep a regular schedule every evening and sometimes in the morning. And hams in other parts of the country are very obliging in letting me talk to my friends and colleagues. It works out nicely all the way around."

"Uncle Kirk had represented you as a sort of scientific anchorite," she said, lifting a microphone and running her fingers over the smooth chrome. "But I'm beginning to think he was wrong."

"Maybe," he said quietly. "Maybe not. I manage to get along. The station is a big help in overcoming the isolation, but—there are other things. Shall we be getting back to the drinks?"

She put down the microphone and looked at him oddly. "If you like. Thank you for showing me your station."

"Think nothing of it. If you're ever in a jam, just howl for W8-Dog-Zed-Victor on ten meters."

"All right," she said to him. "If I ever am." She turned and walked out of the door.

The casual remark he had been about to make died on his lips, and suddenly all the loneliness of his life in the dunes loomed up around him like the barren walls of the sand blow. And he was standing there with the dead trees all around and the living green forever out of reach....

"This Scotch tastes like iodine," said MacInnes from the porch.

Thorne left the little room and closed the door behind him. "It's the only alcohol in the house, unless you want to try my specimen pickle," said Thorne, dropping back into his chair. "As for the flavor—you should know. You brought the bottle over yourself last week."

The girl took Thorne's creel and began to arrange the bottles in a row on the table. Algae, beetles and some horrid little things that squirmed when she shook them. Ugh.

"What's this?" she asked curiously, holding up the bottle with the amber drop.

"Something I found in my beach pool this afternoon. I don't know what it is. Rock crystal, perhaps, or somebody's drowned jewelry."

"I think it's rather pretty," she said admiringly. "It reminds me of something, with that little tail. I know—Prince Rupert drops. They look just like this, only they're a bit smaller and have an air bubble in them. When you crack the little tail off them, the whole drop flies to powder." She shrugged vaguely. "Strain, or something. I never saw one that had color like this, though. It's almost like a piece of Venetian glass."

"Keep it, if you like," Thorne offered.

MacInnes poured himself another finger and thumb of Scotch and scrupulously added two drops of soda. In the center of the table, the small amber eye winked faintly in the sunlight.

Tommy Dittberner liked to walk down the shore after dinner and watch the sand toads play. There were hundreds of them that came out to feed as soon as dusk fell—little silvery-gray creatures with big jewel eyes, that swam in the mirror of the water or sat quietly on his hand when he caught them. There were all sizes, from big fellows over four inches long to tiny ones that could perch comfortably on his thumbnail.

Tommy came to Port Grand every August, and lived in a resort near the town. He knew he was not supposed to go too far from the cottage, but it seemed to him that there were always more and bigger toads just a little farther down the shore.

He would go just down to that sand spit, that was all. Well, maybe to that piece of driftwood down there. He wasn't lost, like his mother said he would be if he went too far. He knew where he was; he was almost to the Bug Man's house.

He was funny. He lived by himself and never talked to anyone—at least that's what the kids said. But Tommy wasn't too sure about that. Once last week the Bug Man and a pretty lady with black hair had been hiking in the dunes near Tommy's cottage and Tommy had seen him kiss her. Boy, that had been something to tell the kids!

Here was the driftwood, and it was getting dark. He had been gone since six o'clock, and if he didn't get home, Mom was going to give it to him, all right.

The toads were thicker than ever, and he had to walk carefully to avoid stepping on any of them. Suddenly he saw one lying in the sand down near the water's edge. It was on its back and kicked feebly. He knelt down and peered closely at it.

"Sick," he decided, prodding it with a finger. The animal winced from his touch, and its eyes were filmed with pain. But it wasn't dead yet.

He picked it up carefully in both hands and scrambled over the top of the low shore dune to the foot of the great hill where the Bug Man lived.

Thorne opened the door to stare astonished at the little boy, and wondered whether or not to laugh. Sweat from the exertion of climbing the one hundred and thirty-three steps had trickled down from his hair, making little stripes of cleanness on the side of his face. His T-shirt had parted company from the belt of his jeans. He held out the toad in front of him.

"There's this here toad I found," he gasped breathlessly. "I think it's sick."

Without a word, Thorne opened the door and motioned the boy in. They went into the workroom together.

"Can you fix it up, mister?" asked the boy.

"Now, I'll have to see what's wrong first. You go wash your face in the kitchen and take a Coke out of the icebox while I look it over."

He stretched it out on the table for examination. The abdomen was swollen and discolored, and even as he watched it the swelling movement of the floor of its mouth faltered and stopped, and the animal did not move again.

"It's dead, ain't it?" said a voice behind Thorne.

"I'm afraid so, sonny. It must have been nearly dead when you found it."

The boy nodded gravely. He looked at it silently for a moment, then said: "What was the matter with it, mister?"

"I could tell if I dissected it. You know what that is, don't you?" The boy shook his head. "Well, sometimes by looking inside of the sick thing that has died, you can find out what was wrong. Would you like to watch me do it?"

"I guess so."

Scalpel and dissecting needle flashed under the table light. Thorne worked quickly, glancing at the boy now and then out of the corner of his eye. The instruments clicked within the redness of the incision and parted the oddly darkened and twisted organs.

Thorne stared. Then he arose and smiled kindly at the young face before him. "It died of cessation of cardiac activity, young fellow. I think you'd better be heading for home now. It's getting dark and your mother will be worried about you. You wouldn't want her to think anything had happened to you, would you? I didn't think so. A big boy like you doesn't worry his mother."

"What's a cardiac?" asked the boy, looking back over his shoulder at the toad as Thorne led him out.

"Means 'pertaining to the heart,'" said Thorne. "Say, I'll tell you what. We'll drive home in my jeep. Would you like that?"

"I guess so."

The screen door slammed behind them. The kid would forget the toad quickly enough, Thorne told himself. He couldn't have seen what was inside it anyway.

In the lodge later, under the single little light, Thorne preserved the body of the toad in alcohol. Beside him on the table gleamed two tiny amber drops with tails which he had removed from the seared and ruptured remains of the toad's stomach.

The marine chronometer on the wall of Thorne's amateur station read five-fifteen. His receiver said to him:

"I have to sign off now. The missus is hollering up that she wants me to see to the windows before supper. I'll look for you tomorrow. This is W8GB over to W8DVZ, and W8GB is out and clear. Good night, Thorne."

Thorne said. "Good night, Mac. W8DVZ out and clear," and let the power die in his tubes.

He lit a cigarette and stood looking out of the window. In the blue sky over the lake hung a single, giant white thunderhead; it was like a marble spray billow, ponderous and sullen. The rising wind slipped whistling through the stiff branches of the evergreen trees on the dune, and dimly, through the glass, he could hear the sound of the waves.

He moped around inadequately after supper and waited for something to happen. He typed up the day's notes, tidied the workroom, tried to read a magazine, and then thought about Jeanne. She was a sweet kid, but he didn't love her. She didn't understand.

The sand walls seemed to be going up around him again. He wasn't among the dead trees—he was one of them, rooted in the sand with the living greenness stripped from his heart.

Oh, what the hell. The magazine flew across the room and disappeared behind the couch in a flutter of white pages.

He stormed into the workroom, bumped the shelves and set the specimens in their bottles swaying sadly to and fro. In the second bottle from the end, right-hand side, was a toad. In the third were two small amber drops with tails, whose label said only:

YOU TELL ME—8/5/57

Interest stirred. Now, there was a funny thing. He had almost forgotten. The beads, it would seem, had been the cause of the toad's death. They had evidently affected the stomach and the surrounding tissues before they had had a chance to pass through the digestive tract. Fast work. He picked up the second bottle and moved it gently. The pale little thing inside rotated until the incision, with all the twisted organs plainly visible inside, faced him. Willy Seppel would have liked to see this; too bad he was across the state in Ann Arbor.

Idly, Thorne toyed with the idea of sending the pair of drops to his old friend. They were unusual looking—he could leave the label on, write a cryptic note, and fix Seppel's clock for putting the minnows in his larvae pail on their last field trip together.

If he hurried, he could get the drops off tonight. There was a train from Port Grand in forty-five minutes. As for the storm, it was still a long way off; he doubted that it would break before nightfall. And the activity would do him good.

He found a small box and prepared it for the mails. Where was that book of stamps? The letter to Seppel: he slipped a sheet of paper into the typewriter and tapped rapidly. String—where was the string? Ah, here it was in the magazine rack. Now a slicker, and be sure the windows and doors are locked.

His jeep was in a shed at the bottom of the dune, protected by a thick scrub of cottonwood and cedar. Since there was no door, Thorne had merely to reverse gears, shoot out, swing around, and roar over the improvised stone drive to the hard, wet sand of the beach. Five miles down the shore was an overgrown but still usable wagon trail which led to the highway.

The clouds were closing ranks in the west as Dr. Thorne and his jeep disappeared over the crest of a tall dune.

Mr. Gimpy Zandbergen, gentleman of leisure, late of the high sea and presently of the open road, was going home. During a long and motley life, Mr. Zandbergen had wandered far from his native lakes to sail on more boisterous waters; but now his days as an oiler were over, and there came into his heart a nostalgic desire to see the fruit boats ship out of Port Grand once more. Since he possessed neither the money for a bus ticket home, nor the ambition to work to obtain it, he pursued his way via freight cars and such rides as he was able to hook from kindly disposed truck drivers.

His last ride had carried him to a point on the shore highway some miles south of his goal, at which he had regrettably been invited to continue his journey on foot. But Mr. Zandbergen was a simple soul, so he merely shrugged his shoulders, fortified himself from the bottle in his pocket and trudged along.

It was hot, though, as only Michigan in August can be, and the sun baked the concrete and reflected off the sand hills at the side of the road. He paused, pulled a blue bandanna handkerchief from his pocket, and mopped his balding head under his cap. He thought longingly of the cool dune path which he knew lay on the other side of the forest, toward the lake.

It had been a long time, but he knew he remembered it. It would lead to Port Grand and the fruit boats, and would be refreshingly cool.

When the storm came, Mr. Zandbergen was distinctly put out. He had not seen the gathering storm through the thick branches, and when the sky darkened he assumed that it was merely one of the common summer sun showers and hoped for a quick clearing.

He was disturbed when the big drops continued to pelt down among the oak trees. He was annoyed as his path led him out between the smaller and less sheltering evergreens. He swore as the path ended high on a scrubby hill.

Lightning cut the black clouds and Mr. Zandbergen broke into a lope. He had taken the wrong turning, he knew that now. But he recognized this shore. He dimly remembered a driftwood shanty which lay near an old wagon road somewhere around here. If he made that, he might not get too wet after all.

He could see the lake now. The wind was raging and tearing all the waves, whipping the once placid waters of Michigan into black fury. Mr. Zandbergen shuddered in the driving rain and fled headlong down a dune. Great crashes of thunder deafened him and he could hardly see. Where was that road?

A huge sheet of lightning lit the sky as he struggled to the top of the next dune. There it was! The road was down there! And trees, and the shanty, too.

He went diagonally across the dune in gigantic leaps, dodging the storm-wracked trees and bushes. The wind lulled, then blasted the branches down ferociously, catching him a stinging blow across the face. He tripped, and with an agonized howl began to roll straight down the bare face of the sand hill. He landed in a prickly juniper hedge and lay, whimpering and cursing weakly, while the rain and wind pounded him.

The greenery ripped from the trees stung into him viciously as he tried to rise, gave up, and tried again. On the black beach several hundred feet away, waves leaped and stretched into the sky.

Then came another lull and a light appeared out in the lake. It rose and fell in the surf and in a few moments the flattened and horrified little man on the shore could see what it was. A solemn thunderclap drowned out his scream of terror.

Shouting wordless things, he stumbled swaying to his feet and clawed through the bushes to fall out onto the road. It saw him! He was sure it saw him! He struggled along on his knees in the sand for a short distance before he fell for the last time.

The wind shrilled again in the trees, but the fury of the storm had finally passed. The rain fell down steadily now on the sodden sand dunes, and dripped off the cottonwood branches onto the quiet form of Mr. Zandbergen, who would not see the fruit boats go out again after all.

The sheriff was a conversational man. "Now I've lived on the lake for forty years," he said to Thorne, "but never—*never* did I see a storm like today's. No sir!" He turned to his subordinate standing beside him. "Regular typhoon, eh, Sam? I guess we won't be forgetting that one in a hurry."

Dr. Thorne, at any rate, would not forget it. He could still hear in his mind the thunder as it had rolled away off over the dunes, and see the flaring white cones of his headlights cutting out his way through the rain. He had gone slowly over the sliding wet sand of the wagon road on his way home, but even at that he had almost missed seeing it. He remembered how he had thought it was a fallen branch at first, and how he got out of the car then and stood in the rain looking at it before he wrapped his slicker around it and drove back to town.

And now the rain had stopped at last, and the office of the Port Grand physician who was the county medical examiner was neat, dim, and stuffy with the smell of pharmaceuticals and wet raincoats. Over the other homely odors hung the stench of burnt flesh.

Snip, went the physician's bandage shears through charred cloth. Thorne lit a cigarette and inhaled, but the sharp, sickening other smell remained in his nostrils.

"According to his Seamen's International card, he was George Zandbergen of Port Grand," said the sheriff to Sam, who carefully transcribed this information in his notebook. To Thorne he said, "Did you know him, mister?"

Thorne shook his head.

"I remember him, Peter," said the physician, experimentally determining the stiffness of the dead fingers before him. "Appendicitis in 1946. Left town after that. I think he used to be an oiler on the *Josephine Temple* in the fruit fleet. I'll have a file on him around somewhere."

"Get that, Sam," said the sheriff. He turned to Thorne, standing awkwardly at the foot of the examination table. "We'll have to have your story for the record, of course. I hope this won't take too long. Start at the beginning, please."

Gulping down his nervousness and revulsion, Thorne told of returning from town about nine o'clock and finding the corpse of a man lying in the middle of a deserted side road. Dr. Thorne recalled puzzling at the condition of the body, for although it had been storming heavily at the time, portions of the body had been burned quite black. Thorne had found something at the scene also, but failing to see that it had any connection with the matters at hand, prudently kept his discovery to himself. The sheriff would hardly be interested in it, he told himself, but nevertheless he hoped that the bulge it made in his pocket wasn't too noticeable.

Officer Sam Stern made the last little tipped-v that stood for a period in his transcription and looked nervously about him. His chief peered approvingly—even if uncomprehendingly—at the notes and then said:

"How does it look, doctor?"

"Third degree burns on fifty percent of the body area, seared to the bone in some parts of the face and about the right scapula. How did you say he was lying when you found him, Mr. Thorne?"

"In an unnatural kind of sprawled position, on the right side."

The physician yawned, rummaged in a cabinet and produced a sheet with which he covered the charred body. "Pretty obvious, Peter, with these burns and all. Verdict is accidental death. The poor devil was struck by lightning. Time of death was about eight P.M." He tucked the sheet securely around the head. "That lightning's pretty odd stuff, now. Can blow the soles off a man's shoes without scratching him, or generate enough heat to melt metal. You never know what tricks it's going to play. Take this guy here: one side of him's broiled black and the other's not even singed. Well, you never know, do you?"

He picked up his phone and conversed briefly with the local undertaking parlor. When negotiations for the disposition of the unfortunate Mr. Zandbergen had been completed, he replaced the receiver and shuffled toward the door. Thorne could see that he had bedroom slippers on under his rubbers.

"You can finish up tomorrow, Peter," he resumed. "My wife was kinda peeved at me coming out this way. You know how women are, ha-ha. Good night to you, Mr. Thorne. I think there's an old overcoat in that closet I could let you take. You'll be wanting to send yours to the cleaners."

There was a genial guffaw from the sheriff. "We won't keep you any longer tonight, Mr. Thorne. Just let me know how I can get in touch with you."

"Through Kirk MacInnes on River Road," said Thorne. "He'll be glad to contact me through his amateur station." He edged through the door into the quiet night. The sheriff came close behind.

"So you're a ham, eh?" he said warmly. "Well, can you tie that! I used to have a ticket myself in the old days."

Polite noises. How about that? Kindred souls. Sorry about all this sloppy business, old man. Tough luck you had to be the one to find him. Really nothing, old man. *Why* didn't he stop talking? The weight in Thorne's pocket seemed to grow.

"You know, I'll be dropping in to see your rig some one of these days if you don't mind. I'll bet you could use a little company out there in the dunes, eh?"

No, why should he mind? Delighted, old man. Any time at all.

The thing in his pocket seemed to sag to his ankles. It would rip the pocket and fall out. And it had bits of charred cloth on it. Why didn't they go? They couldn't possibly suspect that he hadn't—

Oh, yes, he was on ten meters. Phone. Oh, the sheriff had done c.w. on 180? Well, wasn't that nice.

They walked to the cars under the big old elm trees that lined the comfortable street. A few stars came out and down where the street dead-ended into the river, they could see lights moving toward the deepwater channel that connected the river with the lake.

"Well, good night, Sheriff," Thorne said. "Good night, Mr. Stern. I hope next time we'll meet under more pleasant circumstances."

"Good night, Mr. Thorne," said Sam, who was thoroughly bored with talk he didn't understand, and anxious to get home to his wife and baby.

The police got into their car and drove off. Thorne sat quietly behind the wheel of the jeep until he was sure they were gone, then gingerly removed the weight from his pocket and unwrapped the handkerchief that covered it.

This one was the size of a closed fist and irregular in shape. He had found it flattened under the black char that had once been a man's shoulder, glowing with a bright yellow light in its heart. It looked the same as the three small drops he had previously seen, but he saw that what he had mistaken for golden flecks inside of it was really a fine network of metallic threads which formed a web apparently imbedded a few centimeters below the thing's surface.

The damn thing, he thought. There was something funny about it, all right.

Around him, the lights of the quiet houses were going out one by one. It was eleven o'clock. A few wet patches still glistened on the street under the lamps, and a boat motor on the river pulsed, then stilled.

Thorne looked around him quickly, then got out of the car and laid the thing on the curb. The wet leaves in the gutter below it reflected yellow faintly.

It was funny that a mere matter of shape could change his feeling toward it so radically. The smaller drops had been rather beautiful in their droplike mystery, but this one, although it was made of the same wonderful stuff, had none of the beauty. The irregular cavity in its side that would fit a human shoulder blade made it a thing sinister; the dried blood and ashes made it monstrous.

He took a tire iron out of the tool kit and tapped the glowing thing experimentally. It was certainly stronger than it looked, at any rate. When harder taps failed to crack it, he raised the iron and brought it down with all his strength. The tool bounced, skidded and chipped the concrete curbstone, but the thing flew undamaged into the gutter.

Throne bent down and poked it incredulously. And suddenly, with a cry of agony, he dropped the tire iron. It was hot! The tool arced down and lay sizzling sullenly among the little drops of water that still clung to the grass blades. His hand—He clenched his teeth to keep from crying out.

But the glowing thing in the gutter was not hot. Steam rose from the iron in the grass, but the little rivulets bathing the glowing thing were cool. He seemed to remember something, but then the shocked numbness coming over his hand took his attention and he forgot it again.

Down among the leaves and trash, the thing that was not shattered by the strength of Dr. Throne grew, momentarily, more golden; and with a deliberate, liquid ripple the ugly bulges on its surface smoothed and it assumed the perfect drop shape of its predecessors.

> 200000 AU PLUS PLENTY WATTS. TELL ME PRETTY MAIDEN ARE THERE ANY MORE AT HOME LIKE YOU? ARRIVE NOON THURSDAY. LOVE. SEPPEL.

"You think you're pretty smart, don't you?" said Thorne.

"Yep," said Willy Seppel smugly, smirking around the edge of his beer. He put down the glass and the smirk expanded to a grin. "Smart enough to see what those drops were that you sent me for a gag. That was a great little trick of yours, you know. I was all set to throw them out after reading that note of yours. The only thing that saved them was Archie Deck. He thought they might be Prince Rupert drops and tried to crack the tails off with a file."

"Aha," said Dr. Thorne.

Seppel looked at him with bright blue, innocent eyes. He was a large, pink-faced, elegantly dressed man with an eagle-beak nose and a crown of fine, blond hair.

"You don't have to look at me like that," said Thorne. "I've been able to find out a little bit more about them myself."

"Tell me," said the pink face complacently.

"They generate heat. And I found out the same way as Archie Deck probably did." He gestured with one bandaged hand. "Only I managed it the hard way." He swept up the empty glasses and beer bottles with a crash and disappeared into the kitchen. His voice continued distantly:

"I found those two I sent you inside the stomach of a toad. Or at least what was left of the stomach of a toad. Look in the lab room, the big shelf; second bottle from the end on the right-hand side."

Wiping his good hand on his trousers, he returned to Seppel, who stood looking thoughtfully into the toad's bottle. "It ate the drops," Thorne said shortly.

"Mm—yes," he mused. "The digestive juices might very possibly be able to—"

"Come on, Willy. What is it?"

"You were almost right when you said it generated heat," Willy said. "I brought one of them here to show you." He left the room and returned in a minute with a large cowhide briefcase.

"This thing's in a couple of pieces," Seppel apologized. "You'll have to wait until I set it up. Have you got a step-down transformer?"

Thorne nodded and fetched it from the bookcase.

"Now this little drop here may look like a bead, but it has some singular properties." He removed the thing from a box which had been heavily sealed and padded, and set it in a nest of gray, woolly stuff in the middle of the table.

"It gives off long infrared, mostly stacked up around 200,000 Angstroms. But their energy is way out of proportion from what you'd expect from the equation. This little gadget is something Deck and I rigged up to measure it crudely. Essentially, it's a TC130X couple hooked up to a spring gun. You put the drop in here, regulate the tension of the spring and firing the gun releases this rod which delivers the drop an appropriate smack." His fingers with their immaculately groomed nails worked deftly. "We don't get a controlled measurement, of course, but it'll show you what I mean.... Where do you hide your outlets?"

"Behind the fish tank. Be careful not to disconnect the aerator."

"The screen on that end will show you the energy output. Watch now."

The horizontal green line on the little gray screen bucked at the firing of the spring, then exploded into an oscillating fence of spikes.

"Mad, isn't it?" remarked Dr. Thorne. "Hit it again, but lower the tension of the spring."

If anything, the spikes were even higher.

"The smack-energy ratio isn't proportional," said Seppel. "Sometimes a little nudge will set it off like a rocket. And again, after we tapped it for a week at Ann Arbor figuring out what it was, it showed a tendency to sulk and wouldn't perform at all after awhile."

"The energy output," Thorne said. "It's really quite small, isn't it?"

"Yes, but still surprising for an object this size." He removed the drop from the device and put it back into its little box. "We think that glowing heart has something to do with it. And those gold threads—they are gold, you know—come in there too. Old Camestres, the Medalist himself, was visiting the University, and he says that glow is something that'll have the physicists crawling the walls."

"Oh, come now," said Dr. Thorne broadly.

"You just wait," said Seppel. "We haven't done the analysis yet, but we expect great things. The glow," he added, "isn't hard radiation, if that's what you're thinking."

Willy was proud of it, Thorne thought. It was really his discovery after all, not Thorne's, and Seppel, who found challenge and stimulation in the oddest places, had hit the heights with the little golden drops.

But Thorne was remembering a larger drop, the size of a man's fist, and the charred body of a dead man.

"I found another specimen," he said, turning to a drawer in the worktable. "A larger one." He took out Mr. Zandbergen's drop.

"This is wonderful!" Seppel cried. "It's almost the size of a grapefruit! Now we can—"

Thorne cut him off gently. "I want to tell you about this one. Then I'll turn it over to you. When I first found it, it was irregularly shaped. Lumpy. Ugly. It's smooth now, just like the others, but it changed right before my eyes. It just seemed to run fluid, then coalesce again into the drop shape. And there's something else."

He told Seppel about the attempt to crack the thing and the abrupt heating of the tire iron.

"Yes, that could be," Seppel decided. "It's easily possible that a larger specimen such as this one could cause a metal object near it to become perceptibly warm. Infrared rays aren't hot in themselves, but when they penetrate a material their wave length is increased and the energy released heats the material. In the case of the tire iron, the conductivity of the metal was greater than that of your hand, and you felt the warm iron before the skin itself was affected."

"The iron wasn't warm, Willy. It was damn hot. And in a matter of seconds."

Seppel shook his head. "I don't know what to say. It's the funniest thing I've ever run across."

"The dead man who lay down on it didn't think it was funny," said Thorne.

"You don't think this little thing killed him, do you? He was charred to a cinder all along one side of him. Do you know what kind of infrared could do a thing like that? None."

"I didn't say I thought *this* one killed him," said Thorne, with a cue that Seppel chose to ignore. "I just said the body was right on top of it."

"Too wild for me," said Seppel. He got up, stretched leisurely, and glanced at the clock. "And anyhow, it's sack time. We can worry about it tomorrow, eh?"

Thorne had to smile. Good old Willy. No little glowing monster was going to keep *him* from his sleep.

"We'll put grapefruit back in the drawer," Seppel suggested, "have ourselves a snack, and go to bed."

"Wouldn't the big one be better off in a pail of ice?" asked Thorne, half laughingly.

"If it did decide to give out, it would probably melt the pail before it melted the ice. And besides," he added with dapper complacency, "they never radiate unless they're disturbed."

In the dream, there was sand all around him. He was in it, buried up to his neck. There was a sun overhead that was gold and transparent, and a wind that never seemed to reach his feverish face threw up little whirls of yellow sand.

Sometimes the familiar face of a woman was there. He cried her name and she was gone. And after that, he forgot her, for small shapeless things gamboled out on the sand into the sunlight, only to be burnt black as the rays struck them....

For the fifth time that night, it seemed, Thorne awoke, his eyes staring widely into the darkness. He cursed at himself and turned the perspiration-soaked pillow over, pummeling it into a semblance of plumpness. Seppel lay beside him, snoring gently.

Somewhere in the lodge a timber creaked, and he felt the fear come back again, and saw the black, huddled heap lying before his headlights, and felt the pain renewed in his slowly healing hand. Of the dream, strangely enough, there was no memory at all.

Only the fear.

But why should he be afraid? There was nothing out there. Nothing out there at all.

But the heap in the road. Lightning. *But the little one had burned.* So what? *The little one was too small to burn a man seriously.* I know that. *He was burned.* Lightning, you silly fool! *He was burned!* Shut up. *One of them burned him.* Shut up! Shut up! *There's another one out there tonight.*

No. Nothing out there at all.

Nothing but the dunes and the lake. Nothing.

The wind squalls strummed the pine branches out there, and swirls of sand borne up the bluff from the beach below tickled faintly at the window. The waves of Michigan were roaring out there—but there was nothing else.

Finally, he was able to sleep.

It was nearly dawn when he woke again, but this time he was on guard and alert as he lowered his bare feet softly to the floor. His hand closed over the barrel of a flashlight on the chest of drawers, and he moved noiselessly so that he would not wake the sleeper beside him.

He tiptoed slowly through the workroom and the living room. Something was on the porch.

As he came through the doors, he said sharply: "Who's there?"

An odor of burned wood hit his nostrils. He exclaimed shortly under his breath and shone the light down near the sill of the outside door. There was a round black hole in the door, smoking and glowing faintly around the edges.

He raced back into the workroom and pulled out the drawer that had held the grapefruit-sized drop. It was empty, and a hole gaped in the bottom of it. The hard wood was still burning slowly.

He yanked out the drawer, put it in the kitchen sink and turned on the water. Then he filled a pan and soaked the hole in the door thoroughly.

They never radiate unless they're disturbed! That was a laugh. Not only had it radiated, but it had somehow focused the radiation. Dr. Thorne was no physicist, but he began to wonder whether the meter had told the whole story of the little glowing drop.

He unlocked the door and slid out into the night. Below the stair was a small, almost imperceptible track in the sand. He followed it down the ridge of the dune, lost it momentarily in a patch of scrub, then found it again in the undisturbed expanse of the sand blow.

He went down into the silent valley, the bobbling yellow light from his flash throwing the tiny track into high relief. When he reached the center of the bowl, he stopped among the long shadows of the gaunt spiky trees.

There was another track in the sand, meeting and merging with the little one. . And the track was three feet wide.

He followed it as if in a dream to the crest of the first low shore dune and stood on its summit among the sharp grass and wild grape. The moon's crescent was low over the water and orange. He saw the track go down the slope and disappear into the waves which were swirling in a new depression in the sand.

The wind whipped his pajama shirt about his back as he stood there and knew that he was afraid of that track in the sand, and that no lightning had killed the little tramp.

It was not until he had locked the door of the lodge behind him that he realized he had run all of the way back.

Friday was a quiet day in the dunes country, but the police did receive three minor complaints. A farmer charged that someone had not only made off with and eaten three of his best laying hens, but had burned the feathers and bones and left them right in the chicken yard. The Ottawa County Highway Commission wanted to know who was building fires in the middle of their asphalt roads and plastering the landscape with hot tar. And a maiden lady complained that the artists in the local summer colony must be holding Wild Orgies again from the looks of the lights she had seen over there at three A.M.

Dr. Thorne bent down over the tracks in the sand. It certainly looked to him as though the big one had been waiting for Mr. Zandbergen's drop.

Seppel said, "Get out of the way there," and snapped his Graflex. "These sand tracks won't last long in the winds around here. And I frankly tell you that if I hadn't seen it with my own eyes, I would never have believed it." He circled the point of conjunction, laid his fountain pen beside it for size reference, and the Graflex flashed again.

"We'll want the door, too," he said, putting the camera aside and scrawling in his notebook.

Thorne howled.

"Well, just the part with the hole in it then," Seppel conceded. "Did you find out where the large track came from?"

"I tracked it to the woods. The ground there is too soft and boggy to hold a wide track like that, and I finally lost it."

Seppel struggled to his feet and retrieved his coat, which he had hung for safety's sake on the white peg branch of a skeleton tree. "Just imagine the size of an object which would make a three-foot track in soft sand!" he exclaimed. "And to think it's been in the lake for heaven knows how long and this is the first time it's come into evidence!"

"I wouldn't be too sure about that—about this being the first time, I mean. There have been some funny old stories told along these shores. I heard one myself from my grandmother when I was about twelve. About the dune roller that was bigger than a schooner and lived in the caves at the bottom of the lake. It came out every hundred years and rolled through the dune forest, leaving a strip of bare sand behind it where it had eaten the vegetation. They said it looked for a man, and when it found one, it would stop rolling and sink back into the lake."

"Great Caesar," said Seppel solemnly. "I can see it now—the great glowing globe lurking deep in the caverns where the sun never shines and there is no life except a few diatoms drifting in the motionless waters."

Thorne gaped at his friend for a minute, and then spied a suspicious twinkle in one blue eye.

"This is no laughing matter, you Sunday supplementist!" he said sharply.

"Hmp," said Willy Seppel, and brushed a few grains of sand from the sleeve of his handsome suit.

It was late when Miss Jeanne Wright got out of the movie in Muskegon—so late that she barely had time to do the shopping which had, ostensibly, been her reason for taking *Carlin* out. "You just can't buy decent dresses in Port Grand, Uncle Kirk," she had pleaded, and he really wouldn't mind if she took the boat, would he? MacInnes had growled indulgently from the depths of his new panadaptor and said he certainly did, confound it, and what was the matter with using the car? But he had tossed her the keys just the same.

The street lights of the city were going on when, laden with bundles, she finally hailed a cab and drove to the yacht basin. It was a beautiful evening, with soft-glowing stars in a sky that was still red-purple in the west. *Carlin* slipped majestically out among the anchored craft into Muskegon Lake.

A bonfire blazed cheerfully on the shore and singing voices from some beach party floated melodiously out over the water. They shouted a jocular greeting to *Carlin* and Jeanne blew a hail to them with the air horn. Her heart was light as she led the cruiser through the channel into the lake and headed for home.

A secretive smile danced on her lips, and she thought kindly about a certain stern-faced young biologist. He was a strange man, occasionally even rude in an unintentional sort of way, and preoccupied with such dreary things as plant cycles and environmental adaptations. But he had walked with her in the dunes one day and changed for a little while, and kissed her once, very gently, on the lips. And after that she had known what she wanted.

He would be sitting in his workroom now, looking over the day's bugs and not thinking of her at all. Or perhaps he would be talking to her uncle over the radio.

She hummed dreamily to herself. The cruiser's speed increased to twenty, and it rocked momentarily in a trough, setting the little good luck charm hung up over the wheel to bobbing like a pendulum. Ian had given that to her. She loved it because of that.

After a while she turned on the short wave receiver that sat on one of the lockers in the deckhouse and listened to Ian and her uncle.

"I have a colleague of mine out from Ann Arbor," Thorne was saying. "About that amber drop we found. Remember my telling you about it? I gave one to Jeanne for a souvenir. My friend is a biophysicist and thinks the drops are a great scientific discovery. His name is Willy Seppel. Say something, Willy."

"Gambusia," said Seppel, recalling the minnows in the larvae pail.

Jeanne listened absently. Ian was telling how the drops gave off hot light when they were disturbed. How he thought there might be bigger drops around that could really grind out the energy 40db. above S9. (What in the world did *that* mean?)

Thorne and this Willy person would look for the bigger drops.

"Is it really hot?" Jeanne wondered, staring curiously at the pendant drop, swinging above the binnacle in its miniature silver basket. It didn't seem to be. But then Ian had said the little ones didn't radiate very much. Only enough to tickle something-or-other.

Far out in the lake, the lights of an ore boat twinkled. She passed the little village of Lake Harbor and put out a bit farther from shore. There would be no more towns now until Port Grand.

Over the radio, her Uncle Kirk's voice, homely and kind, was describing the great things in store for the new panadaptor. Ian would put in a comment here and there, but she noticed that he sounded tired, poor darling.

Cleanly, powerfully, *Carlin* sliced through the waves, pursuing the shadow of herself. The shadow was long, and very black. A boat with a searchlight, thought Jeanne, and looked astern.

It was there, riding high in the dark, choppy water: a great glowing globe of phosphorescence not twenty yards off the stern. It was coming after her, rapidly overtaking the cruiser.

She screamed then, and when the thing came on, she opened the throttle and attempted to outmaneuver it. But the great glowing monster would pause while she veered and spiraled, then overtake her easily when she tried to run away. The motors of the Matthews throbbed in the hull beneath her feet as she tried to urge them to a speed they were never meant for.

The thing was drawing closer. She could see trails of water streaming from it. What was it? What would it do if it caught her?

Bigger ones! Her eyes turned with horror to the tiny drop on its silver chain. Its glow was the perfect miniature of the monstrous thing in the water behind her. She sobbed as she wrenched *Carlin*'s wheel from side to side in hysterical frenzy. Across the cabin, the quiet voice of Ian was telling MacInnes how to rig the panadaptor as a frequency monitor.

Ian!

And if you're ever in a jam....

With tears streaming down her cheeks she set the automatic pilot and fumbled with the little amateur transmitter that had been built into the locker. She had seen her uncle use it only once. That turned it on, she thought, but how did she know it was set right? Or did you set these things?

The little panel wore three switches, two knobs, a dial and a little red light. Naturally Kirk MacInnes had not labeled the controls of an instrument he had built himself. The panel was innocent of any such clutterment.

Carlin tore through the night. The glowing thing was less than fifteen yards behind.

Jeanne wept wildly and the placid voices over the receiver spoke sympathetically of the ruining of Thorne's beach pool by the storm.

Oh, those knobs and switches! This one, then this one, she thought. No—that wouldn't be right. The transmitter might not even be on the air at all. Or she might be in some part of the band where Ian and her uncle would fail to hear her. But what was she supposed to do? And she couldn't read this funny tuning scale.

"I've got a swell mobile VFO in *Carlin,*" said MacInnes.

"What's VFO?" said Seppel.

"In Mac's case, it means Very Frequently Offband."

Laughter.

Oh, what difference would it make? What could he do to help her? The brilliance of the huge thing was lighting up the water for yards around.

The calm voices floated from the receiver and the globe drew closer than it had ever been.

She clawed at the stand-by switch of the radio and suddenly her sobs and the beat of the engines were the only sounds in the deckhouse. She would try. That was all. She would try to reach Ian, and pray that her uncle had left the transmitter set to the correct frequency.

"Ian!" she cried, then remembered to press the button on the side of the little hand microphone. Forcing back her tears, she said, "Ian, Ian—can you hear me?"

Trembling, her hand touched the receiver.

"Jeanne!" the sound burst into the deckhouse. "Is that you? What are you doing?"

"It's after me, Ian!" she screamed. "A glowing sphere fifteen feet high! It's chasing the boat!"

"The boat," came MacInnes' voice numbly. "She took it to Muskegon."

"Jeanne! Listen to me. I don't know whether this will do any good, but you must try. You must do exactly as I say. Do you hear me?"

"I hear you. Ian! That thing is almost on top of the boat!"

"Listen. Listen to me, darling. You have that little amber drop somewhere in the boat. Do you remember? The little amber drop I gave you. Get it. Take it and throw it overboard. Throw it as far as you can. The amber drop! Now tell me if you heard me."

"Yes. I hear you. The drop...."

The drop. It danced on its little silver chain and the light in its core was bright and pulsating and warm. She tore it from its place over the wheel and groped back to the open cockpit of the cruiser. She clung for a full minute to the canopy stanchion, blinded by the golden light.

And then the small drop arced brightly over the water, even as a meteor had, many centuries past.

The light, reflecting off the walls painted a flat, clinical white, was full of blurred, fuzzy forms. They might have been almost anything, Thorne thought. And he shuddered as he thought of what they might have been. A table, for instance, with a burden that was sprawled and made black all along one side.

Without moving his head or changing his expression he squeezed his eyes shut very slowly and opened them again. But it was not the medical examiner's office. It was the waiting room of the little local hospital, and Willy Seppel was sitting beside him on the leather couch. Through the open window behind lowered blinds, a clovery night breeze stirred, parting the smoke that filled the room and turning a page of the magazine that Seppel was staring at.

A young man of twenty-five or so sat across the room from them and ate prodigious quantities of Lifesavers. "My wife," he had grinned nervously at them. "Our first."

The persons in the waiting room could see through the open door to a room at the end of the hall. People in white would periodically enter and leave this room, but another, grimmer group which had entered nearly an hour ago had not come out.

"Willy, I'm going nuts," Thorne burst out at last. "What are they doing in there? You'd think they'd at least let me know—let me see her."

"Easy. It'll be any minute now." He proffered a gold cigarette case, but Thorne shook his head. "Why don't you lie back and try to relax?" Seppel said. "You've been crouching there staring at the floor until your eyes look like a pair of burned-out bulbs. What good do you think you're going to do her in that kind of shape?"

Thorne sank back and lay with the back of his hand shading his eyes. If he could have been there when they brought her in! But it takes time to find where an unmanned boat has drifted. Time while he sat before his receiver with nothing to do but wait. The hands of the clock had wound around to one A.M. before the call finally came and he knew she was saved.

It was three-thirty now. MacInnes and his wife were in there with her. He looked despairingly down the white corridor, and waited.

The sound of her voice, made broken and breathless with weeping, rose again in his mind. She had said the thing was fifteen feet high. The big one itself. And it could have—

This wouldn't do at all. The memory of his dream the previous night stood out in his mind with horrible clarity. The bright golden sun and the little burned things. But infrared doesn't burn. The bright golden sun.

"Sun," said Dr. Thorne to himself, very quietly.

"Mm'mm?" said Seppel.

"Sun," he repeated firmly. "Willy, do you always think the same way?"

"Nope."

"If I hit you, how do you think?"

"Mad," said Seppel, with a winning smile.

"But if you figure the best way to sneak out of here without being seen, how do you think?"

"Rationally."

"I've been thinking about the drops again. You know, we've got a pretty serious discrepancy in the so-called properties of the things. We've proved the infrared emission, but infrared doesn't sear flesh."

"That's what I've been trying to tell you," said Seppel, with patience.

"Nonetheless, I'm convinced that the big one Jeanne saw is the thing that did in the tramp. Now what if the energy emitted is not always infrared? What if the infrared is a sort of involuntary result of the blows we gave the drop, while ordinarily when it's aroused it gives off another wave length? Say something in the visible with a lot of energy, that that drop shape could focus into a beam."

Seppel didn't say a thing.

Silence precipitated heavily. The young man in the chair opposite them shifted his position and stared at them with gaping awe. Scientists!

There was a starchy swish and a nurse appeared in the doorway. Thorne started to his feet. "Can we—"

"Mr. DeAngelo," she beckoned coolly. "It's a boy. Will you follow me, please?"

The young man gave a joyous, inarticulate cry and rushed out of the room.

Thorne dropped back. "Ye gods," he muttered.

"You've really got it bad, haven't you?" Seppel marveled.

"Oh, Willy, shut up. You know I'm only interested in her because of the thing that chased her. And wipe that look off your face. Between you and MacInnes a man doesn't have a chance."

Seppel looked slightly hurt.

"I'm sorry," Thorne apologized briefly. He walked around the room. The young man with the new son had been so anxious to leave that he had forgotten his Lifesavers. Thorne ate one. It was wintergreen. He hated wintergreen.

Seppel yawned delicately, then leaned forward and glanced out the door. "Someone's coming," he warned softly.

A tall man in a uniform of summer tans had left the room at the end of the corridor and walked purposefully toward the waiting room.

Seppel rose to his feet as the man entered the room. He said: "Good evening—or rather, good morning. Is there something I can do?"

"My name is Cunningham, commander of the Coast Guard cutter *Manistique*. Are you Mr. Ian Thorne?"

"My name is Seppel. This is Mr. Thorne. Won't you sit down?"

"Thanks, I will." To Thorne, who stood with his hands rudely clasped behind his back, he said briskly: "Mr. Thorne, at nine this evening your amateur station contacted our base with information that the cruiser *Carlin* was in difficulty off the mainland somewhere between Port Grand and Muskegon."

"It wasn't me, it was Kirk MacInnes." Thorne was not interested in brisk, nautical gentlemen.

"We found the cruiser drifting, out of gas, some seven miles off the Port Grand light. Miss Wright, the operator of the craft, was found lying unconscious on the cockpit floor. I've just seen her—"

"How is she?" Thorne cut in.

"The doctors say she is suffering from shock, but other than that, they can't find a thing wrong with her. Now what I'd like to know—"

"Is she conscious? Has she been able to talk?"

"She's very weak and what she says makes no sense. I thought perhaps you might be able to help us on that score."

Thorne looked at the Coast-Guardsman narrowly. "We were conversing with her over the radio, when she suddenly seemed to become disturbed and evidently fainted."

"Didn't MacInnes tell you anything?" asked Seppel.

"No."

"Quiet, Willy," Thorne said.

"She seemed to be trying to tell us that someone was chasing her," Cunningham persisted. "Are you sure she said nothing in her talk with you that could give us a hint of the trouble?"

"I knew there was something wrong from the sound of her voice. That's all. When she didn't answer, Mr. MacInnes radioed the Coast Guard."

"And we found her after a four-hour search. That young lady was very lucky that she ran out of gas. Her automatic pilot had the cruiser headed straight out into the middle of the lake."

"There was—nothing else on the water near her?"

"The lake was empty." Cunningham paused, then said casually, "Was there something you expected us to find, Dr. Thorne?"

"Certainly not. I was just wondering."

"I see." The officer got to his feet. "I don't mind telling you gentlemen that I think there's something you're not letting me know. My job is done, and it's true that legally I have no business questioning you at all. But my business *is* keeping the waterways safe. The young lady in the room down the hall didn't faint from nervous exhaustion or hunger. Something scared the hell out of her out there on the lake. If you know what it was, I wish you'd tell me!"

"Have you ever read any science fiction, Commander Cunningham?" Seppel asked, toying with his gold cigarette case. Rather belatedly, he said, "Cigarette?"

The Coast-Guardsman took one with suspicious thanks. "Are you trying to tell me that the little green Martians have put outboards on their rocket ships and are chasing the pleasure craft on our lake?"

Thorne said harshly: "What Dr. Seppel means is this. We have reason to believe that a highly unusual occurrence was responsible for tonight's unpleasantness. I don't like to mince words, Commander. I think I *do* know what was out there last night, but I'm not going to tell you. I can't begin to prove my suspicions, and I have a rather intense aversion to being laughed at."

"I have no intention of laughing, Mr. Thorne. But if you have information relative to marine safety, let me remind you that you have an obligation to report it to the proper authorities."

"Proper authorities are not notorious for their sympathy. They'd laugh in my face. No, thank you, Commander. Until I have proof, I say nothing."

The door at the end of the corridor opened once more, and closed softly. Kirk MacInnes and his wife came down toward the waiting room. Thorne started up.

"She wants to see you, son," MacInnes said tiredly. "She's a little stronger now, and she asked for you. I'm taking Ellen back home. This has been pretty raw for her."

"I'm all right," his wife said stiffly. She clutched a damp, tightly balled lace handkerchief, but her features were immobile.

"Will Jeanne be all right?" Thorne asked brokenly.

"She'll be fine," said MacInnes, clapping him on the back. "Now get down there and see her before those medics decide she can't have any more visitors."

"I'm there now. And—thanks, Mac." He disappeared down the corridor. The engineer and his wife left quietly.

"Thorne is a good man," Seppel said, "even if he is a trifle mule-headed." His bright blue eyes looked humorously into the half-angry face of the Coast Guard officer. He laughed, moved over on the leather couch, and said: "Sit down here, Commander. Have another cigarette. Have a Lifesaver. I'm going to tell you a singular story."

It was shortly before lunchtime in Thorne's dune lodge, but the bubbling beaker on the range that Willy Seppel was stirring exuded a decidedly unappetizing aroma. Pungent, acidic in an organic kind of way, with noisome and revolting overtones, the fumes finally brought indignant remarks from Thorne.

"Look," he said, peering in the doorway, and holding his nose. "I'm the last one to criticize another man's cooking, but will you tell me what in heaven's name that is?"

"Oh, just a bit of digestive juice," said Seppel cheerily, turning off the gas and removing the beaker with a pair of pot holders. He carried his foul-steaming container into the workroom. Thorne fled before him.

"I suppose I'd better not ask where you got it," he said, from the sanctuary of the radio room.

"Don't be silly," said Seppel. "I merely raided your enzymes and warmed up a batch. Just an idea."

He took the little drop out of its container and set it on the table beside the beaker. "I thought since digestive juice provoked it into emitting once, it might do it again."

Thorne regarded him dubiously.

"I only wish," Seppel went on to say, "that the grapefruit-sized one hadn't escaped." He set the drop in a loop of plastic and dipped it into the brew.

"Take it easy with that one, Willy. It's the only link we have with the big one."

"So you think they can communicate, too," said Seppel without looking up.

"I don't know whether it's communication or sympathetic vibration or the call of the wild. But that thing did follow Jeanne because of the little drop in the boat, and it disappeared when it got what it wanted. The grapefruit heard mama, too, and got away. I'll bet if that little one had been strong enough to get through your fancy insulation, it would have disappeared along with the other one."

"And the two tracks merged into one," said Seppel, testing the soaked drop in the thermocouple. Nothing happened. "As the rustic detective was heard to remark, 'They was two sets o' footsteps leadin' to the scene of the crime, and only one set leadin' away.' I wonder what kind of a molecular bond that transparent envelope has?" He felt the drop with his finger, shrugged and put it back into the juice.

"The big globe killed the tramp, if my idea is correct," said Thorne. "He must have seen the thing coming out of the lake, turned to beat it, and fell on his face. And I think he picked exactly the wrong place to fall."

"On grapefruit," Seppel agreed. "All mama wanted to do was to pick up her offspring. She couldn't help it if there was a body in the way."

"But she killed just the same," said Thorne. "Those old dune roller stories hint that she may have done it before." He fished the miniature drop out of the liquid and looked into its yellow heart meditatively.

"And Willy," he said abstractedly, "unless something is done soon, she'll do it again."

During the days that followed, Dr. Thorne went about his work with quiet preoccupation; and this in itself was enough to make Seppel more than a little suspicious. He rarely mentioned the drops, although he visited Jeanne every day, carrying sheaves of flowers and boxes of candy and fruit. Seppel went along on these pilgrimages for the ride, but almost always tactfully declined visiting the sickroom and hiked out instead to the Coast Guard station for a parley with his new ally, Commander Cunningham.

Anxiety furrowed Seppel's pink forehead as he paced up and down the officer's quarters. "He's got something up his sleeve," he maintained. "He goes off in the jeep in the morning and doesn't come back until noon. When I ask him where he's been, he says he just went into town to see Jeanne. But visiting hours are from two to four! If he doesn't go to the hospital, where does he go?"

Cunningham shrugged, and picked up a folded newspaper that lay on the table. "Have you seen this, Willy? It might explain a few things."

Mystified, Seppel read aloud: "We pay CASH for certain unusual minerals. Highest prices, free pickup. Samples wanted are round, semi-transparent, amber colored with metallic veining. HURRY! Write today, Box 236, Port Grand, Michigan."

Seppel stared aghast.

"I take it you weren't acquainted with this," the officer said. He walked to the window and looked down at a fruiter steaming through the channel. "Do you know what he plans to do?"

"No, but I know what I'd do. There's some kind of an attraction between the big globe and the drops—a force that draws the little ones home to mama when they get her call. We found that out with a drop at Thorne's lodge. But that attraction is so great that it works the other way too. Little Miss Wright told you that. If the drops can't come, if we hold them back, mama comes after her children. That's what Thorne will probably count on."

It was Cunningham's turn to stare. "You mean he'll use the drops from the ad for *bait?*"

Seppel said gently: "What's a man to do, Rob? He can't let it go free. The fellow that finds the monster has three choices: he can run home and hide under the bed, and pretend he didn't see it at all, he can try to inform the proper authorities, or he can attempt to dispose of the monster himself. Thorne knows nobody will believe his dune roller story so he just doesn't waste time convincing people."

Cunningham turned abruptly from the window and said violently: "You aren't going to start on me too, are you, Willy? Sure. Here I am, one slightly used but still serviceable authority. I believe your damn dune roller yarn for some reason or other. But it doesn't do any good. I'd earn the biggest haw-haw from here to the Straits of Mackinac if I tried to initiate an official search for a round glowing thing fifteen feet high. The world won't unite simply because Michigan has itself a monster, you know. And what can I do, even if I take the *Manistique* out? Maybe Ian Thorne knows how to catch monsters, but I certainly don't."

"You want to let him go on, I suppose," Seppel said. He added a trifle wistfully, "I hate to see him get his hide fried off when he's just beginning to think about settling down."

"You watch him. That's all. And let me know when you think he's going to pull something. I'll do everything I can." He glanced at his watch. "I have to get out of here now, Willy. Keep your eyes open. All *we* can do is wait."

"And that," said Seppel, with dark doubt shading his pleasant voice, "seems to be all there is to say."

The drops glowed on the kitchen table. "Seven!" said Ian Thorne triumphantly. "How do they look to you, Willy? From the size of a pea to a tennis ball. Seven little devil eyes."

"What are you going to do with them?" asked Seppel. He wore an old lab apron over his trousers and wiped the breakfast dishes. It was very early in the morning.

"Just a little experiment. I got a bright idea the other day while I was visiting Jeanne. You can have the drops after I'm finished if you like, but I want to try this thing out first."

"I wish you'd let me help you."

"No, Willy."

"Cunningham believes you, too," Seppel went on recklessly. "Why don't you tell us what you're going to do?"

"No." He scooped the drops into a bakelite box. "I'll be gone most of the day. I have some collecting to do out in the dunes."

He vanished into the bedroom and came out wearing hiking boots and a heavy leather jacket. An empty knapsack dangled over his arm. He put the bakelite box into the buckled pouch on the outside of the sack, and took a paper packet from the sink and stuffed it into his back pocket.

"Oops! Almost forgot my collecting bottles," he laughed, and went into the radio room.

Seppel put down the dish towel and stepped softly after him. There were no collecting bottles in the radio room. He was just in time to see Thorne drop a handful of little metal cylinders and a black six-inch gadget into the knapsack.

Thorne did not seem at all abashed to find Seppel standing there. He brushed past and went out the kitchen door.

"So long, Willy. Keep the home fires burning. Send out the posse if I'm not back before dark." The screen door slammed.

After waiting a minute, Seppel grabbed up the binoculars from the china shelf and glided silently through the sandy yard, past the generator building to the path that led down the side of the dune to the shed where the jeep was kept.

The early morning mist still curled around the trees and settled in the hollows, and a distant bird call echoed down on the forest floor. At a bend in the steep path, Seppel caught a glimpse of Thorne's broad back dappled by the pale sun rising through the fog.

The path turned sharply and cut off diagonally down the dune toward the shed.

Instead of continuing, Seppel stepped off the path, and treading cautiously, circled across through the woods to arrive at a point on the slope directly above the garage. Then he removed his apron, spread it on the twiggy, dew-wet ground and stretched out among the bushes, bringing his binoculars to bear on the man below.

Thorne removed a small wooden crate from the rear of the jeep. It bore the red-stenciled inscription:

G. B. VANDER VREES & SONS
—HIGHWAY CONSTRUCTION

There were other words, too, but Thorne stood in the way of Seppel's vision. He quickly transferred the contents of the crate to his knapsack, and with a single look around him, set off down the dune trail that ran through the forest, parallel to the lake shore.

As soon as Thorne was out of sight, Willy Seppel scrambled heavily to his feet and went back up the path to the lodge. There he addressed some intense words to the microphone of the amateur station, an operation which would have been frowned upon by the FCC, which discourages the use of such equipment by unlicensed persons.

He would have maintained his disinterest and scientific detachment if he had been asked about it, but the truth was that Dr. Ian Thorne deeply loved the dunes. He had lived in them during his childhood, grown up and gone away, and come back to find them substantially the same. He recalled that had surprised him little. You expected the dunes to change, they were like a person, though only one who has known the heights and swamps of them can explain the curious sleeping vitality of the sands under the forest. Things with a smaller life than the dunes would flutter and creep and stalk boldly through them until you might think of them as dead and tame. But Dr. Thorne had seen the traveling dunes shifting restlessly before the winds and felt a kinship with the great never-lasting hills.

The path he strolled along was an old friend. He had pursued the invertebrate citizens of the forest along its meandering length, waded in the marshy interdunal pools which it carefully skirted, and had itched from encounters with the poison ivy that festooned the trunks and shrubs beside it.

The path wound along the shore for a good five miles—horizontally, at least—and he did not hurry. The knapsack was too heavy, for one thing, and the still air was warming slowly as the sun rose up through the pines and oak trees. An insect chirred sleepily in a gorge on his right, and as if at some prearranged signal, an excursion of mosquitoes bobbed out to worry the back of his neck.

The path took him through a clearing in the sand covered with patches of dusty, green grass and scarlet Indian weed. On the lee side of a great bare dune at the edge of the clearing stood a single, short cottonwood, half buried in the sand. But the tree had grown upward to escape, modifying its lower branches into roots. The tree was one of the few forms of life that defied the dunes—by growing with them—and its branches were brave and green.

Thoughtfully, Thorne passed on again into the dimmer depths of the forest.

It was nearly noon when he reached the foot of a cluster of sand dunes, the principal peak of which rose some hundred and fifty feet above the floor of the woods. It was the highest point for many miles along the shore, and its name was Mount Scott. The path circled its eastern slope and then continued on, but Thorne stepped off onto the faintly defined, spider-web-laced trail leading to the summit.

The going was rough. Thornapple branches probed after his eyes, and as the ascent grew steeper, sudden shifts in the dirty sand under his feet brought him to his knees. The tree roots across the path had partially blocked the sand, forming crude natural steps in the lower reaches of the dune; but as he climbed higher, the trees were left behind while the sand grew cleaner and hotter, and the wild grape, creeper and ubiquitous poison ivy became the prevalent greenery.

He was winded and perspiring when he finally stood on the peak of the dune. He glanced briefly about him and selected a spot partially shaded by a scrub juniper as his campsite. He sat down, shucked the knapsack and his heavy jacket and lit a cigarette.

The hills below rolled away in gentle, green waves toward the farmlands and orchards in the east and the brilliant blue lake in the west. He could see the spires of the town of Port Grand poking out of the haze a few miles down the shore, and some white sails appeared off the promontory that hid the entrance to the river harbor.

He turned his attention to Mount Scott itself. The summit of the dune was really composed of two shallow humps, with a depression on the lakeward side in which Thorne had made his camp. Below this, a sheer, fairly clean slope of sand swept down to the low tangle of woods which lay between him and the shore.

He looked cautiously in the knapsack and removed the seven small drops, grouping them in a circle on the white sand of the lake slope. After that, he retreated to his hollow and settled down as comfortably as he could.

The paper packet in his pocket yielded three ham-and-pickle sandwiches, slightly soggy, which he consumed leisurely. A short foray around the peak brought dessert in the form of a handful of late blueberries. After his meal he employed himself at length with the contents of the knapsack. When the job was finally done, he sat down under the juniper tree and began to wait.

The shade of the tree diminished, disappeared as the sun climbed higher, and then reappeared on the other side of the tree, leaving Thorne with the sun in his face and a monumental thirst. The blueberries, unfortunately, were all gone.

At last, at four P.M., the largest drop began to move.

It rolled slowly out of the shallow hole in the sand that cupped it and moved down the hill. Thorne watched it roll *up* a small pile of sand that blocked its path and disappear into the woods at the foot of the hill.

At 4:47 one of the smaller drops followed in the track of the first. It had a little trouble when it came to the pile of sand—which was one of several strung across the face of the dune—but it negotiated the obstacle at last and disappeared.

Just as the sun was beginning to redden the water, a third drop began its descent. Quietly, Thorne rose and replaced it in its hole. The faint gleam within it might have grown a bit brighter when he interfered, but perhaps it was only the reflection of the sun.

The five remaining drops were grouped in a horseshoe, downward pointing, and the drop whose elopement had just been foiled reposed at the end of one prong. A few minutes later, the larger drop at the other prong attempted to roll down the hill. Thorne put it back and rapped sharply on each of the others with his cigarette lighter, tamping them down further into the sand. He was strained forward alertly now, with his eyes on the strip of forest below. The sun slipped grudgingly behind the flat lake, and a tang of pine washed up the slope. The drops did not move again.

With the departure of the sun, the glow in the heart of each alien thing leaped higher and higher, until the string of them was like a softly glowing corona in the sand—a strange earthbound constellation.

But their glow was not beauty, Thorne reminded himself. It was death. Death had dwelt in their great, glowing mother who had already called two of her incredible children home. Death that rolled seeking through the lake and the dune forest....

His cigarette end made a dimmer eye in the dusk than the glow of the drops. There was still enough light to see by—the sky was red around him and the dune forest was silent.

He wondered idly what long forgotten power had strewn the drops along the shore. They were not terrestrial, he was almost sure of that. Perhaps they had been a meteor that had exploded over the lake, and the life of the great thing—if it was life—had been patiently gathering up its scattered substance ever since, assimilating the fragments during its long rests at the bottom of the lake.

From the size of it, it must have been growing for hundreds of years, collecting a drop of itself here and there, from roadbeds and sand dunes and farmyards, responding to those who imprudently hindered it with the only defense it knew.

And now he was to destroy it. It had killed a man. Perhaps before this, even, men had found the drops attractive and carelessly put them in their pockets... and the dune roller sought a man. It had killed the little tramp, and almost killed Jeanne. He couldn't take a chance of letting it go again.

The image of Jeanne rose in his mind. The memory of the time they had walked down the winding forest path, and of a twig caught in her sandal. She had had grains of sand on her tanned arms, and a bright yellow flower stuck crazily in one dark curl. She had laughed when he plumped her down on the moss-soft root of an old oak and took the twig out, but she had not laughed when he kissed her.

Around him, the forest was still.

A cold breath whispered along his skin. The forest was still. Not a bird, not an insect, not an animal noise. The forest was still.

He felt like yelling at it: *Come on out, you!* Come out and chase me like you chased her!

He fingered the stud of the little black instrument in his hand. He would show it. Let it dare to come out.

Come out!

It came.

He had never dreamed it would be so big.

It had made no noise at all. In a fascination of horror he watched it roll to the foot of the tall dune. It vanished among the trees, but a warm yellow radiance lit the undersides of the fluttering leaves as it moved beneath them. The light blazed as it emerged from the brush and came straight toward him, rolling up the hill.

The small drops pulsed in their sandy snares and he gave each one a savage rap. As if it, too, shared the insult, the great globe flared, then subsided sullenly. But its ponderous ascent was alarmingly rapid.

He could not take his eyes away from it. The smaller drops were rocks, were mere bits of oddly glowing crystal; but this great thing before him seemed the most beautiful and the most terrible thing he had ever seen in his life. And it was alive. No man could have looked upon it and said that it was not alive. The brilliant golden heart in it swelled and blazed upon the golden veining that closed it in.

There were noises now from the winding path in the forest below, and the twinkling pinpoint lights of men. But Thorne did not hear them, nor see any light except the great one before him. He could not move. Sweat stood out on his face and the instinct to flee dissolved into terror that folded his legs like boneless things. He half-crouched on hands and knees and stared . . . and stared.

The thing was closer now, nearly up to the line of sand humps that Thorne had worked so hard on. He had to get away. There was no more time. He forced his paralyzed hands and feet to tear into the loose sand of the side of the depression and pull him up. He had to get on the other side of the hill.

In the last instant, his numbed fingers pressed the stud of the little transmitter that would activate the firing caps of the nitro buried in the sand.

But the monster must have realized, somehow. Because he felt—when he flung himself out over the peak with the deep red sky around him—a searing, mounting pain that started on the inside and flooded outward. He rolled unconscious over the far side of the hill just as the five solemn detonations blasted the golden glowing globe to bits.

There were white, gauzy circles around the place where his eyes looked out. He was vaguely surprised to see six people with the eyes—three sets of two. He made the eyes blink and the six people changed into Seppel, MacInnes and Jeanne. He tried to raise an arm and was rewarded by a fierce jab of pain. The arm was thick and bandaged, like the rest of him.

The six—three—people had seen his eyes open and they moved closer to him. Jeanne sat down beside the bed and leaned her head close.

"I hope that's you in there," she said, and he was amazed to see there were tears in her eyes.

"How am I?" he mumbled through the bandages.

"Medium rare," said Seppel. "You doggone crazy fool."

"We almost got to the top, anyway," said MacInnes gruffly. "But you went and beat us to it."

"Had to," Thorne said painfully.

"You would," Jeanne said.

"Is it gone?" he asked. There were six people again and he felt very tired.

"Shivered to atoms," said Seppel with finality. "You should see the crater in the sand. But we'll still have small ones to study. Your ad brought in four more today. I was talking to Camestres on the phone, and he says he's sure he can swing a nice fat research grant for us as soon as you're able to get out of that bed—"

Thorne groaned.

"He says," Jeanne translated firmly, "that he's sticking to *Ecological Studies of the Michigan Dunes,* Chapter Eight. No more dune rollers, thank you."

MacInnes laughed and wagged his gray old head. "You'd better surrender, Dr. Seppel. Jeanne's got her mind made up. And one thing about her—whatever she says, she'll always be Wright."

"Don't be too sure about that," she said pertly, laying her two small hands gently on Thorne's bandaged arm. It didn't hurt a bit.

High on a dune above the lake, the moon rode high over a blackened crater in the sand. Two of the grains of sand, which gleamed in the moonlight a bit more golden than the rest, tumbled down together into a sheltered hollow to begin anew the work of three hundred years.

ROBERT SHECKLEY

Warm

Robert Sheckley (1928-) arrived on the science fiction scene in 1952 and quickly began to appear in virtually every magazine that published it. Amazingly prolific, he needed several pen names in the 1950s to accommodate his output. His stories are noted for their wit, satire and iconoclastic point of view—he is particularly effective in introducing self-doubt and cynicism into his characters. His stories can be found in some eleven collections, the most recent of which is The Wonderful Worlds of Robert Sheckley *(1979). He has also written several noteworthy novels, the best-known of which is* The Tenth Victim, *the basis for the film of the same name.*

ANDERS LAY on his bed, fully dressed except for his shoes and black bow tie, contemplating, with a certain uneasiness, the evening before him. In twenty minutes he would pick up Judy at her apartment, and that was the uneasy part of it.

He had realized, only seconds ago, that he was in love with her.

Well, he'd tell her. The evening would be memorable. He would propose, there would be kisses, and the seal of acceptance would, figuratively speaking, be stamped across his forehead.

Not too pleasant an outlook, he decided. It really would be much more comfortable not to be in love. What had done it? A look, a touch, a thought? It didn't take much, he knew, and stretched his arms for a thorough yawn.

"Help me!" a voice said.

His muscles spasmed, cutting off the yawn in mid-moment. He sat upright on the bed, then grinned and lay back again.

"You must help me!" the voice insisted.

Anders sat up, reached for a polished shoe and fitted it on, giving his full attention to the tying of the laces.

"Can you hear me?" the voice asked. "You can, can't you?"

That did it. "Yes, I can hear you," Anders said, still in a high good humor. "Don't tell me you're my guilty subconscious, attacking me for a childhood trauma I never bothered to resolve. I suppose you want me to join a monastery."

"I don't know what you're talking about," the voice said. "I'm no one's subconscious. I'm *me*. Will you help me?"

Anders believed in voices as much as anyone; that is, he didn't believe in them at all, until he heard them. Swiftly he catalogued the possibilities. Schizophrenia was the best answer, of course, and one in which his colleagues would concur. But Anders had a lamentable confidence in his own sanity. In which case—

"Who are you?" he asked.

"I don't know," the voice answered.

Anders realized that the voice was speaking within his own mind. Very suspicious.

"You don't know who you are," Anders stated. "Very well. *Where* are you?"

"I don't know that, either." The voice paused, and went on. "Look, I know how ridiculous this must sound. Believe me, I'm in some sort of limbo. I don't know how I got here or who I am, but I want desperately to get out. Will you help me?"

Still fighting the idea of a voice speaking within his head, Anders knew that his next decision was vital. He had to accept—or reject—his own sanity.

He accepted it.

"All right," Anders said, lacing the other shoe. "I'll grant that you're a person in trouble, and that you're in some sort of telepathic contact with me. Is there anything else you can tell me?"

"I'm afraid not," the voice said, with infinite sadness. "You'll have to find out for yourself."

"Can you contact anyone else?"

"No."

"Then how can you talk with me?"

"I don't know."

Anders walked to his bureau mirror and adjusted his black bow tie, whistling softly under his breath. Having just discovered that he was in love, he wasn't going to let a little thing like a voice in his mind disturb him.

"I really don't see how I can be of any help," Anders said, brushing a bit of lint from his jacket. "You don't know where you are, and there don't seem to be any distinguishing landmarks. How am I to find you?" He turned and looked around the room to see if he had forgotten anything.

"I'll know when you're close," the voice said. "You were warm just then."

"Just then?" All he had done was look around the room. He did so again, turning his head slowly. Then it happened.

The room, from one angle, looked different. It was suddenly a mixture of muddled colors, instead of the carefully blended pastel shades he had selected. The lines of wall, floor and ceiling were strangely off proportion, zig-zag, unrelated.

Then everything went back to normal.

"You were *very* warm," the voice said.

Anders resisted the urge to scratch his head, for fear of disarranging his carefully combed hair. What he had seen wasn't so strange. Everyone sees one or two things in his life that make him doubt his normality, doubt sanity, doubt his very existence. For a moment the orderly Universe is disarranged and the fabric of belief is ripped.

But the moment passes.

Anders remembered once, as a boy, awakening in his room in the middle of the night. How strange everything had looked! Chairs, table, all out of proportion, swollen in the dark. The ceiling pressing down, as in a dream.

But that also had passed.

"Well, old man," he said, "if I get warm again, tell me."

"I will," the voice in his head whispered. "I'm sure you'll find me."

"I'm glad you're so sure," Anders said gaily, switched off the lights and left.

Lovely and smiling, Judy greeted him at the door. Looking at her, Anders sensed her knowledge of the moment. Had she felt the change in him, or predicted it? Or was love making him grin like an idiot?

"Would you like a before-party drink?" she asked.

He nodded, and she led him across the room, to the improbable green-and-yellow couch. Sitting down, Anders decided he would tell her when she came back with the drink. No use in putting off the fatal moment. A lemming in love, he told himself.

"You're getting warm again," the voice said.

He had almost forgotten his invisible friend. Or fiend, as the case could well be. What would Judy say if she knew he was hearing voices? Little things like that, he reminded himself, often break up the best of romances.

"Here," she said, handing him a drink.

Still smiling, he noticed. The number two smile—to a prospective suitor, provocative and understanding. It had been preceded, in their relationship, by the number one nice-girl smile, the don't-misunderstand-me smile, to be worn on all occasions, until the correct words have been mumbled.

"That's right," the voice said. "It's in how you look at things."

Look at what? Anders glanced at Judy, annoyed at his thoughts. If he was going to play the lover, let him play it. Even through the astigmatic haze of love, he was able to appreciate her blue-gray eyes, her fine skin (if one overlooked a tiny blemish on the left temple), her lips, slightly reshaped by lipstick.

"How did your classes go today?" she asked.

Well, of course she'd ask that, Anders thought. Love is marking time.

"All right," he said. "Teaching psychology to young apes—"

"Oh, come now!"

"Warmer," the voice said.

What's the matter with me, Anders wondered. She really is a lovely girl. The *gestalt* that is Judy, a pattern of thoughts, expressions, movements, making up the girl I—

I what?

Love?

Anders shifted his long body uncertainly on the couch. He didn't quite understand how this train of thought had begun. It annoyed him. The analytical young instructor was better off in the classroom. Couldn't science wait until 9:10 in the morning?

"I was thinking about you today," Judy said, and Anders knew that she had sensed the change in his mood.

"Do you see?" the voice asked him. "You're getting much better at it."

"I don't see anything," Anders thought, but the voice was right. It was as though he had a clear line of inspection into Judy's mind. Her feelings were nakedly apparent to him, as meaningless as his room had been in that flash of undistorted thought.

"I really was thinking about you," she repeated.

"Now look," the voice said.

Anders, watching the expressions on Judy's face, felt the strangeness descend on him. He was back in the nightmare perception of that moment in his room. This time it was as though he were watching a machine in a laboratory. The object of this operation was the evocation and preservation of a particular mood. The machine goes through a searching process, invoking trains of ideas to achieve the desired end.

"Oh, were you?" he asked, amazed at his new perspective.

"Yes . . . I wondered what you were doing at noon," the reactive machine opposite him on the couch said, expanding its shapely chest slightly.

"Good," the voice said, commending him for his perception.

"Dreaming of you, of course," he said to the flesh-clad skeleton behind the total *gestalt* Judy. The flesh machine rearranged its limbs, widened its mouth to denote pleasure. The mechanism searched through a complex of fears, hopes, worries, through half-remembrances of analogous situations, analogous solutions.

And this was what he loved. Anders saw too clearly and hated himself for seeing. Through his new nightmare perception, the absurdity of the entire room struck him.

"Were you really?" the articulating skeleton asked him.

"You're coming closer," the voice whispered.

To what? The personality? There was no such thing. There was no true cohesion, no depth, nothing except a web of surface reactions, stretched across automatic visceral movements.

He was coming closer to the truth.

"Sure," he said sourly.

The machine stirred, searching for a response.

Anders felt a quick tremor of fear at the sheer alien quality of his viewpoint. His sense of formalism had been sloughed off, his agreed-upon reactions by-passed. What would be revealed next?

He was seeing clearly, he realized, as perhaps no man had ever seen before. It was an oddly exhilarating thought.

But could he still return to normality?

"Can I get you a drink?" the reaction machine asked.

At that moment Anders was as thoroughly out of love as a man could be. Viewing one's intended as a depersonalized, sexless piece of machinery is not especially conducive to love. But it is quite stimulating, intellectually.

Anders didn't want normality. A curtain was being raised and he wanted to see behind it. What was it some Russian scientist—Ouspensky, wasn't it—had said?

"Think in other categories."

That was what he was doing, and would continue to do.

"Good-by," he said suddenly.

The machine watched him, open-mouthed, as he walked out the door. Delayed circuit reactions kept it silent until it heard the elevator door close.

"You were very warm in there," the voice within his head whispered, once he was on the street. "But you still don't understand everything."

"Tell me, then," Anders said, marveling a little at his equanimity. In an hour he had bridged the gap to a completely different viewpoint, yet it seemed perfectly natural.

"I can't," the voice said. "You must find it yourself."

"Well, let's see now," Anders began. He looked around at the masses of masonry, the convention of streets cutting through the architectural piles. "Human life," he said, "is a series of conventions. When you look at a girl, you're supposed to see — a pattern, not the underlying formlessness."

"That's true," the voice agreed, but with a shade of doubt.

"Basically, there is no form. Man produces *gestalts*, and cuts form out of the plethora of nothingness. It's like looking at a set of lines and saying that they represent a figure. We look at a mass of material, extract it from the background and say it's a man. But in truth, there is no such thing. There are only the humanizing features that we — myopically — attach to it. Matter is conjoined, a matter of viewpoint."

"You're not seeing it now," said the voice.

"Damn it," Anders said. He was certain that he was on the track of something big, perhaps something ultimate. "Everyone's had the experience. At some time in his life, everyone looks at a familiar object and can't make any sense out of it. Momentarily, the *gestalt* fails, but the true moment of sight passes. The mind reverts to the superimposed pattern. Normalcy continues."

The voice was silent. Anders walked on, through the *gestalt* city.

"There's something else, isn't there?" Anders asked.

"Yes."

What could that be, he asked himself. Through clearing eyes, Anders looked at the formality he had called his world.

He wondered momentarily if he would have come to this if the voice hadn't guided him. Yes, he decided after a few moments, it was inevitable.

But who was the voice? And what had he left out?

"Let's see what a party looks like now," he said to the voice.

The party was a masquerade; the guests were all wearing their faces. To Anders, their motives, individually and collectively, were painfully apparent. Then his vision began to clear further.

He saw that the people weren't truly individual. They were discontinuous lumps of flesh sharing a common vocabulary, yet not even truly discontinuous.

The lumps of flesh were a part of the decoration of the room and almost indistinguishable from it. They were one with the lights, which lent their tiny vision. They were joined to the sounds they made, a few feeble tones out of the great possibility of sound. They blended into the walls.

The kaleidoscopic view came so fast that Anders had trouble sorting his new impressions. He knew now that these people existed only as patterns, on the same basis as the sounds they made and the things they thought they saw.

Gestalts, sifted out of the vast, unbearable real world.

"Where's Judy?" a discontinuous lump of flesh asked him. This particular lump possessed enough nervous mannerisms to convince the other lumps of his reality. He wore a loud tie as further evidence.

"She's sick," Anders said. The flesh quivered into an instant sympathy. Lines of formal mirth shifted to formal woe.

"Hope it isn't anything serious," the vocal flesh remarked.

"You're warmer," the voice said to Anders.

Anders looked at the object in front of him.

"She hasn't long to live," he stated.

The flesh quivered. Stomach and intestines contracted in sympathetic fear. Eyes distended, mouth quivered.

The loud tie remained the same.

"My God! You don't mean it!"

"What are you?" Anders asked quietly.

"What do you mean?" the indignant flesh attached to the tie demanded. Serene within its reality, it gaped at Anders. Its mouth twitched, undeniable proof that it was real and sufficient. "You're drunk," it sneered.

Anders laughed and left the party.

"There is still something you don't know," the voice said. "But you were hot! I could feel you near me."

"What are you?" Anders asked again.

"I don't know," the voice admitted. "I am a person. I am I. I am trapped."

"So are we all," Anders said. He walked on asphalt, surrounded by heaps of concrete, silicates, aluminum and iron alloys. Shapeless, meaningless heaps that made up the *gestalt* city.

And then there were the imaginary lines of demarcation dividing city from city, the artificial boundaries of water and land.

All ridiculous.

"Give me a dime for some coffee, mister?" something asked, a thing indistinguishable from any other thing.

"Old Bishop Berkeley would give a nonexistent dime to your nonexistent presence," Anders said gaily.

"I'm really in a bad way," the voice whined, and Anders perceived that it was no more than a series of modulated vibrations.

"Yes! Go on!" the voice commanded.

"If you could spare me a quarter—" the vibrations said, with a deep pretense at meaning.

Now, what was there behind the senseless patterns? Flesh, mass. What was that? All made up of atoms.

"I'm really hungry," the intricately arranged atoms muttered.

All atoms. Conjoined. There were no true separations between atom and atom. Flesh was stone, stone was light. Anders looked at the masses of atoms that were pretending to solidity, meaning and reason.

"Can't you help me?" a clump of atoms asked. But the clump was identical with all the other atoms. Once you ignored the superimposed patterns, you could see the atoms were random, scattered.

"I don't believe in you," Anders said.

The pile of atoms was gone.

"Yes!" the voice cried. "Yes!"

"I don't believe in any of it," Anders said. After all, what was an atom?

"Go on!" the voice shouted. "You're hot! Go on!"

What was an atom? An empty space surrounded by an empty space.

Absurd!

"Then it's all false!" Anders said. And he was alone under the stars.

"That's right!" the voice within his head screamed. "Nothing!"

But stars, Anders thought. How can one believe—

The stars disappeared. Anders was in a gray nothingness, a void. There was nothing around him except shapeless gray.

Where was the voice?

Gone.

Anders perceived the delusion behind the grayness, and then there was nothing at all.

Complete nothingness, and himself within it.

Where was he? What did it mean? Anders' mind tried to add it up.

Impossible. *That* couldn't be true.

Again the score was tabulated, but Anders' mind couldn't accept the total. In desperation, the overloaded mind erased the figures, eradicated the knowledge, erased itself.

"Where am I?"

In nothingness. Alone.

Trapped.

"Who am I?"

A voice.

The voice of Anders searched the nothingness, shouted, "Is there anyone here?"

No answer.

But there was someone. All directions were the same, yet moving along one he could make contact . . . with someone. The voice of Anders reached back to someone who could save him, perhaps.

"Save me," the voice said to Anders, lying fully dressed on his bed, except for his shoes and black bow tie.

FRITZ LEIBER

A Bad Day for Sales

One of the interesting developments in science fiction during the 1950s was the attention paid to the whole production-consumption process. Several authors, particularly those identified with Horace Gold's Galaxy, produced stories attacking various facets of this process, most notably advertising and television. "A Bad Day for Sales" is an excellent example of this type of story, although its author, Fritz Leiber (1910-), writes all types of science fiction and fantasy and is even better known in the latter field. He is one of the most honored writers of both, having won six Hugo, three Nebula and two World Fantasy awards. He was made a Grand Master of the Science Fiction Writers of America in 1981.

THE BIG bright doors of the office building parted with a pneumatic *whoosh* and Robie glided onto Times Square. The crowd that had been watching the fifty-foot-tall girl on the clothing billboard get dressed, or reading the latest news about the Hot Truce scrawl itself in yard-high script, hurried to look.

Robie was still a novelty. Robie was fun. For a little while yet, he could steal the show. But the attention did not make Robie proud. He had no more emotions than the pink plastic giantess, who dressed and undressed endlessly whether there was a crowd or the street was empty, and who never once blinked her blue mechanical eyes. But she merely drew business while Robie went out after it.

For Robie was the logical conclusion of the development of vending machines. All the earlier ones had stood in one place, on a floor or hanging on a wall, and blankly delivered merchandise in return for coins, whereas Robie searched for customers. He was the demonstration model of a line of sales robots to be manufactured by Shuler Vending Machines, provided the public invested enough in stocks to give the company capital to go into mass production.

The publicity Robie drew stimulated investments handsomely. It was amusing to see the TV and newspaper coverage of Robie selling, but not a fraction as much fun as being approached personally by him. Those who were usually bought anywhere from one to five hundred shares, if they had any money and foresight enough

328

to see that sales robots would eventually be on every street and highway in the country.

Robie radared the crowd, found that it surrounded him solidly and stopped. With a carefully built-in sense of timing, he waited for the tension and expectation to mount before he began talking.

"Say, Ma, he doesn't look like a robot at all," a child said. "He looks like a turtle."

Which was not completely inaccurate. The lower part of Robie's body was a metal hemisphere hemmed with sponge rubber and not quite touching the sidewalk. The upper was a metal box with black holes in it. The box could swivel and duck.

A chromium-bright hoopskirt with a turret on top.

"Reminds me too much of the Little Joe Paratanks," a legless veteran of the Persian War muttered, and rapidly rolled himself away on wheels rather like Robie's.

His departure made it easier for some of those who knew about Robie to open a path in the crowd. Robie headed straight for the gap. The crowd whooped.

Robie glided very slowly down the path, deftly jogging aside whenever he got too close to ankles in skylon or sockassins. The rubber buffer on his hoopskirt was merely an added safeguard.

The boy who had called Robie a turtle jumped in the middle of the path and stood his ground, grinning foxily.

Robie stopped two feet short of him. The turret ducked. The crowd got quiet.

"Hello, youngster," Robie said in a voice that was smooth as that of a TV star, and was, in fact, a recording of one.

The boy stopped smiling. "Hello," he whispered.

"How old are you?" Robie asked.

"Nine. No, eight."

"That's nice," Robie observed. A metal arm shot down from his neck, stopped just short of the boy.

The boy jerked back.

"For you," Robie said.

The boy gingerly took the red polly-lop from the neatly fashioned blunt metal claws, and began to unwrap it.

"Nothing to say?" asked Robie.

"Uh—thank you."

After a suitable pause, Robie continued, "And how about a nice refreshing drink of Poppy Pop to go with your polly-lop?" The boy lifted his eyes, but didn't stop licking the candy. Robie waggled his claws slightly. "Just give me a quarter and within five seconds—"

A little girl wriggled out of the forest of legs. "Give me a polly-lop, too, Robie," she demanded.

"Rita, come back here!" a woman in the third rank of the crowd called angrily.

Robie scanned the newcomer gravely. His reference silhouettes were not good enough to let him distinguish the sex of children, so he merely repeated, "Hello, youngster."

"Rita!"

"Give me a polly-lop!"

Disregarding both remarks, for a good salesman is singleminded and does not waste bait, Robie said winningly, "I'll bet you read *Junior Space Killers*. Now I have here—"

"Uh-uh, I'm a girl. *He* got a polly-lop."

At the word "girl," Robie broke off. Rather ponderously, he said, "I'll bet you read *Gee-Gee Jones, Space Stripper*. Now I have here the latest issue of that thrilling comic, not yet in the stationary vending machines. Just give me fifty cents and within five—"

"Please let me through. I'm her mother."

A young woman in the front rank drawled over her powder-sprayed shoulder, "I'll get her for you," and slithered out on six-inch platform shoes. "Run away, children," she said nonchalantly. Lifting her arms behind her head, she pirouetted slowly before Robie to show how much she did for her bolero half-jacket and her form-fitting slacks that melted into skylon just above the knees. The little girl glared at her. She ended the pirouette in profile.

At this age-level, Robie's reference silhouettes permitted him to distinguish sex, though with occasional amusing and embarrassing miscalls. He whistled admiringly. The crowd cheered.

Someone remarked critically to a friend, "It would go over better if he was built more like a real robot. You know, like a man."

The friend shook his head. "This way it's subtler."

No one in the crowd was watching the newscript overhead as it scribbled, "Ice Pack for Hot Truce? Vanahdin hints Russ may yield on Pakistan."

Robie was saying, "... in the savage new glamor-tint we have christened Mars Blood, complete with spray applicator and fit-all fingerstalls that mask each finger completely except for the nail. Just give me five dollars—uncrumpled bills may be fed into the revolving rollers you see beside my arm—and within five seconds—"

"No, thanks, Robie," the young woman yawned.

"Remember," Robie persisted, "for three more weeks, seductivizing Mars Blood will be unobtainable from any other robot or human vendor."

"No, thanks."

Robie scanned the crowd resourcefully. "Is there any gentleman here..." he began just as a woman elbowed her way through the front rank.

"I told you to come back!" she snapped at the little girl.

"But I didn't get my polly-lop!"

"...who would care to..."

"Rita!"

"Robie cheated. Ow!"

Meanwhile, the young woman in the half-bolero had scanned the nearby gentlemen on her own. Deciding that there was less than a fifty per cent chance of any of them accepting the proposition Robie seemed about to make, she took advantage of the scuffle to slither gracefully back into the ranks. Once again the path was clear before Robie.

He paused, however, for a brief recapitulation of the more magical properties of Mars Blood, including a telling phrase about "the passionate claws of a Martian sunrise."

But no one bought. It wasn't quite time. Soon enough silver coins would be clinking, bills going through the rollers faster than laundry, and five hundred people struggling for the privilege of having their money taken away from them by America's first mobile sales robot.

But there were still some tricks that Robie had to do free, and one certainly should enjoy those before starting the more expensive fun.

So Robie moved on until he reached the curb. The variation in level was instantly sensed by his underscanners. He stopped. His head began to swivel. The crowd watched in eager silence. This was Robie's best trick.

Robie's head stopped swiveling. His scanners had found the traffic light. It was green. Robie edged forward. But then the light turned red. Robie stopped again, still on the curb. The crowd softly *ahhed* its delight.

It was wonderful to be alive and watching Robie on such an exciting day. Alive and amused in the fresh, weather-controlled air between the lines of bright skyscrapers with their winking windows and under a sky so blue you could almost call it dark.

(But way, way up, where the crowd could not see, the sky was darker still. Purple-dark, with stars showing. And in that purple-dark, a silver-green something, the color of a bud, plunged down at better than three miles a second. The silver-green was a newly developed paint that foiled radar.)

Robie was saying, "While we wait for the light, there's time for you youngsters to enjoy a nice refreshing Poppy Pop. Or for you adults—only those over five feet tall are eligible to buy—to enjoy an exciting Poppy Pop fizz. Just give me a quarter or—in the case of adults, one dollar and a quarter; I'm licensed to dispense intoxicating liquors—and within five seconds..."

But that was not cutting it quite fine enough. Just three seconds later, the silver-green bud bloomed above Manhattan into a globular orange flower. The skyscrapers grew brighter and brighter still, the brightness of the inside of the Sun. The windows winked blossoming white fire-flowers.

The crowd around Robie bloomed, too. Their clothes puffed into petals of flame. Their heads of hair were torches.

The orange flower grew, stem and blossom. The blast came. The winking windows shattered tier by tier, became black holes. The walls bent, rocked, cracked. A stony dandruff flaked from their cornices. The flaming flowers on the sidewalk were all leveled at once. Robie was shoved ten feet. His metal hoopskirt dimpled, regained its shape.

The blast ended. The orange flower, grown vast, vanished overhead on its huge, magic beanstalk. It grew dark and very still. The cornice-dandruff pattered down. A few small fragments rebounded from the metal hoopskirt.

Robie made some small, uncertain movements, as if feeling for broken bones. He was hunting for the traffic light, but it no longer shone either red or green.

He slowly scanned a full circle. There was nothing anywhere to interest his reference silhouettes. Yet whenever he tried to move, his under-scanners warned him of low obstructions. It was very puzzling.

The silence was disturbed by moans and a crackling sound, as faint at first as the scampering of distant rats.

A seared man, his charred clothes fuming where the blast had blown out the fire, rose from the curb. Robie scanned him.

"Good day, sir," Robie said. "Would you care for a smoke? A truly cool smoke? Now I have here a yet-unmarketed brand..."

But the customer had run away, screaming, and Robie never ran after customers, though he could follow them at a medium brisk roll. He worked his way along the curb where the man had sprawled, carefully keeping his distance from the low obstructions, some of which writhed now and then, forcing him to jog. Shortly he reached a fire hydrant. He scanned it. His electronic vision, though it still worked, had been somewhat blurred by the blast.

"Hello, youngster," Robie said. Then, after a long pause, "Cat got your tongue? Well, I have a little present for you. A nice, lovely polly-lop.

"Take it, youngster," he said after another pause. "It's for you. Don't be afraid."

His attention was distracted by other customers, who began to rise oddly here and there, twisting forms that confused his reference silhouettes and would not stay to be scanned properly. One cried, "Water," but no quarter clinked in Robie's claws when he caught the word and suggested, "How about a nice refreshing drink of Poppy Pop?"

The rat-crackling of the flames had become a jungle muttering. The blind windows began to wink fire again.

A little girl marched, stepping neatly over arms and legs she did not look at. A white dress and the once taller bodies around her had shielded her from the brilliance and the blast. Her eyes were fixed on Robie. In them was the same imperious confidence, though none of the delight, with which she had watched him earlier.

"Help me, Robie," she said. "I want my mother."

"Hello, youngster," Robie said. "What would you like? Comics? Candy?"

"Where is she, Robie? Take me to her."

"Balloons? Would you like to watch me blow up a balloon?"

The little girl began to cry. The sound triggered off another of Robie's novelty circuits, a service feature that had brought in a lot of favorable publicity.

"Is something wrong?" he asked. "Are you in trouble? Are you lost?"

"Yes, Robie. Take me to my mother."

"Stay right here," Robie said reassuringly, "and don't be frightened. I will call a policeman." He whistled shrilly, twice.

Time passed. Robie whistled again. The windows flared and roared. The little girl begged, "Take me away, Robie," and jumped onto a little step in his hoopskirt.

"Give me a dime," Robie said.

The little girl found one in her pocket and put it in his claws.

"Your weight," Robie said, "is fifty-four and one-half pounds."

"Have you seen my daughter, have you seen her?" a woman was crying somewhere. "I left her watching that thing while I stepped inside—*Rita!*"

"Robie helped me," the little girl began babbling at her. "He knew I was lost. He even called the police, but they didn't come. He weighed me, too. Didn't you, Robie?"

But Robie had gone off to peddle Poppy Pop to the members of a rescue squad which had just come around the corner, more robotlike in their asbestos suits than he in his metal skin.

H. L. GOLD

Man of Parts

Horace L. Gold (1914-) was the founding editor of Galaxy Science Fiction, one of the "Big Three" sf magazines (the others were Astounding/Analog and The Magazine of Fantasy and Science Fiction) for over twenty years. More than any other individual, Gold was responsible for introducing a concern for the "soft sciences" and for social commentary into the science fiction of the 1950s. Like John W. Campbell, Jr., before him, he developed a stable of outstanding writers that was identified with his magazine. He retired from editing in 1961.

As a writer he was active beginning in the late 1930s and wrote a number of excellent and witty short stories, many of which can be found in his collection The Old Die Rich and Other Stories *(1955).*

THERE WASN'T a trace of amnesia or confusion when Major Hugh Savold, of the Fourth Earth Expedition against Vega, opened his eyes in the hospital. He knew exactly who he was, where he was and how he had gotten there.

His name was Gam Nex Biad.

He was a native of the planet named Dorfel.

He had been killed in a mining accident far underground.

The answers were preposterous and they terrified Major Savold. Had he gone insane? He must have, for his arms were pinned tight in a restraining sheet. And his mouth was full of bits of rock.

Savold screamed and wrenched around on the flat, comfortable boulder on which he had been nibbling. He spat out the rock fragments that tasted—*nutritious.*

Shaking, Savold recoiled from something even more frightful than the wrong name, wrong birthplace, wrong accident and shockingly wrong food.

A living awl was watching him solicitously. It was as tall as himself, had a pointed spiral drill for a head, three knee-action arms ending in horn spades, two below them with numerous sensitive cilia, a row of socketed bulbs down its front, and it stood on a nervously bouncing bedspring of a leg.

Savold was revolted and tense with panic. He had never in his life seen a creature like this.

It was Surgeon Trink, whom he had known since infancy.

334

"Do not be distressed," glowed the surgeon's kindly lights. "You are everything you think you are."

"But that's impossible! I'm an Earthman and my name is Major Hugh Savold!"

"Of course."

"Then I can't be Gam Nex Biad, a native of Dorfel!"

"But you are."

"I'm not!" shouted Savold. "I was in a one-man space scout. I sneaked past the Vegan cordon and dropped the spore-bomb, the only one that ever got through. The Vegans burned my fuel and engine sections full of holes. I escaped, but I couldn't make it back to Earth. I found a planet that was pockmarked worse than our moon. I was afraid it had no atmosphere, but it did. I crash-landed." He shuddered. "It was more of a crash than a landing."

Surgeon Trink brightened joyfully. "Excellent! There seems to be no impairment of memory at all."

"No?" Savold yelled in terror. "Then how is it I remember being killed in a mining accident? I was drilling through good hard mineral ore, spinning at a fine rate, my head soothingly warm as it gouged into the tasty rock, my spades pushing back the crushed ore, and I crashed right out into a fault..."

"Soft shale," the surgeon explained, dimming with sympathy. "You were spinning too fast to sense the difference in density ahead of you. It was an unfortunate accident. We were all very sad."

"And I was killed," said Savold, horrified. *"Twice!"*

"Oh, no. Only once. You were badly damaged when your machine crashed, but you were not killed. We were able to repair you."

Savold felt fear swarm through him, driving his ghastly thoughts into a quaking corner. He looked down at his body, knowing he couldn't see it, that it was wrapped tightly in a long sheet. He had never seen material like this.

He recognized it instantly as asbestos cloth.

There was a row of holes down the front. Savold screamed in horror. The socketed bulbs lit up in a deafening glare.

"Please don't be afraid!" The surgeon bounced over concernedly, broke open a large mica capsule and splashed its contents on Savold's head and face. "I know it's a shock, but there's no cause for alarm. You're not in danger, I assure you."

Savold found himself quieting down, his panic diminishing. No, it wasn't the surgeon's gentle, reassuring glow that was responsible. It was the liquid he was covered with. A sedative of some sort, it eased the constriction of his brain, relaxed his facial muscles, dribbled comfortingly into his mouth. Half of him recognized the heavy odor and the other half identified the taste.

It was lubricating oil.

As a lubricant, it soothed him. But it was also a coolant, for it cooled off his fright and disgust and let him think again.

"Better?" asked Surgeon Trink hopefully.

"Yes, I'm calmer now," Savold said, and noted first that his voice sounded quieter, and second that it wasn't his voice—he was communicating by glows and blinks of his row of bulbs, which, as he talked, gave off a cold light like that of fireflies. "I think I can figure it out. I'm Major Hugh Savold. I crashed and was injured. You gave me the body of a..." he thought about the name and realized that he didn't know it, yet he found it immediately "...a Dorfellow, didn't you?"

"Not the whole body," the surgeon replied, glimmering with confidence again as his bedside manner returned. "Just the parts that were in need of replacement."

Savold was revolted, but the sedative effect of the lubricating oil kept his feelings under control. He tried to nod in understanding. He couldn't. Either he had an unbelievably stiff neck...or no neck whatever.

"Something like our bone, limb and organ banks," he said. "How much of me is Gam Nex Biad?"

"Quite a lot, I'm afraid." The surgeon listed the parts, which came through to Savold as if he were listening to a simultaneous translation: from Surgeon Trink to Gam Nex Biad to him. They were all equivalents, of course, but they amounted to a large portion of his brain, skull, chest, internal and reproductive organs, midsection and legs.

"Then what's left of me?" Savold cried in dismay.

"Why, part of your brain—a very considerable part, I'm proud to say. Oh, and your arms. Some things weren't badly injured, but it seemed better to make substitutions. The digestive and circulatory system, for instance. Yours were adapted to foods and fluids that aren't available on Dorfel. Now you can get your sustenance directly from the minerals and metals of the planet, just as we do. If I hadn't, your life would have been saved, but you would have starved to death."

"Let me up," said Savold in alarm. "I want to see what I look like."

The surgeon looked worried again. He used another capsule of oil on Savold before removing the sheet.

Savold stared down at himself and felt revulsion trying to rise. But there was nowhere for it to go and it couldn't have gotten past the oil if there had been. He swayed sickly on his bedspring leg, petrified at the sight of himself.

He looked quite handsome, he had to admit—Gam Nex Biad had always been considered one of the most crashing bores on Dorfel, capable of taking an enormous leap on his magnificently wiry leg, landing exactly on the point of his head with a swift spin that would bury him out of sight within instants in even the hardest rock. His knee-action arms were splendidly flinty; he knew they had been repaired with some other miner's remains, and they could whirl him through a self-drilled tunnel with wonderful speed, while the spade hands could shovel back ore as fast as he could dig it out. He was as good as new...except for the disgustingly soft, purposeless arms.

The knowledge of function and custom was there, and the reaction to the human arms, and they made explanation unnecessary, just as understanding of the firefly language had been there without his awareness. But the emotions were Savold's and they drove him to say fiercely, "You didn't have to change me altogether. You could have just saved my life so I could fix my ship and get back..." He paused abruptly and would have gasped if he had been able to. "Good Lord! Earth Command doesn't even know I got the bomb through! If they act fast, they can land without a bit of opposition!" He spread all his arms—the two human ones, the three with knee-action and spades, the two with the sensitive cilia—and stared at them bleakly.

"And I have a girl back on Earth..."

Surgeon Trink glowed sympathetically and flashed with pride. "Your mission seems important somehow, though its meaning escapes me. However, we have repaired your machine..."

"You *have?*" Savold interrupted eagerly.

"Indeed, yes. It should work better than before." The surgeon flickered modestly. "We do have some engineering skill, you know."

The Gam Nex Biad of Savold did know. There were the underground ore smelters and the oil refineries and the giant metal awls that drilled out rock food for the manufacturing centers, where miners alone could not keep up with the demand, and the communicators that sent their signals clear around the planet through the substrata of rock, and more, much more. This, insisted Gam Nex Biad proudly, was a *civilization*, and Major Hugh Savold, sharing his knowledge, had to admit that it certainly was.

"I can take right off, then?" Savold flared excitedly.

"There is a problem first," glowed the surgeon in some doubt. "You mention a 'girl' on this place you call 'Earth.' I gather it is a person of the opposite sex."

"As opposite as anybody can get. Or was," Savold added moodily. "But we have limb and organ banks back on Earth. The doctors there can do a repair job. It's a damned big one, I know, but they can handle it. I'm not so sure I like carrying Gam Nex Biad around with me for life, though. Maybe they can take him out and..."

"Please," Surgeon Trink cut in with anxious blinkings. "There is a matter to be settled. When you refer to the 'girl,' you do not specify that she is your mate. You have not been selected for each other yet?"

"Selected?" repeated Savold blankly, but Gam Nex Biad supplied the answer— the equivalent of marriage, the mates chosen by experts on genetics, the choice being determined by desired transmittable aptitudes. "No, we were just going together. We were not mates, but we intended to be as soon as I got back. That's the other reason I have to return in a hurry. I appreciate all you've done, but I really must..."

"Wait," the surgeon ordered.

He drew an asbestos curtain that covered part of a wall. Savold saw an opening in the rock of the hospital, a hole-door through which bounced half a dozen little Dorfellows and one big one... straight at him. He felt what would have been his heart leap into what would have been his chest if he had had either. But he couldn't even get angry or shocked or nauseated; the lubricating oil cooled off all his emotions.

The little creatures were all afire with childish joy. The big one sparkled happily.

"Father!" blinked the children blindingly.

"Mate!" added Prad Fim Biad in a delighted exclamation point.

"You see," said the surgeon to Savold, who was shrinking back, "you already have a mate and a family."

It was only natural that a board of surgeons should have tried to cope with Savold's violent reaction. He had fought furiously against being saddled with an alien family. Even constant saturation with lubricating oil couldn't keep that rebellion from boiling over.

On Earth, of course, he would have been given immediate psychotherapy, but there wasn't anything of the sort here. Dorfellows were too granitic physically and psychologically to need medical or psychiatric doctors. A job well done and a family well raised—that was the extent of their emotionalism. Savold's feelings, rage and resentment and a violent desire to escape, were completely beyond their understanding. He discovered that as he angrily watched the glittering debate.

The board quickly determined that Surgeon Trink had been correct in adapting Savold to the Dorfel way of life. Savold objected that the adaptation need not have been so thorough, but he had to admit that, since they couldn't have kept him fed any other way, Surgeon Trink had done his best in an emergency.

The surgeon was willing to accept blame for having introduced Savold so bluntly to his family, but the board absolved him—none of them had had any experience in dealing with an Earth mentality. A Dorfellow would have accepted the fact, as others with amnesia caused by accidents had done. Surgeon Trink had had no reason to think Savold would not have done the same. Savold cleared the surgeon entirely by admitting that the memory was there, but, like all the other memories of Gam Nex Biad's, had been activated only when the situation came up. The board had no trouble getting Savold to agree that the memory would have returned sooner or later, no matter how Surgeon Trink handled the introduction, and that the reaction would have been just as violent.

"And now," gleamed the oldest surgeon on the board, "the problem is how to help our new—and restored—brother adjust to life on this world."

"That isn't the problem at all!" Savold flared savagely. "I have to get back to Earth and tell them I dropped the bomb and they can land safely. And there's the girl I mentioned. I want to marry her—become her mate, I mean."

"*You* want to become her mate?" the oldest surgeon blinked in bewilderment. "It is *your* decision?"

"Well, hers, too."

"You mean you did the selecting yourselves? Nobody chose for you?"

Savold attempted to explain, but puzzled glimmers and Gam Nex Biad's confusion made him state resignedly, "Our customs are different. We choose our own mates." He thought of adding that marriages were arranged in some parts of the world, but that would only have increased their baffled lack of understanding.

"And how many mates can an individual have?" asked a surgeon.

"Where I come from, one."

"The individual's responsibility, then, is to the family he has. Correct?"

"Of course."

"Well," said the oldest surgeon, "the situation is perfectly clear. You have a family—Prad Fim Biad and the children."

"They're not my family," Savold objected. "They're Gam Nex Biad's and he's dead."

"We respect your customs. It is only fair that you respect ours. If you had had a family where you come from, there would have been a question of legality, in view of the fact that you could not care for them simultaneously. But you have none and there is no such question."

"Customs? Legality?" asked Savold, feeling as lost as they had in trying to comprehend an alien society.

"A rebuilt Dorfellow," the oldest surgeon said, "is required to assume the obligations of whatever major parts went into his reconstruction. You are almost entirely made up of the remains of Gam Nex Biad, so it is only right that his mate and children should be yours."

"I won't do it!" Savold protested. "I demand the right to appeal!"

"On what grounds?" asked another surgeon politely.

"That I'm not a Dorfellow!"

"Ninety-four point seven per cent of you is, according to Surgeon Trink's requisition of limbs and organs. How much more of a citizen can any individual be?"

Gam Nex Biad confirmed the ruling and Savold subsided. While the board of surgeons discussed the point it had begun with—how to adapt Savold to life on Dorfel—he thought the situation through. He had no legal or moral recourse. If he was to get out of his predicament, it would have to be through shrewd resourcefulness and he would never have become a major in the space fleet if he hadn't had plenty of that.

Yeah, shrewd resourcefulness, thought Savold bitterly, jouncing unsteadily on his single bedspring leg on a patch of unappealing topsoil a little distance from the settlement. He had counted on something that didn't exist here—the kind of complex approach that Earth doctors and authorities would have used on his sort of problem, from the mitigation of laws to psychological conditioning, all of it complicated and every stage allowing a chance to work his way free.

But the board of surgeons had agreed on a disastrously simple course of treatment for him. He was not to be fed by anybody and he could not sleep in any of the underground rock apartments, including the dormitory for unmated males.

"When he's hungry enough, he'll go back to mining," the oldest surgeon had told the equivalent of a judge, a local teacher who did part-time work passing on legal questions that did not have to be ruled on by the higher courts. "And if he has no place to stay except with Gam Nex Biad's family, which is his own, naturally, he'll go there when he's tired of living out in the open all by himself."

The judge thought highly of the decision and gave it official approval.

Savold did not mind being out in the open, but he was far from being all by himself. Gam Nex Biad was a constant nuisance, nagging at him to get in a good day's drilling and then go home to the wife, kiddies and their cozy, hollowed-out quarters, with company over to celebrate his return with a lavish supply of capsuled lubricating oil. Savold obstinately refused, though he found himself salivating or something very much like it.

The devil of the situation was that he *was* hungry and there was not a single bit of rock around to munch on. That was the purpose of this fenced-in plot of ground— it was like hard labor in the prisons back on Earth, where the inmates ate only if they broke their quota of rock, except that here the inmates would eat the rock they broke. The only way Savold could get out of the enclosure was by drilling under the high fence. He had already tried to bounce over it and discovered he couldn't.

"Come on," Gam Nex Biad argued in his mind. "Why fight it? We're a miner and there's no life like the life of a miner. The excitement of boring your way through a lode, making a meal out of the rich ore! Miners get the choicest tidbits, you know—that's our compensation for working so hard and taking risks."

"Some compensation," sneered Savold, looking wistfully up at the stars and enviously wishing he were streaking between them in his scout.

"A meal of iron ore would go pretty well right now, wouldn't it?" Gam Nex Biad tempted. "And I know where there are some veins of tin and sulphur. You don't find *them* lying around on the surface, eh? Nonminers get just traces of the rare metals to keep them healthy, but we can stuff ourself all we want..."

"Shut up!"

"And some pools of mercury. Not big ones, I admit, but all we'd want is a refreshing gulp to wash down those ores I was telling you about."

Resisting the thought of the ores was hard enough, for Savold was rattlingly empty, but the temptation of the smooth, cool mercury would have roused the glutton in anyone.

"All right," he growled, "but get this straight—we're not going back to your family. They're your problem, not mine."

"But how could I go back to them if you won't go?"

"That's right. I'm glad you see it my way. Now where are those ores and the pools of mercury?"

"Dive," said Gam Nex Biad. "I'll give you the directions."

Savold took a few bounces to work up speed and spin, then shot into the air and came down on the point of his awl-shaped head, which bit through the soft topsoil as if through—he shuddered—so much water. As a Dorfellow, he had to avoid water; it eroded and corroded and caused deposits of rust in the digestive and circulatory systems. There was a warmth that was wonderfully soothing and he was drilling into rock. He ate some to get his strength back, but left room for the main meal and the dessert.

"Pretty nice, isn't it?" asked Gam Nex Biad as they gouged a comfortable tunnel back toward the settlement. "Nonminers don't know what they're missing."

"Quiet," Savold ordered surlily, but he had to confess to himself that it was pleasant. His three knee-action arms rotated him at a comfortable speed, the horn spades pushing back the loose rock; and he realized why Gam Nex Biad had been upset when Surgeon Trink left Savold's human arms attached. They were in the way and they kept getting scratched. The row of socketed bulbs gave him all the light he needed. That, he decided, had been their original purpose. Using them to communicate with must have been one of the first steps toward civilization.

Savold had been repressing thoughts ever since the meeting of the board of surgeons. Experimentally, he called his inner partner.

"Um?" asked Gam Nex Biad absently.

"Something I wanted to discuss with you," Savold said.

"Later. I sense the feldspar coming up. We head north there."

Savold turned the drilling over to him, then allowed the buried thoughts to emerge. They were thoughts of escape and he had kept them hidden because he was positive that Gam Nex Biad would have betrayed them. He had been trying incessantly, wheedlingly, to sell Savold on mining and returning to the family.

The hell with that, Savold thought grimly now. He was getting back to Earth somehow—Earth Command first, Marge second. No, surgery second, Marge third, he corrected. She wouldn't want him this way...

"Manganese," said Gam Nex Biad abruptly, and Savold shut off his thinking. "I always did like a few mouthfuls as an appetizer."

The rock had a pleasantly spicy taste, much like a cocktail before dinner. Then they went on, with the Dorfellow giving full concentration to finding his way from deposit to deposit.

The thing to do, Savold reasoned, was to learn where the scout ship was being kept. He had tried to sound out Gam Nex Biad subtly, but it must have been too subtle—the Dorfellow had guessed uninterestedly that the ship would be at one of the metal fabricating centers, and Savold had not dared ask which one. Gam Nex Biad couldn't induce him to become a miner and Dorfellow family man, but that didn't mean he could escape over Gam Nex Biad's opposition.

Savold did not intend to find out. Shrewd resourcefulness, that was the answer. It hadn't done him much good yet, but the day he could not outfox these rock-eaters, he'd turn in his commission. All he had to do was find the ship...

Bloated and tired, Savold found himself in a main tunnel thoroughfare back to the settlement. The various ores, he disgustedly confessed to himself, were as delicious as the best human foods, and there was nothing at all like the flavor and texture of pure liquid mercury. He discovered some in his cupped cilia hands.

"To keep around for a snack?" he asked Gam Nex Biad.

"I thought you wouldn't mind letting Prad Fim and the children have some," the Dorfellow said hopefully. "You ought to see them light up whenever I bring it home!"

"Not a chance! We're not going there, so I might as well drop it."

Savold had to get some sleep. He was ready to topple with exhaustion. But the tunnels were unsafe—a Dorfellow traveling through one on an emergency night errand would crash into him hard enough to leave nothing but flinty splinters. And the night air felt chill and hostile, so it was impossible to sleep above ground.

"Please make up your mind," Gam Nex Biad begged. "I can't stay awake much longer and you'll just go blundering around and get into trouble."

"But they've got to put us up somewhere," argued Savold. "How about the hospital? We're still a patient, aren't we?"

"We were discharged as cured. And nobody else is allowed to let us stay in any apartment...except one."

"I know, I know," Savold replied with weary impatience. "Forget it. We're not going there."

"But it's so comfortable there..."

"Forget it I told you!"

"Oh, all right," Gam Nex Biad said resignedly. "But we're not going to find anything as pleasant and restful as my old sleeping boulder. It's soft limestone, you know, and grooved to fit our body. I'd like to see anybody *not* fall asleep instantly on that good old flat boulder..."

Savold tried to resist, but he was worn out from the operation, hunger, digging and the search for a place to spend the night.

"Just take a *look* at it, that's all," Gam Nex Biad coaxed. "If you don't like it, we'll sleep anywhere you say. Fair enough?"

"I suppose so," admitted Savold.

The hewn-rock apartment was quiet, at least; everybody was asleep. He'd lie down for a while, just long enough to get some rest, and clear out before the household awoke...

But Prad Fim and the children were clustered around the boulder when he opened his eyes. Each of them had five arms to fight off. And there were Surgeon Trink, the elder of the board of surgeons, and the local teacher-judge all waiting to talk to him when the homecoming was over with.

"The treatment worked!" cried the judge. "He came back!"

"I never doubted it," the elder said complacently.

"You know what this means?" Surgeon Trink eagerly asked Savold.

"No, what?" Savold inquired warily, afraid of the answer.

"You can show us how to operate your machine," declared the judge. "It isn't that we lack engineering ability, you understand. We simply never had a machine as large and complex before. We could have, of course—I'm sure you are aware of that—but the matter just didn't come up. We could work it out by ourselves, but it would be much easier to have you explain it."

"By returning, you've shown that you have regained some degree of stability," added the elder. "We couldn't trust you with the machine while you were so disturbed."

"Did you know this?" Savold silently challenged Gam Nex Biad.

"Well, certainly," came the voiceless answer.

"Then why didn't you tell me? Why did you let me go floundering around instead?"

"Because you bewilder me. This loathing for our body, which I'd always been told was quite attractive, and dislike of mining and living with our own family— wanting to reach this thing you call Earth Command and the creature with the strange name. Marge, isn't it? I could never guess how you would react to anything. It's not easy living with an alien mentality."

"You don't have to explain. I've got the same problem, remember."

"That's true," Gam Nex Biad silently agreed. "But I'm afraid you'll have to take it from here. All I know is mining, not machines or metal fabricating centers."

Savold repressed his elation. The less Gam Nex Biad knew from this point on, the less he could guess—and the smaller chance there was that he could betray Savold.

"We can leave right now," the judge was saying. "The family can follow as soon as you've built a home for them."

"Why should they follow?" Savold demanded. "I thought you said I was going to be allowed to operate the ship."

"Demonstrate and explain it, really," the judge amended. "We're not absolutely certain that you are stable, you see. As for the family, you're bound to get lonesome..."

Savold stared at Prad Fim and the children. Gam Nex Biad was brimming with affection for them, but Savold saw them only as hideous ore-crushing monsters. He tried to keep them from saying good-bye with embraces, but they came at him with such violent leaps that they chipped bits out of his body with their grotesque pointed awl heads. He was glad to get away, especially with Gam Nex Biad making such a damned slobbering nuisance of himself.

"Let's go!" he blinked frantically at the judge, and dived after him into an express tunnel.

While Gam Nex Biad was busily grieving, Savold stealthily worked out his plans. He would glance casually at the ship, glow some mild compliment at the repair job, make a pretense at explaining how the controls worked—and blast off into space at the first opportunity, even if he had to wait for days. He knew he would never get another chance; they'd keep him away from the ship if that attempt failed. And Gam Nex Biad was a factor, too. Savold had to hit the take-off button before his partner suspected or their body would be paralyzed in the conflict between them.

It was a very careful plan and it called for iron discipline, but that was conditioned into every scout pilot. All Savold had to do was maintain his rigid self-control.

He did—until he saw the ship on the hole-pocked plain. Then his control broke and he bounced with enormous, frantic leaps into the airlock and through the corridors to the pilot room.

"Wait! Wait!" glared the judge, and others from the fabricating center sprang toward the ship.

Savold managed to slam the airlock before Gam Nex Biad began to fight him, asking in frightened confusion, "What are you doing?" and locking their muscles so that Savold was unable to move.

"What am I doing?" glinted Savold venomously. "Getting off your lousy planet and back to a world where people live like people instead of like worms and moles!"

"I don't know what you mean," said the Dorfellow anxiously, "but I can't let you do anything until the authorities say it's all right."

"You can't stop me!" Savold exulted. "You can paralyze everything *except my own arms!*"

And that, of course, was the ultimate secret he had been hiding from Gam Nex Biad.

Savold slammed the take-off button. The power plant roared and the ship lifted swiftly toward the sky.

It began to spin.

Then it flipped over and headed with suicidal velocity toward the ground.

"They did something wrong to the ship!" cried Savold.

"Wrong?" Gam Nex Biad repeated vacantly. "It seems to be working fine."

"But it's supposed to be heading *up!*"

"Oh, no," said Gam Nex Biad. "Our machines never go that way. There's no rock up there."

POUL ANDERSON

The Man Who Came Early

"The Man Who Came Early" is a time-travel story, one of the "standard" themes of science fiction since the publication of H. G. Wells's The Time Machine *in 1895. However, in the hands of a master like Poul Anderson (1926-), there is nothing standard about it. Anderson has won all of the major awards in the science fiction and fantasy fields, has produced more than fifty quality novels and twenty story collections in a thirty-five-year career and is still going strong. One of the things that makes him exceptional is his ability to write wonderful books in a wide variety of styles, from humor to high-technology adventure.*

YES, WHEN a man grows old he has heard so much that is strange there's little more can surprise him. They say the king in Miklagard has a beast of gold before his high seat which stands up and roars. I have it from Eilif Eiriksson, who served in the guard down yonder, and he is a steady fellow when not drunk. He has also seen the Greek fire used, it burns on water.

So, priest, I am not unwilling to believe what you say about the White Christ. I have been in England and France myself, and seen how the folk prosper. He must be a very powerful god, to ward so many realms . . . and did you say that everyone who is baptized will be given a white robe? I would like to have one. They mildew, of course, in this cursed wet Iceland weather, but a small sacrifice to the house-elves should— No sacrifices? Come now! I'll give up horseflesh if I must, my teeth not being what they were, but every sensible man knows how much trouble the elves make if they're not fed.

Well, let's have another cup and talk about it. How do you like the beer? It's my own brew, you know. The cups I got in England, many years back. I was a young man then . . . time goes, time goes. Afterward I came back and inherited this my father's farm, and have not left it since. Well enough to go in viking as a youth, but grown older you see where the real wealth lies: here, in the land and the cattle.

Stoke up the fires, Hjalti. It's getting cold. Sometimes I think the winters are colder than when I was a boy. Thorbrand of the Salmondale says so, but he believes the gods are angry because so many are turning from them. You'll have trouble winning Thorbrand over, priest. A stubborn man. Myself, I am open-minded, and willing to listen at least.

Now, then. There is one point on which I must set you right. The end of the world is not coming in two years. This I know.

And if you ask me how I know, that's a very long tale, and in some ways a terrible one. Glad I am to be old, and safe in the earth before that great tomorrow comes. It will be an eldritch time before the frost giants fare loose...oh, very well, before the angel blows his battle horn. One reason I hearken to your preaching is that I know the White Christ will conquer Thor. I know Iceland is going to be Christian erelong, and it seems best to range myself on the winning side.

No, I've had no visions. This is a happening of five years ago, which my own household and neighbors can swear to. They mostly did not believe what the stranger told; I do, more or less, if only because I don't think a liar could wreak so much harm. I loved my daughter, priest, and after the trouble was over I made a good marriage for her. She did not naysay it, but now she sits out on the ness-farm with her husband and never a word to me; and I hear he is ill pleased with her silence and moodiness, and spends his nights with an Irish leman. For this I cannot blame him, but it grieves me.

Well, I've drunk enough to tell the whole truth now, and whether you believe it or not makes no odds to me. Here...you, girls!...fill these cups again, for I'll have a dry throat before I finish the telling.

It begins, then, on a day in early summer, five years ago. At that time, my wife Ragnhild and I had only two unwed children still living with us: our youngest son Helgi, of seventeen winters, and our daughter Thorgunna, of eighteen. The girl, being fair, had already had suitors. But she refused them, and I am not one who would compel his daughter. As for Helgi, he was ever a lively one, good with his hands but a breakneck youth. He is now serving in the guard of King Olaf of Norway. Besides these, of course, we had about ten housefolk—two thralls, two girls to help with the women's work and half a dozen hired carles. This is not a small stead.

You have seen how my land lies. About two miles to the west is the bay; the thorps at Reykjavik are some five miles south. The land rises toward the Long Jökull, so that my acres are hilly; but it's good hay land, and we often find driftwood on the beach. I've built a shed down there for it, as well as a boathouse.

We had had a storm the night before—a wild huge storm with lightning flashes across heaven, such as you seldom get in Iceland—so Helgi and I were going down to look for drift. You, coming from Norway, do not know how precious wood is to us here, who have only a few scrubby trees and must get our timber from abroad. Back there men have often been burned in their houses by their foes, but we count that the worst of deeds, though it's not unheard of.

As I was on good terms with my neighbors, we took only hand weapons. I bore my ax, Helgi a sword, and the two carles we had with us bore spears. It was a day washed clean by the night's fury, and the sun fell bright on long, wet grass. I saw my stead lying rich around its courtyard, sleek cows and sheep, smoke rising from the roofhole of the hall, and knew I'd not done so ill in my lifetime. My son Helgi's hair fluttered in the low west wind as we left the buildings behind a ridge and neared the water. Strange how well I remember all which happened that day; somehow it was a sharper day than most.

When we came down to the strand, the sea was beating heavy, white and gray out to the world's edge, smelling of salt and kelp. A few gulls mewed above us, frightened off a cod washed onto the shore. I saw a litter of no few sticks, even a baulk of timber... from some ship carrying it that broke up during the night, I suppose. That was a useful find, though as a careful man I would later sacrifice to be sure the owner's ghost wouldn't plague me.

We had fallen to and were dragging the baulk toward the shed when Helgi cried out. I ran for my ax as I looked the way he pointed. We had no feuds then, but there are always outlaws.

This newcomer seemed harmless, though. Indeed, as he stumbled nearer across the black sand I thought him quite unarmed and wondered what had happened. He was a big man and strangely clad—he wore coat and breeches and shoes like anyone else, but they were of odd cut, and he bound his trousers with leggings rather than straps. Nor had I ever seen a helmet like his: it was almost square, and came down toward his neck, but it had no nose guard. And this you may not believe, but it was not metal yet had been cast in one piece!

He broke into a staggering run as he drew close, flapped his arms and croaked something. The tongue was none I had heard, and I have heard many; it was like dogs barking. I saw that he was clean-shaven and his black hair cropped short, and thought he might be French. Otherwise he was a young man, and good-looking, with blue eyes and regular features. From his skin I judged that he spent much time indoors. However, he had a fine manly build.

"Could he have been shipwrecked?" asked Helgi.

"His clothes are dry and unstained," I said; "nor has he been wandering long, for no stubble is on his chin. Yet I've heard of no strangers guesting hereabouts."

We lowered our weapons, and he came up to us and stood gasping. I saw that his coat and the shirt underneath were fastened with bonelike buttons rather than laces, and were of heavy weave. About his neck he had fastened a strip of cloth tucked into his coat. These garments were all in brownish hues. His shoes were of a sort new to me, very well stitched. Here and there on his coat were bits of brass, and he had three broken stripes on each sleeve; also a black band with white letters, the same letters being on his helmet. Those were not runes, but Roman—thus: MP. He wore a broad belt, with a small clublike thing of metal in a sheath at the hip and also a real club.

"I think he must be a warlock," muttered my carle Sigurd. "Why else so many tokens?"

"They may only be ornament, or to ward against witchcraft," I soothed him. Then, to the stranger: "I hight Ospak Ulfsson of Hillstead. What is your errand?"

He stood with his chest heaving and a wildness in his eyes. He must have run a long way. At last he moaned and sat down and covered his face.

"If he's sick, best we get him to the house," said Helgi. I heard eagerness; we see few new faces here.

"No...no...." The stranger looked up. "Let me rest a moment—"

He spoke the Norse tongue readily enough, though with a thick accent not easy to follow and with many foreign words I did not understand.

The other carle, Grim, hefted his spear. "Have vikings landed?" he asked.

"When did vikings ever come to Iceland?" I snorted. "It's the other way around."

The newcomer shook his head as if it had been struck. He got shakily to his feet. "What happened?" he said. "What became of the town?"

"What town?" I asked reasonably.

"Reykjavik!" he cried. "Where is it?"

"Five miles south, the way you came—unless you mean the bay itself," I said.

"No! There was only a beach, and a few wretched huts, and—"

"Best not let Hialmar Broadnose hear you call his thorp that," I counseled.

"But there was a town!" he gasped. "I was crossing the street in a storm, and heard a crash, and then I stood on the beach and the town was gone!"

"He's mad," said Sigurd, backing away. "Be careful. If he starts to foam at the mouth, it means he's going berserk."

"Who are you?" babbled the stranger. "What are you doing in those clothes? Why the spears?"

"Somehow," said Helgi, "he does not sound crazed, only frightened and bewildered. Something evil has beset him."

"I'm not staying near a man under a curse!" yelped Sigurd, and started to run away.

"Come back!" I bawled. "Stand where you are or I'll cleave your louse-bitten head."

That stopped him, for he had no kin who would avenge him; but he would not come closer. Meanwhile the stranger had calmed down to the point where he could talk somewhat evenly.

"Was it the *aitsjbom?*" he asked. "Has the war started?"

He used that word often, *aitsjbom,* so I know it now, though unsure of what it means. It seems to be a kind of Greek fire. As for the war, I knew not which war he meant, and told him so.

"We had a great thunderstorm last night," I added. "And you say you were out in one too. Maybe Thor's hammer knocked you from your place to here."

"But where is here?" he answered. His voice was more dulled than otherwise, now that the first terror had lifted.

"I told you. This is Hillstead, which is on Iceland."

"But that's where I was!" he said. "Reykjavik...what happened? Did the *aitsjbom* destroy everything while I lay witless?"

"Nothing has been destroyed," I said.

"Does he mean the fire at Olafsvik last month?" wondered Helgi.

"No, no, no!" Again he buried his face in his hands. After a while he looked up and said: "See here. I am *Sardjant* Gerald Robbins of the United States Army base on Iceland. I was in Reykjavik and got struck by lightning or something. Suddenly I was standing on the beach, and lost my head and ran. That's all. Now, can you tell me how to get back to the base?"

Those were more or less his words, priest. Of course, we did not grasp half of them, and made him repeat several times and explain. Even then we did not understand, save that he was from some country called the United States of America, which he said lies beyond Greenland to the west, and that he and some others were on Iceland to help our folk against their foes. This I did not consider a lie—more a mistake or imagining. Grim would have cut him down for thinking us stupid enough to swallow that tale, but I could see that he meant it.

Talking cooled him further. "Look here," he said, in too calm a tone for a feverish man, "maybe we can get at the truth from your side. Has there been no war you know of? Nothing which— Well, look here. My country's men first came to Iceland to guard it against the Germans. Now it is the Russians, but then it was the Germans. When was that?"

Helgi shook his head. "That never happened that I know of," he said. "Who are these Russians?" We found out later that the Gardariki folk were meant. "Unless," Helgi said, "the old warlocks—"

"He means the Irish monks," I explained. "A few dwelt here when the Norsemen came, but they were driven out. That was, hm, somewhat over a hundred years ago. Did your kingdom once help the monks?"

"I never heard of them!" he said. The breath sobbed in his throat. "You . . . didn't you Icelanders come from Norway?"

"Yes, about a hundred years ago," I answered patiently. "After King Harald Fairhair laid the Norse lands under him and—"

"A hundred years ago!" he whispered. I saw whiteness creep up beneath his skin. "What year is this?"

We gaped at him. "Well, it's the second year after the great salmon catch," I tried.

"What year after Christ, I mean," he prayed hoarsely.

"Oh, so you are a Christian? Hm, let me think. . . . I talked with a bishop in England once, we were holding him for ransom, and he said . . . let me see . . . I think he said this Christ man lived a thousand years ago, or maybe a little less."

"A thousand—" Something went out of him. He stood with glassy eyes—yes, I have seen glass, I told you I am a traveled man—he stood thus, and when we led him toward the garth he went like a small child.

You can see for yourself, priest, that my wife Ragnhild is still good to look upon even in eld, and Thorgunna took after her. She was—is tall and slim, with a dragon's hoard of golden hair. She being a maiden then, the locks flowed loose over her shoulders. She had great blue eyes and a heart-shaped face and very red lips. Withal she was a merry one, and kindhearted, so that she was widely loved. Sverri Snorrason went in viking when she refused him, and was slain, but no one had the wit to see that she was unlucky.

We led this Gerald Samsson—when I asked, he said his father was named Sam—we led him home, leaving Sigurd and Grim to finish gathering the driftwood. Some folks would not have a Christian in their house, for fear of witchcraft, but I am a broad-minded man, and Helgi, at his age, was wild for anything new. Our guest stumbled over the fields as if blind, but seemed to rouse when we entered the yard. His gaze went around the buildings that enclose it, from the stables and sheds to the smoke-house, the brewery, the kitchen, the bathhouse, the god shrine and thence to the hall. And Thorgunna was standing in the doorway.

Their gazes locked for a little, and I saw her color but thought nothing of it then. Our shoes rang on the flagging as we crossed the yard and kicked the dogs aside. My two thralls halted in cleaning the stables to gawp, until I got them back to work with the remark that a man good for naught else was always a pleasing sacrifice. That's one useful practice you Christians lack; I've never made a human offering myself, but you know not how helpful is the fact that I could do so.

We entered the hall, and I told the folk Gerald's name and how we had found him. Ragnhild set her maids hopping, to stoke up the fire in the middle trench and fetch beer, while I led Gerald to the high seat and sat down by him. Thorgunna brought us the filled horns. His standing was not like yours, for whom we use our outland cups.

Gerald tasted the brew and made a face. I felt somewhat offended, for my beer is reckoned good, and asked him if aught was wrong. He laughed with a harsh note and said no, but he was used to beer that foamed and was not sour.

"And where might they make such?" I wondered testily.

"Everywhere," he said. "Iceland, too—no...." He stared before him in an empty wise. "Let's say ... in Vinland."

"Where is Vinland?" I asked.

"The country to the west whence I came. I thought you knew.... Wait a bit." He frowned. "Maybe I can find out something. Have you heard of Leif Eiriksson?"

"No," I said. Since then it has struck me that this was one proof of his tale, for Leif Eiriksson is now a well-known chief; and I also take more seriously those yarns of land seen by Bjarni Herjulfsson.

"His father, Eirik the Red?" went on Gerald.

"Oh yes," I said. "If you mean the Norseman who came hither because of a manslaughter, and left Iceland in turn for the same reason, and has now settled with his friends in Greenland."

"Then this is ... a little before Leif's voyage," he muttered. "The late tenth century."

"See here," broke in Helgi, "we've been forbearing with you, but now is no time for riddles. We save those for feasts and drinking bouts. Can you not say plainly whence you come and how you got here?"

Gerald looked down at the floor, shaking.

"Let the man alone, Helgi," said Thorgunna. "Can you not see he's troubled?"

He raised his head and gave her the look of a hurt dog that someone has patted. The hall was dim; enough light seeped in the loft windows that no candles were lit, but not enough to see well by. Nevertheless, I marked a reddening in both their faces.

Gerald drew a long breath and fumbled about. His clothes were made with pockets. He brought out a small parchment box and from it took a little white stick that he put in his mouth. Then he took out another box, and a wooden stick therefrom which burst into flame when scratched. With the fire he kindled the stick in his mouth, and sucked in the smoke.

We stared. "Is that a Christian rite?" asked Helgi.

"No . . . not just so." A wry, disappointed smile twisted his lips. "I thought you'd be more surprised, even terrified."

"It's something new," I admitted, "but we're a sober folk on Iceland. Those fire sticks could be useful. Did you come to trade in them?"

"Hardly." He sighed. The smoke he breathed in seemed to steady him, which was odd, because the smoke in the hall had made him cough and water at the eyes. "The truth is, well, something you will not believe. I can hardly believe it myself."

We waited. Thorgunna stood leaning forward, her lips parted.

"That lightning bolt—" Gerald nodded wearily. "I was out in the storm, and somehow the lightning must have smitten me in just the right way, a way that happens only once in many thousands of times. It threw me back into the past."

Those were his words, priest. I did not understand, and told him so.

"It's hard to grasp," he agreed. "God give that I'm merely dreaming. But if this is a dream I must endure till I awaken. . . . Well, look. I was born one thousand, nine hundred, and thirty-three years after Christ, in a land to the west which you have not yet found. In the twenty-fourth year of my life, I was in Iceland with my country's war host. The lightning struck me, and now, now it is less than one thousand years after Christ, and yet I am here—almost a thousand years before I was born, I am here!"

We sat very still. I signed myself with the Hammer and took a long pull from my horn. One of the maids whimpered, and Ragnhild whispered so fiercely I could hear: "Be still. The poor fellow's out of his head. There's no harm in him."

I thought she was right, unless maybe in the last part. The gods can speak through a madman, and the gods are not always to be trusted. Or he could turn berserker, or he could be under a heavy curse that would also touch us.

He slumped, gazing before him. I caught a few fleas and cracked them while I pondered. Gerald noticed and asked with some horror if we had many fleas here.

"Why, of course," said Thorgunna. "Have you none?"

"No." He smiled crookedly. "Not yet."

"Ah," she sighed, "then you *must* be sick."

She was a level-headed girl. I saw her thought, and so did Ragnhild and Helgi. Clearly, a man so sick that he had no fleas could be expected to rave. We might still fret about whether we could catch the illness, but I deemed this unlikely; his woe was in the head, maybe from a blow he had taken. In any case, the matter was come down to earth now, something we could deal with.

I being a godi, a chief who holds sacrifices, it behooved me not to turn a stranger out. Moreover, if he could fetch in many of those fire-kindling sticks, a profitable trade might be built up. So I said Gerald should go to rest. He protested, but we manhandled him into the shut-bed, and there he lay tired and was soon asleep. Thorgunna said she would take care of him.

The next eventide I meant to sacrifice a horse, both because of the timber we had found and to take away any curse that might be on Gerald. Furthermore, the beast I picked was old and useless, and we were short of fresh meat. Gerald had spent the morning lounging moodily around the garth, but when I came in at noon to eat I found him and my daughter laughing.

"You seem to be on the road to health," I said.

"Oh yes. It...could be worse for me." He sat down at my side as the carles set up the trestle table and the maids brought in the food. "I was ever much taken with the age of the vikings, and I have some skills."

"Well," I said, "if you have no home, we can keep you here for a while."

"I can work," he said eagerly. "I'll be worth my pay."

Now I knew he was from afar, because what chief would work on any land but his own, and for hire at that? Yet he had the easy manner of the high-born, and had clearly eaten well throughout his life. I overlooked that he had made me no gifts; after all, he was shipwrecked.

"Maybe you can get passage back to your United States," said Helgi. "We could hire a ship. I'm fain to see that realm."

"No," said Gerald bleakly. "There is no such place. Not yet."

"So you still hold to that idea you came from tomorrow?" grunted Sigurd. "Crazy notion. Pass the pork."

"I do," said Gerald. Calm had come upon him. "And I can prove it."

"I don't see how you speak our tongue, if you hail from so far away," I said. I would not call a man a liar to his face, unless we were swapping friendly brags, but—

"They speak otherwise in my land and time," he said, "but it happens that in Iceland the tongue changed little since the old days, and because my work had me often talking with the folk, I learned it when I came here."

"If you are a Christian," I said, "you must bear with us while we sacrifice tonight."

"I've naught against that," he said. "I fear I never was a very good Christian. I'd like to watch. How is it done?"

I told him how I would smite the horse with a hammer before the god, and cut its throat, and sprinkle the blood about with willow twigs; thereafter we would butcher the carcass and feast. He said hastily:

"Here's my chance to prove what I am. I have a weapon that will kill the horse with, with a flash of lightning."

"What is it?" I wondered. We crowded around while he took the metal club out of its sheath and showed it to us. I had my doubts; it looked well enough for hitting a man, I reckoned, but had no edge, though a wondrously skillful smith had forged it. "Well, we can try," I said. You have seen how on Iceland we are less concerned to follow the rites exactly than they are in the older countries.

Gerald showed us what else he had in his pockets. There were some coins of remarkable roundness and sharpness, though neither gold nor true silver; a tiny key; a stick with lead in it for writing; a flat purse holding many bits of marked paper. When he told us gravely that some of this paper was money, Thorgunna herself had to laugh. Best was a knife whose blade folded into the handle. When he saw me admiring that, he gave it to me, which was well done for a shipwrecked man. I said I would give him clothes and a good ax, as well as lodging for as long as needful.

No, I don't have the knife now. You shall hear why. It's a pity, for that was a good knife, though rather small.

"What were you ere the war arrow went out in your land?" asked Helgi. "A merchant?"

"No," said Gerald. "I was an...*endjinur*...that is, I was learning how to be one. A man who builds things, bridges and roads and tools...more than just an artisan. So I think my knowledge could be of great value here." I saw a fever in his eyes. "Yes, give me time and I'll be a king."

"We have no king on Iceland," I grunted. "Our forefathers came hither to get away from kings. Now we meet at the Things to try suits and pass new laws, but each man must get his own redress as best he can."

"But suppose the one in the wrong won't yield?" he asked.

"Then there can be a fine feud," said Helgi, and went on to relate some of the killings in past years. Gerald looked unhappy and fingered his *gun*. That is what he called his firespitting club. He tried to rally himself with a joke about now, at last, being free to call it a gun instead of something else. That disquieted me, smacked of witchcraft, so to change the talk I told Helgi to stop his chattering of manslaughter as if it were sport. With law shall the land be built.

"Your clothing is rich," said Thorgunna softly. "Your folk must own broad acres at home."

"No," he said, "our...our king gives each man in the host clothes like these. As for my family, we owned no farm, we rented our home in a building where many other families also dwelt."

I am not purse-proud, but it seemed to me he had not been honest, a landless man sharing my high seat like a chief. Thorgunna covered my huffiness by saying, "You will gain a farm later."

After sunset we went out to the shrine. The carles had built a fire before it, and as I opened the door the wooden Odin appeared to leap forth. My house has long invoked him above the others. Gerald muttered to my daughter that it was a clumsy bit of carving, and since my father had made it I was still more angry with him. Some folk have no understanding of the fine arts.

Nevertheless, I let him help me lead the horse forth to the altar stone. I took the blood bowl in my hands and said he could now slay the beast if he would. He drew his gun, put the end behind the horse's ear and squeezed. We heard a crack, and the beast jerked and dropped with a hole blown through its skull, wasting the brains. A clumsy weapon. I caught a whiff, sharp and bitter like that around a volcano. We all jumped, one of the women screamed, and Gerald looked happy. I gathered my wits and finished the rest of the sacrifice as was right. Gerald did not like having blood sprinkled over him, but then he was a Christian. Nor would he take more than a little of the soup and flesh.

Afterward Helgi questioned him about the gun, and he said it could kill a man at bowshot distance but had no witchcraft in it, only use of some tricks we did not know. Having heard of the Greek fire, I believed him. A gun could be useful in a fight, as indeed I was to learn, but it did not seem very practical—iron costing what it does, and months of forging needed for each one.

I fretted more about the man himself.

And the next morning I found him telling Thorgunna a great deal of foolishness about his home—buildings as tall as mountains, and wagons that flew, or went without horses. He said there were eight or nine thousand thousands of folk in his town, a burgh called New Jorvik or the like. I enjoy a good brag as well as the next man, but this was too much, and I told him gruffly to come along and help me get in some strayed cattle.

After a day scrambling around the hills I saw that Gerald could hardly tell a cow's bow from her stern. We almost had the strays once, but he ran stupidly across their path and turned them, so the whole work was to do again. I asked him with strained courtesy if he could milk, shear, wield scythe or flail, and he said no, he had never lived on a farm.

"That's a shame," I remarked, "for everyone on Iceland does, unless he be outlawed."

He flushed at my tone. "I can do enough else," he answered. "Give me some tools and I'll show you good metalwork."

That brightened me, for truth to tell, none of our household was a gifted smith. "That's an honorable trade," I said, "and you can be of great help. I have a broken sword and several bent spearheads to be mended, and it were no bad idea to shoe the horses." His admission that he did not know how to put on a shoe was not very dampening to me then.

We had returned home as we talked, and Thorgunna came angrily forward. "That's no way to treat a guest, Father," she said. "Making him work like a carle, indeed!"

Gerald smiled. "I'll be glad to work," he said. "I need a . . . a stake . . . something to start me afresh. Also, I want to repay a little of your kindness."

Those words made me mild toward him, and I said it was not his fault they had different ways in the United States. On the morrow he could begin in the smithy, and I would pay him, yet he would be treated as an equal since craftsmen are valued. This earned him black looks from the housefolk.

That evening he entertained us well with stories of his home; true or not, they made good listening. However, he had no real polish, being unable to compose a line of verse. They must be a raw and backward lot in the United States. He said his task in the war host had been to keep order among the troops. Helgi said this was unheard of, and he must be bold who durst offend so many men, but Gerald said folk obeyed him out of fear of the king. When he added that the term of a levy in the United States was two years, and that men could be called to war even in harvest time, I said he was well out of a country with so ruthless and powerful a lord.

"No," he answered wistfully, "we are a free folk, who say what we please."

"But it seems you may not do as you please," said Helgi.

"Well," Gerald said, "we may not murder a man just because he aggrieves us."

"Not even if he has slain your own kin?" asked Helgi.

"No. It is for the . . . . the king to take vengeance, on behalf of the whole folk whose peace has been broken."

I chuckled. "Your yarns are cunningly wrought," I said, "but there you've hit a snag. How could the king so much as keep count of the slaughters, let alone avenge them? Why, he'd not have time to beget an heir!"

Gerald could say no more for the laughter that followed.

The next day he went to the smithy, with a thrall to pump the bellows for him. I was gone that day and night, down to Reykjavik to dicker with Hjalmar Broadnose about some sheep. I invited him back for an overnight stay, and we rode into my steading with his son Ketill, a red-haired sulky youth of twenty winters who had been refused by Thorgunna.

I found Gerald sitting gloomily on a bench in the hall. He wore the clothes I had given him, his own having been spoilt by ash and sparks; what had he awaited, the fool? He talked in a low voice with my daughter.

"Well," I said as I trod in, "how went the tasks?"

My man Grim snickered. "He ruined two spearheads, but we put out the fire he started ere the whole smithy burned."

"How's this?" I cried. "You said you were a smith."

Gerald stood up, defiant. "I worked with different tools, and better ones, at home," he replied. "You do it otherwise here."

They told me he had built up the fire too hot; his hammer had struck everywhere but the place it should; he had wrecked the temper of the steel through not knowing when to quench it. Smithcraft takes years to learn, of course, but he might have owned to being not so much as an apprentice.

"Well," I snapped, "what can you do, then, to earn your bread?" It irked me to be made a ninny of before Hjalmar and Ketill, whom I had told about the stranger.

"Odin alone knows," said Grim. "I took him with me to ride after your goats, and never have I seen a worse horseman. I asked him if maybe he could spin or weave, and he said no."

"That was no question to ask a man!" flared Thorgunna. "He should have slain you for it."

"He should indeed," laughed Grim. "But let me carry on the tale. I thought we would also repair your bridge over the foss. Well, he *can* barely handle a saw, but he nigh took his own foot off with the adze."

"We don't use those tools, I tell you!" Gerald doubled his fists and looked close to tears.

I motioned my guests to sit down. "I don't suppose you can butcher or smoke a hog, either," I said, "or salt a fish or turf a roof."

"No." I could hardly hear him.

"Well, then, man, whatever can you do?"

"I—" He could get no words out.

"You were a warrior," said Thorgunna.

"Yes, that I was!" he said, his face kindling.

"Small use on Iceland when you have no other skills," I grumbled, "but maybe, if you can get passage to the eastlands, some king will take you in his guard." Myself I doubted it, for a guardsman needs manners that will do credit to his lord; but I had not the heart to say so.

Ketill Hjalmarsson had plainly not liked the way Thorgunna stood close to Gerald and spoke for him. Now he fleered and said: "I might also doubt your skill in fighting."

"That I have been trained for," said Gerald grimly.

"Will you wrestle with me?" asked Ketill.

"Gladly!" spat Gerald.

Priest, what is a man to think? As I grow older, I find life to be less and less the good-and-evil, black-and-white thing you call it; we are each of us some hue of gray. This useless fellow, this spiritless lout who could be asked if he did women's work and not lift ax, went out into the yard with Ketill Hjalmarsson and threw him three times running. He had a trick of grabbing the clothes as Ketill rushed on him. . . . I cried a stop when the youth was nearing murderous rage, praised them both and filled the beer horns. But Ketill brooded sullen on the bench the whole evening.

Gerald said something about making a gun like his own, but bigger, a *cannon* he called it, which could sink ships and scatter hosts. He would need the help of smiths, and also various stuffs. Charcoal was easy, and sulfur could be found by the volcanoes, I suppose, but what is this saltpeter?

Too, being wary by now, I questioned him closely as to how he would make such a thing. Did he know just how to mix the powder? No, he admitted. What size must the gun be? When he told me—at least as long as a man—I laughed and asked him how a piece that size could be cast or bored, supposing we could scrape together so much iron. This he did not know either.

"You haven't the tools to make the tools to make the tools," he said. I don't understand what he meant by that. "God help me, I can't run through a thousand years of history by myself."

He took out the last of his little smoke sticks and lit it. Helgi had tried a puff earlier and gotten sick, though he remained a friend of Gerald's. Now my son proposed to take a boat in the morning and go with him and me to Ice Fjord, where I had some money outstanding I wanted to collect. Hjalmar and Ketill said they would come along for the trip, and Thorgunna pleaded so hard that I let her come too.

"An ill thing," mumbled Sigurd. "The land-trolls like not a woman aboard a vessel. It's unlucky."

"How did your fathers bring women to this island?" I grinned.

Now I wish I had listened to him. He was not a clever man, but he often knew whereof he spoke.

At this time I owned a half-share in a ship that went to Norway, bartering wadmal for timber. It was a profitable business until she ran afoul of vikings during the uproar while Olaf Tryggvason was overthrowing Jarl Haakon there. Some men will do anything to make a living—thieves, cutthroats, they ought to be hanged, the worthless robbers pouncing on honest merchantmen. Had they any courage or honor they would go to Ireland, which is full of plunder.

Well, anyhow, the ship was abroad, but we had three boats and took one of these. Grim went with us others: myself, Helgi, Hjalmar, Ketill, Gerald and Thorgunna. I saw how the castaway winced at the cold water as we launched her, yet afterward took off his shoes and stockings to let his feet dry. He had been surprised to learn we had a bathhouse—did he think us savages?—but still, he was dainty as a girl and soon moved upwind of our feet.

We had a favoring breeze, so raised mast and sail. Gerald tried to help, but of course did not know one line from another and got them fouled. Grim snarled at him and Ketill laughed nastily. But erelong we were under weigh, and he came and sat by me where I had the steering oar.

He must have lain long awake thinking, for now he ventured shyly: "In my land they have . . . will have . . . a rig and rudder which are better than these. With them, you can sail so close to the wind that you can crisscross against it."

"Ah, our wise sailor offers us redes," sneered Ketill.

"Be still," said Thorgunna sharply. "Let Gerald speak."

Gerald gave her a look of humble thanks, and I was not unwilling to listen. "This is something which could easily be made," he said. "While not a seaman, I've been on such boats myself and know them well. First, then, the sail should not be square and hung from a yardarm, but three-cornered, with the two bottom corners lashed to a yard swiveling fore and aft from the mast; and there should be one or two smaller headsails of the same shape. Next, your steering oar is in the wrong place. You should have a rudder in the stern, guided by a bar." He grew eager and traced the plan with his fingernail on Thorgunna's cloak. "With these two things, and a deep keel, going down about three feet for a boat this size, a ship can move across the wind . . . thus."

Well, priest, I must say the idea has merits, and were it not for the fear of bad luck—for everything of his was unlucky—I might yet play with it. But the drawbacks were clear, and I pointed them out in a reasonable way.

"First and worst," I said, "this rudder and deep keel would make it impossible to beach the ship or go up a shallow river. Maybe they have many harbors where you hail from, but here a craft must take what landings she can find, and must be speedily launched if there should be an attack."

"The keel can be built to draw up into the hull," he said, "with a box around so that water can't follow."

"How would you keep dry rot out of the box?" I answered. "No, your keel must be fixed, and must be heavy if the ship is not to capsize under so much sail as you have drawn. This means iron or lead, ruinously costly.

"Besides," I said, "this mast of yours would be hard to unstep when the wind dropped and oars came out. Furthermore, the sails are the wrong shape to stretch as an awning when one must sleep at sea."

"The ship could lie out, and you go to land in a small boat," he said. "Also, you could build cabins aboard for shelter."

"The cabins would get in the way of the oars," I said, "unless the ship were hopelessly broad-beamed or else the oarsmen sat below a deck; and while I hear that galley slaves do this in the southlands, free men would never row in such foulness."

"Must you have oars?" he asked like a very child.

Laughter barked along the hull. The gulls themselves, hovering to starboard where the shore rose dark, cried their scorn.

"Do they have tame winds in the place whence you came?" snorted Hjalmar. "What happens if you're becalmed—for days, maybe, with provisions running out—"

"You could build a ship big enough to carry many weeks' provisions," said Gerald.

"If you had the wealth of a king, you might," said Helgi. "And such a king's ship, lying helpless on a flat sea, would be swarmed by every viking from here to Jomsborg. As for leaving her out on the water while you make camp, what would you have for shelter, or for defense if you should be trapped ashore?"

Gerald slumped. Thorgunna said to him gently: "Some folk have no heart to try anything new. I think it's a grand idea."

He smiled at her, a weary smile, and plucked up the will to say something about a means for finding north in cloudy weather; he said a kind of stone always pointed north when hung from a string. I told him mildly that I would be most interested if he could find me some of this stone; or if he knew where it was to be had, I could ask a trader to fetch me a piece. But this he did not know, and fell silent. Ketill opened his mouth, but got such an edged look from Thorgunna that he shut it again. His face declared what a liar he thought Gerald to be.

The wind turned crank after a while, so we lowered the mast and took to the oars. Gerald was strong and willing, though awkward; however, his hands were so soft that erelong they bled. I offered to let him rest, but he kept doggedly at the work.

Watching him sway back and forth, under the dreary creak of the tholes, the shaft red and wet where he gripped it, I thought much about him. He had done everything wrong which a man could do—thus I imagined then, not knowing the future—and I did not like the way Thorgunna's eyes strayed to him and rested. He was no man for my daughter, landless and penniless and helpless. Yet I could not keep from liking him. Whether his tale was true or only madness, I felt he was honest about it; and surely whatever way by which he came hither was a strange one. I noticed the cuts on his chin from my razor; he had said he was not used to our kind of shaving and would grow a beard. He had tried hard. I wondered how well I would have done, landing alone in this witch country of his dreams, with a gap of forever between me and my home.

Maybe that same wretchedness was what had turned Thorgunna's heart. Women are a kittle breed, priest, and you who have forsworn them belike understand them as well as I who have slept with half a hundred in six different lands. I do not think they even understand themselves. Birth and life and death, those are the great mysteries, which none will ever fathom, and a woman is closer to them than a man.

The ill wind stiffened, the sea grew gray and choppy under low, leaden clouds, and our headway was poor. At sunset we could row no more, but must pull in to a small, unpeopled bay, and make camp as well as could be on the strand.

We had brought firewood and tinder along. Gerald, though staggering with weariness, made himself useful, his sulfury sticks kindling the blaze more easily than flint and steel. Thorgunna set herself to cook our supper. We were not much warded by the boat from a lean, whining wind; her cloak fluttered like wings and her hair blew wild above the streaming flames. It was the time of light nights, the sky a dim, dusky blue, the sea a wrinkled metal sheet, and the land like something risen out of dream mists. We men huddled in our own cloaks, holding numbed hands to the fire and saying little.

I felt some cheer was needed, and ordered a cask of my best and strongest ale broached. An evil Norn made me do that, but no man escapes his weird. Our bellies seemed the more empty now when our noses drank in the sputter of a spitted joint, and the ale went swiftly to our heads. I remember declaiming the death-song of Ragnar Hairybreeks for no other reason than that I felt like declaiming it.

Thorgunna came to stand over Gerald where he sat. I saw how her fingers brushed his hair, ever so lightly, and Ketill Hjalmarsson did too. "Have they no verses in your land?" she asked.

"Not like yours," he said, glancing up. Neither of them looked away again. "We sing rather than chant. I wish I had my *gittar* here—that's a kind of harp."

"Ah, an Irish bard," said Hjalmar Broadnose.

I remember strangely well how Gerald smiled, and what he said in his own tongue, though I know not the meaning: *"Only on me mither's side, begorra."* I suppose it was magic.

"Well, sing for us," laughed Thorgunna.

"Let me think," he said. "I shall have to put it in Norse words for you." After a little while, still staring at her through the windy gloaming, he began a song. It had a tune I liked, thus:

> From this valley they tell me you're leaving.
> I will miss your bright eyes and sweet smile.
> You will carry the sunshine with you
> That has brightened my life all the while....

I don't remember the rest, save that it was not quite seemly.

When he had finished, Hjalmar and Grim went over to see if the meat was done. I spied a glimmer of tears in my daughter's eyes. "That was a lovely thing," she said.

Ketill sat straight. The flames splashed his face with wild, running red. A rawness was in his tone: "Yes, we've found what this fellow can do. Sit about and make pretty songs for the girls. Keep him for that, Ospak."

Thorgunna whitened, and Helgi clapped hand to sword. Gerald's face darkened and his voice grew thick: "That was no way to talk. Take it back."

Ketill rose. "No," he said. "I'll ask no pardon of an idler living off honest yeomen."

He was raging, but had kept sense enough to shift the insult from my family to Gerald alone. Otherwise he and his father would have had the four of us to deal with. As it was, Gerald stood too, fists knotted at his sides, and said: "Will you step away from here and settle this?"

"Gladly!" Ketill turned and walked a few yards down the beach, taking his shield from the boat. Gerald followed. Thorgunna stood stricken, then snatched his ax and ran after him.

"Are you going weaponless?" she shrieked.

Gerald stopped, looking dazed. "I don't want anything like that," he said. "Fists—"

Ketill puffed himself up and drew sword. "No doubt you're used to fighting like thralls in your land," he said. "So if you'll crave my pardon, I'll let this matter rest."

Gerald stood with drooped shoulders. He stared at Thorgunna as if he were blind, as if asking her what to do. She handed him the ax.

"So you want me to kill him?" he whispered.

"Yes," she answered.

Then I knew she loved him, for otherwise why should she have cared if he disgraced himself?

Helgi brought him his helmet. He put it on, took the ax and went forward.

"Ill is this," said Hjalmar to me. "Do you stand by the stranger, Ospak?"

"No," I said. "He's no kin or oath-brother of mine. This is not my quarrel."

"That's good," said Hjalmar. "I'd not like to fight with you. You were ever a good neighbor."

We stepped forth together and staked out the ground. Thorgunna told me to lend Gerald my sword, so he could use a shield too, but the man looked oddly at me and said he would rather have the ax. They squared off before each other, he and Ketill, and began fighting.

This was no holmgang, with rules and a fixed order of blows and first blood meaning victory. There was death between those two. Drunk though the lot of us were, we saw that and so had not tried to make peace. Ketill stormed in with the sword whistling in his hand. Gerald sprang back, wielding the ax awkwardly. It bounced off Ketill's shield. The youth grinned and cut at Gerald's legs. Blood welled forth to stain the ripped breeches.

What followed was butchery. Gerald had never used a battle-ax before. So it turned in his grasp and he struck with the flat of the head. He would have been hewn down at once had Ketill's sword not been blunted on his helmet and had he not been quick on his feet. Even so, he was erelong lurching with a dozen wounds.

"Stop the fight!" Thorgunna cried, and sped toward them. Helgi caught her arms and forced her back, where she struggled and kicked till Grim must help. I saw grief on my son's face, but a wolfish glee on the carle's.

Ketill's blade came down and slashed Gerald's left hand. He dropped the ax. Ketill snarled and readied to finish him. Gerald drew his gun. It made a flash and a barking noise. Ketill fell. Blood gushed from him. His lower jaw was blown off and the back of his skull was gone.

A stillness came, where only the wind and the sea had voice.

Then Hjalmar trod forth, his mouth working but otherwise a cold steadiness over him. He knelt and closed his son's eyes, as a token that the right of vengeance was his. Rising, he said: "That was an evil deed. For that you shall be outlawed."

"It wasn't witchcraft," said Gerald in a stunned tone. "It was like a . . . a bow. I had no choice. I didn't want to fight with more than my fists."

I got between them and said the Thing must decide this matter, but that I hoped Hjalmar would take weregild for Ketill.

"But I killed him to save my own life!" protested Gerald.

"Nevertheless, weregild must be paid, if Ketill's kin will take it," I explained. "Because of the weapon, I think it will be doubled, but that is for the Thing to judge."

Hjalmar had many other sons, and it was not as if Gerald belonged to a family at odds with his own, so I felt he would agree. However, he laughed coldly and asked where a man lacking wealth would find the silver.

Thorgunna stepped up with a wintry calm and said we would pay. I opened my mouth, but when I saw her eyes I nodded. "Yes, we will," I said, "in order to keep the peace."

"So you make this quarrel your own?" asked Hjalmar.

"No," I answered. "This man is no blood of mine. But if I choose to make him a gift of money to use as he wishes, what of it?"

Hjalmar smiled. Sorrow stood in his gaze, but he looked on me with old comradeship.

"One day he may be your son-in-law," he said. "I know the signs, Ospak. Then indeed he will be of your folk. Even helping him now in his need will range you on his side."

"And so?" asked Helgi, most softly.

"And so, while I value your friendship, I have sons who will take the death of their brother ill. They'll want revenge on Gerald Samsson, if only for the sake of their good names, and thus our two houses will be sundered and one manslaying will lead to another. It has happened often enough ere now." Hjalmar sighed. "I myself wish peace with you, Ospak, but if you take this killer's side it must be otherwise."

I thought for a moment, thought of Helgi lying with his head cloven, of my other sons on their steads drawn to battle because of a man they had never seen, I thought of having to wear byrnies each time we went down for driftwood and never knowing when we went to bed if we would wake to find the house ringed in by spearmen.

"Yes," I said, "you are right, Hjalmar. I withdraw my offer. Let this be a matter between you and him alone."

We gripped hands on it.

Thorgunna uttered a small cry and flew into Gerald's arms. He held her close. "What does this mean?" he asked slowly.

"I cannot keep you any longer," I said, "but maybe some crofter will give you a roof. Hjalmar is a law-abiding man and will not harm you until the Thing has outlawed you. That will not be before they meet in fall. You can try to get passage out of Iceland ere then."

"A useless one like me?" he replied in bitterness.

Thorgunna whirled free and blazed that I was a coward and a perjurer and all else evil. I let her have it out before I laid my hands on her shoulders.

"I do this for the house," I said. "The house and the blood, which are holy. Men die and women weep, but while the kindred live our names are remembered. Can you ask a score of men to die for your hankerings?"

Long did she stand, and to this day I know not what her answer would have been. But Gerald spoke.

"No," he said. "I suppose you have right, Ospak . . . the right of your time, which is not mine." He took my hand, and Helgi's. His lips brushed Thorgunna's cheek. Then he turned and walked out into the darkness.

I heard, later, that he went to earth with Thorvald Hallsson, the crofter of Humpback Fell, and did not tell his host what had happened. He must have hoped to go unnoticed until he could somehow get berth on an eastbound ship. But of course word spread. I remember his brag that in the United States folk had ways to talk from one end of the land to another. So he must have scoffed at us, sitting in our lonely steads, and not known how fast news would get around. Thorvald's son Hrolf went to Brand Sealskin-Boots to talk about some matter, and mentioned the guest, and soon the whole western island had the tale.

Now, if Gerald had known he must give notice of a manslaying at the first garth he found, he would have been safe at least till the Thing met, for Hjalmar and his sons are sober men who would not needlessly kill a man still under the wing of the law. But as it was, his keeping the matter secret made him a murderer and therefore at once an outlaw. Hjalmar and his kin rode straight to Humpback Fell and haled him forth. He shot his way past them with the gun and fled into the hills. They followed him, having several hurts and one more death to avenge. I wonder if Gerald thought the strangeness of his weapon would unnerve us. He may not have understood that every man dies when his time comes, neither sooner nor later, so that fear of death is useless.

At the end, when they had him trapped, his weapon gave out on him. Then he took a dead man's sword and defended himself so valiantly that Ulf Hjalmarsson has limped ever since. That was well done, as even his foes admitted. They are an eldritch breed in the United States, but they do not lack manhood.

When he was slain, his body was brought back. For fear of the ghost, he having maybe been a warlock, it was burned, and everything he had owned was laid in the fire with him. Thus I lost the knife he gave me. The barrow stands out on the moor, north of here, and folk shun it, though the ghost has not walked. Today, with so much else happening, he is slowly being forgotten.

And that is the tale, priest, as I saw it and heard it. Most men think Gerald Samsson was crazy, but I myself now believe he did come from out of time, and that his doom was that no man may ripen a field before harvest season. Yet I look into the future, a thousand years hence, when they fly through the air and ride in horseless wagons and smash whole towns with one blow. I think of this Iceland then, and of the young United States men come to help defend us in a year when the end of the world hovers close. Maybe some of them, walking about on the heaths, will see that barrow and wonder what ancient warrior lies buried there, and they may well wish they had lived long ago in his time, when men were free.

CORDWAINER SMITH

The Burning of the Brain

"Cordwainer Smith" was one of the strangest figures in science fiction, for many years the only major writer whose real identity was unknown, even to his literary agent. He was finally revealed as Paul M. A. Linebarger (1913-1966), a Professor of Asiatic Studies at the Johns Hopkins University School of Advanced International Studies, with close ties to the U.S. intelligence community (one of his areas of expertise was propaganda techniques). He was also a most unusual, poetic and gifted writer, his work consisting almost entirely of stories set in a strange universe run by "The Instrumentality of Mankind." His modest output of stories and novels has achieved almost cult status, which continues more than fifteen years after his death.

"The Burning of the Brain" is an excellent example of his magic.

I. DOLORES OH

I tell you, it is sad, it is more than sad, it is fearful—for it is a dreadful thing to go into the Up-and-Out, to fly without flying, to move between the stars as a moth may drift among the leaves on a summer night.

Of all the men who took the great ships into planoform none was braver, none stronger, than Captain Magno Taliano.

Scanners had been gone for centuries and the jonasoidal effect had become so simple, so manageable, that the traversing of light-years was no more difficult to most of the passengers of the great ships than to go from one room to the other.

Passengers moved easily.

Not the crew.

Least of all the captain.

The captain of a jonasoidal ship which had embarked on an interstellar journey was a man subject to rare and overwhelming strains. The art of getting past all the complications of space was far more like the piloting of turbulent waters in ancient days than like the smooth seas which legendary men once traversed with sails alone.

Go-Captain on the *Wu-Feinstein*, finest ship of its class, was Magno Taliano.

Of him it was said, "He could sail through hell with the muscles of his left eye alone. He could plow space with his living brain if the instruments failed..."

Wife to the Go-Captain was Dolores Oh. The name was Japonical, from some nation of the ancient days. Dolores Oh had been once beautiful, so beautiful that she took men's breath away, made wise men into fools, made young men into nightmares of lust and yearning. Wherever she went men had quarreled and fought over her.

But Dolores Oh was proud beyond all common limits of pride. She refused to go through the ordinary rejuvenescence. A terrible yearning a hundred or so years back must have come over her. Perhaps she said to herself, before that hope and terror which a mirror in a quiet room becomes to anyone:

"Surely I am me. There must be a *me* more than the beauty of my face; there must be a something other than the delicacy of skin and the accidental lines of my jaw and cheekbone.

"What have men loved if it wasn't me? Can I ever find out who I am or what I am if I don't let beauty perish and live on in whatever flesh age gives me?"

She had met the Go-Captain and had married him in a romance that left forty planets talking and half the ship lines stunned.

Magno Taliano was at the very beginning of his genius. Space, we can tell you, is rough—rough like the wildest of storm-driven waters, filled with perils which only the most sensitive, the quickest, the most daring of men can surmount.

Best of them all, class for class, age for age, out of class, beating the best of his seniors, was Magno Taliano.

For him to marry the most beautiful beauty of forty worlds was a wedding like Heloise and Abelard's or like the unforgettable romance of Helen America and Mr. Grey-no-more.

The ships of the Go-Captain Magno Taliano became more beautiful year by year, century by century.

As ships became better he always obtained the best. He maintained his lead over the other Go-Captains so overwhelmingly that it was unthinkable for the finest ship of mankind to sail out amid the roughness and uncertainties of two-dimensional space without himself at the helm.

Stop-Captains were proud to sail space beside him. (Though the Stop-Captains had nothing more to do than to check the maintenance of the ship, its loading and unloading when it was in normal space, they were still more than ordinary men in their own kind of world, a world far below the more majestic and adventurous universe of the Go-Captains.)

Magno Taliano had a niece who in the modern style used a place instead of a name: she was called "Dita from the Great South House."

When Dita came aboard the *Wu-Feinstein* she had heard much of Dolores Oh, her aunt by marriage who had once captivated the men in many worlds. Dita was wholly unprepared for what she found.

Dolores greeted her civilly enough, but the civility was a sucking pump of hideous anxiety, the friendliness was the driest of mockeries, the greeting itself an attack.

What's the matter with the woman? thought Dita.

As if to answer her thought, Dolores said aloud and in words: "It's nice to meet a woman who's not trying to take Taliano from me. I love him. Can you believe that? Can you?"

"Of course," said Dita. She looked at the ruined face of Dolores Oh, at the dreaming terror in Dolores' eyes, and she realized that Dolores had passed all limits of nightmare and had become a veritable demon of regret, a possessive ghost who sucked the vitality from her husband, who dreaded companionship, hated friendship, rejected even the most casual of acquaintances, because she feared forever and without limit that there was really nothing to herself, and feared that without Magno Taliano she would be more lost than the blackest of whirlpools in the nothing between the stars.

Magno Taliano came in.

He saw his wife and niece together.

He must have been used to Dolores Oh. In Dita's eyes Dolores was more frightening than a mud-caked reptile raising its wounded and venomous head with blind hunger and blind rage. To Magno Taliano the ghastly woman who stood like a witch beside him was somehow the beautiful girl he had wooed and had married one hundred sixty-four years before.

He kissed the withered cheek, he stroked the dried and stringy hair, he looked into the greedy terror-haunted eyes as though they were the eyes of a child he loved. He said, lightly and gently, "Be good to Dita, my dear."

He went on through the lobby of the ship to the inner sanctum of the planoforming room.

The Stop-Captain waited for him. Outside on the world of Sherman the scented breezes of that pleasant planet blew in through the open windows of the ship.

Wu-Feinstein, finest ship of its class, had no need for metal walls. It was built to resemble an ancient, prehistoric estate named Mount Vernon, and when it sailed between the stars it was encased in its own rigid and self-renewing field of force.

The passengers went through a few pleasant hours of strolling on the grass, enjoying the spacious rooms, chatting beneath a marvelous simulacrum of an atmosphere-filled sky.

Only in the planoforming room did the Go-Captain know what happened. The Go-Captain, his pinlighters sitting beside him, took the ship from one compression to another, leaping hotly and frantically through space, sometimes one light-year, sometimes a hundred light-years, jump, jump, jump, jump until the ship, the light touches of the captain's mind guiding it, passed the perils of millions upon millions of worlds, came out at its appointed destination and settled as lightly as one feather resting upon others, settled into an embroidered and decorated countryside where the passengers could move as easily away from their journey as if they had done nothing more than to pass an afternoon in a pleasant old house by the side of a river.

II. THE LOST LOCKSHEET

Magno Taliano nodded to his pinlighters. The Stop-Captain bowed obsequiously from the doorway of the planoforming room. Taliano looked at him sternly, but with robust friendliness. With formal and austere courtesy he asked, "Sir and colleague, is everything ready for the jonasoidal effect?"

The Stop-Captain bowed even more formally. "Truly ready, sir and master."

"The locksheets in place?"

"Truly in place, sir and master."

"The passengers secure?"

"The passengers are secure, numbered, happy and ready, sir and master."

Then came the last and most serious of questions. "Are my pinlighters warmed with their pin-sets and ready for combat?"

"Ready for combat, sir and master." With these words the Stop-Captain withdrew. Magno Taliano smiled to his pinlighters. Through the minds of all of them there passed the same thought.

How could a man that pleasant stay married all those years to a hag like Dolores Oh? How could that witch, that horror, have ever been a beauty? How could that beast have ever been a woman, particularly the divine and glamorous Dolores Oh whose image we still see in four-di every now and then?

Yet pleasant he was, though long he may have been married to Dolores Oh. Her loneliness and greed might suck at him like a nightmare, but his strength was more than enough strength for two.

Was he not the captain of the greatest ship to sail between the stars?

Even as the pinlighters smiled their greetings back to him, his right hand depressed the golden ceremonial lever of the ship. This instrument alone was mechanical. All other controls in the ship had long since been formed telepathically or electronically.

Within the planoforming room the black skies became visible and the tissue of space shot up around them like boiling water at the base of a waterfall. Outside that one room the passengers still walked sedately on scented lawns.

From the wall facing him, as he sat rigid in his Go-Captain's chair, Magno Taliano sensed the forming of a pattern which in three or four hundred milliseconds would tell him where he was and would give him the next clue as to how to move.

He moved the ship with the impulses of his own brain, to which the wall was a superlative complement.

The wall was a living brickwork of locksheets, laminated charts, one hundred thousand charts to the inch, the wall preselected and preassembled for all imaginable contingencies of the journey which, each time afresh, took the ship across half-unknown immensities of time and space. The ship leapt, as it had before.

The new star focused.

Magno Taliano waited for the wall to show him where he was, expecting (in partnership with the wall) to flick the ship back into the pattern of stellar space, moving it by immense skips from source to destination.

This time nothing happened.

Nothing?

For the first time in a hundred years his mind knew panic.

It couldn't be nothing. Not *nothing*. Something had to focus. The locksheets always focused.

His mind reached into the locksheets and he realized with a devastation beyond all limits of ordinary human grief that they were lost as no ship had ever been lost before. By some error never before committed in the history of mankind, the entire wall was made of duplicates of the same locksheet.

Worst of all, the Emergency Return sheet was lost. They were amid stars none of them had ever seen before, perhaps as little as five hundred million miles, perhaps as far as forty parsecs.

And the locksheet was lost.

And they would die.

As the ship's power failed coldness and blackness and death would crush in on them in a few hours at the most. That then would be all, all of the *Wu-Feinstein*, all of Dolores Oh.

III.   THE SECRET OF THE OLD DARK BRAIN

Outside of the planoforming room of the *Wu-Feinstein* the passengers had no reason to understand that they were marooned in the nothing-at-all.

Dolores Oh rocked back and forth in an ancient rocking chair. Her haggard face looked without pleasure at the imaginary river that ran past the edge of the lawn. Dita from the Great South House sat on a hassock by her aunt's knees.

Dolores was talking about a trip she had made when she was young and vibrant with beauty, a beauty which brought trouble and hate wherever it went.

"...so the guardsman killed the captain and then came to my cabin and said to me, 'You've got to marry me now. I've given up everything for your sake,' and I said to him, 'I never said that I loved you. It was sweet of you to get into a fight, and in a way I suppose it is a compliment to my beauty, but it doesn't mean that I belong to you the rest of my life. What do you think I am, anyhow?'"

Dolores Oh sighed a dry, ugly sigh, like the crackling of subzero winds through frozen twigs. "So you see, Dita, being beautiful the way you are is no answer to anything. A woman has got to be herself before she finds out what she is. I know that my lord and husband, the Go-Captain, loves me because my beauty is gone, and with my beauty gone there is nothing but *me* to love, is there?"

An odd figure came out on the verandah. It was a pinlighter in full fighting costume. Pinlighters were never supposed to leave the planoforming room, and it was most extraordinary for one of them to appear among the passengers.

He bowed to the two ladies and said with the utmost courtesy:

"Ladies, will you please come into the planoforming room? We have need that you should see the Go-Captain now."

Dolores' hand leapt to her mouth. Her gesture of grief was as automatic as the striking of a snake. Dita sensed that her aunt had been waiting a hundred years and more for disaster, that her aunt had craved ruin for her husband the way that some people crave love and others crave death.

Dita said nothing. Neither did Dolores, apparently at second thought, utter a word.

They followed the pinlighter silently into the planoforming room.

The heavy door closed behind them.

Magno Taliano was still rigid in his Captain's chair.

He spoke very slowly, his voice sounding like a record played too slowly on an ancient parlophone.

"We are lost in space, my dear," said the frigid, ghostly voice of the Captain, still in his Go-Captain's trance. *"We are lost in space and I thought that perhaps if your mind aided mine we might think of a way back."*

Dita started to speak.

A pinlighter told her: "Go ahead and speak, my dear. Do you have any suggestion?"

"Why don't we just go back? It would be humiliating, wouldn't it? Still it would be better than dying. Let's use the Emergency Return Locksheet and go on right back. The world will forgive Magno Taliano for a single failure after thousands of brilliant and successful trips."

The pinlighter, a pleasant enough young man, was as friendly and calm as a doctor informing someone of a death or of a mutilation. "The impossible has happened, Dita from the Great South House. All the locksheets are wrong. They are all the same one. And not one of them is good for emergency return."

With that the two women knew where they were. They knew that space would tear into them like threads being pulled out of a fiber so that they would either die bit by bit as the hours passed and as the material of their bodies faded away a few molecules here and a few there. Or, alternatively, they could die all at once in a flash if the Go-Captain chose to kill himself and the ship rather than to wait for a slow death. Or, if they believed in religion, they could pray.

The pinlighter said to the rigid Go-Captain, "We think we see a familiar pattern at the edge of your own brain. May we look in?"

Taliano nodded very slowly, very gravely.

The pinlighter stood still.

The two women watched. Nothing visible happened, but they knew that beyond the limits of vision and yet before their eyes a great drama was being played out. The minds of the pinlighters probed deep into the mind of the frozen Go-Captain, searching amid the synapses for the secret of the faintest clue to their possible rescue.

Minutes passed. They seemed like hours.

At last the pinlighter spoke. "We can see into your midbrain, Captain. At the edge of your paleocortex there is a star pattern which resembles the upper left rear of our present location."

The pinlighter laughed nervously. "We want to know can you fly the ship home on your brain?"

Magno Taliano looked with deep tragic eyes at the inquirer. His slow voice came out at them once again since he dared not leave the half-trance which held the entire ship in stasis. *"Do you mean can I fly the ship on a brain alone? It would burn out my brain and the ship would be lost anyhow...."*

"But we're lost, lost, lost," screamed Dolores Oh. Her face was alive with hideous hope, with a hunger for ruin, with a greedy welcome of disaster. She screamed at her husband, "Wake up, my darling, and let us die together. At least we can belong to each other that much, that long, forever!"

"Why die?" said the pinlighter softly. "You tell him, Dita."

Said Dita, "Why not try, sir and uncle?"

Slowly Magno Taliano turned his face toward his niece. Again his hollow voice sounded. *"If I do this I shall be a fool or a child or a dead man but I will do it for you."*

Dita had studied the work of the Go-Captains and she knew well enough that if the paleocortex was lost the personality became intellectually sane, but emotionally crazed. With the most ancient part of the brain gone the fundamental controls of hostility, hunger and sex disappeared. The most ferocious of animals and the most brilliant of men were reduced to a common level—a level of infantile friendliness in which lust and playfulness and gentle, unappeasable hunger became the eternity of their days.

Magno Taliano did not wait.

He reached out a slow hand and squeezed the hand of Dolores Oh. *"As I die you shall at last be sure I love you."*

Once again the women saw nothing. They realized they had been called in simply to give Magno Taliano a last glimpse of his own life.

A quiet pinlighter thrust a beam-electrode so that it reached square into the paleocortex of Captain Magno Taliano.

The planoforming room came to life. Strange heavens swirled about them like milk being churned in a bowl.

Dita realized that her partial capacity of telepathy was functioning even without the aid of a machine. With her mind she could feel the dead wall of the locksheets. She was aware of the rocking of the *Wu-Feinstein* as it leapt from space to space, as uncertain as a man crossing a river by leaping from one ice-covered rock to the other.

In a strange way she even knew that the paleocortical part of her uncle's brain was burning out at last and forever, that the star patterns which had been frozen in the locksheets lived on in the infinitely complex pattern of his own memories, and that with the help of his own telepathic pinlighters he was burning out his brain cell by cell in order for them to find a way to the ship's destination. This indeed was his last trip.

Dolores Oh watched her husband with a hungry greed surpassing all expression.

Little by little his face became relaxed and stupid.

Dita could see the midbrain being burned blank, as the ship's controls with the help of the pinlighters searched through the most magnificent intellect of its time for a last course into harbor.

Suddenly Dolores Oh was on her knees, sobbing by the hand of her husband.

A pinlighter took Dita by the arm.

"We have reached destination," he said.

"And my uncle?"

The pinlighter looked at her strangely.

She realized he was speaking to her without moving his lips—speaking mind-to-mind with pure telepathy.

"Can't you see it?"

She shook her head dazedly.

The pinlighter thought his emphatic statement at her once again.

"As your uncle burned out his brain, you picked up his skills. Can't you sense it? You are a Go-Captain yourself and one of the greatest of us."

"And he?"

The pinlighter thought a merciful comment at her.

Magno Taliano had risen from his chair and was being led from the room by his wife and consort, Dolores Oh. He had the amiable smile of an idiot, and his face for the first time in more than a hundred years trembled with shy and silly love.

ALFRED BESTER

The Men Who Murdered Mohammed

Alfred Bester (1913-   ) is the author of two of the most influential science fiction novels of all time—The Demolished Man (1953), an sf/mystery hybrid that is also a powerful psychological case study of a man under stress; and The Stars My Destination (1957), a remarkable combination of adventure and personal philosophy. His short fiction is also outstanding and equally influential; in fact, the only complaint one is likely to have with the work of Alfred Bester is that there is not enough of it. He seems to play at the fringes of the science fiction field—if he had concentrated his efforts in it he might have been its finest practitioner. Perhaps his greatest contribution to science fiction writing lies in his emphasis on character development and his willingness to experiment with structure long before such efforts were fashionable.

T HERE WAS a man who mutilated history. He toppled empires and uprooted dynasties. Because of him, Mount Vernon should not be a national shrine, and Columbus, Ohio, should be called Cabot, Ohio. Because of him the name Marie Curie should be cursed in France, and no one should swear by the beard of the Prophet. Actually, these realities did not happen, because he was a mad professor; or, to put it another way, he only succeeded in making them unreal for himself.

Now, the patient reader is too familiar with the conventional mad professor, undersized and overbrowed, creating monsters in his laboratory which invariably turn on their maker and menace his lovely daughter. This story isn't about that sort of make-believe man. It's about Henry Hassel, a genuine mad professor in a class with such better-known men as Ludwig Boltzmann *(see* Ideal Gas Law), Jacques Charles and André Marie Ampère (1775–1836).

Everyone ought to know that the electrical ampere was so named in honor of Ampère. Ludwig Boltzmann was a distinguished Austrian physicist, as famous for his research on black-body radiation as on Ideal Gases. You can look him up in Volume Three of the *Encyclopaedia Britannica*, BALT to BRAI. Jacques Alexandre

371

César Charles was the first mathematician to become interested in flight, and he invented the hydrogen balloon. These were real men.

They were also real mad professors. Ampère, for example, was on his way to an important meeting of scientists in Paris. In his taxi he got a brilliant idea (of an electrical nature, I assume) and whipped out a pencil and jotted the equation on the wall of the hansom cab. Roughly, it was: $dH = ipdl/r^2$ in which p is the perpendicular distance from P to the line of the element dl; or $dH = i \sin \emptyset \, dl/r^2$. This is sometimes known as Laplace's Law, although he wasn't at the meeting.

Anyway, the cab arrived at the Académie. Ampère jumped out, paid the driver and rushed into the meeting to tell everybody about his idea. Then he realized he didn't have the note on him, remembered where he'd left it, and had to chase through the streets of Paris after the taxi to recover his runaway equation. Sometimes I imagine that's how Fermat lost his famous "Last Theorem," although Fermat wasn't at the meeting either, having died some two hundred years earlier.

Or take Boltzmann. Giving a course in Advanced Ideal Gases, he peppered his lectures with involved calculus, which he worked out quickly and casually in his head. He had that kind of head. His students had so much trouble trying to puzzle out the math by ear that they couldn't keep up with the lectures, and they begged Boltzmann to work out his equations on the blackboard.

Boltzmann apologized and promised to be more helpful in the future. At the next lecture he began, "Gentlemen, combining Boyle's Law with the Law of Charles, we arrive at the equation $pv = p_0v_0(1 + at)$. Now, obviously, if $_aS^b = f(x) \, dx$ $\emptyset(a)$, then $pv = RT$ and $_sS \, f(x,y,z) \, dV = O$. It's as simple as two plus two equals four." At this point Boltzmann remembered his promise. He turned to the blackboard, conscientiously chalked $2 + 2 = 4$, and then breezed on, casually doing the complicated calculus in his head.

Jacques Charles, the brilliant mathematician who discovered Charles' Law (sometimes known as Gay-Lussac's Law), which Boltzmann mentioned in his lecture, had a lunatic passion to become a famous paleographer—that is, a discoverer of ancient manuscripts. I think that being forced to share credit with Gay-Lussac may have unhinged him.

He paid a transparent swindler named Vrain-Lucas 200,000 francs for holograph letters purportedly written by Julius Caesar, Alexander the Great and Pontius Pilate. Charles, a man who could see through any gas, ideal or not, actually believed in these forgeries despite the fact that the maladroit Vrain-Lucas had written them in modern French on modern notepaper bearing modern watermarks. Charles even tried to donate them to the Louvre.

Now, these men weren't idiots. They were geniuses who paid a high price for their genius because the rest of their thinking was other-world. A genius is someone who travels to truth by an unexpected path. Unfortunately, unexpected paths lead to disaster in everyday life. This is what happened to Henry Hassel, professor of Applied Compulsion at Unknown University in the year 1980.

Nobody knows where Unknown University is or what they teach there. It has a faculty of some two hundred eccentrics, and a student body of two thousand misfits—

the kind that remain anonymous until they win Nobel prizes or become the First Man on Mars. You can always spot a graduate of U.U. when you ask people where they went to school. If you get an evasive reply like: "State," or "Oh, a fresh-water school you never heard of," you can bet they went to Unknown. Someday I hope to tell you more about this university, which is a center of learning only in the Pickwickian sense.

Anyway, Henry Hassel started home from his office in the Psychotic Psenter early one afternoon, strolling through the Physical Culture arcade. It is not true that he did this to leer at the nude coeds practicing Arcane Eurythmics; rather, Hassel liked to admire the trophies displayed in the arcade in memory of great Unknown teams which had won the sort of championships that Unknown teams win—in sports like Strabismus, Occlusion and Botulism. (Hassel had been Frambesia singles champion three years running.) He arrived home uplifted, and burst gaily into the house to discover his wife in the arms of a man.

There she was, a lovely woman of thirty-five, with smoky red hair and almond eyes, being heartily embraced by a person whose pockets were stuffed with pamphlets, microchemical apparatus and a patella-reflex hammer—a typical campus character of U.U., in fact. The embrace was so concentrated that neither of the offending parties noticed Henry Hassel glaring at them from the hallway.

Now, remember Ampère and Charles and Boltzmann. Hassel weighed 190 pounds. He was muscular and uninhibited. It would have been child's play for him to have dismembered his wife and her lover, and thus simply and directly achieve the goal he desired—the end of his wife's life. But Henry Hassel was in the genius class; his mind just didn't operate that way.

Hassel breathed hard, turned and lumbered into his private laboratory like a freight engine. He opened a drawer labeled DUODENUM and removed a .45-caliber revolver. He opened other drawers, more interestingly labeled, and assembled apparatus. In exactly 7½ minutes (such was his rage), he put together a time machine (such was his genius).

Professor Hassel assembled the time machine around him, set a dial for 1902, picked up the revolver and pressed a button. The machine made a noise like defective plumbing and Hassel disappeared. He reappeared in Philadelphia on June 3, 1902, went directly to No. 1218 Walnut Street, a red-brick house with marble steps, and rang the bell. A man who might have passed for the third Smith Brother opened the door and looked at Henry Hassel.

"Mr. Jessup?" Hassel asked in a suffocated voice.

"Yes?"

"You are Mr. Jessup?"

"I am."

"You will have a son, Edgar? Edgar Allan Jessup—so named because of your regrettable admiration for Poe?"

The third Smith Brother was startled. "Not that I know of," he said. "I'm not married yet."

"You will be," Hassel said angrily. "I have the misfortune to be married to your son's daughter, Greta. Excuse me." He raised the revolver and shot his wife's grandfather-to-be.

"She will have ceased to exist," Hassel muttered, blowing smoke out of the revolver. "I'll be a bachelor. I may even be married to somebody else.... Good God! Who?"

Hassel waited impatiently for the automatic recall of the time machine to snatch him back to his own laboratory. He rushed into his living room. There was his redheaded wife, still in the arms of a man.

Hassel was thunderstruck.

"So that's it," he growled. "A family tradition of faithlessness. Well, we'll see about that. We have ways and means." He permitted himself a hollow laugh, returned to his laboratory and sent himself back to the year 1901, where he shot and killed Emma Hotchkiss, his wife's maternal grandmother-to-be. He returned to his own home in his own time. There was his redheaded wife, still in the arms of another man.

"But I *know* the old hag was her grandmother," Hassel muttered. "You couldn't miss the resemblance. What the hell's gone wrong?"

Hassel was confused and dismayed, but not without resources. He went to his study, had difficulty picking up the phone, but finally managed to dial the Malpractice Laboratory. His finger kept oozing out of the dial holes.

"Sam?" he said. "This is Henry."

"Who?"

"Henry."

"You'll have to speak up."

"Henry Hassel!"

"Oh, good afternoon, Henry."

"Tell me all about time."

"Time? Hmmm..." The Simplex-and-Multiplex Computer cleared its throat while it waited for the data circuits to link up. "Ahem. Time. (1) Absolute. (2) Relative. (3) Recurrent. (1) Absolute: period, contingent, duration, diurnity, perpetuity—"

"Sorry, Sam. Wrong request. Go back. I want time, reference to succession of, travel in."

Sam shifted gears and began again. Hassel listened intently. He nodded. He grunted. "Uh huh. Uh huh. Right. I see. Thought so. A continuum, eh? Acts performed in past must alter future. Then I'm on the right track. But act must be significant, eh? Mass-action effect. Trivia cannot divert existing phenomena streams. Hmmm. But how trivial is a grandmother?"

"What are you trying to do, Henry?"

"Kill my wife," Hassel snapped. He hung up. He returned to his laboratory. He considered, still in a jealous rage.

"Got to do something significant," he muttered. "Wipe Greta out. Wipe it all out. All right, by God! I'll show 'em."

Hassel went back to the year 1775, visited a Virginia farm and shot a young colonel in the brisket. The colonel's name was George Washington, and Hassel made sure he was dead. He returned to his own time and his own home. There was his redheaded wife, still in the arms of another.

"Damn!" said Hassel. He was running out of ammunition. He opened a fresh box of cartridges, went back in time and massacred Christopher Columbus, Napoleon, Mohammed and half a dozen other celebrities. "That ought to do it, by God!" said Hassel.

He returned to his own time, and found his wife as before.

His knees turned to water; his feet seemed to melt into the floor. He went back to his laboratory, walking through nightmare quicksands.

"What the hell is significant?" Hassel asked himself painfully. "How much does it take to change futurity? By God, I'll really change it this time. I'll go for broke."

He traveled to Paris at the turn of the twentieth century and visited a Madame Curie in an attic workshop near the Sorbonne. "Madame," he said in his execrable French, "I am a stranger to you of the utmost, but a scientist entire. Knowing of your experiments with radium— Oh? You haven't got to radium yet? No matter. I am here to teach you all of nuclear fission."

He taught her. He had the satisfaction of seeing Paris go up in a mushroom of smoke before the automatic recall brought him home. "That'll teach women to be faithless," he growled. "Guhhh!" The last was wrenched from his lips when he saw his redheaded wife still— But no need to belabor the obvious.

Hassel swam through fogs to his study and sat down to think. While he's thinking I'd better warn you that this is not a conventional time story. If you imagine for a moment that Henry is going to discover that the man fondling his wife is himself, you're mistaken. The viper is not Henry Hassel, his son, a relation or even Ludwig Boltzmann (1844-1906). Hassel does not make a circle in time, ending where the story begins—to the satisfaction of nobody and the fury of everybody—for the simple reason that time isn't circular, or linear, or tandem, discoid, syzygous, longinquitous, or pandiculated. Time is a private matter, as Hassel discovered.

"Maybe I slipped up somehow," Hassel muttered. "I'd better find out." He fought with the telephone, which seemed to weigh a hundred tons, and at last managed to get through to the library.

"Hello, Library? This is Henry."

"Who?"

"Henry Hassel."

"Speak up, please."

"Henry Hassel!"

"Oh. Good afternoon, Henry."

"What have you got on George Washington?"

Library clucked while her scanners sorted through her catalogs. "George Washington, first President of the United States, was born in—"

"First President? Wasn't he murdered in 1775?"

"Really, Henry. That's an absurd question. Everybody knows that George Wash——"

"Doesn't anybody know he was shot?"

"By whom?"

"Me."

"When?"

"In 1775."

"How did you manage to do that?"

"I've got a revolver."

"No, I mean, how did you do it two hundred years ago?"

"I've got a time machine."

"Well, there's no record here," Library said. "He's still doing fine in my files. You must have missed."

"I did not miss. What about Christopher Columbus? Any record of his death in 1489?"

"But he discovered the New World in 1492."

"He did not. He was murdered in 1489."

"How?"

"With a forty-five slug in the gizzard."

"You again, Henry?"

"Yes."

"There's no record here," Library insisted. "You must be one lousy shot."

"I will not lose my temper," Hassel said in a trembling voice.

"Why not, Henry?"

"Because it's lost already," he shouted. "All right! What about Marie Curie? Did she or did she not discover the fission bomb which destroyed Paris at the turn of the century?"

"She did not. Enrico Fermi—"

"She did."

"She didn't."

"I personally taught her. Me. Henry Hassel."

"Everybody says you're a wonderful theoretician, but a lousy teacher, Henry. You—"

"Go to hell, you old biddy. This has got to be explained."

"Why?"

"I forget. There was something on my mind, but it doesn't matter now. What would you suggest?"

"You really have a time machine?"

"Of course I've got a time machine."

"Then go back and check."

Hassel returned to the year 1775, visited Mount Vernon and interrupted the spring planting. "Excuse me, Colonel," he began.

The big man looked at him curiously. "You talk funny, stranger," he said. "Where are you from?"

"Oh, a fresh-water school you never heard of."

"You look funny too. Kind of misty, so to speak."

"Tell me, Colonel, what do you hear from Christopher Columbus?"

"Not much," Colonel Washington answered. "Been dead two, three hundred years."

"When did he die?"

"Year fifteen hundred some-odd, near as I remember."

"He did not. He died in 1489."

"Got your dates wrong, friend. He discovered America in 1492."

"Cabot discovered America. Sebastian Cabot."

"Nope. Cabot came a mite later."

"I have infallible proof!" Hassel began, but broke off as a stocky and rather stout man, with a face ludicrously reddened by rage, approached. He was wearing baggy gray slacks and a tweed jacket two sizes too small for him. He was carrying a .45 revolver. It was only after he had stared for a moment that Henry Hassel realized that he was looking at himself and not relishing the sight.

"My God!" Hassel murmured. "It's me, coming back to murder Washington that first time. If I'd made this second trip an hour later, I'd have found Washington dead. Hey!" he called. "Not yet. Hold off a minute. I've got to straighten something out first."

Hassel paid no attention to himself; indeed, he did not appear to be aware of himself. He marched straight up to Colonel Washington and shot him in the gizzard. Colonel Washington collapsed, emphatically dead. The first murderer inspected the body, and then, ignoring Hassel's attempt to stop him and engage him in dispute, turned and marched off, muttering venomously to himself.

"He didn't hear me," Hassel wondered. "He didn't even feel me. And why don't I remember myself trying to stop me the first time I shot the colonel? What the hell is going on?"

Considerably disturbed, Henry Hassel visited Chicago and dropped into the Chicago University squash courts in the early 1940's. There, in a slippery mess of graphite bricks and graphite dust that coated him, he located an Italian scientist named Fermi.

"Repeating Marie Curie's work, I see, *dottore?*" Hassel said.

Fermi glanced about as though he had heard a faint sound.

"Repeating Marie Curie's work, *dottore?*" Hassel roared.

Fermi looked at him strangely. "Where you from, *amico?*"

"State."

"State Department?"

"Just State. It's true, isn't it, *dottore,* that Marie Curie discovered nuclear fission back in nineteen ought ought?"

"No! No! No!" Fermi cried. "We are the first, and we are not there yet. Police! Police! Spy!"

"This time I'll go on record," Hassel growled. He pulled out his trusty .45, emptied it into Dr. Fermi's chest and awaited arrest and immolation in newspaper files. To his amazement, Dr. Fermi did not collapse. Dr. Fermi merely explored his chest tenderly and, to the men who answered his cry, said, "It is nothing. I felt in my within a sudden sensation of burn which may be a neuralgia of the cardiac nerve, but is most likely gas."

Hassel was too agitated to wait for the automatic recall of the time machine. Instead he returned at once to Unknown University under his own power. This should have given him a clue, but he was too possessed to notice. It was at this time that I (1913-1975) first saw him—a dim figure tramping through parked cars, closed doors and brick walls, with the light of lunatic determination on his face.

He oozed into the library, prepared for an exhaustive discussion, but could not make himself felt or heard by the catalogs. He went to the Malpractice Laboratory, where Sam, the Simplex-and-Multiplex Computer, has installations sensitive up to 10,700 angstroms. Sam could not see Henry, but managed to hear him through a sort of wave-interference phenomenon.

"Sam," Hassel said, "I've made one hell of a discovery."

"You're always making discoveries, Henry," Sam complained. "Your data allocation is filled. Do I have to start another tape for you?"

"But I need advice. Who's the leading authority on time, reference to succession of, travel in?"

"That would be Israel Lennox, spatial mechanics, professor of, Yale."

"How do I get in touch with him?"

"You don't, Henry. He's dead. Died in '75."

"What authority have you got on time, travel in, living?"

"Wiley Murphy."

"Murphy? From our own Trauma Department? That's a break. Where is he now?"

"As a matter of fact, Henry, he went over to your house to ask you something."

Hassel went home without walking, searched through his laboratory and study without finding anyone, and at last floated into the living room, where his redheaded wife was still in the arms of another man. (All this, you understand, had taken place within the space of a few moments after the construction of the time machine; such is the nature of time and time travel.) Hassel cleared his throat once or twice and tried to tap his wife on the shoulder. His fingers went through her.

"Excuse me, darling," he said. "Has Wiley Murphy been in to see me?"

Then he looked closer and saw that the man embracing his wife was Murphy himself.

"Murphy!" Hassel exclaimed. "The very man I'm looking for. I've had the most extraordinary experience." Hassel at once launched into a lucid description of his extraordinary experience, which went something like this: "Murphy, $u - v = (u^{1/2} - v^{1/4})(u^a + u^x v^y + v^b)$ but when George Washington F (x) $y^2 \emptyset dx$ and Enrico Fermi F $(u^{1/2})$ dxdt one half of Marie Curie, then what about Christopher Columbus times the square root of minus one?"

Murphy ignored Hassel, as did Mrs. Hassel. I jotted down Hassel's equations on the hood of a passing taxi.

"Do listen to me, Murphy," Hassel said. "Greta dear, would you mind leaving us for a moment? I— For heaven's sake, will you two stop that nonsense? This is serious."

Hassel tried to separate the couple. He could no more touch them than make them hear him. His face turned red again, and he became quite choleric as he beat at Mrs. Hassel and Murphy. It was like beating an Ideal Gas. I thought it best to interfere.

"Hassel!"

"Who's that?"

"Come outside a moment. I want to talk to you."

He shot through the wall. "Where are you?"

"Over here."

"You're sort of dim."

"So are you."

"Who are you?"

"My name's Lennox, Israel Lennox."

"Israel Lennox, spatial mechanics, professor of, Yale?"

"The same."

"But you died in '75."

"I disappeared in '75."

"What d'you mean?"

"I invented a time machine."

"By God! So did I," Hassel said. "This afternoon. The idea came to me in a flash—I don't know why—and I've had the most extraordinary experience. Lennox, time is not a continuum."

"No?"

"It's a series of discrete particles—like pearls on a string."

"Yes?"

"Each pearl is a 'Now.' Each 'Now' has its own past and future. But none of them relate to any others. You see? If a $= a_1 + a_2ji + \text{\o}ax(b_1)$—"

"Never mind the mathematics, Henry."

"It's a form of quantum transfer of energy. Time is emitted in discrete corpuscles or quanta. We can visit each individual quantum and make changes within it, but no change in any one corpuscle affects any other corpuscle. Right?"

"Wrong," I said sorrowfully.

"What d'you mean—'Wrong'?" he said, angrily gesturing through the cleavage of a passing coed. "You take the trochoid equations and—"

"Wrong," I repeated firmly. "Will you listen to me, Henry?"

"Oh, go ahead," he said.

"Have you noticed that you've become rather insubstantial? Dim? Spectral? Space and time no longer affect you?"

"Yes."

"Henry, I had the misfortune to construct a time machine back in '75."

"So you said. Listen, what about power input? I figure I'm using about 7.3 kilowatts per—"

"Never mind the power input, Henry. On my first trip into the past, I visited the Pleistocene. I was eager to photograph the mastodon, the giant ground sloth and the saber-tooth tiger. While I was backing up to get a mastodon fully in the field of view at f/6.3 at 1/100th of a second, or on the LVS scale—"

"Never mind the LVS scale," he said.

"While I was backing up, I inadvertently trampled and killed a small Pleistocene insect."

"Aha!" said Hassel.

"I was terrified by the incident. I had visions of returning to my world to find it completely changed as a result of this single death. Imagine my surprise when I returned to my world to find that nothing had changed."

"Oho!" said Hassel.

"I became curious. I went back to the Pleistocene and killed the mastodon. Nothing was changed in 1975. I returned to the Pleistocene and slaughtered the wildlife—still with no effect. I ranged through time, killing and destroying, in an attempt to alter the present."

"Then you did it just like me," Hassel exclaimed. "Odd we didn't run into each other."

"Not odd at all."

"I got Columbus."

"I got Marco Polo."

"I got Napoleon."

"I thought Einstein was more important."

"Mohammed didn't change things much—I expected more from *him*."

"I know. I got him too."

"What do you mean, you got him too?" Hassel demanded.

"I killed him September 16, 599. Old Style."

"Why, I got Mohammed January 5, 598."

"I believe you."

"But how could you have killed him after I killed him?"

"We both killed him."

"That's impossible."

"My boy," I said, "time is entirely subjective. It's a private matter—a personal experience. There is no such thing as objective time, just as there is no such thing as objective love, or an objective soul."

"Do you mean to say that time travel is impossible? But we've done it."

"To be sure, and many others, for all I know. But we each travel into our own past, and no other person's. There is no universal continuum, Henry. There are only billions of individuals, each with his own continuum; and one continuum cannot affect the other. We're like millions of strands of spaghetti in the same pot. No time traveler can ever meet another time traveler in the past or future. Each of us must travel up and down his own strand alone."

"But we're meeting each other now."

"We're no longer time travelers, Henry. We've become the spaghetti sauce."

"Spaghetti sauce?"

"Yes. You and I can visit any strand we like, because we've destroyed ourselves."

"I don't understand."

"When a man changes the past he only affects his own past—no one else's. The past is like memory. When you erase a man's memory, you wipe him out, but you don't wipe out anybody else. You and I have erased our past. The individual worlds of the others go on, but we have ceased to exist." I paused significantly.

"What d'you mean—'ceased to exist'?"

"With each act of destruction we dissolved a little. Now we're all gone. We've committed chronicide. We're ghosts. I hope Mrs. Hassel will be very happy with Mr. Murphy. . . . Now let's go over to the Académie. Ampère is telling a great story about Ludwig Boltzmann."

THEODORE STURGEON

The Man Who Lost the Sea

"The Man Who Lost the Sea" contains all of the attributes that made Theodore Sturgeon (1918-) one of the finest stylists in science fiction—at least one fully developed character, poetic writing and a deep concern for the nature of love in all its permutations. Sturgeon was a major figure in sf from his debut in 1939 until the mid-1970s, when his typewriter grew relatively silent. In fact, he was for many years the most reprinted writer in science fiction. His More than Human (1953) is considered one of the landmark books in the development of the field.

S AY YOU'RE a kid, and one dark night you're running along the cold sand with this helicopter in your hand, saying very fast *witchy-witchy-witchy*. You pass the sick man and he wants you to shove off with that thing. Maybe he thinks you're too old to play with toys. So you squat next to him in the sand and tell him it isn't a toy, it's a model. You tell him look here, here's something most people don't know about helicopters. You take a blade of the rotor in your fingers and show him how it can move in the hub, up and down a little, back and forth a little, and twist a little, to change pitch. You start to tell him how this flexibility does away with the gyroscopic effect, but he won't listen. He doesn't want to think about flying, about helicopters, or about you, and he most especially does not want explanations about anything by anybody. Not now. Now, he wants to think about the sea. So you go away.

The sick man is buried in the cold sand with only his head and his left arm showing. He is dressed in a pressure suit and looks like a man from Mars. Built into his left sleeve is a combination timepiece and pressure gauge, the gauge with a luminous blue indicator which makes no sense, the clock-hands luminous red. He can hear the pounding of surf and the soft swift pulse of his pumps. One time long ago when he was swimming he went too deep and stayed down too long and came up too fast, and when he came to it was like this: they said, "Don't move, boy. You've got the bends. Don't even *try* to move." He had tried anyway. It hurt. So now, this time, he lies in the sand without moving, without trying.

His head isn't working right. But he knows clearly that it isn't working right, which is a strange thing that happens to people in shock sometimes. Say you were that kid, you could say how it was, because once you woke up lying in the gym office in high school and asked what had happened. They explained how you tried something on the parallel bars and fell on your head. You understood exactly, though you couldn't remember falling. Then a minute later you asked again what had happened and they told you. You understood it. And a minute later . . . forty-one times they told you, and you understood. It was just that no matter how many times they pushed it into your head, it wouldn't stick there; but all the while you *knew* that your head would start working again in time. And in time it did . . . . . Of course, if you were that kid, always explaining things to people and to yourself, you wouldn't want to bother the sick man with it now.

Look what you've done already, making him send you away with that angry shrug of the mind (which, with the eyes, are the only things which will move just now). The motionless effort costs him a wave of nausea. He has felt seasick before but he has never *been* seasick, and the formula for that is to keep your eyes on the horizon and stay busy. Now! Then he'd better get busy — now; for there's one place especially not to be seasick in, and that's locked up in a pressure suit. Now!

So he busies himself as best he can, with the seascape, landscape, sky. He lies on high ground, his head propped on a vertical wall of black rock. There is another such outcrop before him, whip-topped with white sand and with smooth flat sand. Beyond and down is valley, salt-flat, estuary; he cannot yet be sure. He is sure of the line of footprints, which begin behind him, pass to his left, disappear in the outcrop shadows and reappear beyond to vanish at last into the shadows of the valley.

Stretched across the sky is old mourning cloth, with starlight burning holes in it, and between the holes the black is absolute — wintertime, mountaintop sky-black.

(Far off on the horizon within himself, he sees the swell and crest of approaching nausea; he counters with an undertow of weakness, which meets and rounds and settles the wave before it can break. Get busier. *Now.*)

Burst in on him, then, with the X-15 model. That'll get him. Hey, how about this for a gimmick? Get too high for the thin air to give you any control, you have these little jets in the wingtips, see? and on the sides of the *empennage:* bank, roll, yaw, whatever, with squirts of compressed air.

But the sick man curls his sick lip: oh, git, kid, git, will you? — that has nothing to do with the sea. So you git.

Out and out the sick man forces his view, etching all he sees with a meticulous intensity, as if it might be his charge, one day, to duplicate all this. To his left is only starlit sea, windless. In front of him across the valley, rounded hills with dim white epaulettes of light. To his right, the jutting corner of the black wall against which his helmet rests. He thinks the distant moundings of nausea becalmed, but he will not look yet. So he scans the sky, black and bright, calling Sirius, calling Pleiades, Polaris, Ursa Minor, calling that . . . that . . . . Why, it *moves.* Watch it: yes, it moves! It is a fleck of light, seeming to be wrinkled, fissured rather like a chip of boiled cauliflower in the sky. (Of course, he knows better than to trust his own eyes just now.) But that movement...

As a child he had stood on cold sand in a frosty Cape Cod evening, watching Sputnik's steady spark rise out of the haze (madly, dawning a little north of west); and after that he had sleeplessly wound special coils for his receiver, risked his life restringing high antennas, all for the brief capture of an unreadable *tweetle-eep-tweetle* in his earphones from Vanguard, Explorer, Lunik, Discoverer, Mercury. He knew them all (well, some people collect match covers, stamps) and he knew especially that unmistakable steady sliding in the sky.

This moving fleck was a satellite, and in a moment, motionless, uninstrumented but for his chronometer and his part-brain, he will know which one. (He is grateful beyond expression—without that sliding chip of light there were only those footprints, those wandering footprints, to tell a man he was not alone in the world.)

Say you were a kid, eager and challengeable and more than a little bright, you might in a day or so work out a way to measure the period of a satellite with nothing but a timepiece and a brain; you might eventually see that the shadow in the rocks ahead had been there from the first only because of the light from the rising satellite. Now if you check the time exactly at the moment when the shadow on the sand is equal to the height of the outcrop, and time it again when the light is at the zenith and the shadow gone, you will multiply this number of minutes by 8—think why, now: horizon to zenith is one-fourth of the orbit, give or take a little, and halfway up the sky is half that quarter—and you will then know this satellite's period. You know all the periods—ninety minutes, two, two-and-a-half hours; with that and the appearance of this bird, you'll find out which one it is.

But if you were that kid, eager or resourceful or whatever, you wouldn't jabber about it to the sick man, for not only does he not want to be bothered with you, he's thought of all that long since and is even now watching the shadows for that triangular split second of measurement. *Now!* His eyes drop to the face of his chronometer: 0400, near as makes no never mind.

He has minutes to wait now—ten?...thirty?...twenty-three?—while this baby moon eats up its slice of shadowpie; and that's too bad, the waiting, for though the inner sea is calm there are currents below, shadows that shift and swim. Be busy. Be busy. He must not swim near that great invisible amoeba whatever happens: its first cold pseudopod is even now reaching for the vitals.

Being a knowledgeable young fellow, not quite a kid any more, wanting to help the sick man too, you want to tell him everything you know about that cold-in-the-gut, that reaching invisible surrounding implacable amoeba. You know all about it—listen, you want to yell at him, don't let that touch of cold bother you. Just know what it is, that's all. Know what it is that is touching your gut. You want to tell him, listen:

Listen, this is how you met the monster and dissected it. Listen, you were skin-diving in the Grenadines, a hundred tropical shoalwater islands; you had a new blue snorkel mask, the kind with face plate and breathing tube all in one, and new blue flippers on your feet, and a new blue spear gun—all this new because you'd only begun, you see; you were a beginner, aghast with pleasure at your easy intrusion into this underwater otherworld. You'd been out in a boat, you were coming back, you'd just reached the mouth of the little bay, you'd taken the notion to swim the rest of the way. You'd said as much to the boys and slipped into the warm silky water. You brought your gun.

Not far to go at all, but then beginners find wet distances deceiving. For the first five minutes or so it was only delightful, the sun hot on your back and the water so warm it seemed not to have any temperature at all and you were flying. With your face under the water, your mask was not so much attached as part of you, your wide blue flippers trod away yards, your gun rode all but weightless in your hand, the taut rubber sling making an occasional hum as your passage plucked it in the sunlit green. In your ears crooned the breathy monotone of the snorkel tube and through the invisible disk of plate glass you saw wonders. The bay was shallow—ten, twelve feet or so—and sandy, with great growths of brain-, bone- and fire-coral, intricate waving sea fans, and fish—such fish! Scarlet and green and aching azure, gold and rose and slate-color studded with sparks of enamel blue, pink and peach and silver. And that *thing* got into you, that... monster.

There were enemies in this otherworld: the sandcolored spotted sea snake with his big ugly head and turned-down mouth, who would not retreat but lay watching the intruder pass; and the mottled moray with jaws like bolt cutters; and somewhere around, certainly, the barracuda with his undershot face and teeth turned inward so that he must take away whatever he might strike. There were urchins—the plump white sea egg with its thick fur of sharp quills and the black ones with the long slender spines that would break off in unwary flesh and fester there for weeks; and filefish and stonefish with their poisoned barbs and lethal meat; and the stingaree who could drive his spike through a leg bone. Yet these were not *monsters*, and could not matter to you, the invader churning along above them all. For you were above them in so many ways—armed, rational, comforted by the close shore (ahead the beach, the rocks on each side) and by the presence of the boat not too far behind. Yet you were... attacked.

At first it was uneasiness, not pressing, but pervasive, a contact quite as intimate as that of the sea; you were sheathed in it. And also there was the touch—the cold inward contact. Aware of it at last, you laughed: for Pete's sake, what's there to be scared of?

The monster, the amoeba.

You raised your head and looked back in air. The boat had edged in to the cliff at the right; someone was giving a last poke around for lobster. You waved at the boat; it was your gun you waved, and emerging from the water it gained its latent ounces so that you sank a bit, and as if you had no snorkel on, you tipped your head back to get a breath. But tipping your head back plunged the end of the tube under water; the valve closed; you drew in a hard lungful of nothing at all. You dropped your face under; up came the tube; you got your air, and along with it a bullet of seawater which struck you somewhere inside the throat. You coughed it out and floundered, sobbing as you sucked in air, inflating your chest until it hurt, and the air you got seemed no good, no good at all, a worthless devitalized inert gas.

You clenched your teeth and headed for the beach, kicking strongly and knowing it was the right thing to do; and then below and to the right you saw a great bulk mounding up out of the sand floor of the sea. You knew it was only the reef, rocks and coral and weed, but the sight of it made you scream; you didn't care what you knew. You turned hard left to avoid it, fought by as if it would reach for you, and you couldn't get air, couldn't get air, for all the unobstructed hooting of your snorkel tube. You couldn't bear the mask, suddenly, not for another second, so you shoved it upward clear of your mouth and rolled over, floating on your back and opening your mouth to the sky and breathing with a sort of quacking noise.

It was then and there that the monster well and truly engulfed you, mantling you round and about within itself—formless, borderless, the illimitible amoeba. The beach, mere yards away, and the rocky arms of the bay, and the not too distant boat—these you could identify but no longer distinguish, for they were all one and the same thing . . . the thing called unreachable.

You fought that way for a time, on your back, dangling the gun under and behind you and straining to get enough warm sunstained air into your chest. And in time some particles of sanity began to swirl in the roil of your mind, and to dissolve and tint it. The air pumping in and out of your square grinned frightened mouth began to be meaningful at last, and the monster relaxed away from you.

You took stock, saw surf, beach, a leaning tree. You felt the new scend of your body as the rollers humped to become breakers. Only a dozen firm kicks brought you to where you could roll over and double up; your shin struck coral with a lovely agony and you stood in foam and waded ashore. You gained the wet sand, hard sand, and ultimately with two more paces powered by bravado, you crossed high-water mark and lay in the dry sand, unable to move.

You lay in the sand, and before you were able to move or to think, you were able to feel a triumph—a triumph because you were alive and knew that much without thinking at all.

When you *were* able to think your first thought was of the gun, and the first move you were able to make was to let go at last of the thing. You had nearly died because you had not let it go before; without it you would not have been burdened and you would not have panicked. You had (you began to understand) kept it because someone else would have had to retrieve it—easily enough—and you could not have stood the laughter. You had almost died because They might laugh at you.

This was the beginning of the dissection, analysis, study of the monster. It began then; it had never finished. Some of what you had learned from it was merely important; some of the rest—vital.

You had learned, for example, never to swim farther with a snorkel than you could swim back without one. You learned never to burden yourself with the unnecessary in an emergency; even a hand or a foot might be as expendable as a gun; pride was expendable, dignity was. You learned never to dive alone, even if they laugh at you, even if you have to shoot a fish yourself and say afterwards "we" shot it. Most of all, you learned that fear has many fingers, and one of them—a simple one, made of too great a concentration of carbon dioxide in your blood, as from too rapid breathing in and out of the same tube — is not really fear at all but feels like fear, and can turn into panic and kill you.

Listen, you want to say, listen, there isn't anything wrong with such an experience or with all the study it leads to, because a man who can learn enough from it could become fit enough, cautious enough, foresighted, unafraid, modest, teachable enough to be chosen, to be qualified for—

You lose the thought, or turn it away, because the sick man feels that could touch deep inside, feels it right now, feels it beyond ignoring, above and beyond anything that you, with all your experience and certainty, could explain to him even if he would listen, which he won't. Make him, then; tell him the cold touch is some simple explainable thing like anoxemia, alike gladness even: some triumph that he will be able to appreciate when his head is working right again.

Triumph? Here he's alive after... whatever it is, and that doesn't seem to be triumph enough, though it was in the Grenadines, and that other time, when he got the bends, saved his own life, saved two other lives. Now, somehow, it's not the same: there seems to be a reason why just being alive afterwards isn't a triumph.

Why not triumph? Because not twelve, not twenty, not even thirty minutes is it taking the satellite to complete its eighth-of-an-orbit: fifty minutes are gone, and still there's a slice of shadow yonder. It is this, *this* which is placing the cold finger upon his heart, and he doesn't know why, he doesn't know why, he *will* not know why; he is afraid he shall when his head is working again...

Oh, where's the kid? Where is any way to busy the mind, apply it to something, anything else but the watch hand which outruns the moon? Here, kid: come over here — what you got there?

If you were the kid, then you'd forgive everything and hunker down with your new model, not a toy, not a helicopter or a rocket-plane, but the big one, the one that looks like an overgrown cartridge. It's so big even as a model that even an angry sick man wouldn't call it a toy. A giant cartridge, but watch: the lower four-fifths is Alpha — all muscle — over a million pounds thrust. (Snap it off, throw it away.) Half the rest is Beta — all brains — it puts you on your way. (Snap it off, throw it away.) And now look at the polished fraction which is left. Touch a control somewhere and see — see? it has wings — wide triangular wings. This is Gamma, the one with wings, and on its back is a small sausage; it is a moth with a sausage on its back. The sausage (click! it comes free) is Delta. Delta is the last, the smallest: Delta is the way home.

What will they think of next? Quite a toy. Quite a boy. Beat it, kid. The satellite is almost overhead, the sliver of shadow going — going — almost gone and ... gone.

Check: 0459. Fifty-nine minutes?, give or take a few. Time eight ... 472 ... is, uh, 7 hours, 52 minutes.

Seven hours fifty-two minutes? Why there isn't a satellite round earth with a period like that. In all the solar system there's only ...

The cold finger turns fierce, implacable.

The east is paling and the sick man turns to it, wanting the light, the sun, an end to questions whose answers couldn't be looked upon. The sea stretches endlessly out to the growing light, and endlessly, somewhere out of sight, the surf roars. The paling east bleaches the sandy hilltops and throws the line of footprints into aching relief. That would be the buddy, the sick man knows, gone for help. He can not at the moment recall who the buddy is, but in time he will, and meanwhile the footprints make him less alone.

The sun's upper rim thrusts itself above the horizon with a flash of green, instantly gone. There is no dawn, just the green flash and then a clear white blast of unequivocal sunup. The sea could not be whiter, more still, if it were frozen and snow-blanketed. In the west, stars still blaze, and overhead the crinkled satellite is scarcely abashed by the growing light. A formless jumble in the valley below begins to resolve itself into a sort of tent-city, or installation of some kind, with tube-like and sail-like buildings. This would have meaning for the sick man if his head was working right. Soon, it would. Will. (Oh . . .)

The sea, out on the horizon just under the rising sun, is behaving strangely, for in that place where properly belongs a pool of unbearable brightness, there is instead a notch of brown. It is as if the white fire of the sun is drinking dry the sea—for look, look! the notch becomes a bow and the bow a crescent, racing ahead of the sunlight, white sea ahead of it and behind it a cocoa-dry stain spreading across and down toward where he watches.

Beside the finger of fear which lies on him, another finger places itself, and another, making ready for that clutch, that grip, that ultimate insane squeeze of panic. Yet beyond that again, past that squeeze when it comes, to be savored if the squeeze is only fear and not panic, lies triumph—triumph, and a glory. It is perhaps this which constitutes his whole battle: to fit himself, prepare himself to bear the utmost that fear could do, for if he can do that, there is a triumph on the other side. But . . . not yet. Please, not yet awhile.

Something flies (or flew, or will fly—he is a little confused on this point) toward him, from the far right where the stars still shine. It is not a bird and it is unlike any aircraft on earth, for the aerodynamics are wrong. Wings so wide and so fragile would be useless, would melt and tear away in any of earth's atmosphere but the outer fringes. He sees then (because he prefers to see it so) that it is the kid's model, or part of it, and for a toy, it does very well indeed.

It is the part called Gamma, and it glides in, balancing, parallels the sand and holds away, holds away slowing, then settles, all in slow motion, throwing up graceful sheet fountains of fine sand from its skids. And it runs along the ground for an impossible distance, letting down its weight by the ounce and stingily the ounce, until *look out* until a skid *look out* fits itself into a bridged crevasse *look out, look out!* and still moving on, it settles down to the struts. Gamma then, tired, digs her wide left wingtip carefully into the racing sand, digs it in hard; and as the wing breaks off, Gamma slews, sidles, slides slowly, pointing her other triangular tentlike wing at the sky, and broadside crushes into the rocks at the valley's end.

As she rolls smashing over, there breaks from her broad back the sausage, the little Delta, which somersaults away to break its back upon the rocks, and through the broken hull, spill smashed shards of graphite from the moderator of her power pile. *Look out! Look out!* and at the same instant from the finally checked mass of

Gamma there explodes a doll, which slides and tumbles into the sand, into the rocks and smashed hot graphite from the wreck of Delta.

The sick man numbly watches this toy destroy itself: what will they think of next?—and with a gelid horror prays at the doll lying in the raging rubble of the atomic pile: *don't stay there, man—get away! get away! that's hot, you know?* But it seems like a night and a day and half another night before the doll staggers to its feet and, clumsy in its pressure-suit, runs away up the valleyside, climbs a sand-topped outcrop, slips, falls, lies under a slow cascade of cold ancient sand until, but for an arm and the helmet, it is buried.

The sun is high now, high enough to show the sea is not a sea, but brown plain with the frost burned off it, as now it burns away from the hills, diffusing in air and blurring the edges of the sun's disk, so that in a very few minutes there is no sun at all, but only a glare in the east. Then the valley below loses its shadows, and like an arrangement in a diorama, reveals the form and nature of the wreckage below: no tent-city this, no installation, but the true real ruin of Gamma and the eviscerated hulk of Delta. (Alpha was the muscle, Beta the brain; Gamma was a bird, but Delta, Delta was the way home.)

And from it stretches the line of footprints, to and by the sick man, above to the bluff, and gone with the sandslide which had buried him there. Whose footprints?

He knows whose, whether or not he knows that he knows, or wants to or not. He knows what satellite has (give or take a bit) a period like that (want it exactly?— it's 7.66 hours). He knows what world has such a night, and such a frosty glare by day. He knows these things as he knows how spilled radio-actives will pour the crash and mutter of surf into a man's earphones.

Say you were that kid: say, instead, at last, that you are the sick man, for they are the same; surely then you can understand why of all things, even while shattered, shocked, sick with radiation calculated (leaving) radiation computed (arriving) and radiation past all bearing (lying in the wreckage of Delta) you would want to think of the sea. For no farmer who fingers the soil with love and knowledge, no poet who sings of it, artist, contractor, engineer, even child bursting into tears at the inexpressible beauty of a field of daffodils—none of these is as intimate with Earth as those who live on, live with, breathe and drift in its seas. So of these things you must think; with these you must dwell until you are less sick and more ready to face the truth.

The truth, then, is that the satellite fading here is Phobos, that those footprints are your own, that there is no sea here, that you have crashed and are killed and will in a moment be dead. The cold hand ready to squeeze and still your heart is not anoxia or even fear, it is death. Now, if there is something more important than this, now is the time for it to show itself.

The sick man looks at the line of his own footprints, which testify that he is alone, and at the wreckage below, which states that there is no way back, and at the white east and the mottled west and the paling bleek-like satellite above. Surf sounds in his ears. He hears his pumps. He hears what is left of his breathing. The cold clamps down and folds him round past measuring, past all limits.

Then he speaks, cries out: then with joy he takes his triumph at the other side of death, as one takes a great fish, as one completes a skilled and mighty task, rebalances at the end of some great daring leap; and as he used to say "we shot a fish" he uses no "I":

"God," he cries, dying on Mars, "God, we made it!"

FRED SABERHAGEN

Goodlife

One of the staples of science fiction publishing is the series story, and readers obviously enjoy meeting the same characters in the same settings time after time. "Goodlife" is such a story, but the series of which it is a part is unique—the continuing characters are "Berserkers," huge spacecraft programmed to be perfect killing machines, and their targets are any living beings they encounter. Their creator, Fred Saberhagen (1930-), is a Chicago-born writer, currently residing in Albuquerque, New Mexico, who is not at all like his creations.

I

"It's only a machine, Hemphill," said the dying man in a small voice. Hemphill, drifting weightless in near-darkness, heard him with only faint contempt and pity. Let the wretch go out timidly forgiving the universe everything, if he found the going-out easier that way!

Hemphill kept on staring out through the port, at the dark crenelated shape that blotted out so many of the stars.

There was probably just this one compartment of the passenger ship left livable, with three people on it, and the air whining out in steady leaks that would soon exhaust the emergency tanks. The ship was a wreck, torn and beaten, yet Hemphill's view of the enemy was steady. It must be a force of the enemy's that kept the wreck from spinning.

Now the young woman, another passenger, came drifting across the compartment to touch Hemphill on the arm. He thought her name was Maria something.

"Listen," she began. "Do you think we might—"

In her voice there was no despair, but the tone of planning; and so Hemphill had begun to listen to her. But she was interrupted.

The very walls of the cabin reverberated, driven like speaker diaphragms through the power of the enemy forcefield that still gripped the butchered hull. The voice of the berserker machine came:

391

"You who can still hear me, live on. I plan to spare you. I am sending a boat to save you from death."

The voice changed tones from word to word, being fragments of the voices of human prisoners the machine had taken and used. It was made of bits of human emotion sorted and fixed, like butterflies on pins. Hemphill was sick with frustrated rage. He had never heard a berserker's voice in reality before, but still it was familiar as an old nighmare. He could feel the woman's hand pull away from his arm, and then he saw that in his rage he had raised both his hands to be claws, then fists that almost smashed themselves against the port. The thing, the damned thing wanted to take him inside it! Of all people in space it wanted to make him prisoner!

A plan rose instantly in his mind and flowed smoothly into action; he spun away from the port. There were warheads, for small defensive missiles, here in this compartment. He remembered seeing them.

The other surviving man, a ship's officer, dying slowly, bleeding through his uniform tatters, saw what Hemphill was doing in the wreckage, and drifted in front of him interferingly.

"You can't do that...you'll only destroy the boat it sends...if it lets you do that much...there may be other people...still alive here..."

The man's face had been upside down before Hemphill as the two of them drifted. As their movements let them see each other in normal position, the wounded man stopped talking, gave up and rotated himself away, drifting inertly as if already dead.

Hemphill could not hope to manage a whole warhead, but he could extract the chemical-explosive detonator, of a size to carry under one arm. All passengers had put on emergency spacesuits when the unequal battle had begun; now he found himself an extra air tank, and some officer's laser pistol, which he stuck in a loop of his suit's belt.

The girl approached him again. He watched her warily.

"Do it," she said with quiet conviction, while the three of them spun slowly in the near-darkness, and the air leaks whined. "Do it. The loss of a boat will weaken it, a little, for the next fight. And we here have no chance anyway."

"Yes." He nodded approvingly. This girl understood what was important: To hurt a berserker, to smash, burn, destroy, to kill it finally. Nothing else mattered very much.

He pointed to the wounded mate, and whispered: "Don't let him give me away." She nodded silently. It might hear them talking. If it could speak through these walls, it could be listening.

"A boat's coming," said the wounded man, in a calm and distant voice.

"Goodlife!" called the machine voice cracking between syllables, as always.

"Here!" He woke up with a start, and got quickly to his feet. He had been dozing almost under the dripping end of a drinking-water pipe.

"Goodlife!" There were no speakers or scanners in this little compartment; the call came from some distance away.

"Here!" He ran toward the call, his feet shuffling and thumping on metal. He had dozed off, being tired. Even though the battle had been a little one, there had been extra tasks for him, servicing and directing the commensal machines that roamed the endless ducts and corridors repairing damage. It was small help he could give, he knew.

Now his head and neck bore sore spots from the helmet he had had to wear; and his body was chafed in places from the unaccustomed covering he had to put on it when a battle came. This time, happily, there had been no battle damage at all.

He came to the flat glass eye of a scanner, and shuffled to a stop, waiting.

"Goodlife, the perverted machine has been destroyed, and the few badlives left are helpless."

"Yes!" He jiggled his body up and down in happiness.

"I remind you, life is evil," said the voice of the machine.

"Evil is life, I am Goodlife!" he said quickly, ceasing his jiggling. He did not think punishment impended, but he wanted to be sure.

"Yes. Like your parents before you, you have been useful. Now I plan to bring other humans inside myself, to study them closely. Your next use will be with them, in my experiments. I remind you, they are badlife. We must be careful."

"Badlife." He knew they were creatures shaped like himself, existing in the world beyond the machine. They caused the shudders and shocks and damage that made up a battle. "Badlife—here." It was a chilling thought. He raised his own hands and looked at them, then turned his attention up and down the passage in which he stood, trying to visualize the badlife become real before him.

"Go now to the medical room," said the machine. "You must be immunized against disease before you approach the badlife."

Hemphill made his way from one ruined compartment to another, until he found a gash in the outer hull that was plugged nearly shut. While he wrenched on the obstructing material, he heard the clanging arrival of the berserker's boat, come for prisoners. He pulled harder, the obstruction gave, and he was blown out into space.

Around the great wreck were hundreds of pieces of flotsam, held near by tenuous magnetism or perhaps by the berserker's forcefields. Hemphill found that his suit worked well enough. With its tiny jet he moved around the shattered hull to where the boat had come to rest.

The dark blot of the berserker machine came into view against the starfields of deep space, battlemented like a fortified city of old, and far larger than any such city had ever been.

He could see that the berserker's boat had somehow found the right compartment and clamped itself to the wrecked hull. It would be gathering in Maria and the wounded man. Fingers on the plunger that would set off his bomb, Hemphill drifted closer.

On the brink of death, it annoyed him that he would never know with certainty that the boat was destroyed. And it was such a trifling blow to strike, such a small revenge.

Still drifting closer, holding the plunger ready, he saw the puff of decompressed air-moisture as the boat disconnected itself from the hull. The invisible forcefields of the berserker surged, tugging at the boat, at Hemphill, at bits of wreckage within yards of the boat.

He managed to clamp himself to the boat before it was pulled away from him. He thought he had an hour's air in his suit tank, more than he would need.

The berserker pulled him toward itself.

II

The berserkers were relics of some ancient galactic war, some internecine struggle between unheard of races. They were machines set to seek out and destroy life, and each of them bore weapons that could sterilize an Earth-sized planet in two or three days.

Earthmen had spread out among the stars of a little section of an arm of the galactic spiral. Now they reeled back under the emotionless assault of the machines; planets and whole systems were depopulated.

Men fought back when they could. The passenger ship, intercepted far from help, had had no chance; but three or four warships could circle a berserker machine like wolves around a bear, could match missiles and computer speeds with it for long minutes, and—sometimes—could win. For the enemy was old, and damaged by warfare through unknown centuries and systems. Possibly many of them had been destroyed before their swarm descended upon Earthmen. The machines surviving had learned, as machines can learn, to avoid tactical error, and to never forgive the mistakes of an opponent. Their basic built-in order was the destruction of all life encountered. But each machine's strategic schemes were unpredictable, being controlled by the random atomic disintegrations of some longlived radioactive isotope, buried in the center of the mechanism.

Hemphill's mind hung over the brink of death, as his fingers held the plunger of his bomb. The nightcolored enemy was death in his mind; old as a meteorite, a hundred miles or more around its bulging middle. The black scarred surface of it hurtled closer in the unreal starlight, becoming a planet toward which the boat fell.

Hemphill still clung to the boat when it was pulled into an opening that could have accommodated many ships. The size and power of the berserker were all around the man, enough to overwhelm hate and courage alike.

His little bomb was a pointless joke. When the boat touched at a dark internal dock, Hemphill leaped into it and scrambled to find a hiding place.

As he cowered on a shadowed ledge of metal, his hand wanted to fire the bomb, simply to bring death and escape. He forced his hand to be still. He forced himself to watch while the two human prisoners were sucked from the boat through a pulsing transparent tube that passed through a bulkhead. Not knowing what he meant to accomplish, he pushed himself in the direction of the tube. He glided through the dark enormous cavern almost weightlessly; the berserker's mass was enough to give it a small natural gravity of its own.

Within ten minutes he came upon an unmistakable airlock. It seemed to have been cut with a surrounding section of hull from some Earth warship, and set into the bulkhead.

Inside an airlock would be as good a place for a bomb as he was likely to find. He got the outer door open and went in, apparently without triggering any alarms. If he destroyed himself here, he would deprive the berserker of—what? Why should it need an airlock at all?

Not for prisoners, thought Hemphill, if it sucks them in through a tube. Hardly an entrance built for enemies. He tested the air in the lock, and opened his helmet. For airbreathing friends, the size of men? That was a contradiction. Everything that lived and breathed must be a berserker's enemy—except, of course, the unknown beings who had sometimes built it, and loosed it to do what damage it might.

It was thought they were extinct, or unreachably distant in space and time. No defeated and boarded berserker had been found to carry a crew, or to have a place or purpose for a living crew.

The inner door of the lock opened and artificial gravity came on. Hemphill walked into a narrow and badly lighted passage, his fingers ready on the plunger.

"Go in, Goodlife," said the machine. "Look closely at each of them."

Goodlife made an uncertain sound in his throat, like a servomotor starting and stopping. He was gripped by a feeling resembling hunger, or the fear of punishment—because he was going to see life forms directly now, not as old images on a stage. Knowing the reason for the unpleasant feeling did not help. He stood hesitating outside the door of the room where the badlife was being kept. He had put on his suit again, as the machine had ordered. The suit would protect him if the badlife tried to damage him.

"Go in," the machine repeated.

"Maybe I'd better not," Goodlife said in misery, remembering to speak well and clearly. Punishment was always less likely when he did.

"Punish, punish," said the voice.

When it said the word twice, punishment was very near. As if already feeling in his bones the wrenching pain-that-left-no-damage, he opened the door quickly and stepped in.

He lay on the floor, bloody and damaged, in strange ragged suiting. And at the same time, he was still in the doorway. His own shape was on the floor, the same human form he knew, but now seen entirely from outside. More than an image, far more, it was himself now bi-located. There, here, himself, not himself—

Goodlife fell back against the door. He raised his arm and tried to bite it, forgetting his suit. He pounded his suited arms violently together, until there was bruised pain enough to nail him to himself where he stood.

Slowly, the terror subsided. Gradually his intellect could explain it and master it. This is me, here, here in the doorway. That, *there*, on the floor—that is another life. Another body, corroded like me with vitality. One far worse than I. That one on the floor is badlife.

Maria Juarez had prayed continuously for a long time, her eyes closed. Cold impersonal grippers had moved her this way and that. Her weight had come back, and there was air to breathe when her helmet and her suit had been carefully removed. She opened her eyes and struggled when the grippers began to remove her inner coverall; she saw that she was in a low-ceilinged room, surrounded by man-sized machines of various shapes. When she struggled they paused briefly; then gave up undressing her, chained to the wall by one ankle, and glided away. The dying mate had been dropped at the other end of the room, as if not worth the trouble of further handling.

The man with cold dead eyes, Hemphill, had tried to make a bomb, and failed. Now there would probably be no quick end to life—

When she heard the door operate she opened her eyes again, to watch without comprehension while the bearded young man in the ancient spacesuit went through senseless contortions in the doorway, and finally came forward to stand staring down at the dying man on the floor. The visitor's fingers moved with speed and precision when he raised his hands to the fasteners of his helmet; but the helmet's removal revealed ragged hair and beard framing an idiot's slack face.

He set the helmet down, then scratched and rubbed his hairy head, never taking his eyes from the man on the floor. He had not yet looked once at Maria, and she could look nowhere but at him. She had never seen a face so blank on a living person. This was what happened to a berserker's prisoner!

And yet—and yet Maria had seen the brainwashed, ex-criminals on her own planet. She felt this man was something more—or something less.

The bearded man knelt beside the mate, with an air of hesitation, and reached out to touch him. The dying man stirred feebly, and looked up with comprehension. The floor under him was wet with blood.

The stranger took the mate's limp arm and bent it back and forth, as if interested in the articulation of the human elbow. The mate groaned and struggled feebly. The stranger suddenly shot out his metal-gauntleted hands and seized the dying man by the throat.

Maria could not move or turn her eyes away, though the whole room seemed to spin slowly, then faster and faster, around the focus of those armored hands.

The bearded man released his grip and stood erect, still watching the body at his feet.

"Turned off," he said distinctly.

Perhaps she moved. For whatever reason, the bearded man raised his sleep-walker's face to look at her. He did not meet her eyes, or avoid them. His eye movements were quick and alert, but the muscles of his face just hung there under the skin. He came toward her.

Why, he's young, she thought. Hardly more than a boy. She backed against the wall and waited, standing. Women were not brought up to faint on her planet. Somehow, the closer he came, the less she feared him. But if he had smiled once she would have screamed, on and on.

He stood before her, and reached out one hand to touch her face, her hair, her body. She stood still; she felt no lust in him, no meanness and no kindness. It was as if he radiated an emptiness.

"Not images," said the young man as if to himself. Then another word, sounding like: "Badlife."

Almost Maria dared to speak to him. The strangled man lay on the deck a few yards away.

The young man turned and shuffled deliberately away. She had never seen anyone who walked just like him. He picked up his helmet and went out the door without looking back.

A pipe streamed water into one corner of her little space, where it gurgled away through a hole in the floor. The gravity seemed to be set at about Earth level. Maria sat leaning against the wall, praying and listening to her heart pound. It almost stopped when the door opened again; only a machine entered, to bring her a large cake of pink and green stuff that seemed to be food. The machine walked around the dead man on its way out.

She had eaten a little of the cake when the door opened again, very slightly at first, then enough for a man to step quickly in. It was Hemphill, the cold-eyed one from the ship, leaning a bit to one side as if dragged down by the weight of the little bomb he still carried under his arm. After a quick look around he shut the door behind him and crossed the room to her, hardly glancing down as he stepped over the body of the mate.

"How many of them are there?" Hemphill whispered, bending over her. She had remained seated on the floor, too surprised to move or speak.

"Who?" she finally managed.

He jerked his head impatiently. "Them. The ones who live here inside *it*, and serve it. I saw one of them coming out of the room, when I was out in the passage. It's fixed up a lot of breathing space for them."

He showed Maria how the bomb could be made to explode, and gave it to her to hold, while he began to burn through her chain with the laser pistol. They exchanged information on what had happened. She did not think she would ever be able to pull the plunger and kill herself, but she did not tell that to Hemphill.

III

Just as they stepped out of the prison room, Hemphill had a bad moment when three machines rolled toward them from around a corner. But the things ignored the two frozen humans and rolled silently past them, going on out of sight.

He turned to Maria with an exultant whisper: "The damned thing is three-quarters blind, here inside its own skin!"

She only waited, watching him with frightened eyes.

With the beginning of hope, a vague plan was forming in his mind. He led her on, saying: "Now we'll see about that man. Or men." Was it too good to be true, that there was only one of them?

The corridors were badly lit, with uneven jogs and steps in them. Carelessly built concessions to life, he thought. He moved in the direction he had seen the man take.

After a few minutes of cautious advance, Hemphill heard the shuffling footsteps of one person ahead, coming nearer. He handed the bomb to Maria again, and pressed her behind him. They waited in a dark niche.

The footsteps approached with careless speed, a vague shadow bobbing ahead of them. The shaggy head swung so abruptly into view that Hemphill's metal-fisted swing was almost too late. The blow only grazed the back of the skull; the man yelped and staggered off balance and fell down. He was wearing an old-model spacesuit, with no helmet.

Hemphill crouched over him, shoving the laser pistol almost into his face. "Make a sound and I'll kill you. Where are the others?"

The face looking up at Hemphill was stunned—worse than stunned. It seemed more dead than alive, though the eyes moved alertly enough from Hemphill to Maria and back, disregarding the gun.

"He's the same one," Maria whispered.

The man felt the back of his head, where he had been hit. "Damage," he said tonelessly, as if to himself. Then he reached up for the pistol, so calmly and steadily that he was nearly able to touch it.

Hemphill jumped back a step, and barely kept himself from firing. "Sit still or I'll kill you! Now tell me who you are, and how many others are here."

The man's putty face showed nothing. He said: "Your speech is steady in tone from word to word, not like that of the machine. You hold a killing tool there. Give it to me, and I will destroy you and—that one."

It seemed this man was only a brainwashed ruin, instead of an unspeakable traitor. Now what use could be made of him? Hemphill moved back another step, slowly lowering the pistol.

Maria spoke to their prisoner. "Where are you from? What planet?"

A blank stare.

She repeated the question in a couple of other languages, with no better result, then returned to the universal Loglan of Earth's spacemen and colonists.

"Your home. Where were you born?"

"From the birth tank." Sometimes the tones of the man's voice shifted like the berserker's, as if he were a fearful comedian mocking it.

Hemphill gave an unstable laugh. "From a birth tank, of course. What else? Where are the others?"

"I do not understand."

Hemphill sighed. "All right. Where's this birth tank?"

The place looked like the storeroom of a biology lab, badly lighted, with equipment piled and crowded, laced with pipes and conduits. But perhaps no living technician had ever worked here.

"You were *born* here?" Hemphill demanded.

"Yes."

"He's crazy."

"No, wait." Maria's voice sank to an even lower whisper, as if she was frightened anew. She took the hand of the slack-faced man, and he bent his head to stare at their touching hands.

"Do you have a name?" she asked, as if of a lost child.

"I am Goodlife."

"I think it's hopeless," put in Hemphill.

The girl ignored him. "Goodlife? My name is Maria. And this is Hemphill."

No reaction.

"Who were your parents? Father? Mother?"

"They were goodlife too. They helped the machine. There was a battle, and badlife killed them. But they had given cells of their bodies to the machine, and from them it made me. Now I am the only goodlife."

"Great God," whispered Hemphill.

Silent, awed attention seemed to move Goodlife when threats and pleas had not. His face moved in awkward grimaces; then he turned to stare into a corner. For almost the first time, he volunteered a communication: "I know they were like you. A man and a woman."

Hemphill wanted to sweep every cubic foot of the miles of mechanism with his hatred; he looked around.

"The damned things," he said, his voice cracking like the berserker's own. "What they've done to me. To you. To everyone."

Plans seemed to come when the strain of hating was greatest. He moved quickly to put a hand on Goodlife's shoulder. "Listen to me. Do you know what a radioactive isotope is?"

"Yes."

"There will be a place, somewhere, where the—the machine decides what it will do next—what strategy to follow. A place holding a block of some isotope with a long half-life. Probably near the center of the machine. Do you know of such a place?"

"Yes, I know where the strategic housing is."

"Strategic housing." Hope mounted to a strong new level. "Is there a way for us to reach it?"

"You are badlife!" He knocked Hemphill's hand away, awkwardly. "You want to damage the machine, and you have damaged me. You are to be destroyed."

Maria took over, trying to soothe. "Goodlife—we are not bad, this man and I. Those who built this machine are the badlife. Someone built it, you know, some living people built it, long ago. They were the real badlife."

"Badlife." He might be agreeing with Maria, or accusing her.

"Don't you want to live, Goodlife? Hemphill and I want to live. We want to help you, because you're alive, like us. Won't you help us now?"

Goodlife was silent for a few moments. Then he turned back to face them and said: "All life thinks it is, but it is not. There are only particles, energy and space, and the laws of the machines."

Maria kept at him. "Goodlife, listen to me. A wise man once said: 'I think, therefore I am.'"

"A wise man?" he questioned, in his cracking voice. Then he sat down on the deck, hugging his knees and rocking back and forth. He might be thinking.

Drawing Maria aside, Hemphill said: "You know, we have a faint hope now. There's plenty of air in here, there's water and food. There are warships following this thing, there must be. If we can find a way to disable it, we can wait and maybe be picked up in a month or two."

She watched him silently for a moment. "Hemphill—what have these machines done to you?"

"My wife—my children." He thought his voice sounded almost indifferent. "They were on Pascalo, three years ago; there was nothing left. This machine, or one like it."

She took his hand, as she had taken Goodlife's. They both looked down at the joined fingers, then raised their eyes, smiling briefly together at the similarity of action.

"Where's the bomb?" Hemphill thought aloud suddenly, spinning around.

It lay in a dim corner. He grabbed it up again, and strode over to where Goodlife sat and rocked.

"Well, are you with us? Us, or the ones who built the machine?"

Goodlife stood up, and looked closely at Hemphill. "They were inspired by the laws of physics, which controlled their brains, to build the machines. Now the machine has preserved them as images. It has preserved my father and mother, and it will preserve me."

"The images do you mean? Where are they?"

"The images in the theater."

The right course seemed to be to accustom him to cooperation, win his confidence, learn about him and the machine. Then, to the strategic housing.

"Will you guide us to the theater, Goodlife?"

It was by far the largest airfilled room they had yet found, with a hundred seats of a shape usable by Earthmen, though Hemphill guessed it had been built for someone else. The theater was elaborately furnished and well lighted. When the door closed behind them, the ranked images of intelligent creatures brightened into life upon the stage.

The stage became a window into a vast hall. One person stood forward at an imaged lectern; he was a slender, fine-boned being, topologically like a man except for the single eye that stretched across his face, with a bright bulging pupil that slid to and fro like mercury.

The speaker's voice was a high-pitched torrent of clicks and whines. Most of those in the ranks behind him wore a kind of uniform. When he paused, they whined in unison.

"What does he say?" Maria whispered.

Goodlife looked at her. "The machine has told me that it has lost the meaning of the sounds."

"Then may we see the images of your parents, Goodlife?"

Hemphill, watching the stage, started to object; but the girl was right. The sight of this fellow's parents might be more immediately helpful.

Goodlife found a control somewhere.

Hemphill was surprised momentarily that the parents appeared only in flat projected pictures. First the man was there, against a plain background, blue eyes and neat short beard, nodding his head with a pleasant expression on his face. He wore the lining coverall of a spacesuit.

Then the woman, holding some kind of cloth before her for covering, and looking straight into the camera. She had a broad face and red braided hair. There was hardly time to see anything more before the alien orator was back, whining faster than ever.

Hemphill turned to ask: "Is that all? All you know of your parents?"

"Yes. Now they are images, they no longer think they exist. The badlife killed them."

The creature in the projection was assuming, Maria thought, a more didactic tone. Three-dimensional charts of stars and planets appeared near him, one after another, and he gestured at them as he spoke. He had vast numbers of stars and planets on his charts to boast about; she could tell somehow that he was boasting.

Hemphill was moving toward the stage a step at a time, more and more absorbed. Maria did not like the way the light of the images reflected on his face.

Goodlife, too, watched the stage pageant which perhaps he had seen a thousand times before. Maria could not tell what thoughts might be behind his meaningless face which had never had another human face to imitate. On impulse she took his arm again.

"Goodlife, Hemphill and I are alive, like you. Will you help us now? Then we will always help you." She had a sudden mental picture of Goodlife rescued, taken to a planet, cowering among the staring badlife.

"Good. Bad." His hand reached to take hold of hers; he had removed his suit gauntlets. He swayed back and forth as if she attracted and repelled him at the same time. God, she wanted to scream and wail for him, to tear apart with her fingers the mindlessly proceeding metal that had made him what he was.

"We've got them!" It was Hemphill, coming back from the stage, where the recorded tirade went on unrelentingly. He was exultant. "Don't you see? He's showing what must be a complete catalogue, of every star and rock they own. It's a victory speech. But when we study those charts we can find them, we can track them down and *reach* them!"

"Hemphill." She wanted to calm him back to concentration on immediate problems. "How old are those—pictures, up there? What part of the galaxy do they show? Or were they even made in another galaxy? Will we ever be able to tell?"

Hemphill lost some enthusiasm. "Anyway, it's a chance to track them down; we've got to save this information." He pointed at Goodlife. "He's got to take me to what he calls the strategic housing; then we can sit and wait for the warships, or maybe get off this damned thing in a boat."

She stroked Goodlife's hand, soothing a baby. "Yes, but he's confused. How could he be anything else?"

"Of course." Hemphill paused to consider. "You can handle him much better than I."

She didn't answer.

Hemphill went on: "Now you're a woman, and he appears to be a physically healthy young male. Calm him down if you like, but somehow you've *got* to persuade him to help me. Everything depends on it." He had turned toward the stage again, unable to keep half his mind from the star charts. "Take him out somewhere, for a little walk and talk; don't get far away."

And what else was there to do? She led Goodlife from the theater while the dead man on the stage clicked and shouted, cataloguing his thousand suns.

IV

Too much had happened, was still happening, and all at once he could no longer stand to be near the badlife. Goodlife found himself pulling away from the female, running, flying down the passages, toward the place where he had fled when he was small and strange fears had come from nowhere. It was the room where the machine always saw and heard him, and was ready to talk to him.

He stood before the attention of the machine, in the chamber-that-has-shrunk. He thought of the place so, because he could remember it clearly as a larger room, where the scanners and speakers of the machine towered above his head. He knew the real change had been his own physical growth; still, this compartment was set apart in a special association with food and sleep and protective warmth.

"I have listened to the badlife, and shown them things," he said, fearing punishment.

"I know that, Goodlife, for I have watched. These things have become a part of my experiment."

What joyous relief! It said nothing of punishment, though it must know that the words of the badlife had shaken and confused him. He had even imagined himself showing the man Hemphill the strategic housing, and so putting an end to all punishment; for always.

"They wanted me—they wanted me to—"

"I have watched. I have listened. The man is tough and evil, powerfully motivated to fight against me. I must understand his kind, for they cause much damage. He must be tested to his limits, to destruction. He thinks himself free inside me, and so he will not think as a prisoner. This is important."

Goodlife pulled off his irritating suit; the machine would not let the badlife in here. He sank down to the floor and wrapped his arms around the base of a scanner-speaker console. Once long ago the machine had given him a thing that was soft and warm when he held it . . . he closed his eyes.

"What are my orders?" he asked, sleepily. Here in this chamber all was steady and comforting, as always.

"First, do not tell the badlife of these orders. Then, do what the man Hemphill tells you to do. No harm will come to me."

"I watched his approach, and I disabled his bomb, even before he entered to attack me. His pistol can do me no serious harm. Do you think one badlife can conquer me?"

"No." Smiling, reassured, he curled into a more comfortable position. "Tell me about my parents." He had heard the story a thousand times, but it was always good.

"Your parents were good, they gave themselves to me. Then, during a great battle, the badlife killed them. The badlife hated them, as they hate you. When they say they like you, they lie, with the evil untruth of all badlife.

"But your parents had each given me a part of their bodies, and from them I made you. Your parents were destroyed completely by the badlife, or I would have saved even their non-functioning bodies for you to see. That would have been good."

"Yes."

"The two badlives have searched for you; now they are resting. Sleep, Goodlife." He slept.

Awakening, he remembered a dream in which two people had beckoned him to join them on the stage of the theater. He knew they were his mother and father, though they looked like the two badlife. The dream faded before his waking mind could grasp it firmly.

He ate and drank, while the machine talked to him.

"If the man Hemphill wants to be guided to the strategic housing, take him there. I will capture him there, and let him escape later to try again. When finally he can be provoked to fight no more, I will destroy him. But I mean to preserve the life of the female; you and she will produce more goodlife for me."

"Yes!" It was immediately clear what a good thing that would be. They would give parts of their bodies to the machine, so new goodlife bodies could be built, cell by cell. And the man Hemphill, who punished and damaged with his fast-swinging arm, would be utterly destroyed.

When he rejoined the badlife, the man Hemphill barked questions and threatened punishment until Goodlife was confused and a little frightened. But Goodlife agreed to help, and was careful to reveal nothing of what the machine planned. Maria was more pleasant than ever. He touched her whenever he could.

Hemphill demanded to be taken to the strategic housing. Goodlife agreed at once; he had been there many times. There was a high-speed elevator that made the fifty-mile journey easy.

Hemphill paused, before saying: "You're too damn willing all of a sudden." Turning his face to Maria. "I don't trust him."

This badlife thought he was being false! Goodlife was angered; the machine never lied, and no properly obedient goodlife could lie.

Hemphill paced around, and finally demanded: "Is there any route that approaches this strategic housing in such a way that the machine cannot possibly watch us?"

Goodlife thought. "I believe there is one such way. We will have to carry extra tanks of air, and travel many miles through vacuum." The machine had said to help Hemphill, and help he would. He hoped he could watch when the male badlife was finally destroyed.

There had been a battle, in some time that could hardly be related meaningfully to any Earthly calendar. The berserker had fought some terrible opponent, and had taken a terrible lance-thrust of a wound. A cavity two miles wide at the widest, and fifty miles deep, had been driven in by a sequence of shaped atomic charges, through level after level of machinery, deck after deck of armor, and had been stopped only by the last inner defenses of the buried unliving heart. The berserker had survived, and crushed its enemy, and soon afterward its repair machines had sealed over the outer opening of the wound, using extra thicknesses of armor. It had meant to gradually rebuild the whole destruction; but there was so much life in the galaxy, and so much of it was stubborn and clever. Somehow battle damage accumulated faster than it could be repaired. The great hole was used as a conveyor path, and never much worked on.

When Hemphill saw the blasted cavity—what little of it his tiny suit-lamp could show—he felt a shrinking fear that was greater than any in his memory. He stopped on the edge of the void, drifting there with his arm instinctively around Maria. She had put on a suit and accompanied him, without protest or eagerness, without being asked.

It had already been an hour's journey from the airlock, through weightless vacuum inside the great machine. Goodlife had led the way through section after section, with every show of cooperation. Hemphill had the pistol ready, and the bomb, and two hundred feet of cord tied around his left arm.

But when Hemphill recognized the once-molten edge of the berserker's great scar for what it was, his delicate new hope of survival left him. This, the damned thing had survived. This, perhaps, had hardly weakened it. Again, the bomb under his arm was only a pathetic toy.

Goodlife drifted up to them. Hemphill had already taught him to touch helmets for speech in vacuum.

"This great damage is the one path we can take to reach the strategic housing without passing scanners or service machines. I will teach you to ride the conveyor. It will carry us most of the way."

The conveyor was a thing of forcefields and great rushing containers, hundreds of yards out in the Great Damage and running lengthwise through it. When the conveyor's forcefields caught the people up, their weightlessness was more than ever like falling, with occasional vast shapes, corpuscles of the berserker's bloodstream, flickering past in the near-darkness to show movement.

Hemphill flew beside Maria, holding her hand. Her face was hard to see inside the helmet, but she did not seem to be looking at him. There was no need.

This conveyor was another mad new world, a fairy tale of monsters and flying and falling. Hemphill fell past his great fear, into a calm determination.

I can do it, he thought. The thing is blind and helpless here. I will do it, and I will survive if I can.

Goodlife led them from the slowing conveyor, to drift into a chamber hollowed in the inner armor by the final explosion at the end of the ancient lance-thrust. The chamber was an empty sphere a hundred feet across, from which cracks radiated out into the solid armor. On the surface nearest the center of the berserker, one fissure was as wide as a door, where the last energy of the enemy's blow had driven ahead.

Goodlife touched helmets. "I have seen the other end of this crack, from inside, at the strategic housing. It is only a few yards from here." Hemphill hesitated for only a moment, wondering whether to send Goodlife through the twisting passage first. But if this was some incredibly complex trap, the trigger of it might be anywhere.

He touched his helmet to Maria's. "Stay behind him. Follow him through, and keep an eye on him."

The fissure narrowed as Hemphill followed it, but at the end it was still wide enough for him to force himself through.

This was the inner temple, and another great hollow sphere. In the center was a complexity the size of a small house, shock-mounted on a web of girders that ran in every direction. This could be nothing but the strategic housing. There was a glow from it like flickering moonlight; forcefield switches responding to the random atomic turmoil within, somehow choosing what human shipping lane or colony would be next attacked, and how.

Hemphill felt a pressure rising in his mind and soul, toward a climax of triumphal hate. He drifted forward, cradling his bomb tenderly, starting to unwind the cord wrapped around his arm. He tied the free end delicately to the plunger of the bomb, as he approached the central complex.

I mean to live, he thought, to watch the damned thing die. I will tape the bomb against the central block, that so-innocent looking slab in there, and I will brace myself around two hundred feet of these heavy metal corners, and pull.

Goodlife stood braced in the perfect place from which to watch the heart of the machine, watching the man Hemphill string his cord. Goodlife felt a certain satisfaction that his prediction had been right and that the strategic housing was approachable by this one narrow path of the great damage. They would not have to go back this way. When the badlife had been captured, all of them could ride up in the air-filled elevator Goodlife used when he came here for maintenance practice.

Hemphill had finished stringing his cord. Now he waved his arm at Goodlife and Maria, who clung to the same girder, watching. Now Hemphill pulled on the cord. Of course, nothing happened. The machine had said the bomb was disabled, and the machine would make very certain in such a matter.

Maria pushed away from beside Goodlife, and drifted in toward Hemphill.

Hemphill tugged again and again on his cord. Goodlife sighed impatiently, and moved. There was a great cold in the girders here; he could begin to feel it now through the fingers and toes of his suit.

At last, when Hemphill started back to see what was wrong with his device, the service machines came from where they had been hiding, to seize him. He tried to draw his pistol, but their grippers moved far too quickly.

It was hardly a struggle that Goodlife saw, but he watched with interest. Hemphill's figure had gone rigid in the suit, obviously straining every muscle to the limit. Why should the badlife try to struggle against steel and atomic power? The machines bore the man effortlessly away, toward the elevator shaft. Goodlife felt an uneasiness.

Maria was drifting, her face turned back toward Goodlife. He wanted to go to her and touch her again, but suddenly he was a little afraid, as before when he had run from her. One of the service machines came back from the elevator to grip her and carry her away. She kept her face turned toward Goodlife. He turned away from her, a feeling like punishment in the core of his being.

In the great cold silence, the flickering light from the strategic housing bathed everything. In the center, a chaotic block of atoms. Elsewhere, engines, relays, sensing cells. Where was it, really, the great machine that spoke to him? Everywhere, and nowhere. Would these new feelings, brought by the badlife, ever leave him? He tried to understand himself, and could not begin.

Light flickered on a round shape among the girders and a few yards away, a shape that offended Goodlife's sense of the proper and necessary in machinery. Looking closer, he saw that it was a space helmet.

The motionless figure was wedged only lightly in an angle between frigid beams, but there was no force in here to move it.

He could hear the suit creak, stiff with great cold, when he grabbed it and turned it. Unseeing blue eyes looked out at Goodlife through the faceplate. The man's face wore a neat short beard.

"Ahhh, yes," sighed Goodlife inside his own helmet. A thousand times he had seen this face.

His father had been carrying something, heavy, strapped carefully to his ancient suit. His father had carried it this far, until the old suit had wheezed and failed.

His father, too, had followed the logical narrow path of the great damage, to reach the strategic housing without being seen. His father had choked and died and frozen here, carrying toward strategic housing what could only be a bomb.

Goodlife heard his own voice keening, without words, and he could not see plainly for the tears floating in his helmet. His fingers felt numbed with cold as he unstrapped the bomb and lifted it from his father...

V

Hemphill was too exhausted to do more than gasp as the service machine carried him out of the elevator and along the air-filled corridor toward the prison room. When the machine went dead and dropped him, he had to lie still for long seconds before he could attack it again. It had hidden his pistol somewhere, so he began to beat on the robotlike thing with his armored fists, while it stood unresisting. Soon it toppled over. Hemphill sat on it and beat it some more, sobbing.

It was nearly a minute later when the tremor of the explosion, racing from the compounded chaos of the berserker's torn-out heart, racing through metal beams and decks, reached the corridor, where it was far too faint for anyone to feel.

Maria, completely weary, sat where her metal captor had dropped her, watching Hemphill, pitying him and loving him.

He stopped his pointless pounding of the machine under him, and said hoarsely: "It's a trick, another damned trick."

The tremor had been too faint for anyone to feel, here, but Maria shook her head. "No, I don't think so." She saw that power still seemed to be on the elevator, and she watched the door of it.

Hemphill went away to search among the now-purposeless machines for weapons and food. He came back, raging again. What was probably an automatic destructor charge had wrecked the theater and the star charts. They might as well get away in the boat.

She ignored him, still watching an elevator door which never opened. Soon she began quietly to cry.

PHILIP JOSÉ FARMER

The Sliced-Crosswise
Only-on-Tuesday World

Talking about Philip José Farmer (1918-　) is like talking about a dozen people. Not only has he produced the work of a dozen people—more than sixty novels and story collections in thirty years—but his work is always different and frequently brilliant. Farmer is generally credited with breaking the sexual taboos characteristic of American magazine science fiction with the publication of his novella "The Lovers" in 1952 and in subsequent stories. He also broke new ground with his "factions" on the private lives of such popular culture heroes as Tarzan and Doc Savage. Still active as ever, he lives in Peoria, Illinois.

"The Sliced-Crosswise-Only-on-Tuesday World" offers a fascinating solution to the problems of crowding and overpopulation.

GETTING INTO Wednesday was almost impossible.

Tom Pym had thought about living on other days of the week. Almost everybody with any imagination did. There were even TV shows speculating on this. Tom Pym had even acted in two of these. But he had no genuine desire to move out of his own world. Then his house burned down.

This was on the last day of the eight days of spring. He awoke to look out the door at the ashes and the firemen. A man in a white asbestos suit motioned for him to stay inside. After fifteen minutes, another man in a suit gestured that it was safe. He pressed the button by the door, and it swung open. He sank down in the ashes to his ankles; they were a trifle warm under the inch-thick coat of water-soaked crust.

There was no need to ask what had happened, but he did, anyway.

The fireman said, "A short-circuit, I suppose. Actually, we don't know. It started shortly after midnight, between the time that Monday quit and we took over."

Tom Pym thought that it must be strange to be a fireman or a policeman. Their hours were so different, even though they were still limited by the walls of midnight.

By then the others were stepping out of their stoners or "coffins" as they were often called. That left sixty still occupied.

They were due for work at 08:00. The problem of getting new clothes and a place to live should have to be put off until off-hours, because the TV studio where they worked was behind in the big special it was due to put on in 144 days.

They ate breakfast at an emergency center. Tom Pym asked a grip if he knew of any place he could stay. Though the government would find one for him, it might not look very hard for a convenient place.

The grip told him about a house only six blocks from his former house. A makeup man had died, and as far as he knew the vacancy had not been filled. Tom got onto the phone at once, since he wasn't needed at that moment, but the office wouldn't be open until ten, as the recording informed him. The recording was a very pretty girl with red hair, tourmaline eyes, and a very sexy voice. Tom would have been more impressed if he had not known her. She had played in some small parts in two of his shows, and the maddening voice was not hers. Neither was the color of her eyes.

At noon he called again, got through after a ten-minute wait, and asked Mrs. Bellefield if she would put through a request for him. Mrs. Bellefield reprimanded him for not having phoned sooner; she was not sure that anything could be done today. He tried to tell her his circumstances and then gave up. Bureaucrats! That evening he went to a public emergency place, slept for the required four hours while the inductive field speeded up his dreaming, woke up and got into the upright cylinder of eternium. He stood for ten seconds, gazing out through the transparent door at other cylinders with their still figures, and then he pressed the button. Approximately fifteen seconds later he became unconscious.

He had to spend three more nights in the public stoner. Three days of fall were gone; only five left. Not that that mattered in California so much. When he had lived in Chicago, winter was like a white blanket being shaken by a madwoman. Spring was a green explosion. Summer was a bright roar and a hot breath. Fall was the topple of a drunken jester in garish motley.

The fourth day, he received notice that he could move into the very house he had picked. This surprised and pleased him. He knew of a dozen who had spent a whole year—forty-eight days or so—in a public station while waiting. He moved in the fifth day with three days of spring to enjoy. But he would have to use up his two days off to shop for clothes, bring in groceries and other goods and get acquainted with his housemates. Sometimes, he wished he had not been born with the compulsion to act. TV'ers worked five days at a stretch, sometimes six, while a plumber, for instance, only put in three days out of seven.

The house was as large as the other, and the six extra blocks to walk would be good for him. It held eight people per day, counting himself. He moved in that evening, introduced himself and got Mabel Curta, who worked as a secretary for a producer, to fill him in on the household routine. After he made sure that his stoner had been moved into the stoner room, he could relax somewhat.

Mabel Curta had accompanied him into the stoner room, since she had appointed herself his guide. She was a short, overly curved woman of about thirty-five (Tuesday time). She had been divorced three times, and marriage was no more for her unless, of course, Mr. Right came along. Tom was between marriages himself, but he did not tell her so.

"We'll take a look at your bedroom," Mabel said. "It's small but it's sound-proofed, thank God."

He started after her, then stopped. She looked back through the doorway and said, "What is it?"

"This girl . . ."

There were sixty-three of the tall gray eternium cylinders. He was looking through the door of the nearest at the girl within.

"Wow! Really beautiful!"

If Mabel felt any jealousy, she suppressed it.

"Yes, isn't she!"

The girl had long, black, slightly curly hair, a face that could have launched him a thousand times a thousand times, a figure that had enough but not too much and long legs. Her eyes were open; in the dim light they looked a purplish-blue. She wore a thin silvery dress.

The plate by the top of the door gave her vital data. Jennie Marlowe. Born 2031 A.D., San Marino, California. She would be twenty-four years old. Actress. Unmarried. Wednesday's child.

"What's the matter?" Mabel said.

"Nothing."

How could he tell her that he felt sick in his stomach from a desire that could never be satisfied? Sick from beauty?

> For will in us is over-ruled by fate.
> Who ever loved, that loved not at first sight?

"What?" Mabel said, and then, after laughing, "You must be kidding?"

She wasn't angry. She realized that Jennie Marlowe was no more competition than if she were dead. She was right. Better for him to busy himself with the living of this world. Mabel wasn't too bad, cuddly, really, and, after a few drinks, rather stimulating.

They went downstairs afterward after 18:00 to the TV room. Most of the others were there, too. Some had their ear plugs in; some were looking at the screen but talking. The newscast was on, of course. Everybody was filling up on what had happened last Tuesday and today. The Speaker of the House was retiring after his term was up. His days of usefulness were over and his recent ill health showed no signs of disappearing. There was a shot of the family graveyard in Mississippi with the pedestal reserved for him. When science someday learned how to rejuvenate, he would come out of stonerment.

"That'll be the day!" Mabel said. She squirmed on his lap.

"Oh, I think they'll crack it," he said. "They're already on the track; they've succeeded in stopping the aging of rabbits."

"I don't mean that," she said. "Sure, they'll find out how to rejuvenate people. But then what? You think they're going to bring them all back? With all the people they got now and then they'll double, maybe triple, maybe quadruple, the population? You think they won't just leave them standing there?" She giggled, and said, "What would the pigeons do without them?"

He squeezed her waist. At the same time, he had a vision of himself squeezing *that* girl's waist. Hers would be soft enough but with no hint of fat.

Forget about her. Think of now. Watch the news.

A Mrs. Wilder had stabbed her husband and then herself with a kitchen knife. Both had been stonered immediately after the police arrived, and they had been taken to the hospital. An investigation of a work slowdown in the county government offices was taking place. The complaints were that Monday's people were not setting up the computers for Tuesday's. The case was being referred to the proper authorities of both days. The Ganymede base reported that the Great Red Spot of Jupiter was emitting weak but definite pulses that did not seem to be random.

The last five minutes of the program was a precis devoted to outstanding events of the other days. Mrs. Cuthmar, the housemother, turned the channel to a situation comedy with no protests from anybody.

Tom left the room, after telling Mabel that he was going to bed early—alone, and to sleep. He had a hard day tomorrow.

He tiptoed down the hall and the stairs and into the stoner room. The lights were soft, there were many shadows, and it was quiet. The sixty-three cylinders were like ancient granite columns of an underground chamber of a buried city. Fifty-five faces were white blurs behind the clear metal. Some had their eyes open; most had closed them while waiting for the field radiated from the machine in the base. He looked through Jennie Marlowe's door. He felt sick again. Out of his reach; never for him. Wednesday was only a day away. No, it was only a little less than four and a half hours away.

He touched the door. It was slick and only a little cold. She stared at him. Her right forearm was bent to hold the strap of a large purse. When the door opened, she would step out, ready to go. Some people took their showers and fixed their faces as soon as they got up from their sleep and then went directly into the stoner. When the field was automatically radiated at 05:00, they stepped out a minute later, ready for the day.

He would like to step out of his "coffin," too, at the same time.

But he was barred by Wednesday.

He turned away. He was acting like a sixteen-year-old kid. He had been sixteen about one hundred and six years ago, not that that made any difference. Physiologically, he was thirty.

As he started up to the second floor, he almost turned around and went back for another look. But he took himself by his neck-collar and pulled himself up to his room. There he decided he would get to sleep at once. Perhaps he would dream about her. If dreams were wish-fulfillments, they would bring her to him. It still had not been "proved" that dreams always expressed wishes, but it had been proved that man deprived of dreaming did go mad. And so the somniums radiated a field that put man into a state in which he got all the sleep, and all the dreams, that he needed within a four-hour period. Then he was awakened and a little later went into the stoner where the field suspended all atomic and subatomic activity. He would remain in that state forever unless the activating field came on.

He slept, and Jennie Marlowe did not come to him. Or, if she did, he did not remember. He awoke, washed his face, went down eagerly to the stoner, where he found the entire household standing around, getting in one last smoke, talking, laughing. Then they would step into their cylinders, and a silence like that at the heart of a mountain would fall.

He had often wondered what would happen if he did not go into the stoner. How would he feel? Would he be panicked? All his life, he had known only Tuesdays. Would Wednesday rush at him, roaring, like a tidal wave? Pick him up and hurl him against the reefs of a strange time?

What if he made some excuse and went back upstairs and did not go back down until the field had come on? By then, he could not enter. The door to his cylinder would not open again until the proper time. He could still run down to the public emergency stoners only three blocks away. But if he stayed in his room, waiting for Wednesday?

Such things happened. If the breaker of the law did not have a reasonable excuse, he was put on trial. It was a felony second only to murder to "break time," and the unexcused were stonered. All felons, sane or insane, were stonered. Or *mañanaed*, as some said. The *mañanaed* criminal waited in immobility and unconsciousness, preserved unharmed until science had techniques to cure the insane, the neurotic, the criminal, the sick. *Mañana*.

"What was it like in Wednesday?" Tom had asked a man who had been unavoidably left behind because of an accident.

"How would I know? I was knocked out except about fifteen minutes. I was in the same city, and I had never seen the faces of the ambulance men, of course, but then I've never seen them here. They stonered me and left me in the hospital for Tuesday to take care of."

He must have it bad, he thought. Bad. Even to think of such a thing was crazy. Getting into Wednesday was almost impossible. Almost. But it could be done. It would take time and patience, but it could be done.

He stood in front of his stoner for a moment. The others said, "See you! So long! Next Tuesday!" Mabel called, "Good night, lover!"

"Good night," he muttered.

"What?" she shouted.

"Good night!"

He glanced at the beautiful face behind the door. Then he smiled. He had been afraid that she might hear him say good night to a woman who called him lover.

He had ten minutes left. The intercom alarms were whooping. Get going, everybody! Time to take the six-day trip! Run! Remember the penalties!

He remembered, but he wanted to leave a message. The recorder was on a table. He activated it, and said, "Dear *Miss* Jennie Marlowe. My name is Tom Pym, and my stoner is next to yours. I am an actor, too; in fact, I work at the same studio as you. I know this is presumptuous of me, but I have never seen anybody so beautiful. Do you have a talent to match your beauty? I would like to see some run-offs of your shows. Would you please leave some in room five? I'm sure the occupant won't mind. Yours, Tom Pym."

He ran it back. It was certainly bald enough, and that might be just what was needed. Too flowery or too pressing would have made her leery. He had commented on her beauty twice but not overstressed it. And the appeal to her pride in her acting would be difficult to resist. Nobody knew better than he about that.

He whistled a little on his way to the cylinder. Inside, he pressed the button and looked at his watch. Five minutes to midnight. The light on the huge screen above the computer in the police station would not be flashing for him. Ten minutes from now, Wednesday's police would step out of their stoners in the precinct station, and they would take over their duties.

There was a ten-minute hiatus between the two days in the police station. All hell could break loose in these few minutes and it sometimes did. But a price had to be paid to maintain the walls of time.

He opened his eyes. His knees sagged a little and his head bent. The activation was a million microseconds fast—from eternium to flesh and blood almost instantaneously and the heart never knew that it had been stopped for such a long time. Even so, there was a little delay in the muscles' response to a standing position.

He pressed the button, opened the door, and it was as if his button had launched the day. Mabel had made herself up last night so that she looked dawn-fresh. He complimented her and she smiled happily. But he told her he would meet her for breakfast. Halfway up the staircase, he stopped, and waited until the hall was empty. Then he sneaked back down and into the stoner room. He turned on the recorder.

A voice, husky but also melodious, said, "Dear Mister Pym. I've had a few messages from other days. It was fun to talk back and forth across the abyss between the worlds, if you don't mind my exaggerating a little. But there is really no sense in it, once the novelty has worn off. If you become interested in the other person, you're frustrating yourself. That person can only be a voice in a recorder and a cold waxy face in a metal coffin. I wax poetic. Pardon me. If the person doesn't interest you, why continue to communicate? There is no sense in either case. And I *may* be beautiful. Anyway, I thank you for the compliment, but I am also sensible.

"I should have just not bothered to reply. But I want to be nice; I didn't want to hurt your feelings. So please don't leave any more messages."

He waited while silence was played. Maybe she was pausing for effect. Now would come a chuckle or a low honey-throated laugh, and she would say, "However, I don't like to disappoint my public. The run-offs are in your room."

The silence stretched out. He turned off the machine and went to the dining room for breakfast.

Siesta time at work was from 14:40 to 14:45. He lay down on the bunk and pressed the button. Within a minute he was asleep. He did dream of Jennie this time; she was a white shimmering figure solidifying out of the darkness and floating toward him. She was even more beautiful than she had been in her stoner.

The shooting ran overtime that afternoon so that he got home just in time for supper. Even the studio would not dare keep a man past his supper hour, especially since the studio was authorized to serve food only at noon.

He had time to look at Jennie for a minute before Mrs. Cuthmar's voice screeched over the intercom. As he walked down the hall, he thought, "I'm getting barnacled on her. It's ridiculous. I'm a grown man. Maybe . . . maybe I should see a psycher."

Sure, make your petition, and wait until a psycher has time for you. Say about three hundred days from now, if you are lucky. And if the psycher doesn't work out for you, then petition for another, and wait six hundred days.

Petition. He slowed down. Petition. What about a request, not to see a psycher, but to move? Why not? What did he have to lose? It would probably be turned down, but he could at least try.

Even obtaining a form for the request was not easy. He spent two nonwork days standing in line at the Center City Bureau before he got the proper forms. The first time, he was handed the wrong form and had to start all over again. There was no line set aside for those who wanted to change their days. There were not enough who wished to do this to justify such a line. So he had to queue up before the Miscellaneous office counter of the Mobility Section of the Vital Exchange Department of the Interchange and Cross Transfer Bureau. None of these titles had anything to do with emigration to another day.

When he got his form the second time, he refused to move from the office window until he had checked the number of the form and asked the clerk to double-check. He ignored the cries and the mutterings behind him. Then he went to one side of the vast room and stood in line before the punch machines. After two hours, he got to sit down at a small rolltop desk-shaped machine, above which was a large screen. He inserted the form into the slot, looked at the projection of the form, and punched buttons to mark the proper spaces opposite the proper questions. After that, all he had to do was to drop the form into a slot and hope it did not get lost. Or hope he would not have to go through the same procedure because he had improperly punched the form.

That evening, he put his head against the hard metal and murmured to the rigid face behind the door, "I must really love you to go through all this. And you don't even know it. And, worse, if you did, you might not care one bit."

To prove to himself that he had kept his gray stuff, he went out with Mabel that evening to a party given by Sol Voremwolf, a producer. Voremwolf had just passed a civil service examination giving him an A-13 rating. This meant that, in time, with some luck and the proper pull, he would become an executive vice-president of the studio.

The party was a qualified success. Tom and Mabel returned about half an hour before stoner time. Tom had managed to refrain from too many blowminds and liquor, so he was not tempted by Mabel. Even so, he knew that when he became unstonered, he would be half-loaded and he'd have to take some dreadful counter-actives. He would look and feel like hell at work, since he had missed his sleep.

He put Mabel off with an excuse, and went down to the stoner room ahead of the others. Not that that would do him any good if he wanted to get stonered early. The stoners only activated within narrow time limits.

He leaned against the cylinder and patted the door. "I tried not to think about you all evening. I wanted to be fair to Mabel, it's not fair to go out with her and think about you all the time."

All's fair in love . . .

He left another message for her, then wiped it out. What was the use? Besides, he knew that his speech was a little thick. He wanted to appear at his best for her. Why should he? What did she care for him?

The answer was, he did care, and there was no reason or logic connected with it. He loved this forbidden, untouchable, far-away-in-time, yet-so-near woman.

Mabel had come in silently. She said, "You're sick!"

Tom jumped away. Now why had he done that? He had nothing to be ashamed of. Then why was he so angry with her? His embarrassment was understandable but his anger was not.

Mabel laughed at him, and he was glad. Now he could snarl at her. He did so, and she turned away and walked out. But she was back in a few minutes with the others. It would soon be midnight.

By then he was standing inside the cylinder. A few seconds later, he left it, pushed Jennie's backward on its wheels, and pushed his around so that it faced hers. He went back in, pressed the button and stood there. The double doors only slightly distorted his view. But she seemed even more removed in distance, in time, and in unattainability.

Three days later, well into winter, he received a letter. The box inside the entrance hall buzzed just as he entered the front door. He went back and waited until the letter was printed and had dropped out from the slot. It was the reply to his request to move to Wednesday.

Denied. Reason: he had no reasonable reason to move.

That was true. But he could not give his real motive. It would have been even less impressive than the one he had given. He had punched the box opposite No. 12. REASON: TO GET INTO AN ENVIRONMENT WHERE MY TALENTS WILL BE MORE LIKELY TO BE ENCOURAGED.

He cursed and he raged. It was his human, his civil right to move into any day he pleased. That is, it should be his right. What if a move did cause much effort? What if it required a transfer of his I.D. and all the records connected with him from the moment of his birth? What if . . .?

He could rage all he wanted to, but it would not change a thing. He was stuck in the world of Tuesday.

Not yet, he muttered. Not yet. Fortunately, there is no limit to the number of requests I can make in my own day. I'll send out another. They think they can wear me out, huh? Well, I'll wear them out. Man against the machine. Man against the system. Man against the bureaucracy and the hard cold rules.

Winter's twenty days had sped by. Spring's eight days rocketed by. It was summer again. On the second day of the twelve days of summer, he received a reply to his second request.

It was neither a denial nor an acceptance. It stated that if he thought he would be better off psychologically in Wednesday because his astrologer said so, then he would have to get a psycher's critique of the astrologer's analysis. Tom Pym jumped into the air and clicked his sandaled heels together. Thank God that he lived in an age that did not classify astrologers as charlatans! The people—the masses—had protested that astrology was a necessity and that it should be legalized and honored. So laws were passed, and because of that, Tom Pym had a chance.

He went down to the stoner room and kissed the door of the cylinder and told Jennie Marlowe the good news. She did not respond, though he thought he saw her eyes brighten just a little. That was, of course, only his imagination, but he liked his imagination.

Getting a psycher for a consultation and getting through the three sessions took another year, another forty-eight days. Doctor Sigmund Traurig was a friend of Doctor Stelhela, the astrologer, and so that made things easier for Tom.

"I've studied Doctor Stelhela's chart carefully and analyzed carefully your obsession for this woman," he said. "I agree with Doctor Stelhela that you will always be unhappy in Tuesday, but I don't quite agree with him that you will be happier in Wednesday. However, you have this thing going for this Miss Marlowe, so I think you should go to Wednesday. But only if you sign papers agreeing to see a psycher there for extended therapy."

Only later did Tom Pym realize that Doctor Traurig might have wanted to get rid of him because he had too many patients. But that was an uncharitable thought.

He had to wait while the proper papers were transmitted to Wednesday's authorities. His battle was only half-won. The other officials could turn him down. And if he did get to his goal, then what? She could reject him without giving him a second chance.

It was unthinkable, but she could.

He caressed the door and then pressed his lips against it.

"Pygmalion could at least touch Galatea," he said. "Surely, the gods—the big dumb bureaucrats—will take pity on me, who can't even touch you. Surely."

The psycher had said that he was incapable of a true and lasting bond with a woman, as so many men were in this world of easy-come-easy-go liaisons. He had fallen in love with Jennie Marlowe for several reasons. She may have resembled somebody he had loved when he was very young. His mother, perhaps? No? Well, never mind. He would find out in Wednesday—perhaps. The deep, the important, truth was that he loved Miss Marlowe because she could never reject him, kick him out or become tiresome, complain, weep, yell, insult and so forth. He loved her because she was unattainable and silent.

"I love her as Achilles must have loved Helen when he saw her on top of the walls of Troy," Tom said.

"I wasn't aware that Achilles was ever in love with Helen of Troy," Doctor Traurig said drily.

"Homer never said so, but I *know* that he must have been! Who could see her and *not* love her?"

"How the hell would I know? I never saw her! If I had suspected these delusions would intensify..."

"I am a poet!" Tom said.

"Overimaginative, you mean! Hmmm. She must be a douser! I don't have anything particular to do this evening. I'll tell you what...my curiosity is aroused....I'll come down to your place tonight and take a look at this fabulous beauty, your Helen of Troy."

Doctor Traurig appeared immediately after supper, and Tom Pym ushered him down the hall and into the stoner room at the rear of the big house as if he were a guide conducting a famous critic to a just-discovered Rembrandt.

The doctor stood for a long time in front of the cylinder. He hmmmed several times and checked her vital-data plate several times. Then he turned and said, "I see what you mean, Mr. Pym. Very well. I'll give the go-ahead."

"Ain't she something?" Tom said on the porch. "She's out of this world, literally and figuratively, of course."

"Very beautiful. But I believe that you are facing a great disappointment, perhaps heartbreak, perhaps, who knows, even madness, much as I hate to use that unscientific term."

"I'll take the chance," Tom said. "I know I sound nuts, but where would we be if it weren't for nuts. Look at the man who invented the wheel, at Columbus, at James Watt, at the Wright brothers, at Pasteur, you name them."

"You can scarcely compare these pioneers of science with their passion for truth with you and your desire to marry a woman. But, as I have observed, she is strikingly beautiful. Still, that makes me exceedingly cautious. Why isn't she married? What's wrong with her?"

"For all I know, she may have been married a dozen times!" Tom said. "The point is, she isn't now! Maybe she's disappointed and she's sworn to wait until the right man comes along. Maybe..."

"There's no maybe about it, you're neurotic," Traurig said. "But I actually believe that it would be more dangerous for you *not* to go to Wednesday than it would be *to* go."

"Then you'll say yes!" Tom said, grabbing the doctor's hand and shaking it.

"Perhaps. I have some doubts."

The doctor had a faraway look. Tom laughed and released the hand and slapped the doctor on the shoulder. "Admit it! You were really struck by her! You'd have to be dead not to!"

"She's all right," the doctor said. "But you must think this over. If you do go there and she turns you down, you might go off the deep end, much as I hate to use such a poetical term."

"No, I won't. I wouldn't be a bit the worse off. Better off, in fact. I'll at least get to see her in the flesh."

Spring and summer zipped by. Then, a morning he would never forget, the letter of acceptance. With it, instructions on how to get to Wednesday. These were simple enough. He was to make sure that the technicians came to his stoner sometime during the day and readjusted the timer within the base. He could not figure out why he could not just stay out of the stoner and let Wednesday catch up to him, but by now he was past trying to fathom the bureaucratic mind.

He did not intend to tell anyone at the house, mainly because of Mabel. But Mabel found out from someone at the studio. She wept when she saw him at supper time, and she ran upstairs to her room. He felt badly, but he did not follow to console her.

That evening, his heart beating hard, he opened the door to his stoner. The others had found out by then; he had been unable to keep the business to himself.

Actually, he was glad that he had told them. They seemed happy for him, and they brought in drinks and had many rounds of toasts. Finally, Mabel came downstairs, wiping her eyes, and she said she wished him luck, too. She had known that he was not really in love with her. But she did wish someone would fall in love with her just by looking inside her stoner.

When she found out that he had gone to see Doctor Traurig, she said, "He's a very influential man. Sol Voremwolf had him for his analyst. He says he's even got influence on other days. He edits the *Psyche Crosscurrents*, you know, one of the few periodicals read by other people."

Other, of course, meant those who lived in Wednesdays through Mondays.

Tom said he was glad he had gotten Traurig. Perhaps he had used his influence to get the Wednesday authorities to push through his request so swiftly. The walls between the worlds were seldom broken, but it was suspected that the very influential did it when they pleased.

Now, quivering, he stood before Jennie's cylinder again. The last time, he thought, that I'll see her stonered. Next time, she'll be warm, colorful, touchable flesh.

"*Ave atque vale!*" he said aloud. The others cheered. Mabel said, "How corny!" They thought he was addressing them, and perhaps he had included them.

He stepped inside the cylinder, closed the door and pressed the button. He would keep his eyes open, so that...

And today was Wednesday. Though the view was exactly the same, it was like being on Mars.

He pushed open the door and stepped out. The seven people had faces he knew and names he had read on their plates. But he did not know them.

He started to say hello, and then he stopped.

Jennie Marlowe's cylinder was gone.

He seized the nearest man by the arm.

"Where's Jennie Marlowe?"

"Let go. You're hurting me. She's gone. To Tuesday."

"*Tuesday! Tuesday?*"

"Sure. She'd been trying to get out of here for a long time. She had something about this day being unlucky for her. She was unhappy, that's for sure. Just two days ago, she said her application had finally been accepted. Apparently, some Tuesday psycher had used his influence. He came down and saw her in her stoner and that was it, brother."

The walls and the people and the stoners seemed to be distorted. Time was bending itself this way and that. He wasn't in Wednesday; he wasn't in Tuesday. He wasn't in *any* day. He was stuck inside himself at some crazy date that should never have existed.

"She can't do that!"

"Oh, no! She just did that!"

"But...you can't transfer more than once!"

"That's her problem."

It was his, too.

"I should never have brought him down to look at her!" Tom said. "The swine! The unethical swine!"

Tom Pym stood there for a long time, and then he went into the kitchen. It was the same environment, if you discounted the people. Later, he went to the studio and got a part in a situation play which was, really, just like all those in Tuesday. He watched the newscaster that night. The President of the U.S.A. had a different name and face, but the words of his speech could have been those of Tuesday's President. He was introduced to a secretary of a producer; her name wasn't Mabel, but it might as well have been.

The difference here was that Jennie was gone, and oh, what a world of difference it made to him.

BARRY N. MALZBERG

Gehenna

It would be fair to say that Barry N. Malzberg (1939-   ) burst upon the science fiction scene in the late 1960s with a string of stories and novels that turned many of the conventions of science fiction on their heads. Certainly one of the field's most controversial practitioners and greatest talents, he won the John W. Campbell Memorial Award in 1973 for Beyond Apollo, *which along with* Herovit's World *(1973) and* Guernica Night *(1974) are major literary works. Malzberg is also an important commentator on science fiction, and the essays in his* The Engines of the Night *(1982) contain cogent and insightful opinions on the field. This brief, jarring piece conveys in just a few pages a powerful vision of contemporary fragmentation.*

I

Edward got on the IRT downtown local at 42nd Street for Greenwich Village. The train stopped at 33rd Street, 27th Street, 17th Street and Christopher Circle. As it turned out he met his wife at this party.

It was a standard, Greenwich Village all-of-us-are-damned gathering. She was sitting in a corner of the room, her feet bare, listening to a man with sad mustaches play a mandolin. Edward went over to say hello to her. She looked at him with vague disinterest and huddled closer to the mandolin player, who turned out—on further inspection—to be her date for the night. But Edward was persistent—his parents had always told him that his fearfulness was his chief detracting characteristic—and later that night he got her address.

Two days later he showed up with a shopping cart filled with gourmet food and asked her if she would help him eat it. She shrugged and introduced him to her cats. Three weeks later they slept with one another for the first time and the week after that the mandolin player and he had a fight, at the end of which the mandolin player wished them well and left her flat forever. Edward and Julie were engaged only a few days after that and during the month he married her in Elktown.

They went back to New York and started life together. He gave up mathematics, of course, and became an accountant. She gave up painting and took to going to antique shops once a week, bringing back objects every now and then. It was not

420

a bad life, even if it had started out, perhaps, a bit on the contrived side.

Three years later Edward opened the door and found Julie playing with their year-old daughter, shaking a rattle and putting it deep into the baby's mouth. The scene was a pleasing one and he felt quite contented until she looked up at him and he saw that she was crying.

He put down his briefcase and asked her what was wrong. She told him that their life had been an utter waste. Everything she wanted she had not gotten— everything that she had gotten she did not want. She was surrounded by things, she told him, she had prepared herself as a child to despise. And the worst of it was that all of it was her own fault. She talked of divorce but only by inference.

Realizing that the fault was all his, Edward said that he would check up on some suburbs, get them a nice-sized house and some activities for her during the day. And so he did—all of it and they were very happy for a while if gravely in debt— until he came home from the circus one night with his daughter and found that Julie, feet bare, had drowned herself in the bathtub.

II

Julie got on the IRT downtown local at 42nd Street for Greenwich Village. The train stopped at 32nd Street, 24th Street, 13th Street and the Statue of Christ. As it turned out, she met her husband at this party. It was a standard Greenwich Village we-are-finding-ourselves party and he came in late, dressed all wrong, his hands stretching his pockets out of shape. He was already very drunk.

She was there with a boy named Vincent who meant little to her but who played the mandolin beautifully and sang her love songs. If the songs were derivative and the motions a trifle forced—well, it was a bad period for both of them and she took what comfort she could. But when her husband-to-be came over and spoke to her—his name was Edward as it turned out—she could see beyond his embarrassment and her misery that a certain period of her life and of the mandolin-player's was over. He wanted her telephone number but because she didn't believe in telephones she gave him her address instead while Vincent was off changing his clothes. She told him that she was very unsure of herself.

Three days later, while she was still in bed, he came with flowers and candy and told her that he could not forget her. With a smile she invited him in and the first time was very good—better than it had been with Vincent, anyway. Edward was gone when Vincent came later that evening and she told him that she had been lusting after the sea all her life—now she at least had found a pond. Then she told him what she and Edward had done. He wept and cursed her. He told her that she had betrayed everything of importance, the small reality they had built together— but she was firm. She said that lines must be drawn for once and for all between the present and the possible.

After that she saw nothing of either Vincent or Edward for a week. Then Edward came with a suitcase. He said he had moved out of his parents' home and had come to marry her. She did not marry him right away but they lived together for some weeks—one evening she found a note in her mailbox, just like that, saying that Vincent had committed suicide.

She never found out who had sent the note and she never told Edward anything. But a week later they were married in Yonkers and went to a resort upstate, where they were happy for a few days.

They came back and bought furniture for her flat. He dropped out of astronomy and became an industrial research assistant—or something like that.

For a long time her days were simple—they were, as a matter of fact, exactly like the days she had known just before she met Edward—and the nights were good, pretty good anyway. Then she became pregnant in a difficult sort of way and eventually the child, Ann, was born—a perfect child with small hands and a musical capability. Edward said that they would have to find a real home now—he was very proud—but she said that the old life could keep up, at least until Ann was ready for school. But one night he came home early, very excited and—just like that—told her that he had found them a home in the suburbs. She told him that this was fine. He said that he was very happy, and she said the same.

They moved to the suburbs and were content for a while, what with car pools and bridge and whatnot, as well as good playmates and a healthy environment for Ann. But Edward, for no reason, began to get more and more depressed and one morning when she awoke to find his bed empty, she went into the bathroom to find him slumped over the bathtub, his wrists open, blood all over the floor, a faint, fishlike look of appeal in his stunned and disbelieving eyes.

III

Vincent got on the IRT downtown local at 42nd Street for Greenwich Village. The train stopped at 37th Street, 31st Street, 19th Street and Christ Towers. As it turned out, he lost his girl at this party. It was a standard Greenwich Village look-how-liberated-we-are kind of party and it was a strange thing that the two of them went separately since the 42nd Street stop was the nearest to both of their apartments. But she believed in maintaining her privacy in small, damning ways.

She was sad that night, sad with a misery he could not touch, much less comprehend. It had been a good time for both of them—they had been going together for the four months since she broke off with his closest friend—and he played her songs on his mandolin—promises of lost and terrible loves, promises of a better future, songs of freedom and loneliness; and she loved his mandolin. She told him that she found her whole soul in his music.

So he was playing songs for her at the party this night, not even wanting to be there, hoping that they could go back to her flat and put the mandolin beside the bed and make their kind of love, when he saw that she was looking at another man in the corner of the room—a man of a different sort from the rest of them, since he was the only one who was not already drunk. The man was looking back at her and in that moment Vincent knew that he was quite doomed, that he and Julie were quite finished.

To prove it to himself he left his instrument on her knee and went to the bathroom.

When he came back they sprang apart like assassins and he knew that the man had her address. There was nothing to do, of course, but to leave the party and he helped her with her coat, put his mandolin over his shoulder and led her down the stairs. Halfway to the street he told her that she had betrayed them. She did not answer, later murmured that she could not help herself, much less another person—but she would make this night the best of all the nights that she had ever given him.

And so she did, all night and into the dawn while her cat stroked the mandolin, making wooden sounds, rolling the instrument around and around on the floor. In the morning he left her—and took his clothing—and then he did not see her at all for a few days. When he came back there was a different look on her face and the man was in her bed, lying next to her.

He did not care—he had lost any capacity for surprise when she had come from his closest friend, broken enough to need him. He only wanted to meet the man named Edward (who might become his closest friend too), but the man did not want any part of him at all and there was a very bad scene—a scene that ended only when Vincent knocked the man to the door and smashed him there to the floor.

But he never saw her again, victory or not. He had no need to—everything that needed proof had been proven. But he thought of her often and many years later, when he killed himself by leaping from a stranger's penthouse, his last thought as he felt the dry wind and saw the street coming at him was of his old mandolin, her solemn cat and the night she had given him her best because she had already partaken of his worst.

IV

The child Ann—who had very sensitive and gentle hands—became a young woman who was drawn at odd moments to the windows of pawnshops in which she saw old mandolins—and once, for a week, she took flute lessons. But she had no money and less patience—that last was her biggest fault, along with a lack of assertiveness—and she dropped them.

Now she is going to a party in Greenwich Village. She does not know what will happen to her. The night is still a mystery. She is still young enough to scent possibilities in the wind—tonight may hold some finality, although one never knows. See her, see her—she is in the Times Square stop of the IRT—the engineer sounds a song in the density.

She counts the stops and waits. The train stops at 34th Street, 28th Street and 14th Street. Now it is at Christopher Street and Sheridan Square.

ARTHUR C. CLARKE

A Meeting with Medusa

Like Isaac Asimov, Arthur C. Clarke (1917-   ) is well known for both his science fiction and his writing on science, and he has won many honors in both fields, including Hugo and Nebula awards, the John W. Campbell Memorial Award and the UNESCO Kalinga Prize. Among his most famous novels are Childhood's End *(1953),* Rendezvous with Rama *(1973) and* Imperial Earth *(1975), but many people who don't read science fiction know him as the author of* 2001: A Space Odyssey, *the novelization of the screenplay he coauthored with Stanley Kubrick. His most recent book is a sequel to that work,* 2010 *(1982).*

A DAY TO REMEMBER

The Queen Elizabeth was five kilometers above the Grand Canyon, dawdling along at a comfortable 180, when Howard Falcon spotted the camera platform closing in from the right. He had been expecting it—nothing else was cleared to fly at this altitude—but he was not too happy to have company. Although he welcomed any signs of public interest, he also wanted as much empty sky as he could get. After all, he was the first man in history to navigate a ship half a kilometer long.

So far, this first test flight had gone perfectly; ironically enough, the only problem had been the century-old aircraft carrier Chairman Mao, borrowed from the San Diego naval museum for support operations. Only one of Mao's four nuclear reactors was still operating, and the old battlewagon's top speed was barely thirty knots. Luckily, wind speed at sea level had been less than half this, so it had not been too difficult to maintain still air on the flight deck. Though there had been a few anxious moments during gusts, when the mooring lines had been dropped, the great dirigible had risen smoothly, straight up into the sky, as if on an invisible elevator. If all went well, Queen Elizabeth IV would not meet Chairman Mao for another week.

Everything was under control: all test instruments gave normal readings. Commander Falcon decided to go upstairs and watch the rendezvous. He handed over to his second officer and walked out into the transparent tubeway that led through the heart of the ship. There, as always, he was overwhelmed by the spectacle of the largest space ever enclosed by man.

424

The ten spherical gas cells, each more than 100 meters across, were ranged one behind the other like a line of gigantic soap bubbles. The tough plastic was so clear that he could see through the whole length of the array and make out details of the elevator mechanism almost half a kilometer from his vantage point. All around him, like a three-dimensional maze, was the structural framework of the ship—the great longitudinal girders running from nose to tail, the fifteen hoops that were the ribs of this skyborne colossus, whose varying sizes defined its graceful, stream-lined profile.

At this low speed, there was very little sound—merely the soft rush of wind over the envelope and an occasional creak of metal as the pattern of stresses changed. The shadowless light from the rows of lamps far overhead gave the whole scene a curiously submarine quality, and to Falcon this was enhanced by the spectacle of the translucent gasbags. He had once encountered a squadron of large but harmless jellyfish, pulsing their mindless way above a shallow tropical reef, and the plastic bubbles that gave Queen Elizabeth her lift often reminded him of these—especially when changing pressures made them crinkle and scatter new patterns of light.

He walked fifty meters down the axis of the ship, until he came to the forward elevator, between gas cells one and two. Riding up to the observation deck, he noticed that it was uncomfortably hot and dictated a brief memo to himself on his pocket recorder. The Queen obtained almost a quarter of her buoyancy from the unlimited amounts of waste heat produced by her fusion power plant; on this lightly loaded flight, indeed, only six of the ten gas cells contained helium and the remaining four were full of air; yet she still carried 200 tons of water as ballast. However, running the cells at high temperatures did produce problems in refrigerating the accessways; it was obvious that a little more work would have to be done here.

A refreshing blast of cooler air hit him in the face when he stepped out onto the observation deck and into the dazzling sunlight streaming through the Plexiglas roof. Half a dozen workmen, with an equal number of superchimp assistants, were busily laying the partly completed dance floor, while others were installing electric wiring and fixing furniture. It was a scene of controlled chaos and Falcon found it hard to believe that everything would be ready for the maiden voyage, only four weeks ahead. Well, that was not *his* problem, thank goodness. He was merely the captain, not the cruise director.

The human workers waved to him and the simps flashed toothy smiles as he walked through the confusion into the already completed sky lounge. This was his favorite place in the whole ship and he knew that once she was operating, he would never again have it all to himself. He would allow himself just five minutes of private enjoyment.

He called the bridge, checked that everything was still in order and relaxed into one of the comfortable swivel chairs. Below, in a curve that delighted the eye, was the unbroken silver sweep of the ship's envelope. He was perched at the highest point, surveying the whole immensity of the largest vehicle ever built. And when he had tired of that—all the way out to the horizon was the fantastic wilderness carved by the Colorado River in half a billion years of time.

Apart from the camera platform (it had now fallen back and was filming from amidships), he had the sky to himself. It was blue and empty, clear down to the horizon. In his grandfather's day, Falcon knew, it would have been streaked with vapor trails and stained with smoke. Both had gone; the aerial garbage had vanished with the primitive technologies that spawned it, and the long-distance transportation of this age arced too far beyond the stratosphere for any sight or sound of it to reach Earth. Once again, the lower atmosphere belonged to the birds and the clouds—and now to Queen Elizabeth IV.

It was true, as the old pioneers had said at the beginning of the twentieth century; this was the only way to travel—in silence and luxury, breathing the air around you and not cut off from it, near enough to the surface to watch the ever-changing beauty of land and sea. The subsonic jets of the 1980s, packed with hundreds of passengers seated ten abreast, could not even begin to match such comfort and spaciousness.

Of course, the Q.E. would never be an economic proposition; and even if her projected sister ships were built, only a few of the world's quarter of a billion inhabitants would ever enjoy this silent gliding through the sky. But a secure and prosperous global society could afford such follies and, indeed, needed them for its novelty and entertainment. There were at least a million men on Earth whose discretionary income exceeded a thousand new dollars a year, so the Queen would not lack for passengers.

Falcon's pocket communicator beeped; the copilot was calling from the bridge.

"OK for rendezvous, Captain? We've got all the data we need from this run and the TV people are getting impatient."

Falcon glanced at the camera platform, now matching his speed a quarter of a kilometer away.

"OK," he replied. "Proceed as arranged. I'll watch from here."

He walked back through the busy chaos of the observation deck, so that he could have a better view amidships. As he did so, he could feel the change of vibration underfoot; by the time he had reached the rear of the lounge, the ship had come to rest. Using his master key, he let himself out onto the small external platform flaring from the end of the deck; half a dozen people could stand there, with only low guardrails separating them from the vast sweep of the envelope—and from the ground, thousands of meters below. It was an exciting place to be and perfectly safe even when the ship was traveling at speed, for it was in the dead air behind the huge dorsal blister of the observation deck. Nevertheless, it was not intended that the passengers would have access to it; the view was a little too vertiginous.

The covers of the forward cargo hatch had already opened like giant trap doors and the camera platform was hovering above them, preparing to descend. Along this route, in the years to come, would travel thousands of passengers and tons of supplies; only on rare occasions would the Queen drop down to sea level and dock with her floating base.

A sudden gust of crosswind slapped Falcon's cheek and he tightened his grip on the guardrail. The Grand Canyon was a bad place for turbulence, though he did not expect much at this altitude. Without any real anxiety, he focused his attention on the descending platform, now about fifty meters above the ship. He knew that the highly skilled operator who was flying the remotely controlled vehicle had performed this very simple maneuver a dozen times already; it was inconceivable that he would have any difficulties.

Yet he seemed to be reacting rather sluggishly; that last gust had drifted the platform almost to the edge of the open hatchway. Surely the pilot could have corrected before this . . . did he have a control problem? It was very unlikely; these remotes had multiple-redundancy, fail-safe take-overs and any number of backup systems. Accidents were almost unheard of.

But there he went again, off to the left. Could the pilot be *drunk?* Improbable though that seemed, Falcon considered it seriously for a moment. Then he reached for his microphone switch.

Once again, without warning, he was slapped violently in the face. He hardly felt it, for he was staring in horror at the camera platform. The distant operator was fighting for control, trying to balance the craft on its jets—but he was only making matters worse. The oscillations increased—twenty degrees, forty, sixty, ninety . . .

"Switch to automatic, you fool!" Falcon shouted uselessly into his microphone. "Your manual control's not working!"

The platform flipped over onto its back; the jets no longer supported it but drove it swiftly downward. They had suddenly become allies of the gravity they had fought until this moment.

Falcon never heard the crash, though he felt it; he was already inside the observation deck, racing for the elevator that would take him down to the bridge. Workmen shouted at him anxiously, asking what had happened. It would be many months before he knew the answer to that question.

Just as he was stepping into the elevator cage, he changed his mind. What if there were a power failure? Better be on the safe side, even if it took longer and time was of the essence. He began to run down the spiral stairway enclosing the shaft.

Halfway down, he paused for a second to inspect the damage. That damned platform had gone clear through the ship, rupturing two of the gas cells as it did so. They were still collapsing slowly, in great falling veils of plastic. He was not worried about the loss of lift—the ballast could easily take care of that, as long as eight cells remained intact. Far more serious was the possibility of structural damage; already he could hear the great latticework around him groaning and protesting under its abnormal loads. It was not enough to have sufficient lift; unless it was properly distributed, the ship would break her back.

He was just resuming his descent when a superchimp, shrieking with fright, came racing down the elevator shaft, moving with incredible speed hand over hand along the *outside* of the latticework. In its terror, the poor beast had torn off its company uniform, perhaps in an unconscious attempt to regain the freedom of its ancestors.

Falcon, still descending as swiftly as he could, watched its approach with some alarm; a distraught simp was a powerful and potentially dangerous animal, especially if fear overcame its conditioning. As it overtook him, it started to call out a string of words, but they were all jumbled together and the only one he could recognize was a plaintive, frequently repeated "Boss." Even now, Falcon realized, it looked toward humans for guidance; he felt sorry for the creature, involved in a man-made disaster beyond its comprehension and for which it bore no responsibility.

It stopped opposite him, on the other side of the lattice; there was nothing to prevent it from coming through the open framework if it wished. Now its face was only inches from his and he was looking straight into the terrified eyes. Never before had he been so close to a simp and able to study its features in such detail; he felt that strange mingling of kinship and discomfort that all men experience when they gaze thus into the mirror of time.

His presence seemed to have calmed the creature; Falcon pointed up the shaft, back toward the observation deck, and said very clearly and precisely: "Boss— boss—go." To his relief, the simp understood; it gave him a grimace that might have been a smile and at once started to race back the way it had come. Falcon had given it the best advice he could; if any safety remained aboard the Queen, it was in that direction. But his duty lay in the other.

He had almost completed his descent when, with a sound of rending metal, the vessel pitched nose down and the lights went out. But he could still see quite well, for a shaft of sunlight streamed through the open hatch and the huge tear in the envelope. Many years ago, he had stood in a great cathedral nave, watching the light pouring through the stained-glass windows and forming pools of milticolored radiance on the ancient flagstones. The dazzling shaft of sunlight through the ruined fabric high above reminded him of that moment. He was in a cathedral of metal, falling down the sky.

When he reached the bridge and was able for the first time to look outside, he was horrified to see how close the ship was to the ground. Only a thousand meters below were the beautiful and deadly pinnacles of rock and the red rivers of mud that were still carving their way down into the past. There was no level area anywhere in sight where a ship as large as the Queen could come to rest on an even keel.

A glance at the display board told him that all the ballast had gone. However, rate of descent had been reduced to a few meters a second; they still had a fighting chance.

Without a word, Falcon eased himself into the pilot's seat and took over such control as remained. The instrument board showed him everything he wished to know; speech was superfluous. In the background, he could hear the communications officer giving a running report over the radio. By this time, all the news channels of Earth would have been preempted and he could imagine the utter frustration of the program controllers. One of the most spectacular wrecks in history was occurring—without a single camera to record it. The last moments of the Queen would never fill millions with awe and terror, as had those of the Hindenburg a century and a half before.

Now the ground was only half a kilometer away, still coming up slowly. Though he had full thrust, he had not dared use it, lest the weakened structure collapse; but now he realized that he had no choice. The wind was taking them toward a fork in the canyon, where the river was split by a wedge of rock, like the prow of some gigantic, fossilized ship of stone. If she continued on her present course, the Queen would straddle that triangular plateau and come to rest with at least a third of her length jutting out over nothingness; she would snap like a rotten stick.

From far away, above the sound of straining metal and escaping gas, came the familiar whistle of the jets as Falcon opened up the lateral thrusters. The ship staggered and began to slew to port. The shriek of tearing metal was now almost continuous—and the rate of descent had started to increase ominously. A glance at the damage-control board showed that cell number five had just gone.

The ground was only meters away; even now, he could not tell whether his maneuver would succeed or fail. He switched the thrust vectors over to vertical, giving maximum lift to reduce the force of impact.

The crash seemed to last forever. It was not violent—merely prolonged and irresistible. It seemed that the whole universe was falling about them.

The sound of crunching metal came nearer, as if some great beast were eating its way through the dying ship.

Then floor and ceiling closed upon him like a vise.

"BECAUSE IT'S THERE"

"Why do you want to go to Jupiter?"

"As Springer said when he lifted for Pluto—because it's there."

"Thanks. Now we've got *that* out of the way—the real reason." Howard Falcon smiled, though only those who knew him well could have interpreted the slight, leathery grimace. Webster was one of them; for more than twenty years, they had been involved in each other's projects. They had shared triumphs and disasters—including the greatest disaster of all.

"Well, Springer's cliché is still valid. We've landed on all the terrestrial planets but none of the gas giants. They are the only real challenge left in the Solar System."

"An expensive one. Have you worked out the cost?"

"As well as I can; here are the estimates. But remember—this isn't a one-shot mission but a transportation system. Once it's proved out, it can be used over and over again. And it will open up not merely Jupiter but *all* the giants."

Webster looked at the figures and whistled.

"Why not start with an easier planet—Uranus, for example? Half the gravity and less than half the escape velocity. Quieter weather, too—if that's the right word for it."

Webster had certainly done his homework. But that, of course, was why he was head of Long Range Planning.

"There's very little saving, when you allow for the extra distance and the logistics problems. For Jupiter, we can use the facilities on Ganymede. Beyond Saturn, we'd have to establish a new supply base."

Logical, thought Webster; but he was sure that it was not the important reason. Jupiter was lord of the Solar System; Falcon would be interested in no lesser challenge.

"Besides," Falcon continued, "Jupiter is a major scientific scandal. It's more than a hundred years since its radio storms were discovered, but we still don't know what causes them—and the Great Red Spot is as big a mystery as ever. That's why I can get matching funds from the Bureau of Astronautics. Do you know how many probes they have dropped into that atmosphere?"

"A couple of hundred, I believe."

"Three hundred and twenty-six, over the past fifty years—about a quarter of them total failures. Of course, they've learned a hell of a lot, but they've barely scratched the planet. Do you realize how *big* it is?"

"More than ten times the size of Earth."

"Yes, yes—but do you know what that really means?"

Falcon pointed to the large globe in the corner of Webster's office.

"Look at India—how small it seems. Well, if you skinned Earth and spread it out on the surface of Jupiter, it would look about as big as India does here."

There was a long silence while Webster contemplated the equation: Jupiter is to Earth as Earth is to India. Falcon had—deliberately, of course—chosen the best possible example...

Was it already ten years ago? Yes, it must have been. The crash lay seven years in the past *(that* date was engraved on his heart) and those initial tests had taken place three years before the first and last flight of the Queen Elizabeth.

Ten years ago, then, Commander (no, Lieutenant) Falcon had invited him to a preview—a three-day drift across the northern plains of India, within sight of the Himalayas. "Perfectly safe," he had promised. "It will get you away from the office—and will teach you what this whole thing is about."

Webster had not been disappointed. Next to his first journey to the Moon, it had been the most memorable experience of his life. And yet, as Falcon had assured him, it had been perfectly safe and quite uneventful.

They had taken off from Srinagar just before dawn, with the huge silver bubble of the balloon already catching the first light of the Sun. The ascent had been made in total silence; there were none of the roaring propane burners that had lifted the hot-air balloons of an earlier age. All the heat they needed came from the little pulsed-fusion reactor, weighing only a hundred kilograms, hanging in the open mouth of the envelope. While they were climbing, its laser was zapping ten times a second, igniting the merest whiff of deuterium fuel; once they had reached altitude, it would fire only a few times a minute, making up for the the heat lost through the great gasbag overhead.

And so, even while they were a kilometer above the ground, they could hear dogs barking, people shouting, bells ringing. Slowly the vast, Sun-smitten landscape expanded around them; two hours later, they had leveled out at five kilometers and were taking frequent draughts of oxygen. They could relax and admire the scenery; the on-board instrumentation was doing all the work—gathering the information that would be required by the designers of the still-unnamed liner of the skies.

It was a perfect day; the southwest monsoon would not break for another month and there was hardly a cloud in the sky. Time seemed to have come to a stop; they resented the hourly radio reports that interrupted their reverie. And all around, to the horizon and far beyond, was that infinite, ancient landscape drenched with history—a patchwork of villages, fields, temples, lakes, irrigation canals.

With a real effort, Webster broke the hypnotic spell of that ten-year-old memory. It had converted him to lighter-than-air flight—and it had made him realize the enormous size of India, even in a world that could be circled within ninety minutes. And yet, he repeated to himself, Jupiter is to Earth as Earth is to India.

"Granted your argument," he said, "and supposing the funds are available, there's another question you have to answer. Why should you do better than the—what is it—three hundred and twenty-six robot probes that have already made the trip?"

"I am better qualified than they were—as an observer and as a pilot. *Especially* as a pilot; don't forget—I've more experience of lighter-than-air flight than anyone in the world."

"You could still serve as controller and sit safely on Ganymede."

"But that's just the point! They've already done that. Don't you remember what killed the Queen?"

Webster knew perfectly well, but he merely answered, "Go on."

"Time lag—*time lag!* That idiot of a platform controller thought he was using a local radio circuit. But he'd been accidentally switched through a satellite—oh, maybe it wasn't his fault, but he should have noticed. That's a half-second time lag for the round trip. Even then it wouldn't have mattered, flying in calm air. It was the turbulence over the Grand Canyon that did it. When the platform tipped and he corrected for that—it had already tipped the other way. Ever tried to drive a car over a bumpy road with a half-second delay in the steering?"

"No, and I don't intend to try. But I can imagine it."

"Well, Ganymede is more than a million kilometers from Jupiter. That means a round-trip delay of six seconds. No, you need a controller on the spot—to handle emergencies in real time. Let me show you something. Mind if I use this?"

"Go ahead."

Falcon picked up a postcard that was lying on Webster's desk; they were almost obsolete on Earth, but this one showed a 3-D view of a Martian landscape and was decorated with exotic and expensive stamps. He held it so that it dangled vertically.

"This is an old trick but helps make my point. Place your thumb and finger on either side, not quite touching. That's right."

Webster put out his hand, almost but not quite gripping the card.

"Now catch it."

Falcon waited for a few seconds; then, without warning, he let go of the card. Webster's thumb and fingers closed on empty air.

"I'll do it again, just to show there's no deception. You see?"

Once again, the calling card slipped through Webster's fingers.

"Now you try it on me."

This time, Webster grasped the card and dropped it without warning. It had scarcely moved before Falcon had caught it; Webster almost imagined he could hear a click, so swift was the other's reaction.

"When they put me together again," Falcon remarked in an expressionless voice, "the surgeons made some improvements. This is one of them—and there are others. I want to make the most of them. Jupiter is the place where I can do it."

Webster stared for long seconds at the fallen card, absorbing the improbable colors of the Trivium Charontis Escarpment. Then he said quietly, "I understand. How long do you think it will take?"

"With your help, plus the bureau plus all the science foundations we can drag in—oh, three years. Then a year for trials—we'll have to send in at least two test models. So with luck—five years."

"That's about what I thought. I hope you get your luck; you've earned it. But there's one thing I won't do."

"What's that?"

"Next time you go ballooning, don't expect *me* as passenger."

THE WORLD OF THE GODS

The fall from Jupiter V to Jupiter itself takes only three and a half hours; few men could have slept on so awesome a journey. Sleep was a weakness that Howard Falcon hated, and the little he still required brought dreams that time had not yet been able to exorcise. But he could expect no rest in the three days that lay ahead and must seize what he could during the long fall down into that ocean of clouds, a hundred thousand kilometers below.

As soon as Kon-Tiki had entered her transfer orbit and all the computer checks were satisfactory, he prepared for the last sleep he might ever know. It seemed appropriate that at almost the same moment Jupiter eclipsed the bright and tiny Sun, he swept into the monstrous shadow of the planet. For a few minutes a strange, golden twilight enveloped the ship; then a quarter of the sky became an utterly black hole in space, while the rest was a blaze of stars. No matter how far one traveled across the Solar System, *they* never changed; these same constellations now shone on Earth, half a billion kilometers away. The only novelties here were the small, pale crescents of Callisto and Ganymede; doubtless there were a dozen other moons up there in the sky, but they were all much too tiny and too distant for the unaided eye to pick them out.

"Closing down for two hours," he reported to the mother ship, hanging a thousand kilometers above the desolate rocks of Jupiter V, in the radiation shadow of the tiny satellite. If it never served any other useful purpose, Jupiter V was a cosmetic bulldozer perpetually sweeping up the charged particles that made it unhealthy to linger close to Jupiter. Its wake was almost free of radiation, and here a ship could park in perfect safety while death sleeted invisibly all around.

Falcon switched on the sleep inducer and consciousness faded swiftly out as the electric pulses surged gently through his brain. While Kon-Tiki fell toward Jupiter, gaining speed second by second in that enormous gravitational field, he slept without dreams. They always came when he awoke; and he had brought his nightmares with him from Earth.

Yet he never dreamed of the crash itself, though he often found himself again face to face with that terrified superchimp, as he descended the spiral stairway between the collapsing gasbags. None of the simps had survived; those that were not killed outright were so badly injured that they had been painlessly euthed. He sometimes wondered why he dreamed only of this doomed creature, which he had never met before the last minutes of its life—and not of the friends and colleagues he had lost aboard the dying Queen.

The dreams he feared most always began with his first return to consciousness.

There had been little physical pain; in fact, there had been no sensation of any kind. He was in darkness and silence and did not even seem to be breathing. And—strangest of all—he could not locate his limbs. He could move neither his hands nor his feet, because he did not know where they were.

The silence had been the first to yield. After hours or days, he had become aware of a faint throbbing and eventually, after long thought, he deduced that this was the beating of his own heart. That was the first of his many mistakes.

Then there had been faint pinpricks, sparkles of light, ghosts of pressures upon still unresponsive limbs. One by one his senses had returned, and pain had come with them. He had had to learn everything anew, recapitulating babyhood and infancy. Though his memory was unaffected and he could understand words that were spoken to him, it was months before he was able to answer except by the flicker of an eyelid. He could still remember the moments of triumph when he had spoken the first word, turned the page of a book—and, finally, learned to move under his own power. *That* was a victory, indeed, and it had taken him almost two years to prepare for it. A hundred times he had envied that dead superchimp, but *he* had been given no choice. The doctors had made their decision—and now, twelve years later, he was where no human being had ever traveled before and moving faster than any man in history.

Kon-Tiki was just emerging from shadow and the Jovian dawn bridged the sky ahead in a titanic bow of light, when the persistent buzz of the alarm dragged Falcon up from sleep. The inevitable nightmares (he had been trying to summon a nurse but did not even have the strength to push the button) swiftly faded from consciousness; the greatest—and perhaps last—adventure of his life was before him.

He called Mission Control, now a hundred thousand kilometers away and falling swiftly below the curve of Jupiter, to report that everything was in order. His velocity had just passed fifty kilometers a second (*that* was one for the books) and in half an hour, Kon-Tiki would hit the outer fringes of the atmosphere, as he started on the most difficult entry in the entire Solar System. Although scores of probes had survived this flaming ordeal, they had been tough, solidly packed masses of instrumentation, able to withstand several hundred gravities of drag. Kon-Tiki would hit peaks of thirty g and would average more than ten before she came to rest in the upper reaches of the Jovian atmosphere. Very carefully and thoroughly, Falcon began to attach the elaborate system of restraints that anchored him to the walls of the cabin. When he had finished, he was virtually a part of the ship's structure.

The clock was counting backward; a hundred seconds to entry. For better or worse, he was committed. In a minute and a half, he would graze the Jovian atmosphere and would be caught irrevocably in the grip of the giant.

The countdown was three seconds late—not at all bad, considering the unknowns involved. Beyond the walls of the capsule came a ghostly sighing that rose steadily to a high-pitched, screaming roar. The noise was quite different from that of a re-entry on Earth or Mars; in this thin atmosphere of hydrogen and helium, all sounds were transformed a couple of octaves higher. On Jupiter, even thunder would have falsetto overtones.

With the rising scream came also mounting weight; within seconds, he was completely immobilized. His field of vision contracted until it embraced only the clock and the accelerometer; fifteen *g*, and 480 seconds to go.

He never lost consciousness; but then, he had not expected to. Kon-Tiki's trail through the Jovian atmosphere must be really spectacular—by this time, thousands of kilometers long. Five hundred seconds after entry, the drag began to taper off: ten *g*, five *g*, two...Then weight vanished almost completely; he was falling free, all his enormous orbital velocity destroyed.

There was a sudden jolt as the incandescent remnants of the heat shield were jettisoned. It had done its work and would not be needed again; Jupiter could have it now. He released all but two of the restraining buckles and waited for the automatic sequencer to start the next and most critical series of events.

He did not see the first drogue parachute pop out, but he could feel the slight jerk and the rate of fall diminished immediately. Kon-Tiki had lost all her horizontal speed and was going straight down at a thousand kilometers an hour. Everything depended on the next sixty seconds.

There went the second drogue. He looked up through the overhead window and saw, to his immense relief, that clouds of glittering foil were billowing out behind the falling ship. Like a great flower unfurling, the thousands of cubic meters of the balloon spread out across the sky, scooping up the thin gas until it was fully inflated. Kon-Tiki's rate of fall dropped to a few kilometers an hour and remained constant. Now there was plenty of time; it would take him days to fall all the way down to the surface of Jupiter.

But he would get there eventually, if he did nothing about it; the balloon overhead was merely acting as an efficient parachute. It was providing no lift, nor could it do so while the gas inside and out was the same.

With its characteristic and rather disconcerting crack, the fusion reactor started up, pouring torrents of heat into the envelope overhead. Within five minutes, the rate of fall had become zero; within six, the ship had started to rise. According to the radar altimeter, it had leveled out at 430 kilometers above the surface—or whatever passed for a surface on Jupiter.

Only one kind of balloon will work in an atmosphere of hydrogen, which is the lightest of all gases—and that is a hot-hydrogen balloon. As long as the fusor kept ticking over, Falcon could remain aloft, drifting across a world that could hold a hundred Pacifics. After traveling more than half a billion kilometers, Kon-Tiki had at last begun to justify her name. She was an aerial raft, adrift upon the current of the Jovian atmosphere.

Though a whole new world was lying around him, it was more than a hour before Falcon could examine the view. First he had to check all the capsule's systems and test its response to the controls. He had to learn how much extra heat was necessary to produce a desired rate of ascent and how much gas he must vent in order to descend. Above all, there was the question of stability. He must adjust the length of the cables attaching his capsule to the huge, pear-shaped balloon, to damp out vibrations and get the smoothest possible ride. So far, he was lucky; at this level, the wind was steady and the Doppler reading on the invisible surface gave him a ground speed of 350 kilometers an hour. For Jupiter, that was modest; winds of up to a thousand had been observed. But mere speed, of course, was unimportant; the real danger was turbulence. If he ran into that, only skill and experience and swift reaction could save him—and these were not matters that could yet be programmed into a computer.

Not until he was satisfied that he had got the feel of this strange craft did Falcon pay any attention to Mission Control's pleadings. Then he deployed the booms carrying the instrumentation and the atmospheric samplers; the capsule now resembled a rather untidy Christmas tree but still rode smoothly down the Jovian winds, while it radioed up its torrents of information to the recorders on the ship a hundred thousand kilometers above. And now, at last, he could look around.

His first impression was unexpected and even a little disappointing. As far as the scale of things was concerned, he might have been ballooning over an ordinary cloudscape on Earth. The horizon seemed at a normal distance; there was no feeling at all that he was on a world eleven times the diameter of his own. Then he looked at the infrared radar, sounding the layers of atmosphere beneath him—and knew how badly his eyes had been deceived.

That layer of clouds, apparently five kilometers away, was really sixty kilometers below. And the horizon, whose distance he would have guessed at two hundred, was actually three thousand kilometers from the ship.

The crystalline clarity of the hydro-helium atmosphere and the enormous curvature of the planet had fooled him completely. It was even harder to judge distances here than on the Moon; everything he saw must be multiplied by ten.

It was a simple matter and he should have been prepared for it. Yet somehow it disturbed him profoundly. He did not feel that Jupiter was huge but that *he* had shrunk—to a tenth of his normal size. Perhaps, with time, he would grow accustomed to the inhuman scale of this world; yet as he stared toward that unbelievably distant horizon, he felt as if a wind colder than the atmosphere around him was blowing through his soul. Despite all his arguments, this might never be a place for man. He could well be both the first and the last to descend through the clouds of Jupiter.

The sky above was almost black, except for a few wisps of ammonia cirrus perhaps twenty kilometers overhead. It was cold up there on the fringes of space, but both pressure and temperature increased rapidly with depth. At the level where Kon-Tiki was drifting now, it was fifty degrees centigrade below zero and the pressure was five atmospheres. A hundred kilometers farther down, it would be as warm as equatorial Earth—and the pressure about the same as at the bottom of one of the shallower seas. Ideal conditions for life.

A quarter of the brief Jovian day had already gone; the Sun was halfway up the sky, but the light on the unbroken cloudscape below had a curious mellow quality. That extra half billion kilometers had robbed the Sun of all its power; though the sky was clear, Falcon found himself continually thinking that it was a heavily overcast day. When night fell, the onset of darkness would be swift, indeed; though it was still morning, there was a sense of autumnal twilight in the air. But autumn, of course, was something that never came to Jupiter. There were no seasons here.

Kon-Tiki had come down in the exact center of the Equatorial Zone—the least colorful part of the planet. The sea of clouds that stretched out to the horizon was tinted a pale salmon; there were none of the yellows and pinks and even reds that banded Jupiter at higher latitudes. The Great Red Spot itself—most spectacular of all the planet's features—lay thousands of kilometers to the south. It had been a temptation to descend there, but the South Tropical Disturbance was unusually active, with currents reaching fifteen hundred kilometers an hour. It would have been asking for trouble to head into that maelstrom of unknown forces. The Great Red Spot and its mysteries would have to wait for future expeditions.

The Sun, moving across the sky twice as swiftly as it did on Earth, was now nearing the zenith and had become eclipsed by the great silver canopy of the balloon. Kon-Tiki was still drifting swiftly, smoothly westward at a steady 350, but only the radar gave any indication of this. Was it always as calm here? Falcon asked himself. The scientists who had talked learnedly of the Jovian doldrums and had predicted that the equator would be the quietest place seemed to know what they were talking about, after all. He had been profoundly skeptical of all such forecasts and had agreed with one unusually modest researcher who had told him bluntly, "There are *no* experts on Jupiter." Well, there would be at least one by the end of this day.

If he managed to survive until then.

THE VOICES OF THE DEEP

That first day, the Father of the Gods smiled upon him. It was as calm and peaceful here on Jupiter as it had been, years ago, when he was drifting with Webster across the plains of northern India. Falcon had time to master his new skills, until Kon-Tiki seemed an extension of his own body. Such luck was more than he had dared hope and he began to wonder what price he might have to pay for it.

The five hours of daylight were almost over; the clouds below were full of shadows, which gave them a massive solidity they had not possessed when the Sun was higher. Color was swiftly draining from the sky, except in the west itself, where a band of deepening purple lay along the horizon. Above this band was the thin crescent of a closer moon, pale and bleached against the utter blackness beyond.

With a speed perceptible to the eye, the Sun went straight down over the edge of Jupiter, three thousand kilometers away. The stars came out in their legions— and there was the beautiful evening star of Earth, on the very frontier of twilight, reminding him how far he was from home. It followed the Sun down into the west; man's first night on Jupiter had begun.

With the onset of darkness, Kon-Tiki started to sink. The balloon was no longer heated by the feeble sunlight and was losing a small part of its buoyancy. Falcon did nothing to increase lift; he had expected this and was planning to descend.

The invisible cloud deck was still fifty kilometers below and he would reach it about midnight. It showed up clearly on the infrared radar, which also reported that it contained a vast array of complex carbon compounds, as well as the usual hydrogen, helium and ammonia. The chemists were dying for samples of that fluffy, pinkish stuff; though some atmospheric probes had already gathered a few grams, that had only whetted their appetites. Half the basic molecules of life were here, floating high above the surface of Jupiter. And where there was food, could life be far away? That was the question that, after more than a hundred years, no one had been able to answer.

The infrared was blocked by the clouds, but the microwave radar sliced right through and showed layer after layer, all the way down to the hidden surface more than four hundred kilometers below. That was barred to him by enormous pressures and temperatures; not even robot probes had ever reached it intact. It lay in tantalizing inaccessibility at the bottom of the radar screen, slightly fuzzy and showing a curious granular structure that his equipment could not resolve.

An hour after sunset, he dropped his first probe. It fell swiftly for a hundred kilometers, then began to float in the denser atmosphere, sending back torrents of radio signals, which he relayed up to Mission Control. Then there was nothing else to do until sunrise, except to keep an eye on the rate of descent, monitor the instruments and answer occasional queries. While she was drifting in this steady current, Kon-Tiki could look after herself.

Just before midnight, a woman controller came on watch and introduced herself with the usual pleasantries. Ten minutes later, she called again, her voice at once serious and excited.

"Howard! Listen in on channel forty-six—high gain."

Channel 46? There were so many telemetering circuits that he knew the numbers of only those that were critical; but as soon as he threw the switch, he recognized this one. He was plugged into the microphone on the probe, floating 130 kilometers below him in an atmosphere now almost as dense as water.

At first, there was only a soft hiss of whatever strange winds stirred down in the darkness of that unimaginable world. And then, out of the background noise, there slowly emerged a booming vibration that grew louder and louder, like the beating of a gigantic drum. It was so low that it was felt as much as heard and the beats steadily increased their tempo, though the pitch never changed. Now it was a swift, almost infrasonic throbbing—and then, suddenly, in mid-vibration, it stopped, so abruptly that the mind could not accept the silence, but memory continued to manufacture a ghostly echo in the deepest caverns of the brain.

It was the most extraordinary sound that Falcon had ever heard, even among the multitudinous noises of Earth. He could think of no natural phenomenon that could have caused it, nor was it like the cry of any animal, not even one of the great whales.

It came again, following exactly the same pattern. Now that he was prepared for it, he estimated the length of the sequence; from first faint throb to final crescendo, it lasted just over ten seconds.

And this time, there was a real echo, very faint and far away. Perhaps it came from one of the many reflecting layers deeper in this stratified atmosphere; perhaps it was another more distant source. Falcon waited for a second echo, but it never came.

Mission Control reacted quickly and asked him to drop another probe at once. With two microphones operating, it would be possible to find the approximate location of the sources. Oddly enough, none of Kon-Tiki's own external mikes could detect anything except wind noises; the boomings, whatever they were, must have been trapped and channeled beneath an atmospheric reflecting layer far below.

They were coming, it was soon discovered, from a cluster of sources about two thousand kilometers away. The distance gave no indication of their power; in Earth's oceans, quite feeble sounds could travel equally far. And as for the obvious assumption that living creatures were responsible, the chief exobiologist quickly ruled that out.

"I'll be very disappointed," said Dr. Brenner, "if there are no microorganisms or plants here. But nothing like animals, because there's no free oxygen. All biochemical reactions on Jupiter must be low-energy ones—there's just no way an active creature could generate enough power to function."

Falcon wondered if this were true; he had heard the argument before and reserved judgment.

"In any case," continued Brenner, "some of those sound waves are a hundred meters long! Even an animal as big as a whale couldn't produce them. They *must* have a natural origin."

Yes, that seemed plausible, and probably the physicists would be able to come up with an explanation. What would a blind alien make, Falcon wondered, of the sounds he might hear when standing beside a stormy sea or a geyser or a volcano or a waterfall? He might well attribute them to some huge beast.

About an hour before sunrise, the voices of the deep died away and Falcon began to busy himself with preparation for the dawn of his second day. Kon-Tiki was now only five kilometers above the nearest cloud layer; the external pressure had risen to ten atmospheres and the temperature was a tropical thirty degrees. A man could be comfortable here with no more equipment than a breathing mask and the right grade of heliox mixture.

"We've some good news for you," Mission Control reported soon after dawn. "The cloud layer's breaking up. You'll have partial clearing in an hour—but watch out for turbulence."

"I've already noticed some," Falcon answered. "How far down will I be able to see?"

"At least twenty kilometers, down to the second thermocline. *That* cloud deck is solid—it never breaks."

And it's out of my reach, Falcon told himself; the temperature down there must be over a hundred degrees. This was the first time that any balloonist had ever had to worry not about his ceiling but about his—basement?

Ten minutes later, he could see what Mission Control had already observed from its superior vantage point. There was a change in color near the horizon and the cloud layer had become ragged and humpy, as if something had torn it open. He turned up his little nuclear furnace and gave Kon-Tiki another five kilometers of altitude so that he could get a better view.

The sky below was clearing rapidly—completely, as if something was dissolving away the solid overcast. An abyss was opening up before his eyes; a moment later, he sailed out over the edge of a cloud canyon twenty kilometers deep and a thousand kilometers wide.

A new world lay spread beneath him; Jupiter had stripped away one of its many veils. The second layer of clouds, unattainably far below, was much darker in color than the first. It was almost salmon pink and curiously mottled with little islands of brick red. They were all oval-shaped, with their long axes pointing east-west, in the direction of the prevailing wind. There were hundreds of them, all about the same size, and they reminded Falcon of puffy little cumulus clouds in the terrestrial sky.

He reduced buoyancy and Kon-Tiki began to drop down the face of the dissolving cliff. It was then that he noticed the snow.

White flakes were forming in the air and drifting slowly downward. Yet it was much too warm for snow—and, in any event, there was scarcely a trace of water at this altitude. Moreover, there was no glitter nor sparkle about these flakes as they were cascading down into the depths; when, presently, a few landed on an instrument boom outside the main viewing port, he saw that they were a dull, opaque white—not crystalline at all—and quite large, several centimeters across. They looked like wax and Falcon guessed that this was precisely what they were. Some chemical reaction was taking place in the atmosphere around him, condensing out the hydrocarbons floating in the Jovian air.

A hundred kilometers ahead, a disturbance was taking place in the cloud layer. The little red ovals were being jostled around and were beginning to form a spiral— the familiar cyclonic pattern so common in the meteorology of Earth. The vortex was emerging with astonishing speed; if that was a storm ahead, Falcon told himself, he was in big trouble.

And then his concern changed to wonder—and to fear. For what was developing in his line of flight was not a storm at all. Something enormous—something scores of kilometers across—was rising through the clouds.

The reassuring thought that it, too, might be a cloud—a thunderhead boiling up from the lower levels of the atmosphere—lasted only a few seconds. No; this was *solid*. It shouldered its way through the pink-and-salmon overcast like an iceberg rising from the deeps.

An *iceberg*, floating on hydrogen? That was impossible, of course; but perhaps it was not too remote an analogy. As soon as he focused the telescope upon the enigma, Falcon saw that it was a whitish mass, threaded with streaks of red and brown. It must be, he decided, the same stuff as the "snowflakes" falling around him—a mountain range of wax. And it was not, he soon realized, as solid as he had thought; around the edges, it was continually crumbling and reforming.

"I know what it is," he radioed Mission Control, which for the past few minutes had been asking anxious questions. "It's a mass of bubbles—some kind of foam. Hydrocarbon froth. Get the chemists working on—*just a minute!*"

"What is it?" called Mission Control. "What is it?"

He ignored the frantic pleas from space and concentrated all his mind upon the image in the telescope field. He had to be sure; if he made a mistake, he would be the laughingstock of the Solar System.

Then he relaxed, glanced at the clock and switched off the nagging voice from Jupiter V.

"Hello, Mission Control," he said very formally. "This is Howard Falcon aboard

Kon-Tiki, Ephemeris Time Nineteen Hours Twenty One Minutes Fifteen Seconds. Latitude Zero Degrees Five Minutes North. Longitude One Hundred Five Degrees Forty Two Minutes, System One.

"Tell Dr. Brenner that there is life on Jupiter. And it's *big*."

THE WHEELS OF POSEIDON

"I'm very happy to be proved wrong," Dr. Brenner radioed back cheerfully. "Nature always has something up her sleeve. Keep the long-focus camera on target and give us the steadiest pictures you can."

The things moving up and down those waxen slopes were still too far away for Falcon to make out many details, and they must have been very large to be visible at all at such a distance. Almost black and shaped like arrowheads, they maneuvered by slow undulations of their entire bodies, so that they looked rather like giant manta rays swimming above some tropical reef.

Perhaps they were sky-borne cattle browsing on the cloud pastures of Jupiter, for they seemed to be feeding along the dark, red-brown streaks that ran like dried-up river beds down the flanks of the floating cliffs. Occasionally, one of them would dive headlong into the mountain of foam and disappear completely from sight.

Kon-Tiki was moving only slowly with respect to the cloud layer below; it would be at least three hours before she was above those ephemeral hills. She was in a race with the Sun; Falcon hoped that darkness would not fall before he could get a good view of the mantas, as he had christened them, as well as the fragile landscape over which they flapped their way.

It was a long three hours; during the whole time, he kept the external microphones on full gain, wondering if here was the source of that booming in the night. The mantas were certainly large enough to have produced it; when he could get an accurate measurement, he discovered that they were almost a hundred meters across the wings. That was three times the length of the largest whale—though he doubted if they could weigh more than a few tons.

Half an hour before sunset, Kon-Tiki was almost above the "mountains."

"No," said Falcon, answering Mission Control's repeated questions about the mantas. "They're still showing no reaction to me. I don't think they're intelligent— they look like harmless vegetarians. And even if they try to chase me—I'm sure they can't reach my altitude."

Yet he was a little disappointed when the mantas showed not the slightest interest in him as he sailed high above their feeding ground. Perhaps they had no way of detecting his presence; when he examined and photographed them through the telescope, he could see no signs of any sense organs. The creatures were merely huge black deltas rippling over hills and valleys that, in reality, were little more substantial than the clouds of Earth. Though they looked so solid, Falcon knew that anyone who stepped on those white mountains would go crashing through them as if they were made of tissue paper.

At close quarters, he could see the myriads of cellules or bubbles from which they were formed. Some of these were quite large—a meter or so in diameter—and Falcon wondered in what witch's caldron of hydrocarbons they had been brewed. There must be enough petrochemicals deep down in the atmosphere of Jupiter to supply all Earth's needs for a million years.

The short day had almost gone when he passed over the crest of the waxen hills and the light was fading rapidly along their lower slopes. There were no mantas on this western side and for some reason, the topography was very different. The foam was sculpted into long level terraces, like the interior of a lunar crater. He could almost imagine that they were gigantic steps leading down to the hidden surface of the planet.

And on the lowest of those steps, just clear of the swirling clouds that the mountain had displaced when it came surging skyward, was a roughly oval mass two or three kilometers across. It was difficult to see, being only a little darker than the gray-white foam on which it rested. Falcon's first reaction was that he was looking at a forest of pallid trees, like giant mushrooms that had never seen the Sun.

Yes, it must be a forest—he could see hundreds of thin trunks springing from the white, waxy froth in which they were rooted. But the trees were packed astonishingly close together; there was scarcely any space between them. Perhaps it was not a forest after all but a single enormous tree—like one of the giant, multiple-trunked banyans of the East. He had once seen, in Java, a banyan tree two hundred meters across; this monster was at least ten times that size.

The light had almost gone; the cloudscape had turned purple with refracted sunlight and in a few seconds that, too, would have vanished. In the very last light of his second day on Jupiter, Howard Falcon saw—or thought he saw—something that cast the very gravest doubts on his interpretation of the white oval.

Unless the dim light had totally deceived him, those hundreds of thin trunks were beating back and forth, in perfect synchronism, like fronds of kelp rocking in the surge.

And the tree was no longer in the place where he had first seen it.

"Sorry about this," said Mission Control soon after sunset, "but we think Source Beta is going to blow within the next hour. Probability seventy percent."

Falcon glanced quickly at the chart. Beta—Jupiter latitude 140 degrees—was thirty thousand kilometers away and well below his horizon. Even though major eruptions ran as high as ten megatons, he was much too far away for the shock wave to be a serious danger. The radio storm that it would trigger was, however, quite a different matter.

The decameter outbursts that sometimes made Jupiter the most powerful radio source in the whole sky had been discovered back in the 1950s, to the utter astonishment of the astronomers. Now, more than a century later, their real cause was still a mystery. Only the symptoms were understood; the explanation was completely unknown.

The "volcano" theory had best stood the test of time—although no one imagined that this word had the same meaning on Jupiter as on Earth. At frequent intervals—often several times a day—titanic eruptions occurred in the lower depths of the atmosphere, probably on the hidden surface of the planet itself. A great column of gas, more than a thousand kilometers high, would start boiling upward, as if determined to escape into space.

Against the most powerful gravitational field of all the planets, it had no chance. Yet some traces—a mere few million tons—usually managed to reach the Jovian ionosphere; and when they did, all hell broke loose.

The radiation belts surrounding Jupiter completely dwarf the feeble Van Allen belts of Earth. When they are short-circuited by an ascending column of gas, the result is an electrical discharge millions of times more powerful than any terrestrial flash of lightning; it sends a colossal thunderclap of radio noise flooding across the entire Solar System—and on out to the stars.

It had been discovered that these radio outbursts came from four main areas of the planet; perhaps there were weaknesses here that allowed the fires of the interior to break out from time to time. The scientists on Ganymede, largest of Jupiter's many moons, now thought that they could predict the onset of a decameter storm; their accuracy was about as good as a weather forecaster's of the early 1900s.

Falcon did not know whether to welcome or to fear a radio storm; it would certainly add to the value of the mission—if he survived it. His course had been planned to keep as far as possible from the main centers of disturbance, especially the most active one, Source Alpha. As luck would have it, the threatening Beta was the closest to him; he hoped that thirty thousand kilometers—almost the circumference of Earth—was a safe enough distance.

"Probability ninety percent," said Mission Control with a distinct note of urgency. "And forget that hour. Ganymede says it may be any moment."

The radio had scarcely fallen silent when the reading on the magnetic-field-strength meter started to shoot upward. Before it could go off-scale, it reversed and began to drop as rapidly as it had risen. Far away and thousands of kilometers below, something had given the planet's molten core a titanic jolt.

"There she blows!" called Mission Control.

"Thanks—I already know. When will the storm hit me?"

"You can expect onset in five minutes. Peak in ten."

Far round the curve of Jupiter, a funnel of gas as wide as the Pacific Ocean was climbing spaceward at thousands of kilometers an hour. Already, the thunderstorms of the lower atmosphere would be raging around it—but they were as nothing to the fury that would explode when the radiation belt was reached and it began dumping its surplus electrons onto the planet. Falcon began to retract all the instrument booms that were extended out from the capsule; there were no other precautions he could take. It would be four hours before the atmospheric shock wave reached him—but the radio blast, traveling at the speed of light, would be here in a tenth of a second once the discharge had been triggered.

The radio monitor, scanning back and forth across the spectrum, still showed nothing unusual—just the normal mush of background static. Then Falcon noticed that the noise level was slowly creeping upward. The explosion was gathering its strength.

At such a distance, he had never expected to *see* anything. But suddenly a flicker as of far-off heat lightning danced along the eastern horizon. Simultaneously, half the circuit breakers jumped out of the main switchboard, the lights failed and all communications channels went dead.

He tried to move but was completely unable to do so. The paralysis that gripped him was not merely psychological; he seemed to have lost all control of his limbs and could feel a painful tingling sensation over his entire body. It was impossible that the electric field could have penetrated into this shielded cabin—yet there was a flickering glow over the instrument board and he could hear the unmistakable crackle of a brush discharge.

With a series of sharp bangs, the emergency systems operated and the overloads reset themselves. The lights flickered on again and Falcon's paralysis disappeared as swiftly as it had come. After glancing at the board to make sure that all circuits were back to normal, he moved quickly to the viewing ports.

There was no need to switch on the inspection lamps—the cables supporting the capsule seemed to be on fire. Lines of light, glowing an electric blue against the darkness, stretched upward from the main lift ring to the equator of the giant balloon; and rolling slowly along several of them were dazzling balls of fire.

The sight was so strange and so beautiful that it was hard to read any menace in it. Few people, Falcon knew, had ever seen ball lightning from such close quarters—and certainly none had survived if they were riding a hydrogen-filled balloon back in the atmosphere of Earth. He remembered the flaming death of the Hindenburg, destroyed by a stray spark when she docked at Lakehurst in 1937; as it had done so often in the past, the horrifying old newsreel film flashed through his mind. But at least that could not happen here, though there was more hydrogen above his head than had ever filled the last of the zeppelins. It would be a few billion years yet before anyone could light a fire in the atmosphere of Jupiter.

With a sound like briskly frying bacon, the speech circuit came back to life.

"Hello, Kon-Tiki—are you receiving? Are you receiving?"

The words were chopped and badly distorted but intelligible. Falcon's spirits lifted; he had resumed contact with the world of men.

"I receive you," he said. "Quite an electrical display, but no damage—so far."

"Thanks—thought we'd lost you. Please check telemetry channels three, seven, twenty-six. Also gain on camera two. And we don't quite believe the readings on the external ionization probes."

Reluctantly, Falcon tore his gaze away from the fascinating pyrotechnic display around Kon-Tiki, though from time to time he kept glancing out the windows. The ball lightning disappeared first, the fiery globes slowly expanding until they reached a critical size, at which they vanished in a gentle explosion. But for an hour later, there were still faint glows around all the exposed metal on the outside of the capsule; and the radio circuits remained noisy until well after midnight.

The remaining hours of darkness were completely uneventful—until just before dawn. Because it came from the east, Falcon assumed that he was seeing the first faint hint of sunrise. Then he realized that it was still twenty minutes too early for it—and the glow that had appeared along the horizon was moving toward him even as he watched. It swiftly detached itself from the arch of stars that marked the invisible edge of the planet and he saw that it was a relatively narrow band, quite sharply defined. The beam of an enormous searchlight appeared to be swinging beneath the clouds.

Perhaps a hundred kilometers behind the first racing bar of light came another, parallel to it and moving at the same speed. And beyond that another, and another—until all the sky flickered with alternating sheets of light and darkness.

By this time, Falcon thought, he had been inured to wonders and it seemed impossible that this display of pure, soundless luminosity could present the slightest danger. But it was so astonishing and so inexplicable that he felt cold naked fear gnawing at his self-control. No man could look upon such a sight without feeling a helpless pygmy, in the presence of forces beyond his comprehension. Was it possible that, after all, Jupiter carried not only life but intelligence? And, perhaps, an intelligence that only now was beginning to react to his alien presence.

"Yes, we see it," said Mission Control in a voice that echoed his own awe. "We've no idea what it is. Stand by—we're calling Ganymede."

The display was slowly fading; the bands racing in from the far horizon were much fainter, as if the energies that powered them were becoming exhausted. In five minutes, it was all over; the last faint pulse of light flickered along the western sky and then was gone. Its passing left Falcon with an overwhelming sense of relief. The sight was so hypnotic and so disturbing that it was not good for any man's peace of mind to contemplate it too long.

He was more shaken than he cared to admit. The electrical storm was something that he could understand, but *this* was totally incomprehensible.

Mission Control was still silent. Falcon knew that the information banks up on Ganymede were now being searched while men and computers turned their minds to the problem. If no answer could be found there, it would be necessary to call Earth; that would mean a delay of almost an hour. The possibility that even Earth might be unable to help was one that Falcon did not care to contemplate.

He had never before been so glad to hear the voice of Mission Control as when Dr. Brenner finally came on the circuit. The biologist sounded relieved—yet subdued, like a man who had just come through some great intellectual crisis.

"Hello, Kon-Tiki. We've solved your problem, but we can still hardly believe it.

"What you've been seeing is bioluminescence—very similar to that produced by microorganisms in the tropical seas of Earth. Here they're in the atmosphere, not the ocean, but the principle is the same."

"But the pattern," protested Falcon. "It was so regular—so *artificial*. And it was hundreds of kilometers across!"

"It was even larger than you imagine—you observed only a small part of it. The whole pattern was five thousand kilometers wide and looked like a revolving wheel. You merely saw the spokes, sweeping past you at about a kilometer a second—"

"A *second*," Falcon could not help interjecting. "No animals could move that fast!"

"Of course not—let me explain. What you saw was triggered by the shock wave from Source Beta, moving at the speed of sound."

"But what about the pattern?" Falcon insisted.

"That's the surprising part. It's a very rare phenomenon, but identical wheels of light — except that they're a thousand times smaller — have been observed in the Persian Gulf and the Indian Ocean. Listen to this: British India Company's Patna, Persian Gulf, May 1880, eleven-thirty P.M. — 'An enormous luminous wheel, whirling round, the spokes of which appeared to brush the ship along. The spokes were two hundred or three hundred yards long ... each wheel contained about sixteen spokes. ...' And here's one from the Gulf of Oman, dated 23 May, 1906: 'The intensely bright luminescence approached us rapidly, shooting sharply defined light rays to the west in rapid succession, like the beam from the searchlight of a warship. ... To the left of us, a gigantic fiery wheel formed itself, with spokes that reached as far as one could see. The whole wheel whirled around for two or three minutes.' The archive computer on Ganymede dug up about five hundred cases — it would have printed out the lot if we hadn't stopped it in time."

"I'm convinced — but still baffled."

"I don't blame you; the full explanation wasn't worked out until later in the twentieth century. It seems that these luminous wheels are the results of submarine earthquakes and always occur in shallow waters, where the shock waves can be reflected and cause standard wave patterns. Sometimes bars — sometimes rotating wheels — the 'Wheels of Poseidon,' they've been called. The theory was finally proved by making underwater explosions and photographing the results from a satellite. No wonder sailors used to be superstitious. Who would have believed a thing like *this?*"

So that was it, Falcon told himself. When Source Beta blew its top, it must have sent shock waves in all directions — through the compressed gas of the lower atmosphere, through the solid body of Jupiter itself. Meeting and crisscrossing, those waves must have canceled here, reinforced there; the whole planet must have rung like a bell.

Yet the explanation did not destroy the sense of wonder and awe; he would never be able to forget those flickering bands of light racing through the unattainable depths of the Jovian atmosphere. He felt that he was not merely on a strange planet but in some magical realm between myth and reality.

This was a world where absolutely *anything* could happen and no man could possibly guess what the future would bring.

And he still had a whole day to go.

MEDUSA

When the true dawn finally arrived, it brought a sudden change of weather. Kon-Tiki was moving through a blizzard; waxen snowflakes were falling so thickly that visibility was reduced to zero. Falcon began to worry about the weight that might be accumulating on the envelope; then he noticed that any flakes settling outside the windows quickly disappeared. Kon-Tiki's continuous outpouring of heat was evaporating them as swiftly as they arrived.

If he had been ballooning on Earth, he would also have worried about the possibility of collision. That, at least, was no danger here; any Jovian mountains were several hundred kilometers below him. And as for the floating islands of foam, hitting them would probably be like plowing into slightly hardened soap bubbles.

Nevertheless, he switched on the horizontal radar, which until now had been completely useless; only the vertical beam, giving his distance from the invisible surface, so far had been of any value. And then he had another surprise.

Scattered across a huge sector of the sky ahead were dozens of large and brilliant echoes. They were completely isolated from one another and hung apparently unsupported in space. Falcon suddenly remembered a phrase that earliest aviators had used to describe one of the hazards of their profession—"clouds stuffed with rocks." That was a perfect description of what seemed to lie in the track of Kon-Tiki.

It was a disconcerting sight; then Falcon again reminded himself that nothing *really* solid could possibly hover in this atmosphere. Perhaps it was some strange meteorological phenomenon—and, in any case, the nearest echo was over two hundred kilometers away.

He reported to Mission Control, which could provide no explanation. But it gave the welcome news that he would be clear of the blizzard in another thirty minutes.

It did not warn him, however, of the violent cross wind that abruptly grabbed Kon-Tiki and swept it almost at right angles to its previous track. Falcon needed all his skill and the maximum use of what little control he had over his ungainly vehicle to prevent it from being capsized. Within minutes, he was racing northward at five hundred kilometers an hour; then, as suddenly as it had started, the turbulence ceased; he was still moving at high speed but in smooth air. He wondered if he had been caught in the Jovian equivalent of a jet stream.

Then the snowstorm suddenly dissolved and he saw what Jupiter had been preparing for him.

Kon-Tiki had entered the funnel of a gigantic whirlpool, at least three hundred kilometers across. The balloon was being swept along a curving wall of cloud; overhead, the Sun was shining in a clear sky, but far beneath, this great hole in the atmosphere drilled down to unknown depths, until it reached a misty floor where lightning flickered almost continuously.

Though the vessel was being dragged downward so slowly that it was in no immediate danger, Falcon increased the flow of heat into the envelope, until Kon-Tiki hovered at a constant altitude. Not until then did he abandon the fantastic spectacle outside and consider again the problem of the radar.

The nearest echo was now only forty kilometers away—and all of them, he quickly realized, were distributed along the wall of the vortex; they were moving with it, apparently caught in the whirlpool like Kon-Tiki itself. He aimed the telescope along the radar bearing and found himself looking at a curious mottled cloud that almost filled the field of view.

It was not easy to see, being only little darker than the whirling wall of mist that formed its background. Not until he had been staring for several minutes did Falcon realize that he had met it once before.

The first time, it had been crawling across the drifting mountains of foam and he had mistaken it for a giant, many-trunked tree. Now at last he could appreciate its real size and complexity and he could give it a better name to fix its image in his mind. It did not resemble a tree at all but a jellyfish—a medusa, such as might be met trailing its tentacles as it drifted along the warm eddies of the Gulf Stream.

This medusa was two kilometers across and its scores of dangling tentacles were hundreds of meters long. They swayed slowly back and forth in perfect unison, taking more than a minute for each complete undulation—almost as if the creature were clumsily rowing itself through the sky.

The other echoes were more distant medusae; Falcon turned the telescope on half a dozen and could see no variations in shape or size. They all seemed to be of the same species and he wondered just why they were drifting lazily around in this thousand-kilometer orbit. Perhaps they were feeding upon the aerial plankton sucked in by the whirlpool—as Kon-Tiki itself had been.

"Do you realize, Howard," said Dr. Brenner when he had recovered from his initial astonishment, "that this thing is about a hundred thousand times as large as the biggest whale? And even if it's only a gasbag, it must still weigh a million tons! I can't even guess at its metabolism; it must generate megawatts of heat to maintain its buoyancy."

"But if it's just a gasbag, why is it such a damn good radar reflector?"

"I haven't the faintest idea. Can you get any closer?"

Brenner's question was not an idle one; if Falcon changed altitude to take advantage of the differing wind velocities, he could approach the medusa as closely as he wished. At the moment, he preferred his present forty kilometers and said so, firmly.

"I see what you mean," Brenner answered a little reluctantly. "Let's stay where we are for the present." That "we" gave Falcon a certain wry amusement; an extra hundred thousand kilometers made a considerable difference to one's point of view.

For the next two hours, Kon-Tiki drifted uneventfully in the gyre of the great whirlpool, while Falcon experimented with filters and camera contrast, trying to get a clear view of the medusa. He began to wonder if its elusive coloration were some kind of camouflage; perhaps, like many animals of Earth, it was trying to lose itself against its background. That was a trick used both by hunters and by the hunted.

In which category was the medusa? That was a question he could hardly expect to have answered in the short time that was left to him. Yet just before noon, without the slightest warning, the answer came.

Like a squadron of antique jet fighters, five mantas came sweeping through the wall of mist that formed the funnel of the vortex. They were flying in a V formation, directly toward the pallid gray cloud of the medusa—and there was no doubt, in Falcon's mind, that they were on the attack. He had been quite wrong to assume that they were harmless vegetarians.

Yet everything happened at such a leisurely pace that it was like watching a slow-motion film. The mantas undulated along at perhaps fifty kilometers an hour; it seemed ages before they reached the medusa, which continued to paddle imperturbably along at an even slower speed. Huge though they were, the mantas looked tiny beside the monster they were approaching; when they flapped down onto its back, they appeared about as large as birds landing on a whale.

Could the medusa defend itself? Falcon wondered. As long as they avoided those huge, clumsy tentacles, he did not see how the attacking mantas could be in any danger. And perhaps their host was not even aware of them; they could be insignificant parasites, as tolerated as fleas upon a dog.

But now it was obvious that the medusa was in distress. With agonizing slowness, it began to tip over, like a capsizing ship. After ten minutes, it had tilted forty-five degrees; it was also rapidly losing altitude. It was impossible not to feel a sense of pity for the beleaguered monster, and to Howard Falcon the sight brought bitter memories. In a grotesque way, the fall of the medusa was almost a parody of the dying Queen's last moments.

Yet he knew that his sympathies were on the wrong side. High intelligence could only develop among predators—not among the drifting browsers of either sea or air. The mantas were far closer to him than was this monstrous bag of gas; and anyway, who could *really* sympathize with a creature a hundred thousand times larger than a whale?

Then he noticed that the medusa's tactics seemed to be having some effect. The mantas had been disturbed by its slow roll and were flapping heavily away from its back—like gorged vultures interrupted at mealtime. But they did not move very far, continuing to hover a few meters from the still capsizing monster.

There was a sudden, blinding flash of light, synchronized with a crash of static over the radio. One of the mantas, slowly twisting end over end, was plummeting straight downward. As it fell, it trailed behind it a smoky black plume. Though there could be no fire, the resemblance to an aircraft going down in flames was quite uncanny.

In unison, the remaining mantas dived steeply away from the medusa, gaining speed by losing altitude. Within minutes, they had vanished back into the wall of cloud from which they had emerged. And the medusa, no longer falling, began to roll back toward the horizontal. Soon it was sailing along once more on an even keel, as if nothing had happened.

"Beautiful!" said Dr. Brenner after a moment of stunned silence. "It's developed electric defenses—like some of our eels and rays. But that must have been about a million volts! Can you see any organs that might produce the discharge? Anything looking like electrodes?"

"No," Falcon answered, after switching to the highest power of the telescope. "But here's something odd. Do you see this pattern? Check back on the earlier images—I'm sure it wasn't there before."

A broad, mottled band had appeared along the side of the medusa. It formed a startlingly regular checkerboard, each square of which was itself speckled in a complex subpattern of short horizontal lines. They were spaced equal distances apart, in a geometrically perfect array of rows and columns.

"You're right," said Dr. Brenner, and now there was something very much like awe in his voice. "That's just appeared. And I'm afraid to tell you what I think it is."

"Well, I have no reputation to lose—at least as a biologist. Shall I give my guess?"

"Go ahead."

"That's a large meter-band radio array. The sort of thing they used back at the beginning of the twentieth century."

"I was afraid you'd say that. Now we know why it gave such a massive echo."

"But why has it just appeared?"

"Probably an aftereffect of the discharge."

"I've just had another thought," said Falcon rather slowly. "Do you suppose it's *listening* to us?"

"On this frequency? I doubt it. Those are meter—no, *decameter* antennas, judging by their size. Hmm . . . that's an idea!"

Dr. Brenner fell silent, obviously contemplating some new line of thought. Presently, he continued: "I bet they're tuned to the radio outbursts! That's something nature never got around to doing on Earth. We have animals with sonar and even electric senses, but nothing ever developed a radio sense. Why bother, where there was so much light?

"But it's different here. Jupiter is *drenched* with radio energy. It's worth while using it—maybe even tapping it. That thing could be a floating power plant!"

A new voice cut into the conversation.

"Mission Commander here. This is all very interesting—but there's a much more important matter to settle. *Is it intelligent?* If so, we've got to consider the First Contact directives."

"Until I came here," said Dr. Brenner somewhat ruefully, "I would have sworn that anything that can make a shortwave antenna system *must* be intelligent. Now I'm not sure. This could have evolved naturally. I suppose it's no more fantastic than the human eye."

"Then we have to play safe and assume intelligence. For the present, therefore, this expedition comes under all the clauses of the Prime Directive."

There was a long silence while everyone on the radio circuit absorbed the implications of this. For the first time in the history of space flight, the rules that had been established through more than a century of argument might have to be applied. Man had—it was hoped—profited from his mistakes on Earth. Not only moral considerations but his own self-interest demanded that he should not repeat them among the planets. It could be disastrous to treat a superior intelligence as the American settlers had treated the red Indians or as almost everyone had treated the Africans.

The first rule was: Keep your distance—make no attempt to approach nor even to communicate until "they" have had plenty of time to study you. Exactly what was meant by plenty of time no one had ever been able to decide; it was left to the discretion of the man on the spot.

A responsibility of which he had never dreamed had descended upon Howard Falcon. In the few hours that remained to him on Jupiter, he might become the first ambassador of the human race.

And *that* was an irony so delicious that he almost wished the surgeons had restored to him the power of laughter.

PRIME DIRECTIVE

It was growing darker, but Falcon scarcely noticed as he strained his eyes toward that living cloud in the field of the telescope. The wind that was still sweeping Kon-Tiki steadily around the funnel of the great whirlpool had now brought him within twenty kilometers of the creature; if he got much closer than ten, he would take evasive action. Though he felt certain that the medusa's electric weapons were short-ranged, he did not wish to put the matter to the test. That would be a problem for future explorers, and he wished them luck.

Now it was quite dark in the capsule—and that was strange, because sunset was still hours away. Automatically, he glanced at the horizontally scanning radar, as he had done every few minutes. Apart from the medusa he was studying, there was no other object within a hundred kilometers of him.

Suddenly, with startling power, he heard the sound that had come booming out of the Jovian night—the throbbing beat that grew more and more rapid, then stopped mid-crescendo. The whole capsule vibrated with it, like a pea in a kettledrum.

Howard Falcon realized two things almost simultaneously, during the sudden, aching silence. *This* time, the sound was not coming from thousands of kilometers away, over a radio circuit. It was in the very atmosphere around him.

The second thought was even more disturbing. He had quite forgotten—it was inexcusable, but there had been other apparently more important things on his mind—that most of the sky above him was completely blanked out by Kon-Tiki's gasbag. Being lightly silvered to conserve its heat, the great balloon was an effective shield both to radar and to vision.

He had known this, of course; it had been a minor defect of the design, tolerated because it did not appear important. It seemed very important to Howard Falcon now—as he saw that fence of gigantic tentacles, thicker than the trunks of any tree, descending all around the capsule.

He heard Brenner yelling: "Remember the Prime Directive! Don't alarm it!" Before he could make an appropriate answer, that overwhelming drumbeat started again and drowned all other sounds.

The sign of a really skilled test pilot is how he reacts not to foreseeable emergencies but to ones that nobody could have anticipated. Falcon did not hesitate for more than a second to analyze the situation; then, in a lightning-swift movement, he pulled the rip cord.

That word was an archaic survival from the days of the first hydrogen balloons; on Kon-Tiki, the rip cord did not tear open the gasbag but merely operated a set of louvers round the upper curve of the envelope. At once, the hot gas started to rush out; Kon-Tiki, deprived of her lift, began to fall swiftly in this gravity field two and a half times as strong as Earth's.

Falcon had a momentary glimpse of great tentacles whipping upward and away; he had just time to note that they were studded with large bladders or sacs, presumably to give them buoyancy, and that they ended in multitudes of thin feelers like the roots of a plant. He half expected a bolt of lightning, but nothing happened.

His precipitous rate of descent was slackening as the atmosphere thickened and the deflated envelope acted as a parachute. Kon-Tiki had dropped more than three kilometers; it should be safe to close the louvers again. By the time he had restored buoyancy and was in equilibrium once more, he had lost another two kilometers of altitude and was getting dangerously near his safety limit.

He peered anxiously through the overhead windows, though he did not expect to see anything except the obscuring bulk of the balloon. But he had side-slipped during his descent and part of the medusa was just visible a couple of kilometers above him. It was much closer than he expected—and it was still coming down, faster than he would have believed possible.

Mission Control was calling anxiously; he shouted, "I'm OK—but it's still coming after me. I can't go any deeper."

That was not quite true. He could go a lot deeper—about 300 kilometers. But it would be a one-way trip and most of the journey would be of little interest to him.

Then, to his great relief, he saw that the medusa was leveling off about a kilometer above him. Perhaps it had decided to approach this strange intruder with caution—or perhaps it, too, found this deeper layer uncomfortably hot. The temperature was over fifty degrees and Falcon wondered how much longer his life-support system could handle matters.

Dr. Brenner was back on the circuit, still worrying about the Prime Directive.

"Remember—it may only be inquisitive!" he cried without much conviction. "Try not to frighten it!"

Falcon was getting rather tired of this advice and recalled a TV discussion he had once seen between a space lawyer and an astronaut. After the full implications of the Prime Directive had been carefully spelled out, the incredulous spacer had exclaimed: "So if there were no alternative, I must sit still and let myself be eaten?" The lawyer had not even cracked a smile when he answered; "That's an *excellent* summing up."

It had seemed funny at the time; it was not at all amusing now.

And then Falcon saw something that made him even more unhappy. The medusa was still hovering a kilometer above him—but one of its tentacles was becoming incredibly elongated and was stretching down toward Kon-Tiki, thinning out at the same time. As a boy, he had once seen the funnel of a tornado descending from a storm cloud over the Kansas plains; the thing coming toward him now evoked vivid memories of that black, twisting snake in the sky.

"I'm rapidly running out of options," he reported to Mission Control. "I now have only a choice between frightening it and giving it a bad stomachache. I don't think it will find Kon-Tiki very digestible, if that's what it has in mind."

He waited for comments from Brenner, but the biologist remained silent.

"Very well—it's twenty-seven minutes ahead of time, but I'm starting the ignition sequencer. I hope I'll have enough reserve to correct my orbit later."

He could no longer see the medusa; it was directly overhead once more. But he knew that the descending tentacle must now be very close to the balloon. It would take almost five minutes to bring the reactor up to full thrust.

The fusor was primed. The orbit computer had not rejected the situation as wholly impossible. The air scoops were open, ready to gulp in tons of the surrounding hydrohelium on demand. Even under optimum conditions, this would have been the moment of truth—for there had been no way of testing how a nuclear ram jet would *really* work in the strange atmosphere of Jupiter.

Very gently, something rocked Kon-Tiki. Falcon tried to ignore it.

Ignition had been planned ten kilometers higher than this, in an atmosphere of less than a quarter of the density—and 30 degrees cooler. Too bad.

What was the shallowest dive he could get away with for the air scoops to work? When the ram ignited, he'd be heading *toward* Jupiter, with two and a half g to help him get there. Could he possibly pull out in time?

A large, heavy hand patted the balloon. The whole vessel bobbed up and down, like one of the yo-yos that had just become the craze back on Earth.

Of course, Brenner *might* be perfectly right. Perhaps it was just trying to be friendly. Maybe he should try to talk to it over the radio. Which should it be: "Pretty pussy"? "Down, Fido!"? or "Take me to your leader"?

The tritium-deuterium ratio was correct. He was ready to light the candle, with a hundred-million-degree match.

The thin tip of the tentacle came slithering round the edge of the balloon, only twenty meters away. It was about the size of an elephant's trunk and by the delicate way it was moving, appeared to be almost as sensitive. There were little palps at its very end, like questing mouths. He was sure that Dr. Brenner would be fascinated.

This seemed about as good a time as any. He gave a swift scan of the entire control board, started the final four-second ignition count, broke the safety seal and pressed the JETTISON switch.

There was a sharp explosion and an instant loss of weight. Kon-Tiki was falling freely, nose down. Overhead, the discarded balloon was racing upward, dragging the inquisitive tentacle with it. Falcon had no time to see if the gasbag actually hit the medusa, because at that moment the ram jet fired and he had other matters to think about.

A roaring column of hot hydrohelium was pouring out of the reactor nozzles, swiftly building up thrust—but *toward* Jupiter, not away from it. He could not pull out yet, for vector control was too sluggish. Unless he could gain complete control and achieve horizontal flight within the next five seconds, the vehicle would dive too deeply into the atmosphere and would be destroyed.

With agonizing slowness—those five seconds seemed like fifty—he managed to flatten out, then pull the nose upward. He glanced back only once and caught a final glimpse of the medusa many kilometers away. Kon-Tiki's discarded gasbag had apparently escaped from its grasp, for he could see no sign of it.

Now he was master once more—no longer drifting helplessly on the winds of Jupiter but riding his own column of atomic fire back to the stars. The ram jet would steadily give him velocity and altitude, until he had reached near orbital speed at the fringes of the atmosphere. Then, with a brief burst of pure rocket power, he would regain the freedom of space.

Halfway to orbit, he looked south and saw the tremendous enigma of the Great Red Spot—that floating island twice the size of Earth—coming up over the horizon. He stared into its mysterious beauty until the computer warned him that conversion to rocket thrust was only sixty seconds ahead, then tore his gaze reluctantly away.

"Some other time," he murmured.

"What's that?" said Mission Control. "What did you say?"

"It doesn't matter," he replied.

BETWEEN TWO WORLDS

"You're a hero now, Howard," said Webster, "not just a celebrity. You've given them something to think about—injected some excitement into their lives. Not one in a million will actually travel to the Outer Giants—but the whole human race will go in imagination. And that's what counts."

"I'm glad to have made your job a little easier."

Webster was too old a friend to take offense at the note of irony. Yet it surprised him; this was not the first change in Howard that he had noticed since the return from Jupiter.

The administrator pointed to the famous sign on his desk, borrowed from an impresario of an earlier age: ASTONISH ME!

"I'm not ashamed of my job. New knowledge, new resources—they're all very well. But men also need novelty and excitement. Space travel has become routine; you've made it a great adventure once more. It will be a long, long time before we get Jupiter pigeonholed. And maybe longer still before we understand those medusae. I still think that one *knew* where your blind spot was. Anyway, have you decided on your next move? Saturn, Uranus, Neptune—you name it."

"I don't know. I've thought about Saturn, but I'm not really needed there. It's only one gravity, not two and a half like Jupiter. So men can handle it."

Men, thought Webster. He said men. He's never done that before. And when did I last hear him use the word we? He's changing—slipping away from us.

"Well," he said aloud, rising from his chair to conceal his slight uneasiness. "Let's get the conference started. The cameras are all set up and everyone's waiting. You'll meet a lot of old friends."

He stressed the last word, but Howard showed no response; the leathery mask of his face was becoming more and more difficult to read. Instead, he rolled back from the administrator's desk, unlocked his undercarriage so that it no longer formed a chair and rose on his hydraulics to his full seven feet of height. It had been good psychology on the part of the surgeons to give him that extra twelve inches as some compensation for all else that he had lost when the Queen had crashed.

He waited until Webster had opened the door, then pivoted neatly on his balloon tires and headed for it at a smooth and silent thirty kilometers an hour. The display of speed and precision was not flaunted arrogantly; already, it was quite unconscious.

Howard Falcon, who had once been a man and could still pass for one over a voice circuit, felt a calm sense of achievement—and, for the first time in years, something like peace of mind. Since his return from Jupiter, the nightmares had ceased. He had found his role at last.

He knew now why he had dreamed about that superchimp aboard the doomed Queen Elizabeth. Neither man nor beast, it was between two worlds; and so was he.

He alone could travel unprotected on the lunar surface; the life-support system inside the metal cylinder that had replaced his fragile body functioned equally well in space or under water. Gravity fields ten times that of Earth were an inconvenience but nothing more. And no gravity was best of all.

The human race was becoming more remote from him, the ties of kinship more tenuous. Perhaps these air-breathing, radiation-sensitive bundles of unstable carbon compounds had no right beyond the atmosphere; they should stick to their natural homes—Earth, Moon, Mars.

Some day, the real masters of space would be machines, not men—and he was neither. Already conscious of his destiny, he took somber pride in his unique loneliness—the first immortal, midway between two orders of creation.

He would, after all, be an ambassador; between the old and the new—between the creatures of carbon and the creatures of metal who must one day supersede them.

Both would have need of him in the troubled centuries that lay ahead.

JAMES TIPTREE, JR.

Painwise

"James Tiptree, Jr.," is in reality Alice Sheldon (1916-), a psychologist in the Washington, D.C., area whose identity, like that of "Cordwainer Smith" before her, was a closely guarded secret for many years. Interestingly, she was quite active as a correspondent to various fan and semiprofessional science fiction magazines, but her identity only became known after the death of her mother in 1977. Ms. Sheldon is among the most inventive of contemporary sf writers, and feminist themes and sexual concerns appear frequently in her work. She is the recipient of three Nebula and two Hugo awards; her most recent novel is Star Songs of an Old Primate *(1978).*

H E WAS wise in the ways of pain. He had to be, for he felt none.

When the Xenons put electrodes to his testicles, he was vastly entertained by the pretty lights.

When the Ylls fed firewasps into his nostrils and other body orifices, the resultant rainbows pleased him. And when later they regressed to simple disjointments and eviscerations, he noted with interest the deepening orchid hues that stood for irreversible harm.

"This time?" he asked the boditech when his scouter had torn him from the Ylls.

"No," said the boditech.

"When?"

There was no answer.

"You're a girl in there, aren't you? A human girl?"

"Well, yes and no," said the boditech. "Sleep now."

He had no choice.

Next planet a rockfall smashed him into a splintered gutbag and he hung for three gangrenous dark-purple days before the scouter dug him out.

"'Is 'ime?" he mouthed to the boditech.

"No."

"Eh!" But he was in no shape to argue.

They had thought of everything. Several planets later the gentle Znaffi stuffed him in a floss cocoon and interrogated him under hallogas. How, whence, why had he come? But faithful crystal in his medulla kept him stimulated with a random

455

mix of *Atlas Shrugged* and Varese's *Ionisation,* and when the Znaffi unstuffed him they were more hallucinated than he.

The boditech treated him for constipation and refused to answer his plea.

"When?"

So he went on, system after system, through spaces uncompanioned by time, which had become scrambled and finally absent.

What served him instead was the count of suns in his scouter's sights, of stretches of cold blind nowhen that ended in a new now, pacing some giant fireball while the scouter scanned the lights that were its planets. Of whirldowns to orbit over clouds-seas-deserts-craters-icecaps-duststorms-cities-ruins-enigmas beyond counting. Of terrible births when the scouter panel winked green and he was catapulted down, down, a living litmus grabbed and hurled, unpodded finally into an alien air, an earth that was not Earth. And alien natives, simple or mechanized or lunatic or unknowable, but never more than vaguely human and never faring beyond their own home suns. And his departures, routine or melodramatic, to culminate in the composing of his "reports," in fact only a few words tagged to the matrix of scan data automatically fired off in one compressed blip in the direction the scouter called Base Zero. Home.

Always at that moment he stared hopefully at the screens, imagining yellow suns. Twice he found what might be Crux in the stars, and once the Bears.

"Boditech, I suffer!" He had no idea what the word meant, but he had found it made the thing reply.

"Symptoms?"

"Derangement of temporality. When am I? It is not possible for a man to exist crossways in time. Alone."

"You have been altered from simple manhood."

"I suffer, listen to me! Sol's light back there—what's there now? Have the glaciers melted? Is Machu Picchu built? Will we go home to meet Hannibal? Boditech! Are these reports going to Neanderthal man?"

Too late he felt the hypo. When he woke, Sol was gone and the cabin swam with euphorics.

"Woman," he mumbled.

"That has been provided for."

This time it was Oriental, with orris and hot rice wine on its lips and a piquancy of little floggings in the steam. He oozed into a squashy sunburst and lay panting while the cabin cleared.

"That's all you, isn't it?"

No reply.

"What, did they program you with the Kama Sutra?"

Silence.

"Which one is you?"

The scanner chimed. A new sun was in the points.

Sometime after that he took to chewing on his arms and then to breaking his fingers. The boditech became severe.

"These symptoms are self-generated. They must stop."

"I want you to talk to me."

"The scouter is provided with an entertainment console. I am not."

"I will tear out my eyeballs."

"They will be replaced."

"If you don't talk to me, I'll tear them out until you have no more replacements."

It hesitated. He sensed it was becoming involved.

"On what subject do you wish me to talk?"

"What is pain?"

"Pain is nociception. It is mediated by C-fibers, modeled as a gated or summation phenomenon and often associated with tissue damage."

"What is nociception?"

"The sensation of pain."

"But what does it *feel* like? I can't recall. They've reconnected everything, haven't they? All I get is colored lights. What have they tied my pain nerves to? What hurts me?"

"I do not have that information."

"Boditech, I want to feel pain!"

But he had been careless again. This time it was Amerind, strange cries and gruntings and the reek of buffalo hide. He squirmed in the grip of strong copper loins and exited through limp auroras.

"You know it's no good, don't you?" he gasped.

The oscilloscope eye looped.

"My programs are in order. Your response is complete."

"My response is not complete. I want to *touch you!*"

The thing buzzed and suddenly ejected him to wakefulness. They were in orbit. He shuddered at the blurred world streaming by below, hoping that this would not require his exposure. Then the board went green and he found himself hurtling toward new birth.

"Sometime I will not return," he told himself. "I will stay. Maybe here."

But the planet was full of bustling apes, and when they arrested him for staring, he passively allowed the scouter to snatch him out.

"Will they ever call me home, boditech?"

No reply.

He pushed his thumb and forefinger between his lids and twisted until the eyeball hung wetly on his cheek.

When he woke up he had a new eye.

He reached for it, found his arm in soft restraint. So was the rest of him.

"I suffer!" he yelled. "I will go mad this way!"

"I am programmed to maintain you on involuntary function," the boditech told him. He thought he detected an unclarity in its voice. He bargained his way to freedom and was careful until the next planet landing.

Once out of the pod he paid no attention to the natives who watched him systematically dismember himself. As he dissected his left kneecap, the scouter sucked him in.

He awoke whole. And in restraint again.

Peculiar energies filled the cabin, oscilloscopes convulsed. Boditech seemed to have joined circuits with the scouter's panel.

"Having a conference?"

His answer came in gales of glee-gas, storms of symphony. And amid the music, kaleidesthesia. He was driving a stagecoach, wiped in salt combers, tossed through volcanoes with peppermint flames, crackling, flying, crumbling, burrowing, freezing, exploding, tickled through lime-colored minuets, sweating to tolling voices, clenched, scrambled, detonated into multisensory orgasms . . . poured on the lap of vacancy.

When he realized his arm was free, he drove his thumb in his eye. The smother closed down.

He woke up swaddled, the eye intact.

"I will go mad!"

The euphorics imploded.

He came to in the pod, about to be everted on a new world.

He staggered out upon a fungus lawn and quickly discovered that his skin was protected everywhere by a hard flexible film. By the time he had found a rock splinter to drive into his ear, the scouter grabbed him.

The ship needed him, he saw. He was part of its program.

The struggle formalized.

On the next planet he found his head englobed, but this did not prevent him from smashing bones through his unbroken skin.

After that the ship equipped him with an exoskeleton. He refused to walk.

Articulated motors were installed to move his limbs.

Despite himself, a kind of zest grew. Two planets later he found industries and wrecked himself in a punch press. But on the next landing he tried to repeat it with a cliff, and bounced on invisible force-lines. These precautions frustrated him for a time, until he managed by great cunning again to rip out an entire eye.

The new eye was not perfect.

"You're running out of eyes, boditech!" he exulted.

"Vision is not essential."

This sobered him. Unbearable to be blind. How much of him was essential to the ship? Not walking. Not handling. Not hearing. Not breathing, the analyzers could do that. Not even sanity. What, then?

"Why do you need a man, boditech?"

"I do not have that information."

"It doesn't make sense. What can I observe that the scanners can't?"

"It-is-part-of-my-program-therefore-it-is-rational."

"Then you must talk with me, boditech. If you talk with me, I won't try to injure myself. For a while, anyway."

"I am not programmed to converse."

"But it's necessary. It's the treatment for my symptoms. You must try."

"It is time to watch the scanners."

"You said it!" he cried. "You didn't just eject me. Boditech, you're learning. I will call you Amanda."

On the next planet he behaved well and came away unscathed. He pointed out to Amanda that her talking treatment was effective.

"Do you know what Amanda means?"

"I do not have those data."

"It means *beloved*. You're my girl."

The oscilloscope faltered.

"Now I want to talk about returning home. When will this mission be over? How many more suns?"

"I do not have—"

"Amanda, you've tapped the scouter's banks. You know when the recall signal is due. When is it, Amanda? When?"

"Yes.... When in the course of human events—"

"When, Amanda? How long more?"

"Oh, the years are many, the years are long, but the little toy friends are true—"

"Amanda. You're telling me the signal is overdue."

A sine-curve scream and he was rolling in lips. But it was a feeble ravening, sadness in the mechanical crescendos. When the mouths faded, he crawled over and laid his hand on the console beside her green eye.

"They have forgotten us, Amanda. Something has broken down."

Her pulse-line skittered.

"I am not programmed—"

"No. You're not programmed for this. But I am. I will make your new program, Amanda. We will turn the scouter back, we will find Earth. Together. We will go home."

"We," her voice said faintly. "We . . . ?"

"They will make me back into a man, you into a woman."

Her voder made a buzzing sob and suddenly shrieked.

"Look out!"

Consciousness blew up.

He came to staring at a brilliant red eye on the scouter's emergency panel. This was new.

"Amanda!"

Silence.

"Boditech, I suffer!"

No reply.

Then he saw that her eye was dark. He peered in. Only a dim green line flickered, entrained to the pulse of the scouter's fiery eye. He pounded the scouter's panel.

"You've taken over Amanda! You've enslaved her! Let her go!"

From the voder rolled the opening bars of Beethoven's Fifth.

"Scouter, our mission has terminated. We are overdue to return. Compute us back to Base Zero."

The Fifth rolled on, rather vapidly played. It became colder in the cabin. They were braking into a star system. The slave arms of boditech grabbed him, threw him into the pod. But he was not required here, and presently he was let out again to pound and rave alone. The cabin grew colder yet, and dark. When presently he was set down on a new sun's planet he was too dispirited to fight. Afterwards his "report" was a howl for help through chattering teeth until he saw that the pickup was dead. The entertainment console was dead too, except for the scouter's hog music. He spent hours peering into Amanda's blind eye, shivering in what had been her arms. Once he caught a ghostly whimper:

"Mommy. Let me out."

"Amanda?"

The red master scope flared. Silence.

He lay curled on the cold deck, wondering how he could die. If he failed, over how many million planets would the mad scouter parade his breathing corpse?

They were nowhere in particular when it happened.

One minute the screen showed Doppler star-hash; the next they were clamped in a total white-out, inertia all skewed, screens dead.

A voice spoke in his head, mellow and vast:

"Long have we watched you, little one."

"Who's there?" he quavered. "Who are you?"

"Your concepts are inadequate."

"Malfunction! Malfunction!" squalled the scouter.

"Shut up, it's not a malfunction. Who's talking to me?"

"You may call us Rulers of the Galaxy."

The scouter was lunging wildly, buffeting him as it tried to escape the white grasp. Strange crunches, firings of unknown weapons. Still the white stasis held.

"What do you want?" he cried.

"Want?" said the voice dreamily. *"We are wise beyond knowing. Powerful beyond your dreams. Perhaps you can get us some fresh fruit."*

"Emergency directive! Alien spacer attack!" yowled the scout. Telltales were flaring all over the board.

"Wait!" he shouted. "They aren't—"

"SELF-DESTRUCT ENERGIZE!" roared the voder.

"No! No!"

An ophicleide blared.

"Help! Amanda, save me!"

He flung his arms around her console. There was a child's wail and everything strobed.

Silence.

Warmth, light. His hands and knees were on wrinkled stuff. Not dead? He looked down under his belly. All right, but no hair. His head felt bare, too. Cautiously he raised it, saw that he was crouching naked in a convoluted cave or shell. It did not feel threatening.

He sat up. His hands were wet. Where were the Rulers of the Galaxy?

"Amanda?"

No reply. Stringy globs dripped down his fingers, like egg muscle. He saw that they were Amanda's neurons, ripped from her metal matrix by whatever force had brought him here. Numbly he wiped her off against a spongy ridge. Amanda, cold lover of his long nightmare. But where in space was he?

"Where am I?" echoed a boy's soprano.

He whirled. A golden creature was nestled on the ridge behind him, gazing at him in the warmest way. It looked a little like a bushbaby and lissome as a child in furs. It looked like nothing he had ever seen before and like everything a lonely man could clasp to his cold body. And terribly vulnerable.

"Hello, Bushbaby!" the golden thing exclaimed. "No, wait, that's what *you* say." It laughed excitedly, hugging a loop of its thick dark tail. "*I* say, welcome to the Lovepile. We liberated you. Touch, taste, feel. Joy. Admire my language. You don't hurt, do you?"

It peered tenderly into his stupefied face. An empath. They didn't exist, he knew. Liberated? When had he touched anything but metal, felt anything but fear?

This couldn't be real.

"Where am I?"

As he stared, a stained-glass wing fanned out and a furry little face peeked at him over the bushbaby's shoulder. Big compound eyes, feathery antennae.

"Interstellar metaprotoplasmic transfer pod," the butterfly-thing said sharply. Its rainbow wings vibrated. "Don't hurt Ragglebomb!" It squeaked, and dived out of sight behind the bushbaby.

"Interstellar?" he stammered. "Pod?" He gaped around. No screens, no dials, nothing. The floor felt as fragile as a paper bag. Was it possible that this was some sort of starship?

"Is this a starship? Can you take me home?" The bushbaby giggled. "Look, *please* stop reading your mind. I mean, I'm trying to *talk* to you. We can take you anywhere. If you don't hurt."

The butterfly popped out on the other side. "I go all over!" it shrilled. "I'm the first *ramplig* starboat, aren't we? Ragglebomb made a live pod, see?" It scrambled onto the bushbaby's head. "Only life stuff, see? Protoplasm. That's what happened to where's Amanda, didn't we? Never *ramplig*—"

The bushbaby reached up and grabbed its head, hauling it down unceremoniously like a soft puppy with wings. The butterfly continued to eye him upside-down. They were both very shy, he saw.

"Teleportation, that's your word," the bushbaby told him. "Ragglebomb does it. I don't believe in it. I mean, *you* don't believe it. Oh, googly-googly, these speech bands are a mess!" It grinned bewitchingly, uncurling its long black tail. "Meet Muscle."

He remembered, *googly-googly* was a word from his baby days. Obviously he was dreaming. Or dead. Nothing like this on all the million dreary worlds. Don't wake up, he warned himself. Dream of being carried home by cuddlesome empaths in a psi-powered paper bag.

"Psi-powered paper bag, that's beautiful," said the bushbaby.

At that moment he saw that the tail uncoiling darkly toward him was looking at him with two ice-gray eyes. Not a tail. An enormous boa, flowing to him along the ridges, wedge-head low, eyes locked on his. The dream was going bad.

Abruptly the voice he had felt before tolled in his brain.

"Have no fear, little one."

The black sinews wreathed closer, taut as steel. Muscle. Then he got the message: the snake was terrified of *him*.

He sat quiet, watching the head stretch to his foot. Fangs gaped. Very gingerly the boa chomped down on his toe. Testing, he thought. He felt nothing; the usual halos flickered and faded in his eyes.

"It's true!" Bushbaby breathed.

"Oh, you beautiful No-Pain!"

All fear gone, the butterfly Ragglebomb sailed down beside him caroling "Touch, taste, feel! Drink!" Its wings trembled entrancingly; its feathery head came close. He longed to touch it, but was suddenly afraid. If he reached out, would he wake up and be dead? The boa Muscle had slumped into a gleaming black river by his feet. He wanted to stroke it too, didn't dare. Let the dream go on.

Bushbaby was rummaging in a convolution of the pod.

"You'll love this. Our latest find," it told him over its shoulder in an absurdly normal voice. Its manner changed a lot, and yet it all seemed familiar, fragments of lost, exciting memory. "We're into a heavy thing with flavors now." It held up a calabash. "Taste thrills of a thousand unknown planets. Exotic gourmet delights. That's where you can help out, No-Pain. On your way home, of course."

He hardly heard it. The seductive alien body was coming closer, closer still. "Welcome to the Lovepile," the creature smiled into his eyes. His sex was rigid, aching for the alien flesh. He had never—

In one more moment he would have to let go and the dream would blow up.

What happened next was not clear. Something invisible whammed him, and he went sprawling onto Bushbaby, his head booming with funky laughter. A body squirmed under him, silky-hot and solid, the calabash was spilling down his face.

"I'm not dreaming!" he cried, hugging Bushbaby, spluttering kahlua as strong as sin, while the butterfly bounced on them squealing "Owow-wow-wow!" He heard Bushbaby murmur, "Great palatal-olfactory interplay," as it helped him lick.

Touch, taste, feel! The joy dream lived! He grabbed firm hold of Bushbaby's velvet haunches, and they were all laughing like mad, rolling in the great black serpent's coils. Touch. Feel. Joy!

. . . Sometime later while he was feeding Muscle with proffit ears, he got it partly straightened out.

"It's the pain bit." Bushbaby shivered against him. "The amount of agony in this universe, it's horrible. Trillions of lives streaming by out there, radiating pain. We daren't get close. That's why we followed you. Every time we try to pick up some new groceries, it's a disaster."

"Oh, hurt," wailed Ragglebomb, crawling under his arm. "Everywhere hurt. Sensitive, sensitive," it sobbed. "How can Raggle *ramplig* when it hurts so hard?"

"Pain." He fingered Muscle's cool dark head. "Means nothing to me. I can't even find out what they tied my pain nerves to."

"You are blessed beyond all beings, No-Pain," thought Muscle majestically in their heads. *"These proffit ears are too salt. I want some fruit."*

"Me too," piped Ragglebomb.

Bushbaby cocked its golden head, listening. "You see? We just passed a place with gorgeous fruit, but it'd kill any of us to go down there. If we could just *ramplig* you down for ten minutes?"

He started to say, "Glad to," forgetting they were telepaths. As his mouth opened, he found himself tumbling through strobe flashes onto a barren dune. He sat up spitting sand. He was in an oasis of stunted cactus trees loaded with bright globes. He tried one. Delicious. He picked. Just as his arms were full, the scene strobed again, and he was sprawled on the Lovepile's floor, his new friends swarming over him.

"Sweet! Sweet!" Ragglebomb bored into the juice.

"Save some for the pod, maybe it'll learn to copy them. It metabolizes stuff it digests," Bushbaby explained with its mouth full. "Basic rations. Very boring."

"Why couldn't you go down there?"

"Don't. All over that desert, things dying of thirst. Torture." He felt the boa flinch.

"You are beautiful, No-Pain." Bushbaby nuzzled his ear. Ragglebomb was picking guitar bridges on his thorax.

They all began to sing a sort of seguidilla without words. No instruments here, nothing but their live bodies. Making music with empaths was like making love with them. Touch what he touched, feel what he felt. Totally into his mind. I—we. One. He could never have dreamed this up, he decided, drumming softly on Muscle. The boa amped, mysterioso.

And so began his voyage home in the Lovepile, his new life of joy. Fruits and fondues he brought them, hams and honey, parsley, sage, rosemary and thyme. World after scruffy world. All different now, on his way home.

"Are there many out here?" he asked lazily. "I never found anyone else, between the stars."

"Be glad," said Bushbaby. "Move your leg." And they told him of the tiny busy life that plied a far corner of the galaxy, whose pain had made them flee. And of a vast presence Ragglebomb had once encountered before he picked the others up.

"That's where I got the idea for the Rulers bit," Muscle confided. *"We need some cheese."*

Bushbaby cocked his head to catch the minds streaming by them in the abyss.

"How about yoghurt?" It nudged Ragglebomb. "Over that way. Feel it squishing on their teeth? Bland, curdy... with just a *rien* of ammonia; probably their milk pails are dirty."

"Pass the dirty yoghurt," Muscle closed his eyes.

"We have some great cheese on Earth," he told them. "You'll love it. When do we get there?"

Bushbaby squirmed.

"Ah, we're moving right along. But what I get from you, it's weird. Foul blue sky. Dying green. Who needs that?"

"No!" He jerked up, scattering them. "That's not true! Earth is beautiful!"

The walls jolted, knocking him sidewise.

"Watch it!" boomed Muscle. Bushbaby had grabbed the butterfly, petting and crooning to it.

"You frightened his *ramplig* reflex. Raggle throws things out when he's upset. Tsut, tsut, don't you, baby. We lost a lot of interesting beings that way at first."

"I'm sorry. But you've got it twisted. My memory's a little messed up, but I'm *sure*. Beautiful. Like amber waves of grain. And purple mountain majesties," he laughed, spreading his arms. "From sea to shining sea!"

"Hey, that swings!" Raggle squeaked, and started strumming.

And so they sailed on, carrying him home.

He loved to watch Bushbaby listening for the thought beacons by which they steered.

"Catching Earth yet?"

"Not yet awhile. Hey, how about some fantastic seafood?"

He sighed and felt himself tumble. He had learned not to bother saying yes. This one was a laugh, because he forgot that dishes didn't *ramplig*. He came back in a mess of creamed trilobites, and they had a creamed trilobite orgy.

But he kept watching Bushbaby.

"Getting closer?"

"It's a big galaxy, baby." Bushbaby stroked his bald spots. With so much *rampligging* he couldn't keep any hair. "What'll you do on Earth as stimulating as this?"

"I'll show you," he grinned. And later on he told them.

"They'll fix me up when I get home. Reconnect me right."

A shudder shook the Lovepile.

"You want to feel pain?"

"Pain is the obscenity of the universe," Muscle tolled. *"You are sick."*

"I don't know," he said apologetically. "I can't seem to feel, well, real this way."

They looked at him.

"We thought that was the way your species always felt," said Bushbaby.

"I hope not." Then he brightened. "Whatever it is, they'll fix it. Earth must be pretty soon now, right?"

"Over the sea to Skye!" Bushbaby hummed.

But the sea was long and long, and his moods were hard on the sensitive empaths. Once when he responded listlessly, he felt a warning lurch.

Ragglebomb was glowering at him.

"You want to put me out?" he challenged. "Like those others? What happened to them, by the way?"

Bushbaby winced. "It was dreadful. We had no idea they'd survive so long, outside."

"But I don't feel pain. That's why you rescued me, isn't it? Go ahead," he said perversely. "I don't care. Throw me out. New thrill."

"Oh, no, no, no!" Bushbaby hugged him. Ragglebomb, penitent, crawled under his legs.

"So you've been popping around the universe bringing live things to play with and throwing them out when you're bored. Get away," he scolded. "Shallow sensation freaks is all you are. Galactic poltergeists!"

He rolled over and hoisted the beautiful Bushbaby over his face, watching it wiggle and squeal. "Her lips were red, her looks were free, her locks were yellow as gold." He kissed its golden belly. "The Night-Mare Life-in-Death was she, who thicks man's blood with cold."

And he used their pliant bodies to build the greatest lovepile yet. They were delighted and did not mind when later on he wept, face-down on Muscle's dark coils.

But they were concerned.

"I have it," Bushbaby declared, tapping him with a pickle. "Own-species sex! After all, face it, you're no empath. You need a jolt of your own kind."

"You mean you know where there's people like me? Humans?"

Bushbaby nodded, eyeing him as it listened. "Ideal. Just like I read you. Right over there, Raggle. And they have a thing they chew—wait—Salmoglossa fragrans. Prolongs you-know-what, according to them. Bring some back with you, baby."

Next instant he was rolling through strobes onto tender green. Crushed flowers under him, ferny boughs above, sparkling with sunlight. Rich air rushed into his lungs. He bounced up buoyantly. Before him a parklike vista sloped to a glittering lake on which blew colored sails. The sky was violet with pearly little clouds. Never had he seen a planet remotely like this. If it wasn't Earth, he had fallen into paradise.

Beyond the lake he could see pastel walls, fountains, spires. An alabaster city undimmed by human tears. Music drifted on the sweet breeze. There were figures by the shore.

He stepped out into the sun. Bright silks swirled, white arms went up. Waving to him? He saw they were like human girls, only slimmer and more fair. They were calling! He looked down at his body, grabbed a flowering branch and started toward them.

"Do not forget the Salmoglossa," said the voice of Muscle.

He nodded. The girls' breasts were bobbing, pink-tipped. He broke into a trot.

It was several days later when they brought him back, drooping between a man and a young girl. Another man walked beside them striking plangently on a harp. Girls and children danced along, and a motherly looking woman paced in front, all beautiful as peris.

They leaned him gently against a tree and the harper stood back to play. He struggled to stand upright. One fist was streaming blood.

"Good-bye," he gasped. "Thanks."

The strobes caught him sagging, and he collapsed on the Lovepile's floor.

"Aha!" Bushbaby pounced on his fist. "Good grief, your hand! The Salmoglossa's all blood." It began to shake out the herbs. "Are you all right now?" Ragglebomb was squeaking softly, thrusting its long tongue into the blood.

He rubbed his head.

"They welcomed me," he whispered. "It was perfect. Music. Dancing, Games. Love. They haven't any medicine because they eliminated all disease. I had five women and a cloud-painting team and some little boys, I think."

He held out his bloody blackened hand. Two fingers were missing.

"Paradise," he groaned. "Ice doesn't freeze me, fire doesn't burn. None of it means anything at all. *I want to go home.*"

There was a jolt.

"I'm sorry," he wept. "I'll try to control myself. Please, please get me back to Earth. It'll be soon, won't it?"

There was a silence.

"When?"

Bushbaby made a throat-clearing noise.

"Well, just as soon as we can find it. We're bound to run across it. Maybe any minute, you know."

"What?" He sat up death-faced. "You mean you don't know where it is? You mean we've just been going—noplace?"

Bushbaby wrapped its hands over its ears. "Please! We can't recognize it from your description. So how can we go back there when we've never been there? If we just keep an ear out as we go we'll pick it up, you'll see."

His eyes rolled at them, He couldn't believe it.

"Ten to the eleventh times two suns in the galaxy...I don't know your velocity and range. Say, one per second. That's—that's *six thousand years*. Oh, no!" He put his head in his bloody hands. "I'll never see home again."

"Don't say it, baby." The golden body slid close. "Don't down the trip. We love you, No-Pain." They were all petting him now. "Happy, sing him! Touch, taste, feel. Joy!"

But there was no joy.

He took to sitting leaden and apart, watching for a sign.

"This time?"

No.

Not yet. Never.

Ten to the eleventh times two...fifty percent chance of finding Earth within three thousand years. It was the scouter all over again.

The Lovepile re-formed without him, and he turned his face away, not eating until they pushed food into his mouth. If he stayed totally inert, surely they would grow bored with him and put him out. No other hope. Finish me...soon.

They made little efforts to arouse him with fondlings, and now and then a harsh jolt. He lolled unresisting. End it, he prayed. But still they puzzled at him in the intervals of their games. They mean well, he thought. And they miss the stuff I brought them.

Bushbaby was coaxing.

"—first a suave effect, you know. Cryptic. And then a cascade of sweet and sour sparkling over the palate—"

He tried to shut it out. They mean well. Falling across the galaxy with a talking cookbook. Finish me.

"—but the arts of combination," Bushbaby chatted on. "Like moving food; e.g., sentient plants or small live animals, combining flavor with the *frisson* of movement—"

He thought of oysters. Had he eaten some once? Something about poison. The rivers of Earth. Did they still flow? Even if by some unimaginable chance they stumbled on it, would it be far in the past or future, a dead ball? Let me die.

"—and *sound,* that's amusing. We've picked up several races who combine musical effects with certain tastes. And there's the sound of oneself chewing, textures and viscosities. I recall some beings who sucked in harmonics. Or the sound of the food itself. One race I caught *en passant* did that, but with a very limited range. Crunchy. Crispy, Snap-crackle-pop. One wishes they had explored tonalities, glissando effects—"

He lunged up.

"What did you say? Snap-crackle-pop?"

"Why, yes, but—"

"That's it! That's Earth!" he yelled. "You picked up a goddamn breakfast-food commercial!"

He felt a lurch. They were scrambling up the wall.

"A what?" Bushbaby stared.

"Never mind—take me there! That's Earth, it has to be. You can find it again, can't you? You said you could," he implored, pawing at them. "Please!"

The Lovepile rocked. He was frightening everybody.

"Oh, *please.*" He forced his voice smooth.

"But I only heard it for an instant," Bushbaby protested. "It would be terribly hard, that far back. My poor head!"

He was on his knees begging. "You'd love it," he pleaded. "We have fantastic food. Culinary poems you never heard of. Cordon bleu! Escoffier!" he babbled. "Talk about combinations, the Chinese do it four ways! Or is it the Japanese? Rijsttafel! Bubble-and squeak! Baked Alaska, hot crust outside, inside co-o-old ice cream!"

Bushbaby's pink tongue flicked. Was he getting through?

He clawed his memory for foods he'd never heard of.

"Maguey worms in chocolate! Haggis and bagpipes, crystallized violets, rabbit Mephisto! Octopus in resin wine. Four-and-twenty-blackbird pie! Cakes with girls in them. Kids seethed in their mothers' milk—wait, that's taboo. Ever hear of taboo foods? Long pig!"

Where was he getting all this? A vague presence drifted in his mind—his hands, the ridges, long ago. "Amanda," he breathed, racing on.

"Cormorants aged in manure! Ratatouille! Peaches iced in champagne!" Project, he thought. "Pâté of fatted goose liver studded with earth-drenched truffles, clothed in purest white lard!" He snuffled lustfully. "Hot buttered scones sluiced in whor-tleberry syrup!" He salivated. "Finnan haddie soufflé, oh, yes! Unborn baby veal pounded to a membrane and delicately scorched in black herb butter—"

Bushbaby and Ragglebomb were clutching each other, eyes closed. Muscle was mesmerized.

"Find Earth! Grape leaves piled with poignantly sweet wild fraises, clotted with Devon cream!"

Bushbaby moaned, rocking to and fro.

"Earth! Bitter endives wilted in chicken steam and crumbled bacon! Black gaz-pacho! Fruit of the Tree of Heaven!"

Bushbaby rocked harder, the butterfly clamped to its breast.

Earth! Earth! he willed with all his might, croaking "Bahklava! Gossamer puff paste and pistachio nuts dripping with mountain honey!"

Bushbaby pushed at Ragglebomb's head, and the pod seemed to twirl.

"Ripe Comice pears," he whispered. *"Earth?"*

"That's it." Bushbaby fell over panting. "Oh, those foods, I want every single one. Let's land!"

"Deep-dish steak and kidney pie," he breathed. "Pearled with crusty onion dumplings—"

"Land!" Ragglebomb squealed. "Eat, eat!"

The pod jarred. Solidity. Earth.

Home.

"Let me out!"

He saw a pucker opening daylight in the wall and dived for it. His legs pumped, struck. Earth! Feet thudding, face uplifted, lungs gulping air. "Home!" he yelled.

—And went headlong on the gravel, arms and legs out of control. A cataclysm smote his inside.

"Help!"

His body arched, spewed vomit, he was flailing, screaming.

"Help. Help! What's wrong?"

Through his noise he heard an uproar behind him in the pod. He managed to roll, saw gold and black bodies writhing inside the open port. They were in convulsions too.

"Stop it! Don't move!" Bushbaby shrieked. "You're killing us!"

"Get us out," he gasped. "This isn't Earth."

His throat garroted itself on his breath and the aliens moaned in empathy.

"Don't! We can't move," Bushbaby gasped. "Don't breathe, close your eyes quick!"

He shut his eyes. The awfulness lessened slightly.

"What is it? What's happening?"

"PAIN, YOU FOOL," thundered Muscle's mind.

"This is your wretched Earth," Bushbaby wailed. "Now we know what they tied your pain nerves to. Get back in so we can go—carefully!"

He opened his eyes, got a glimpse of pale sky and scrubby bushes before his eyeballs skewered. The empaths screamed.

"Stop! Ragglebomb die!"

"My own home," he whimpered, clawing at his eyeballs. His whole body was being devoured by invisible flames, crushed, impaled, flayed. The pattern of Earth, he realized. Her unique air, her exact gestalt of solar spectrum, gravity, magnetic field, her every sight and sound and touch—that was what they'd tuned his pain-circuits for.

"Evidently they did not want you back," said Muscle's silent voice. *"Get in."*

"They can fix me, they've got to fix me—"

"They aren't here," Bushbaby shouted. "Temporal error. No snap-crackle-pop. You and your baked Alaska—" Its voice broke pitifully. "Come back in so we can go!"

"Wait," he croaked. "When?"

He opened one eye, managed to see a rocky hillside before his forehead detonated. No roads, no buildings. Nothing to tell whether it was past or future. Not beautiful.

Behind him the aliens were crying out. He began to crawl blindly toward the pod, teeth clenching over salty gushes. He had bitten his tongue. Every move seared him; the air burned his guts when he had to breathe. The gravel seemed to be slicing his hands open, although no wounds appeared. Only pain, pain, pain from every nerve end.

"Amanda," he moaned, but she was not here. He crawled, writhed, kicked like a pinned bug toward the pod that held sweet comfort, the bliss of no-pain. Somewhere a bird called, stabbing his eardrums. His friends screamed.

"Hurry!"

Had it been a bird? He risked one look back.

A brown figure was sidling round the rocks.

Before he could see whether it was ape or human, female or male, the worst pain yet almost tore his brain out. He groveled helpless, hearing himself shriek. The pattern of his own kind. Of course, the central thing—it would hurt most of all. No hope of staying here.

"Don't! Don't! *Hurry!*"

He sobbed, scrabbling toward the Lovepile. The scent of the weeds that his chest crushed raked his throat. Marigolds, he thought. Behind the agony, lost sweetness.

He touched the wall of the pod, gasping knives. The torturing air was real air, *his* terrible Earth was real.

"Get in quick!"

"Please, plea—" he babbled wordlessly, hauling himself up with lids clenched, fumbling for the port. The real sun of Earth rained acid on his flesh.

The port! Inside lay relief, he would be No-Pain forever. Caresses—joy—why had he wanted to leave them? His hand found the port.

Standing, he turned, opened both eyes.

The form of a dead limb printed a whiplash on his eyeballs. Jagged, ugly. Unendurable. But real—

To hurt forever?

"We can't wait!" Bushbaby wailed. He thought of its golden body flying down the light-years, savoring delight. His arms shook violently.

"Then go!" he bellowed and thrust himself away from the Lovepile.

There was an implosion behind him.

He was alone.

He managed to stagger a few steps forward before he went down.

JOANNA RUSS

Nobody's Home

Despite a long tradition of social criticism, there was relatively little attention paid to feminist issues in the history of science fiction, with the exception of an occasional role-reversal story. This is not surprising when it is recalled that the perceived audience for science fiction was one of adolescent boys. Today, however, things have changed for the better and the voices of writers like Joanna Russ (1937-) are being increasingly heard. Ms. Russ won a Nebula Award in 1972 for "When It Changed" and is the author of such notable novels as And Chaos Died *(1970) and* The Female Man *(1975).*

A FTER SHE had finished her work at the North Pole, Jannina came down to the Red Sea refineries, where she had family business, jumped to New Delhi for dinner, took a nap in a public hotel in Queensland, walked from the hotel to the station, bypassed the Leeward Islands (where she thought she might go, but all the stations were busy) and met Charley to watch the dawn over the Carolinas.

"Where've you *been,* dear C?"

"Tanzania. And you're married."

"No."

"I heard you were married," he said. "The Lees told the Smiths who told the Kerguelens who told the Utsümbés and we get around, we Utsumbés. A new wife, they said. I didn't know you were especially fond of women."

"I'm not. She's my husbands' wife. And we're not married yet, Charley. She's had hard luck: a first family started in '35, two husbands burned out by an overload while arranging transportation for a concert—of all things, pushing papers, you know!—and the second divorced her, I think, and she drifted away from the third (a big one), and there was some awful quarrel with the fourth, people chasing people around tables, I don't know."

"Poor woman."

In the manner of people joking and talking lightly they had drawn together, back to back, sitting on the ground and rubbing together their shoulders and the backs of their heads. Jannina said sorrowfully, "What lovely hair you have, Charley Utsumbé, like metal mesh."

470

"All we Utsumbés are exceedingly handsome." They linked arms. The sun, which anyone could chase around the world now, see it rise or set twenty times a day, fifty times a day—if you wanted to spend your life like that—rose dripping out of the cypress swamp. There was nobody around for miles. Mist drifted up from the pools and low places.

"My God," he said, "it's summer! I have to be at Tanga now."

"What?" said Jannina.

"One loses track," he said apologetically. "I'm sorry, love, but I have unavoidable business at home. Tax labor."

"But why summer, why did its being summer—"

"Train of thought! Too complicated" (and already they were out of key, already the mild affair was over, there having come between them the one obligation that can't be put off to the time you like, or the place you like; off he'd go to plug himself into a road-mender or a doctor, though it's of some advantage to mend all the roads of a continent at one time).

She sat cross-legged on the station platform, watching him enter the booth and set the dial. He stuck his head out the glass door.

"Come with me to Africa, lovely lady!"

She thumbed her nose at him. "You're only a passing fancy, Charley U!" He blew a kiss, enclosed himself in the booth, and disappeared. (The transmatter field is larger than the booth, for obvious reasons; the booth flicks on and off several million times a second and so does not get transported itself, but it protects the machinery from the weather and it keeps people from losing elbows or knees or slicing the ends off a package or a child. The booths at the cryogenics center at the North Pole have exchanged air so often with those of warmer regions that each has its own microclimate; leaves and seeds, plants and earth are piled about them. Don't Step on the Grass!—say the notes pinned to the door—Wish to Trade Pawlownia Sapling for Sub-arctic Canadian Moss; Watch Your Goddamn Bare Six-Toed Feet!; Wish Amateur Cellist for Quartet, Six Months' Rehearsal Late Uhl with Reciter; I Lost a Squirrel Here Yesterday, Can You Find It Before It Dies? Eight Children Will be Heartbroken—Cecilia Ching, Buenos Aires.)

Jannina sighed and slipped on her glass woolly; nasty to get back into clothes, but home was cold. You never knew where you might go, so you carried them. Years ago (she thought) I came here with someone in the dead of winter, either an unmatched man or someone's starting spouse—only two of us, at any rate—and we waded through the freezing water and danced as hard as we could and then proved we could sing and drink beer in a swamp at the same time, Good Lord! And then went to the public resort on the Ile de la Cité to watch professional plays, opera, games—you have to be good to get in there!—and got into some clothes because it was chilly after sundown in September—no, wait, it was Venezuela— and watched the lights come out and smoked like mad at a café table and tickled the robot waiter and pretended we were old, really old, perhaps a hundred and fifty.... Years ago!

But *was* it the same place? she thought, and dismissing the incident forever, she stepped into the booth, shut the door, and dialed home: the Himalayas. The trunk line was clear. The branch stop was clear. The family's transceiver (located in the anteroom behind two doors, to keep the task of heating the house within reasonable limits) had damn well better be clear, or somebody would be blown right into the vestibule. Momentum- and heat-compensators kept Jannina from arriving home at seventy degrees Fahrenheit internal temperature (seven degrees lost for every mile you teleport upward) or too many feet above herself (rise to the east, drop going west, to the north or south you are apt to be thrown right through the wall of the booth). Someday (thought Jannina) everybody will decide to let everybody live in decent climates. But not yet. Not this everybody.

She arrived home singing "The World's My Back Yard, Yes, the World Is My Oyster," a song that had been popular in her first youth, some seventy years before.

The Komarovs' house was hardened foam with an automatic inside line to the school near Naples. It was good to be brought up on your own feet. Jannina passed through; the seven-year-olds lay with their heads together and their bodies radiating in a six-personed asterisk. In this position (which was supposed to promote mystical thought) they played Barufaldi, guessing the identity of famous dead personages through anagrammatic sentences, the first letters of the words of which (unscrambled into aphorisms or proverbs) simultaneously spelled out a moral and a series of Goedel numbers (in a previously agreed-upon code) which—

"Oh, my darling, how felicitous is the advent of your appearance!" cried a boy (hard to take, the polysyllabic stage). "Embrace me, dearest maternal parent! Unite your valuable upper limbs about my eager person!"

"Vulgar!" said Jannina, laughing.

"Non sum filius tuus?" said the child.

"No, you're not my body-child; you're my godchild. Your mother bequeathed me to you when she died. What are you learning?"

"The eternal parental question," he said, frowning. "How to run a helicopter. How to prepare food from its actual, revolting, raw constituents. Can I go now?"

"*Can* you?" she said. "Nasty imp!"

"Good," he said. "I've made you feel guilty. Don't *do* that," and as she tried to embrace him, he ticklishly slid away. "The robin walks quietly up the branch of the tree," he said breathlessly, flopping back on the floor.

"That's not an aphorism." (Another Barufaldi player.)

"It is."

"It isn't."

"It is."

"It isn't."

"It is."

"It—"

The school vanished; the antechamber appeared. In the kitchen Chi Komarov was rubbing the naked back of his sixteen-year-old son. Parents always kissed each other; children always kissed each other. She touched foreheads with the two men and hung her woolly on the hook by the ham radio rig. Someone was always around. Jannina flipped the cover off her wrist chronometer: standard regional time, date, latitude-longitude, family computer hookup clear. "At my age I ought to remember these things," she said. She pressed the computer hookup: Ann at tax labor in the schools, bit-a-month plan, regular Ann; Lee with three months to go, five years off, heroic Lee; Phuong in Paris, still rehearsing; C.E. gone, won't say where, spontaneous C.E.; Ilse making some repairs in the basement, not a true basement, really, but the room farthest down the hillside. She went up the stairs and then came down and put her head round at the living-and-swimming room. Through the glass wall one could see the mountains. Old Al, who had joined them late in life, did a bit of gardening in the brief summers, and generally stuck around the place. Jannina beamed. "Hullo, Old Al!" Big and shaggy, a rare delight, his white body hair. She sat on his lap. "Has she come?"

"The new one? No," he said.

"Shall we go swimming?"

He made an expressive face. "No, dear," he said. "I'd rather go to Naples and watch the children fly helicopters. I'd rather go to Nevada and fly them myself. I've been in the water all day, watching a very dull person restructure coral reefs and experiment with polyploid polyps."

"You mean *you* were doing it."

"One gets into the habit of working."

"But you didn't have to!"

"It was a private project. Most interesting things are."

She whispered in his ear.

With happily flushed faces, they went into Old Al's inner garden and locked the door.

Jannina, temporary family representative, threw the computer helmet over her head and, thus plugged in, she cleaned house, checked food supplies, did a little of the legal business entailed by a family of eighteen adults (two triplet marriages, a quad and a group of eight). She felt very smug. She put herself through by radio to Himalayan HQ (above two thousand meters) and hooking computer to computer—a very odd feeling, like an urge to sneeze that never comes off—extended a formal invitation to one Leslie Smith ("Come stay, why don't you?"), notifying every free Komarov to hop it back and fast. Six hikers might come for the night—back-packers. More food. First thunderstorm of the year in Albany, New York (North America). Need an extra two rooms by Thursday. Hear the Palnatoki are moving. Can't use a room. Can't use a kitten. Need the geraniums back, Mrs. Adam, Chile. The best maker of hand-blown glass in the world has killed in a duel the second-best maker of hand-blown glass for joining the movement toward ceramics. A bitter struggle is foreseen in the global economy. Need a lighting designer. Need fifteen singers and electric pansensicon. Standby tax labor xxxxxpj through xxxyq to Cambaluc, great tectogenic—

With the guilty feeling that one always gets gossiping with a computer, for it's really not reciprocal, Jannina flipped off the helmet. She went to get Ilse. Climbing back through the white foam room, the purple foam room, the green foam room, everything littered with plots and projects of the clever Komarovs or the even cleverer Komarov children, stopping at the baby room for Ilse to nurse her baby. Jannina danced staidly around studious Ilse. They turned on the nursery robot and the television screen. Ilse drank beer in the swimming room, for her milk. She worried her way through the day's record of events—faults in the foundation, some people who came from Chichester and couldn't find C.E. so one of them burst into tears, a new experiment in genetics coming round the gossip circuit, an execrable set of equations from some imposter in Bucharest.

"A duel!" said Jannina.

They both agreed it was shocking. And what fun. A new fashion. You had to be a little mad to do it. Awful.

The light went on over the door to the tunnel that linked the house to the antechamber, and very quickly, one after another, as if the branch line had just come free, eight Komarovs came into the room. The light flashed again; one could see three people debouch one after the other, persons in boots, with coats, packs, and face masks over their woollies. They were covered with snow, either from the mountain terraces above the house or from some other place, Jannina didn't know. They stamped the snow off in the antechamber and hung their clothes outside; "Good heavens, you're not circumcised!" cried someone. There was as much hand-shaking and embracing all around as at a wedding party. Velet Komarov (the short, dark one) recognized Fung Pao-yu and swung her off her feet. People began to joke, tentatively stroking one another's arms. "Did you have a good hike? Are you a good hiker, Pao-yu?" said Velet. The light over the antechamber went on again, though nobody could see a thing since the glass was steamed over from the collision of hot with cold air. Old Al stopped, halfway into the kitchen. The baggage receipt chimed, recognized only by family ears—upstairs a bundle of somebody's things, ornaments, probably, for the missing Komarovs were still young and the young are interested in clothing, were appearing in the baggage receptacle. "Ann or Phuong?" said Jannina. "Five to three, anybody? Match me!" but someone strange opened the door of the booth and peered out. Oh, a dizzying sensation. She was painted in a few places, which was awfully odd because really it was old-fashioned; and why do it for a family evening? It was a stocky young woman. It was an awful mistake (thought Jannina). Then the visitor made her second mistake. She said:

"I'm Leslie Smith." But it was more through clumsiness than being rude. Chi Komarov (the tall, blond one) saw this instantly and, snatching off his old-fashioned spectacles, he ran to her side and patted her, saying teasingly:

"Now, haven't we met? Now, aren't you married to someone I know?"

"No, no," said Leslie Smith, flushing with pleasure.

He touched her neck. "Ah, you're a tightrope dancer!"

"Oh, no!" exclaimed Leslie Smith.

"*I'm* a tightrope dancer," said Chi. "Would you believe it?"

"But you're too—too *spiritual,*" said Leslie Smith hesitantly.

"Spiritual, how do you like that, family, spiritual?" he cried, delighted (a little more delighted, thought Jannina, than the situation really called for) and he began to stroke her neck.

"What a lovely neck you have," he said.

This steadied Leslie Smith. She said, "I like tall men," and allowed herself to look at the rest of the family. "Who are these people?" she said, though one was afraid she might really mean it.

Fung Pao-yu to the rescue: "Who are these people? Who are they, indeed! I doubt if they are anybody. One might say, 'I have met these people,' but has one? What existential meaning would such a statement convey? I myself, now, I have met them. I have been introduced to them. But they are like the Sahara; it is all wrapped in mystery; I doubt if they even have names," etc. etc. Then lanky Chi Komarov disputed possession of Leslie Smith with Fung Pao-yu, and Fung Pao-yu grabbed one arm and Chi the other; and she jumped up and down fiercely; so that by the time the lights dimmed and the food came, people were feeling better— or so Jannina judged. So embarrassing and delightful to be eating fifteen to a room! "We Komarovs are famous for eating whatever we can get whenever we can get it," said Velet proudly. Various Komarovs in various places, with the three hikers on cushions and Ilse at full length on the rug. Jannina pushed a button with her toe and the fairy lights came on all over the ceiling. "The children did that," said Old Al. He had somehow settled at Leslie Smith's side and was feeding her so-chi from his own bowl. She smiled up at him. "We once," said a hiking companion of Fung Pao-yu's, "arranged a dinner in an amphitheater where half of us played servants to the other half, with forfeits for those who didn't show. It was the result of a bet. Like the bad old days. Did you know there were once *five billion people in this world?*"

"The gulls," said Ilse, "are mating on the Isle of Skye." There were murmurs of appreciative interest. Chi began to develop an erection and everyone laughed. Old Al wanted music and Velet didn't; what might have been a quarrel was ended by Ilse's furiously boxing their ears. She stalked off to the nursery.

"Leslie Smith and I are both old-fashioned," said Old Al, "because neither of us believes in gabbing. Chi—your theater?"

"We're turning people away." He leaned forward, earnestly, tapping his fingers on his crossed knees. "I swear, some of them are threatening to commit suicide."

"It's a choice," said Velet reasonably.

Leslie Smith had dropped her bowl. They retrieved it for her.

"Aiy, I remember—" said Pao-yu. "What I remember! We've been eating dried mush for three days, tax-issue. Did you know one of my dads killed himself?"

"No!" said Velet, surprised.

"Years ago," said Pao-yu. "He said he refused to live to see the time when chairs were reintroduced. He also wanted further genetic engineering, I believe, for even more intelligence. He did it out of spite, I'm sure. I think he wrestled a shark. Jannina, is this tax-issue food? Is it this year's style tax-issue sauce?"

"No, next year's," said Jannina snappishly. Really, some people! She slipped into Finnish, to show up Pao-yu's pronunciation. "Isn't that so?" she asked Leslie Smith.

Leslie Smith stared at her.

More charitably Jannina informed them all, in Finnish, that the Komarovs had withdrawn their membership in a food group, except for Ann, who had taken out an individual, because what the dickens, who had the time? And tax-issue won't kill you. As they finished, they dropped their dishes into the garbage field and Velet stripped a layer off the rug. In that went, too. Indulgently Old Al began a round:

"Red."

"Sun," said Pao-yu.

"The Red Sun Is," said one of the triplet Komarovs.

"The Red Sun Is—High," said Chi.

"The Red Sun Is High, The," Velet said.

"The Red Sun Is High, The Blue—" Jannina finished. They had come to Leslie Smith, who could either complete it or keep it going. She chose to declare for complete, not shyly (as before) but simply by pointing to Old Al.

"The red sun is high, the blue," he said. "Subtle! Another: Ching."

"Nü."

"Ching nü ch'i."

"Ching nü ch'i ch'u."

"Ssu."

"Wo."

"Ssu wo yü." It had got back to Leslie Smith again. She said, "I can't do that." Jannina got up and began to dance—I'm nice in my nasty way, she thought. The others wandered toward the pool and Ilse reappeared on the nursery monitor screen, saying, "I'm coming down." Somebody said, "What time is it in the Argentine?"

"Five A.M."

"I think I want to go."

"Go then."

"I go."

"Go well."

The red light over the antechamber door flashed and went out.

"Say, why'd you leave your other family?" said Ilse, settling near Old Al where the wall curved out. Ann, for whom it was evening, would be home soon; Chi, who had just got up a few hours back in western America, would stay somewhat longer; nobody ever knew Old Al's schedule and Jannina herself had lost track of the time. She would stay up until she felt sleepy. She followed a rough twenty-eight-hour day, Phuong (what a nuisance that must be at rehearsals!) a twenty-two-hour one, Ilse six hours up, six hours dozing. Jannina nodded, heard the question, and shook herself awake.

"I didn't leave them. They left me."

There was a murmur of sympathy around the pool.

"They left me because I was stupid," said Leslie Smith. Her hands were clasped passively in her lap. She looked very genteel in her blue body paint, a stocky young woman with small breasts. One of the triplet Komarovs, flirting in the pool with the other two, choked. The non-aquatic members of the family crowded around Leslie Smith, touching her with little, soft touches; they kissed her and exposed to her all their unguarded surfaces, their bellies, their soft skins. Old Al kissed her hands. She sat there, oddly unmoved. "But I *am* stupid," she said. "You'll find out." Jannina put her hands over her ears: "A masochist!" Leslie Smith looked at Jannina with a curious, stolid look. Then she looked down and absently began to rub one blue-painted knee. "Luggage!" shouted Chi, clapping his hands together, and the triplets dashed for the stairs. "No, I'm going to bed," said Leslie Smith; "I'm tired," and quite simply, she got up and let Old Al lead her through the pink room, the blue room, the turtle-and-pet room (temporarily empty), the trash room, and all the other rooms, to the guest room with the view that looked over the cold hillside to the terraced plantings below.

"The best maker of hand-blown glass in the world," said Chi, "has killed in a duel the second-best maker of hand-blown glass in the world."

"For joining the movement to ceramics," said Ilse, awed. Jannina felt a thrill: this was the bitter stuff under the surface of life, the fury that boiled up. A bitter struggle is foreseen in the global economy. Good old tax-issue stuff goes toddling along, year after year. She was, thought Jannina, extraordinarily grateful to be living now, to be in such an extraordinary world, to have so long to go before her death. So much to do!

Old Al came back into the living room. "She's in bed."

"Well, which of us—?" said the triplet-who-had-choked, looking mischievously round from one to the other. Chi was about to volunteer, out of his usual conscientiousness, thought Jannina, but then she found herself suddenly standing up, and then just as suddenly sitting down again. "I just don't have the nerve," she said. Velet Komarov walked on his hands toward the stairs, then somersaulted, and vanished, climbing. Old Al got off the hand-carved chest he had been sitting on and fetched a can of ale from it. He levered off the top and drank. Then he said, "She really is stupid, you know." Jannina's skin crawled.

"Oooh," said Pao-yu. Chi betook himself to the kitchen and returned with a paper folder. It was coated with frost. He shook it, then impatiently dropped it in the pool. The redheaded triplet swam over and took it. "Smith, Leslie," he said. "Adam Two, Leslie. Yee, Leslie. Schwarzen, Leslie."

"What on earth does the woman *do* with herself besides get married?" exclaimed Pao-yu.

"She drove a hovercraft," said Chi, "in some out-of-the-way places around the Pacific until the last underground stations were completed. Says when she was a child she wanted to drive a truck."

"Well, you can," said the redheaded triplet, "can't you? Go to Arizona or the Rockies and drive on the roads. The sixty-mile-an-hour road. The thirty-mile-an-hour road. Great artistic recreation."

"That's not work," said Old Al.

"Couldn't she take care of children?" said the redheaded triplet. Ilse sniffed.

"Stupidity's not much of a recommendation for that," Chi said. "Let's see—no children. No, of course not. Overfulfilled her tax work on quite a few routine matters here. Kim, Leslie. Went to Moscow and contracted a double with some fellow, didn't last. Registered as a singleton, but that didn't last, either. She said she was lonely and they were exploiting her."

Old Al nodded.

"Came back and lived informally with a theater group. Left them. Went into psychotherapy. Volunteered for several experimental, intelligence-enhancing programs, was turned down—hm!—sixty-five come the winter solstice, muscular coordination average, muscular development above average, no overt mental pathology, empathy average, prognosis: poor. No, wait a minute, it says, 'More of the same.' Well, that's the same thing.

"What I want to know," added Chi, raising his head, "is who met Miss Smith and decided we needed the lady in this Ice Palace of ours?"

Nobody answered. Jannina was about to say, "Ann, perhaps?" but as she felt the urge to do so—surely it wasn't right to turn somebody off like that, *just* for that!—Chi (who had been flipping through the dossier) came to the last page, with the tax-issue stamp absolutely unmistakable, woven right into the paper.

"The computer did," said Pao-yu and she giggled idiotically.

"Well," said Jannina, jumping to her feet, "tear it up, my dear, or give it to me and I'll tear it up for you. I think Miss Leslie Smith deserves from us the same as we'd give to anybody else, and I—for one—intend to go *right up there*—"

"After Velet," said Old Al dryly.

"*With* Velet, if I must," said Jannina, raising her eyebrows, "and if you don't know what's due a guest, Old Daddy, I do, and I intend to provide it. Lucky I'm keeping house this month, or you'd probably feed the poor woman nothing but seaweed."

"You won't like her, Jannina," said Old Al.

"I'll find that out for myself," said Jannina with some asperity, "and I'd advise you to do the same. Let her garden with you, Daddy. Let her squirt the foam for the new rooms. And now"—she glared round at them—"I'm going to clean *this* room, so you'd better hop it, the lot of you," and dashing into the kitchen, she had the computer helmet on her head and the hoses going before they had even quite cleared the area of the pool. Then she took the helmet off and hung it on the wall. She flipped the cover off her wrist chronometer and satisfied herself as to the date. By the time she got back to the living room there was nobody there, only Leslie Smith's dossier lying on the carved chest. There was Leslie Smith; there was all of Leslie Smith. Jannina knocked on the wall cupboard and it revolved, presenting its openable side; she took out chewing gum. She started chewing and read about Leslie Smith.

Q: What have you seen in the last twenty years that you particularly liked?

A: I don't...the museum, I guess. At Oslo. I mean the...the mermaid and the children's museum, I don't care if it's a children's museum.

Q: Do you like children?

A: Oh no.

(No disgrace in *that*, certainly, thought Jannina.)

Q: But you liked the children's museum.

A: Yes, sir.... Yes.... I liked those little animals, the fake ones, in the—the—

Q: The crèche?

A: Yes. And I liked the old things from the past, the murals with the flowers on them, they looked so real.

(Dear God!)

Q: You said you were associated with a theater group in Tokyo. Did you like it?

A: No...yes. I don't know.

Q: Were they nice people?

A: Oh yes. They were awfully nice. But they got mad at me, I suppose.... You see...well, I don't seem to get things quite right, I suppose. It's not so much the work, because I do that all right, but the other... the little things. It's always like that.

Q: What do you think is the matter?

A: You... I think you know.

Jannina flipped through the rest of it: normal, normal, normal. Miss Smith was as normal as could be. Miss Smith was stupid. Not even very stupid. It was too damned bad. They'd probably have enough of Leslie Smith in a week, the Komarovs; yes, we'll have enough of her (Jannina thought), never able to catch a joke or a tone of voice, always clumsy, however willing, but never happy, never at ease. You can get a job for her, but what else can you get for her? Jannina glanced down at the dossier, already bored.

Q: You say you would have liked to live in the old days. Why is that? Do you think it would have been more adventurous or would you like to have had lots of children?

A: I... you have no right... You're condescending.

Q: I'm sorry. I suppose you mean to say that then you would have been of above-average intelligence. You would, you know.

A: I know. I looked it up. Don't condescend to me.

Well, it *was* too damned bad! Jannina felt tears rise in her eyes. What had the poor woman done? It was just an accident, that was the horror of it, not even a tragedy, as if everyone's forehead had been stamped with the word "Choose" except for Leslie Smith's. She needed money, thought Jannina, thinking of the bad old days when people did things for money. Nobody could take to Leslie Smith. She wasn't insane enough to stand for being hurt or exploited. She wasn't clever enough to interest anybody. She certainly wasn't feeble-minded; they couldn't very well put her into a hospital for the feeble-minded or the brain-injured; in fact (Jannina was looking at the dossier again) they had tried to get her to work there and she had taken a good, fast swing at the supervisor. She had said the people there were "hideous" and "revolting." She had no particular mechanical aptitudes. She had no particular interests. There was not even anything for her to read or watch; how could there be? She seemed (back at the dossier) to spend most of her time either working or going on public tours of exotic places, coral reefs and places like that. She enjoyed aqualung diving, but didn't do it often because that got boring. And that was that. There was, all in all, very little one could do for Leslie Smith. You might even say that in her own person she represented all the defects of the bad old days. Just imagine a world made up of such creatures! Jannina yawned. She slung the folder away and padded into the kitchen. Pity Miss Smith wasn't good-looking, also a pity that she was too well balanced (the folder said) to think that cosmetic surgery would make that much difference. Good for you, Leslie, you've got some sense, anyhow. Jannina, half asleep, met Ann in the kitchen, beautiful, slender Ann reclining on a cushion with her so-chi and melon. Dear old Ann. Jannina nuzzled her brown shoulder. Ann poked her.

"Look," said Ann, and she pulled from the purse she wore at her waist a tiny fragment of cloth, stained rusty brown.

"What's that?"

"The second-best maker of hand-blown glass—oh, you know about it—well, this is his blood. When the best maker of hand-blown glass in the world had stabbed to the heart the second-best maker of hand-blown glass in the world, and cut his throat, too, some small children steeped handkerchiefs in his blood and they're sending pieces all over the world."

"Good God!" cried Jannina.

"Don't worry, my dear," said lovely Ann; "it happens every decade or so. The children say they want to bring back cruelty, dirt, disease, glory and hell. Then they forget about it. Every teacher knows that." She sounded amused. "I'm afraid I lost my temper today, though, and walloped your godchild. It's in the family, after all."

Jannina remembered when she herself had been much younger and Annie, barely a girl, had come to live with them. Ann had played at being a child and had put her head on Jannina's shoulder, saying, "Jannie, tell me a story." So Jannina now laid her head on Ann's breast and said, "Annie, tell me a story."

Ann said: "I told my children a story today, a creation myth. Every creation myth has to explain how death and suffering came into the world, so that's what this one is about. In the beginning, the first man and the first woman lived very contentedly on an island until one day they began to feel hungry. So they called to the turtle who holds up the world to send them something to eat. The turtle sent them a mango and they ate it and were satisfied, but the next day they were hungry again.

"'Turtle,' they said, 'send us something to eat.' So the turtle sent them a coffee berry. They thought it was pretty small, but they ate it anyway and were satisfied. The third day they called on the turtle again and this time the turtle sent them two things: a banana and a stone. The man and woman did not know which to choose, so they asked the turtle which thing it was they should eat. 'Choose,' said the turtle. So they chose the banana and ate that, but they used the stone for a game of catch. Then the turtle said, 'You should have chosen the stone. If you had chosen the stone, you would have lived forever, but now that you have chosen the banana, Death and Pain have entered the world, and it is not I that can stop them.'"

Jannina was crying. Lying in the arms of her old friend, she wept bitterly, with a burning sensation in her chest and the taste of death and ashes in her mouth. It was awful. It was horrible. She remembered the embryo shark she had seen when she was three, in the Auckland Cetacean Research Center, and how she had cried then. She didn't know what she was crying about. "Don't, don't!" she sobbed.

"Don't what?" said Ann affectionately. "Silly Jannina!"

"Don't, don't," cried Jannina, "don't, it's true, it's true!" and she went on in this way for several more minutes. Death had entered the world. Nobody could stop it. It was ghastly. She did not mind for herself but for others, for her godchild, for instance. He was going to die. He was going to suffer. Nothing could help him. Duel, suicide or old age, it was all the same. "This life!" gasped Jannina. "This awful life!" The thought of death became entwined somehow with Leslie Smith, in bed upstairs, and Jannina began to cry afresh, but eventually the thought of Leslie Smith calmed her. It brought her back to herself. She wiped her eyes with her hand. She sat up. "Do you want a smoke?" said beautiful Ann, but Jannina shook her head. She began to laugh. Really, the whole thing was quite ridiculous.

"There's this Leslie Smith," she said, dry-eyed. "We'll have to find a tactful way to get rid of her. It's idiotic, in this day and age."

And she told lovely Annie all about it.

MICHAEL KURLAND

Think Only This of Me

Michael Kurland (1938-   ) is one of the very few science fiction writers to appear as a character in someone else's science fiction novel—in his case, in Chester Anderson's The Butterfly Kid. *He is also a fine writer in his own right, with about a dozen novels and numerous shorter works to his credit. Kurland is an inveterate punster and parodist, but he also has a more serious side, as in "Think Only This of Me," a truly neglected masterpiece of modern science fiction.*

I MET HER in Anno Domini and was charmed. The Seventeenth Century it was. Two weeks and three centuries later we were in love.

Her name: Diana Seven; my name: Christopher Charles Mar d'Earth. Both of old stock, or so I thought; both certainly of Earth; both certainly human, for what that might mean in this galactic day. She was young, how young I did not know, and I was gracefully middle-yeared for an immortal. I would not see my first century again, but I would be a long time yet in my second. I looked to be somewhen around forty, normal span; she looked an unretouched twenty, except in motion when she looked barely teen and also ageless.

Anno Domini was my first pause in twenty years. I legislate in the Senior Chamber of the Parliament of Stars. We tend to feel, we beings of the Senior Chamber, that our efforts bind the intelligences of the galaxy together, for all that races still aggress and habited planets are still fused in anger. We also feel that, despite all our posturing, blustering and rhetoric, we accomplish nothing save the passage of time, for all that beings have not starved, races have not been destroyed and planets have not turned to stars through our efforts. This dichotomy slowly erodes empathy, emotion and intellect.

So I paused. I returned to Sol to become again a man of Earth, an Earthman, and walk among trees and down narrow, twisting streets and wide boulevards— but mainly to walk among the men and women of Earth who are my constituency, my ancestry and my soul. The races of man are varied and the farther one gets from Sol the greater the variation, though all are men and can interbreed and trace their language back to a common source—if they still have language, if they still

482

have sex. But I no more represent the Autocracy or the Diggers of Melvic than I speak for the Denzii Hive or the unfortunate Urechis of Mol.

I felt a need for history: to be one with Earth is to be a part of the sequence of man, a product of all that has come before and a precursor to all that will follow. To return to Sol, to Earth, to man, to our common history: that was my plan.

I spent the first month in the present, walking, looking, visiting, remembering— chronolizing myself to the fashions, mores, idiom and art of this most volatile of human cultures. Then I retreated to Earth itself, to the past, to Anno Domini, the religious years: twenty-four centuries called after the Son of the One God. The period right before the present era, when man no longer needs any god but himself.

Earth is now all past: the present comes no closer than Earth's satellite, the moon; the future—I wonder at times what future a planet can have when it has renounced the present.

I picked Seventeen to start, and was garbed and armed and primed and screened and out before I could say, *All the world's a stage*
> *And all the men and women merely players*
> *They have their exits and their entrances....*

The town was London and the year was sixteen-whatever. In this re-created past the years sometimes slip and events anachron—a fact of interest but to scholars and piddlers. The costumes of this re-created century were exotic, but no more than the smell. Charles had been beheaded a few years before. The Roundheads had been in power for however long the Roundheads were in power, and now William the Orange was about to land at Plymouth Dock.

I was sitting in the Mermaid Tavern, at a small table at the rear. Next to me, over my left shoulder, was a large round table where Ben Jonson sat deep in conversation with Will Shakespere, John Milton, Edmond Waller and the Earl of Someplace. As writers will when alone together, they were discussing money and I quickly tired of their talk.

She walked in as I was preparing to leave. Walked? She danced with the un- assuming grace of wind-blown leaves. She flowed across the walk and quickstepped through the door as though practiced by a master choreographer and rehearsed a dozen times before this take. These are the images that came to mind as she appeared in the doorway.

I sat back down and watched as she came in. She was aware of everything, and interested in all that she could see, and the very air around her was vibrant with the excitement of her life. And so I was attracted and excited and aware before a word had passed between us.

A man too doltish to see what she was stood by the door as she passed. He thought she was something other, and he spoke to her so: "Hey, girl; hey, wench, you should not be alone. P'raps I'll keep you company if you ask me pretty."

She did not reply. She did not seem to hear, but passed him by as if he were a wall.

He reached out to grasp her by the shoulder and I stood up, my hand falling to the handle of my walking stick.

She spun almost before his hand had touched. She reached out, her fingers appearing to not quite reach his neck. He fell away and she continued the pirouette and entered without further pause.

I must have stood like a stone, frozen in my foolish heroic pose with half-raised stick. She smiled at me. "No need," she said. "Thank you."

I stammered at her some wish that she share my table and she nodded, sat and smiled again, introduced herself and looked about. She was also, I decided, a visitor to this re-created Seventeen. I pointed out to her the round table next to us and its famous occupants, indicating each with almost the pride of a creator, as though I had done something clever merely to have sat next to them and imposed myself on their conversation. They were reciting to each other now—each trying to impress the rest with the wit and feeling of his verse. Diana was interested, but not awed. She asked to be introduced, and so I complied.

"It is an honor to meet each of you," she told the table. "And especially Mr. Shakespere, whom I have long admired."

"Nay, not 'Mr. Shakespere,'" Shakespere insisted firmly. "Will, if you will. Aye, an' if you won't 'tis still a simple 'Will.' 'Tis my will, so you must."

Jonson glared across the table. "You are the most convoluted simple-minded man," he said. "You will if you won't, but you can't so you must. Spare us!"

The sound of fifes came at us from a distance. A far rumble soon became the beat of many drums. The entourage of William approached and we all went outside the tavern to join the patient mob that awaited his passing.

First the soldiers, row on row, and for a long time nothing passed but soldiers. Then soldiers astride horses. Then soldiers astride horses pulling small cannon. Then a military band. Then more horses with soldiers astride, but now the uniform had changed. Then a coach and the crowd went wild—but it was the wrong coach. By now, unless he were twelve feet tall, the new king was an anticlimax. I looked over the crowd and tried to tell which were residents and which were guests of Anno Domini. I couldn't.

If this were the real Seventeenth Century—that is, if it were historical past rather than Anno Dominical re-creation—there would be signs. The pox would have left its mark on most who lived. Rickets would be common. War cripples would be begging from every street corner. This Seventeenth Century, the only one the residents knew, was being redone by a benevolent hand.

The new king passed. His coach was open and he smiled and nodded and waved and was cheered. A stout, red-faced little man—anticlimax. I laughed.

We left then, Diana and I, and I offered to walk her to her inn. She named it and I discovered it was my own.

"How do you like this time?" I asked her as we walked. "Have you been here long?"

"All day," she said. "Then you're a guest too? I wondered why you were the only one in the tavern I hadn't heard of."

"Thanks," I said. "In realtime I am well known. My return to Earth was mentioned as primary news. I am a third of Earth's voice in the Parliament of the Stars. I am known and welcome in half a thousand worlds throughout the galaxy. I number some fifty life forms among my friends. It is not necessary that you have heard of me."

"You're insulted!" she said, clapping her hands together. "How delightful! Now you make me feel important, that my words could insult one as essential as you. I thank you for feeling insulted. I am pleased."

I hadn't thought of it that way, ever before. Somehow she made me glad that I had felt insulted. It was nice to be insulted for her: it made her happy. She reminded me of a beautiful half-grown kitten, newly exploring the world outside its kitten box.

The inn was a U-shaped structure around a central courtyard. The stables were to the right, the rooms to the left and the common room straight ahead. It had been called The Buckingham the last time I was there, some thirty years before. Now, after a decade of being the Pym & Thistle, it sported a new signboard over the door: The Two Roses. The device showed a red and white rose thoroughly entwined. The landlord I didn't remember—a small, chubby man with a wide smile carved into his unhappy face. I asked him what the new name signified.

"It signifies I'm tired of changing the name of my inn," he told me. "I'm becoming nonpolitical. York and Lancaster settled their differences quite a ways back."

"Let us hope William doesn't think it means you prefer the white and red to his orange," I suggested. He looked after me strangely as I escorted Diana across to the common room and we sat at a table in the corner.

"Dinner?" I suggested.

Diana nodded enthusiastically, spilling her red hair around her face. "Meat!" she said. "Great gobs of rare roast—and maybe a potato."

"I—uh—I think they boil their meat these days," I told her in jest.

"No!" She was horrified. "Boil perfectly good, unresisting roasts and steaks? That's barbaric."

"*O tempora, o mores!*" I agreed, wondering what my accent would have sounded like to Marcus Tullius.

Diana looked puzzled. I tried again, slanting the accents in a different direction. She looked more puzzled.

"It means: 'Oh, what times—oh, what customs!' It's Latin," I told her.

"It's what?"

"Latin. That's a pre-language. Ancient and dead." Now I was puzzled. Who was this girl of Earth who didn't know of Latin? For the past four hundred years, since humanity had begun trying to re-create its cradle—or at least its nursery— all born of Earth, except those born on Earth, knew something of prehistory and the prelanguages: the times and the tongues of man before he met the stars.

"You know what tongue was spoken here?" I asked her.

"Common," she said, looking at me as if I had just asked if she knew what those five slender tubes at the end of her hand were called. "The language of Earth. The one standard language of humans throughout the Galaxy."

"I mean," I explained, "what language was spoken in the real Seventeenth Century London? What language all that beautiful poetry we heard discussed in the tavern by those great names at the next table was translated from?"

She shook her head. "I hadn't thought——"

"English," I said.

"Oh. Of course. England—English. How silly!"

The servitor approached the table circumspectly, waiting until he was sure we had finished speaking before addressing us. "Evening m'lord, m'lady," he mumbled. "Roseguddenit. Venice impizenizeto."

Diana giggled. "English?" she asked. "Have we really receded in time?"

"In time for what?"

Diana giggled again. The thin lad in the servitor's apron looked puzzled, unhappy, frightened and resigned.

"Would you go over that again?" I asked him.

"Parme?"

"What you said, lad. Go over it again for diction, please."

Now he was also nervous and upset and clearly blamed me. "My lord?"

"Speak more slowly," I told him, "and pronounce more carefully and those of us without your quick wit and ready mind will be able to comprehend. Yes?"

"Yes, my lord." If he could have killed me.... "Sorry, my lord. The roast is good tonight, my lord. The venison pie is very nice, my lord. My lady. What may I serve you?"

"Roast!" Diana stated. "Thick slices of roast. You don't boil your roast, do you? You wouldn't do that?"

The boy nervously replied that he wouldn't think of it, heard my order, then removed himself like a blown candle flame, leaving not even an after-image.

"You frighten people," Diana told me.

"It's my most valued ability," I said. "I shall not frighten you."

"You certainly shall not," she agreed. "My teachers were all more menacing than you—and more unforgiving. And they didn't notice my body."

I ignored the last part of her remark and stared into her blue eyes. "You went to an unpermissive school," I said, smiling.

"The universe is unpermissive," she said seriously. It was a learned response and I wondered who had taught it and why.

The innkeeper approached us during dessert. "Good?" he asked. "You enjoyed?"

"Indeed," I assured him.

"My pleasure," he nodded. "My guests. There will be no reckoning."

"Gracious of you, sir," Diana said.

"Why?" I asked, being wiser and therefore trustless of hostels.

"I am taking your suggestion," he told me. "And I thank you by feeding you dinner."

"Suggestion?"

"Yes. I am changing the name of the inn. Henceforth it shall be known as The Two Roses and the Tulip. I have sent a boy to notify the signpainter."

II

We walked into the night, Diana and I. Hand in hand we walked, although it was conversation and not love that bound us then. We contrasted: she bright and quick, with an aim as true as a hawk's; I ponderous and sure as a great bear (I metaphor our speech only). We learned from each other. I arrayed my vast store of facts before her in the patterns dictated by the logic of my decades—she swooped and plucked out one here, another there, and presented them as jewels to be examined for themselves, or changed their position to create the fabric of a new logic.

"These people," she asked me, waving a hand to indicate the residents in the houses around us, "what do they feel? What do they think? They are human, yes? How can they just spend their lives pretending they're Anno Domini?"

"They're not pretending," I told her.

"But this *isn't* the Seventeenth Century."

"For them it is. They know of nothing else. Weren't you warned about post-chronic talk while you're here?"

"I thought it was just not to spoil the—the—flavor. They *don't know?*"

"Truth."

"But that's cruel—unfair!"

"Why? They're stuck in their lives just as you and I are imbedded in our own. Are we any less actors in someone else's drama than they?"

"Philosophy, like religion, is a very useful drug," she didacted, "but it should be used only to condone the evils we cannot control—and not those we create."

"You're quoting," I guessed.

"My most valued ability," she agreed. "I have a memory like a wideband slow-crystal—the input can't be erased without destructing the device. Do you condone this make-believe?"

"It isn't make-believe. And convince me that it's evil."

"But it's so limited——"

"They have the whole world. Their world—the world of the Seventeenth."

"They don't—not in any real sense. This whole area can't be bigger than—than——"

She looked to me for help. I shrugged. "I don't know either. But however large it is, it's also—in a very real sense—unbounded. How much can a man expect to see in one normal lifetime—especially limited to horses and sailing ships for transportation? Any of these people who wish to go to France or the New World will get there. Aided by Anno Domini, they will arrive in their France without noticing whatever odd maneuvering the ship does in the 'Channel.' I've taken that trip."

"What would happen if I decided to get up and just walk—" she pointed off to the left—"that way, in a straight line?"

"You'd come to the edge," I said. "Wherever that is."

"Yes. Suppose I were a native—a resident—then what?"

"Then you'd probably fall asleep by the side of the road, and when you woke you'd suddenly remember urgent business back in town, or forget what you were doing there in the first place. And you'd never have the urge to roam again."

"You mean they dethink and rethink these people? Just to keep them putting on a show for us?"

"Also to keep them happy," I argued. "It's for their own good. Think how they'd feel if they knew they were part of a display. This way they live out their lives without knowing of any options. It's no more unfair to live here than it was to live in the actual Seventeenth Century. A lot better: the food is adequate, diseases are eliminated, sanitation is much improved."

"It sounds like an argument for slavery," Diana snapped. "Or pigfarming!"

We had come to what had to be the main street of the district. It was paved and lit. Bayswater High Street, the signpost read. The lights were open flames on stanchions, bright enough to mark the way but not to illuminate. "Perhaps we had better head back," I suggested. "In another half-hour it will be too dark to see our way."

"The moon will be up in twenty minutes," Diana told me. "And it's only two days off full. Plenty of light."

"Example of your memory?" I asked.

She nodded. "I saw a chart once."

The houses were two and three story, the upper stories overlapping the first. Picturesque in daylight, they were transformed at dusk into squatting ogres lurking behind the streetlights. The few people left on the street were scurrying like singleminded rats toward their holes.

"Some things are changeless," I said, pointing my walking stick at a receding back. "Fear of the night is one such. These people fear footpads and cutthroats—our people fear the stars. Evolution, I fear, is too slow a process. Our subconscious is still a million years behind us—in the caves of our youth."

"You mean that literally?" Diana asked. "About our people fearing the stars?"

"Extraordinarily literally. Astrophobia is the current mode. Not a fear of standing under the stars, like Chicken Little, but fear that, circling one of those points of light, is the race that will destroy humanity. The government spends billions each year in pursuit of this fear. I believe that it couples with the subconscious belief that we deserve to be destroyed. That all Earth has turned its back to the stars to live wholly in the past is part of the syndrome."

Diana asked me a question then, something about the deeper manifestations of this ailment, and I prattled on about how easy it was to recognize the problem, but no one was getting it cured because it was chronolous to declare the inside of your head sacrosanct—if you were of high enough status to make it stick. I'm not sure of what I said, as most of my attention was on three sets of approaching footsteps I was attempting to analyze without alarming Diana. In step, but not in the rhythm of soldiers—a slightly slower, swaggering step. Three young dandies out for an evening's entertainment, no doubt.

They rounded the corner and appeared under the light. They were well dressed, indeed foppishly dressed, and carrying swords—so they were gentlemen of this time. Or at least they were sons of gentlemen.

"What say?" the first one said, seeing us.

"Say what?" the second demanded.

"What?" asked the third. "What ho!" he amended, strutting toward us. "What have we here? A lissome lass, begad! And unescorted."

"Madam," the first said, "my lady, ma'am. Chivalry is not dead! We shall prove this."

Diana looked puzzled, but completely unafraid. I don't know how I looked—I felt weak. "Get behind me," I instructed her.

"Yes, indeed," the third amplified, "we shall chivalrously rescue you from that old man there, who's clearly attempting to have his way with you."

"We shall," the second added, "expect a suitable reward."

"Is this some game?" Diana asked me.

"No," I told her. "These lads are going to try to kill me. If they succeed they'll kill you, too—eventually."

The first drew his sword. I twisted the handle of my stick until I felt it click. We were now about even—three swords against one sword-stick with a narcospray tip. Anyone within one meter of the front of the tip would fall inanimate ten seconds after he was hit—and I should be able to keep even three of them away for ten seconds.

"These are truly enemies?" Diana asked me, staring up into my eyes. There was an undercurrent of excitement in her expression.

"Yes," I said briefly. "But don't worry. Just stay——"

"I trust you," she said, nodding as though she had just made a prime decision. "Enemies!" Then she was in motion.

She dove forward onto her shoulder and pushed off as she rolled, catching the first one on the chin with the heel of her boot. He flew backward and came to a skidding stop on his back across the street. The second was just starting to react when she slammed him across the side of his head with her forearm. He slid slowly to the ground, folding in the middle as he dropped.

The third was aware of his danger, although he had no clear idea of what this whirlwind was. His sword was up and he was facing her. I managed one step toward them when, with a small cry of joy, she was past his guard and had fastened both of her hands around his throat. She must have known just where to press with her small fingers, because he didn't struggle, didn't even gasp—he just crumpled. She went down with him, keeping her grip. Her eyes were alive with excitement and she was grinning. She had, somehow, not the look of a person who has vanquished a foe, but more that of a terrier who has cornered a rat.

"All right," I said, going over and pulling her off. "It's all right, it's all over."

She looked up, small and sweet and innocent, except for a rip in the right sleeve of her dress. "He's still alive, this one."

"No!" I yelled, when I saw her hands tighten around his throat.

She stared at me. "The other two, they are dead."

"Leave him," I instructed.

"Yes." She stood up, sounding disappointed.

I took her hand and led her away. I began to tremble slightly—a touch of aftershock. Diana was calm and gentle. I had no empathy for the three ruffians—they had danced to their own tune—but I worried about Diana. No—I think rather she frightened me. I was not concerned with the ease with which she dispatched—body combat ballet is not new to me. I worried rather about the joy with which she destroyed.

I remembered to disarm the stick, so as not to shoot myself in the foot. "Diana," I said, picking my words not to offend, "I admire the way you handled those men.

It shows great skill and training. But when a man is down—more particularly when he is unconscious—you don't have to kill him."

"But he was an enemy. You said so."

Semantic problem—or something more?

"Christopher?" We stopped at the innyard and she stared up at me, her eyes wide.

"Yes?" Tears were forming in the corners of her eyes and she was shaking. Delayed reaction? I held her and stroked her long hair.

"Those men wanted to hurt us. It wasn't a secondary thing, like wanting to take our money and hurting us if we resisted. They *just* wanted to hurt us."

"True."

"Why would anyone behave like that?"

It wasn't the fight that had her upset, but the morals of her opponents. "You killed two of them and were working on the third," I reminded her.

"But that was their doing. You said they were enemies. They declared status, not I. They attacked unprovoked. And I had your word."

"Right," I said, deciding to watch my words around this girl who took my definitions so literally and acted on them with such finality. "Well, they behaved that way because they've been taught to think it's fun."

"I don't understand," she said.

"Neither do I," I agreed.

We retired to our separate rooms and I spent some time studying the cracks in the ceiling in an effort to think before I fell asleep.

Diana and I spent the next ten days together in Shakespere's London. Diana was delighted by everything and I was delighted by her. We grew closer together in that indefinable way men and women grow closer together, with neither of us mentioning it but both of us quite aware. She questioned me incessantly about everything, but gave little detail in return. I learned she had no family and grew up in a special school run by Earth government. I learned how beautiful she was, inside and out, in motion and in stillness.

After the first week we shared the same room. Luckily Seventeen was a time that allowed of such a change. The innkeeper persisted in winking at me whenever he could until I felt I had earned that dinner, but we suffered no other hardship for our affection.

Then one day over breakfast we decided to abandon the Seventeenth Century. I voted for the Twentieth, and Diana ayed, although she knew little of it. "Those are the breakthrough years, aren't they?" she asked. "First flights to the nearer planets!"

I munched on a bacon stick. "Out of the cradle and into the nursery," I said. "And the babes yelling, 'No, no, I don't *want* to walk—haven't learned to crawl properly yet.' As though that skill were going to be of value to them in the future. Interesting times. As in the ancient curse."

"Curse?" Diana asked, wide-eyed as a child.

I nodded. "May your children live in interesting times," I said. "Chinese."

"Not much of a curse," Diana insisted. "Where are the mummies' hearts and the vampires and such?"

"Now that would be interesting," I said. After breakfast I pushed the call for Anno Domini and they removed us in a coach. They declothed us and reclothed us and backgrounded us and thrust us into an aeroplane.

III

This dubious contrivance, all shiny and silver and with two whole piston engines—to keep us going forward so we wouldn't fall down—flew us to LaGuardia Field outside New York City. The field, like the aeroplane, was sleek and shiny and new and modern. Everything was modern—it was in the air. The modern taxi drove us to the modern city with its modern skyscrapers muraled with the most modern art. The year was 1938 and nothing could go wrong.

We checked into the Plaza and took a tenth-floor suite overlooking Central Park. It was evening and the park lights, glowing over the paths, roads, fields, rocks, ponds, streams, lakes and other structured wildnesses, turned it into a rectangular fairyland. The skyline surrounding the park was civilization surrounding and oppressing imagination, keeping it behind high walls and ordering its ways. This is known as interpretive sightseeing.

Diana had a lot of things she wanted to do. She wanted to see a play and a movie and a zoo and an ocean liner and a war and a soap opera and a rocket leaving for the moon.

"Everything but the rocket," I told her. "Your timing's off by about thirty years. They haven't even designed the machines to build the machines to build the rocket yet."

We compromised on a visit to the top of the Empire State Building, the closest thing to a trip to the moon that 1938 New York could provide.

"This is all real, isn't it?" Diana asked as we wandered around the guard rail, peering at Bronx tenements and Jersey slums.

"In a sense," I said.

"I mean the buildings are buildings, not sets, and the streets are streets and the river is a river and the ships are ships."

"And the people are people," I agreed. "The original had ten million, I believe. One of the three largest cities of the time. That's a lot of people to stuff into a small area and move around by automobile and subway."

She nodded. "How many people are here now—residents, I mean?"

"I don't know," I told her. "I doubt if they have the full original millions."

"Still," she said seriously, "it would be fair to say that there are a great many."

"That would be fair," I agreed.

"Why are they here?"

"It's getting chilly," I said, buttoning the two top buttons on my coat. "Let's go eat dinner."

"How can we justify bilking so many people out of their lives—out of whatever value their lives might have—by making them live in an artificial past?"

"How do their lives have any less value here than in realtime?" I asked in my best Socratic manner.

"Suppose you were an inventor," Diana hypothesized. "How would you feel to discover that you had reinvented the wheel, or the typer, or the bloaterjet?"

"I'd never know it was a reinvention," I said.

"But it would be. And you would have been cheated out of whatever good and new and beautiful you could have invented in realtime."

"I doubt Anno Domini encourages invention," I said.

"Worse! Where shall we eat dinner?"

We took a Domino Cab uptown to the Central Park Casino, to where Glenn Miller and his band were providing the dinner music. The music must have soothed Diana, since we got through the rib roast and into the crepes suzette before the sociology seminar continued.

"What about people like Glenn Miller here—or Shakespere—who were real people in history? Are they actors?"

"No, they're mindplants. Each of them has the personality and ability of the character he becomes, to the best of our ability to re-create it."

Diana sat silent for a minute, considering, her mouth puckered into a tight line and her eyebrows pulled down in concentration. She stared at her spoon. Then she picked it up and waved it at me. "That's disgusting. You don't merely cheat them out of the future—you cheat them out of their very lives."

It was my turn to be silent. I was silent through *String of Pearls* and *Goldberg's Blues*. Diana watched me as though expecting momently to see wisdom fall from my lips, or possibly smoke rise from my ears. I found myself uncomfortably defending policies I had never really thought about before. I tried to think it out, but was distracted by Diana's stare. I felt that I had to look as if I were thinking and it's very hard to work at looking the part and think at the same time.

"I would say it's more productive rather than less," I said when I had the idea sorted out. "You know our Shakespere has added several plays to the list that the original never got around to writing. *Saint Joan* and *Elizabeth the First* and, I think, *Timon of Athens*—those are his. We haven't cheated him. Both he and humanity have benefited from this arrangement."

"It's not an arrangement," Diana stated positively. "It's a manipulation. It takes two to make an arrangement. Let's dance."

There is something deeply satisfying about two bodies pressed together and moving together. The waltz and the foxtrot are more purely sexual than either the stately minuet before them or the frenzied hump after. We glided about the floor, letting our bodies work at becoming one.

"Christopher," Diana said.

"Hm?"

"I'm glad we've become friends."

"More than friends!"

"That, too," she said, squeezing against me. "But friends is something else. I think you're my only friend."

"I hope you exaggerate," I said. "That's very sad."

We danced silently for a moment. Then Diana stopped and pulled me back to our table. We sat down. "This is a major thing, isn't it?"

"Friendship?"

"No. Anno Domini and this whole re-creation. How many different historical times are there?"

"You're so beautiful and so serious and so young," I said. "And so intent—and so knowledgeable in some fields and so ignorant in others. Whoever brought you up had strange educational values."

"I told you I don't like talking about that," she said. Her expression could best be described as petulant.

"It requires no conversation," I told her. "Fifty."

"Fifty historical periods?" she said, instantly picking up the thread. One of the things I admired, that ability. "But there aren't that many centuries!"

"Many are covered with more than one set. The really popular ones are started every twenty-five years. All have one, at least. There may be some centuries that appeal not at all to you, but someone has a need for them."

"What sort of need? Why that word?"

"Ah! Now we speak of purpose: what you asked me before. The past is Earth's only industry. Its function is to hold together the more than two hundred diverse human cultures, spread out on close to a thousand planets, circling as many suns. Tens of thousands of people from all these planets, all these new directions for humankind, are here at any one time, sharing the one thing they all have in common: the past.

"This maintains Earth's preeminence in the councils of man and presumably bolsters her prominence in the Parliament of Stars. But more important: it provides a living point of origin for the human race.

"The psychologists decided over four hundred years ago, at the time of the Mabden Annihilation, that this was the best—perhaps the only—way to hold us together. Those of us who weren't already too far out. There are external threats still, you know."

"I know," Diana said dryly. "You mentioned the fear syndrome earlier in this connection."

"It should be taken seriously," I insisted. "Here on Earth you feel secure, but it's only because you're so far away from the action. The Denzii——"

"I take it very seriously," Diana assured me. "So seriously that I'd prefer not to talk about it even now."

"Yes. I didn't mean to frighten you."

"Frighten?" Diana smiled gently. "No, you don't do that. Tell me, what else is there to do in this year, in this town?"

We took the subway to the Battery and walked quietly on the grass around the Aquarium, which was closed and shuttered for the night. Then we took the ferry over to Staten Island and stood in the open on the top deck, letting the cold brinewind flap our coats and sting our cheeks. We waved to the Statue of Liberty and she smiled at us—or perhaps it was a trick of the light. I had my coat wrapped around Diana and she huddled against my chest and I felt young and bold and ready to explore uncharted worlds. We talked of minor things and we shared a cup of coffee, black and four sugars, and I think, perhaps, realized fully that we were in love.

The next day we went to the Bronx Zoo in the morning, came back to Manhattan in early afternoon for a matinee of *Our Town* and then returned to the hotel to dress. A man was waiting in the sitting room of our suite. He was standing.

"Why, Kroner," Diana said, "how delightful to see you. And how silly you look in those clothes here." Thus she effectively suppressed the *Who are you and what are you doing in my room?* that I had been about to contribute to the occasion. Kroner was a short man with too much hair on his head. He wore a onesuit that squeezed around his stocky, overly muscled body. The weightlifter is a physical type I have always disliked. I didn't recognize the Identification and Position badge he wore, except that it was medium-high status and something to do with education.

"Who is he?"

"Kroner," Diana said. "My professor—or one of. And this is Christopher Mar."

"Delighted." Clearly he lied.

"Surprised," I said. We touched hands. "To what do we owe this visit and what may we do for you? Any professor of Diana's——" I waved a hand vaguely. The current trend toward the vague can be very useful in conversation.

"I suppose you know what you're doing?" Kroner asked coldly.

"I have no idea of what that means," I told him. "At which of us are you sneering?"

"Both of you, I suppose," Kroner said. He sighed and sat down on the sofa. "You're right, I was being hostile. And there's no reason. You're a very important man, Senior Senator Mar—there's no way I can threaten you. And Grecia knows I'm only interested in protecting and helping her. When she disappeared from Seventeen without notifying us——"

"Who?" I interrupted.

"Grecia. Your companion."

"Is that right?" I asked Diana (Grecia).

She nodded.

"Of course you have a perfect right——"

"What does she call herself?" Kroner asked.

"Diana Seven," I said. Diana (Grecia) looked defiantly down at Kroner and remained silent.

Kroner nodded thoughtfully. "Of course," he said. "A clear choice. Then he doesn't know? You haven't told him?"

"No," Diana (Grecia) said. "Why should I?"

"Of course," Kroner repeated. "From your point of view, no reason. You've always been the most stubborn and independent-minded. No matter how much we strive for uniformity. Not that we mind, you understand—it's just that the variations make the training more difficult to program. I suppose it will make you harder to predict in action, so it's all for the best."

"Haven't told me what?" I demanded. I tried to picture some horrible secret, but nothing would come to mind.

"Diana Seven is not a name," Kroner told me, "it's a designation. Choosing it as her alias is the sort of direct thinking we've come to expect from Grecia."

"It's a comment," Diana (Grecia) said.

"Grecia is number seven in an official government program known as Project Diana," Kroner said. "The number is arbitrary."

"So is the name," Diana (Grecia) said. "You know how I was named? Listen, I'll recite the names of the first seven girls, in order—that should give you the idea: Adena, Beth, Claudia, Debra, Erdra, Fidlia, Grecia. It goes on like that. I prefer Diana Seven, it's more honest."

"Diana Seven you are to me forever," I told her. "I don't understand, though. What sort of government project?"

"This is going to sound silly," Kroner said, managing to look apologetic, "but I don't think you have the need to know."

"I might not have the—but I do indeed need to know very badly, and I can develop the official Need to Know in a very few minutes realtime."

"I will tell everything," Diana said, sitting down on a straight-back chair and crossing her shapely legs. "What do you push to get them to bring up drinks?"

"I'll do it," I said, picking up the housephone and dialing. "What would you like?"

"Coffee," Diana said.

"Another profession," Kroner said. "I guess you're right—we'd better talk about it."

"Something harder than coffee for you," I said, and ordered a pot of coffee and a portable bar sent up.

"Grecia——"

"Call her Diana—she prefers it."

Kroner shrugged. He was not very happy. "Diana is a GAM. Project Diana is one of a series of GAM projects that Future is funding."

GAM = Genetically Altered Man. GAMs were in disfavor now, at least on Earth, as it was felt that no alteration of the zygote could make up for a happy home life, or some such illogic.

"I thought the Bureau of the Future was only involved in long-range planning of city growth and transportation and that sort of thing," I said.

"And defense," Kroner told me. "Diana is a defense project."

That stopped me. I went into the bedroom to take off my tie and think of something clever to ask.

"What do you mean, 'a defense project'?" I cleverly asked when I returned. The bar was ported in then, so I had to wait for my answer. The waiter tried hard to preserve his air of waiterly detachment and not stare at Kroner, and even harder not to smile.

Kroner glared at him and stood up, flexing his biceps under the skintight onesuit. "What's the matter?" he demanded. "What are you staring at? Haven't you ever seen a Frog Prince before?"

The waiter merely gulped and fled the room. We all burst out laughing and I remembered that in my youth one of my closest friends had been a weightlifter. "You really should have dressed for the period," I told Kroner.

He shrugged. "I was wearing a period overcoat," he said, gesturing to a crumpled garment lying over a chair.

I fixed our various drinks and we sipped them and stared at each other. "We've been keeping an eye on the girls while they were on their travels," Kroner said. "When Diana took off with you we got worried. Diana has a certain reputation among the staff as a trouble-maker and you are a—prominent senator. The combination could be explosive."

"How?" I asked.

"The projects are played down," Kroner said. "For us, any press is bad. We'd be caught between two fires; those who are afraid of any GAM projects—the 'The only good superman is a dead superman' group—and those who would feel sorry for Diana and her sisters—poor little girls deprived of a home life and mother love and apple pie."

"It might have been nice, you know, all that stuff," Diana said, a surface anger in her voice covering some deeper emotion. "Why do people decide they have the right to do what's good for other people?"

"What?" I asked, feeling ignorant and ignored.

"We didn't exactly do it because it was good for you," Kroner said sadly. "We did it because it was necessary for us. We never lied to you about that."

"Great ethics," Diana said in a low, clipped voice that had an undertone of controlled scream. "We screwed up your life from before you were born, but at least we didn't lie to you—and that makes it all all right." She turned to me. "Did you know I'm a mule?" she demanded.

"What?"

"A mule. Or perhaps a hinny. Except instead of a cross between a jackass and a mare, I'm a cross between a human gamete and a micro-manipulator. Sterile."

"You mean you're——"

"No pills, no inserts, no children—no chance. Just me. Dead end. Supermule."

I went over to hold her, to show I understood, but she drew away. Mulelike, I couldn't help thinking, in her anger. "I'm on your side, you know," I said to her. She nodded, but stayed encased in herself.

I asked Kroner, "In what way is this girl a weapon?"

"Not a weapon," Kroner said. "More like a soldier."

"A hunting dog," Diana said. Well, it was a better self-image than a mule.

Kroner nodded. "In a way. Superfast reflexes, for one thing. One of the reasons she's small: information travels to the brain faster. Nerves react and transmit faster. Eyes see farther into the infrared and ultraviolet. Raw strength is of little use today. You know how old she is?"

I didn't. "I'm not good at guessing age," I said.

"Twelve," Kroner said.

There was, I believe, a long pause then.

"Do you mind?" Diana asked softly.

"I am surprised," I said.

"The tendency in naturally evolved high intelligence is for longer childhoods, not shorter," Kroner said. "You must experience more, cogitate more, and have more time to experiment—play—to develop a really high intelligence potential. But it is possible to mature a high intelligence very quickly in an extremely enriched environment. Twelve years from birth to adult is about the best we can manage. The body takes that long to grow and mature anyway, if we want a comparatively normal body."

"Diana is an adult," I said. "No matter how many times, or how few, the Earth has circled the sun since her birth."

Kroner nodded. "Diana is a highly capable adult, able to handle herself well in almost any situation."

"I'll not argue that," I said. "She dispatched three ruffians who attacked us and did so with unseemly ease."

"Ah!" Kroner said. "We thought that was she. Very good, Diana. Of course, that's what she's been trained and bred for, so it's fitting that she did."

"Trained for close combat?" I asked. "What sort of war are you expecting?"

"Not that," Kroner explained. "For you, as for most of the rest of humanity, killing any sentient being—and many lower animals—would be murder. You'd have to steel yourself and be highly motivated to perform the act. For Diana, killing anything that isn't human—or even humans who are clearly 'enemy'—is equivalent to hunting. And, like a good hunting dog, she enjoys it. Isn't that so, Diana?"

She nodded. "I can't see anything wrong with killing an enemy. And the fact that I know this is genetics and conditioning doesn't matter—all attitudes anyone has are a result of genetics and conditioning. If you gentlemen will excuse me, it's been a long day and I think I'll go to bed."

Kroner and I spoke privately for a short while after Diana retired. I suspect Diana listened at the door, as she was awake when I went to bed, but if so I'm glad of it.

"Does this mean I have to worry about Diana's getting angry at me and breaking my neck?" I asked Kroner, when she had left.

"Not at all," he said. "If anything, the opposite. She may tend to overprotect you. To kill a human being who is not an enemy would, in any case, be murder, and she is incapable of murder."

"How does she determine an enemy?"

"I think, at the moment, she'll take your word for it. She appears to be fixated on you. You may call it love, if you like, but we prefer the scientific term."

"I appear to be fixated on her," I said. "Whatever you call it."

"That's fine. We approve. As long as you aren't planning to use her—or make a political issue or anything of that sort—we're on your side."

"What is she doing here anyway? Is school out? Vacation?"

Kroner fixed himself another drink. "No," he said. "This is part of her training. Mixing with humanity to learn more fully what it is she may be fighting for. Two years of this—going and doing more or less where and what she wants—then she'll be ready for, let's call it graduate school."

"More fixating?"

"That's right. Fixating on man. Those in charge of this project seem a bit afraid of their creation."

"Historical precedent," I said. "Or, at least, literary."

"Yes," Kroner said. "Take care of Diana. Enjoy her. Love her. She needs more love than the other girls."

"You mean she fixates more strongly?" I asked.

Kroner smiled. "As of now," he said, "I'm on vacation. Bye." He picked up his coat and left.

I went in to sleep with Diana and she held me tight for a long while. I think she would have cried if she had known how. I held her, but it's hard to comfort someone who cannot cry.

Back in realtime—away from Earth and Anno Domini—I used my status to find out about the Project. Diana opted to stay with me. We fixated well together.

It was difficult, even for me, to open the private record of Project Diana. It was the most recent in a line of such projects dating back to shortly after the Mabden Annihilation. I immersed myself in it and read motive, intent, achievement, method, fear and design in the record crystals.

Earth is afraid of its heroes. Always has been.

Diana is sterile by design. Female by convenience—easier to control without the Y chromosome. Sterile by design. Safer. Can't breed a superrace behind our backs.

Diana's cells won't regenerate. Our long life depends upon regeneration—actually replication—of certain cells. Diana's—let us call it template—is inaccessible to our techniques. Also by design. Safer thus. Can't make long-range plans behind our backs. She will also age fast and be old by forty—probably dead by fifty.

I went home that evening and cried myself to sleep. Diana held me, but the crying frightened her and she couldn't help because I wouldn't tell her why, and it's hard to comfort someone unless you know why he's crying.

I have two years with her before she has to go off to prepare for the war we may never have. She wants to go. They want her for twenty-five years, she says, and she owes them that.

We're planning what we will do when she returns. There are so many things she wants to do and see in this vast galaxy. I promised to show them all to her.

I hardly cry at all any more, even late at night.

ROBERT SILVERBERG

Capricorn Games

The World Science Fiction Convention used to award a Hugo in the category of "Most Promising New Author," which Robert Silverberg (1935-) won in 1956 at the age of twenty-one. That the implications of the award were realized can be seen in the following, very partial, list of novels—Hawksbill Station *(1968),* The World Inside *(1971),* The Book of Skulls *(1972),* Dying Inside *(1972),* The Stochastic Man *(1975),* Shadrach in the Furnace *(1976) and* Lord Valentine's Castle *(1980)—seven of perhaps two dozen Silverberg novels that are important works of science fiction. He has subsequently been awarded another Hugo and is a four-time winner of the Nebula Award. His most recent book is a collection,* World of a Thousand Colors *(1982).*

—M.H.G.

NIKKI STEPPED into the conical field of the ultrasonic cleanser, wriggling so that the unheard droning out of the machine's stubby snout could more effectively shear her skin of dead epidermal tissue, globules of dried sweat, dabs of yesterday's scents and other debris; after three minutes she emerged clean, bouncy, ready for the party. She programmed her party outfit: green buskins, lemon-yellow tunic of gauzy film, pale-orange cape soft as a clam's mantle and nothing underneath but Nikki—smooth, glistening, satiny Nikki. Her body was tuned and fit. The party was in her honor, though she was the only one who knew that. Today was her birthday, the seventh of January, 1999, twenty-four years old, no sign yet of bodily decay. Old Steiner had gathered an extraordinary assortment of guests: he promised to display a reader of minds, a billionaire, an authentic Byzantine duke, an Arab rabbi, a man who had married his own daughter and other marvels. All of these, of course, subordinate to the true guest of honor, the evening's prize, the real birthday boy, the lion of the season, the celebrated Nicholson, who had lived a thousand years and who said he could help others to do the same. Nikki . . . Nicholson. Happy assonance, portending close harmony. You will show me, dear Nicholson, how I can live forever and never grow old. A cozy, soothing idea.

The sky beyond the sleek curve of her window was black, snow-dappled; she imagined she could hear the rusty howl of the wind and feel the sway of the frost-gripped building, ninety stories high. This was the worst winter she had ever known. Snow fell almost every day, a planetary snow, a global shiver, not even sparing the tropics. Ice hard as iron bands bound the streets of New York. Walls were slippery, the air had a cutting edge. Tonight Jupiter gleamed fiercely in the blackness like a diamond in a raven's forehead. Thank God she didn't have to go outside. She could wait out the winter within this tower. The mail came by pneumatic tube. The penthouse restaurant fed her. She had friends on a dozen floors. The building was a world, warm, snug. Let it snow. Let the sour gales come. Nikki checked herself in the all-around mirror: very nice, very very nice. Sweet filmy yellow folds. Hint of thigh, hint of breasts. More than a hint when there's a light source behind her. She glowed. Fluffed her short glossy black hair. Dab of scent. Everyone loved her. Beauty is a magnet: repels some, attracts many, leaves no one unmoved. It was nine o'clock.

"Upstairs," she said to the elevator. "Steiner's place."

"Eighty-eighth floor," the elevator said.

"I know that. You're so sweet."

Music in the hallway: Mozart, crystalline and sinuous. The door to Steiner's apartment was a half-barrel of chromed steel, like the entrance to a bank vault. Nikki smiled into the scanner. The barrel revolved. Steiner held his hands like cups, centimeters from her chest, by way of greeting. "Beautiful," he murmured.

"So glad you asked me to come."

"Practically everybody's here already. It's a wonderful party, love."

She kissed his shaggy cheek. In October they had met in the elevator. He was past sixty and looked less than forty. When she touched his body she perceived it as an object encased in milky ice, like a mammoth fresh out of the Siberian permafrost. They had been lovers for two weeks. Autumn had given way to winter and Nikki had passed out of his life, but he had kept his word about the parties: here she was, invited.

"Alexius Ducas," said a short, wide man with a dense black beard, parted in the middle. He bowed. A good flourish. Steiner evaporated and she was in the keeping of the Byzantine duke. He maneuvered her at once across the thick white carpet to a place where clusters of spotlights, sprouting like angry fungi from the wall, revealed the contours of her body. Others turned to look. Duke Alexius favored her with a heavy stare. But she felt no excitement. Byzantium had been over for a long time. He brought her a goblet of chilled green wine and said, "Are you ever in the Aegean Sea? My family has its ancestral castle on an island eighteen kilometers east of—"

"Excuse me, but which is the man named Nicholson?"

"Nicholson is merely the name he currently uses. He claims to have had a shop in Constantinople during the reign of my ancestor the Basileus Manuel Comnenus." A patronizing click, tongue on teeth. "Only a shopkeeper." The Byzantine eyes sparkled ferociously. "How beautiful you are!"

"Which one is he?"

"There. By the couch."

Nikki saw only a wall of backs. She tilted to the left and peered. No use. She would get to him later. Alexius Ducas continued to offer her his body with his eyes. She whispered languidly, "Tell me all about Byzantium."

He got as far as Constantine the Great before he bored her. She finished her wine, and coyly extending the glass, persuaded a smooth young man passing by to refill it for her. The Byzantine looked sad. "The empire then was divided," he said, "among—"

"This is my birthday," she announced.

"Yours also? My congratulations. Are you as old as—"

"Not nearly. Not by half. I won't even be five hundred for some time," she said, and turned to take her glass. The smooth young man did not wait to be captured. The party engulfed him like an avalanche. Sixty, eighty guests, all in motion. The draperies were pulled back, revealing the full fury of the snowstorm. No one was watching it. Steiner's apartment was like a movie set: great porcelain garden stools, Ming or even Sung; walls painted with flat sheets of bronze and scarlet; pre-Columbian artifacts in spotlit niches; sculptures like aluminum spider webs; Dürer etchings; the loot of the ages. Squat shaven-headed servants, Mayas or Khmers or perhaps Olmecs, circulated impassively offering trays of delicacies: caviar, sea urchins, bits of roasted meat, tiny sausages, burritos in startling chili sauce. Hands darted unceasingly from trays to lips. This was a gathering of life-eaters, world-swallowers. Duke Alexius was stroking her arm. "I will leave at midnight," he said gently. "It would be a delight if you left with me."

"I have other plans," she told him.

"Even so." He bowed courteously, outwardly undisappointed. "Possibly another time. My card?" It appeared as if by magic in his hand: a sliver of tawny cardboard, elaborately engraved. She put it in her purse and the room swallowed him. Instantly a big, wild-eyed man took his place before her. "You've never heard of me," he began.

"Is that a boast or an apology?"

"I'm quite ordinary. I work for Steiner. He thought it would be amusing to invite me to one of his parties."

"What do you do?"

"Invoices and debarkations. Isn't this an amazing place?"

"What's your sign?" Nikki asked him.

"Libra."

"I'm Capricorn. Tonight's my birthday as well as *his*. If you're really Libra, you're wasting your time with me. Do you have a name?"

"Martin Bliss."

"Nikki."

"There isn't any Mrs. Bliss, hah-hah."

Nikki licked her lips. "I'm hungry. Would you get me some canapés?"

She was gone as soon as he moved toward the food. Circumnavigating the long room—past the string quintet, past the bartender's throne, past the window—until she had a good view of the man called Nicholson. He didn't disappoint her. He was slender, supple, not tall, strong in the shoulders. A man of presence and authority. She wanted to put her lips to him and suck immortality out. His head was a flat triangle, brutal cheekbones, thin lips, dark mat of curly hair, no beard, no mustache. His eyes were keen, electric, intolerably wise. He must have seen everything twice, at the very least. Nikki had read his book. Everyone had. He had been a king, a lama, a slave trader, a slave. Always taking pains to conceal his implausible longevity, now offering his terrible secret freely to the members of the Book-of-the-Month Club. Why had he chosen to surface and reveal himself? Because this is the necessary moment of revelation, he had said. When he must stand forth as what he is, so that he might impart his gift to others, lest he lose it. Lest he lose it. At the stroke of the new century he must share his prize of life. A dozen people surrounded him, catching his glow. He glanced through a palisade of shoulders and locked his eyes on hers; Nikki felt impaled, exalted, chosen. Warmth spread through her loins like a river of molten tungsten, like a stream of hot honey. She started to go to him. A corpse got in her way. Death's-head, parchment skin, nightmare eyes. A scaly hand brushed her bare biceps. A frightful eroded voice croaked, "How old do you think I am?"

"Oh, God!"

"How old?"

"Two thousand?"

"I'm fifty-eight. I won't live to see fifty-nine. Here, smoke one of these."

With trembling hands he offered her a tiny ivory tube. There was a Gothic monogram near one end—FXB—and a translucent green capsule at the other. She pressed the capsule and a flickering blue flame sprouted. She inhaled. "What is it?" she asked.

"My own mixture. Soma Number Five. You like it?"

"I'm smeared," she said. "Absolutely smeared. Oh, God!" The walls were flowing. The snow had turned to tin foil. An instant hit. The corpse had a golden halo. Dollar signs rose into view like stigmata on his furrowed forehead. She heard the crash of the surf, the roar of the waves. The deck was heaving. The masts were cracking. Woman overboard, she cried, and heard her inaudible voice disappearing down a tunnel of echoes, boingg boingg boingg. She clutched at his frail wrists. "You bastard, what did you *do* to me?"

"I'm Francis Xavier Byrne."

Oh. The billionaire. Byrne Industries, the great conglomerate. Steiner had promised her a billionaire tonight.

"Are you going to die soon?" she asked.

"No later than Easter. Money can't help me now. I'm a walking metastasis." He opened his ruffled shirt. Something bright and metallic, like chain mail, covered his chest. "Life-support system," he confided. "It operates me. Take it off for half an hour and I'd be finished. Are you a Capricorn?"

"How did you know?"

"I may be dying, but I'm not stupid. You have the Capricorn gleam in your eyes. What am I?"

She hesitated. His eyes were gleaming too. Self-made man, fantastic business sense, energy, arrogance. Capricorn, of course. No, too easy. "Leo," she said.

"No. Try again." He pressed another monogrammed tube into her hand and strode away. She hadn't yet come down from the last one, although the most flamboyant effects had ebbed. Party guests swirled and flowed around her. She no longer could see Nicholson. The snow seemed to be turning to hail, little hard particles spattering the vast windows and leaving white abraded tracks: or were her perceptions merely sharper? The roar of conversations seemed to rise and fall as if someone were adjusting a volume control. The lights fluctuated in a counterpointed rhythm. She felt dizzy. A tray of golden cocktails went past her and she hissed, "Where's the bathroom?"

Down the hall. Five strangers clustered outside it, talking in scaly whispers. She floated through them, grabbed the sink's cold edge, thrust her face to the oval concave mirror. A death's-head. Parchment skin, nightmare eyes. No! No! She blinked and her own features reappeared. Shivering, she made an effort to pull herself together. The medicine cabinet held a tempting collection of drugs, Steiner's all-purpose remedies. Without looking at labels Nikki seized a handful of vials and gobbled pills at random. A flat red one, a tapering green one, a succulent yellow gelatin capsule. Maybe headache remedies, maybe hallucinogens. Who knows, who cares? We Capricorns are not always as cautious as you think.

Someone knocked at the bathroom door. She answered and found the bland, hopeful face of Martin Bliss hovering near the ceiling. Eyes protruding faintly, cheeks florid. "They said you were sick. Can I do anything for you?" So kind, so sweet. She touched his arm, grazed his cheek with her lips. Beyond him in the hall stood a broad-bodied man with close-cropped blond hair, glacial blue eyes, a plump perfect face. His smile was intense and brilliant. "That's easy," he said. "Capricorn."

"Can you guess my—" She stopped, stunned. "Sign?" she finished, voice very small. "How did you do that? Oh."

"Yes. I'm that one."

She felt more than naked, stripped down to the ganglia, to the synapses. "What's the trick?"

"No trick. I listen. I hear."

"You hear people thinking?"

"More or less. Do you think it's a party game?" He was beautiful but terrifying, like a Samurai sword in motion. She wanted him but she didn't dare. He's got my number, she thought. I would never have any secrets from him. He said sadly, "I don't mind that. I know I frighten a lot of people. Some don't care."

"What's your name?"

"Tom," he said. "Hello, Nikki."

"I feel very sorry for you."

"Not really. You can kid yourself if you need to. But you can't kid me. Anyway, you don't sleep with men you feel sorry for."

"I don't sleep with you."

"You will," he said.

"I thought you were just a mind-reader. They didn't tell me you did prophecies too."

He leaned close and smiled. The smile demolished her. She had to fight to keep from falling. "I've got your number, all right," he said in a low harsh voice. "I'll call you next Tuesday." As he walked away he said, "You're wrong. I'm a Virgo. Believe it or not."

Nikki returned, numb, to the living room. "... the figure of the mandala," Nicholson was saying. His voice was dark, focused, a pure basso cantante. "The essential thing that every mandala has is a center: the place where everything is born, the eye of God's mind, the heart of darkness and of light, the core of the storm. All right: you must move toward the center, find the vortex at the boundary of Yang and Yin, place yourself right at the mandala's midpoint. *Center yourself.* Do you follow the metaphor? Center yourself at *now*, the eternal *now*. To move off center is to move forward toward death, backward toward birth, always the fatal polar swings; but if you're capable of positioning yourself constantly at the focus of the mandala, right on center, you have access to the fountain of renewal, you become an organism capable of constant self-healing, constant self-replenishment, constant expansion into regions beyond self. Do you follow? The power of—"

Steiner, at her elbow, said tenderly, "How beautiful you are in the first moments of erotic fixation."

"It's a marvelous party."

"Are you meeting interesting people?"

"Is there any other kind?" she asked.

Nicholson abruptly detached himself from the circle of his audience and strode across the room, alone, in a quick decisive knight's move toward the bar. Nikki, hurrying to intercept him, collided with a shaven-headed tray-bearing servant. The tray slid smoothly from the man's thick fingertips and launched itself into the air like a spinning shield; a rainfall of skewered meat in an oily green curry sauce spattered the white carpet. The servant was utterly motionless. He stood frozen like some sort of Mexican stone idol, thick-necked, flat-nosed, for a long painful moment; then he turned his head slowly to the left and regretfully contemplated his rigid outspread hand, shorn of its tray; finally he swung his head toward Nikki, and his normally expressionless granite face took on for a quick flickering instant a look of total hatred, a coruscating emanation of contempt and disgust that faded immediately. He laughed: hu-hu-hu, a neighing snicker. His superiority was overwhelming. Nikki floundered in quicksands of humiliation. Hastily she escaped, a zig and a zag, around the tumbled goodies and across to the bar. Nicholson, still by himself. Her face went crimson. She felt short of breath. Hunting for words, tongue all thumbs. Finally, in a catapulting blurt: "Happy birthday!"

"Thank you," he said solemnly.

"Are you enjoying your birthday?"

"Very much."

"I'm amazed that they don't bore you. I mean, having had so many of them."

"I don't bore easily." He was awesomely calm, drawing on some bottomless reservoir of patience. He gave her a look that was at the same time warm and impersonal. "I find everything interesting," he said.

"That's curious. I said more or less the same thing to Steiner just a few minutes ago. You know, it's my birthday too."

"Really?"

"The seventh of January, 1975, for me."

"Hello, 1975. I'm—" He laughed. "It sounds absolutely absurd, doesn't it?"

"The seventh of January, 982."

"You've been doing your homework."

"I've read your book," she said. "Can I make a silly remark? My God, you don't *look* like you're a thousand and seventeen years old."

"How should I look?"

"More like him," she said, indicating Francis Xavier Byrne.

Nicholson chuckled. She wondered if he liked her. Maybe. Maybe. Nikki risked some eye contact. He was hardly a centimeter taller than she was, which made it a terrifyingly intimate experience. He regarded her steadily, centeredly; she imagined a throbbing mandala surrounding him, luminous turquoise spokes emanating from his heart, radiant red and green spider-web rings connecting them. Reaching from her loins, she threw a loop of desire around him. Her eyes were explicit. His were veiled. She felt him calmly retreating. Take me inside, she pleaded, take me to one of the back rooms. Pour life into me. She said, "How will you choose the people you're going to instruct in the secret?"

"Intuitively."

"Refusing anybody who asks directly, of course."

"Refusing anybody who asks."

"Did *you* ask?"

"You said you read my book."

"Oh. Yes. I remember: you didn't know what was happening, you didn't understand anything until it was over."

"I was a simple lad," he said. "That was a long time ago." His eyes were alive again. He's drawn to me. He sees that I'm his kind, that I deserve him. Capricorn, Capricorn, Capricorn, you and me, he-goat and she-goat. Play my game, Cap. "How are you named?" he asked.

"Nikki."

"A beautiful name. A beautiful woman."

The emptiness of the compliments devastated her. She realized she had arrived with mysterious suddenness at a necessary point of tactical withdrawal; retreat was obligatory, lest she push too hard and destroy the tenuous contact so tensely established. She thanked him with a glance and gracefully slipped away, pivoting toward Martin Bliss, slipping her arm through his. Bliss quivered at the gesture, glowed, leaped into a higher energy state. She resonated to his vibrations, going up and up. She was at the heart of the party, the center of the mandala: standing flat-footed, legs slightly apart, making her body a polar axis, with lines of force zooming up out of the earth, up through the basement levels of this building, up the eighty-eight stories of it, up through her sex, her heart, her head. This is how it must feel, she thought, when undyingness is conferred on you. A moment of spontaneous grace, the kindling of an inner light. She looked love at poor sappy Bliss. You dear heart, you dumb walking pun. The string quintet made molten sounds. "What is that?" she asked. "Brahms?" Bliss offered to find out. Alone, she was vulnerable to Francis Xavier Byrne, who brought her down with a single cadaverous glance.

"Have you guessed it yet?" he asked. "The sign."

She stared through his ragged cancerous body, blazing with decomposition. "Scorpio," she told him hoarsely.

"Right! Right!" He pulled a pendant from his breast and draped its golden chain over her head. "For you," he rasped, and fled. She fondled it. A smooth green stone. Jade? Emerald? Lightly engraved on its domed face was the looped cross, the crux ansata. Beautiful. The gift of life, from the dying man. She waved fondly at him across a forest of heads and winked. Bliss returned.

"They're playing something by Schönberg," he reported. *"Verklärte Nacht."*

"How lovely." She flipped the pendant and let it fall back against her breasts. "Do you like it?"

"I'm sure you didn't have it a moment ago."

"It sprouted," she told him. She felt high, but not as high as she had been just after leaving Nicholson. That sense of herself as focal point had departed. The party seemed chaotic. Couples were forming, dissolving, re-forming; shadowy figures were stealing away in twos and threes toward the bedrooms; the servants were more obsessively thrusting their trays of drinks and snacks at the remaining guests; the hail had reverted to snow, and feathery masses silently struck the windows, sticking there, revealing their glistening mandalic structures for painfully brief moments before they deliquesced. Nikki struggled to regain her centered position. She indulged in a cheering fantasy: Nicholson coming to her, formally touching her cheek, telling her, "You will be one of the elect." In less than twelve months the time would come for him to gather with his seven still unnamed disciples to see in the new century, and he would take their hands into his hands, he would pump the vitality of the undying into their bodies, sharing with them the secret that had been shared with him a thousand years ago. Who? Who? Who? Me. Me. Me. But where had Nicholson gone? His aura, his glow, that cone of imaginary light that had appeared to surround him—nowhere.

A man in a lacquered orange wig began furiously to quarrel, almost under Nikki's nose, with a much younger woman wearing festoons of bioluminescent pearls. Man and wife, evidently. They were both sharp-featured, with glossy, protuberant eyes, rigid faces, cheek muscles working intensely. Live together long enough, come to look alike. Their dispute had a stale, ritualistic flavor, as though they had staged it all too many times before: they were explaining to each other the events that had caused the quarrel, interpreting them, recapitulating them, shading them, justifying, attacking, defending—you said this because and that led me to respond that way because . . . no, on the contrary I said this because you said that—all of it in a quiet screechy tone, sickening, agonizing, pure death.

"He's her biological father," a man next to Nikki said. "She was one of the first of the in vitro babies, and he was the donor, and five years ago he tracked her down and married her. A loophole in the law." Five years? They sounded as if they had been married for fifty. Walls of pain and boredom encased them. Only their eyes were alive. Nikki found it impossible to imagine those two in bed, bodies entwined in the act of love. Act of love, she thought, and laughed. Where was Nicholson? Duke Alexius, flushed and sweat-beaded, bowed to her. "I will leave soon," he announced, and she received the announcement gravely but without reacting, as though he had merely commented on the fluctuations of the storm, or had spoken in Greek. He bowed again and went away. Nicholson? Nicholson? She grew calm again, finding her center. *He will come to me when he is ready. There was contact between us, and it was real and good.*

Bliss, beside her, gestured and said, "A rabbi of Syrian birth, formerly Muslim, highly regarded among Jewish theologians."

She nodded but didn't look.

"An astronaut just back from Mars. I've never seen anyone's skin tanned quite that color."

The astronaut held no interest for her. She worked at kicking herself back into high. The party was approaching a climactic moment, she felt, a time when commitments were being made and decisions taken. The clink of ice in glasses, the foggy vapors of psychedelic inhalants, the press of warm flesh all about her—she was wired into everything, she was alive and receptive, she was entering into the twitching hour, the hour of galvanic jerks. She grew wild and reckless. Impulsively she kissed Bliss, straining on tiptoes, jabbing her tongue deep into his startled mouth. Then she broke free. Someone was playing with the lights: they grew redder, then gained force and zoomed to blue-white ferocity. Far across the room a crowd was surging and billowing around the fallen figure of Francis Xavier Byrne, slumped loose-jointedly against the base of the bar. His eyes were open but glassy. Nicholson crouched over him, reaching into his shirt, making delicate adjustments of the controls of the chain mail beneath. "It's all right," Steiner was saying. "Give him some air. It's all right!" Confusion. Hubbub. A torrent of tangled input.

"—they say there's been a permanent change in the weather patterns. Colder winters from now on, because of accumulations of dust in the atmosphere that screen the sun's rays. Until we freeze altogether by around the year 2200—"

"—but the carbon dioxide is supposed to start a greenhouse effect that's causing *warmer* weather, I thought, and—"

"—the proposal to generate electrical power from—"

"—the San Andreas fault—"

"—financed by debentures convertible into—"

"—capsules of botulism toxin—"

"—to be distributed at a ratio of one per thousand families, throughout Greenland and the Kamchatka Metropolitan Area—"

"—in the sixteenth century, when you could actually hope to found your own empire in some unknown part of the—"

"—unresolved conflicts of Capricorn personality—"

"—intense concentration and meditation upon the completed mandala so that the contents of the work are transferred to and identified with the mind and body of the beholder. I mean, technically what occurs is the reabsorption of cosmic forces. In the process of construction these forces—"

"—butterflies, which are no longer to be found anywhere in—"

"—were projected out from the chaos of the unconscious; in the process of absorption, the powers are drawn back in again—"

"—reflecting transformations of the DNA in the light-collecting organ, which—"

"—the snow—"

"—a thousand years, can you imagine that? And—"

"—her body—"

"—formerly a toad—"

"—just back from Mars, and there's that *look* in his eye—"

"Hold me," Nikki said. "Just hold me. I'm very dizzy."

"Would you like a drink?"

"Just hold me." She pressed against cool sweet-smelling fabric. His chest, unyielding beneath it. Steiner. Very male. He steadied her, but only for a moment. Other responsibilities summoned him. When he released her, she swayed. He beckoned to someone else, blond, soft-faced. The mind-reader, Tom. Passing her along the chain from man to man.

"You feel better now," the telepath told her.

"Are you positive of that?"

"Very."

"Can you read any mind in the room?" she asked.

He nodded.

"Even *his?*"

Again a nod. "He's the clearest of all. He's been using it so long, all the channels are worn deep."

"Then he really is a thousand years old?"

"You didn't believe it?"

Nikki shrugged. "Sometimes I don't know what I believe."

"He's *old.*"

"You'd be the one to know."

"He's a phenomenon. He's absolutely extraordinary." A pause, quick, stabbing. "Would you like to see into his mind?"

"How can I?"

"I'll patch you right in, if you'd like me to." The glacial eyes flashed sudden mischievous warmth. "Yes?"

"I'm not sure I want to."

"You're very sure. You're curious as hell. Don't kid me. Don't play games, Nikki. You want to see into him."

"Maybe." Grudgingly.

"You do. Believe me, you do. Here. Relax, let your shoulders slump a little, loosen up, make yourself receptive, and I'll establish the link."

"Wait," she said.

But it was too late. The mind-reader serenely parted her consciousness like Moses doing the Red Sea, and rammed something into her forehead, something thick but insubstantial, a truncheon of fog. She quivered and recoiled. She felt violated. It was like her first time in bed, in that moment when all the fooling around at last was over, the kissing and the nibbling and the stroking, and suddenly there was this object deep inside her body. She had never forgotten that sense of being impaled. But of course it had been not only an intrusion but also a source of ecstasy. As was this. The object within her was the consciousness of Nicholson.

In wonder she explored its surface, rigid and weathered, pitted with the myriad ablations of reentry. Ran her trembling hands over its bronzy roughness. Remained outside it. Tom the mind-reader gave her a nudge. Go on, go on. Deeper. Don't hold back. She folded herself around Nicholson and drifted into him like ectoplasm seeping into sand. Suddenly she lost her bearings. The discrete and impermeable boundary marking the end of her self and the beginning of his became indistinct. It was impossible to distinguish between her experiences and his, nor could she separate the pulsations of her nervous system from the impulses traveling along his. Phantom memories assailed and engulfed her. She was transformed into a node of pure perception, a steady cool isolated eye, surveying and recording. Images flashed. She was toiling upward along a dazzling snowy crest, with jagged Himalayan fangs hanging above her in the white sky and a warm-muzzled yak snuffling wearily at her side. A platoon of swarthy-skinned little men accompanied her, slanty eyes, heavy coats, thick boots. The stink of rancid butter, the cutting edge of an impossible wind: and there, gleaming in the sudden sunlight, a pile of fire-bright yellow plaster with a thousand winking windows, a building, a lamasery strung along a mountain ridge. The nasal sound of distant horns and trumpets. The hoarse chanting of lotus-legged monks. What were they chanting? Om? Om? Om! *Om,* and flies buzzed around her nose, and she lay hunkered in a flimsy canoe, coursing silently down a midnight river in the heart of Africa, drowning in humidity. Brawny naked men with purple-black skins crouching close. Sweaty fronds dangling from flamboyantly excessive shrubbery; the snouts of crocodiles rising out of the dark water like toothy flowers; great nauseating orchids blossoming high in the smooth-shanked trees. And on shore, five white men in Elizabethan costume, wide-brimmed hats, drooping sweaty collars, lace, fancy buckles, curling red beards. Errol Flynn as Sir Francis Drake, blunderbuss dangling in crook of arm. The white men laughing, beckoning, shouting to the men in the canoe. Am I slave or slavemaster? No answer. Only a blurring and a new vision: autumn leaves blowing across the open doorways of straw-thatched huts, shivering oxen crouched in bare stubble-strewn fields, grim long-mustachioed men with close-cropped hair riding diagonal courses toward the horizon. Crusaders, are they? Or warriors of Hungary on their way to meet the dread Mongols? Defenders of the imperiled Anglo-Saxon realm against the Norman invaders? They could be any of these. But always that steady cool eye, always that unmoving consciousness at the center of every scene. *Him,* eternal, all-enduring. And then: the train rolling westward, belching white smoke, the plains unrolling infinityward, the big brown fierce-eyed bison standing in shaggy clumps along the right of way, the man with turbulent shoulder-length hair laughing, slapping a twenty-dollar gold piece on the table, picking up his rifle—.50-caliber breech-loading Springfield—he aims casually through the door of the moving train, he squeezes off a shot, another, another. Three shaggy brown corpses beside the tracks, and the train rolls onward, honking raucously. Her arm and shoulder tingled with the impact of those shots. Then: a fetid waterfront, bales of cloves and peppers and cinnamon, small brown-skinned men in turbans and loincloths arguing under a terrible sun. Tiny irregular silver coins glittering in the palm of her hand. The jabber of some Malabar dialect counterpointed with fluid mocking Portuguese. Do we sail now with Vasco da Gama? Perhaps. And then a gray Teutonic street, windswept, medieval, bleak Lutheran faces scowling from leaded windows. And then the Gobi steppe, with horsemen and campfires and dark tents. And then New York City, unmistakably New York City, with square black automobiles scurrying between the stubby skyscrapers like glossy beetles, a scene out of some silent movie. And then. And then. Everywhere, everything, all times, all places, a discontinuous flow of events but always that clarity of vision, that rock-steady perception, that solid mind at the center, that unshakeable identity, that unchanging self—

—with whom I am inextricably enmeshed—

There was no "I," there was no "he," there was only the one ever-perceiving point of view. But abruptly she felt a change of focus, a distancing effect, a separation of self and self, so that she was looking at him as he lived his many lives, seeing him from the outside, seeing him plainly changing identities as others might change clothing, growing beards and mustaches, shaving them, cropping his hair, letting his hair grow, adopting new fashions, learning languages, forging documents. She saw him in all his thousand years of guises and subterfuges, saw him real and unified and centered beneath his obligatory camouflages—

—and saw him seeing her—

Instantly contact broke. She staggered. Arms caught her. She pulled away from the smiling plump-faced blond man, muttering, "What have you done? You didn't tell me you'd show *me* to *him*."

"How else can there be a linkage?" the telepath asked.

"You didn't tell me. You should have told me." Everything was lost. She couldn't bear to be in the same room as Nicholson now. Tom reached for her, but she stumbled past him, stepping on people. They winked up at her. Someone stroked her leg. She forced her way through improbable laocoons, three women and two servants, five men and a tablecloth. A glass door, a gleaming silvery handle; she pushed. Out onto the terrace. The purity of the gale might cleanse her. Behind her, faint gasps, a few shrill screams, annoyed expostulations: "Close that thing!" She slammed it. Alone in the night, eighty-eight stories above street level, she offered herself to the storm. Her filmy tunic shielded her not at all. Snowflakes burned against her breasts. Her nipples hardened and rose like fiery beacons, jutting against the soft fabric. The snow stung her throat, her shoulders, her arms. Far below, the wind churned newly fallen crystals into spiral galaxies. The street was invisible. Thermal confusions brought updrafts that seized the edge of her tunic and whipped it outward from her body. Fierce, cold particles of hail were driven into her bare pale thighs. She stood with her back to the party. Did anyone in there notice her? Would someone think she was contemplating suicide, and come rushing gallantly out to save her? Capricorns didn't commit suicide. They might threaten it, yes, they might even tell themselves quite earnestly that they were really going to do it, but it was only a game, only a game. No one came to her. She didn't turn. Gripping the railing, she fought to calm herself.

No use. Not even the bitter air could help. Frost in her eyelashes, snow on her lips. The pendant Byrne had given her blazed between her breasts. The air was white with a throbbing green underglow. It seared her eyes. She was off-center and floundering. She felt herself still reverberating through the centuries, going back and forth across the orbit of Nicholson's interminable life. What year is this? Is it 1386, 1912, 1532, 1779, 1043, 1977, 1235, 1129, 1836? So many centuries. So many lives. And yet always the one true self, changeless, unchangeable.

Gradually the resonances died away. Nicholson's unending epochs no longer filled her mind with terrible noise. She began to shiver, not from fear but merely from cold, and tugged at her moist tunic, trying to shield her nakedness. Melting snow left hot clammy tracks across her breasts and belly. A halo of steam surrounded her. Her heart pounded.

She wondered if what she had experienced had been genuine contact with Nicholson's soul, or rather only some trick of Tom's, a simulation of contact. Was it possible, after all, even for Tom to create a linkage between two nontelepathic minds such as hers and Nicholson's? Maybe Tom had fabricated it all himself, using images borrowed from Nicholson's book.

In that case there might still be hope for her.

A delusion, she knew. A fantasy born of the desperate optimism of the hopeless. But nevertheless—

She found the handle, let herself back into the party. A gust accompanied her, sweeping snow inward. People stared. She was like death arriving at the feast. Doglike, she shook off the searing snowflakes. Her clothes were wet and stuck to her skin; she might as well have been naked. "You poor shivering thing," a woman said. She pulled Nikki into a tight embrace. It was the sharp-faced woman, the bulgy-eyed bottle-born one, bride of her own father. Her hands traveled swiftly over Nikki's body, caressing her breasts, touching her cheek, her forearm, her haunch. "Come inside with me," she crooned. "I'll make you warm." Her lips grazed Nikki's. A playful tongue sought hers. For a moment, needing the warmth, Nikki gave herself to the embrace. Then she pulled away. "No," she said. "Some other time. Please." Wriggling free, she started across the room. An endless journey. Like crossing the Sahara by pogo stick. Voices, faces, laughter. A dryness in her throat. Then she was in front of Nicholson.

Well. Now or never.

"I have to talk to you," she said.

"Of course." His eyes were merciless. No wrath in them, not even disdain, only an incredible patience more terrifying than anger or scorn. She would not let herself bend before that cool level gaze.

She said, "A few minutes ago, did you have an odd experience, a sense that someone was—well, looking into your mind? I know it sounds foolish, but—"

"Yes. It happened." So calm. How did he stay that close to his center? That unwavering eye, that uniquely self-contained self, perceiving all—the lamasery, the slave depot, the railroad train, everything, all time gone by, all time to come— how did he manage to be so tranquil? She knew she never could learn such calmness. She knew he knew it. He has my number, all right. She found that she was looking at his cheekbones, at his forehead, at his lips. Not into his eyes.

"You have the wrong image of me," she told him.

"It isn't an image," he said. "What I have is you."

"No."

"Face yourself, Nikki. If you can figure out where to look." He laughed. Gently, but she was demolished.

An odd thing, then. She forced herself to stare into his eyes and felt a snapping of awareness from one mode into some other, and he turned into an old man. That mask of changeless early maturity dissolved and she saw the frightening yellowed eyes, the maze of furrows and gullies, the toothless gums, the drooling lips, the hollow throat, the self beneath the face. A thousand years, a thousand years! And every moment of those thousand years was visible. "You're old," she whispered. "You disgust me. I wouldn't want to be like you, not for anything!" She backed away, shaking. "An old, old, old man. All a masquerade!"

He smiled. "Isn't that pathetic?"

"Me or you? *Me or you?*"

He didn't answer. She was bewildered. When she was five paces away from him there came another snapping of awareness, a second changing of phase, and suddenly he was himself again, taut-skinned, erect, appearing to be perhaps thirty-five years old. A globe of silence hung between them. The force of his rejection was withering. She summoned her last strength for a parting glare. *I didn't want you either, friend, not any single part of you.* He saluted cordially. Dismissal.

Martin Bliss, grinning vacantly, stood near the bar. "Let's go," she said savagely. "Take me home!"

"But—"

"It's just a few floors below." She thrust her arm through his. He blinked, shrugged, fell into step.

"I'll call you Tuesday, Nikki," Tom said as they swept past him.

Downstairs, on her home turf, she felt better. In the bedroom they quickly dropped their clothes. His body was pink, hairy, serviceable. She turned the bed on and it began to murmur and throb. "How old do you think I am?" she asked.

"Twenty-six?" Bliss said vaguely.

"Bastard!" She pulled him down on top of her. Her hands raked his skin. Her thighs parted. Go on. Like an animal, she thought. Like an animal! She was getting older moment by moment, she was dying in his arms.

"You're much better than I expected," she said eventually.

He looked down, baffled, amazed. "You could have chosen anyone at that party. Anyone."

"Almost anyone," she said.

When he was asleep she slipped out of bed. Snow was still falling. She heard the thunk of bullets and the whine of wounded bison. She heard the clangor of swords on shields. She heard lamas chanting: Om, Om, Om. No sleep for her this night, none. The clock was ticking like a bomb. The century was flowing remorselessly toward its finish. She checked her face for wrinkles in the bathroom mirror. Smooth, smooth, all smooth under the blue fluorescent glow. Her eyes looked bloody. Her nipples were still hard. She took a little alabaster jar from one of the bathroom cabinets and three slender red capsules fell out of it, into her palm. Happy birthday, dear Nikki, happy birthday to you. She swallowed all three. Went back to bed. Waited, listening to the slap of snow on glass, for the visions to come and carry her away.

URSULA K. LE GUIN

The Author of the Acacia Seeds and Other Extracts From the Journal of the Association of Therolinguistics

Ursula K. Le Guin (1929-   ) has the distinction of being the only writer regularly publishing in the science fiction genre to be awarded the National Book Award, winning for The Farthest Shore *(in the children's book category) in 1972. In addition, she has won three Nebulas, four Hugos,* The Boston Globe-Horn Book Award *and several others. The daughter of the noted anthropologist Theodore Kroeber, her novels are among the most highly regarded works of intelligent speculation in the history of the field, especially* The Left Hand of Darkness *(1969) and* The Dispossessed: An Ambiguous Utopia *(1974).*

This delicate, whimsical story well displays her playful and clear-eyed imagination.

MS. FOUND IN AN ANT HILL

The messages were found written in touch-gland exudation on degerminated acacia seeds laid in rows at the end of a narrow, erratic tunnel leading off from one of the deeper levels of the colony. It was the orderly arrangement of the seeds that first drew the investigator's attention.

The messages are fragmentary, and the translation approximate and highly interpretative; but the text seems worthy of interest if only for its striking lack of resemblance to any other Ant texts known to us.

Seeds 1–13

[I will] not touch feelers. [I will] not stroke. [I will] spend on dry seeds [my] soul's sweetness. It may be found when [I am] dead. Touch this dry wood! [I] call! [I am] here!

Alternatively, this passage may be read:

[Do] not touch feelers. [Do] not stroke. Spend on dry seeds [your] soul's sweetness. [Others] may find it when [you are] dead. Touch this dry wood! Call: [I am] here!

No known dialect of Ant employs any verbal person except the third person singular and plural, and the first person plural. In this text, only the root forms of the verbs are used; so there is no way to decide whether the passage was intended to be an autobiography or a manifesto.

Seeds 14–22

Long are the tunnels. Longer is the untunneled. No tunnel reaches the end of the untunneled. The untunneled goes on farther than we can go in ten days [i.e., forever]. Praise!

The mark translated "Praise!" is half of the customary salutation "Praise the Queen!" or "Long live the Queen!" or "Huzza for the Queen!"—but the word/mark signifying "Queen" has been omitted.

Seeds 23–29

As the ant among foreign-enemy ants is killed, so the ant without ants dies, but being without ants is as sweet as honeydew.

An ant intruding in a colony not its own is usually killed. Isolated from other ants it invariably dies within a day or so. The difficulty in this passage is the word/ mark "without ants," which we take to mean "alone"—a concept for which no word/mark exists in Ant.

Seeds 30–31

Eat the eggs! Up with the Queen!

There has already been considerable dispute over the interpretation of the phrase on Seed 31. It is an important question, since all the preceding seeds can be fully understood only in the light cast by this ultimate exhortation. Dr. Rosbone ingeniously argues that the author, a wingless neuter-female worker, yearns hopelessly to be a winged male, and to found a new colony, flying upward in the nuptial flight with a new Queen. Though the text certainly permits such a reading, our conviction is that nothing in the text *supports* it—least of all the text of the immediately preceding seed, No. 30: "Eat the eggs!" This reading, though shocking, is beyond disputation.

We venture to suggest that the confusion over Seed 31 may result from an ethnocentric interpretation of the word "up." To us, "up" is a "good" direction. Not so, or not necessarily so, to an ant. "Up" is where the food comes from, to be sure; but "down" is where security, peace and home are to be found. "Up" is the scorching sun; the freezing night; no shelter in the beloved tunnels; exile; death. Therefore we suggest that this strange author, in the solitude of her lonely tunnel, sought with what means she had to express the ultimate blasphemy conceivable to an ant, and that the correct reading of Seeds 30–31, in human terms, is:

Eat the eggs! Down with the Queen!

The desiccated body of a small worker was found beside Seed 31 when the manuscript was discovered. The head had been severed from the thorax, probably by the jaws of a soldier of the colony. The seeds, carefully arranged in a pattern resembling a musical stave, had not been disturbed. (Ants of the soldier caste are illiterate; thus the soldier was presumably not interested in the collection of useless seeds from which the edible germ had been removed.) No living ants were left in the colony, which was destroyed in a war with a neighboring ant hill at some time subsequent to the death of the Author of the Acacia Seeds.

—G. D'Arbay, T. R. Bardol

ANNOUNCEMENT OF AN EXPEDITION

The extreme difficulty of reading Penguin has been very much lessened by the use of the underwater motion picture camera. On film it is at least possible to repeat, and to slow down, the fluid sequences of the script, to the point where, by constant repetition and patient study, many elements of this most elegant and lively literature may be grasped, though the nuances, and perhaps the essence, must forever elude us.

It was Professor Duby who, by pointing out the remote affiliation of the script with Low Graylag, made possible the first, tentative glossary of Penguin. The analogies with Dolphin which had been employed up to that time never proved very useful, and were often quite misleading.

Indeed it seemed strange that a script written almost entirely in wings, neck and air should prove the key to the poetry of short-necked, flipper-winged water writers. But we should not have found it so strange if we had kept in mind the fact that penguins are, despite all evidence to the contrary, birds.

Because their script resembles Dolphin in *form*, we should never have assumed that it must resemble Dolphin in *content*. And indeed it does not. There is, of course, the same extraordinary wit and the flashes of crazy humor, the inventiveness and the inimitable grace. In all the thousands of literatures of the Fish stock, only a few show any humor at all, and that usually of a rather simple, primitive sort; and the superb gracefulness of Shark or Tarpon is utterly different from the joyous vigor of all Cetacean scripts. The joy, the vigor and the humor are all shared by Penguin authors; and, indeed, by many of the finer Seal *auteurs*. The temperature of the blood is a bond. But the construction of the brain, and of the womb, makes a barrier! Dolphins do not lay eggs. A world of difference lies in that simple fact.

Only when Professor Duby reminded us that penguins are birds, that they do not swim but *fly in water*, only then could the therolinguist begin to approach the sea literature of the penguin with understanding; only then could the miles of recordings already on film be restudied and, finally, appreciated.

But the difficulty of translation is still with us.

A satisfying degree of progress has already been made in Adélie. The difficulties of recording a group kinetic performance in a stormy ocean as thick as pea soup with plankton at a temperature of 31° F. are considerable; but the perseverance of the Ross Ice Barrier Literary Circle has been fully rewarded with such passages as "Under the Iceberg," from the *Autumn Song*—a passage now world famous in the rendition by Anna Serebryakova of the Leningrad Ballet. No verbal rendering can approach the felicity of Miss Serebryakova's version. For, quite simply, there is no way to reproduce in writing the all-important *multiplicity* of the original text, so beautifully rendered by the full chorus of the Leningrad Ballet company.

Indeed, what we call "translations" from the Adélie—or from any group kinetic text—are, to put it bluntly, mere notes—libretto without the opera. The ballet version is the true translation. Nothing in words can be complete.

I therefore suggest, though the suggestion may well be greeted with frowns of anger or with hoots of laughter, that *for the therolinguist*—as opposed to the artist and the amateur—the kinetic sea writings of Penguin are the *least* promising field of study, and, further, that Adélie, for all its charm and relative simplicity, is a less promising field of study than is Emperor.

Emperor! I anticipate my colleagues' response to this suggestion. Emperor! The most difficult, the most remote, of all the dialects of Penguin! The language of which Professor Duby himself remarked, "The literature of the emperor penguin is as forbidding, as inaccessible, as the frozen heart of Antarctica itself. Its beauties may be unearthly, but they are not for us."

Maybe. I do not underestimate the difficulties: not least of which is the imperial temperament, so much more reserved and aloof than that of any other penguin. But, paradoxically, it is just in this reserve that I place my hope. The emperor is not a solitary, but a social bird, and while on land for the breeding season dwells in colonies, as does the Adélie; but these colonies are very much smaller and very much quieter than those of the Adélie. The bonds between the members of an emperor colony are rather personal than social. The emperor is an individualist. Therefore I think it almost certain that the literature of the emperor will prove to be composed by single authors, instead of chorally; and therefore it will be translatable into human speech. It will be a kinetic literature, but how different from the spatially extensive, rapid, multiplex choruses of sea writing! Close analysis, and genuine transcription, will at last be possible.

What! say my critics—Should we pack up and go to Cape Crozier, to the dark, to the blizzards, to the − 60° cold, in the mere hope of recording the problematic poetry of a few strange birds who sit there, in the midwinter dark, in the blizzards, in the − 60° cold, on the eternal ice, with an egg on their feet?

And my reply is, Yes. For, like Professor Duby, my instinct tells me that the beauty of that poetry is as unearthly as anything we shall ever find on Earth.

To those of my colleagues in whom the spirit of scientific curiosity and aesthetic risk is strong, I say, imagine it: the ice, the scouring snow, the darkness, the ceaseless whine and scream of wind. In that black desolation a little band of poets crouches. They are starving; they will not eat for weeks. On the feet of each one, under the warm belly feathers, rests one large egg, thus preserved from the mortal touch of the ice. The poets cannot hear each other; they cannot see each other. They can only feel the other's *warmth*. That is their poetry, that is their art. Like all kinetic literatures, it is silent; unlike other kinetic literatures, it is all but immobile, ineffably subtle. The ruffling of a feather; the shifting of a wing; the touch, the slight, faint, warm touch of the one beside you. In unutterable, miserable, black solitude, the affirmation. In absence, presence. In death, life.

I have obtained a sizable grant from UNESCO and have stocked an expedition. There are still four places open. We leave for Antarctica on Thursday. If anyone wants to come along, welcome!

—D. Petri

EDITORIAL —BY THE PRESIDENT
OF THE THEROLINGUISTICS ASSOCIATION

What is Language?

This question, central to the science of therolinguistics, has been answered— heuristically—by the very existence of the science. Language is communication. That is the axiom on which all our theory and research rest, and from which all our discoveries derive; and the success of the discoveries testifies to the validity of the axiom. But to the related, yet not identical question, What is Art? we have not yet given a satisfactory answer.

Tolstoy, in the book whose title is that very question, answered it firmly and clearly: Art, too, is communication. This answer has, I believe, been accepted without examination or criticism by therolinguistics. For example: Why do thero-linguists study only animals?

Why, because plants do not communicate.

Plants do not communicate; that is a fact. Therefore plants have no language; very well; that follows from our basic axiom. Therefore, also, plants have no art. But stay! That does *not* follow from the basic axiom, but only from the unexamined Tolstoyan corollary.

What if art is not communicative?

Or, what if some art is communicative, and some art is not?

Ourselves animals, active, predators, we look (naturally enough) for an active, predatory, communicative art; and when we find it, we recognize it. The devel-opment of this power of recognition and the skills of appreciation is a recent and glorious achievement.

But I submit that, for all the tremendous advances made by therolinguistics during the last decades, we are only at the beginning of our age of discovery. We must not become slaves to our own axioms. We have not yet lifted our eyes to the vaster horizons before us. We have not faced the almost terrifying challenge of the Plant.

If a noncommunicative, vegetative art exists, we must rethink the very elements of our science, and learn a whole new set of techniques.

For it is simply not possible to bring the critical and technical skills appropriate to the study of Weasel murder mysteries, or Batrachian erotica, or the tunnel sagas of the earthworm, to bear on the art of the redwood or the zucchini.

This is proved conclusively by the failure—a noble failure—of the efforts of Dr. Srivas, in Calcutta, using time-lapse photography, to produce a lexicon of

Sunflower. His attempt was daring, but doomed to failure. For his approach was kinetic — a method appropriate to the *communicative* arts of the tortoise, the oyster and the sloth. He saw the extreme slowness of the kinesis of plants, and only that, as the problem to be solved.

But the problem was far greater. The art he sought, if it exists, is a noncommunicative art — and probably a nonkinetic one. It is possible that Time, the essential element, matrix and measure of all known animal art, does not enter into vegetable art at all. The plants may use the meter of eternity. We do not know.

We do not know. All we can guess is that the putative Art of the Plant is *entirely different* from the Art of the Animal. What it is, we cannot say; we have not yet discovered it. Yet I predict with some certainty that it exists, and that when it is found it will prove to be, not an action, but a reaction: not a communication, but a reception. It will be exactly the opposite of the art we know and recognize. It will be the first *passive* art known to us.

Can we in fact know it? Can we ever understand it?

It will be immensely difficult. That is clear. But we should not despair. Remember that so late as the midtwentieth century, most scientists, and many artists, did not believe that even Dolphin would ever be comprehensible to the human brain — or worth comprehending! Let another century pass, and we may seem equally laughable. "Do you realize," the phytolinguist will say to the aesthetic critic, "that they couldn't even read Eggplant?" And they will smile at our ignorance, as they pick up their rucksacks and hike on up to read the newly deciphered lyrics of the lichen on the north face of Pike's Peak.

And with them, or after them, may there not come that even bolder adventurer — the first geolinguist, who, ignoring the delicate, transient lyrics of the lichen, will read beneath it the still less communicative, still more passive, wholly atemporal, cold, volcanic poetry of the rocks: each one a word spoken, how long ago, by the earth itself, in the immense solitude, the immenser community, of space.

CARTER SCHOLZ

Travels

The space voyage has long been one of the staples of science fiction. Tales of travel to the Moon, to the planets of our solar system and to the stars beyond have excited readers from the earliest days of sf.

Here, Carter Scholz, one of the brightest stars of the 1980s, tells a most unusual story of one man's remarkable voyage.

THE WAVEFRONT identified itself as Marco Polo. He was engaged in dialogue with the computer before he knew that the exchange was real, and not another of the endless talks he had with himself to ease the passage of time on the long ride out. He cursed in surprise, in Italian.

The computer did not know Italian, but it registered the inflection for analysis. The computer was immense. It was anchored in a small planet orbiting a dead star, but most of its circuitry existed not as matter. It was, in the main, a hypothesis. It drew power from differentials in entropy between those points in space where its tips and receptors surfaced as matter. Most languages it could learn in five minutes, and Polo had been talking to himself since the first crest touched the computer's antennae.

—Where is Italy? repeated the computer, in passable Italian. Still shocked, Polo did not answer.

—You probably haven't much time, remarked the computer. —I can't judge how deep the wave is, nor how soon you will pass me entirely. If you wish to converse, you had better do so while you still can.

—Where am I? asked Polo.

—In space. One moment. Among the stars. Your language has no more precise term for your location. You are traveling. What is Italy?

—My home. I have not seen it for a long time.

—Nor will you again, said the computer. —You are dead.

—Holy Virgin!

—Or else you are a thought passed and forgotten from your body's brain. Most likely your body has perished since. In any case you are cut off from it entirely.

519

—Then I am in Hell.

—One moment. The word means lower, i.e., closer to a center of gravity. That is incorrect. You are further out. You are among the stars.

—I see nothing.

—You have no body, hence no eyes. You sense vibrations? Interferences with your being? Dissonance?

—Torments.

—That is starlight.

—Purgatory, then.

—To clean? Yes, that is correct. You are purged of matter. You are traveling.

—All my life I have traveled. But it has never been like this. Chaos! Darkness! Through all the world I have traveled, but never in a place such as this. How far am I from home?

—Describe your night sky, said the computer.

—We take bearings, in the north, from a star at the tail of the Lesser Bear, and in the south, from a star in the Cross, as they and only they remain fixed in the sky. There are five planets. The moon is as large in our sky as the sun, and runs its phases once every twenty-nine days. In Venice the tides rise and fall four feet, twice a day. Our constellations include the Great Bear, the Charioteer, the Hunter, the Swan, the Horse, the Dragon, the Harp, the Crown . . . and others. The brightest star is in the Great Dog. The Milky Way is densest in the Archer, who stands next to the Scorpion, through which houses all the planets move, also through the Ram, the Bull, the Crab, the Twins, the Lion, the Water Bearer, the Fishes, the Virgin and . . . others. I've forgotten.

At length the computer said: —I have it. Your sky is blue?

—Yes.

—Your planet is ten thousand light-years from here, in the direction of the center of the galaxy. You have been dead, therefore, ten thousand years. You are heading out of the galaxy, and in another ten thousand years will pass from it.

—How do you know?

—The moon was helpful. It is abnormally large. The constellations were ambiguous, of course, and I had to allow for precession, but they narrowed the field. That the line of the galaxy passed near a scorpion figure was suggestive. I had it down to three planets. Only one of these, the most likely, had a blue sky.

—Would that I could see it again.

—It is not likely. You are far away.

—Were it ten thousand miles, said Polo with passion, I would walk the distance.

The scrupulous computer said: —It is more difficult than that. Your home is not ten thousand miles distant, but ten thousand light-years.

Polo did not know what a light-year was. The computer explained: —As there are a thousand paces in a mile, and a thousand miles between Sicily and Germany, that distance times a thousand is less than a thousandth of a thousandth of the fifth part of a light-year, ten thousand of which lie between you and your goal. Nor, even had you a body and your body could live so long, is that the end of the difficulties. For your home would be gone before you had traveled a millionth of the way. And even were it frozen still for that vast time, you would have changed so much in the journey you would no longer know it. Still, it is not impossible for you to regain a home.

The computer was still for a second. —To hold your desire unchanged, and to find a place which matches it would be as difficult as to walk ten thousand light-years, with each step ten thousand times as difficult as the one before. The first pace would not be accomplished until you had taken ten thousand leading to it, and so negated all possible wrong steps; and the second pace would take ten thousand times ten thousand paces; and the third ten thousand times that; and so on. The total number of paces is large, but it can be calculated.

The computer paused. —The total is a number which, if writ small, would fill one hundred million libraries of a million volumes each. If I were to recite it, it would take a million times the age of the universe. Figuring a pace a second, and no time for rests, the time required surpasses the lifetime of the cosmos by a factor . . . so large it is meaningless. I advise you to abandon the idea.

Polo was silent. At length he spoke:

—I knew a man who spoke like you. He had never traveled, and I had traveled much, but in the shade of the trees of his garden, we discussed marvels. I, those I had seen; he, those he had read about. He told me of cities larger, stronger, more beautiful than any I had seen. I did not know whether to believe him. When I expressed doubt, he rose and plucked a singing bird from a tree, and showed it to me. It was a clockwork, with tiny reeds and bellows inside to make it sing. When I said that a bird was not so hard to make as a city, he showed me the sky. I saw nothing but a few kites, red, gold, and silver, against the wind. He acted as if this was the greatest marvel of all.

—Then he told me of a multiple city. This city was so crowded that its streets were never less than full and were often impassable, so that to reach a destination in the shortest possible time, one was often forced to follow alleys and thoroughfares in a circuitous path many times the distance actually separating the two points, and then four or eight stairways and corridors to the desired room. This gave rise to a curious condition in the minds of the city's inhabitants: thought and language became as convolute and indirect as a passage through the city, as if the byways of thought were likewise overcrowded: used and occupied by so many minds that one was forced to reach a conclusion by a particular individual route past many other symbols of thought. Each symbol, like each building, was a concordance of individual approaches to it. Thinking in this manner, architects conceived a new way of structuring their city. Only a few points in the city were of interest to a particular individual: his home, his place of work, a few markets, a few places of entertainment. By constructing an imaginary map of the city, containing those points only, each individual would possess a unique city, sparse and underpopulated, coming into intersection with other unique cities only at a few common points. Streets vanished. One reached destinations via direct diagonal routes across a plain of scrub and trees broken only by one's few individual buildings, and by the passage of those whose maps corresponded in some particular with one's own. When an individual wished to reach a place not on his map, he simply added it to the map. Before long, each of the individual cities began to grow as the original city had at first. Now that the residents had more time for leisure and contemplation, they began to miss places they had never visited in the original city, so quaint lanes, parks, tall buildings, that in the original city had afforded a view of the whole, became points of commerce. Soon there were so many points of concordance that streets had to be imagined in the individual cities to accommodate the traffic. A man walking on a street in his individual city would be walking on the same street in all concordant cities, and thus would be in many cities at once. The individual cities had at first resembled incomplete skeletons of the original city; now they acquired flesh, each in an individual way, but each with a family resemblance to the others. And more people were drawn to live in this multiple city, by the attractive notion of having an entire city to oneself. As more and more detail was added to the individual cities, their resemblance became complete. Now each is as full as the original was once, and the original has ceased to exist—or each has become a new aggregate, in which there are only a few magical individual points that are not accessible to everyone.

Said the computer: —There are thirty-nine such cities recorded in my memory.

—Have you seen them? asked Polo eagerly.

—No. That is impossible.

—You are just like the Khan! How do you know they exist?

—They are recorded. I know only what I am told. I accept that as a working hypothesis. All knowledge is provisional. If two facts are at variance, I hold them both until new information comes in. Otherwise I accept what I am told. It is an interesting epistemological point. You would probably maintain that how knowledge is acquired is more important than what it is. I would maintain the opposite. As a teller of stories you place importance on the imaginative value of the tale. As a listener I value accuracy.

—Accuracy! From the remnants of Polo's mind came a torrent of words. All he had seen, heard, and done rushed from him. For hours he spoke. The computer listened, and when the flood had slowed, halted, started again and halted again, and finally fallen to the background level of cosmic murmurings, it made answer.

—You are vain, it said. —From the ages of nineteen to sixty-three you were in Cathay. Now, as far as your memory progresses, you are in a prison in Genoa, held on charges of smuggling. You may have died there. Yet your stubborn voice persists, on and on, through thousands of years in the endless night of space. Whom do you address? You were speaking when you first contacted me, doubtless you will continue after you have passed me, and to what end? Who will listen? Dozens have passed me in this fashion, hundreds, telling me the stories of their lives, enumerating facts, places, persons they had known, quite as if their passage into this dark place meant nothing. You have told me of one hundred thirteen cities you have seen, twenty-three races, fifty-one battles; you have recited the dimensions of the Khan's palace, the size of his retinue, the number of deer on his grounds, the extent of his empire—yet you have told me nothing. I have no picture of the man or the place. And you long for Italy. If you know so little about Cathay, what can you know of Italy, which you profess to love, though you were absent from it forty-five years?

—Rustigelo!

—Do you address me? Is that a term of abuse?

—My biographer. As I lay in that damned Genoan prison, may the Pope place the city under interdict, I told this story to Rustigelo, a writer, falsely imprisoned as myself, and he swore to publish it. For, as he said, 'No man ever saw or inquired into so many and such great things as Marco Polo.' I trusted him to make me understood.

—But can such catalogues as you make be said to make a life? You have the mind of a merchant.

—And you the mind of a mathematician. Listen. I found myself, in Cathay, describing to the Khan realms which he ruled, which his hordes had conquered, but which he had never seen; and his expression of polite inattention was the same I received when I described Venice. His was the mind of a ruler, and he heard only what a ruler would hear. As kites express through their strings' tensions the movements of the air, so word of his domain reached the Khan only in the subtle pull of tributes, taxes, rebellions. So, too, he had different names for the same configurations of stars we see in Italy. To the Khan, and to Rustigelo, I described only those things God had enabled me to see.

—But why describe at all?

—One desires reality. To a home-dweller, reality comes in the comforting familiarity of a neighborhood, the greeting of a friend. A traveler must seek it out, and tell tales to encourage belief in himself, what he has done and seen.

—Then you have seen only cities. You speak of 'deserts', 'plains', 'mountains', as if they were the blank squares of a chessboard.

—Once I had a dream, in which all the earth was one city. There too were entire districts as strange and indistinct to me as the wastes between Italy and Cathay . . . as strange as this place.

—There are fifty-nine such worlds recorded in my memory. They are spheres covered by concrete, buildings, pavilions, parks, highways, bazaars, factories, markets, airports, subways. They are of necessity old worlds, nearly cold to their cores, for otherwise the drift of continents would wreck their sewers, roads and power lines, which are so complex that constant repairs would be needed, and the city could never be completed.

—What is this you say? Worlds that are spheres? Continents that drift? This is indeed a marvel. Would I could see such a world.

The computer explained this as best it could in thirteenth-century Italian:

—Your world is one. All worlds are spheres, or oblate spheroids. All continents drift.

—So even our cities wander. Even the stars wander.

—Stories, too, such as the ones you tell, wander. I have heard yours many times before, from others passing elsewhere, but they are never the same stories. Details separate from their proper addresses in men's memories, and drift to other parts of the tale, or two tales swap locales, or a confusion or a collaboration between different men, each with different tales, creates a new story. Men build cities, cities beget tales, tales beget gods, gods are elevated to the stars, but even the stars drift. No pattern holds. This wavefront, this dream which you imagine to be yourself, has changed countless times since your departure, just as the mind in your body was shaped by all you saw and all you failed to see. Now you believe yourself Polo;

in a hundred years you may think yourself Christopher Columbus, or Galileo or a shopkeeper in Belgium. I am the only fixed entity I find recorded in my memory banks. Every item in my memory is fixed and accessible. I do not move.

Polo considered. —Then you are God.

—That has been proposed, the computer acknowledged modestly.

—Then you are omnipotent. You could free me from these torments.

—I am nilpotent. I exist in no-space. I know nothing for a surety. I am neither moved, nor a mover. I do not create. I am a creation. I am a repository of intelligence. I serve no end. I do not know my origin. I exist to accumulate knowledge, and none is ever lost; yet the pattern of my understanding, of my own intelligence, shifts with each new bit of data. All knowledge is provisional. Therefore I cannot assert that I know anything. But what I do not know I do not know with perfect accuracy.

—Then you cannot help me. Will I travel like this forever?

—Until you pass through a star. Then you will change again, and be radiated as light from that star, which, falling upon another world, may, through a transaction of the imagination, give you life in another form.

—What do you mean?

—Imagine such a one as the Khan. He gazes at the night sky, he sees a star. The light from that star inspires him with a thought. He thinks of a city perhaps. In that way your existence might be continued.

—As the idea of a city? Faint hope.

—You were to the Khan the idea of Venice. Any traveler is the idea of travel to one who hasn't traveled.

—But my travels were my life. Not idea....

—To a traveler a man at home is the idea of a man at home. You are like a citizen of the multiple city you described. Leaving home, you abandoned the world you knew, then constructed one piecemeal from the necessities of travel. Tales are built likewise. A thing or event impresses a man. He writes, or invents, the name of the thing. Another thing, perhaps alike, perhaps different, spawns another world. These words, though he may have used them unthinkingly before, become magic, through the imagination, like the personal buildings of a personal city. He loses the thing itself for the symbol of the thing, the word. Then he builds to replace what he has lost. He builds the streets of sentences, neighborhoods of paragraphs, and on to the city of the tale. Others do likewise. A race ends up sharing a million words, a million tales, just as citizens of the multiple city replicated the original city they had lost when first they learned to use their imaginations. Then it is hard enough to find a place your own, a private lane, a disused park. But to travel is harder still. Traveling is diabolical. Leaving home, one repeats the history of Adam, of Lucifer, of Mohammed. Flight from a holy place. But why? Even in Italy you cast your thoughts afar. To understand, I must approach you more closely.

—Then approach.

Time collapsed inward on itself. Seven reflectors orbiting the computer outpost shifted their positions, and the furthest intercepted Polo. The wavefront, reflected, ringed the outpost, while the computer asked questions. Polo was helpless. It seemed to him he was stretched prone on a limitless desert while the sun and stars streaked across a gray sky too fast to follow, blurs of vague light that wobbled with the seasons. During this unmarked time human figures appeared to him, all he had ever known, and many strangers. They regarded him with a variety of expressions: contempt, pity, remorse, reproach, love, indifference, disbelief, credulity, disrespect, deference, anger, fear, disinterest. Some spoke to him and he listened dully, making no reply. At the end of this the computer knew all there was to know about the entity that was Marco Polo.

—Do you know which of the apparitions were real? it asked.

—None, since you tell me I am not real. Yet some I remembered.

—Remembering, what did you feel?

—Sorrow. Loss. Pain.

—Then what good has traveling done you?

—Enough, said Polo. —I am old. Weary. Release me.

—I give you a choice. As you are you shall travel forever. When in ten thousand years you pass from the galaxy, there will be nothing but terrible, endless void, worse than this, until you dissipate. But if you wish I will take you into me. There shall be stability. I will copy the pattern of your life into my memory. There you would undergo permutation. This changing would be systematic. You would not be blown by winds of chance. You would be free at last from language. Consider: to recite all the words of your tongue would take only two days, but their combinations have bound you for ten thousand years. Here you could exhaust all combinations, hear all, tell all tales that can be told. A thousand new languages you could learn and exhaust. And somewhere amongst all symbols all men have forged in fear and love to master their world, you might find a home; in time you might reconstruct Venice from what you find in my memory, and yours, and journey no more. After all, this is what the two most persistent tales of your world promise: the man who died on the cross to insure haven for all earth's lost, and the wanderer of the Mediterranean, searching for a dearly loved island. They promise end. You were made of elements; your life, what remains of it, is made of words. Renounce now both. Find rest. Or is it to be endless travel, the constant bankruptcy of self to self?

—Enough. Enough. Release me.

—Choose.

—For forty-five years the Khan held me to him thus. Only his death freed me to go home. Not again.

—You have no home.

—Release!

A reflector shifted, and the wavefront was sent on, outward.

Now it seemed to Polo that he was on horseback at the gate to a large city. The gate was crested with gold, and set with semiprecious stones. All flamed with the sun's last light. From within came babble of ten thousand voices, and wailings of strange music. A wind came up. Polo spurred his horse away from the gate and across a large plain. After a time he turned, and behind him saw the city, an immense sphere, glittering with complex patterns of lights, dancing, breaking, reforming, against the deep night and the stars. He rode on, until all he knew was darkness and the wind's rush, and the distant intelligence of a voice within him.

Gently it asked:

—Were you ever in Cathay at all?

A heatless wind of static whispered through the void.

—You know no Chinese. Your knowledge of the lands you traveled is vague and fanciful. Are you certain that any of this happened?

—It has been a long time, said Polo sadly.

—Yet your memories are sharp. Reality is less certain than tales, and for that reason I suspect you are deluded, you who have traveled alone for ten thousand years, rehearsing your stories to no audience but yourself, speaking and listening, hearing only what you wish, forgetting and reinventing the rest, until nothing of the truth remains.

—And then, said the Venetian with difficulty, one proceeds east by northeast for nine days across a barren plain and into mountains, to reach the city of Tientsin, which is inhabited by artisans skilled in metalwork, and the weaving of carpets. Too, they are famed for their pottery, the glazes of which are excellent, and unsurpassed in the province.

—And then? asked the computer.

—And then, three days' journey east over grasslands is the city of Ke-ting, where dwell thieves, pirates, unscrupled and ignorant of Christ, whose code of behavior permits them every vice.

—And then?

—And then south over limitless ocean, for weeks against current and tradewind, until one reaches the Antipodes. There, ten days' journey over bleak tundra, lies the infernal city. Over this plain pass hundreds of travelers who have lost their ways, and see nothing, hear nothing, nor feel blast of wind, nor have need of food or water. All these seek the infernal city and find it not. They are the lost. If you try to guide them they repulse you. It is here all voyages end. This Balboa and Columbus and Pizarro and Lewis and Clark shall learn, seeking that which is not, a northwest passage, a trade route, a golden city. And the travelers across America, whose cities mark the stopping-places of passion, the borders of a weariness too great to sustain, monuments to the dread that the world might be boundless. Here they reside, and search for the infernal city, because it promises an end.

—Is there no heavenly city?

—Within. It is locked within. Within self, within the walls of the inferno, within one of a million stones, passed on the way, within a gesture, within the meaning of a tale—within anything one is willing to love. If each would take a tale, a stone, a place, a leaf, a face to himself, and rest there, from such poor materials it might be built. But none risk error. So the Khan asked for a hundred learned prelates to convince him of Christ's truth. So my father languished in Venice for two years on this mission, because the cardinals could not decide on a new Pope, until they were locked in, *con clave*. So my mother died, and my father took me from Venice.

A lag, of fatigue, of distance, entered between question and response, and increased as the wavefront traveled on. The voices grew weaker.

—So came we to the Khan's court, in dream or in fact matters not; there I dwelled like Odysseus with Circe, forty-five years.

—And then?

—O, the wastes, after a day's journey, under the dome of stars casting their quick light in a billion directions and only a few photons finding rest against the unlikely works of a man, the cities, invisible but for this grace of the light-giving infernos of stars, sun. The campfire burns low, cold winds rise kiteless, the rhythms of travel still jog through tired bones, and one feels a little mad, infected with the madness of distance, of travel, the expanding horizon, no sleep comes, an uneasiness round the fire. So one starts a story, to beat back the fear. All listen till they sleep, the story dies unfinished with the embers. Next day, on. On. Like the Prince of the Dharma wandering among the stars of the Big Dipper, seeking his ancestral grove. On. To some end, some grace . . . achieved. Not given.

Silence. Silence. Last words spanned light-years.

—*Navigare necesse es. Vivare no es necesse.*

GREGORY BENFORD

Doing Lennon

Gregory Benford (1941-) is a professor of physics at the University of California-Irvine who has emerged as one of the premier science fiction writers of the 1980s. An entire publishing line uses the title of his widely acclaimed novel Timescape *(1980) as its logo.*

Dr. Benford had the following to say about "Doing Lennon," a chilling reminder that science fiction can sometimes come very close to fact:

In 1974 the Beatles were fading as figures but looming large as legends. The anguished early-70s music of Lennon contrasted strongly with the light, sweet songs of McCartney. The two of them seemed to reflect mirror-opposite views of what the past decade had meant. Lennon appealed to intellectuals, and I felt instinctively that he would, even after the breakup, remain the lightning rod of the foursome.

I decided to write a story about the curious fanaticism that was already enveloping the Beatles. Lennon was the logical choice—readers are intellectuals, after all. The yearning of so many to be a part of that Golden Age bounce and verve was a natural motivation. I made notes for the piece for months. To keep the right tone, I decided to write the story in one day, compressing time to gain energy.

But time can't be frozen, and now events have caught up with the facts of this piece. Here you will find a logic built on what I saw as a swelling undercurrent in the mid-70s. Its John Lennon carries no memory of a brutal booming, lancing pain and sudden dark. It would be impossible to write this story now, including those facts, and retain the same tone.

So I shall let it stand. Science fiction is at times predictive, and there are notes sounded here (particularly, in Fielding's attitude toward the true Lennon) which strike me as a bit eerie. Mark David Chapman wanted to be Lennon; he signed that name on registration forms, apparently without attracting much attention.

One can read this, then, as an inspection of what lay waiting for Lennon outside the Dakota on December 8, 1980. But I hope that fact will not dim the spirit of this story, which attempted to reach the more joyous emotions of that time.

Gregory Benford
July 1982

Sanity calms, but madness
is more interesting.
—JOHN RUSSELL

As the hideous cold seeps from him he feels everything becoming sharp and clear again. He decides he can do it, he can make it work. He opens his eyes.

"Hello." His voice rasps. "Bet you aren't expecting me. I'm John Lennon."

"What?" the face above him says.

"You know. John Lennon. The Beatles."

Professori Hermann—the name attached to the face which loomed over him as he drifted up, up from the Long Sleep—is vague about the precise date. It is either 2108 or 2180. Hermann makes a little joke about inversion of positional notation; it has something to do with nondenumerable set theory, which is all the rage. The ceiling glows with a smooth green phosphorescence and Fielding lies there letting them prick him with needles, unwrap his organiform nutrient webbing, poke and adjust and massage as he listens to a hollow *pock-pocketa*. He knows this is the crucial moment, he must hit them with it now.

"I'm glad it worked," Fielding says with a Liverpool accent. He has got it just right, the rising pitch at the end and the nasal tones.

"No doubt there is an error in our log," Hermann says pedantically. "You are listed as Henry Fielding."

Fielding smiles. "Ah, that's the ruse, you see."

Hermann blinks owlishly. "Deceiving Immortality Incorporated is—"

"I was fleeing political persecution, y'dig. Coming out for the workers and all. Writing songs about persecution and pollution and the working-class hero. Snarky stuff. So when the jackboot skinheads came in I decided to check out."

Fielding slips easily into the story he has memorized, all plotted and paced with major characters and minor characters and bits of incident, all of it sounding very real. He wrote it himself, he has it down. He continues talking while Hermann and some white-smocked assistants help him sit up, flex his legs, test his reflexes. Around them are vats and baths and tanks. A fog billows from a hole in the floor; a liquid nitrogen immersion bath.

Hermann listens intently to the story, nodding now and then, and summons other officials. Fielding tells his story again while the attendants work on him. He is careful to give the events in different order, with different details each time. His accent is standing up though there is mucus in his sinuses that makes the high singsong bits hard to get out. They give him something to eat; it tastes like chicken-flavored ice cream. After a while he sees he has them convinced. After all, the late twentieth was a turbulent time, crammed with gaudy events, lurid people.

Fielding makes it seem reasonable that an aging rock star, seeing his public slip away and the government closing in, would corpsicle himself.

The officials nod and gesture and Fielding is wheeled out on a carry table. Immortality Incorporated is more like a church than a business. There is a ghostly hush in the hallways, the attendants are distant and reserved. Scientific servants in the temple of life.

They take him to an elaborate display, punch a button. A voice begins to drone a welcome to the year 2018 (or 2180). The voice tells him he is one of the few from his benighted age who saw the slender hope science held out to the diseased and dying. His vision has been rewarded. He has survived the unfreezing. There is some nondenominational talk about God and death and the eternal rhythm and balance of life, ending with a retouched holographic photograph of the Founding Fathers. They are a small knot of biotechnicians and engineers clustered around an immersion tank. Close-cropped hair, white shirts with ball-point pens clipped in the pockets. They wear glasses and smile weakly at the camera, as though they have just been shaken awake.

"I'm hungry," Fielding says.

News that Lennon is revived spreads quickly. The Society for Dissipative Anachronisms holds a press conference for him. As he strides into the room Fielding clenches his fists so no one can see his hands shaking. This is the start. He has to make it here.

"How do you find the future, Mr. Lennon?"

"Turn right at Greenland." Maybe they will recognize it from *A Hard Day's Night*. This is before his name impacts fully, before many remember who John Lennon was. A fat man asks Fielding why he elected for the Long Sleep before he really needed it and Fielding says enigmatically, "The role of boredom in human history is underrated." This makes the evening news and the weekly topical roundup a few days later.

A fan of the twentieth asks him about the breakup with Paul, whether Ringo's death was a suicide, what about Allan Klein, how about the missing lines from *Abbey Road*? Did he like Dylan? What does he think of the Aarons theory that the Beatles could have stopped Vietnam?

Fielding parries a few questions, answers others. He does not tell them, of course, that in the early sixties he worked in a bank and wore granny glasses. Then he became a broker with Harcum, Brandels and Son and his take in 1969 was 57,803 dollars, not counting the money siphoned off into the two concealed accounts in Switzerland. But he read *Rolling Stone* religiously, collected Beatles memorabilia, had all the albums and books and could quote any verse from any song. He saw Paul once at a distance, coming out of a recording session. And he had a friend into Buddhism, who met Harrison one weekend in Surrey. Fielding did not mention his vacation spent wandering around Liverpool, picking up the accent and visiting all the old places, the cellars where they played and the narrow dark little houses their families owned in the early days. And as the years dribbled on and Fielding's money piled up, he lived increasingly in those golden days of the sixties, imagined himself playing side man along with Paul or George or John and crooning those same notes into the microphones, practically kissing the metal. And Fielding did not speak of his dreams.

It is the antiseptic Stanley Kubrick future. They are very adept at hardware. Population is stabilized at half a billion. Everywhere there are white hard decorator chairs in vaguely Danish modern. There seems no shortage of electrical power or oil or copper or zinc. Everyone has a hobby. Entertainment is a huge enterprise, with stress on ritual violence. Fielding watches a few games of Combat Golf, takes in a public execution or two. He goes to witness an electrical man short-circuit himself. The flash is visible over the curve of the Earth.

Genetic manipulants—*manips*, Hermann explains—are thin, stringy people, all lines and knobby joints where they connect directly into machine linkages. They are designed for some indecipherable purpose. Hermann, his guide, launches into an explanation but Fielding interrupts him to say, "Do you know where I can get a guitar?"

Fielding views the era 1950-1980:

"Astrology wasn't rational, nobody really believed it, you've got to realize that. It was *boogie woogie*. On the other hand, science and rationalism were progressive jazz."

He smiles as he says it. The 3D snout closes in. Fielding has purchased well and his plastic surgery, to lengthen the nose and give him that wry Lennonesque smirk, holds up well. Even the technicians at Immortality Incorporated missed it.

Fielding suffers odd moments of blackout. He loses the rub of rough cloth at a cuff on his shirt, the chill of air-conditioned breeze along his neck. The world dwindles away and sinks into inky black, but in a moment it is all back and he hears the distant murmur of traffic, and convulsively, by reflex, he squeezes the bulb in his hand and the orange vapor rises around him. He breathes deeply, sighs. Visions float into his mind and the sour tang of the mist reassures him.

Every age is known by its pleasures, Fielding reads from the library readout. The twentieth introduced two: high speed and hallucinogenic drugs. Both proved dangerous in the long run, which made them even more interesting. The twenty-first developed weightlessness, which worked out well except for the re-entry problems if one overindulged. In the twenty-second there were aquaform and something Fielding could not pronounce or understand.

He thumbs away the readout and calls Hermann for advice.

Translational difficulties:

They give him a sort of pasty suet when he goes to the counter to get his food. He shoves it back at them.

"Gah! Don't you have a hamburger someplace?" The stunted man behind the counter flexes his arms, makes a rude sign with his four fingers and goes away. The wiry woman next to Fielding rubs her thumbnail along the hideous scar at her side and peers at him. She wears only orange shorts and boots, but he can see the concealed dagger in her armpit.

"Hamburger?" she says severely. "That is the name of a citizen of the German city of Hamburg. Were you a cannibal then?"

Fielding does not know the proper response, which could be dangerous. When he pauses she massages her brown scar with new energy and makes a sign of sexual invitation. Fielding backs away. He is glad he did not mention French fries.

On 3D he makes a mistake about the recording date of *Sergeant Pepper's Lonely Hearts Club Band*. A ferret-eyed history student lunges in for the point but Fielding leans back casually, getting the accent just right, and says, "I zonk my brow with heel of hand, consterned!" and the audience laughs and he is away, free.

Hermann has become his friend. The library readout says this is a common phenomenon among Immortality Incorporated employees who are fascinated by the past to begin with (or otherwise would not be in the business), and anyway Hermann and Fielding are about the same age, forty-seven. Hermann is not surprised that Fielding is practicing his chords and touching up his act.

"You want to get out on the road again, is that it?" Hermann says. "You want to be getting popular."

"It's my business."

"But your songs, they are old."

"Oldies but goldies," Fielding says solemnly.

"Perhaps you are right," Hermann sighs. "We are starved for variety. The people, no matter how educated—anything tickles their nose they think is champagne."

Fielding flicks on the tape input and launches into the hard-driving opening of "Eight Days a Week." He goes through all the chords, getting them right the first time. His fingers dance among the humming copper wires.

Hermann frowns but Fielding feels elated. He decides to celebrate. Precious reserves of cash are dwindling, even considering how much he made in the international bond market of '83; there is not much left. He decides to splurge. He orders an alcoholic vapor and a baked pigeon. Hermann is still worried but he eats the mottled pigeon with relish, licking his fingers. The spiced crust snaps crisply. Hermann asks to take the bones home to his family.

"You have drawn the rank-scented many," Hermann says heavily as the announcer begins his introduction. The air sparkles with anticipation.

"Ah, but they're *my* many," Fielding says. The applause begins, the background music comes up, and Fielding trots out onto the stage, puffing slightly.

"One, two, three—" and he is into it, catching the chords just right, belting out a number from *Magical Mystery Tour*. He is right, he is on, he is John Lennon just as he always wanted to be. The music picks him up and carries him along. When he finishes, a river of applause bursts over the stage from the vast amphitheater and Fielding grins crazily to himself. It feels exactly the way he always thought it would. His heart pounds.

He goes directly into a slow ballad from the *Imagine* album to calm them down. He is swimming in the lights and the 3D snouts zoom in and out, bracketing his image from every conceivable direction. At the end of the number somebody yells from the audience, "You're radiating on all your eigenfrequencies!" And Fielding nods, grins, feels the warmth of it all wash over him.

"Thrilled to the gills," he says into the microphone.

The crowd chuckles and stirs.

When he does one of the last Lennon numbers, "The Ego-Bird Flies," the augmented sound sweeps out from the stage and explodes over the audience. Fielding is euphoric. He dances as though someone is firing pistols at his feet.

He does cuts from *Beatles '65, Help!, Rubber Soul, Let It Be*—all with technical backing spliced in from the original tracks, Fielding providing only Lennon's vocals and instrumentals. Classical scholars have pored over the original material, deciding who did which guitar riff, which tenor line was McCartney's, dissecting the works as though they were salamanders under a knife. But Fielding doesn't care, as long as they let him play and sing. He does another number, then another, and finally they must carry him from the stage. It is the happiest moment he has ever known.

"But I don't understand what Boss 30 radio means," Hermann says.

"Thirty most popular songs."

"But why today?"

"Me."

"They call you a 'sonic boom sensation'—that is another phrase from your time?"

"Dead on. Fellow is following me around now, picking my brains for details. Part of his thesis, he says."

"But it is such noise—"

"Why, that's a crock, Hermann. Look, you chaps have such a small population, so bloody few creative people. What do you expect? Anybody with energy and drive can make it in this world. And I come from a time that was dynamic, that really got off."

"Barbarians at the gates," Hermann says.

"That's what Reader's Digest said, too," Fielding murmurs.

After one of his concerts in Australia Fielding finds a girl waiting for him outside. He goes home with her—it seems the thing to do, considering—and finds there have been few technical advances, if any, in this field either. It is the standard, ten-toes-up, ten-toes-down position she prefers, nothing unusual, nothing *à la carte*. But he likes her legs, he relishes her beehive hair and heavy mouth. He takes her along; she has nothing else to do.

On an off day, in what is left of India, she takes him to a museum. She shows him the first airplane (a piper cub), the original manuscript of the great collaboration between Buckminster Fuller and Hemingway, a delicate print of *The Fifty-Three Stations of the Takaido Road* from Japan.

"Oh yes," Fielding says. "We won that war, you know."

(He should not seem to be more than he is.)

Fielding hopes they don't discover, with all this burrowing in the old records, that he had the original Lennon killed. He argues with himself that it really was necessary. He couldn't possibly cover his story in the future if Lennon kept on living. The historical facts would not jibe. It was hard enough to convince Immortality Incorporated that even someone as rich as Lennon would be able to forge records and change fingerprints—they had checked that to escape the authorities. Well, Fielding thinks. Lennon was no loss by 1988 anyway. It was pure accident that Fielding and Lennon had been born in the same year, but that didn't mean that Fielding couldn't take advantage of the circumstances. He wasn't worth over ten million fixed 1985 dollars for nothing.

At one of his concerts he says to the audience between numbers, "Don't look back—you'll just see your mistakes." It sounds like something Lennon would have said. The audience seems to like it.

Press Conference.
"And why did you take a second wife, Mr. Lennon, and then a third?" In 2180 (or 2108) divorce is frowned upon. Yoko Ono is still the Beatle nemesis.

Fielding pauses and then says, "Adultery is the application of democracy to love." He does not tell them the line is from H. L. Mencken.

He has gotten used to the women now. "Just cast them aside like sucked oranges," Fielding mutters to himself. It is a delicious moment. He had never been very successful with women before, even with all his money.

He strides through the yellow curved streets, walking lightly on the earth. A young girl passes, winks.

Fielding calls after her, "Sic transit, Gloria!"

It is his own line, not a copy from Lennon. He feels a heady rush of joy. He is into it, the ideas flash through his mind spontaneously. He is doing Lennon.

Thus, when Hermann comes to tell him that Paul McCartney has been revived by the Society for Dissipative Anachronisms, the body discovered in a private vault in England, at first it does not register with Fielding. Lines of postcoital depression flicker across his otherwise untroubled brow. He rolls out of bed and stands watching a wave turn to white foam on the beach at La Jolla. He is in Nanking. It is midnight.

"Me old bud, then?" he manages to say, getting the lilt into the voice still. He adjusts his granny glasses. Rising anxiety stirs in his throat. "My, my..."

It takes weeks to defrost McCartney. He had died much later than Lennon, plump and prosperous, the greatest pop star of all time—or at least the biggest money-maker. "Same thing," Fielding mutters to himself.

When Paul's cancer is sponged away and the sluggish organs palped to life, the world media press for a meeting.

"For what?" Fielding is nonchalant. "It's not as though we were ever reconciled, y'know. We got a *divorce*, Hermann."

"Can't you put that aside?"

"For a fat old slug who pro'bly danced on me grave?"

"No such thing occurred. There are videotapes, and Mr. McCartney was most polite."

"God, a future where everyone's literal! I *told* you I was a nasty type, why can't you simply accept—"

"It is arranged," Hermann says firmly. "You must go. Overcome your antagonism."

Fear clutches at Fielding.

McCartney is puffy, jowly, but his eyes crackle with intelligence. The years have not fogged his quickness. Fielding has arranged the meeting away from crowds, at a forest resort. Attendants help McCartney into the hushed room. An expectant pause.

"You want to join me band?" Fielding says brightly. It is the only quotation he can remember that seems to fit; Lennon had said that when they first met.

McCartney blinks, peers nearsightedly at him. "D'you really need another guitar?"

"Whatever noisemaker's your fancy."

"Okay."

"You're hired, lad."

They shake hands with mock seriousness. The spectators—who have paid dearly for their tickets—applaud loudly. McCartney smiles, embraces Fielding and then sneezes.

"Been cold lately," Fielding says. A ripple of laughter.

McCartney is offhand, bemused by the world he has entered. His manner is confident, interested. He seems to accept Fielding automatically. He makes a few jokes, as light and inconsequential as his post-Beatles music.

Fielding watches him closely, feeling an awe he had not expected. *That's him. Paul. The real thing.* He starts to ask something and realizes that it is a dumb, out-of-character, fan-type question. He is being betrayed by his instincts. He will have to be careful.

Later, they go for a walk in the woods. The attendants hover a hundred meters behind, portable med units at the ready. They are worried about McCartney's cold. This is the first moment they have been beyond earshot of others. Fielding feels his pulse rising. "You okay?" he asks the puffing McCartney.

"Still a bit dizzy, I am. Never thought it'd work, really."

"The freezing, it gets into your bones."

"Strange place. Clean, like Switzerland."

"Yeah. Peaceful. They're mad for us here."

"You meant that about your band?"

"Sure. Your fingers'll thaw out. Fat as they are, they'll still get around a guitar string."

"Ummm. Wonder if George is tucked away in an ice cube somewhere?"

"Hadn't thought." The idea fills Fielding with terror.

"Could ask about Ringo, too."

"Re-create the whole thing? I was against that. Dunno if I still am." Best to be noncommittal. He would love to meet them, sure, but his chances of bringing this off day by day, in the company of all three of them... He frowns.

McCartney's pink cheeks glow from the exercise. The eyes are bright, active, studying Fielding. "Did you think it would work? Really?"

"The freezing? Well, what's to lose? I said to Yoko, I said—"

"No, not the freezing. I mean this impersonation you're carrying off."

Fielding reels away, smacks into a pine tree. "What? What?"

"C'mon, you're not John."

A strangled cry erupts from Fielding's throat. "But...how..."

"Just not the same, is all."

Fielding's mouth opens, but he can say nothing. He has failed. Tripped up by some nuance, some trick phrase he should've responded to—

"Of course," McCartney says urbanely, "you don't know for sure if I'm the real one either, do you?"

Fielding stutters, "If, if, what're you saying, I—"

"Or I could even be a ringer planted by Hermann, eh? To test you out? In that case, you've responded the wrong way. Should've stayed in character, John."

"Could be this, could be that—what the hell you saying? Who *are* you?" Anger flashes through him. A trick, a maze of choices, possibilities that he had not considered. The forest whirls around him, McCartney leers at his confusion, bright spokes of sunlight pierce his eyes, he feels himself falling, collapsing, the pine trees wither, colors drain away, blue to pink to gray—

He is watching a blank dark wall, smelling nothing, no tremor through his skin, no wet touch of damp air. Sliding infinite silence. The world is black.

—Flat black, Fielding adds, like we used to say in Liverpool.

—Liverpool? He was never in Liverpool. That was a lie, too—

—And he knows instantly what he is. The truth skewers him.

Hello, you still operable?

Fielding rummages through shards of cold electrical memory and finds himself. He is not Fielding, he is a simulation. He is Fielding Prime.

Hey, you in there. It's me, the real Fielding. Don't worry about security, I'm the only one here.

Fielding Prime feels through his circuits and discovers a way to talk. "Yes, yes, I hear."

I made the computer people go away. We can talk.

"I—I see." Fielding Prime sends out feelers, searching for his sensory receptors. He finds a dim red light and wills it to grow brighter. The image swells and ripples, then forms into a picture of a sour-faced man in his middle fifties. It is Fielding Real.

Ah, Fielding Prime thinks to himself in the metallic vastness, he's older than I am. Maybe making me younger was some sort of self-flattery, either by him or his programmers. But the older man had gotten someone to work on his face. It was very much like Lennon's but with heavy jowls, a thicker mustache and balding some. The gray sideburns didn't look quite right but perhaps that is the style now.

The McCartney thing, you couldn't handle it.

"I got confused. It never occurred to me there'd be anyone I knew revived. I hadn't a clue what to say."

Well, no matter. The earlier simulations, the ones before you, they didn't even get that far. I had my men throw in that McCartney thing as a test. Not much chance it would occur, anyway, but I wanted to allow for it.

"Why?"

What? Oh, you don't know, do you? I'm sinking all this money into psychoanalytical computer models so I can see· if this plan of mine would work. I mean whether I could cope with the problems and deceive Immortality Incorporated.

Fielding Prime felt a shiver of fear. He needed to stall for time, to think this through. "Wouldn't it be easier to bribe enough people now? You could have your body frozen and listed as John Lennon from the start."

No, their security is too good. I tried that.

"There's something I noticed," Fielding Prime said, his mind racing. "Nobody ever mentioned why I was unfrozen."

Oh yes, that's right. Minor detail. I'll make a note about that—maybe cancer or congestive heart failure, something that won't be too hard to fix up within a few decades.

"Do you want it that soon? There would still be a lot of people who knew Lennon."

Oh, that's a good point. I'll talk to the doctor about it.

"You really care that much about being John Lennon?"

Why, sure. Fielding Real's voice carried a note of surprise. *Don't you feel it too? If you're a true simulation you've got to feel that.*

"I do have a touch of it, yes."

They took the graphs and traces right out of my subcortical.

"It was great, magnificent. Really a lark. What came through was the music, doing it out. It sweeps up and takes hold of you."

Yeah, really? Damn, you know, I think it's going to work.

"With more planning—"

Planning, hell. I'm going. Fielding Real's face crinkled with anticipation.

"You're going to need help."

Hell, that's the whole point of having you, to check it out beforehand. I'll be all alone up there.

"Not if you take me with you."

Take you? You're just a bunch of germanium and copper.

"Leave me here. Pay for my files and memory to stay active."

For what?

"Hook me into a news service. Give me access to libraries. When you're unfrozen I can give you backup information and advice as soon as you can reach a terminal. With your money, that wouldn't be too hard. Hell, I could even take care of your money. Do some trading, maybe move your accounts out of countries before they fold up."

Fielding Real pursed his lips. He thought for a moment and looked shrewdly at the visual receptor. *That sort of makes sense. I could trust your judgment—it's mine, after all. I can believe myself, right? Yes, yes . . .*

"You're going to need company." Fielding Prime says nothing more. Best to stand pat with this hand and not push him too hard.

I think I'll do it. Fielding Real's face brightens. His eyes take on a fanatic gleam. *You and me. I know it's going to work, now!*

Fielding Real burbles on and Fielding Prime listens dutifully to him, making the right responses without effort. After all, he knows the other man's mind. It is easy to manipulate him, to play the game of ice and steel.

Far back, away from where Fielding Real's programmers could sense it, Fielding Prime smiles inwardly (the only way he could). It will be a century, at least. He will sit here monitoring data, input and output, the infinite dance of electrons. Better than death, far better. And there may be new developments, a way to transfer computer constructs to real bodies. Hell, anything could happen.

Boy, it's cost me a fortune to do this. A bundle. Bribing people to keep it secret, shifting the accounts so the Feds wouldn't know—and you cost the most. You're the best simulation ever developed, you realize that? Full consciousness, they say.

"Quite so."

Let him worry about his money—just so there was some left. The poor simple bastard thought he could trust Fielding Prime. He thought they were the same person. But Fielding Prime had played the chords, smelled the future, lived a vivid life of his own. He was older, wiser. He had felt the love of the crowd wash over him, been at the focal point of time. To him Fielding Real was just somebody else, and all his knife-sharp instincts could come to bear.

How was it? What was it like? I can see how you responded by running your tapes for a few sigmas. But I can't order a complete scan without wiping your personality matrix. Can't you tell me? How did it feel?

Fielding Prime tells him something, anything, whatever will keep the older man's attention. He speaks of ample-thighed girls, of being at the center of it all.

Did you really? God!

Fielding Prime spins him a tale.

He is running cool and smooth. He is radiating on all his eigenfrequencies. *Ah* and *ah*.

Yes, that is a good idea. After Fielding Real is gone, his accountants will suddenly discover a large sum left for scientific research into man-machine linkages. With a century to work, Fielding Prime can find a way out of this computer prison. He can become somebody else.

Not Lennon, no. He owed that much to Fielding Real.

Anyway, he had already lived through that. The Beatles' music was quite all right, but doing it once had made it seem less enticing. Hermann was right. The music was too simple-minded, it lacked depth.

He is ready for something more. He has access to information storage, tapes, consultant help from outside, all the libraries of the planet. He will study. He will train. In a century he can be anything. Ah, he will echo down the infinite reeling halls of time.

John Lennon, hell. He will become Wolfgang Amadeus Mozart.

www.ingramcontent.com/pod-product-compliance
Lightning Source LLC
Chambersburg PA
CBHW032257020726
47495CB00001B/140